ECHOES OF THE ANCESTORS.

Geoff King

To Gill
in friendship

Geoff King

To my lifelong love and partner Fuggo
for her unfailing love and support
and to our son Robert for showing me the way.

PROLOGUE.

Slowly and carefully, the solemn butler led his two masters as they shuffled disconsolately across the gravel to the black Bentley that waited on the drive. In the starless night, the highly polished surface of the car mirrored flickering images of the blaze upon which they had just been encouraged to turn their crooked backs. The reflections flashed like a scattering of dim, erratic hazard lights on the pale, papery skin of their faces. Their feeble limbs resembled fragile bent sticks, the muscles having atrophied through great age and inactivity. The attendant chauffeur, a hulking giant who dwarfed his employers, opened first one and then the other door as their butler assisted the elderly gentlemen into the back seats of the vehicle. All four figures were dressed in black suits as if knowingly attending the cremation of the building. As the servants took their places in the front of the car, the frail diminutive twins, whose loose clothing was the most faded and worn, looked miserably at the burning mansion. An enormous column of billowing smoke, a churning cloud of orange and black, disgorged into the inky sky, carrying with it the essence of their home and all their belongings. Three fire crews were attempting to douse the huge fire with jets of water from their powerful, barely restrained hoses. Yet compared to the massive flames, they seemed to be ineffectual squirts from water pistols and the brothers had already realised that the manor was lost. However, it was the contents of their home that were of more concern to Belum Asar and Belum Ki. In truth, they felt that the loss of one item in particular was utterly catastrophic.

'I fear,' muttered Asar dejectedly, 'that we do not have very much time remaining to acquire a replacement.'

'Indeed,' agreed his brother with a heavy sigh, 'but we must spare no effort in the attempt.'

Their breathy voices rasped softly in the muffled interior of the car, seemingly cushioned by the upholstery, like their corpses might be in their coffins in the not too distant future.

1

'Nasaru,' they called in unison.

'Yes my lords?' replied the butler deferentially, craning his undersized head on its wrinkled, stick-like neck. The rims of his small, round spectacles and the flinty grey eyes behind them twinkled with reflected flames.

Belum Ki licked his parched lips, 'You must fly to Switzerland immediately,' he instructed urgently in a croaky voice.

'To retrieve the blueprints from the bank vault,' added Asar without a pause.

'Right away, my lords,' replied Nasaru with a nod. He returned his gaze to the driveway ahead as the car began to move slowly along it and away from the scene of devastation behind them.

'Meanwhile,' continued Ki, 'we shall endeavour to locate an artisan with the necessary skills required to fashion the replacement.'

'But we must hurry,' stressed Belum Asar, twisting a lock of his white beard agitatedly with twig-like fingers, 'we do not know how much time we have remaining.'

'Very little I fear,' said the brother with a fleeting look, his eyes disclosing his apprehension. He raised his voice slightly to instruct the chauffeur. 'Zikar, drive us to the Royal Hotel...and then take Nasaru to the airport....there is no time to waste....'

'No time to waste...,' echoed his twin shaking his head unhappily, thus causing his long beard to sway a little in sympathy, '....and we cannot stress enough...the importance of this matter....' The speech of the two men had slowed considerably, as if driven by running-down clockwork.

Reaching a straighter section of the avenue Zikar increased their speed, driving further from their former residence and leaving the unquenchable inferno behind. Above the scrunch of the tyres on the gravel of the long drive and the deep but gentle purr of the flawless engine, their whispery voices were barely audible.

'Perhaps we should contact the Network,' suggested Ki wearily, 'they could provide us with vessels...'

'But we have sworn never to resort to that,' his brother reminded him grimly, 'it is both immoral and dangerous.'

'Nevertheless, the situation is desperate....it need only be as an *insurance*....should we be unable to follow our...customary procedure.'

'I suppose you are right,' conceded Asar reluctantly, 'but it must only be as a last resort.....and I'm afraid the price could be prohibitive, especially considering our current circumstances....I fear we may only be able afford one, so we will have to share.'

'If it must be so,' said the other grimly, 'then it must be so.' He shook his head sadly.

'And then,' added Asar, a hollow chill creeping into his voice, 'we will stop at nothing to find the culprit responsible for this.....*atrocity!* And punish him severely....'

'Well, we have a fairly good idea of who it is,' said Belum Ki knotting his gnarly fingers angrily, 'and I will enjoy making him suffer.'

'But he's particularly elusive, despite his feeble mind and body,' said Asar.

'The Network could help us there too...' proposed his twin weakly.

'But at what price? Our funds are not without end brother.'

'You are right of course....this is indeed a terrible day...' uttered Ki. He scratched his head with his ridged yellowing fingernails, thereby dislodging a few flakes of dead skin that floated down to join the others dusting the shoulders of his dark suit. 'Nasaru..,' he continued haltingly, '...by the time you return....the embers should have cooled sufficiently for you to retrieve the stones...*they* are virtually irreplaceable.'

'You will need to recruit.....a team of helpers of course,' added Asar, his shallow breath now labouring with the effort of speech, 'there will be a lot to search through...the manor was extensive...but they *must* find the stones.'

'And they must never speak of what they find,' said Ki.

'*Never,*' emphasised Asar.

'I understand,' responded Nasaru levelly. 'In the current economic climate it is easy to find um....*disposable* workers. I will organise it without delay.'

The man servant reached into the inside pocket of his jacket, pulled out a smart phone and began to tap the screen with a bony finger. Looking askance, the driver smirked to himself. It greatly amused him whenever he saw Nasaru use a piece of modern technology. It seemed absurd when the butler's character and demeanour were so old fashioned in every other way, like a character from a Dickens novel or something. He didn't like the man either. He scorned his toadying and unquestioning obedience to *their lordships*. Zikar only grudgingly followed his orders. He was merely chauffeuring these old fools for the money, the wages were good after all - in fact the best he had earned since coming to this country ten years previously, but he held them in contempt as he did all those who were "born" into their wealth rather than earning it by hard graft. Still, he enjoyed driving the Bently and got to use it in his spare time too – something he had done to his advantage several times when trying to impress an attractive woman. The large, luxurious and comfortable back seats provided an ideal environment for an easy seduction. The fact that he could get away with this behind his masters' backs gave him even more cause for self satisfaction. Speeding up as he reached the tarmac of the main road he began wondering which of his female acquaintances he would visit later that evening.

In the darkness behind him, Belum Asar and Belum Ki exchanged brief angry glances. They did not need to speak of their displeasure at their present circumstances. Their paired temperaments typically reacted to adversity with a rapidly growing irascibility that often targeted anyone and everyone unfortunate enough to cross their path. Their own employees and those at the hotel were likely to fall foul of their petulance until the old men had gained satisfaction through merciless vengeance.

PART 1

CHAPTER ONE.

Charlie loved the sky. And here, on this flat horn of land pointing crookedly into the cold grey slab of the North Sea, the sky was huge. The peninsula thrust away from the throng of alluring hills yet, like an arthritic finger plunged into an icy pool, it recoiled slightly as if reluctant to fully commit to its course. However, the contorted coastline did nothing to diminish the extent of the sky. Visitors from the city often became troubled, even threatened by the expanse, almost feeling that they could lose themselves in the enormity or be crushed by the weight, as if its mass was proportional to its size. Charlie experienced the opposite. In an urban environment he felt hemmed in by the intimidating cram of hard, hulking angular structures, crowding out the sky and leaning threateningly over him. In the narrow streets the press of the surrounding humanity was stifling. He loved people but in smaller numbers and at times when he chose to be with them; how could so many seethe chaotically around in a muddle of oppositely flowing streams? The confusing melee left him dizzy and panicky. His own surroundings, with the open reach to the heavens and at night to the infinity beyond the uncountable stars, gave him a wondrous sense of freedom. He sensed that the immensity outside of him somehow allowed his inner being to expand, escaping the limits of his flesh-and-bone frame to coalesce with all existence. These thoughts were as close to spirituality as he got, generally thinking of himself as being a fairly down to earth kind of guy and it was why, as often as possible, he would walk from his beloved home, past the docile sheep, across the otherwise empty fields to the tranquil shore of the small sandy estuary, direct his gaze upwards or out to the horizon, breathe in the distances and give space to his random thoughts. Beyond the windblown moor and across the Dornoch Firth, the familiar profile of the northern hills' undulating mounds regularly changed colour with the frequent fluctuations in the Highland maritime climate. It often struck him just how much was happening in the sky above. The east coast weather married to the effects of the nearby mountains and the northern latitude collaborated to create an ever changing, awe-inspiring and unpredictable spectacle. Even when the sky was overcast the clouds competed for originality, collectively manifesting a hundred shades of grey.

One early morning in late February 2011, trudging over the rough pasture to the beach Charlie felt that with no breeze to speak of, he could detect a little warmth from the sun's rays. He noticed the first skylarks of the year chittering madly in the air for terrestrial territory; their seemingly random trilling somehow produced a melodious rhapsody lifting his spirits with their giddy ascendance. What a shame, he thought, that humans couldn't resolve their disputes by singing to each other. The skies here were too often filled with a noise that drowned out the birdsong and served as a constant reminder of the human race's failure to comply to his ideals. Today he was too early for the fighter jets, which practiced low flying and bombing over a range on the moor, but he knew that they flew regularly and was thankful that he was fortunate not to be living in those countries whose people were the unwilling victims of the indiscriminate cargo. What a catastrophic effect it must have, he thought, on the lives of the bulk of the population who were non-combatants but usually formed the majority of the casualties, sometimes for years later when their farmland and ruined towns were still littered with unexploded ordnance. To live in constant fear of your life and the lives of your family would surely result in a devastating impact on one's psyche and probably on the collective consciousness of the entire population of the terrorised nation. He shook his head to free himself of his thoughts. He tried not to dwell on these notions for long – after all what could he do about it?

Noticing the pungent odour of a fox's scent he paused at the stile over the rusty barbed wire fence that separated fields from dunes, although the vegetation did not conform to such a sudden demarcation. The coarse winter-bleached grassland gradually intermingled with a vibrant sward of moss and patches of rabbit cropped turf, which in turn progressively yielded to the straw coloured marram, tinted golden by the newly risen sun. The whole area was punctured by scrapes and burrows, scooped out from the underlying sand and peppered with the droppings of both sheep and rabbits. The tide was half way in and today without a whisper of wind the water, protected from the open ocean by a wide sandbar, was mirror flat and perfectly reflecting the pastel pale blue of the sky. A little further along the strand, oystercatchers piped shrilly and scurried over the mussel beds, seizing their last chance to probe the area for titbits before the sea reclaimed the area for another few hours. On the inlet's opposite shoreline crowds of waders massed in unsteady ranks, occasionally shuffling to retreat from the rising sea.

Charlie climbed over the stile, tramped down the dune to the beach and started wandering along the sandy, windswept foreshore towards the estuary's outlet. Out of habit he glanced down at the sand and was thrilled to see a line of otter tracks. He rarely managed to glimpse one of the elusive creatures but it was gratifying just to know that they were about. Disturbed from their buffet by his advance, the oystercatchers took flight and fled in a trilling clamour across the channel. The commotion alarmed the waders causing them to flock swirling into the air. They swarmed low across the water and then wheeled as one in a broad wave, almost skimming the surface, their beating wings generating an audible rush of air. He watched captivated by the sight as they suddenly swept upwards turning in unison, pale white undersides flashing in the sunlight as a shimmering wave passed from side to side of the flock. Each time they swung around, a rapid undulation pulsed through the host as if some signal passed between them guiding a choreographed dance. How did they communicate, he wondered? For so many birds to act simultaneously and collectively, seemingly without a leader, there must be some sort of telepathic link between them. It could be seen in schools of fish too and swarms of bees. With such miniscule brains how could they accomplish any kind of thought transference? Surely then, the human mind being so much more complex, should be able to perform even greater psychic feats. There was "crowd mentality" of course, as displayed amongst football fans and he'd heard of psychologists (was one of them Jung?) who talked about a "collective unconscious", though he wasn't quite sure what it was. Most people had experienced those moments of mild surprise when the person they were just thinking of telephones out of the blue. Usually this is dismissed light-heartedly as coincidence, but it happened too often to go unremarked. Charlie had experienced it himself on numerous occasions, particularly with his brother, his mother and especially with his wife Bess. Scientists have asserted that three-fifths of the brain seems to go unused – could this be site of long-lost mental abilities, vestigial remnants diminished through lack of use? He had read somewhere that experiments had been done to test for telekinetic aptitude in humans but the results were inconclusive or, when they did show promise, the mainstream scientific community vilified them or insufficient funding was available for comprehensive studies to be completed because there were no commercial or political interests to be served. Sometimes it seemed that the narrow-minded dogma and orthodoxy of the "scientific method" left no room for innovative experiment. Certainly the weight of anecdotal evidence seemed to suggest that there were mental phenomena yet to be explained and understood. Charlie shook his head, a habit he employed in an attempt to clear his mind, causing the loose black curls of his shoulder length hair to flutter about his ears. Metaphysics interested him up to a point but he couldn't find enough enthusiasm to actually care very much about it. Even if he did understand more of the mysteries of life and the universe, would it make much difference to his day-to-day life? He doubted it.

His empty stomach brought him back to reality as it was beginning to complain at the fact that he had carelessly neglected breakfast in favour of an early walk. He had reached the burn just before the "white sands", as the next costal tract was referred to by the locals, so he decided it was a good place to turn back. This stretch of beach was topped by high hummocky dunes which, only partly supported by a bank of stones, were collapsing from the ravages of the wind, the tide and the eager excavations of rabbits. With an elongated shadow marching ahead of him, his eyes glided over the wave-rounded rocks and pebbles at the top of the strand as he strode past, enjoying the collage of sizes, shapes and colours. One large stone in particular caught his attention, so he stooped and picked it up for closer inspection. It was dark green, incredibly smooth and glossy, yet seemingly run through with a network of almost imperceptible veins, as if it was a conglomerate of smaller, irregular pieces united by incredible forces. He had never seen anything quite like it before and he felt a tingle run down his spine, as it always did when he felt awe at a wonder of nature. Pleased with his find, he put it in his coat pocket with the intention of adding it to his modest collection of "special" stones he had gathered on his bedside table in an untidy miniature henge.

As he wandered home across the fields, his thoughts rambled once more. He noticed an early bumblebee creeping slowly over the grass, waiting for the sun's warmth to sufficiently stimulate its flight muscles. Fascinated by this remarkable creature, Charlie sank to his hands and knees for a closer look and took pleasure in the feel of the dewy grass and soft spongy moss beneath his fingers. The slightly chilly dampness was a stimulating sensation. He lifted his hands and rubbed his fingers with his thumbs, spreading the moisture. Returning his eyes to the bee, he wondered in what way it was aware of its environment and how its senses worked. Was it even aware of him? He often wondered whether animals felt a part of the planet in the same way that he did. He was sure there must be some kind of link between himself and the world other than just gravity and a breathable atmosphere. Maybe all living things were part of the same pool of life force that formed both the world and its biosphere. He knew that a lot of tribal peoples had a very strong connection with the Earth. The Australian aborigines for example, not only understood their environment completely but they also were able to "sing" their way through the wilderness. Bess had once told him of a book she'd read in which an anthropologist was relating his experiences with the Bushmen of the Kalahari Desert. Apparently, they could tell from afar when another member of the tribe was returning from a successful hunt. They would light a cooking fire in preparation for the arrival of the meat. In some way he believed he too could feel a sense of belonging to the land, to this location. Although he wasn't born here and neither were his parents, his grandfather and his forebears had been. Maybe this was why he got a powerful sense of coming home when he moved to the Highlands fifteen years previously. He also held a deep respect for the Earth, for nature, for all living things, for this place and for this landscape. He felt bound by a kind of duty of care, though not an onerous one. It was a blissful responsibility. When he was doing voluntary conservation work, planting trees, gardening or even just feeding the birds it was always done with joy. The wonders of nature enthralled him. Scientists could explain how a tiny seed could grow into the largest tree on earth and he understood that, but to him it was still magic. Science was just how the human race had chosen to explain the magic. It was not that he believed in enchantment, sorcery or even creation. He merely felt that life in all its forms and in fact the universe itself was so totally amazing that it was actually beyond the ability of human beings to fully understand it. He didn't waste any of his valuable time on this planet by getting involved in trying to explain the inexplicable. He was here now and he was going to make the most of it. This included, he reminded himself, going to work at the job he loved so that he could make beautiful things for others to enjoy - and earn money in the process. This in turn would enable him to pay the bills to keep up his lifestyle in the wonderful home he shared with his fabulous wife in this amazing landscape. Yes, he thought, I do actually have a lot to be grateful for.

#

An indistinct shape moved slowly and silently through the night's shadows in the grounds of Southampton University's School of Humanities. A large banner in front of the building proudly declared the hosting of an international conference of prehistoric archaeology and an exhibition celebrating Sumerian artefacts. A faint breeze stirred the sign and agitated the sparse vegetation that stood forlornly in the bare earth of the unkempt border by the short, scuffed moonlit turf. The black-clad figure stopped behind a brick pillar, adjusted the straps on a small but heavy backpack and surveyed the empty paved space in front of the dimly illuminated foyer. The weak yellowish light spilled out onto the bare concrete paving slabs through the large panes of glass, now typical of entrances to institutions the worldwide, but made little difference to that cast by the full moon.

It was two o'clock in the morning. Consequently, the security guard had slumped in his chair, asleep in front of a television screen displaying images from a channel showing the world's news all night long to many other dozing night staff such as him. The silhouette just outside moved stealthily towards the door despite its slightly hobbling gait, but then paused glancing up at the sight of a security camera aimed towards the entrance where he now crouched. Somewhat belatedly, the prowler tugged at the edges of the hood surrounding his face as if to further conceal his features and then shuffled over to the keypad on the metal frame. He entered the correct code and the door opened smoothly and noiselessly. The sound of the television was now audible as the intruder stayed low and crept past the counter. The watchman remained immobile, slumbering deeply. Like most in his profession, he also had a day job to provide enough for a demanding wife and family who wanted, like everyone else, to benefit fully from the consumerist delights of the twenty-first century. At least here he could sleep in peace.

'Eight Croatian workers died in Scotland yesterday in a tragic road accident,' announced the newsreader from the screen. 'A spokesman for the Lothian and Border's Police Department said that their vehicle, a fifteen year old Ford Transit minibus, left the carriageway on a sharp bend and plunged into a disused quarry. An eyewitness said that the vehicle did not seem to slow down and it appeared that the driver made no attempt to steer around the bend. Police experts are investigating the roadworthiness of the minibus and the possibility that the safety barrier was in a poor state of repair. It is also suspected that the group may have been employed illegally by a gang-master in the area. No other vehicles were involved in the incident.'

The trespasser crossed the atrium, past a two and a half metre high replica of a megalith, quietly pushed open another door, this one unlocked, and slipped unnoticed into the corridor beyond, moving towards his goal.

#

Charlie yelled and woke, panting and sweating, tangled in clammy sheets. Bess was clutching his wrist, having just shaken him awake.

'Are you alright Charlie? You were jerking and writhing about like you were having a fit,' she said, 'I was worried. Was it another nightmare?'

Her features showed concern but also the bleariness of one recently woken suddenly from deep sleep. To Charlie, struggling to reach full consciousness, the beam of bright spring sunshine cutting across her face seemed for a moment to be slicing it in two. Although his pounding heart and breathing had slowed, the harrowing images from his dream remained vividly imprinted on his mind.

'Aye, sort of,' he replied, rubbing his eyes and shaking his head in an attempt to clear his thoughts. Bess turned to face him and propped herself up on one elbow, raking the curtain of tangled black hair from her sleep-puffed face.

'God, Charlie, that's five in the last week isn't it?' she asked, 'Are you O.K.? Do you want to tell me about it?'

'Er, aye sure, O.K.' he muttered half-heartedly, 'Um, well it started pretty much like the others, you know, there were all these people in some kind of ancient looking city, like some kind of, I don't know, er...ancient Peruvian place and they were all rushing around in a panic...dark skies, earth shaking...,' he paused, trying to translate the images into words, '....some kind of fire I think, or a volcano...and an earthquake. But this time it was different – it was horrible because they weren't just running away, not all of them anyway, some of them were attacking anyone who came within reach, women, children...anyone. It was like they'd been gripped by some kind of collective madness, or they were possessed or something. It was like you'd imagine a kind of vision of hell or something....kind of like that painting by what's his name...Hieronymus Bosch.'

'Sounds awful,' murmured Bess, still not completely awake, reaching over to stroke his hair and comfort him.

'Aye, it was a bit,' he admitted, 'Every time I dream this it gets more detailed, more vivid, more like a memory....but it gets worse. This time, I started walking through the crowd, stepping over the bodies of the dead and injured but ignoring their calls for help, stumbling because of the tremors....I felt irresistibly drawn to an open doorway in a building on the other side of the square. I went through it and down a stone staircase lit by flickering torches. I came to a gloomy chamber, some kind of cellar or vault and in the middle was a plinth with an intricately carved and gilded casket on it – a sarcophagus or something, embedded with big jewels and stones. There was dust falling from the ceiling as the earth shook and I looked up to see these cracks in the stonework, like it was becoming unstable. I knew I should leave but I couldn't help moving closer to the coffin thing. I felt kind of compelled to look inside, you know, even though I dreaded what I might find. So, slowly, I gripped the edge of the lid, expecting it to be heavy, but I lifted it easily. Inside was a body, some really ancient wrinkled old guy. He was bald but had a long white beard and an emaciated kind of pasty, blue-grey face and sort of Middle Eastern. As I was looking at him he suddenly opened his eyes and grabbed my wrist, really tightly. His eyes were icy and evil looking too - I wanted to scream, but I couldn't - and that's when I woke and you were holding my arm.'

'God, that's awful.' said Bess sympathetically. 'Do you want a hug?'

'Yeah, please,' replied Charlie and snuggled into the familiar comfort of her soft, warm body, gently inhaling her reassuring scent. He sighed and consciously calmed his breathing. After a couple of minutes he lifted his head to peer at the glowing red digits on the bedside clock.

'I might as well get up,' he said with a sigh, 'I'd have to be up in half an hour anyway. I won't get back to sleep now.'

He reluctantly disentangled himself from Bess' embrace and turned on his side, then rose to sit on the edge of the bed. Getting dressed he said, 'Shall I bring you a cup of tea?'

'Mmm, yes please,' she replied, wriggling deeper into the cosiness of the warm bedding, 'but don't hurry.'

Cycling to work, almost oblivious to the soft sunlight of late March and its mild heartening warmth, Charlie couldn't quite rid himself of the traumatic images in his mind. It had been so real. It was like he had actually been there, like he was one of the people, felt their madness and pain. Why was he getting these recurring nightmares now? And why did they seem more and more *real*? For the past few weeks his sleep was becoming more frequently disturbed. As far as he could remember there had been nothing like it since he was a small child. He was certainly more deeply shaken and affected than he had been by any other dream or nightmare previously...and that old guy's *eyes,* he just couldn't erase that image from his mind, they were so *piercing,* as if they had peered into his soul and examined every detail.

He freewheeled into the yard of the workshop and propped his bike between a huge stack of air-drying two-inch thick oak slabs and the firm's new van, sign-written with "Fantasy Furniture" and colourfully embellished with images of castles, fairies and dragons. Pausing briefly, as was his habit on arrival, he took in the trees surrounding and sheltering the premises and noticed the gentle birdsong. It was a little late in the day for the full dawn chorus, but still there were some birds giving voice to their claims. The willows were starting to leaf up and their branches displayed long whip-like twigs adorned with fuzzy flowers. Below them the buds on the hawthorns were just beginning to open and clusters of daffodils boasted their early blooms. The sky was an intense blue, the air clean and fresh. Taking a deep satisfying breath, Charlie took his lunch from the saddlebags and headed for the door, the gravel crunching beneath the tread of his cycling shoes.

'You're early!' chirped Rhona, his boss, emerging from her office and smiling pleasantly as he climbed into his over-alls. Formerly a star student at the acclaimed Scottish School of Furniture Design in Glasgow, Rhona spent only three years gaining experience in the sector and then in the space of just four more built up a very successful business of her own. Now aged thirty-two, she employed six craftsmen including Charlie, her seventeen-year-old niece Rowan as apprentice and Flora the part-time secretary, a feisty mature woman of late middle-age with a no-nonsense approach to both life and work.

'Er, aye,' responded Charlie vaguely, 'I woke early, so I thought I might as well come in and do something useful.'

Rhona's dainty figure, accompanied by her elfin features and startling blue eyes seemed to hold a disproportionate amount of energy and enthusiasm. Her self-confidence, positive attitude and vision all contributed to her success in her chosen field. She habitually wore black jeans and a red lumberjack shirt – in fact Charlie could not remember seeing her in anything else, so guessed she must possess a wardrobe containing several of each.

'That's great Charlie,' she said, still smiling, 'because we've got to start the "dragons" dining set soon, so it'd be great if you could try to finish the fairy cabinet a.s.a.p.'

Beneath her rampant mane of bushy red hair, which she loved but at work attempted to contain with a "scrunchy" and a fistful of clips, her eyes shone radiantly, brimming with her eagerness and vitality.

'I'll give you Rowan today,' she added, 'she needs to learn about spray finishing anyway, so this is the ideal opportunity.'

On cue, Rowan appeared from the office clad in a bright orange boiler suit. Turning her phone off in compliance with workshop rules, she placed it in her top pocket and buttoned the flap.

'Hi Rowan,' said Charlie amicably. He liked the girl in a protective, paternal kind of way. He had a twenty-year-old son, but would have liked to have had a daughter too. 'How are you today?'

'Hi Charlie,' she replied sleepily, yawning, 'Not bad, apart from like a sore nose – my new piercing's totally gone septic.' When she spoke, the young woman's voice rose towards the end of the sentence as if asking a question rather than making a statement. It was something that used to annoy Charlie, but since getting to know Rowan he had got used to it. Anyway, it was a trend that seemed to be infiltrating the adult population now too.

'Bummer,' he commiserated, looking at the pretty face beneath the shock of spiky purple- and red-streaked black hair. He couldn't help thinking that her looks had been somewhat spoiled by the multiple piercing of her eyebrows, lower lip, tongue and most recently her nose. The dozen or so studs and rings in each ear he could handle, but the rest did nothing to improve the pale, pasty complexion and dark rimmed eyes of one whom he saw as a dedicated teenage late night party-goer. As a matter of fact, she rarely socialised except with a small handful of friends who usually preferred to gather in each other's homes, drink tea, eat biscuits and chat whilst listening to music. However, she had grown accustomed to people making assumptions about her lifestyle from her appearance and in Charlie's case she didn't mind because he was such a nice bloke and she couldn't be bothered to correct him. Actually she quite liked the idea that she might be seen as a bit of a hedonist - it suited her image and was certainly considered "cooler" by others her age than the early-to-bed bookworm she really was.

'It'll clear up soon, no bother,' she said with a shrug. 'And how are you today?'

'Och, no' bad,' he replied automatically, then added, 'aye, good.'

She regarded him dubiously in an oddly disconcerting manner. Sometimes he imagined that she could see right into his mind.

'Er…right, let's get started,' he said, leading the way towards the spray booth, 'with any luck we can finish this today. I'll cover the dreaded "health and safety" thing first.'

The other craftsmen trickled in. First came Brian, whose arrival was announced by the unmistakable sound of his trusty old Citroen 2CV, whirring like an aged washing machine on spin cycle. His bespectacled and hirsute features were slightly amusing to behold: his eyes protruded, his hair and beard were wispy and he had bucked teeth. It was as if he had just walked off the set of a comedy sketch show. His character too was rather unusual. He was a forty-something Glaswegian Francophile who wrote romantic poetry and listened only to Opera. He was soon followed by Grant, the newest recruit, who had recently moved north from Basingstoke – a swaggering tabloid-reading Jack-the-lad with an over-inflated estimation of his attractiveness to women and an affected devil-may-care attitude to the opinions of everyone else. He drove a Ford Mondeo fitted with a thumping sound-system, the "sports" body kit and finished in striking tonic blue, an inadequate tribute to the vehicle used by James Bond in "Casino Royale". He imagined that this made him appear "cool".

'Mornin' all,' he greeted the room in general, then turning to Rowan asked with a toothy grin, 'What colour are they today love?' referring to her underwear. It was an ongoing "joke" on his part, but he didn't expect an answer, knowing that the girl did not appreciate his sense of humour. To her, his short black hair and thick over-hanging eyebrows made all of his facial expressions seem menacing. As he turned his back she pulled a face at him, poking out her tongue and causing Charlie to smile. He liked the girl and he didn't much like Grant, so was totally sympathetic to her, especially as he disapproved of the macho posturing of the arrogant male, even if supposedly done in jest.

Hamish and Dougie MacLeod entered next, inseparable but dissimilar brothers in their mid-thirties and the only born-and-bred locals on the workforce. This they did not mind, however, being blessed with a combination of a generous dose of traditional Highland hospitality and genuine good nature. Grant called them "Little and

Large" due to the disparity in their size. Hamish was a tiny man, only five feet tall with thinning ginger hair, his whiskers and features mouse-like, whereas his brother's resemblance was that of a bear. Dougie was a tall, broad and powerful with a large dark beard and a shock of hair to match. Last to arrive, but by no means late was Rory, a tall, cheery type from Fife with a long wavy beard and whose frizzy shock of blonde hair was only half tamed by being raked back into a ponytail. Although only in his mid-twenties it was his belief, until quite recently, that good music stopped with the demise of progressive rock music at the end of the nineteen-seventies and was happy to discuss this theory for hours, given the chance, illustrating his argument with countless examples from his encyclopaedic knowledge of his preferred genre. Thanks to a trip to visit family down under the previous year, he was now a convert to contemporary Australian blues and jazz. He always walked to work, living as he did on the edge of town and typically entered the workshop with a spring in his step.

'Hey, guess what?' he asked with a broad grin, exposing a mouthful of perfectly even but yellowing teeth, 'I've just won a hundred quid on a scratch card! Good eh?'

They all agreed that it was and then proceeded to climb into overalls or don aprons according to their preferences in order to begin the day's work.

At lunchtime the staff usually gathered to eat their sandwiches in what Rhona liked to refer to as "The Lizard Lounge". As a great believer in the benefits to business of a happy, even pampered workforce, she had furnished the spacious room with a couple of three-piece suites arranged around low tables, a good quality sound system with a stack of CDs, a kettle and a coffee-maker. Flora, the secretary, was the only one to go home for lunch. Now approaching retirement age, she stubbornly adhered to the convention of her forty-year marriage of returning to cook for "my Angus" as she called him, a good meal to keep him going on the allotment. When Rhona once suggested that "her Angus" should cook his own lunch, Flora was adamant.

'Och no!' she exclaimed, 'He grows it, I cook it! It's only fair. After all, you would nae catch me out in all weathers, breaking my back wi' digging and up tae my knees in muck!'

Not long after he joined the firm Grant had once suggested that they might go for a pint some lunchtimes, but Rhona forbade it. It was about the only time she had put her foot down and asserted her authority.

'No way is anybody here going to operate woodworking machinery after a drink!' she announced, 'I can't afford to have one of you in hospital for weeks with fingers cut off. I'm sorry, but I've got a limited use for amputees here *and* I don't want blood getting all over some ornate piece of furniture that I've paid somebody a lot of money to carve!'

As they all filed in to The Lizard Lounge today, Charlie flopped into the armchair by the window and gazed distractedly at a chaffinch perched in the seed-hung branches of the ash tree waving slightly in the gentle breeze. Once they had started on their lunch, the others produced their phones and started texting, except for Grant who preferred to look at his paper, first admiring page three before turning to the sports section at the back. Rory had reached the hi-fi first so was entitled to play his choice of music, so he selected the latest album by The John Butler Trio. Oblivious to the music, Charlie absent-mindedly chewed on his sandwiches as he brooded over his nightmare. Working with and teaching Rowan at the same time had required all of his concentration so had kept Charlie's mind fully occupied throughout the morning, but now that he had stopped work he began getting flashes of the horrific vision of destruction and violence from his dream. Neither could he get rid of the image of the old man's eyes seeming to burrow into his mind. What could it mean? He'd never really attached much significance to the content of his dreams, but in the last few weeks they had become more and more vivid and increasingly scary. Why should they appear now? Currently in his mid forties, he was happy with his life and his work. He was still very much in love with Bess after 25 years together. His son, Luke, had turned into a great guy, had excelled at his studies and was now spending a gap year helping at an AIDS orphanage in Kenya. Charlie had the ideal job too. After twenty years of struggling to make half a living as a self-employed woodcarver and gilder, along came the position with Rhona whom Bess had met at yoga class. The wages were really good because the clients were all rich and they valued good craftsmanship, as did Rhona. The work was interesting, varied, fulfilling and fun – carving fantasy figures, applying gold leaf to bespoke furniture *and* getting paid well for it was like a dream come true. Bess was also happy. She alternated teaching yoga with growing organic fruit and herbs, which she supplied to local hotels and restaurants. Her high quality produce was very much in demand so her "little sideline" was thriving. They had also created a beautiful home in "The Haven", as they had named their renovated croft house and smallholding. Life couldn't be much better really. Maybe he was reading too much into it – they *were* only dreams after all.

Rhona's voice startled him from his reverie.

'Something on your mind Charlie?' she enquired as she sat in the chair opposite him on the other side of the window, 'You look miles away.'

'Oh, er, yes, I mean no, not really,' he stammered haltingly, sitting himself up straighter in his chair.

'Something you want to talk about?' she persevered amiably, raising her eyebrows slightly.

'No. I'm fine. Really. But thanks anyway,' he replied. He realised he still had a banana remaining in his lunchbox so he picked it up and started to peel it.

'O.K.' she said, 'then in that case can I ask your advice? Something work related.'

'Sure, if you like,' assented Charlie, attempting to give her his full attention, 'I'll do my best.' He bit into his banana and chewed slowly as he listened.

'Right,' she said, leaning forward, 'you know why I employed you, don't you Charlie?' she began, 'I mean apart from you being the best woodcarver and gilder in the Highlands.'

'Because Bess is your best friend?' he suggested wryly, then looking around the room at the others reading their newspapers or books 'Or because you like to surround yourself with bearded men?'

'Hah!' she exclaimed, laughing heartily, 'It may be true that five out of six of you guys have beards, but I think that merely reflects a tendency amongst woodworkers to have a preference for facial hair – it's nothing to do with my taste in men!' She paused, composing herself.

'No, Charlie,' she continued levelly, 'It's *also* because I highly value the wisdom and experience you bring with your years of running your own business.'

Charlie seemed slightly amused. He swallowed his last mouthful.

'Oh, you mean *you* can learn from *my* mistakes?' he ventured with a smile.

'Well....sure, a bit,' she concurred, 'But seriously Charlie, you were in business for two decades, dealing with customers and their orders, organising the whole show. Even though you didn't get rich, you survived, which is more than can be said for a lot of small firms.'

As she paused, Charlie put in, 'Yeah, but the reason I got out when I did was because I was no businessman and the stress got to me. I must be a bit thick if it took me twenty years to realise I wasn't cut out for it.'

Rhona smiled fondly at his humility.

'Come on mate, you're being too modest,' she said, 'and I really do value your opinion. Anyway, that's why I want you to come into my office. I've got something I want to talk to you about and something to show you.'

Charlie raised his bristly eyebrows, 'Top secret, eh?' he whispered playfully.

'Um…sort of, yes,' she replied evenly, getting up and glancing sidelong at the others, 'for the moment at least.'

Curious, Charlie stood. 'O.K.,' he said, 'lead the way.' He followed as she rose and left the room.

The rest of the staff seemed oblivious to their conversation and movements, apart from Rowan who was looking up from the book she had starting reading after sending a text to her best friend Jenny. Charlie noticed her gaze following Rhona but she looked down again quickly when she became aware of his glance. He wondered how much of the conversation she had heard. Not that there was anything confidential in what was said – it just seemed odd that she would be so curious.

They walked through the workshop towards the office. Glancing at the components and skeletons of furniture in the making and the figures of half-carved wizards, fairies, elves and dragons, Charlie reflected on just how much fun it was to work here. Rhona was such a cool boss too. She was more of a team member – she was good at all the skills required of her staff, she was flexible, respectful, considerate and a good listener too. The reason he'd been self-employed for so long was because he hated working for other people. Now he realised that it was all down to how you were treated by your employer. What a rare gem Rhona was. All her workers knew it too – none had left since the start and nobody had any intention of doing so either. They were a good bunch too, apart from Grant, who was a dickhead. But maybe, Charlie mused generously, he would settle in after a few more weeks, after all it wasn't that long since he joined – perhaps he was just being defensive with his false bravado and in-your-face bigotry. Or maybe not. Time would tell.

Charlie followed Rhona into the office where she indicated that he should close the door behind them. The office was very tidy and immaculately organised, with separate shelves for box files, rolled up drawings and reference books. Only a small window on the north side of the building illuminated the room, so she switched on the overhead fluorescent light and walked over to her desk. Its' surface was clear apart from a phone, a "pen tidy", an angle poise lamp and a large roll of paper, which Charlie assumed to be some kind of plan or drawing.

'Take a seat,' she offered, indicating Flora's chair at the other desk where the computer hummed quietly in screen saver mode. Charlie turned it around to face Rhona and sat down.

'So what's on your mind?' he asked easily, always comfortable in Rhona's presence.

'It's this new job that's come in,' she began slowly, 'I haven't accepted it yet – I wanted to speak to you first.'

She seemed uncharacteristically hesitant and was nervously fiddling with her pen, avoiding eye contact.

'That's odd,' commented Charlie, 'you don't usually turn work down, though some *clients* do when they see your prices...*and* you've never consulted me before accepting work in the past. You have all the training and technical expertise – I'm self-taught, what do I know?'

'Well,' continued Rhona, still seeming uneasy but finally meeting his eyes, 'this one's a bit weird and so are the clients – or rather their *"representative"*.'

'Their *"representative"*?' repeated Charlie curiously, frowning.

'Yes, these guys are so rich and secretive they sent some kind of servant to approach me'

'So what was weird about him?'

She sighed and looked to the side as if the answer was amongst the box files on the shelf. Charlie had not seen here like this before. She was faltering and edgy, possibly even a little apprehensive.

'Right,' she began slowly, 'it was yesterday after you'd all gone home apart from Rowan and I stayed on to work on the new logo. There was a knock on the office door and this old guy came in dressed like a funeral director with little round specs perched on the end of his nose and a grey, stony face. He was really tall and thin and stooped – looked like a praying mantis or something.' She was scrutinizing her pen again as if it held her memories. 'Anyway, without a smile or an introduction or anything he just handed over the drawings and an envelope and kind of intoned like a robot, "You are to make this item exactly as specified in the drawings, from the materials listed",' Rhona said, imitating a dry, hollow, deep voice, ' "It must be completed by one craftsman only, your best – a Mr. Charles Mackay I believe is the only one with a high enough level of skill in both carving and gilding   – and it will be collected on the fifth of June at midday. No-one but you and the selected staff member may see the drawings or the artefact at any stage neither in its construction nor on completion." '

'He asked for *me*?' said Charlie incredulously.

'Well you *are* my finest craftsman,' she stated matter-of-factly.

'But how did he know about me?' He was puzzled and felt slightly uneasy, feeling flustered by being singled out and "known" by strangers, yet simultaneously gratified by the appraisal.

'Buggered if I know, Charlie, but anyhow I tried to interrupt but he just droned on and on as if he was reciting some centuries old document – totally emotionless and expressionless. Anyway then he said, "Neither of you will communicate any details of any sort to anyone else at any time before, during or after the undertaking. Failure to comply with these conditions will not be tolerated."

"Are you threatening me?" I asked. I couldn't believe it, some stuffy old skeleton coming in to my office uninvited, threatening *me* if I don't do what he says! I wasn't going to stand for any of that. But he just stood there like I was beneath him and sort of sniffed in a superior stuck-up butler kind of a way and said, "We hope that won't be necessary."

"You've got a cheek coming in here and making demands and threats - I haven't even looked at the job yet, let alone accepted it."

"You will," he said, "the cheque is in with the instructions. My employers are very generous."

'So I looked down at the envelope for a couple of seconds, wondering whether to open it there and then or chuck it back in his face but when I looked up he was gone! I didn't even hear the door close, but it was shut all the same.' She looked up at Charlie, finally losing interest in her pen.

'Weird,' was all that Charlie could manage, trying to absorb the strangeness of her experience.

'Bloody weird,' agreed Rhona.

'So, er, are you going to take it on?' he asked trying to sound as if there was nothing out of the ordinary.

'Well, it's up to you Charlie. You're the bloody "chosen one",' she said, smiling humourlessly.

'But what about the whole cloak and dagger thing?' asked Charlie, 'I mean, it would be difficult to keep it secret from the other guys wouldn't it?'

'Well, you *could* do it in the old storage shed,' she replied, 'there's not much in there now and the weather's warming up so you wouldn't need heating. And if I tell the guys the clients specified confidentiality I'm sure they'd respect it.'

Charlie thought for a moment. He wouldn't feel entirely comfortable having to work in isolation. He enjoyed the camaraderie of the workshop, the shared anecdotes, the playful banter, even the times when everyone was just working in companionable silence he still felt part of a team.

'But before you say anything, Charlie,' added Rhona, 'I've got to tell you – it's a tight deadline for the work involved. There's a lot of intricate and accurate carving *and* the whole thing has to be gilded, which is why they chose you I suppose – you're the only one north of the border with the skills to do both to such a high standard. So it will mean overtime, which I know you don't like....'

'You're telling me!' he responded, 'that's half the reason I packed in my own business – I resented the long hours away from home. I want to spend my evenings and weekends with Bess or in the garden.'

'Let's see if you two love birds have got a price then shall we – they've paid up front with a *very* large cheque. For this job I can double your wages, double *that* for overtime and give you a one thousand pound bonus on completion. *Provided* of course, that you meet the deadline.' Rhona sat back and regarded him questioningly, one eyebrow raised and a half smile on her face, waiting to see if he would be tempted. Charlie's mouth hung open - he was astonished at the amount being offered to him. He thought and scratched his head. He *really* didn't like overtime and didn't actually *need* the money, though he and Bess *were* trying to save for a once-in-a-lifetime trip to New Zealand and this would certainly help a lot...in fact it might be the only way they could realistically make the trip if they wanted to do it before retiring.

'O.K.,' he said, 'I'll need to talk to Bess first, but you might as well show me the drawings.'

She unrolled the plans on her desk, weighing down the corners with the pen tidy, a couple of books and a calculator. Charlie came around to her side to join her and view the details the right way up.

'Bloody hell!' he exclaimed when he saw it, totally aghast, 'I don't believe it.' He suddenly felt a sickening lurch of fear.

Rhona, taken aback by his reaction, turned her head to see the look of shock and disbelief that had appeared on his face.

'What Charlie?' she asked, troubled by his demeanour. 'What's the matter? Have you seen this before?'

'Yes,' he replied, visibly shaken and obviously very perturbed, 'I saw it in a dream I had last night!'

CHAPTER TWO

It was cool for the time of year. The sky was uniformly slate grey and the chill damp air shivered down the street, stirring the fragmented remnants of last autumn's fallen leaves that had managed to survive the winter. Some became trapped in murky puddles where those that had previously suffered the same fate languished, slowly disintegrating. Adam loped shabbily along the quiet avenue, his listless eyes oblivious to the featureless pavement passing below. He trod his customary route out of habit, inattentive to where he was or what was going on around him. An occasional parked car sulked against the curb beneath reluctantly budding trees that clung possessively to their trembling twigs. With scuffed white trainers emerging from the threadbare fringes of his faded blue jeans he kicked absent-mindedly at a crumpled cigarette packet, sending it scuttling into the grimy gutter. He had the greasy collar of his worn wax jacket turned up in an attempt to shield his pale, thin neck from the unwelcome draught. His long, lank brown hair swung in time with his stride where it issued from beneath a discoloured woollen hat pulled down over his ears. There was something reminiscent of a small mammal about him, more meerkat than weasel, though some thought that his large eyes brought to mind the face of a startled deer.

Usually he would have been more furtive, peering over one of his tensed shoulders to see if he was being watched or followed, convinced that his activities were being monitored. Every passing pedestrian was judged by the look in their eye, the manner of their gait or the perceived suspiciousness of their behaviour. His paranoia had diminished somewhat over the years, but it was so ingrained into his psyche that it had become an unshakeable habit. He believed he was hypersensitive to moods and to the underlying ambience in a room, feeling able to perceive more in the demeanour of others than most other people could. He put it down to the fact that his mother had taken LSD whilst he was developing in the womb, thus opening exceptional doors in his mind before he was even born. He felt it was a difficult burden to bear and was often inclined to isolate himself from others so as not to drown in what he imagined he could tell of their thoughts and feelings towards him.

Today however, Adam was preoccupied, too much lost in thought to be influenced by his usual neuroses. Thus it was that he failed to notice two indistinct figures sitting motionless behind the clouds reflected in the windscreen of a dark executive saloon parked across the road. Heedless to his surroundings, he automatically pushed through a weathered wooden gate, its dry aged hinges creaking in protest and, leaving it open behind him, made his way up the cracked weed-ridden path towards a large dilapidated three-storey Victorian house. Although still occupied, the building showed the usual signs of a city landlord's careless neglect. Drab curtains lurked behind the uneven surfaces of ancient glass that forlornly mirrored the dreary sky, framed by peeling paintwork. By contrast the roof was alive with a thriving mosaic of lichen and rich green moss exuding from the cracks between the dull slates above brave colonies of grass that waved jauntily in the breeze from their precarious perches in corroded, leaky gutters.

Adam skirted the ramshackle building to a rusty wrought iron staircase at the back. As he tramped robotically up the steps, his echoing footfall beat out a rhythmic, plodding and discordant tune as each tread struck a different note. At the top he was greeted by the reassuring sight of the colourfully painted door to Nick and Lynn's flat. The surface was adorned with vibrant images of mushrooms, fairies and a caterpillar smoking a hookah beneath a rainbow in a starry sky. He pounded loudly on the door to make himself heard above the blaring sound system within, which was belting out the unmistakeable strains of Jimi Hendrix's guitar. On his second attempt, his fist missed the door as it swung inwards to reveal a moustached, stubbly face surmounted by a heap of dishevelled and dreadlocked mousy hair. The vacant, sleepy expression was suddenly enlivened by a grin.

'Hey Adam, how you doin'?' said Nick good-humouredly as he stood back to let him in. He wore a green Glastonbury Festival 2008 t-shirt and faded jeans. His tall broad-shouldered figure seemed cramped in the small entrance of the low-ceilinged flat as if he had taken the first bite of Alice's "eat me" cake.

'Oh not bad, you know....,' responded Adam vaguely as he entered. Without further preamble he asked, 'Got anything to smoke?'

'Yeah, sure,' replied Nick matter-of-factly as he shambled into the cosy, cluttered lounge, 'haven't I always? Stuff's on the table. Why don't you skin up while I make some coffee?'

'Cheers.'

Two minutes later Adam had just lit up when Nick returned with the drinks. He put the steaming mugs on the coffee table and turned down the volume of the music to facilitate conversation.

'So, what brings you round so early man?' he enquired, settling into a worn armchair, 'not just desperation for a fucking smoke, surely?'

'Er, well, kind of,' admitted Adam uneasily, 'I just needed to calm myself down a bit, you know?' He took a deep lungful of the pungent fumes before continuing, 'I had a really heavy weird dream last night that kind of freaked me out a bit.........well, a lot actually.' He noisily exhaled a thick blue-grey plume.

'Well, you know you're always welcome mate,' responded Nick amiably, 'though you were lucky to find me up at this time on a Saturday – Lynn's still dead to the world.' He took a sip from his coffee and then accepted the joint proffered by Adam. 'Anyway, what was this dream about?' he asked.

Adam said nothing for a moment, as if unwilling to resurrect the previous night's experience and when he spoke he was hesitant, appearing edgy and uneasy. He kept his dull brown eyes on the coffee table as if he could see a vision of his dream played out there. He related it with some difficulty, but tried to portray the images, the feelings and the dismay they had caused him.

'Yeah well, it's over now mate. Forget about it,' said Nick heartily, passing back the reefer. Adam accepted it automatically and continued smoking out of habit, his mind still wallowing in turmoil. You could always rely on Nick to be rational and down to earth, but that wasn't always satisfactory.

'Yeah, but that's the thing though,' he said gravely after a minute, 'I can't get it out of my head. It's really stuck in my mind, like a memory or something, like I was actually *there*. I reckon it means something, you know? Like some karma trip? I could've inadvertently done something really bad, maybe even in a previous life and I'm subconsciously punishing myself to alleviate the guilt.'

'Nah, bollocks!' responded Nick in a light-hearted tone. He was of the opinion that Adam had a tendency to distort the interpretation of his experiences, thinking that it was amazing what some people would believe given the right combination of superstition, gullibility and wishful thinking. 'You probably just ate too much fucking cheese or something before going to bed, right?' he added.

'No, I didn't though,' asserted Adam fervently and passing the last of the smoke to Nick. 'Maybe something's happening in my charts at the moment, some astrological shift, you know? You remember that planetary alignment two years ago? That was when I broke my leg after Julia dumped me.'

'Well, you know I don't believe any of that shit,' stated Nick unemotionally. He only trusted proven facts in his view of the world. He never read fiction, considering novels to be merely "story books" but could spend hours scrutinising volumes related to engineering, mechanics or science. 'Stuff happens man - that's life,' he continued, 'you've got to accept it, deal with it and then move on. Your problem is you're too fucking *cerebral* - you start to psychoanalyse everything and it'll fuck you up, right? You'll end up like Acid Mick if you're not careful.' He stubbed out the roach as he spoke, each word emitting a puff of smoke. 'Julia dumped you because she couldn't handle your paranoia and you broke your leg because you fell off your fucking bike when you got rat-arsed trying to drown your sorrows. End of.'

Noticing Adams doleful expression he added, 'Tell you what mate - roll up another doobie. I've just scored some amazing green - it's crystallised buds from those er..., hydroponic plants, you know – all organic too.'

'Oh right, yeah I've heard about that,' said Adam, 'isn't it grow in that New Age community on the Isle of Wight with a spiritual approach, like everything done mindfully and consciously with heart and soul?'

'Well I don't know about that, man,' said Nick, 'I'm all for the chemical-free methods and everything and if it's grown and cured properly it'll be fucking good weed, but I don't reckon they can make it any better by loving it to bits or sticking it up some hippie's arse while he's meditating! What I *can* guarantee is that this will totally mellow you out, right?' He rummaged in the bureau drawer and pulled out a tobacco tin decorated with cannabis leaf design.

'Here,' he said, offering it to Adam, 'smoke some of that, put on some Steve Hillage or something and just chill for a bit while I pop down the corner shop for some biccies.'

As Nick pulled his timeworn leather jacket over his t-shirt and headed out the door, Adam did as was suggested, reflecting that you could always rely on Nick to calm him down or straighten him out. Lying back on the sofa and deeply inhaling the sweet, satisfying smoke, he let the music massage his mind.

Five minutes later, feeling considerably more relaxed and immersed in following the spiralling notes of the familiar tunes as colourful patterns in his mind, he had forgotten that Lynn was at home. Consequently he was startled when her sleepy voice called 'Nick love, make us a cuppa,' and even more astonished when her naked figure appeared through the bedroom door.

'Oh, hi Adam,' she said, smiling sweetly, 'I didn't know you was 'ere.'

Adam sat bolt upright and gawped momentarily at her luscious, honey-coloured curves exclaiming 'Shit!' before quickly looking away mortified. 'Oops, er, sorry…' he muttered lamely, uncomfortable with embarrassment though secretly thrilled to have glimpsed Lynn's gorgeous body.

'It's O.K. Adam,' she reassured him lightly and amused by his discomfort, 'Put the kettle on will you while I just get dressed, yeah?'

She reappeared moments later clad simply in a pink tie-died t-shirt and baggy orange trousers. To Adam she looked every bit the Turkish princess she claimed was in her ancestry, despite the fact that her uncombed raven-black hair hung in greasy rat-tails around her face. Her dark indigo, almond-shaped eyes seemed to him to glow with an alluring and lustful invitation, but he knew it was just his imagination re-interpreting reality in an attempt to fulfil his desires.

'Blimey, you're up and about early ain't you?' she remarked, having glanced at the clock and noticing there was still an hour until midday. 'We don't often see you much before lunchtime!'

Despite her intelligence and good looks, Lynn had never attempted to refine the North London accent she grew up with and even though she excelled at physics and maths at school, seemingly without effort and much to the annoyance of her patronising teachers, she spurned further education as a waste of time. She saw no reason for it and didn't care whether or not anyone else judged her – that was *their* problem; one of her favourite quotes was, "What other people think of me is none of my business." She *had* managed a year at Art College, but that was mostly for a laugh. As far as Lynn was concerned she painted for her own enjoyment, not so that some pretentious psuedo-intellectual twat could criticise and dissect her technique or interpret the inner workings of her soul, claiming to know how she was commenting on some colossal social defects in twenty-first century society.

Adam quickly overcame his embarrassment thanks to Lynn's easy manner, but still held a mental image of her unclothed to cherish in future moments. Having made the tea, he told her about his dream. She rolled a joint whilst listening sympathetically.

'Blimey, that sounds horrible,' she consoled, crumbling some resin onto the line of teased-out tobacco, 'what do you think it means? Is there something bothering you or something? Have you been like, arguing with your dad again or have the social been giving you hassle?'

'No, nothing like that,' replied Adam, 'it wasn't like a normal dream anyway, it felt way too real, almost like experiencing a particularly vivid memory. I thought it might be past life stuff or something.'

Lynn considered this. He watched as she deftly rolled the spliff between her fingers and licked the gummed edge with the tip of her tongue and then moistened her lips. Yearning for her was now such a habitual part of his nature that a tingle went down his spine and prickled his loins. He took a deep breath and forced himself to look out the window.

'Could be....' she granted, 'What's happening in your chart at the moment?' She tore off a piece of card from an empty tampon packet and rolled it into a roach, which she then poked into the end of the joint. Holding the paper at the other end she shook it to compact the contents, twisted and tore off the surplus.

'Well...' Adam began, about to confess that this was not the first time he had suffered these nightmares, but at that point the door swung open and Nick bustled cheerily in.

'I come bearing munchies!' he proclaimed grandly, dumping a heap of biscuit packets on the table, ' 'allo darlin'!' he added giving Lynn a hug and squeezing her buttocks as she stood to greet him.

'Aren't I the luckiest bloke on earth?' he said rhetorically, his face beaming with a wide self-satisfied smile. Adam secretly agreed but kept his thoughts to himself.

'I've got to get something more healthy inside me before I tuck into those,' Lynn asserted indicating the biscuits with a wave of her hand. She lit up, inhaled the smoke deeply with the practiced ease of a regular stoner and said, 'I'm gonna get myself some muesli. More tea?'

'Coffee please,' replied Adam.

'Yeah, me too love,' agreed Nick, settling comfortably into his scruffy, yielding recliner and giving a satisfied sigh, 'and give us a toke on that number will you?'

'Hang on a minute, I've only just lit it!' she protested, 'give us a chance, yeah?'

Lynn took another couple of puffs then passed it over to Nick before heading off to the kitchen. He paused briefly to draw on the spliff and then exhaled as he spoke.

'So Adam,' he said though the emerging cloud, 'what happened at your grilling with The Department of Swindling Scumbags then?'

Adam groaned.

'Bastards have booked me on one of those compulsory back-to-work schemes. They said I wasn't looking hard enough for a job to deserve my dole money. So, I've got to go or I lose my benefit.'

'Fuckers,' sympathised Nick, 'What about the doctor? Couldn't you convince him you were mental?'

'No. He said paranoia wasn't enough to persuade him I was mad. I reckon he thought I was putting it on so I could stay signed on.'

'Well, he was right there,' said Nick, grinning.

'Maybe,' sighed Adam, 'Anyway, I'm not paranoid, there really *are* people out there watching me, I'm sure of it!'

'Don't be a plonker!' recommended Nick, 'What the fuck would they want to watch *you* for anyway, whoever *they* are?' He passed the joint over.

'Ta,' said Adam, accepting it, 'I reckon they know I suspect them, you know, government secret services and the alien conspiracy? All that stuff about the cover-up at Roswell, the crop circles, those ancient ruins too advanced even for modern man to make…I've been looking it up on the Internet, subscribing to underground magazines… I reckon they follow anyone who's getting close to the truth to make sure they don't spill the beans. They'll have my profile anyway from all that business with my professor from uni.'

'Not all that crap again!' mocked Nick scornfully, 'you *are* fucking mad! Go back to the doctor and tell him all that…on second thoughts, you'd better not, they'll put you in the loony bin! That stuff with your prof' was years ago anyway and he was bonkers too!'

Lynn reappeared with the coffee.

'What you need Adam,' she advised through a mouthful of muesli, 'is a good holiday, yeah? You know, like totally get out of the city for a bit, back to nature and all that. It'd be good for you, help you relax.'

'You're probably right,' he admitted dolefully, 'I'd love to, but I can't afford it.'

He sat with a glum face whilst they drank their coffee and ate biscuits, pondering his misfortune and slowly getting more stoned. After a few minutes' reflection Nick's face lit up.

'Tell you what,' he declared triumphantly, 'me and Lynn are getting a budget flight to Poland next month, you know, hire a car, check out the mountains, go camping in the woods, that sort of thing, right?. Why don't you come with us? You'd be welcome mate.'

'I told you - I can't afford it,' he replied dejectedly.

'It's really fucking cheap just after Easter though, right?' responded his friend. 'The holidays are just over, it's a long time to the summer – they're desperate to get people on those planes!'

'Have you forgotten what it's like surviving on the dole?' countered Adam, exasperated, 'they don't even give you enough to cover the bills, let alone foreign holidays – even if they *are* cheap.'

'Oh yeah, sorry mate.' Nick's wages as a mechanic were quite adequate for his needs and Lynn was working too. He thought for a moment longer.

'Have you still got that old Gibson bass?' he enquired.

'Yeah,' replied Adam, 'but what's that got to do with it?'

'Well you never play the fucking thing do you?' stated Nick. 'It's a rare vintage that and I know a guy who's looking for one. I reckon you could get five hundred quid for it, easy, maybe even six. That'll be more than enough.'

'I don't know…' responded Adam uncertainly, 'I thought I might take it up again one day…'

'Bollocks! You've been saying that ever since I met you, that must be five years and you've shown no sign of doing it. Flog it mate and have a fucking good holiday! What do you say?'

Adam thought for a minute. He could certainly do with a break and to get away somewhere different, especially if he was going to have to survive a job-dodgers' punishment scheme. He had to admit that Nick was right - he was unlikely to play the instrument again. He looked up at Lynn, seeking her approval. She nodded, smiling.

'Come on, Adam,' she urged, 'it'll be great, yeah? You *are* our best mate after all.'

'O.K. then,' he relented, a happy grin uncharacteristically creasing his face, 'I'll do it! I'll sell the bass and come on holiday!'

'Yay!' cried his friends in unison.

#

Rhona gaped at Charlie who had backed unsteadily into Flora's chair.

'What do mean you've dreamed about this box?' she asked incredulously, 'how could you have dreamed about this box? You've never seen it before!'

'I don't know,' he replied, disconcerted and feeling a little shaky, 'I'm as baffled as you are – worried actually – this is a bit too weird for me. I've never been one to attach any significance to dreams. I don't know how to deal with this.'

'It's pretty creepy, I'll give you that,' muttered Rhona, 'especially with that character from the bloody "Adams Family" coming in........Do you want to leave it then?'

'Leave what?' asked Charlie, confused.

'The *job* Charlie.'

'Oh, er, yeah,' he replied vaguely, 'for now, at least. I'll need to think about it...talk to Bess, you know, um about the overtime....and the dream.' He paused and stared at the wall for a moment as if lost in thought.

'Can I tell you tomorrow?' he asked.

'Is that long enough?'

'Er, end of the week then?'

'O.K.,' agreed Rhona, 'let me know at the end of the week.'

'Right,' he said and stood to leave.

'And let me know if you have any more strange dreams,' she added.

'Oh. Yeah. Sure.'

That afternoon Charlie was so preoccupied that he was hardly able to concentrate.

'Charlie?' coaxed Rowan the third time his voice trailed off in mid sentence, 'you're not quite here are you?'

'What? Oh, um sorry Rowan,' he responded distantly, and then perked up as if suddenly becoming aware of his surroundings. 'Er, yes I am a little distracted actually. Something on my mind. Do you mind if we leave this til tomorrow? I think I'll knock off early.'

'Sure, no problem' she answered cheerfully, always happy for an excuse to take a break, even though she quite enjoyed her job. However, she'd never known Charlie to be like this before. He was usually so focused and dedicated to the work, but it was quite clear that this afternoon he needed some time to think things through.

Cycling home, habitually following his well travelled route, Charlie pondered the significance of anonymous clients with a cadaverous retainer commissioning a casket *exactly* like the one in his dream and specifying that it must be him who make it. Always eager to accept coincidence as an explanation of bizarre happenings, he couldn't quite reconcile that view with the present circumstances. He had to grudgingly admit that there was something very out of the ordinary going on. He was extremely uncomfortable with that thought. Entering the cottage kitchen, he was greeted by Nimbus, their ginger tomcat always chancing his luck at an extra feed, and the welcome aroma of baking bread – one of his favourite smells. It got his mouth watering immediately.

'Bess?' he called noticing her absence from the room and hearing the sound of Nick Harper's "Blood Songs" in the distance. It reminded him of Luke – it was an album he had introduced them too – and he wondered how he was getting on.

'I'm on the 'pooter, ' she called from the office along the corridor.

He followed the music, now discerning the tapping of a keyboard, entered the room and kissed her affectionately on the cheek.

'You're home early,' she observed but continuing to type. He never understood how she could talk and type simultaneously.

'Aye, I'll tell you about it when you've finished,' he said, 'what are you up to?' He peered over her shoulder at the screen.

'Oh, just some emails for the yoga class,' she replied, 'I'll be with you in a minute.'

'Anything from Luke?'

'No, he only messaged us last week.'

'O.K. I'll put the kettle on.'

Whilst Charlie was making the drinks the ever-hopeful Nimbus rubbed himself against his legs.

'It's too early, Nimbo mate,' he told the cat and put it out of the door saying, 'go and do your job – catch a mouse!'

Five minutes later Bess joined him in the kitchen and they embraced familiarly but eagerly. It was great, Charlie often thought, that they could still wholeheartedly enjoy the physical side of their relationship after so many years together. He knew of other couples who admitted to going for *months* sometimes without making love. He couldn't understand how it could come to that.

'How was your day?' she enquired conversationally, walking over to the Rayburn. 'Did you get sent home early for bad behaviour?' she added with a wry smile whilst stirring a simmering pot on the hotplate.

'Work was O.K.' he said, 'but I've been a bit preoccupied by that dream last night, especially since Rhona showed me the new job that's come in.'

'Why? What's that got to do with it?' she asked looking round.

'It's an intricately carved gilded sarcophagus,' he replied, 'just like the one in my dream – identical.'

'Jesus, that's weird!' exclaimed Bess.

'You said it. I really don't know *what* to think.'

He then related Rhona's account of the visit she'd had from the strange old man the previous day.

'But how could that happen? How could you dream of that casket the day before you'd seen it? And what is it anyway – some kind of coffin?' Bess was nonplussed. She absent-mindedly stirred the soup again.

'Buggered if I know, though it looks like one,' he commented and then, in a half-hearted attempt to lighten the mood, added in a jokey voice, 'I've got a bad feeling about this.' Then he stood up and started pacing the room.

'Well, you don't have to take the job do you?' she asked.

'No, but the money is *very* good so I told Rhona I'd think about it and talk to you. But if I don't...or even if I do, what's going to happen about these dreams? If any more bits of them start cropping up in real life, it's going to do my head in.'

'I don't know, Charlie. Maybe it was just a one off.' She inspected the bread in the oven and then considering it not to be ready, closed the stove's door. 'There's no guarantee that it will happen again,' she added uncertainly. She went over to him and gave him a long tender hug.

'I'm a bit scared, Bess,' he admitted, 'nothing like this has ever happened to me before.'

'I know,' she said, 'it *is* a bit freaky, but I'm sure everything will be fine.' She wasn't certain she believed it though, or even had any grounds to assume that this would be the case, but she felt it was the right thing to say. They stood quietly in each other's arms for a few moments and then Bess slowly pulled away.

'Why don't you phone your brother?' suggested Bess, 'He's always talking about dreams and bizarre experiences.'

'Aye, he certainly does that, right enough, but he's bonkers, you know that,' replied Charlie, '*and* he's stoned all the time – he's in cloud cuckoo land. He'll probably say I've contracted some alien virus that's expanded my mental powers or something.'

Bess smiled but persevered. 'You never know,' she said, 'he may have some insight into this – it's a pretty surreal situation after all.'

'Aye, maybe you're right,' he conceded reluctantly, 'it's about time I called him anyway – we haven't spoken for months.'

'If that doesn't help, Rhona knows a dream therapist in Dingwall who might be able to throw some light on it.'

'A dream therapist? I don't even know what that is. Hmm, that doesn't really sound like my cup of tea anyway –I think I'll leave that for now.'

'You never know until you try it.'

'That's true,' he admitted, 'but I'll speak to Adam first.'

Bess shrugged. 'O.K.' she said, but then a minute later added, 'look, I can cancel the yoga class tonight if you want me to stay with you,' she offered.

'Er….no, it's alright, I'll be fine. But thanks,' he said knowing that she would not have made the offer lightly. She was very loyal to her class and would only ever call it off in extreme circumstances.

'I don't mind. Really.'

'Thanks, but it's O.K. You go, I'll phone Adam.'

#

Even if the sun could penetrate the grubby window through the curtain of ivy and layer of city grime, it would do little to enliven the cluttered low-ceilinged room. The walls had been painted dark green a decade previously and the shabby furniture was virtually hidden beneath the covering of scattered and heaped possessions. Only one seat of the three-piece suite was free for its intended purpose and it faced the corner that was occupied by a dormant television with a dusty screen. Under the window, Adam flicked through a pile of books acquired from the library that morning. All afternoon he had sat at the scratched Formica-topped table in his basement flat scrutinizing their pages. He had just put on a CD of Ludovico Einaudi as pleasing and relaxing background music but now realised that he was tensely hunched, squinting over the text in the diminishing light, so he switched on the angle poise lamp. Closing the cover of "Dreams or Visions? – The Subconscious Manifestation of Psychic Phenomena" he sighed, unhappy with the day's findings. Picking up the next book from the pile, he read the title: "Dreamworld – The True Meaning of Your Inner Reality". He frowned disapprovingly, but turned to the index nonetheless. Five minutes later, this volume was also discarded. The following tome was the thickest yet. It claimed to be "The *Complete* Encyclopaedia of Dreams". He doubted it and rejected it out of hand. *No*, he thought, *I need a tea break*. He rubbed his tired sore eyes, rose from his chair stiffly, arched his back and then stretched his arms ceiling wards, yawning. With shuffling feet he weaved his familiar route to the cramped kitchenette where he proceeded to make his drink.

So far he hadn't managed to come up with a satisfactory explanation of his dream. It reminded him uncomfortably of some he'd had a few years back – so real, so disturbing and so much like a memory of an actual experience that he felt he *had* to understand. One book postulated that fighting usually symbolizes anger and confusion that comes about in times of change. If nothing is changing in your life, it may be a clue that a change is needed or that you want to change internally. Well, that would require some deep self-analysis that he did not feel up to at the moment. Why was it that the times when such contemplation would be most useful were just the times when one felt least inclined to ruminate? Another volume had hypothesized that visions of brutality predicted a revisit to scenes of childhood. Why that should be, he couldn't imagine. He remembered having a relatively happy time as a boy, although the family moved a little too often for his liking for he had not been happy with changing schools. It seemed that once he had finally settled in a new place and made friends it was time to move on and say goodbye. However, he had always had his brother to keep him company in each new place and he was grateful for that. That reminded him that he hadn't heard from Charlie for a while and wondered how he was. He's probably all right, he thought; he's made a pretty good life for himself up there in the Highlands with Bess. He was about to select some more music when a sudden ring tone startled him from his thoughts. The kettle had boiled unnoticed, so he had yet to make the tea. He walked over to the bedside table and picked up his mobile phone. Seeing his brother's name on the display he answered straight away.

'Hey Charlie!' he chirped happily, 'that's weird, I was just thinking about you. How's it going? How are you?'

'Och, no bad, you know…fine…O.K., kind of plodding along as usual. And you?'

'Er, cool. Yeah, could be worse. Better than most. It's good to hear your voice. How's life up in bonny Scotland? What are you up to these days?'

'Oh, still carving away, you know.'

'Still enjoying it?'

'Aye. Yeah of course. I love it, the dragons, the fairies, bits of gilding – it's different every time.'

'So how's Bess? And Luke, How's he getting on in Africa?'

'Bess is very well, still teaching the yoga and growing stuff. We had a postcard from Luke last week – he says it's all going well out there. Once he got over the culture shock he really felt like he was making a difference and enjoys helping the kids. He's got a blog too, so we follow that.'

'Cool, I'll have to check it out.'

'What about you? Anything new?'

Adam sat on his bed and sighed. 'Well, I just got hauled in by the Social to go on one of those bloody "New Start" schemes. I'm not looking forward to it, but if I don't go, they'll stop my money. It's all about making the statistics look good, they've all just got to achieve targets nowadays, not results – apart from that it's a waste of everybody's time.'

'What happened about that course you were going to apply for?' asked Charlie, 'anthropology wasn't it?'

'No - ethnology,' corrected Adam, 'and I missed the deadline for the application so it never happened.'

'God Adam, you're so untogether!' exclaimed his brother, 'you had months to get that in. Your problem is you smoke too much dope.'

'No, it's not that. I just forgot, you know. I got involved in organising a party and then the washing machine broke and flooded the flat and I had to sort that out. Before I knew it, I'd missed my chance.'

'Well Adam, there are people who go bumbling along from one day to the next just letting life happen to them and never getting anywhere and there are others who seize their chances and make things happen for them. You definitely belong in the former camp and I'm sure being stoned all the time doesn't help.'

'Oh come on Charlie, lay off!' pleaded Adam, 'and don't get all preachy on me. We haven't spoken for months and you start nagging within the first five minutes! I know you're the older brother, but we're not kids anymore. Anyway, you know it's not going to work now we're adults.'

'I seem to remember that it didn't work when we were kids either,' said Charlie wryly.

'That's true. And anyway, *you* used to be a dope smoker too.'

'Right, so I'm giving you the benefit of my experience,' Charlie professed, 'I just know that after ten years of toking I was getting paranoid and psychotic and then when I gave it up when Luke was born, I got better. I've heard other people say the same too.'

'Hey Charlie, don't lay that heavy shit on me. There's nothing worse than someone who's "seen the light" and gone all evangelical and superior. Patronising git.'

'Aye, sorry Ad,' said Charlie meekly, realising that he had been harping on a bit, 'old habits die hard eh? It's your life after all.' He paused, remembering why he had called. 'Anyway, that's not what I rang you about.' He took a moment to collect his thoughts. He was unsure how to start, in fact he felt a little foolish now, as if he had to admit some kind of weakness to his younger brother. This was not an easy thing to do for the sibling who had always been in charge or led the way in their relationship previously. 'Er, well,' he started uncertainly, 'weirdly, I wanted to talk to you about this strange dream I had last night.'

'Yeah, that *is* weird,' agreed Adam, 'I had a strange dream last night too. What was yours about?'

'Well, they're always in some kind of ancient city…' Charlie began.

'What do you mean *"always"* Charlie?' interrupted Adam.

'Well, there have been about a dozen or so over the last few weeks…'

'Oh, right. Recurring dream – far out…O.K. Then what?'

'Each time I get a little further – it starts with an erupting volcano, lava and ash and fiery rocks falling from the sky. There are people running all over the place panicking and screaming, getting hit by rocks and crushed under falling walls because there's an earthquake too - the ground's shaking violently and making buildings fall down. As if that wasn't enough, some of the people are actually attacking *each other* too. It's really horrible and scary too because I *really* feel like I'm there – it's more real than other dreams I've had.'

Adam listened with increasing amazement. 'Wow! Bloody hell, that sounds just like *my* dream….' he said.

'That is odd,' commented Charlie uneasily, 'but there's more….' He hesitated, put off by what Adam had said. He tried to collect his thoughts and put them into words. He was finding that every time he recounted the experience, he remembered more details. 'I notice an open doorway in a wall on the other side of the square and I feel drawn towards it, but until last night I never made it there – I always woke when someone grabbed my ankle or something. I stagger across the courtyard, the ground shaking like a jelly, trying to step over the dead and injured....some of them plead for my help, clawing at my legs, but I shake them off, feeling guilty even though I know there's nothing I can do to help them. I can't stop – I don't know why, but I've just *got* to get to that doorway. Then last night I did.'

'This is getting weirder and weirder,' remarked Adam nervously, 'that all kind of happened to me - I was there too! Except I was following – I saw someone go through the door ahead of me....'

'You're having me on, right?' Charlie asked apprehensively.

'Nope – I was there.'

'Bugger me, that *is* spooky,' Charlie muttered, feeling even more disconcerted, 'but hear me out, then we'll compare notes....er, I went through the doorway,' he continued, trying to focus on his story instead of yet another rather worrying coincidence, 'and down a torch lit staircase to a cellar where there was this kind of intricately carved and gilded sarcophagus on a plinth...'

'With big gemstones set into it?'

'Aye....and anyway, I went over to it and opened the lid and inside was some ancient old guy who I thought was dead but he suddenly opened his eyes and grabbed my wrist, so I screamed and woke up. It was kind of....disturbing you know, especially as it seemed so real, not like a dream at all.'

When Charlie stopped, Adam was too shaken to speak. He sat on his bed, incredulous, at the other end of the phone.

'Adam?' prompted his brother. 'Are you there?'

'What? Oh yeah.' Adam exhaled noisily, shaking his head. 'I'm blown away Charlie, I don't know what to say really,' he said, 'I mean, it's just too bloody weird you know? All of that was in *my* dream too.'

'Really? *All* of it?'

'Yep.'

'Er...,' Charlie didn't know what to say either, or think, and he was feeling a little panicky. 'Shit, this is a bit difficult to accept. So, um...you were following me?'

'Yeah – I felt I had to stop you, but I don't know why.' The details were becoming clearer to Adam now too, the more he thought about it. 'I got into that crypt place just as that guy grabbed you and then you disappeared in front of my eyes. I looked into the coffin but it was empty and I felt this awful sense of failure, you know? Like I should have got there a minute earlier and I could have saved you. Then I felt the presence of someone else in the room and this robed, hooded figure came out of the shadows. When the torchlight caught her face I saw it was a woman, middle-aged, but still quite attractive looking. I got the impression that she was really wise or something and then she smiled slightly as if to reassure me....but then the ground shook again and the ceiling cracked and bits of dust started falling from it. I freaked out, scared shitless and panicked and I ran back up the steps, but as I tried to climb them, they started moving down like an escalator – the faster I ran, the faster they moved until I got swallowed up by the ground. That's when I woke up.'

It was Charlie's turn to sit in stunned silence. 'How many times have you dreamt this?' he managed eventually.

'First time recently,' said Adam, 'but I had something similar once before – a few years ago...'

'Damn. I phoned you to get some kind of reassurance, you know? I thought you were into reading about all that kind of...weird shit and you might be able to kind of explain what it all meant. Now I'm even more worried than I was before. Do you have *any* ideas about what it might mean?'

'Er....no, not really. I got some dream books out of the library but they didn't help much. I know all this seems kind of wacky, but I've always thought that families have some kind of telepathic connection, right? Just like when you phoned – I was thinking of you at exactly the same time. It's happened with mum too. I guess the dream sharing thing must just be a more powerful manifestation of that, right?'

'Um...maybe...aye...O.K., I can just about grasp that,' accepted Charlie, 'but you haven't heard the weirdest yet. Listen to this - at work today, Rhona my boss called me into her office to show me a new job that's just come in. She felt a bit odd about it because the guy who came in was like a kind of Frankenstein character or something and his whole manner was totally weird – Jeez, I can't believe how many times I've said "weird" today...anyway she unrolled the drawings to show me the job and it was *the same box* as in the dream – *and* they wanted it gilded and set with the jewels. *Exactly* the bloody same.'

'Holy shit Charlie!'

'Precisely.'

'Wow, this is like, totally amazing,' jabbered Adam breathlessly, 'you must be developing really powerful telepathic or psychic powers or something.....you either saw into the future in your dreams or you picked up on the thoughts of those customers from the collective subconscious.....*or* they're like powerful telepaths themselves and they've been feeding stuff into your dreams or....I don't know...but *shit*, this is pretty incredible!'

'Aye, well, to tell you the truth I'm finding it all a bit too frightening actually,' Charlie confessed, 'I was hoping to find some kind of rational explanation, but there doesn't appear to be one. I'm feeling inclined to refuse this job and try to forget all about it, you know? I don't think I can handle the idea of other people messing about in my head or even me seeing into theirs.'

'I don't know about the job, Charlie, but you may not have a choice about what your subconscious is doing or what other people might be doing with it. I mean like, these dreams have come unbidden haven't they? It's not like you can control your dreams or anything…or not yet anyway….Wow! This could be an amazing opportunity to hone your psychic abilities, you know, why not embrace it and explore it. You could end up doing some really far out stuff! Come to think of it, so could I….' Adam seemed far less perturbed than Charlie felt, which is what he'd expected, but he had hoped to find more reassurance by speaking to his brother.

'Come on Adam, you know me. I don't want to do "really far out stuff". I just want to get back to my normal, happy life. I've never been into all that paranormal crap like you have – I've never believed *any* of it to tell you the truth.' He was becoming more and more perturbed and starting to gabble. 'There must be some other explanation like a kind of hormonal or biochemical imbalance brought on by something like, I don't know, like pollutants in the environment or in food – there's all sorts of shit out there – even what they put in the water, for Christ's sake…I could get an allergy test….or maybe I've got a brain tumour or I'm going schizophrenic or something…maybe I'll go to the doctor and ask for a brain scan…'

'Whoa, slow down there, bruv,' urged Adam, 'you're sounding a bit panicky now. I reckon you should think about it for a few days, you know, let it sink in. Like I said, this could be great if you just chill out – you might be able to do some amazingly cool stuff if you tried - like, I don't know, er….avoid a lot of trouble…if there's muggers on the street or someone's trying to sell you dodgy goods…or if the pigs are coming round to bust you…'

'Come on Adam, none of that's in my life, nor is it likely to be living where I do. But you're right, I should think it over, let it sink in and see if I can make sense of it *and* see if anything else happens.'

'Let me know how it goes will you?'

'Aye, sure. And thanks for talking me through it…although I'm not sure it helped. If anything, I'm even more worried now.' He paused, took a couple of deep breaths and decided to change the subject. '....um, anyway, anything else happening with you?'

Adam took a moment to realign his wits. 'Oh yeah, I nearly forgot – I'm going to Poland!'

'What?!'

'Yeah, my friends Nick and Lynn were going anyway, so they invited me along – two week's holiday - catching the sights, you know?'

'That's great Adam, but are they paying for you? You haven't got any money.'

'Have now. Or will have soon anyway. I'm selling that old Gibson bass I've had for years – I should get five or six hundred quid for it – it's a classic limited edition - very sought after.'

'Shame to lose it though.'

'Not really. In a way it was a shame to have it sitting there unused, a nice instrument like that. At least this way it'll get played. I realised I was very unlikely to play it again – I was never any good at it and anyway I couldn't be arsed with all the practice. '

'I'm with you there – the same happened with me and the guitar. So, when are you going?'

'Next month some time.'

'Cool.'

'Yeah, I'm really looking forward to it – I haven't been away on holiday for donkey's years.'

'Aye, it'll be nice right enough – spring flowers and everything. Are you going to the countryside or the city?'

'Countryside mostly I expect, camping, walking in the forests and mountains and all that stuff - Nick's a keen bird watcher. We'll probably pop into a few towns or villages, markets, see some castles, that kind of thing you know – a bit of culture.'

'Sounds great. Look, I'd better go now. It's been really good talking to you. Let me know if you have any more dreams about that box or those ruins, or any other revelations about what it might mean…but anyway, if I don't speak to you before you go, have a great holiday!'

'Cheers. Take care – love to Bess.'

CHAPTER THREE

Rhona was at Bess' yoga class so Rowan sat alone in her bedroom listening to the latest release by "Gogol Bordello" on her mp3 player. Cross-legged on the bed she was wearing jeans and a black t-shirt decorated with the image of a fairy caught in a spider web crying tears of blood. She was bent over a sketchpad in her lap and was carefully drawing with a pencil. She felt more relaxed and freer just to be herself when she was on her own. Ever since she was a small child she felt somehow different to those around her. Whilst at school her numerous efforts to try to fit in, as her aunt urged her to be more outgoing and make friends, just met with derision and ridicule from the other children. Even though she didn't *look* that unusual at the time, her peers seemed to be able to sense some peculiarity and used it as a motive to alternately taunt or ignore her. She knew what they were thinking though. Their own fear of rejection caused them to attack the weak or different from the safety of their cowardly mobs. Sometimes she would hide behind the bike sheds at break time or lock herself in a toilet cubicle, where in order to diminish her feelings of fear and despair, she would bite hard into her arm or punch herself in the head. Although this didn't make the problems go away, it was a part of her life she could control and it allowed her to have an outlet for the build up of emotional pressure. The pain was also a distraction, giving her something else upon which to focus. Nevertheless she had usually managed to find one or two easy-going or kind-hearted individuals, oblivious to the influence of crowd mentality, who became her companions for a while and saved her from complete unhappiness. Now that she had left school, she had a small circle of friends with whom she met up on weekends to listen to favourite CDs, share ideas or discus issues that concerned them. Even so, Rowan still found on occasion that she had to leave early, especially if a discussion threatened to turn into an argument, oversensitive as she was to the thoughts and feelings saturating the atmosphere.

She had tried speaking to her mother about it once, but it seemed to make her uncomfortable - she hurriedly changed the subject and then, soon after made her excuses and left the room. Rosalind had become pregnant with Rowan aged fifteen after a drunken one-night-stand at a party and always felt too young to be a mother. Mostly she abandoned the care of her baby to her parents or her twin sister Rhona, who ended up spending so much of her time child minding that she missed out on most of the opportunities for boyfriends and fun. At the age of seventeen Rosalind married a wealthy man twice her age who was very happy to find such a young and nubile partner. He seemed willing to treat Rowan as his own daughter and thus she came to call him "daddy" for a while. The relationship was doomed to fail though, as inevitably he sought to be the authority figure to his rebellious and headstrong young wife. He might as well have tried to hang on to the tail of a comet. After the divorce, Rosalind bought a house in the Highlands with Rhona, using the money they had inherited from their maternal grandfather. She then dedicated her life to building up her career and subsequently her business as a clothing designer. Consequently, she spent most of her time attending fashion shows in Europe and North America or working in her London office, so Rowan rarely saw her. Even when she did return for a fleeting weekend she seemed to want to substitute love and attention with lavish and superficial gifts. Remaining aloof, she would plead fatigue. 'It's been *such* a mad season darling, I've been rushed off my feet'. Or she would go out socialising with old friends. 'I simply *must* see Monica, she's such a sweetie and I haven't seen her for absolutely *ages*.'

As a result, Rhona had become a substitute; a sort of foster mother combined with an aunt and a friend, yet so much more than that and Rowan had a great affection for her. She was not judgemental, respectful of Rowan's needs, willing to listen and fun to be with. In a way she was like an older sister but without the sibling rivalry, so they had become very close.

To begin with, coming to work at her aunt's workshop had been particularly challenging. It was her first and only place of employment, so being in close proximity to five men was initially a bit of a shock, especially as her father had left the home when she was so young. It was extremely unsettling to notice that they were all surreptitiously appraising her and Rhona's bodies but she soon came to realise that this was actually quite normal for most men she encountered and knew she was in no danger from them. When Grant came however, it was different. He had had numerous liaisons with different women and saw each one as a challenge, something to conquer and he was *literally* only after one thing. He would boast to the other guys that his "fuck 'em and chuck 'em" technique was the best way to approach relationships – keeping it simple to avoid all those "emotional complications". Every time he looked at Rowan, she felt him undressing her with his eyes. Although she couldn't be certain that he would ever actually try anything, she knew he had imagined it, so she didn't want to give him a chance. Accordingly, she avoided him as much as possible and made sure they were never alone together. She had once broached the subject with Rhona, who whilst sympathetic, was more pragmatic and at any rate had not witnessed any of his lecherous looks or lewd remarks, so assumed that Rowan's inexperience, immaturity and imagination were exaggerating the situation. Her aunt believed that to get anywhere in this world as a woman you had to harden yourself to sexism and the mindless leering of some men, which no amount of legislation could prevent.

'There will always be some tosser like Grant around,' she had said matter-of-factly, 'so you've got to learn to deal with it. It's a kind of bullying, so like any bully, if they know they've got to you, they'll do it all the more – it gives them a sense of power. That's what they crave, because really they're basically insecure, so lashing out at others makes them feel safe – you know, like "attack is the best form of defence". Don't let them know it affects you, just ignore them or give as good as you get. Then you're using their own weakness against them and it totally disarms them.'

Rowan knew her aunt was right, but she just wasn't cut out for it herself – she just felt she didn't have the self-confidence to carry it off convincingly.

'As long as Grant only makes occasional idiotic comments, there's not a lot I can do,' said Rhona, 'I can't sack him for what you imagine he's thinking. Don't worry though, the workshop's full of people and I will make sure I never team you up with him. If however, he makes persistent and/or unacceptable remarks witnessed by other staff members or if he dares to touch you, *then* I can do something about it.'

It was all right for Rhona. She was a strong willed, independent, assertive woman. But Rowan felt young, vulnerable, timid and insecure; she didn't know how to be confident and self-assured. There were times when in her helplessness and frustration, she resorted to her old habit of self-harm. Sometimes she imagined that she was hurting Grant instead, thereby making the process more satisfying. Over the years she had devised ways to keep her coping mechanism a secret from Rhona, knowing that it would worry her. Certainly, since she had been old enough to bathe herself and then grown out of swimming lessons, she just had to make sure her scars were small and covered by clothing. At the moment though, the situation seemed to have settled down. Rowan managed to steer clear of him most of the time and she did really enjoy the work. She particularly enjoyed Charlie's company. She felt totally safe with him. He treated her with respect, was never patronising, had a dry wit, a subtle sense of humour and only had eyes for Bess.

When the music finished she took her headphones off and looked at her sketchpad. She had drawn from memory a copy of the unusual casket from the plans she had perused in the office at work when Rhona had nipped out, except she had coloured in the gold and fitted large gemstones into the sockets. She had perceived the unease in both Charlie and Rhona regarding the curious nature of the job. Although she was more accepting than most to the occurrence of what appeared to be in the realm of the bizarre, she nonetheless felt uncomfortable about the old man who had brought the drawings. There was something about him that sent a shiver down her spine. The way he walked through the workshop, totally expressionless and detached had left her cold and uneasy. He hadn't made eye contact but she could detect a sinister intensity in his focus that led her to believe he would embrace any methods necessary to fulfil his purpose.

She stood, dropping the pad onto the bed and walked over to her room's large single window through which the evening sun was brightening the untidy bookshelves. Old school books, C.S.Lewis and Harry Potter leaned against more recent acquisitions: Robin Hobb's "Liveship" trilogy, the "Twilight Saga", Terry Pratchett books and some graphic novels. Looking down into the garden below she noticed their cat, Goethe, stalking a pied wagtail on the lawn. Rowan was a vegan and couldn't bear it when he brought in the twitching half dead body of a small frail creature to play with. She knew he couldn't help himself, it was in his nature to be a hunter after all, but he was well fed and rarely ate more than a mouthful of his victims. Suddenly the cat yelped in surprise and leaped in the air, turning to see what had poked him from behind. Noticing nothing, he looked again for his prey but it had taken flight, startled by his noise and movement. Seemingly unperturbed, he sat and began to lick his paw nonchalantly. Rowan chuckled to herself, amused by Goethe's attempt at feigning indifference.

#

Charlie sat on the sofa, gazing into space and lost in thought. The television was on, showing the late evening news but he was oblivious to it. After his phone call to Adam he was even more disturbed than he had been before. How could his brother be having such similar dreams? He had never heard of that happening to anyone else. After all the years he had shared with Bess they could finish each other's sentences, often correctly; one would say something that the other had just been thinking; they could sense each other's moods and knew when to comfort unspoken distress, but they had never to his knowledge shared a dream and nor had anything that had first appeared in a dream then manifested in real life. That was the most worrying aspect – not just as it was outside his normal experience but also because it opened the door for other things to come through. He needed to know how it could happen and how it was possible for Adam to also have such a comparable experience. In fact it seemed more like they were both players *within* the same dream rather than actually dreaming the same thing. Floundering in his mystification and anxiety, he was unaware that Bess had returned. As she was unsure whether or not he was awake, she had tiptoed softly along the passage and quietly eased open the door. Charlie was jerked form his reverie, startled by her sudden appearance.

'Gordon Bennet!' he exclaimed, 'You nearly gave me a heart attack.'

'Sorry love,' she said guiltily, 'I thought you might have nodded off.' She leant down and pecked him affectionately on the lips. 'Are you O.K.?'

'Um, yes. Just a bit preoccupied with this dream and casket stuff,' he replied using the remote control to turn off the television, 'I rang Adam and he'd had a similar dream too.'

'Really?' said Bess, 'You're joking!'

She sat on the edge of the couch and stared at him, openmouthed.

'Aye. And he seemed to think I was undergoing some kind of "psychic awakening" or something – you know what he's like.' Charlie sighed heavily. 'I think I'm going to have to turn this job down,' he said, 'I know the money would come in handy for the New Zealand trip, but it's just too weird, I don't think I can handle it. But I *will* ask

Rhona about her dream therapist friend – maybe I'll get some help there.'

Passing through the sun-silvered landscape the next morning, Charlie was a little more aware of his surroundings. Surprisingly he had managed to get a good sleep the night before. Bess had given him a massage to relieve some of the tension that had somehow transferred from his mind to his muscles, arising as tight knots in his back, neck and shoulders. They had then made love and he fell into a deep, calm and mercifully dreamless slumber. As he freewheeled down the gentle brae, he could hear the mellifluous voices of skylarks twittering above, staking their claim to an unmarked patch of turf in the pasture below. There were other birds singing too, but apart from the characteristic wheeping of the lapwings he was unable to identify them from their calls alone, unlike his grandfather who had been a true countryman. Having grown up on or around Aberdeenshire farms as part of a travelling family in the 1920s, Billy MacKay had learned with his six siblings to supplement their meagre diet from the surrounding countryside. He had learned the calls of all the birds, the tracks of the animals and acquired a deep respect for the complex web of nature not often found amongst the landowners, who mostly seemed to regard it as their right to exploit or subdue the natural world. Billy had passed this outlook on to the young Charlie when he came to stay every summer holiday, who was consequently always happy out in the country, but somehow never managed to master discerning the differences between all the avian voices. Maybe it was because he was tone deaf: he certainly knew most of them by sight, being familiar with their markings, outlines and flight characteristics. Adam wasn't so attracted to bird watching. He had developed an interest in wild food and learned as much as he could from their grandfather before he left home. Since then he had lived mostly in cities so hadn't had much opportunity to use his knowledge. As Charlie's thoughts fixed on his younger brother, he remembered their conversation of the previous evening and found himself fretful once more. He could neither fathom the meaning behind their shared experience nor let go of attempting to figure it out. His usual predilection for leaving the mystifying unsolved didn't seem to be satisfactory on this occasion because it was now deeply ingrained in his own personal experience. He shook his head as if this would fling the unwanted ideas out and tried to focus on the world around him. He noticed with delight that the first buds were beginning to swell slightly on the admirable wych elms that were ranked regularly along this rare stretch of Highland hedgerow. Between and beneath these worthy trees, the blackthorn bushes were already displaying their early presentation of fresh blossom. He even imagined he could smell the evaporating dew as the sun reclaimed it from the grass for the sky's benefit.

At the end of his ride, Charlie rolled into the car park and immediately noticed that Rhona's vehicle was absent. This was extraordinary because she was always the first to arrive and in the five years that he had been working there he had never known her to be late, to have a day off sick or come to think of it, to have any time off for any reason at all. He had his own key for those rare occasions when he stayed late to complete an almost finished task, so since he was the first to arrive this morning he used it now. As he pushed the door open, Brian arrived in his droning Citroen. He was followed closely by Grant who entered the gates far too quickly, skidding his car on the gravel as he braked, thereby sending up a cloud of dust. He emerged chewing gum and wearing mirror "shades".

'Wanker,' muttered Brian under his breath, shaking his head.

Removing his sunglasses, Grant perused the yard and noticed the absence of Rhona's ever-present Volks Wagon Beetle.

'Boss not here yet?' he enquired unnecessarily in his Hampshire accent. 'Bloody hell, that's a first isn't it? Maybe she's got herself a bloke at last.'

Beneath the veneer of his attempts to be jokey, it was easy to tell that Grant maintained the view that for a woman to be normal she had to be in a relationship with a man - ideally one like him. In spite of the fact that Grant's sexist banter was intended to be light-hearted, Charlie still found that it greatly annoyed him – more so than it did Rhona in fact, who was so self-assured and quick witted that such comments were usually promptly and confidently dismissed with a good-natured put-down. Such behaviour often endeared her to characters such as Grant, or at least made them view her with a grudging respect even if they couldn't understand this unusual attitude. They could take comfort in the fact that she was "one of the lads" and therefore no threat to their masculinity.

Setting out his tools for the day, Charlie guessed that Rhona must be ill and would probably phone soon to let them know. Rowan couldn't come alone as it was too far to walk and she had not yet learned to drive. Neither did she have a bicycle, generally not being at all keen on exercise. Rory breezed in next, his fresh Fifean face, or what was visible of it between his long hair and beard, beamed with his customary good morning cheer. He was followed shortly thereafter by

Dougie and Hamish. Flora did not start until ten. Whilst preparing for work the men speculated briefly about their employer's whereabouts.

Fifteen minutes later, Rhona finally arrived with Rowan trailing languorously in her wake. Rhona's face bore the signs of sleeplessness and Charlie noticed an uncharacteristically troubled look in her eyes.

'Allo allo, what's this then?' Grant piped up cheekily, making an over-exaggerated show of looking at his watch. 'Did you have one over the eight last night, or have you found yourself a lover-boy at last?'

'Both actually Grant', quipped Rhona wearily and unenthusiastically, 'I picked up a squaddie, we got rat-arsed on vodka and stayed up all night shagging like rabbits.' The atypically half-hearted and humourless tone of her response took the wind out of his sails. The exchange left his wish for what he saw as witty repartee strangely unfulfilled. He attempted an 'Oo-er,' and looked uneasily at the others but saw that they too were surprised by Rhona's lack of gusto.

She glanced briefly at Charlie.

'Will you come into the office for a minute?' she requested.

'Hey...steady on! Not had enough eh?' said Grant in a pathetic attempt to regain what he saw as the humorous high-ground. To his additional discomfort this didn't raise the hoped for laugh and everyone ignored him. Rowan kept her eyes lowered and took her place reluctantly at her workbench. Charlie followed Rhona, both curious and perturbed by her behaviour. He had never seen her like this before. She had a troubled, almost anxious expression and lacked her usual level-headed business-like manner. Shutting the door he faced the desk behind which she had installed herself in a chair.

'What's up?' he asked, seating himself slowly on the opposite side of the desk as he watched her face for any clues. She hesitated and kept her eyes averted. He could tell that she was unsure how to begin.

'Er... did you have another dream last night?' she ventured hesitantly.

'No,' he replied, 'in fact, I managed to get a good night's sleep for the first time in ages. Why? What's happened?'

She ignored his question and asked him another.

'I know I said you could let me know at the end of the week but did you decide yet whether or not you wanted to take on that casket job?' she enquired.

'Ah, well, aye...um,' he started uncertainly, 'Actually, I decided to phone my brother to talk about it because he's a bit of a.....um, hippy-type, so I thought he'd know about dreams, but er, it seems he had a dream almost identical to mine, which totally freaked me out, so I decided I don't want to touch that job with a barge-pole.'

'O.K.' commented Rhona evenly, meeting his eyes at last, 'that *is* extremely odd, but you had better prepare yourself because it's about to get stranger.'

Charlie nodded wordlessly.

'*I* dreamed about that casket last night too,' she stated.

Charlie's heart leapt into his mouth, but he managed to control himself using the force of reason.

'Aye, well...I expect it's because we'd been talking about it,' he said feigning an air of confidence, 'and then I told you about my dream and it must have kind of planted itself in your subconscious or something.'

'I'd like to think that was the case, Charlie,' she said, 'but this didn't feel like a normal dream. It almost felt like I was...' She hesitated nervously, '"...taken" somewhere...and it was like a message or something. It was *so* vivid, not at all dreamlike.'

'Do you want to tell me about it?' he asked.

'No, I'd rather forget all about it, but I think I should.'.

Rhona looked at the desktop and paused to collect her thoughts. She slowly traced a scratch in the surface with her forefinger.

'Right, here goes,' she began, taking a deep breath, 'I dreamt I woke up in this huge, plush bedroom in a mansion or something. It was so tangible, I thought I really had woken up, you know? I felt the velvet drapes on the four-poster, the thick warm carpet, smelt the roses in a vase on the table. I noticed the wallpaper, the dark oak panelling, the William Morris curtains – even the immaculately tended gardens out of the window. Then the door opened and that same guy came in - you know, the one who brought the drawings – and he told me to follow him. So I got up off the bed...,' at this point she stood and started pacing the office, '....I was in pyjamas just like at home....and I followed him along a lavishly decorated hallway hung with old portraits like in an old stately home. He took me into another room and there were two weird old men, really ancient looking and almost totally identical – they must have been twins or something. I remember it being stifling in there – really hot and airless – and these guys were sitting next to a blazing fire. On the mantel piece was a row of big gemstones or something.

'"Ah Miss Flemming," said one, "so nice of you to join us."

'Then the other one spoke, though his voice sounded the same, "We brought you here to convince you of the importance of the commission we have given to you."

'They took it in turns to speak a sentence, almost like they were just one person or something. I was too shocked to speak – how did they know my name?

'"You see Miss Flemming," said the first one, "tomorrow, your employee, Mr. MacKay will tell you that he has decided not to undertake this assignment and we will need you to persuade him otherwise."

'Then the other one spoke again, "It is too late for us to find anyone else now and to be honest, there are not very many craftsmen left in this country with the necessary level or combination of skills."

'I told them to hold their horses. It is definitely not for me to force any of my staff to do something they don't want to – it's entirely up to them. Then they told me to watch a little "presentation" to help me understand.

'Suddenly I got a load of pictures in my head. It was really weird, like a film but projected into my brain. It showed one of the old guys lying in a casket – the one in the drawings – in a crypt or cellar and he looked dead, like a kind of empty husk, but I could see he was just breathing. Then their butler came over, shut the lid and nodded to a figure in the shadows. It moved forwards into the torchlight and I saw it was a woman, maybe about fortyish, in a hooded robe like a priestess. She went over to the box and put huge gemstones into the sockets, like the ones on their mantelpiece, and then fit what looked like a gold bar into another recess on top. She started chanting in a foreign language, holding her hands over the casket and then the stones started to glow. The gold bar sank into the lid, like it was being *absorbed* and the whole box started glowing and pulsing. After a couple of minutes it stopped and the woman took the gems out and put them inside her robe. She nodded to the servant and slipped back into the shadows. The guy walked over and opened the lid.'

Rhona paused and bit her lower lip, then sat down. 'Inside was a young man, maybe in his mid twenties. He opened his eyes, sat up and smiled.'

After another moment she continued hurriedly, to get it over with.

'Then I was back in that room with the two old weirdoes.

'One of them said, "So you see how important this is to us?"

'Then the other one: "Our survival depends upon it."

'"And we are prepared to go to *any* lengths to make sure it happens."

'Before I had a chance to comment the scene faded and I woke up at home.'

Rhona looked up at Charlie who had remained silent and immobile throughout the telling of her experience. He had listened with an increasing unease and astonishment. Once she had finished, he realised he was holding his breath so exhaled noisily, shaking his head and frowning.

'This is just too bloody weird,' he commented quietly.

'And scary,' added Rhona.

'Aye, *bloody* scary,' agreed Charlie. 'You think it was more than just a dream then?'

'Absolutely,' she replied emphatically, 'I've never had a dream anything like that before – it felt like my mind was being invaded or...*interfered* with – it was bloody horrible.'

'Hmm, yeah, I know what you mean.'

'So you felt like that after your dream?'

'Aye, all of them.'

'*All of them?*' gasped Rhona, astonished, 'you mean to tell me you've had more than one?'

'Oh. Er, yes they started a few weeks ago actually,' Charlie admitted.

'And you didn't tell me?'

'Well, they were just a bunch of strange dreams, as far as I knew,' he said defensively and beginning to get flustered, 'I didn't have any reason to tell you. It wasn't until I saw the drawings yesterday that I knew that they had anything to do with work and that was the first time the box had appeared in them anyway and then it was only just now that you told me about your dream...or whatever it was.'

'O.K., O.K.' Rhona said placatingly, 'I'm just feeling a little panicky – not a sensation I'm used to.'

'But you don't seriously think that this is some kind of rejuvenation device,' said Charlie, 'I mean - I find that hard to believe.'

'Yes, me too, but...'

'There's still a chance that it's all a bizarre coincidence,' Charlie ventured hopefully.

'Aye right and I've got a pet haggis at home.' She smiled humourlessly, 'No Charlie, too much of this ties up for this just to be random chance. Calling it a coincidence is just a way of sticking your head in the sand and avoiding the issue.'

'So, what are we going to do?'

'Have you spoken to Bess about this?'

'Yes, of course.'

'What did she say?'

'Well, other than phoning my brother she suggested seeing a dream therapist – she said that you knew someone.'

'I do,' she said simply and then, making an immediate decision, 'let's go there now. Together.'

'What *right* now? What about work?'

Even in his current state of uneasiness, Charlie was slightly taken aback. Rhona never took time out from work.

'Come on, Charlie, do you think either of us would be able to concentrate with all this going on in our heads?'

'I suppose not, no.'

'Right let's go.' She stood and started towards the door.

'Er, don't we need to phone first?' ventured Charlie.

'No point,' she stated facing him briefly, 'she never answers, just listens to the messages to decide who she wants to speak to. Come on.'

She turned and marched out of the office, grabbing her jacket on the way. Charlie followed in her wake.

'Rory,' she said briskly, 'Charlie and I have to go out. Anything needs doing, you're in charge.'

'Er, sure,' he agreed, a little surprised.

The staff all gazed perplexed at this unprecedented behaviour as the two of them strode from the workshop. Rowan's face remained impassive, but inside she felt deeply unsettled. She had known the reason for Rhona's disquietude that morning and was bewildered by the turn of events. She needed to think without any distractions.

'I need some fresh air,' she told Rory and quietly slipped outside.

#

Adam sat on his bed pondering the call from Charlie that he had received the previous night. Slightly stooped so that his hair formed a curtain across his face, he stared down at his hands in his lap. He had suspected for some time that he and his brother were somehow psychically linked, but to his knowledge they had never before shared any dreams. None of the books from the library had helped in any way that he could make out. Not only did the meanings ascribed to objects and events seem totally arbitrary and irrelevant, he also couldn't find any references to shared dreams at all. He was becoming more convinced that this was somehow linked to a past-life experience, but what it meant and why it had arisen just now he hadn't the slightest inkling. He was unaccustomed to being awake at this hour of the morning and still felt dozy, having been wrenched from his sleep only thirty minutes ago by the startling and unfamiliar sound of the alarm on his phone. He lifted his head and flicked the hair from his face, then rose slowly and rummaged in his box of ancient tapes. He found a recording of Yussef Lateef's "Morning" and put in his cassette player. It was the only jazz record he knew of that was possible to listen to before nightfall. Absent-mindedly scratching his unshaven chin he looked up to the grimy window in the wall opposite. The morning sunshine seemed muted and flattened by its journey through the dirty glass, doing little to stimulate his mind. He was suddenly roused by a loud knock at the door, which reminded him why he was up so early. It was Nick accompanied by the man interested in buying Adam's bass.

'This is Mark,' said Nick, introducing a short, stocky, balding character in his mid-thirties clothed in far too much faded denim.

'Oh yeah. Right. Hi. Come on in,' said Adam blearily.

They followed as he led the way into his bed-sitting room. As Adam extracted a large guitar case from behind an armchair, Mark took in his surroundings. Indicating the books on the table he said, 'I see you're into dreams 'n' stuff Adam,' and started idly turning the pages of the uppermost volume.

'Er, yeah, kind of,' he replied. 'Just recently I've been having some really weird ones, so I thought I'd get some books from the library and look them up.'

'Any of these help then?' asked Mark, reading some of the titles.

Adam always felt defensive in his own space, as if his security was threatened, and this stranger appraising his home and possessions made him uncomfortable. All the same he answered the question - it was in his nature to be polite.

'No, not really,' he admitted, 'I reckon there *is* a lot of meaning in dreams, but these people seem to make up any old rubbish just to get a book published. Maybe it's best to figure it out for yourself.'

'You should go on the interweb man,' asserted Mark, 'do a search for dream meanings and you'll find there's masses of stuff on there.'

'Yeah?' said Adam unenthusiastically. This guy was starting to annoy him now, telling him what he 'should' do.

'Yeah, hundreds of sites. It'll take you a while, but I'm sure you'll turn up something useful.' Mark was now nodding earnestly, pleased to be of assistance.

'Oh, right. O.K. I'll do that next time I go to the library, cheers.' Of course Adam had no intention of doing so but couldn't say it.

'No worries.'

'So anyway, here's the Gibson,' he said, opening the case.

'Allo, my beauty! Cor, she looks like a nice one,' declared Mark eagerly whilst rubbing his hands together, 'you got an amp so I can try her out?'

Fifteen minutes later, Adam was five hundred pounds richer and Mark had left happily with his new instrument. Nick, who had stayed behind for a coffee and a celebratory joint, browsed through the dream books.

'Ha!' he scoffed, 'I told you this stuff was all bollocks!' He announced, stabbing an open volume with a critical finger to indicate the selected entry.

'Listen to this,' he said, ' "If you dream of picking up a hitch-hiker, it *portends* that you will be approached by a creditor." How the fuck did they work that out?'

Adam shrugged non-committally. He agreed that the books were not particularly good but he did believe that there was definitely some meaning to be found in dreams.

'And then there's this one,' continued Nick smirking disdainfully, ' "If you dream you are wearing earrings it *portends*," again, "that you will win some money on the lottery." Jesus, who writes this stuff? It's easy money if you ask me – anyone can think up shit like that!'

'You're probably right, Nick, but you never know. Why don't you look up something you've dreamt recently?' suggested Adam.

'O.K.' agreed Nick, 'this'll be a laugh. Let me think....'

He scratched his chin for a few seconds and then held up his index finger, 'Oh yeah, I know – last night I dreamt that the D.S. kicked down the door and raided the flat, but that's probably just paranoia. You know all about that.'

He paused thoughtfully again.

'Er....oh, how about this – a couple of nights ago I dreamt I was playing a broken, out of tune cello in a flooded cellar. I was up to my knees in water......and er, there were all these rats swimming about....and I knew that I had to keep playing or the little fuckers would come and get me. It was a bit scary actually. I guess that's why I remembered it.'

'Look it up then,' urged Adam, 'there's got to be something about some of that. Let's see what we can unearth from your disturbed sub-conscious.'

'Right, let's have a look,' said Nick, thumbing through the pages, 'I'll start with cellar and cello 'cos they'll be next to each other. Here we go, "Cellar – if you dream you are in a damp cellar it *portends*," don't they just love that word? "a period of fearful depression." O.K. next, cello.... here, blimey it's even got out of tune *and* broken. "To play a cello out of tune means that there will be disharmony in your life." Well, that's bleeding obvious isn't it? .....and um "A broken cello warns of forthcoming illness."'

He looked up and raised his eyebrows.

'So far then, I've got to look forward to fearful depression, disharmony and illness,' he surmised, 'Boy, whoever wrote this happy little number must be the life and soul of the fucking party! Anyway, to continue....let's try "flood". Here we go, "This means you should guard against unscrupulous characters, criminals and other malicious persons." Fuck me, it doesn't get any better does it? What about rats....'
He flipped the pages to find the right place. '"To dream of rats foretells some kind of sickness. It cautions you to safeguard your health."'

'So that's two references to illness then,' contributed Adam gravely, 'maybe you should be careful.'

'What, by avoiding drinking from the fucking sewer?' mocked Nick sarcastically, 'I'd better change my habits then, hadn't I?'

'Well, there might be something in it,' said Adam defensively, even though he gave no credence to the books when he had referred to them for himself.

'Listen, I could just about handle the idea that something that I've *already* experienced might come into a dream, though that is definitely not the case here, but there's no way they can contain anything that's going to happen in the fucking future.'

'Whatever,' said Adam shrugging, 'I guess we'll find out if it does.'

'Yeah right.' Nick laughed. 'Anyway, I'd better be off.'

He picked up his leather jacket from the back of the chair and slipped it on casually.

'Thanks for the coffee. I'll see you soon, right?'

'Yeah,' agreed Adam, 'and thanks for bringing Mark around – it's great to have that cash.' He waved the wad of notes in the air with a happy grin.

'No worries, I had the day off anyway. Don't spend it all at once will you?' teased Nick, 'Half a kilo of Count Chunkula and there'll be none left for Poland.'

Adam smiled. 'Don't worry, I'll resist the temptation,' he responded. 'It's my first chance of a foreign holiday for years so I'm not about to blow it and I want to make it a trip to remember.'

'That's the spirit! S'later.'

Shutting the door behind Nick, Adam turned the key in the lock and slid the bolt across. It was an old habit he found difficult to break and in this city - you just never knew if or when some unwelcome visitors might burst through the door irrespective of which side of the law they were on. He shuffled back to the table where he flicked through a couple of the library books unenthusiastically before sighing and pushing them aside. Pondering his own dream again he tried to recall more details that might give clues to its meaning....the weather...the landscape....the people....anything. He often wrote down his dreams to aid his memory but this time it had remained vividly in his mind. It was unsettling alike some of the ones he had had before. He tried picturing the buildings and the way they were constructed. He closed his eyes and visualised the huge closely interlocking stones. There was definitely something familiar about it. He had a niggling sense of recognition of somewhere he couldn't quite place. He didn't think he had been there but he was sure he knew it, though not from the previous dreams – he was sure they had been set somewhere else. He *had* seen those buildings before...but where? Frowning, he probed his mind further and then suddenly and shockingly it came to him. Abruptly he opened his eyes and stood as he matched the memories, but he had to be certain. He hurried to the wardrobe in the corner of the room and wrenched open the door. Rummaging beneath the heap of clothes that had slumped from the hangers and flinging them over his shoulder he unearthed a cardboard box. With some difficulty, Adam wrested the box from the cupboard. It was heavy and only just narrow enough to drag out through the gap. Thick marker pen identified the contents as "Archaeology books", which had been packed away and hauled from bedsit to bedsit for the last ten years. He somehow could not quite bring himself to get rid of them, even though he no longer looked at them. Opening the folded flaps of the lid he carefully pulled out the weighty hardbacks one at a time, giving each a cursory glance before discarding it on the carpet. The tenth book proved to be the one he was looking for: "Lost Civilisations – Mysteries of the Ancient World". Taking it to the table, he switched on the lamp and started quickly flicking through the pages looking for the colour plates. There it was! A full page, full colour photograph showed the courtyard and the doorway in the wall through which Charlie had passed in his dream. Suddenly it struck him that there was a slight difference. There was no doubt that it was the same place, the same building, the same entrance and the same section of wall, but the picture in the book showed an ancient ruin, a time-worn structure, dilapidated by the passing of the ages. In Adams' dream however, the building had been complete, undamaged and more alarmingly, *new*.

He sat stunned for a few minutes gazing blankly at the wall, but occasionally frowning and glancing back to the photograph as if to make certain that it hadn't altered when his eyes left it. Gently biting the knuckle of his index finger he tried to analyse the evidence before him, to puzzle through this bizarre situation that didn't make any sense in the context of his experience or knowledge. How could he dream of a perfect version of a building that had been in ruin for centuries? Perhaps it was a vision from a previous life – he had sort of half believed in reincarnation for some time. Now it seemed even more plausible. Surely he couldn't recreate the complex structure he had seen in his dream from his long-buried memories of a picture he hadn't cast his eyes on for ten years? On the other hand, maybe he could. After all, the human brain is an amazing and complex organ that is nowhere near fully understood by neurologists or psychologists. As far as Adam was concerned it could be equally capable of containing ancestral or past life memories as it could envisage a faultless edifice from a ruin. Whatever the explanation, he realised that he had little chance of discovering it by weaving complex webs of thought from the utter confusion within his head. He decided to see what he could learn about the place, so he checked the reference beneath the illustration in the book and turned to the correct page. There was a whole chapter on the site in question, so he moved to the armchair to read it in comfort.

CHAPTER FOUR.

It was Charlie's first time as a passenger in Rhona's car and he was more than a little wary of her driving as she accelerated along the A9 southbound towards Dingwall. He was, however, uncertain of mentioning it because he was well aware of how tetchy some drivers could get if they felt they were being criticised. As she overtook a lorry on a blind bend, he closed his eyes, held his breath and gripped the dashboard. Realising that they had survived the manoeuvre he released his grip, exhaled and looked at the empty road ahead.

'I hear they're going to put speed traps along here now,' he ventured hesitantly, attempting a conversational tone.

She glanced quickly at him and smiled slightly.

'Am I scaring you Charlie?' she asked.

'A little,' he admitted.

'Sorry mate, I forgot myself.'

She slowed the vehicle to comply with the speed limit.

'I'm a bit preoccupied, you know,' she added, 'with all this dream business.'

'Aye, sure.'

After a few minutes silence, he asked, 'What's he like then, this dream therapist?'

'He's a she,' corrected Rhona, 'and she's really nice. Her name's Mandisa and I've known her for years. I met her in Glasgow when we were both students.'

'Unusual name,' observed Charlie, 'where's she from?'

'Born in Dingwall actually but her parents are South African. It means "sweet" in the Xhosa language – that's her mother's people. Her father was a white doctor working in the villages of the Eastern Cape where he met her mother who was a nurse and they fell in love. It was years ago, before the release of Nelson Mandela and he'd already been in trouble with the authorities for his anti-apartheid opinions, so when they wanted to get married they fled to Britain.'

'So has she told you what your dreams mean before?' he asked.

Rhona negotiated a roundabout before answering.

'Mandi likes to keep work and pleasure strictly divided, but I *have* seen her in her professional capacity before. She doesn't tell you what your dreams mean though. She tries to help you find a way of interpreting them yourself.'

'Oh aye, that sounds like those counsellors who get you to work out your own problems,' said Charlie sceptically, 'couldn't you do that by yourself?'

'Not really,' she replied evenly, 'it's very useful to have a supportive and detached, non-judgemental observer to sort of guide you through the process and help you examine the symbolism. It really worked for me last time.'

'O.K., I'll take your word for it,' he conceded dubiously but trying to remain open-minded, 'though last time would have been just an ordinary dream, right? I wonder what she'll make of this.'

'Well, we'll soon find out. This is it.'

She turned off the road on the edge of town, which was lined with large Victorian detached houses, onto a gravelled parking area in front of an impressive residence built from cut local stone. It sat grandly in an ornate, beautifully kept garden that boasted a fine collection of specimen trees and flowering shrubs. A fountain spurted from the mouth of a leaping dolphin statue in the centre of a circular, stone-edged fishpond that graced the manicured front lawn. The trees, moving gently in the breeze cast slowly dancing shadows on to the grass and neat flowerbeds. Charlie clambered gratefully out of the car, pleased to be in control of his own fate again, and looked around.

'Blimey,' he muttered, 'she does alright for herself from this dream therapy stuff.'

Rhona sighed and tutted wearily. 'It's her parent's house, you plonker. A few years in the NHS and her dad landed himself a nice job as a consultant neurologist, so he could easily afford a place like this now he's retired. After uni` Mandi decided to move back until she'd paid off a good whack of her student loan. Needless to say, that's taking quite some time.'

Charlie stood enjoying the warmth of the sun and admiring the trees while Rhona rang the doorbell. It was answered by a tall, elegant woman of about sixty with short, slightly greying hair and shiny ebony skin. She wore a brightly coloured and beaded dress, a matching headscarf and a huge friendly smile.

'Rhona, how nice to see you!' she enthused. 'How are you...and who is your handsome friend?'

'I'm fine thanks Zola and this is Charlie – he works for me.'

Zola looked him up and down appraisingly and nodded.

'Well, he's a fine catch my dear,' she teased, 'you hang on to him.'

'You can quit your matchmaking Zola – he's married to my best friend. Although he is my finest carver so I won't let him leave his job.'

'Nice to meet you Charlie. Come on in both of you.' She stood back to let them past and pointed to the stairway. 'Mandisa's upstairs in her office. She's alone, so you can go on up. I'll bring some tea in a few minutes.'

Rhona tapped on Mandi's door and hearing a "Come in!" they entered.

'Rhona, hi!' said Mandisa from behind a polished oak desk as a huge smile creased her smooth round face. In contrast to her mother, she was short and stocky and dressed in a loose black trouser suit. Her shoulder-length beaded plaits swung as she rose and came round to hug her friend affectionately.

'How are you?' she asked, 'I haven't seen you for ages. Busy I guess, running your business and all.' Her wide, bright eyes clearly reflected her good nature and open heartedness. There was an MP3 player in a speaker dock producing the rich, soothing tones of a male a cappella group. Charlie recognised it as Ladysmith Black Mambazo. Rhona introduced him and they were invited to sit on the two-seater cane settee, which was situated in the bay window to catch the sun. To one side was a psychiatrist's couch and behind it a large bookcase lined the wall.

After exchanging pleasantries, Mandisa looked at Rhona and asked, 'So, what brings you here then? It must be important to drag *you* away from work.'

'Actually, it's in your professional capacity that we need to see you,' admitted Rhona, 'Sorry we didn't make an appointment.'

'Don't be silly. *You* don't need an appointment.' She looked from one to the other suspiciously. 'It's unusual for two people to come together...unless they're a couple...?'

'Well we're not,' stated Rhona emphatically, peeved at this having been assumed twice in five minutes. 'Charlie is my best friend Bess' husband and this *is* a very unusual situation....'

There was a tap at the door so she paused. Mandisa went over to admit her mother who was carrying a tray laden with tea and scones.

'I'll let you pour,' said Zola placing the tray on the low table by the settee. She left closing the door behind her.

'Charlie's been having these weird dreams,' continued Rhona, 'which subsequently linked to real life and then last night I had one that was connected too. What we really want to know is what they mean, how they're connected and why bits of them are coming true.'

Mandi could tell that her friend was worried by the expression on her face.

'Right, I'll need you to tell me all about it,' she said slowly as she started pouring the tea, 'but first, I think I should remind you what the role of a dream therapist is because I may not be able to fulfil your expectations.'

She sat behind her desk again and steepled her fingers.

'Dreams are messengers from the soul,' she said, her voice adopting a calm, professional tone, 'When we sleep our spirit takes flight, released from the body and free to enter the timeless world of the unseen universe. Sometimes they just re-run a jumbled mix of our lives' daily episodes and thoughts; other times there can be mysterious or puzzling symbolism, or surreal images whose meanings can only be guessed at. If we are lucky, there *can* be truly astounding revelations. In dreams, we can meet the dead, converse with beings from other dimensions or times and undergo feats or overcome obstacles that we are not normally capable of.

'However, it is not for me to interpret each individual's enigma, nor will any book decode the truths that are unearthed from our subconscious "otherworld". Rather, my job is to help the dreamer find the meanings for themselves by using my skills to guide the investigation. Only *they* can know the inner workings of their own minds and the intimate details of their lives which puts them in context, so only *they* can decipher the messages that the soul brings back from the ethereal realms.'

Charlie looked at Rhona for some response. He was on unfamiliar territory here and wasn't quite sure if anything was required of him. In fact he had been on unfamiliar territory since he first saw the drawings of that casket. Rhona sipped her tea quietly.

'You first, Charlie,' said Mandisa, sliding a notebook in front of her and picking up a pen. 'Give me as much detail as you can remember and pay particular attention to the emotions you felt at the time.'

#

Once Adam started imagining that government agents were contaminating the water supply with a mind-altering substance he realised that he had probably taken things a little too far once more. He still had the "Lost Civilisations" book open on his lap but his thoughts had long wandered from it. He was being paranoid again, but couldn't remember the train of thoughts that had led him from the ancient city in his dreams to this conspiracy theory. He looked back at the book and recalled then that it was the association of this volume with his time in further education that had started it.

Adam's perpetual state of paranoia had first arisen whilst studying archaeology at university. As a keen student of the subject he had befriended the head of department, a Professor Thomas Oakley, and subsequently started helping him with his research. The professor was exploring the possibility of the existence of ancient, prehistoric civilisations that had attained advanced levels of technology. To Adam, already fascinated by the paranormal, conspiracy theories and the possibility that extra-terrestrial life had visited earth in the past, the work was enthralling. The Professor Oakley was highly sceptical about any alien influence but the deeper he delved the more evidence emerged for his own theories. He sought out relevant publications and papers by experts in the field, but soon realised that this subject was not only very unpopular, but in fact derided by mainstream historians and archaeologists. It just did not fit with the accumulated knowledge of the past few centuries of study and very few academics were willing to consider any challenge to the accepted world view: the first civilisation emerged in Sumeria around 3000 BC and progressed with gradual increases in technological advancement up to the present day. The very concept of sophisticated culture prior to this was laughable and the academic community vilified anybody, no matter how notable his or her career, who had the audacity to propose such a thing, regardless of what they saw as "circumstantial" evidence.

Unperturbed, Oakley persevered with his research. The more he discovered, the more his suspicions were aroused that there was some kind of conspiracy to cover up this information and keep it confined to the so-called "lunatic fringes". With Adam's help, he started hunting out the discredited archaeologists and historians to find out more. Most were guarded, distrustful of his declared motives; others seemed fearful and unwilling to either meet or talk with them. Nevertheless, there were a handful who welcomed their approaches and although they were willing to discuss the subject, they wished to remain anonymous, swore them to secrecy and warned them not to publish.

The professor was so convinced by the growing body of evidence that he took a twelve-month sabbatical to study some of the ancient sites himself. Although Adam had to stay behind to continue his studies, Oakley kept him up to date with developments through regular correspondence. Everywhere he went he interviewed field archaeologists, geologists, academics, folklorists and local people to learn as much as he could. His discoveries were so convincing that he returned in no doubt that his theories were correct: there *had* been highly sophisticated *prehistoric* civilisations at various sites throughout the world with technology sufficiently advanced to erect architectural structures so complex as to baffle modern engineers; they were highly competent cartographers who had been able to navigate and travel across the oceans to visit and settle other continents; they had a greatly developed knowledge and understanding of astronomy, mathematics, medicine, agriculture, metallurgy and science, virtually the equal of, if not superior to that of the twenty-first century.

To Thomas Oakley, these revelations were so exciting that he felt compelled to share it with the world. He published all his accumulated evidence, wrote to journals, contacted newspaper editors and television executives. Despite the fact that press and peers alike ridiculed those who had tried before, it still astonished him when he received the same treatment. Nonetheless, he remained undaunted and determined to continue his campaign – the resistance to it somehow toughening his resolve.

That was when the reprisals started. Firstly there were personal attacks on his work, character and integrity. This was followed by break-ins and vandalism to his property, theft of documents and computer equipment. Then he lost his job. He was told that his views were "incompatible" with running a department at a high-profile university and that his presence, now that he had created a very public and controversial persona, was likely to deter potential candidates of the calibre required to uphold the academic reputation of such a prestigious institution. Finally he suffered a vicious assault whilst alone at his country house, leaving him hospitalised for eight weeks and permanently crippled by a shattered kneecap. The culprits were never identified.

Through his friendship with Oakley and as his research assistant, Adam found he was guilty by association and although not physically assaulted himself, the threats and intimidation were enough to force him to drop out of university and send him fleeing to the relative anonymity of the city. A recreational dope smoker from the age of sixteen, Adam now increased his cannabis use in an attempt to forget and escape the memories. It became a daily habit and eventually he found himself bumbling happily along, taking each day as it came, reading, listening to music and making superficial friendships within the soft-drug subculture. Invariably, the conversation occasionally turned to speculation of more philosophical questions: the nature of life and the universe; the possibility of the existence of extra-terrestrial beings and whether or not they had visited Earth and not least, cover-ups and conspiracy theories. After such times Adam's thoughts were often drawn to his troubled past and his mind wove complex webs of connections. The more he contemplated these concepts, the more interrelations emerged, rekindling his paranoia. One day, returning to his bedsit, he noticed two grim looking men in dark suits loitering outside the corner shop on the opposite side of the road. One was reading a newspaper, the other perusing the notices on the door. Seeing them there two days running, induced him into a panic move – a moonlight flit to a squat on the other side of the city. Once ensconced in his new abode, he smoked even more hash in an attempt to calm his nerves. However, the more he smoked the more his suspicions were aroused, until he viewed everyone he saw or met with mistrust. Eventually, after narrowly escaping being run down by a bus because his intoxicated mind was too preoccupied looking out for potential pursuers, he realised he was verging on psychosis. He decided to make a clean break and moved to a different city, way down on the south coast where nobody knew him. He drastically cut down on toking, took regular walks in the park, swam on a weekly basis and resolved to start looking for a job.

That was ten years ago and although the paranoia had never completely left him, being so deeply ingrained, it had diminished to a tolerable level. He managed to find work occasionally, but was always dismissed within a few months due to his unreliability and habitual tardiness.

'I just don't seem to be able to get up in the mornings,' he had once admitted to Nick, who had managed to stay in the same job as a mechanic for the last ten years.

'It's just a question of breaking the old habit and starting a new one,' advised his friend. 'You've got to go to bed earlier to get up earlier, right? You know, establish a new biorhythm.'

'It's not that easy though,' Adam had responded dolefully, 'I get lost in reading a book, or my mind gets carried away exploring crazy ideas and I can't get to sleep.'

'You're too fucking brainy for your own good mate,' Nick had stated. 'Here, have a toke on that,' he offered and handed over a bong, the bowl of which he had just packed with crumbled black resin.

Adam smiled at the memory. That was Nick's answer to everything: 'have a toke on that' and he had to admit that he was not displeased by it. Bimbling along in a mostly contented, bemused condition was a pretty easy life really. It could be worse, for sure.

He looked back at the book in his lap. The reason the image was so familiar to him was because of his fascination with it in his student days. It was associated with the exciting time just before Professor Oakley was discredited, when they both studied late into the night and enthused at descriptions by long-forgotten Victorian explorers of incredible and inexplicable finds. The ruin of Puma Punku is one of four sites in the ancient city of Tiahuanaco in Bolivia. They are believed to be the oldest (estimated by some to be *at least* 17,000 years old) and most puzzling ruins on the face of the Earth. Twenty-first century scholars, even with so much technology and information at their disposal, are confounded by the mysteries that lie within them. Puma Punku is the most fascinating, and most perplexing of all. It seems to be the work of a people who had completely mastered an architecture for which there can be found no infancy, no period of development and of which there are no other examples. The stones used in these structures were granite and diorite. In order to shape these today we would have to use diamond tools. If the people who built this place didn't use diamonds to cut these stones, then what did they use? They were cut somehow, and finely cut. Not only that, but the cuts are perfectly straight. The holes bored into them are faultless and all of equal depth. All of the blocks are fashioned so that they closely interlock and fit together like a jigsaw puzzle - all without the use of mortar. How is it that these ancient people were able to work rock in this way? Not only were some of them exceptionally hard to cut, they are also extremely heavy, weighing up to eight hundred tonnes. How did they move these blocks to form a structure with them? Even with the expertise that we currently have today, it would be virtually impossible recreate the site. If we can't do it now, then how did these ancient people, possibly even during the last Ice Age, accomplish this task? These supposedly "primitive" humans must have been very sophisticated, with an advanced understanding of astronomy, geomancy, and mathematics. To build a place like Puma Punku, would also have required extensive planning, drawing and writing, yet no record of this has been found. Some have suggested, and this is a theory that particularly appealed to Adam, that there must have been benevolent extra-terrestrial visitors who used alien technology to help accelerate human development. However, all that remains today are megalithic ruins, which seem to have been destroyed during a catastrophic event in history. There has certainly been some volcanic activity in the past and some say there is evidence indicating the occurrence of a devastating flood that could have happened as early as twelve thousand years ago. Tools, bones, and other material found within the alluvia show that a civilized people were there prior to the inundation. Any ancient records must been obliterated in the floodwaters and the survivors, if there were any, would have had to start civilization all over again.

Adam was both excited and confused as to the reasons this place had emerged in his dreams. If it was before the city's destruction, it meant that he was able to see back over twelve millennia! He would have to phone Charlie back and share this news with him. Filled with awe at this development, he celebrated by smoking his last tiny bit of weed, his emergency stash. It was a flower head from some particularly smooth sensimillia, or so he'd been told, that he'd been saving for a special occasion. Within minutes he felt quite euphoric and then had a sudden urge to chomp on a few of biscuits and wash them down with another cup of tea. Remembering that he had no milk left, he resolved to make a trip to the supermarket. Even that could be a relatively enjoyable outing when stoned....if you weren't in a hurry.

#

Mandisa sat silently for a few minutes looking at her desk and chewing her bottom lip. She had heard the recent history of Charlie's recurring dreams and his conversation with Adam, followed by Rhona's experience of the night before and how it related to the commission for crafting the sarcophagus. Eventually Charlie spoke.

'So, what do you think it means then?' he asked.

Mandi looked at him levelly. 'I told you I can't tell you what your dreams mean, Charlie,' she replied, 'but these are no ordinary dreams.'

She slowly rose from her seat and started pacing the room.

'You said that they felt more "real" than dreams, more like memories.'

Charlie nodded.

'Well, I think that's a little closer to the truth,' she added.

'What?' exclaimed Charlie incredulously. 'Do you mean like past-life stuff? I'm not sure I believe in any of that.'

'Not exactly past-life stuff, Charlie. More like ancestral memories. In the culture of my mother's people, the Xhosa, ancestors are worshiped and consulted on a wide range of subjects. Some believe that the ancient ones are spirits who can contact the living or be contacted by shamans or healers. Others say that the memories of the ancestors are passed down through the generations. For you, it might be easier if I explain it in different terms.' Mandisa paused by the desk and sipped her tea. 'You know how our DNA retains all the information required to build a complete working human from one generation to the next?'

'Sure,' he nodded, wondering where she was going with this.

'Well,' she continued earnestly, pacing the room once more, 'for some time it has been accepted that other details are transferred, for example a predisposition for diabetes or heart problems. Research has *now* started to show that some seemingly psychological traits are also carried in the code, such as alcoholism, violent behaviour and so forth. Not only that, but evidence has been emerging of heart transplant recipients acquiring some memories from their donors, particularly the last moments of their lives possibly because of the intensity of emotions in some trauma. So, if memory can be stored or retained in the heart, it doesn't seem too far-fetched that it could also be stored in DNA and if that is the case, then there is no reason to suppose that they can't be passed on down through the generations.' As she spoke and warmed to her subject she became more and more expressive, using her hands to emphasise her words. 'I think your dreams may have manifested out of ancestral memory stored in your DNA from some time of great upheaval in ancient history. As to how or why they've been triggered at this moment in time is beyond me.' She stopped and stared directly into Charlie's eyes. 'Has there been any powerful emotional event in the last few months? A death or birth in your close family?'

He shook his head wordlessly, somewhat taken aback by the hypothesis proposed and the growing intensity of her focus.

'Well, think about it,' suggested Mandisa sternly. She quickly turned to Rhona. 'Now,' she said, 'your dream is altogether different. It may have been "just a dream" triggered by the worry about the importance of this job and whether or not Charlie would accept it *or* by hearing about Charlie's dream and being freaked by it seeming to project into the future, but I get the feeling that there's more to it than that. There are too many coincidences and it was too clear and powerful a message - not ephemeral or otherworldly in character.'

She stared fixedly into Rhona's eyes.

'Have you ever had a telepathic experience?' Mandisa demanded passionately pointing a finger at her as if in accusation. Her eyes seemed to shine with the fire of her intensity.

'Oh, um...' mumbled Rhona, looking at the finger, 'maybe, yes, but only with my sister - we're identical twins. More often when one of is in some kind of trouble, usually Roz.'

'Yes, that's quite common with twins.' She slowed a little, becoming more pensive. 'I was just thinking that your experiences sounded like it involved some kind of thought transference from someone else's mind. Charlie's too – I guess you are quite close, working together and friends with Bess...even Charlie and his brother's link makes sense for the same reason but these other guys in your dream.... I'm not sure about them.'

'But that could have been just a dream bit, right?' suggested Charlie hopefully. 'People can't get inside your head like that, control your dreams...' Rhona shook her head. She knew what she had felt. The intrusion was too raw, too real.

'Telepathy and dream journeys are well known amongst the Xhosa,' Mandisa informed them. 'Some are especially trained in those skills and can achieve remarkable psychic feats. There is no reason to suppose that these phenomena should be restricted to one people.'

Charlie shifted in his seat. He was physically comfortable but the turmoil in his mind was now affecting his body.

'So, let me get this right,' he started and then paused to try to gather his thoughts, scratching his beard. 'If these old guys are real people, then you're saying that they are some kind of wizards who can enter people's dreams and give them messages and that they need this carved coffin as a way to regenerate their failing bodies. It all seems a bit far-fetched to me.'

'I don't know really, Charlie – I *am* a bit out of my depth,' Mandi admitted, 'but it's possible. Calling them "wizards" won't really help here – think of them more as shamans maybe. Or it could be Rhona was just picking up on their dreams and desires – some people have desperate thoughts when they're reaching the end of their lives.'

Suddenly Rhona's mobile phone rang, causing them all to jump.

'Sorry,' she said meekly, 'I forgot to turn it off.'

She looked at the display to see who was calling.

'It's my sister, Rosalind,' she said, puzzled, 'she never calls my mobile. Especially not from Italy! I'd better take this, excuse me.'

She stood and walked towards the door, answering the phone on the way.

'Hi Roz, what's up?' she asked leaving for the relative privacy of the landing, then shut the door behind her.

Charlie looked at Mandi.

'So, what do you reckon about this job we've been given?' he asked, 'Rhona and I don't really feel like doing it with all this weird stuff going on in our dreams – it's *way* too spooky. But will they stop if we refuse to do it?'

'I'm not sure,' said Mandi slowly, 'I've never come across anything like this before. Could be they'll just find someone else to do it but it sounds to me like there might not be anyone else this side of Hadrian's wall who *can* do it and they do sound pretty desperate. But at the end of the day you have to do what feels right for you, Charlie.'

'Have you ever experienced telepathy before?' he asked.

'No more than the usual that everyone gets,' she replied, 'you know, you just think of someone and then they ring five minutes later, that kind of thing but my mother has told me stories from the Xhosa tradition where it is widely accepted. Maybe it doesn't have a chance to manifest for most of us with our brains full with all the distractions and worries of modern living...'

Just then, Rhona returned clutching the phone to her chest and looking white as a sheet.

'Bad news?' asked Charlie, getting to his feet.

'Not exactly,' she responded, 'just more weirdness - as if we need it.'

'Well, what's happened?' prompted Mandisa.

'Rosalind has been trying to reach me at the workshop and at home – she was worried about a strange dream she had last night....' She paused and looked from one to the other. 'Then she told me about it. It was almost exactly the same as mine!'

#

The mind-numbing muzak was becoming increasingly annoying and the heavy burden within the shopping basket caused it to cut painfully into Adam's arm. He realised he should have taken a trolley. Why did he always do this? He just came in here to buy a carton of milk but somehow found that he filled up with items he hadn't realised he'd wanted until he saw them posing provocatively from the shelves accompanied by bright little signs declaring their low price. He giggled to himself, still feeling quite stoned. He scratched his head, contemplating either putting some things back or upgrading to the wheeled option. Making this decision took longer than he'd anticipated so he placed the basket on the floor and rubbed his sore arm. He became distracted by the astonishing range of teas and coffees on the shelf in front of him and his mind began to wander. Ideally, he would rather source his groceries from the co-operatively run community whole food shop, but with only his benefit for income, he couldn't afford the luxury. This situation imbued him with an enduring undercurrent of guilt for his involuntary support of a multinational company whose distribution and supply network added so many food miles to his shopping. It was a state of affairs that had caused him to resolve never to fly, thereby perhaps counterbalancing the effects of his purchases. Except that now of course he had just been persuaded to take the plane to Poland with Nick and Lynn on a budget airline – another source of shame. Still, at least he wasn't jetting off all over the world every year for his holidays, which a lot of people seemed to be doing nowadays. Surely, he told the eco-warrior he felt inside himself, he was entitled to *one* foreign trip in his life. It was only fair – after all, if everyone else stuck to that, the planet would be in a much better state.

Adam moved further down the aisle and continued to browse the shelves half-heartedly, suddenly bewildered by the dizzying array of "everyday" choice soups. He shook his head, thinking it best to stop looking and then went back to pick up his basket. As he made his way slowly to the checkout he glimpsed someone he thought he recognised walk past the end of the aisle ahead. He quickened his pace to try to get another look because he couldn't quite believe his eyes. Weaving his way through the flocks of dull-eyed shoppers he finally caught up with the once familiar figure of Professor Oakley by the breakfast cereals.

'Tom!' he called as he approached smiling, 'Professor Oakley! Hi! Wow, what a surprise to see you here! It must be ten years, surely. How are you?'

To Adam's surprise, Oakley seemed panic-stricken at the sight of him, backing away with a look of horror on his face. He looked older too, although Adam supposed he would be, considering it was a decade since they last met, but also careworn and shabby. Suddenly and without a word, the professor dropped his basket and fled hurriedly away, encumbered only slightly his limp.

'Wait!' Adam called after him, 'Professor Oakley! Tom! Don't you remember? It's me - Adam Mackay,' but the old archaeologist had disappeared around the end of the shelves. Adam hastily followed, only to see him dash past the checkout and through the entrance into the milling shoppers beyond. Pushing his way past a queue, Adam was hampered by his heavy basket so he dumped it on the floor and scuttled towards the exit.

'Hey!' called a shop assistant, 'You can't leave that there!'

'Sorry!' he yelled back and sped through the door. He glanced quickly around the busy car park and saw Oakley disappear into an alley. He ran after him again calling 'Professor!' as he went. He couldn't believe that his old mentor didn't want to see him. They had been so close in the past that they were jokingly referred to as "Tweedle-dum & Tweedle-dee" by other students in the department. Adam reached the entrance to the alley panting heavily with his heart beating fast and a pulse thumping in his temples. He hadn't exercised much for ages and his sedentary lifestyle combined with a smoking habit was no doubt having an effect on his ability to run. Leaning against the wall he watched as the professor hobbled to its' exit and into the road beyond. He set off again as fast as he could manage and felt that he must now be gaining on his quarry, who was lame and much older than he was. Emerging from the alleyway into an empty residential street, he saw Oakley glace back over his shoulder as he fled, slowing considerably and with a look of panic in his eyes. Forcing himself on, Adam easily caught up and grabbed the professor's arm to stop him.

'Tom,' he gasped, panting for breath, 'what's wrong? Why are you running away from me?' He was shocked by the look of anguish and desperation on the man's face.

Oakley, too was breathing heavily from the exertion. 'Leave me alone!' he pleaded, 'It's not safe. They're watching. They're after me!' He tried to wrench himself free from Adam's grip. 'Let me go!'

'Who's after you?' demanded Adam, 'Why isn't it safe? What's going on?'

'I can't tell you, Adam,' he insisted. 'It's better that way. You don't want to get caught up in this.' He quickly looked up and down the road.

'Just leave me alone,' he hissed, pulling his arm free of Adam's grip, 'and forget you saw me!' He shuffled away, surveying the street nervously. Adam stood bewildered, watching him limping slowly across to the other pavement, unable to comprehend the professor's behaviour. His former tutor hobbled around a corner and disappeared from view. Adam scratched and shook his head, then turned to wander pensively back to the shop.

#

On the drive back to the workshop, Rhona and Charlie were both quiet and introspective. Although the sun still shone on this stunning spring day, they hardly noticed, their thoughts being so preoccupied with the dream therapy session. Rhona drove much more slowly but nonetheless still almost allowed the car to wander onto the verge at one point. The vehicle behind her sounded its horn and overtook impatiently.

'Concentrate will you please?' requested Charlie, 'this is almost as bad as your high speed driving.'

'Sorry,' she replied and frowned at the road as if this might force her mind to focus, 'I think I need some time to let all this sink in,' she added and wound down her window to admit some fresh air. 'I've probably been a bit more open than you in the past in accepting a range of esoteric ideas, but boy this really pushes the boat out!' She bit her bottom lip and then exhaled loudly.

'Aye, you said it,' agreed Charlie turning to look at her, 'and to extend your metaphor - I feel like I don't have a life jacket, oars or a compass...*and* it's foggy. Shit creek would be a welcome change, I can tell you.' He noticed her hair fluttering slightly in the draught and realising he was hot, opened his own window. 'In the past I've been happy to accept that there's some stuff about the world and life in general that I just don't understand, but now that it's personal and affecting my life directly, I really feel like I've got to kind of get my head around it, you know? I've been so used to being in control of my life. Now I'm not and the stuff that's happening is...well, frightening to be honest.'

'Yes, I know what you mean,' Rhona said bleakly whilst nervously drumming her fingers on the steering wheel, 'but I don't know if we are going to be able to understand all this or take control of it either. We might just have to acknowledge that there's a whole lot of weirder stuff possible than we had previously thought and that some of it is happening to us.'

'Aye, but when it does happen, we've got to learn how to cope with it.'

'Sure, somehow….but I don't think we should let it throw us too much. Let's just get back to the workshop and get on with the day. We don't have to decide anything in a hurry. We can just let it sink in over the next couple of days whilst trying to carry on as normal and then see how we feel. Okay?'

'Okay,' agreed Charlie, but he would rather have been able to rewind the clock and erase this unwelcome chain of events.

They arrived back at "Fantasy Furniture" just after the others had finished their lunch break. On Rhona's instructions, Charlie went into the lizard lounge to eat his sandwiches whilst she headed for the office to eat hers at the desk. As she walked through the workshop she noticed her niece's absence.

'Brian, where's Rowan?' she called to him, 'wasn't she supposed to be helping you?'

'She's gone home,' he replied, 'I gave her a lift just before lunch. She said she wasn't feeling well.'

'Oh right, okay,' said Rhona, 'I suppose she did look a bit peaky this morning,' and entered her office.

Five minutes later, Charlie took his place at his bench and organised his tools, still chewing – he was very conscientious and didn't like taking extra time off. In front of him there was a large rectangle of one-inch thick walnut that was to become the centre panel of the door to a huge wardrobe. Brian and Rowan had already fielded the edges on the spindle-moulder that morning and then Rowan had finished off with the cabinet scraper before transferring the design for relief carving. He subconsciously stroked the smooth surface of the wood heedless of the improvement in the young apprentice's work. He was thinking about Rhona's phone call from Rosalind and wondering how their dream related to his and how odd it was that two pairs of siblings could have a similar experience at roughly the same time. He made another attempt to focus. With a detailed drawing as a reference, he studied the panel before him. The picture showed the ruins of a castle being assailed by two fire-breathing dragons. He inhaled deeply and blew the air out through his mouth. He realised he would have to concentrate on his work. The carving was quite intricate and the dragons' wings had to be undercut to accentuate the foreshortened third dimension.

Grant unexpectedly calling across the room startled him.

'What've you and the boss been up to then?' he sneered, 'I always thought you and her had something going on but sneaking out for a shag when you should be working – that's taking it a bit far, don't you reckon? Eh? Eh?' He chuckled loudly and lewdly.

Charlie had been becoming increasingly annoyed by Grant's snide and unfunny remarks and was about to say so but in the moment it took him to try to formulate his reply, Hamish piped up.

'Shut it will you Grant!' he barked, scowling fiercely, 'You're really starting to get up my bloody nose.'

Grant was instantly affronted. 'Oh yeah? You gonna make me?' he blustered gruffly, putting down his tools and standing up straight whilst clenching his fists and puffing out his chest like an outsized cockerel.

'Don't be a tosser Grant,' suggested Dougie in a deep growl as he straightened to his full height. 'You haven't made any friends here, so don't give me an excuse to break you in half.'

'Ha ha, only joking lads!' insisted Grant feigning cheeriness. 'No need to get your knickers in a twist.' He shrugged nonchalantly and picked up his tools to resume his work.

The others exchanged glances and shook their heads before continuing where they had left off. Charlie tried to once more to apply himself but found that now his irritation with Grant was too distracting. The man was a fly in the ointment, he thought, no two ways about it. Before he had arrived, the staff had enjoyed five years without one cross word between them. His macho posturing, sexist remarks and recurrent, outspoken bigoted opinions had been progressively blighting the once happy atmosphere. It had been mentioned to Rhona who had in turn spoken to Grant, but he had claimed that it was all just good-natured sparring and suggested that none of them could take a joke. In any case there wasn't really anything she could do.

Noticing that everyone else had gone back to their work, Charlie selected a chisel and tested its sharpness by shaving a few hairs from the back of his hand. When Rowan was first learning on the practice tools she certainly struggled with getting a good edge but now it seemed that the young apprentice was becoming quite proficient at tool sharpening. He picked up his mallet and started to chip away at the wood. Soon he was absorbed in the task, carefully removing the waste and enjoying the sweet, tangy smell of walnut released by the fresh cuts.

#

Later that day, Adam felt the need to talk things over so went to visit Lynn. He thought she might be at home as she worked mostly afternoons and evenings. Nick would be at work though and Adam couldn't help relishing the thought of spending some time alone with her. It aroused mixed emotions in him. It involved the exquisite thrill of laying eyes on her beautiful face and stunning body and the agony of knowing that she was unavailable and untouchable. Nevertheless, that was not the entirety of his feelings. He still regarded her as a good friend and was able to enjoy her company in that respect. He was only too aware that he should give no hint of his inner desires to Lynn or Nick. He had to guard against gazing dreamily into her dazzling indigo eyes or staring agog at her superb and braless breasts. He knew that he had to learn to get over his feelings and with a conscious effort, tried his best. He had however, only found one girlfriend once since moving to Portsmouth, but when Julia left him he had lost what little self-confidence he'd possessed and felt unable to approach anyone else since. He had first met Lynn soon after arriving in the city six years previously. She worked in what he defined as a "head shop" sited on the same street as his bedsit. The establishment, frequented by a growing subculture of "retro-hippies" offered the full range of sought-after paraphernalia. The place was packed with incense, cheap imported colourful clothes and crafts, jewellery and all of the accessories desired for the intake of cannabis: bongs, pipes, chillums, rolling papers and a choice of stash tins in three sizes decorated with designs depicting Bob Marley, mushrooms, dragons, pyramids, mystical signs and cannabis leaves. The owner, Martina, a brittle-looking middle-aged wasp of a woman, had named the shop "High de High", much to her own amusement. A former drug-dealer, she had a shrewd head for business, so only paid her staff minimum wage to keep her prices "keen" and had increased her share of the market to such an extent that she was now supplying to trade nationwide from a nearby warehouse. Adam had heard that when scoring from her in the past, people would watch in disbelief as Martina shaved tiny pieces from a lump of hash with a razor blade, so that after the decimal point on the digital display on her scales, sensitive to a one-hundredth of a gram, it would read exactly zero and no more. This was definitely not in the spirit of goodwill that Adam had customarily come to associate with the greater pot-smoking "family". His philosophy, shared by most of those within the circles he moved, was very much in the vein of the comic book "Fabulous Furry Freak Brothers" who famously extolled: "Dope gets you through times of no money better than money gets you through times of no dope". Lynn did not like her employer, describing her as "bitter and twisted", but Martina rarely came in to the shop these days and anyway. Lynn liked the shop and the customers though and enjoyed being able to play her choice from the extensive selection of CDs. As a result of his regular visits Adam discovered that he and Lynn shared similar tastes in books, films and music. When the shop wasn't too busy they would often discus these topics at length. Usually shy with women, he found himself able to talk easily and animatedly with her. It wasn't long before he knew he was deeply in love with her. He visited the store more and more often, usually without even making a purchase, just so he could spend further time in her company. After a few months on tenterhooks he eventually plucked up the courage to ask her out, the butterflies in his stomach metamorphosing into seagulls and then dragons as he approached the moment. He was devastated to find out that she was already involved with someone else. He couldn't believe that this piece of information had not come up in their previous conversations. In fact, she had already been living with Nick for two years at the time and seemed oblivious of the effect that someone with her looks had on men. She told Adam that she was really touched that he had asked, saying he was "cute and really sweet", which made him cringe, and assured him that it would not affect their friendship. He soon came to terms with it, having a fairly fatalistic attitude and low self-esteem. In fact, he would have been amazed if she'd accepted his offer – what *had* he been thinking? She was *way* too good for the likes of him.

One evening soon after that, he met Nick at the shop. Following the introductions Adam was duly invited round for a smoke and a firm friendship was established. Nick was a breath of fresh air in Adam's hitherto lonely life in the city. Up to that point he had made no real friends other than Lynn and it was great to have another bloke to spend time with. Nick was happy-go-lucky, always up for a laugh, reassuringly rational and had a welcome ability to get Adam grounded whenever he got too wound up by the convolutions of his own mind. The companionship with his newfound friends acted like a medicine to his tortured mind and was hugely instrumental in his recovery from the psychoses with which he had arrived in the city. He still sometimes felt like he was being watched or imagined he was being followed, but nothing ever happened, so he tried not to worry too much.

He arrived at the flat to discover that Lynn had painted a new design on the door. A grinning bear flew across a background of blue black scattered with stars and planets. Noticing the "Wet Paint" sign pinned to the frame, he rapped on the thick frosted glass panel that occupied the top third of the door. Lynn answered quickly and let Adam in with a smile. Her recently washed hair shone luxuriantly around her glowing face. She wore a loose blue hooded sweatshirt and tight jeans, both spattered with dots of paint.

'Love the door!' he enthused as he stepped over the threshold, his mood lifting at the sight of her.

'Yeah, thanks. I had a burst of inspiration this morning,' she said brightly. He followed her into the living room where "Yellfire" by Michael Franti was thumping out of the stereo.

'Here, are you getting excited about the holiday?' she asked as she turned the music down. 'I know I am. I've never been to Poland before - I am *so* looking forward to it.'

'Er, yeah, kind of,' he replied half-heartedly, then seeing the look of disappointment on her face added hastily, 'No, I mean yes I am really, I've just been distracted by some weird happenings.'

'What again? Right, sit down,' instructed Lynn firmly, 'just let me make a cuppa and then I'll be all ears, yeah?'

Two minutes later and cradling a hot mug of tea, Adam tried to collect his thoughts.

'Right - fire away,' she said, blowing and sipping gingerly at her own drink, her eyes keen with curiosity.

'Okay. Right. Well, you know that crazy real-as-life dream I had the other day?'

Lynn nodded.

'My brother Charlie phoned and he'd had a dream just like it, except it was actually the same dream but we were both in it and it was *him* I was following and that casket in the cellar turned out to be one that he was shown a drawing of the *next day* as a new job for him to do.' Adam found the words tumbling unstoppably from him as he rambled, hardly pausing for breath. '*Then* I thought I'd seen that city or whatever before and found a picture of it *as a ruin today* in one of my old archaeology books and this morning I bumped into my old professor from uni – you know, the one who was hounded into hiding – there he was in the supermarket and I haven't seen him in the ten years since I left London and he was terrified and scarpered, but I caught up with him and he said that he was being watched or followed and it wasn't safe because *they* were after him whoever they are and...'

'Whoa, Adam! Slow down won't you?' interrupted Lynn, holding up her hands as if to halt the flow, 'I can't take it all in at that pace and you're not making *any* sense at all!'

'Sorry, you're right,' he agreed, 'I need to calm down. But it's all so confusing and scary, I feel like I'm going mad, you know?' He sipped his tea pensively.

'You're not going mad Adam,' she reassured him calmly, 'it's not surprising that you're totally freaked out. A load of like really weird and crazy stuff's happened and it's difficult to make sense of, that's all.'

'That's all?' he said, 'It feels like a lot to me and it might even link back to when I was hassled for helping the prof. Could it *all* be connected or is it just a random and bizarre set of circumstances?'

'It could just be a coincidence that you ran into him round about the same time as your dream...'

'Somebody once said, I think I read it somewhere actually, that the more you use the word "coincidence", the more you are likely to evade rather than seek the truth...or something like that anyway.'

'Well, okay. Why don't you go through it slowly,' suggested Lynn. 'Start at the beginning and tell me everything you can like remember and we'll see if we can't puzzle it out, yeah?'

'Can I cadge a smoke first?' he requested. 'It might help calm me down.' Adam knew that Nick and Lynn always had some dope.

'Course you can,' she replied obligingly and walked over to the bureau. 'I better not give you that wicked weed though, else you'll make even less sense, yeah?'

She selected a tin bearing the face of Bob Marley from the drawer and handed it to him. While his well-practiced fingers rolled a joint, Lynn picked a Tim Wheater CD and pressed play. The gentle sounds of calming New Age music filled the room, the liquid tones of the flute seeming to weave a blanket of reassurance for Adam's troubled mind. He lit up, inhaled deeply and tried to collect his thoughts. He didn't know where to start. Lynn regarded him expectantly for a minute.

'Well?' she said.

'Oh yeah, right. Okay. Firstly, I had a phone call from my brother, Charlie.' He paused to sip his tea and take another toke. 'He was spooked by these dreams he'd been having and then the last one was just like the one *I* had that I told you about the other day and *he* was the other guy in it who I was following!' He held up the joint for Lynn but she shook her head. Adam was baffled. 'What? I've never known you refuse a smoke before. Are you alright?'

'Yeah, fine,' she replied nonchalantly, 'just don't feel like it, that's all.'

Adam frowned, not sure he could believe his ears but then lowered his arm and shrugged.

'Go on then,' she urged.

He related the full details of the phone call to her whilst she sat in rapt attention. The combination of unburdening himself and smoking an entire joint mellowed him considerably. The situation now seemed more intriguing than worrying.

'I always knew that there was some amazing stuff going on with the human mind,' he enthused eagerly, 'but apart from being sensitive to atmospheres and stuff I'd never really experienced anything much personally til now.'

'Yeah, it sounds pretty far out Adam,' agreed Lynn. 'But it's always fascinated me - you know I like to paint from my dreams, yeah? I remember when I was a kid, my Turkish grandma telling me stories about like dreams and stuff that came true.'

'I reckon loads of old folk tales are based on the truth,' said Adam. 'Maybe originally it was a way of passing on knowledge and wisdom before everyone could read and write.'

'Yeah, could be...'

After a thoughtful pause during which Adam became fascinated by the wood grain on the coffee table, Lynn spoke again.

'What was it you were saying about bumping into your old prof'?' she prompted.

'Oh yeah, that was pretty random too,' he said, 'I haven't seen the guy in ten years and he was totally freaked out. He saw me and then scarpered! I ran after him and finally caught up but I had to grab his arm to stop him. He said, "It's not safe, leave me alone, they're watching, they're after me!" And then he ran off again.'

'Sounds like he's gone cuckoo to me,' commented Lynn.

'Well he did seem a bit manic, I have to admit,' said Adam, 'but don't you remember what I said about his research when I was with him and how he got discredited and his career was ruined? And then when he didn't give up he got threatened and they wrecked all his stuff and beat him up. Maybe they're still after him, especially if he carried on investigating. It wasn't like him to give up.'

'Hmm, maybe,' said Lynn doubtfully, 'or maybe losing his reputation cracked him and now he's gone bonkers...'

'Yeah, maybe...' Adam gazed out the window, watching a starling take food to its chicks under the eaves of the roof on the house opposite.

'Anyway, sorry to bore you with my crazy life again,' he said, 'that's twice in the same week.'

'Don't be daft, Adam,' responded Lynn, 'You've got to tell your troubles to someone haven't you? After all, that's what mates are for innit?'

'Well, partly,' he admitted, 'but there's got to be a balance hasn't there? So tell me what's been happening for you. Have you done any painting recently? Apart from the door that is.'

'Funny you should mention it,' she said, 'I've had a particularly creative phase recently and I've finished three pictures in the last couple of weeks – all inspired by my dreams as it happens.'

'Well, I hope the dreams haven't been as disturbing as mine!'

'No, not at all. In fact, totally the opposite. They've all been in like amazing places which is why I felt I had to paint them, yeah?'

'Cool. Can I see?'

'Yeah, sure.'

She led him into the bedroom and up the ladder to the attic, which Nick had illicitly converted into a studio for her. Adam couldn't help watching her backside swaying above him as he followed. He castigated himself and felt the familiar pang of guilt before habitually burying it in what he termed the "shame pit" in his mind. The loft space had two skylights in the north-facing slope of the roof, so it was the perfect place for Lynn's artwork. Although her style was slightly impressionist, the canvas on the easel clearly depicted the courtyard of a grey stone castle. The scene was lit by a soft warm glow of sunshine diffused through the tops of the tall trees that stood outside the walls. Within the courtyard two young women stood facing each other and holding hands. She had cleverly created an effect that suggested that the blonde hair and pale yellow robes of the figures might be emitting a gentle radiance over and above that caused by the natural light.

'Wow, that's amazing Lynn!' gasped Adam, genuinely taken aback. He had always admired her work, but it seemed to just get better and better. 'The way the sunlight plays on those women and the soft warm colours.... it's more than just a picture. It's like I can almost *feel* the atmosphere...it's kind of happy and sad at the same time, but I don't know why...'

'Well, in my dream, right,' said Lynn, 'these were two sisters, like really, really close with a totally amazing love between them, but they were having to say goodbye because they were going to be parted for a while. It's when there's some kind of strong emotion that I really engage with the dream and like, really remember it, yeah?'

'Yeah, that's it,' agreed Adam, 'even though you can't see the expressions on their faces, you've somehow really managed to catch the emotion of the moment. It's bloody brilliant!'

'Thanks, mate,' she said appreciatively, 'I was actually quite pleased with it myself as it happens but it means a lot when someone else likes it.'

'Well, Nick must have seen it.'

'Yeah, but he's no judge – apart from having fairly lowbrow tastes, he just says he likes everything I paint anyway. But I don't think he sees any more than a pretty picture.'

Adam gazed at the painting a while longer in silence. 'Can I see the next one?' he asked eventually.

'O.K., but I'll have to leave that one on the easel 'cos the paint's still wet, yeah?'

Lynn's preferred medium was oil – she felt it gave her greater flexibility than the quicker drying paints and allowed for more of the colour blending typical of her style. She picked up another canvas that was leaning against and facing the wall. She propped it on the chair but had to hold the top because, like the first, it was quite a large painting.

The scene depicted was illuminated by the same kind of glow as in the previous one but brighter and more intense, as if the sun was higher in the sky. However, the main features of the picture seemed to absorb, rather than reflect light. In a large depression surrounded by verdant forest, stood uneven ranks of hundreds of huge, smoothly sculpted dark green monoliths. Whatever material they were carved from also formed the floor of the crater so that they seemed to grow from the ground and cast no shadows. This time there were three figures in the scene. In the background a woman seemed to be hiding behind one of the stones watching a couple in the foreground who were touching the surface of another.

'Wow!' was Adam's response again, looking from the painting to Lynn and back again. 'It's like a massive, gothic, psychedelic Stonehenge! What *is* that place?'

'Dunno really,' she replied tipping her head to one side as she regarded the picture, 'In the dream I got like an overpowering sense of awe – not fear exactly, but a kind of reverence for something powerful and totally beyond my understanding, you know? So it was that strong emotional thing again that made it stick in my mind. I also felt a bit nervous, like I was being watched, so when I heard voices I hid behind that stone.'

'So that's you there?' asked Adam pointing. Lynn nodded. 'Do you know who the others are?'

'No.' she shook her head, 'I saw their faces, but I didn't recognise them, though I think they were newcomers to the place too. I stayed hidden though 'cos I felt a bit like a trespasser, yeah? Like I didn't belong there.'

'And what about those stones?' continued Adam, 'Do you know what they are or what they're for?'

'Nope, but when I saw the others touch one, I plucked up the courage and touched one too.'

'So, what happened? What was it like?'

'It was pretty scary actually,' said Lynn, 'It was like suddenly being plugged into some kind of virtual fairground ride, but like the wildest you can imagine and like totally in the dark and with no warning. As soon as I touched the stone my head was totally filled with like a million voices, yeah? Like I was possessed or something.... and then everything went dark and I felt like I was being sucked backwards through a black hole, you know, like falling and spinning and then I woke up totally tangled up in the covers and stuff.'

'Amazing!' commented Adam, deeply impressed. 'Also a brilliant painting. You should have an exhibition.'

'Yeah, I guess I'm working up to it, but I'm not *entirely* comfortable with the idea. I don't really give a shit what anyone thinks about them really, but, you know, 'cos of the emotional content I feel like I'd be exposing my heart and soul to the world and that makes me feel strangely vulnerable actually.' She put the painting back and then uncharacteristically, started biting her fingernails as she gazed thoughtfully out the window. 'Anyway,' she continued after a moment, 'it's tricky fitting it in sometimes, what with work and everything.'

'Everything?'

'Well, work then. The two til ten shift is a bummer – I don't know why she has to open in the evenings. Well I do actually – she knows her customers and wants every penny she can get. Some of them are working and like to go in after that and others, you know musos and students and unemployed and that spend most of the day in bed, so...anyway, by the time I get home, I'm knackered and just want to slob out for a bit before going to bed – I certainly don't feel creative. Then by the time I've had my breakfast there isn't really time to get into the artistic mood, you know?'

'Except recently?'

'Exactly,' she agreed, 'After these dreams I've just felt like *so* totally compelled to paint that I've been missing breakfast and going into the studio fully energised.'

'Careful you don't starve yourself Lynn,' cautioned Adam with concern, 'it's not like you've got any surplus weight to lose.'

'Thanks Adam, but no worries there. I've been making up for it at lunchtime *and* stuffing myself silly when I get home from work. In fact I've been ravenous recently.'

'Let me see the third picture,' he requested.

She produced an even larger canvas which had been facing another wall and because of its size, had to stand it on the floor. Adam stood back and gasped. He pointed wordlessly at the painting open-mouthed as his eyes darted over the scene.

'What?' asked Lynn, a little perturbed. 'What is it Adam?'

'That's the place in *my* dream!' he blurted looking at her in shock.

'What? No way!'

He nodded quickly. 'Except in my dream there was a volcano erupting and it was full of people panicking everywhere – but it was *definitely* the same place.'

Lynn looked back at her work. She had painted part of a beautiful stone built city in an unusual architectural style – almost like a hybrid of Inca, Egyptian and futuristic. It also looked very clean and new, perhaps even quite recently constructed. It portrayed a peaceful idyll. Children played happily beneath neatly pruned trees, whilst men and women of all ages sat beside ornate fountains laughing and chatting or strolling between manicured hedges and well-tended flower beds.

'Are you sure it's the exact same place?' she asked.

He nodded mutely, unable to speak.

She looked at him askance. 'Are you like *totally* sure,' she pressed, 'I mean without a shadow of a doubt?'

'Absolutely,' insisted Adam, 'even down to that doorway I went through, there.' He pointed.

'Blimey…so now that's like, three of us who've dreamt about the same place innit? How could that have happened?' wondered Lynn. 'And why was yours and your brother's all full of death and destruction and violence when mine is like total paradise?'

'Buggered if I know,' said Adam, 'but you are a generally happier person than me, on the whole.'

'I'd hate to think that my city was about to get like, totally ruined and all these people hurt or killed,' said Lynn sadly.

'Well, that was only in my dream,' he said attempting to reassure her.

'*And* Charlie's' she added.

'Oh, yeah...' he agreed. 'But it was also in my book – it's an actual place. It's called Puma Punku in the ruins of Tiahuanaco in Bolivia. They reckon it's the oldest and most puzzling ruins on the face of the Earth. At least seventeen thousand years old or something...'

'Wow!'

They stood pensively for a while, each trying to make sense of their own thoughts. Unable to devise a satisfactory explanation for the strange coincidence, Adam's shock gradually began to transform into a growing sense of disquiet and apprehension. Even for him there were just too many bizarre happenings in a short space of time.

'Let's have another cuppa,' suggested Lynn eventually, her tone significantly less cheery than when Adam had first arrived, 'Might help get our brains in gear, yeah?'

'Hmm, maybe,' he responded uncertainly, 'a drink would be good anyway.'

One cup of tea later, they were no closer to a convincing explanation. Adam had rolled himself another smoke to see things from a different perspective, but had only managed to confuse himself further.

'Bloody hell, is that the time,' remarked Lynn suddenly looking at the clock and then getting to her feet, 'I've got a doctor's appointment, I'd better go. You can stay if you like - have another cup of tea....smoke...whatever.'

'Doctor? Are you O.K.?' asked Adam in concern.

'Oh, yeah. Nothing to worry about – just routine women's stuff, you know?'

'Oh, right. Good. I'll have one more cuppa and then I think I'll go home and have another look at those dream books.'

As Lynn was taking off her hoodie and putting on her denim jacket, Adam was trying not to look at the jiggling mounds beneath her t-shirt.

'Oh, by the way,' she said, 'come round for dinner tomorrow, yeah? Nick's cooking up something special – we've got something to celebrate.'

'Really? What's that?'

She tapped her nose. 'That'd be telling wouldn't it? You'll just have to wait til tomorrow. Come about seven-thirty, yeah?'

'Sure, I'll be there,' said Adam. He watched her leave and went to put the kettle on again.

CHAPTER FIVE.

A spiral of pungent fumes coiled from the smouldering ember at the tip of the incense stick. Rowan wiped the wetness from her cheeks and blew on it, watching the red glow intensify as the smoke streamed away. She breathed deeply and then bit her lip as once more she pressed the searing point into the soft tender skin inside her upper arm. She winced, but held it steady for five seconds before pulling it away, whimpering slightly. A few more tears leaked from her reddened eyes. The pain gave her mind something else upon which to fix her attention. Somehow physical suffering was easier to bear than emotional distress. She could understand how and why *this* hurt and it was in her control. She braced herself for a repeat of the process, but suddenly stopped and looked up. She hurriedly pushed the joss stick into its holder and pulled her shirt on, then tried to rub away her tears with the back of her hand, spreading the already smudged makeup even further. There was the noise of a vehicle crunching on gravel and coming to a stop. The car door slammed, the house side door opened and Rhona entered the kitchen briskly, dumping her handbag and keys on the table. Rowan hurriedly selected an "Anti-flag" CD and put it on at high volume, hoping that her aunt would not disturb her.

Rhona came into the hallway. 'Rowan?' she called. Hearing no reply she trotted up the stairs and knocked on Rowan's door before entering. Her niece was sitting on the end of the bed, her back to the door and head bowed. A haze of incense filled the room, slightly obscuring the numerous posters of "Goth" bands. In a corner on the floor a huddle of soft toys lay forlornly, as if stupefied by the fumes.

'Hi there,' said Rhona, 'hmm, funny smell, what's that you're burning?' There was no response so she turned the music down and continued, 'Are you all right love? Rory said you were ill.'

Rowan didn't turn, just mumbled, 'No, I'm fine.'

There was no fooling her aunt though - she knew her too well. Rhona walked around the bed to face her. 'Look at me,' she urged gently. Rowan raised her head slowly to reveal the red eyes and smeared eye-liner. 'Oh, Ro love, what's the matter?' she asked tenderly. She sat down next to the girl and circled her shoulders with a consoling arm. Rowan rested her against Rhona's chest. 'Blimey, you're all hot and sweaty,' she noted, 'have you got a temperature?'

'No, it's Grant,' she said in a small, trembling voice. Why is it, she thought, that when there is someone to comfort me, I just start to fall apart?

'Not again,' Rhona sighed.

'I know we've talked about it before,' continued Rowan miserably, trying to hold back her tears but making her voice high and strained in the attempt, 'about how I should stand up to him and try to be an assertive, independent woman like you, but I just can't do it! I'm not like that and whenever I think "right I'm totally going to try this time", I get all shaky and my chest tightens up and I get all breathless and I can't think what to say or anything. I just can't help it. Anyway, this time it was much worse....'

She sobbed quietly whilst Rhona rocked her saying softly, 'It's all right, you're right, I'm sorry if I've tried to pressure you into being someone you're not. I just thought you'd find life easier to cope with that way, but just because it worked for me, doesn't mean it will work for you. I'm sorry.' She stroked Rowan's head and squeezed her shoulder reassuringly. 'Now, tell me what happened today.'

'O.K.' said Rowan straightening up and sniffing back her tears whilst using her sleeve to dry her cheeks and eyes. She blew her nose on the proffered tissue, took a deep breath and exhaled before starting her account. 'Just after you left I went outside for a bit of fresh air, you know, but I'd only been out for like a minute when Grant followed. He was like, "having a crafty fag, eh?" or something, you know, trying to be funny because he knows I don't smoke. So I ignored him and he's like, "Oh ho, playing hard to get are we?" and he came a bit closer and said, "come on, give us a kiss love, you know you want to." So I said, "Fuck off!" and went to push him out of the way as I ran back into the workshop but I totally missed and it was weird because he staggered back and like fell over anyway.' She paused to gather her thoughts and took another deep breath before continuing. 'So later on I was working with Brian on the spindle moulder, like you said and just before lunch he sent me to the store room to get the silicon spray to like lubricate the fence and stuff. So I went in and found the spray but like, when I turned round, there was Grant again, totally looking at me in that real creepy way of his. It was horrible 'cos I knew he really wanted to molest me...'

'You *thought* he did,' interrupted Rhona.

'No, I *know* what he's thinking,' insisted Rowan earnestly, so Rhona held her tongue as her niece continued. 'So I was terrified and backed away and he just like, came slowly closer. I wanted to scream but I couldn't, I just froze. Like I said, my chest tightens up and I couldn't breathe.' She was becoming more distraught whilst relating the event, as if she was reliving it. 'He got close enough for me to feel his hot smelly breath – it was disgusting, it made me want to puke so I turned my face away, then he whispered, "I'm gonna screw you before the end of the week" and then he gave me this evil grin and left. It was horrible...' She broke into tears again and sobbed on Rhona's shoulder.

After a few seconds Rhona said, 'did anyone else see or hear this?'

Rowan shook her head.

'Well, don't worry, I'll give him a bloody good talking to tomorrow. I can't sack him yet, but I can give him an official warning. I'll tell him that if *anything* like that happens again he *will* lose his job and I *will* call the police, even if there are no witnesses.'

'But I so don't want to come back to work while he's there,' pleaded Rowan raising her head, 'I just can't stand him. I feel he's like, *abusing* me every time he looks at me. I feel totally...*violated*. And I'm *so* scared in case he *does* do something.' She shuddered at the thought.

'I'm sorry Ro,' apologised Rhona, 'I've got to give him a warning before I can sack him, especially without any witnesses.' She gently stroked Rowan's hair as she spoke. 'The law on sexual harassment says that, "for action to be taken, the conduct must be sufficiently frequent or severe to create a hostile work environment" or something like that. Unless he touches you. He didn't did he?' Rowan shook her head. 'Take a couple of days off then and hopefully my warning will be sufficient to make him behave himself.'

'I'll think about it.'

'When you come back I'll just make sure that there's never an opportunity for him to be alone with you and I'll talk to the others individually to keep an eye out for you.'

'O.K.'

'Now, how about a cup of tea? I'll put the kettle on and you can wash your face before you come down.' Rhona's matter-of-fact tone indicated that it was time to get back to normal and stop dwelling on something that had been dealt with. Rowan sighed heavily, feeling that it had not.

#

That night Charlie dreamed again. He stood motionless under a hot sun, gazing at a huge sphinx towering above him. He felt in awe of its imposing presence and he believed that this new monument would help his people to focus on the colossal task of rebuilding their once mighty civilisation. This great stone edifice rose from a vast savannah, richly green from the recent rains. The fresh smell of damp grass filled his nostrils as he took a deep breath, thankful for this fertile land and the chance of a new beginning. In the distance he saw the woodlands that showed the edge of the great river's flood plain. A flock of flamingos flew overhead – a sure sign that the rainy season was upon them, even though he stood at the moment in blazing sunshine. Charlie heard a call from behind him and turned to see a figure beckoning from a low timber building. He realised it must be time to get back to work, so he walked over to the structure and entered through the open door. On his workbench lay a large slab of timber, marked out with an intricate pattern for piercing and carving. On the floor nearby was an even larger piece, roughly hewn from a tree trunk. He knew that the two men working on it were hollowing it out to make the body of the sarcophagus, the lid of which was his job to craft. As he picked up his tools, the overseer entered the workshop.

'Your progress is too slow!' he castigated angrily, 'The Belums are nearing their time!'

'But we've not long had the timber delivered,' protested one of the adze-men.

'I don't need excuses, I need results,' snapped the overseer impatiently. 'You'll have to work extra time with no days off until it's finished!'

Charlie looked at the work in front of him. 'But that will be weeks!' he objected. 'It all has to be gilded too and I've got a field of barley to plant now the rains have started – not to mention the goats to milk and all the other jobs at home.'

'You've got a wife haven't you?' said the man, 'and those three boys of yours must be big enough to help. Everyone has to work harder at times like these. It is vitally important that the casket must be finished as soon as possible.' He turned and marched out.

'Filthy scum,' muttered Charlie, fuming. His sons were aged four, five and seven and his wife was six months pregnant. The demands on him and his family seemed so unreasonable. And for what? So that two selfish old men could prolong their lives again.

'Why can't they just get some more carvers in?' he wondered aloud.

'There's not enough up to standard yet, not around here anyway,' answered a workmate, 'and you know how many we lost. *We* can hack the waste out of this no problem, but you're the only one who can do the carving and gilding.'

Charlie knew he was right, but didn't like it. He sighed heavily and got on with his work.

When he woke, he did so retaining a strong sense of the injustice in the situation. He then realised that the casket in the dream was again the same as the commission recently received at work.

What is going on? he wondered. *This is getting more and more mystifying.*

He got out of bed trying not to disturb Bess who was sleeping soundly and walked through to the shower. As he automatically soaped himself he puzzled over the unsettling thoughts and images in his mind. The interview with Mandisa wasn't really very helpful. It left him feeling that there must be some un-dealt with issue in his subconscious that he should be scrutinising for the furtherance of his personal development. He had never been any good at self-examination and any kind of metaphorical symbolism just seemed to go right over his head. The other angle relating to ancestral memories hadn't made any sense to him either. He had heard *something* about some recipients of heart transplants getting a kind of "shadow memory" from the donor, which was quite amazing, but at least in those cases there was a large chunk of someone else's body put inside them. But memories getting attached to DNA? Wasn't the whole point that the DNA passed on unchanged except for occasional random mutations? And anyway, when only one strand was passed from each parent in each generation, wouldn't it all get too diluted?

Bess had risen whilst he showered so he talked it over with her as they had breakfast.

'That's how homeopathy works,' she stated.

'What?' said Charlie frowning quizzically, unable to see the connection. 'What's homeopathy got to do with DNA?'

'No, silly, I mean the dilution,' explained Bess patiently, 'The active ingredient is diluted many times until there is only a trace left in the remedy, like an energy imprint, but it still *works*. You can't deny that – you've benefited from it yourself.'

Charlie looked at her levelly and finished chewing his mouthful of muesli. 'So you reckon,' he said, 'that memories can be passed down from parent to child over and over down the years, possibly over *thousands* of years and then just randomly pop into your dreams for no apparent reason?'

'Could be,' she replied matter-of-factly, 'or maybe there *is* a reason…. some kind of trigger that sets it off.'

He looked out the window for a few moments, watching the greenfinches squabble over seeds. It had started drizzling and droplets of water slowly wriggled down the glass.

'If what you say is true,' he speculated thoughtfully but without conviction, 'then this casket has been cropping up throughout history in some way associated with my ancestors…but I still don't understand how I could dream it before I saw it or knew about it and why now? And why did Adam dream the same and what about Rhona's dream? How does that fit into this?'

'Well…' started Bess, '*her* dream came after she'd seen the drawings and heard about yours, so maybe in her case it really *was* just triggered by events…and Adam…well he *is* your brother, so there might be some kind of telepathic link, you know like when you think of someone and then the next minute there they are on the doorstep?'

Charlie sighed and scratched his beard. 'Aye, maybe…' he said doubtfully. After a minute's silence during which they drank tea and ate toast, he said, 'I definitely don't want to do this job. The whole thing's just too weird you know? I reckon if we tell them no then we can just get back to normal and forget the whole thing.'

'That's totally fine Charlie, it's for you to choose.'

'I wonder if Luke has had any weird dreams or anything related to this…'

'Well it's a bit difficult to ask him at the moment – except by email, but it could be a while before he answered.'

'Yeah, I wonder how he's doing…'

He looked up to see Bess' face wet with tears.

'I still really miss him, you know?' she said.

Charlie got up and went to her, giving her a comforting hug. 'Aye me too,' he admitted. They had both found Luke's departure difficult and had shared their feelings, but they tried not to dwell on it too much – after all what difference would worrying make? At least he sent them personal emails rather than expect them to rely on his blog or intermittent and brief Facebook posts.

'It's just that Africa seems so far away, so....*dangerous*...and so *unreachable* if anything were to happen to him...'

'I know, I know, but I reckon he'll be fine. You know how our views of abroad are distorted by the negative newsmongers. Anyway, Kenya's pretty safe. He's doing a great thing and we should be proud of him.'

Bess dried her eyes. 'Mostly I'm fine about it,' she said, 'I think I've just been a bit unnerved lately and it's made me feel more vulnerable.'

'I know what you mean...,' said Charlie, but it was the first time she had admitted to him that she was also somewhat disturbed by recent events.

'You should get to work,' she told him.

'Will you be okay?'

'Sure. I've got a lot of new cuttings to transplant. You know how calming I find handling plants.'

#

Rowan had decided to be brave and accompanied Rhona to work the next morning. As she entered the workshop to the cheerful greetings of her workmates, Grant was facing the other way and remained so whilst he put on his apron. He leaned over his bench and started setting out his tools. Rowan glared in his direction, daggers in her eyes. She had never hated anyone else before and really didn't enjoy the sensation in any way but felt she had no control over it. Grant straightened abruptly, stifling a curse and putting a hand to his back.

'Ouch! Sudden twinge,' he said by way of explanation to no one in particular.

A few minutes later Rhona called him into her office.

'Now what?' he muttered impatiently under his breath as if this were a common enough occurrence to have become a nuisance.

'Shut the door behind you,' she said as he entered.

He did so, turned to face her where she sat behind the desk and put his hands in his pockets.

'What's up boss?' he asked casually through his gum chewing.

'You really upset Rowan yesterday Grant,' she stated.

'Oh, I didn't mean to,' he said defensively, 'it was just a bit of light hearted banter, you know?'

'That's not how she put it,' Rhona said firmly. 'She said that you cornered her in the storeroom and said "I'm going to screw you before the end of the week." '

'Well, I'm not sure those were my *exact* words,' he said nonchalantly, 'and she wasn't really *cornered* as such, but like I said, it was a joke, you know, just a bit of teasing.'

'She's only *seventeen* for Christ's sake,' Rhona reminded him, becoming increasingly annoyed with his impertinence, although she knew that a lot of the "page three girls" he drooled over weren't much older, '*and* she felt it came across as more of a threat actually, Grant, but in any event it constitutes sexual harassment!' She was trying to remain calm, knowing that to completely lose her temper would also lose her the sense of authority. She could tell he knew this too and saw it as a weakness.

'Well, how was I to know she was hypersensitive?' he said impatiently, 'She needs to learn how to take a joke! This is just more bloody political correctness gone mad.'

Seething with rage, Rhona spoke through clenched teeth. 'She is *not* hypersensitive Grant. *Any* woman would be upset by that kind of obnoxious behaviour. *And* it has nothing to do with political correctness.' She took a deep breath in an attempt to retain a level of composure. 'Political correctness is just about changing the way things are described for fear of upsetting people. This situation is about one member of staff acting in a highly inappropriate manner so as to greatly offend and upset another.'

'Whatever.' He shrugged and smiled derisively, chewing his gum and glancing at the clock. 'I guess some people are more easily upset than others.'

'I'm serious, Grant!' Rhona allowed her voice to rise, but now felt in control of her anger. 'This is an official warning – leave Rowan alone or you're out. I won't have that kind of behaviour here – it's totally unacceptable. Just once more and you're fired. Now get back to work!'

Grant's face betrayed his fury at what he felt was unfair and unjustified treatment. His eyes narrowed and he stopped chewing as his jaw muscles tightened, causing a twitch in his neck, but he kept quiet. Rhona could see that he didn't want to show that he was bothered and in that moment she was slightly disconcerted, thinking she detected a hint of either malice or madness in his gaze, or perhaps both. He took a deep breath, started chewing again slowly, then turned wordlessly and walked briskly from the office leaving the door open. He returned to his bench fuming. He just did not understand women and he certainly didn't like being told what to do by one. He was particularly incensed by the threat too. If that sex-starved prick-teasing little bitch hadn't squealed to her aunt like some puny, spoilt, miserable, snivelling schoolgirl, he wouldn't have had to put up with the indignity of that dressing down. Still, at least the other guys hadn't witnessed it. If his mates down south knew he was working under the thumb of some spiteful feminist finger-wagger he'd never live it down. He almost felt that he didn't care about keeping this job anyway. He hadn't exactly been made to feel welcome by the other blokes. It was probably a racist Scottish thing, he thought. Whenever England were playing another country at football, they would always support the other side, no matter who it was – even the bloody French! He was not sure if they just did it to wind him up or whether they really did hate the English, but either way he'd had enough. Maybe he'd just pack it in and go back down south where at least he had some good mates who thought the same way he did. Yes, the idea of quitting this den of tartan tossers was becoming more appealing. He glared icily across at Rowan and caught her eyes as she hastily looked away from him. The fact that she knew that he had been castigated infuriated him even more. Before he left he was going to find a way of getting back at the vindictive little minx. Instead of resuming work he went outside for a cigarette in an attempt to calm down.

Rhona called Charlie from her office. 'Can I have a word?' she requested.

'Sure,' he said, putting down his mallet and chisel.

As he shut the door behind himself she said, 'I've just given Grant an official warning – he's been harassing Rowan. Yesterday when we got back – she hadn't gone home sick, she was really upset because Grant had cornered her in the storeroom and made obscene suggestions.'

'Bastard!' commented Charlie with feeling.

'Quite,' she agreed. 'Anyway, one more time and he's out.'

'He's totally out of place here you know – the whole ambience has changed since he arrived. We used to be such a happy bunch, but his sexist comments and redneck opinions have been getting everyone's backs up. He's an unfunny chauvinistic bigot and he's really soured the atmosphere.'

'I know,' admitted Rhona, 'but I didn't realise what he was like when I took him on. He had glowing references from his last place down south and he was very polite in the interview. Also he was the only applicant and the workload meant that I really needed to take someone else on. He's a good cabinetmaker too. I think that for the moment at least, we'll have to put up with him.' She sighed heavily. 'Anyway, Charlie, will you keep an eye on him? I mean with Rowan, just in case he tries anything, you know? Make sure he doesn't get a chance to be alone with her again.'

'Yes, of course,' he replied intently, 'and if he does try anything, I'll thump him.'

Rhona smiled humourlessly, 'Thanks. Though of course I could *never* condone an act of violence in the workplace. However, if I happen to be looking the other way at the time.... Anyway, I'm going to tell the others about this too. Can you send Rory in, I might as well start with him.'

'Sure,' said Charlie, but he didn't move. 'Er....'

'What?'

'Well, while I'm here.... this um, coffin job....'

'Yes, what about it?'

'I just wanted to confirm that I *really* don't want to do it. It's just all too crazy for me.'

'More dreams?'

'Aye. Last night – different time, different place, same box. You?'

'No, but I agree. I say sod them. I don't care if these weirdoes can influence our dreams or not. If they can, then I feel kind of...*interfered* with and I don't like it. I'm not going to be pushed around. If not, well then it's just hard luck for them. Besides, I don't like the way they send in some creature from the crypt to order me around, imposing unrealistic deadlines and issuing half-veiled threats. No, you're right, let's have nothing to do with them. It's not like we need the work anyway.'

'You're right there. Anyway I think...' started Charlie, but he was interrupted by Rowan's voice screaming 'Fuck off!' followed immediately by the sound of a man's loud yell of pain and a resounding chorus of cheers. Rhona and Charlie looked at each other then dashed out of the office and into the workshop. They stood open-mouthed and staring at the scene before them. Everyone was looking at Grant who was bent double with his face in his hands. Blood was oozing between his fingers and dripping onto the floor. Rowan was biting her lower lip and massaging her right hand.

'Bitch – you broke my fucking nose,' Grant mumbled angrily through his hands.

Rowan was livid. Panting hard and shaking her clenched fists as if she was going to punch him again, her pent up fury explode from her mouth as she yelled, 'You deserve worse, you bastard! You're a...a fucking cunt and a...a festering, creepy, repugnant....turd!'

The rest of the staff stood in stunned silence but with an odd mixture of astonishment, humour and anger on their faces. Rowan was usually fairly quiet, polite and unassuming. They had never seen the girl lose her temper before and certainly never heard her use language like that; but they were also shocked and outraged by Grant's behaviour whilst simultaneously being impressed by Rowan's.

Rhona found her voice. 'What's going on?' she demanded shrilly.

Grant remained silent, nursing his nose. Rowan turned to face her aunt. 'I can't believe it,' she seethed, 'the fucking bastard actually squeezed my tit!'

'Aye, I saw it too,' confirmed Brian, 'he just came up behind her, reached round and groped. I would have clobbered him myself, but I didn't have to – young Rowan here has done a fine job.'

'Right, that's it! Get out now Grant!' ordered Rhona categorically. She found it hard to believe that he could behave like this so soon after she had berated him in her office. It felt good to finally shout at him. 'Take your tools, go and don't *ever* come back! Before I'm tempted to follow Rowan's fine example. I never want to see you here again. I shall be calling the police to report this as a case of sexual abuse, so you can expect a visit from them.'

Trusting her team to ensure his departure, Rhona went to Rowan and led her slowly into the office with her arm around her shoulder.

'Are you okay?' she asked tenderly.

'Yeah, fine actually,' responded Rowan as if she were only just realising it herself, 'and it felt *so good* to punch him on the nose.' She giggled briefly but then suddenly found herself shaking uncontrollably so lowered herself unsteadily into Flora's chair and started crying.

'Here, drink this,' suggested Rhona, handing her a bottle of water. Rowan took it and drank in small sips until she had calmed down. She dried her eyes and flexed her hand.

'Well, it's good to see you standing up for yourself at last,' Rhona said with a grin, causing a small laugh to escape from her niece. 'How's your hand?' she continued.

'It's a bit sore,' Rowan informed her, rubbing it, 'but I think it'll be all right. I've never hit anyone before,' she admitted, 'I didn't realise it was going to hurt *me* too.'

'Well there you go, that's the price you pay for resorting to violence,' said Rhona in a mock nagging tone. She went to the first aid kit, selected a small bottle of rescue remedy and put a few drops on Rowan's tongue.

'You see,' she said quietly, 'I reckon if you had stood up to him from the first day, it would never have come to this.'

'Yeah, but then we'd still have him here and I'd have to put up with him undressing me with his eyes and playing out sex scenes in his mind.'

'You really think you can read his mind don't you?'

'Yep.'

'You're probably right, but you mustn't always assume that someone's outside behaviour is a manifestation of what's in their mind. In fact, most of the time, it probably isn't.'

'I *know!*' insisted Rowan emphatically, 'You see, I...'

'Sorry, love, I've slipped into "patronising aunt" mode again,' said Rhona appeasingly, 'I just do it because I care about you.'

'I know that too,' said Rowan quietly, 'thanks. And I really do appreciate all the stuff you've done for me. You've been more like a mother than Rosalind has, but even better than that too. I know how much you gave up for me when I was little...' She paused briefly. Having been considering it for some time she decided that now might be the right time to make a confession, but before she could, Rhona spoke again.

'I think I get it from my mother, you know,' she said, 'I grew up thinking "I'm not going to talk to *my* children like that" and then when I started looking after you, it just started happening....forcing its way out of my subconscious, I guess.'

'Well, at least you're aware of it and *try* to stop yourself,' said Rowan. Thinking again that now was a good a time as any for her revelation, she opened her mouth to speak but then wasn't quite sure how to start.

'I've got...'

'Hmm....maybe. I hope so at least,' Rhona interrupted. 'Anyway, I'm forgetting myself - do you want some arnica for that hand? I think there's a tube of ointment in the first aid box.'

'Yeah, thanks, it'll help stop the bruising.' Whilst Rhona got the arnica, Rowan thought again about the best way to disclose her secret, but whilst she faltered, she began to doubt the decision. Maybe it wasn't the right time after all. Perhaps, she thought, it would be better if she were more prepared, rather than in a state of shock. She wouldn't want to blurt it out and get it all wrong. And someone might come into the office. Anyway, it would probably involve all sorts of questions and explanations that would require more time to go through. Thus she convinced herself to postpone it a little longer.

'Right, I'm going to phone the police,' declared Rhona, handing over the ointment. 'We can get that bastard done for this.'

'What? No, don't,' said Rowan hastily. Her aunt raised her eyebrows in surprise. 'I'm just glad to see the back of him. I don't want to have to turn up in court and testify in front of him and everyone else.'

'But I don't think you'll have to. I'm sure in cases like this you can do it all by video link now – you won't have to see anybody and they won't have to see you.'

'No, really, I just want to forget the whole thing.'

'Oh. O.K.' Rhona shrugged, but not really understanding. After all Rowan had been complaining about Grant for months. 'Think about it for a couple of hours and I'll ask you again. If he can be prosecuted then it might stop him doing it to someone else. Will you be alright to work or do you want to take the rest of the day off?'

'I think I'll be alright, thanks. I don't want to go home alone anyway.'

'No, of course. Well, at least have a cup of tea first, then try using your hand and see how it feels. You can always sit and read in the lizard lounge if you want.'

#

Early that evening, Adam phoned his brother to tell him about his discovery of the location of the city in their dreams. Charlie seemed interested, but distracted. He described his most recent dream to Adam and seemed slightly disappointed that it was not another shared experience. He also told him about the visit with Mandisa and Rhona's phone call from her sister. Adam was intrigued by Charlie's dream, wondering again if these were memories of previous incarnations and was fascinated by the dream therapist's insights. The news of the call from Rosalind excited him further. Unlike Charlie, who seemed to be getting more and more worried by the unfolding events, Adam was thrilled to have so much "far out stuff" validated by his own and his brother's experiences.

Now, however, he had other thoughts to occupy his mind. In the five years since Adam had befriended Lynn and Nick he had never known them to celebrate anything other than birthdays and Christmas, so he was intrigued as to the reason for this evening's forthcoming feast. As he walked through the darkening streets, he speculated as to what the reasons might be. Perhaps they were going to get married, he wondered. No, he knew that they didn't believe in marriage. "Who needs a piece of paper from the government to prove your commitment?" Lynn had once said, "If you love each other and trust each other, what difference will it make?"

Adam turned up the collar on his jacket and shivered. He had hung up his winter coat in the belief that spring was finally here, but now he realised this decision had been premature – there would probably be a frost tonight. Passing a kebab shop, he felt a wave of heat lap at him from the open door. The smell of cooking food reminded him of how hungry he was. He hadn't eaten since breakfast to make sure he had plenty of appetite for tonight's meal – Nick was an excellent cook. Maybe a rich uncle had died leaving one of them a huge inheritance, or maybe they had won a large sum on the lottery, he thought. He then remembered that as far as he knew, neither of them had any wealthy relatives, despite Lynn's claim to have royal lineage, nor did they ever buy lottery tickets. "Voluntary tax," Nick called it. "Exploiting the needy and greedy in society is what I reckon." By the time Adam reached the flat it had become completely dark. He noticed an unfamiliar black car parked opposite, but couldn't see if there was anyone inside. He visited his friends here so often that he knew most of the vehicles that were usually stationed in this road. He then became aware of the fact that the entire street was full – there was not one empty parking space. At that point he realised that there was a football match on this evening and despite the fact that the new ground had an extensive car park there was still not enough room for all the vehicles, so inevitably the adjacent area suffered from the overspill, especially where permits were not required. Walking up the back steps he glanced up at the sky. Although there were no clouds, he couldn't even see one star piercing the eerie red gloom of the city-lit night. It's a shame, he thought, if there's one thing I miss about living in the countryside it's not seeing the stars above. He reached the top of the staircase and turned to look behind himself to habitually check that he had not been followed. Naturally there was no one there – there never was, but he did notice the full moon emerging from behind a chimneystack, bright enough to penetrate the urban illumination. He smiled. He loved the full moon. It always made him feel a little light hearted and light headed which was a great mood to be in when celebrating with friends. As usual he had to knock loudly to compete with the music. The thumping beats of the Afro-Celt Sound System shook the frosted glass panel at the top of the door, so he had to bang arhythmically to make himself heard. Lynn opened the door with a grin and ushered him in. She looked fantastic. Uncharacteristically she had forsaken her usual jeans and t-shirt for a bright red, low-cut figure-hugging dress. Adam's heart skipped a beat before he pulled himself together and handed over the bottle of wine he had been clutching, trying not to stare below her neck. As she turned and led the way to the lounge Adam wondered if perhaps she had put on a little weight. He was so familiar with her figure, having stolen so many glances at it, that he couldn't help thinking that her shapely hips and too-visible breasts might be a slightly larger. But then again, maybe it could just be due to the tight dress and his lunar madness. In the living room she turned the volume down on the hi-fi, opened a bottle of beer for him and passed it over, smiling demurely.

'Nick's in the kitchen,' she said, 'cooking up something special.'

The table in the bay window was laid ready for a meal with candles adding to the flickering glow cast by the unrealistic "coal-effect" gas fire.

'Hi Nick!' Adam called in the direction of the kitchen, 'hard at work I hope.'

'You betcha mate!' Nick shouted back cheerfully, 'Skin up will you, I'm kind of tied up at the moment!'

Adam dutifully sat on the sofa and started rolling up on the coffee table where he found the familiar stash tin. 'So, not working this evening then?' he asked Lynn as she sat opposite, then realised the stupidity of the question as he looked up at her smile. 'Ah, no, of course you're not, otherwise you wouldn't be here would you? And you wouldn't have invited me round. What I meant was that you must have taken the evening off.'

'That's right, Adam,' she replied. 'Six years in the same job and at long last the evil bitch lets me have some time off.'

'Blimey, what came over her?' Adam had met Martina a number of times and knew that she did not treat her staff or her customers well. It was a mystery to him why Lynn had stayed there so long.

'She's finally realised that I'm totally indispensable,' she said, 'so when I told her I was leaving she suddenly turned nice and tried to like butter me up and stuff. She offered me a twenty percent pay rise, an extra evening off each week and an extra week's holiday.'

'Well, she's probably realised that most of her customers only come in because you work there – the male ones at least. So....are you really packing it in?'

'Abso-fucking-lutely!' It was the broadest grin Adam had seen on Lynn's face for quite some time.

'That's great! I'm amazed you haven't left before, the way she treats you. You're certainly capable of getting work that will be much more fulfilling than that.' He paused while he lit the joint. 'That must be why we're celebrating! Yay! Cool. Have you got another job lined up?'

'No, I haven't – I just decided it was time to leave and yes, it is one of the reasons we're celebrating.'

'You mean there's more? I can't wait!'

'Well, you'll have to. We shall reveal all when dinner's ready and we're all sat at the table together, yeah?'

Adam offered her the joint but she shook her head. 'I think you ought to take it to the chef,' she suggested, 'the poor man's been slaving over a hot stove for like, the last three hours.'

He did as he was told and said to Nick, 'did Lynn tell you about her painting of that place in my dream?'

'Yeah, freaky eh?' Nick responded distractedly, preoccupied with the cooking and savouring the joint, 'Bit of a coincidence, I 'spose, right?'

'It's got to be more than that, though,' said Adam earnestly, 'I mean, the place was *exactly* the same!'

'Whatever,' said Nick, unimpressed, 'you probably both saw the same picture somewhere.'

'But what about my brother dreaming it too?' persisted Adam.

'Well, you didn't actually *see* what he dreamt did you?' countered Nick. Then added, 'here, take these plates through would you mate?'

Five minutes later, they were seated before an impressive array of delicacies that were steaming from the dishes on the table. Adam was glad of having something to drag his eyes away from Lynn's cleavage. He certainly didn't want to be noticed ogling like a schoolboy. He and Nick each had a glass of the cheap red wine that Adam had brought, but Lynn unexpectedly, had only water.

'I would like to propose a toast,' Nick declared holding up his drink with a mischievous look on his face. 'Here's to our best friend Adam for sharing this little celebration with us!'

'Yay!' agreed Lynn raising her water too.

'To you two as well. Sláinte!' said Adam as they chinked glasses. He was still curious as to the other reason for tonight's merriment, but was very happy just to be with his favourite people in the world. He felt totally relaxed in their company and knew he could just be himself because they liked and accepted him just as he was.

'*And…*,' continued Nick significantly as he put his arm around Lynn's shoulders, '..to us, our future and the little bastard that's growing in Lynn's tummy!'

'What? You're pregnant?' gasped Adam, genuinely amazed and nearly choking on his wine.

'Don't look so surprised, mate,' chuckled Nick, 'it's pretty easy really.'

'Bloody hell! I mean congratulations!' he stammered. Suddenly he smiled, stood up and circled the table to hug them both. 'Wow, I really am gob-smacked – not that I thought you couldn't, but I never thought you *would*. I always saw you as the eternal couple, I never imagined you with a child. You just don't seem like parental types.'

'Nobody *seems* like a parent until they've got children, Adam,' giggled Lynn, 'and anyway, we've been together seven years now and I'm not getting any younger. They reckon that once you're over thirty childbirth gets more difficult if it's your first, with more chance of complications and stuff. I'm twenty-eight, so I got in with a couple of years to spare. Might even have another one.'

'Hey, steady on love,' cautioned Nick jokingly, 'let's not rush things, eh? You might have fucking twins!'

'Oh God,' Lynn gasped merrily, 'I hadn't thought of that.'

'Come on, eat up!' instructed Nick, 'I didn't spend all afternoon cooking all this lovely grub just so it could go cold!'

As he helped himself to a couple of stuffed vine leaves, Adam realised that his long-held and improbable fantasy must finally be put to rest. Even though he dearly loved them both, he had half-hoped that one day, maybe Nick and Lynn might drift apart, amicably of course, leaving him with a chance for his dream romance. In a way it was a relief. At least now he would find more of an incentive to curtail his secret and shameful thoughts. He drained his glass, refilled it and started eating.

'So that's why you're leaving the shop…' he said, having only just come to that understanding. 'When's it due?'

'Not til November,' replied Lynn, 'but we want to be settled into our new home by then.'

'You're moving too? Bloody hell!' exclaimed Adam taken aback again, 'I never imagined you leaving this flat either, you've lived here as long as I've known you.'

'Yeah, well, I reckon seven years is long enough in a place like this,' commented Nick refilling Adam's glass, 'It's nice enough, but it's too small to raise a family – yes, there will probably be more than one eventually – and think of all those iron steps going down to the garden when you've got a buggy, not to mention when the thing starts toddling – fucking nightmare!'

'Yeah, right, I see your point,' agreed Adam, 'Got anywhere in mind? Somewhere with a garden? Southsea? Milton?' Nick and Lynn both shook their heads. 'Further? Not North End surely? Definitely not Leigh Park!' They shook their heads again, smiling. Nick looked at Lynn and nodded for her to answer.

'Prepare yourself for another shock, Adam,' she said slowly, 'we're leaving the Portsmouth area altogether. It's a shit-hole and I *so* don't want to bring up my baby here.'

'Bloody hell!' said Adam again. 'Nobody ever leaves Portsmouth! Well, not many anyway. It's like a black hole, once you're in, you're trapped. I know people who've been talking about leaving for years, but none of them have. And you were born here Nick, you've never known anything else or lived anywhere else – you're the archetypal Pompey lad, down to earth, unchanging…'

'It's never too late to change mate,' asserted Nick, 'I'm only thirty-eight, same as you, so I'm not in my fucking grave yet, far from it. I'm looking forward to it an' all – new life, new place, new start, having a family…yeah, it's all quite exciting really.'

'Well, I wish you all the best,' said Adam raising his glass and taking a gulp. It suddenly dawned on him that he was soon to be deprived of his only friends. The prospect was so terrifying that his heart seemed to stop for a moment. 'God, I'm really going to miss you guys,' he uttered sadly and felt his eyes moisten at the thought. Recognizing that he was being selfish, he cleared his throat and said, 'So, where are you going anyway?'

Again Nick and Lynn exchanged glances. Nick leaned forwards and said 'Well Adam, we would miss you too…which is why we were going to ask you if you wanted to come with us.'

'Blimey!' he responded in amazement.

'Well that makes a change from "bloody hell",' commented Lynn wryly.

'But won't you want to just your own little private family unit?' asked Adam, 'I mean, you won't want other people hanging around and getting in your way...you know "two's company" and all that – you'll have enough on your hands as it is.'

'Of all people, Adam, *you* will not be in the way,' Lynn assured him. She reached across the table, took his hands and looked into his eyes. 'We love you mate,' she said affectionately.

This was too much for him and this time, genuinely touched, he could not hold back his tears. He squeezed her hands wordlessly, and then took his back to wipe his eyes.

'Anyway,' added Nick light-heartedly, trying to ease his embarrassment, 'we need a live-in baby sitter! Not that I'm trying to put you off or anything. Think about it at least, will you?' He stood and began collecting the starter plates. 'I'll get the main course.' Lynn stood to lend her assistance.

Adam sat in stunned silence. All this news was a lot to take in. It meant big changes in his life, even if he didn't go with them. Go where exactly? They hadn't actually said, had they? He unconsciously emptied his glass again. As Nick carefully put the moussaka on the table and replenished Adam's drink, Lynn brought the salad.

'You didn't tell me where you were moving,' he said swigging some more wine. 'Have you found somewhere?'

'Ah, yes. Well spotted my man,' started Nick as he sat down again. 'Help yourself,' he said, indicating the dishes and as Adam did so he continued, 'All the time Lynn's been working she's been saving a little bit every month and whilst I was dealing I built up a good little nest egg from my ill-gotten gains, so we reckon we've probably got enough to buy a nice little croft or something to do up, hopefully with a bit of land to grow fruit and veg, maybe a few chickens....you know, all that "Good Life" hippy shit, right? You'll love it!'

'Yeah, I have always wanted to have a go at that....' said Adam pensively, '...but you *still* haven't told me where...hang on, you said "croft" not cottage. Does that mean Scotland, the seat of my ancestors? That cold and distant land of rain and wind and ice and snow and mad bag-piping, haggis-hunting, whisky-drinking, deep-fried Mars Bar eaters? I thought all you could grow there were sheep, oats and hardened arteries.'

'You guessed right,' confirmed Lynn with a grin, 'but I think you *totally* need to revise your stereotypes, yeah? Anyway, the whole of Scotland doesn't have the same weather. I've got an old school friend who lives up there. Have you heard of the Findhorn Foundation?' Adam shook his head chewing a mouthful of food. 'I'm surprised! It's a famous international spiritual community and eco-village, yeah? Anyway, it's one of the sunniest places in Britain and they produce these like, huge vegetables and that just on sand and compost – you'd be amazed at what they can grow there. I went there once to like, see it for myself. It was great, really nice vibe too and lovely people, but I so would not want to live there mind. I think I'd find community living a bit claustrophobic and I want to move somewhere quieter – they get thousands of visitors from all over and they do courses and everything and loads more just come to have a look around. No, we were actually thinking of somewhere a bit further north but on the east coast, which is drier than the west and doesn't get so many midges. Your brother is up there somewhere isn't he?'

'Yeah, but I've only been once since he moved up,' Adam replied. 'He was actually born there, Scotland I mean, er... somewhere near Stirling, before our parents moved south – they were always moving. He's older than me, but we always got on O.K. It's just that it seems so far away....'

'And so peaceful,' added Nick. 'Wouldn't you like to get away from all the fucking traffic and pollution?'

'Yeah, I guess...' he said uncertainly. He wasn't sure if he liked the idea or not. Of course he would love to be with his only friends in the world and possibly closer to Charlie too, but such a big change was a bit daunting. He had found himself quite a comfortable rut in Portsmouth. However, he realised now that that is what it was, a rut. Sometimes it is easier to do nothing than change, even if your situation is not ideal. He knew that was how a lot of people bumbled through their lives, putting up with the status quo, not taking any risks and becoming...well *boring* if the truth be told. Maybe it *was* time for a change, he thought. He then remembered the strange things that had been happening recently and the astounding news he had heard here this evening. Change was happening anyway, without any action on his part, so maybe he should just leap aboard and enjoy the ride.

'Promise you'll think about it?' urged Lynn with genuine affection.

'Yeah, of course,' he responded, 'but it might take me a little while to get my head around it.' He washed down more food with more wine and noticed that his glass was empty again. He picked up the bottle but was surprised to find that was empty too. He looked up at Lynn. 'Did you have some?' he asked her, but she shook her head. 'Blimey have I drunk all that?' he wondered aloud.

'No, I've been helping you out mate,' said Nick, 'I'll open another.'

'Lovely grub by the way,' said Adam, tucking in enthusiastically, although he realised he hadn't fully appreciated it whilst receiving his friends' startling news. They finished the main course in silence, Adam absorbed in thought and the others allowing him to be so.

'I think I need a break before the pudding. How about an inter-coursal joint?' suggested Nick.

'Shall I do the honours?' asked Adam. He fetched the tin from the coffee table and started sticking the papers together.

'We've got a favour to ask you mate,' said Lynn. He looked up briefly and nodded 'Uh-huh?' before spreading out the tobacco. 'You know we're not like, religious types or anything,' she continued, 'but we quite like the idea of our child having a kind of mentor or guardian, you know, like a godfather, but not that - maybe an *un*-godfather. Whether you decide to come with us or not, we'd really like you to be that person, Adam. Would you be up for it? You can think about it if you like.'

Adam smiled warmly. 'No need to think about it,' he said sincerely, ' 'course I'll do it. I'd be honoured. Any kid from you two is going to be pretty far out anyway.'

'Cheers mate,' said Nick grinning, 'I knew you'd say yes!'

'I'll drink to that!' said Adam and did so.

Lynn declined the joint when it was offered. 'I've got to go to the bathroom,' she said. The two men had smoked it all between them by the time she returned. 'Shall we have pud then?' she proposed.

Nick took the empty dishes back to the kitchen and reappeared announcing, 'And now, the pièce de resistance!' He placed a covered dish on the table, and then removed the lid. 'Iced Chocolate Indulgence!' he declared.

'Wow!' exclaimed Adam and Lynn simultaneously.

'Looks amazing,' added Adam.

'It'd better bloody taste it too,' commented Nick, 'it took fucking ages to make and I expect we'll scoff it in five minutes!'

Tucking in, they all made noises of ecstatic appreciation. Adam sucked each spoonful slowly so he could to extend the pleasure as long as possible.

'It's exquisite Nick,' Lynn told him, 'you've surpassed yourself!'

'Yep it is pretty bloody good isn't it?' he agreed, 'even if I say so myself.'

'Mmmm,' was all that Adam could manage, so totally absorbed was he in the flavour.

Ten minutes later they were seated comfortably on the sofa, hands on their distended stomachs feeling like bloated Buddhas. Adam sipped his Irish coffee, savouring the taste and then offered Lynn the after dinner smoke. She declined, so he passed it to Nick.

'That's the third joint you've refused this evening,' he remarked, 'I've never known you to pass one over before. Are you alright?'

'I'm fine Adam,' she replied, 'I've just given up that's all – you know, for the baby.'

'Bloody hell,' he said, 'I never thought I'd see the day. It was always you who could smoke anyone under the table....'

'And I'll be next,' added Nick forlornly, savouring the acrid fumes and looking fondly at the reefer he held between his fingers, 'my days of indulging my vice are numbered...solidarity and all that, you know?'

'Bloody hell *again!*' exclaimed Adam, truly alarmed, 'No fucking way! I don't know if I can take any more of this! You two have taken my whole world, turned it upside down and shaken it all about. There are only so many surprises a guy can be expected to take in any one day. I'll have to have some more wine to dilute the effect. Anyone else?'

Nick held his glass up.

'Not for me,' said Lynn.

'Hang on – you've given up drinking as well!' realised Adam. 'You used to drink everyone under the table as well. What *is* the world coming to?'

'That's the power of maternal instincts for you,' she stated matter-of-factly, 'last week I wouldn't have believed it myself, but as soon as I found out I was up the duff - wham! The health of my baby became totally the most important thing on earth, yeah?'

'Blimey,' commented Adam, 'well, here's to you. To all three of you – live long and prosper!' He lifted his glass in salute and drank deeply, having reached the point whereby he had forgotten the consequences of the excessive imbibing of alcohol, especially when mixed with dope smoking.

'I'll drink to that!' echoed Nick, who despite having a higher tolerance was himself approaching a similar state.

Adam had a worrying thought. 'Is all this going to affect the trip to Poland?' he asked.

'No way!' Nick assured him, 'I bought the tickets this morning – including yours. It's months before Lynn wouldn't be able to fly. This is going to be our last chance for a foreign holiday for a while. A final fling before the new adventure!'

'I'll drink to that!' said Adam and guzzled more wine, much to Lynn's amusement. She realised for the first time just how different it would be when in the company of the stoned and drunk when not in the same condition herself.

In fact, Adam was not accustomed to drinking much more than the occasional beer or glass of wine. Generally he found that he much preferred just getting stoned having learned long ago that his constitution couldn't cope with too much alcohol. Soon, the combination of inebriants were colluding to blur and fuzzy his senses. He realised too late that he had drunk too much and he started feeling queasy. Suddenly he knew he was going to throw up and rushed to the bathroom as fast as his unsteady legs and swimming head would allow him. His shoulder smacked into the doorframe as he entered spinning him round so that he fell with his head hanging over the bath instead of the toilet. He retched loudly, vomited until his stomach was empty and then sat on the floor sweating, panting and groaning.

He made a feeble attempt at washing the bath, but the lumps of undigested food were clogging the plughole, even when he tried poking it weakly with his forefinger. He gave up, his head pounding and turned to the basin where he splashed his face and washed out his mouth. He emerged a couple of minutes later, wobbling slightly, his face pale and pasty.

'Sorry about that,' he managed to mumble as he slumped back on the settee.

'What a waste of good food,' commented Nick, shaking his head in mock sorrow.

'Yeah, it tasted better first time round too,' Adam muttered.

'Here, you'd better drink some water,' suggested Lynn sensibly offering him her glass. 'You ought to stay tonight too,' she added, 'you can kip on the sofa.'

'Yeah, thanks, I might just do that,' he replied and without changing position, closed his eyes and became unconscious.

'Uh-oh, white-out,' observed Nick. 'He will *not* feel good in the morning.'

'And you won't be much better either,' said Lynn, glad to be sober.

CHAPTER SIX.

Charlie sat in a comfortable armchair beside a large blazing fire. The logs cracked and spat as the searing flames slowly consumed them. He loved staring into an open fire. When he was a child, time spent at his grandparent's house often involved long interludes of inactivity during which he would gaze into the smouldering coals and imagine deep dwarfish mines and dragon's dens. He smiled at the memory and then momentarily became engrossed in the range of colours emanating from the burning wood. He could see yellow, green, red, blue, mauve and orange as the logs and the gasses released from them were incinerated. It was a welcome distraction from his current dilemma and his worries regarding the increasingly bizarre happenings.

He looked down at his hands where they rested in his lap and noticed with a sense of curiosity and slight uneasiness that they had begun to resemble those of an older person. He was only in his mid-forties, hardly even middle-aged. He didn't feel ready to face the physical decline normally associated with the advancing years, not yet anyway. He frowned and lifted his hands for a closer inspection. There was no doubt that they showed the signs of someone who worked with hand tools. There were calluses and a few scars, but the fingers appeared to be thinner and paler than he remembered, the knuckles more pronounced, the skin looser. How could this have come about so quickly? It was quite worrying that this could happen without him having noticed before. With a rising sense of panic he watched the process of deterioration accelerate before his eyes. In astonishment and dismay, he saw his hands age rapidly, fingers curling up to become claw-like, their joints swelling and beginning to throb with pain. Now extremely alarmed, he tried to stand but found it more difficult than usual. His back was stiff and sore, his knees weak and his muscles ached uncharacteristically. He forced himself upright by pulling on the mantelpiece and as he straightened he looked into the mirror above the fireplace. An ancient, unfamiliar face stared back at him with an expression of shock. Thin wisps of white hair topped a high wrinkled brow, below which watery, sunken eyes peered from dry, colourless and papery skin. Shaking in horror, he raised his hands to touch his cheeks and saw the reflection do the same. He suddenly felt immensely sad that he had become so old so quickly and sensed he had so little of his lifespan left. He loved life and wasn't ready for it to end so soon. Tears welled up in his eyes and he began to whimper. He collapsed into his chair, utterly devastated and started sobbing uncontrollably.

He woke crying into his pillow, the overwhelming sorrow still consuming him. He looked at Bess' face resting peacefully beside him. Suddenly she opened her eyes wide and her face contorted into an unfamiliar expression. Her mouth opened and rasped in the voices of two old men, 'Now you know how we feel!' they declared, 'You must make the casket to save us from this fate.' Charlie yelled and leaped from the bed, waking again as he hit the floor. This time Bess' voice was her own. 'Oh, you poor love,' she said softly seeing his tears as he climbed back beneath the covers, 'another bad dream? Do you want to tell me about it?'

To begin with he just needed to comfort himself in her warm and reassuring embrace. She held him close, kissed him gently on the brow and stroked his head lovingly, whispering, 'It's alright, it was just a dream.' However, she was becoming increasingly disconcerted by these recurring nightmares of his and worried that they were both seemingly helpless to reduce their frequency or severity.

Eventually Charlie relaxed his grip and pulled away slightly. He sighed, exhaling heavily. 'Wow, that was pretty intense,' he said. And then explained his dream to her as they lay in each other's arms.

'It's got to be something to do with this bloody casket and those old men in Rhona's dream,' he concluded, 'she was shown that it was some kind of rejuvenation device and now I'm being clued-up on what feels like to be ancient and near the end of my life. Somehow these guys are getting into my head and messing with my dreams and they seem to be getting increasingly desperate.'

'Maybe....' Bess conceded uncertainly, 'but it could be that you're just getting carried away by it all, you know, getting a bit stressed and letting your thoughts spiral out of control?' This was what she hoped in any case and was unwilling to face the ramifications involved in accepting that there were strangers interfering with Charlie's mind. 'I mean, you don't *really* think this casket can make them younger do you?'

'No, of course not,' he replied, but then added, 'I don't know....I'm tired and confused and my brain feels like it's...all kind of scrambled up with thought's I can't control. I don't know what to think.'

He looked at the clock and groaned. It was still early. Sighing heavily, he sat up and said, 'I'm going for a walk to the beach before breakfast. The fresh air might help clear my head.'

It was a chilly morning. Slowly drifting mist had frozen and coated everything with tiny white crystals of ice, which although beautiful, also looked hauntingly eerie in the dim grey light. A pulsing orange glow moved steadily towards the village half a mile away as a gritting lorry rumbled slowly along the single-track road. Charlie opened the garden gate, his breath fogging the air in front of him and hastened across the fields at a pace designed to keep him warm. The grass scrunched under Charlie's feet as if fragile sugar sculptures were disintegrating beneath his marching boots. The air cleared as he approached the coast to reveal that where the dawn brightened the east, a watery, almost translucent sky merged with the serene surface of the ocean so that there was no discernible horizon between the tip of the peninsula and the distant cliffs of Caithness. Striding along the beach, deep in thought, he shivered and stuffed his hands in his pockets, wishing he'd brought his gloves with him. Every spring he seemed to forget that it could still get cold again and carelessly cast aside his winter-wear too soon. Small piles of frost-edged bladder wrack, heaped up and then half covered by the last storm, broke through the sand at regular intervals. A few lazy ripples lapped gently at the shore, hardly making a sound and even the small handful of gulls flapped slowly and quietly as if still half-asleep at this early hour. Charlie hopped across the burn on the scattering of rocks that nature had provided as stepping-stones and climbed to the top of the tallest sand dune. He hadn't been this far along for a few months and noticed with sadness that recreational vehicles had seriously eroded this fragile habitat. He recognised what fun it would be to race up and down the beach and over the dunes on a quad or scrambling bike, but he wished that they would do it elsewhere. Looking down he saw that the sea was also rapidly eating its way into the dunes and had to acknowledge that, whilst sometimes seemingly catastrophic when related to a human lifespan, the activities of humankind on the Earth would become insignificant in terms of geological ages. Yet here he was with, as far as he was aware, just the one lifetime to himself, to follow his path, to live out his dreams, to chose his own personal destiny and it was being stolen from him. His own fate was now being interfered with by other people, control over his actions was being taken out of his hands. It just was not fair and the injustice of it rankled him. Why had he been singled out? He deeply resented it, but couldn't decide whether just to do their bidding and get it over with so things would go back to normal or stubbornly stick his heels in and tough it out. He looked across to Sutherland. A thick mist remained over the middle of the firth, obscuring the opposite coast like his own future was hidden from him. Only the hills showed above harr, topped by a fresh fall of snow, clear and crisp against the sky. Sighing heavily, he could only hope that such clarity would eventually emerge in his thoughts. He turned from the view and trudged slowly home.

'Why don't we get away for a few days?' Bess suggested tactfully over breakfast, 'It would give you time to think. A change would do us both good. You're still owed some holiday time aren't you?'

'Aye, three or four days I think,' replied Charlie.

'Well, it's Friday - we could at least have a long weekend, maybe go to the west coast or somewhere.....what about Skye?'

He thought for a moment and soon realised the good sense of the suggestion.

'Good idea,' he said, 'I'll ask Rhona this morning. It might help to have a wee break. Maybe my imagination has just been playing tricks on me. The mind's a funny thing you know....'

#

The blurred image of Charlie crumbling with age vanished abruptly. Adam only just managed to distinguish the difference between the pounding inside his head and the hammering outside it before the door was kicked in, the frame splintering as the lock-keep broke away with a chunk of wood still attached.

'What the....' He managed before a uniformed policeman grabbed his shoulder and roughly wrenched him into a seated position. He was not ready for this. It was far too early in the morning and he was suffering severely from the effects of last night's overindulgence. His vision swam and the pain in his head ballooned sickeningly with pressure. Vomit surged from his gullet and spewed from his mouth like a discharging sewerage outflow, drenching the crotch of the constable in front of him. The man yelled in revulsion, let go his hold and belatedly stepped back out of range, looking down in disgust at his trousers. Adam flopped back into a recumbent position, his face a pale, waxy grey, the colour of wet pastry left too long exposed to the air. He saw through half-open eyes, five other police officers, one of them female, bustling into the room. Two of the men, no doubt of senior rank, were in "plain clothes", the younger, shorter one wearing a leather jacket and the taller one with a tweed overcoat. The man in leather flung the curtains open to reveal a clear, bright early morning. The other man walked over and looked out of the window. The shade of his matt, silvery hair looked unnatural, the colour of a zinc-galvanised bucket, and he stood with stooped shoulders as if his height had always been a burden to him. The constable with the spattered uniform went to the bathroom to clean up, muttering irritably.

'What the fuck's going on?' demanded Nick angrily, emerging dishevelled from his bedroom and dressed only in boxer shorts. Lynn appeared behind him, just wearing a long t-shirt. Squinting in the light, she looked dazed and confused.

'On the sofa you two,' ordered leather-jacket brusquely. Too stunned to move of their own accord and too tired to respond, they were herded by two of the uniformed officers, but noticing the pool of sick just in time they managed to avoid stepping in it before being thrust roughly onto the sofa next to Adam.

'Oi, watch it you, I'm bloody pregnant,' snapped Lynn indignantly when she was pushed, provoked into recovering her voice. 'You can't just barge in here and shove us around!' she continued irately, 'I know my rights – you need a warrant *and* you've broken my bloody door, you ignorant thugs! I only just painted it an' all! It's no wonder people don't have any respect for you bastards, behaving like that.'

'Well darlin', we did knock first,' leather-jacket responded facetiously, obviously enjoying himself, 'except you didn't answer, so we had to let ourselves in. And here's the warrant,' he said waving a folded piece of paper he had just fished from his pocket. The top of his head was balding, with the few greasy strands of black hair that lingered there plastered to his sweaty scalp; his beer-belly hung over his belt, barely contained by the yellow nylon shirt.

'Let me see that!' insisted Nick. Snatching the document from the man's fingers, he started to scrutinise it.

'Don't you worry, son – it's all in order,' he said in a gleeful and patronising tone, 'we had no trouble getting it knowing your past record and seeing as how you've been associating with the miscreant Mr. Mackay here, who has been behaving *very* suspiciously of late.'

'What? No way,' protested Adam weakly through his suffering, 'I don't know what you're talking about….I haven't done anything.'

The man gave orders to the uniformed officers to search the flat.

'You won't find anything,' asserted Lynn, confident that she had burned all the roach-ends and safely concealed the stash - this had been her customary night-time routine since Nick was convicted of selling dope three years ago.

'You must know I stopped dealing after I was busted,' added Nick, 'you're not that fucking stupid and neither am I. What's really going on? Are you after a new pair of boots or something?' He returned his attention to the warrant and noticed something for the first time. 'Hang on, you must have got this wrong. It says here that you're acting under the auspices of the Prevention of Terrorism Act, and you are "authorised to search for evidence or materials that may be used in conspiring to cause an explosion." You are most definitely barking up the wrong fucking tree mate. There's no way we've got anything to do with that that kind of shit.'

'Let's just say we have some information from a very reliable source,' said the leather-jacketed man, taking back the warrant and sitting in the armchair opposite with a smug expression. His glassy eyes looked tiny in proportion to his large rounded face, like marbles dropped into risen dough. Deep creases surrounded his stubby nose as if it had been pushed on as an afterthought. Meanwhile the policewoman was searching the bedroom, the sound of opening and emptying drawers coming through to the living room. The man who was puked upon investigated the ashtray, rubbing the ashes between his fingers before sniffing them, causing him to sneeze loudly. Nick smiled cheerlessly and shook his head in bemusement. A third officer was rifling the drawers of the desk and the forth was in the kitchen from whence the sound of clattering and crashing indicated the deliberate lack of care going into the search.

'Oi, careful you!' shouted Lynn. 'You aren't allowed to break our stuff! I'm gonna put in a complaint, you bastards!'

'Now, now dearie,' cautioned the detective condescendingly, 'don't get your knickers in a twist!' Then he added with a chuckle, 'Though I couldn't help noticing you weren't wearing any…ha ha….'

Lynn blushed angrily and pulled her t-shirt down lower, keeping her knees together. '...and you don't want to go putting a complaint in either – the word of six upstanding police officers will carry a lot more weight than that of three dirty hippies, especially when one of them's a convicted drug dealer.'

'God, it's no wonder you lot are called the bloody "filth" ' fumed Lynn, 'you're not doing yourselves any favours you know, people would be a lot more cooperative if you treated them with respect, yeah?' She crossed her arms and sulked, knowing that she shouldn't let him get to her, but unable to suppress her sour mood. She hated getting woken early in the morning at the best of times, but having the door kicked in, followed by the careless treatment of their belongings and this indignity, was really too much. Nick was quietly seething by her side. However, with tremendous and uncharacteristic self-control, he kept his mouth shut, realising that he was at their mercy. He was certain that they would find nothing, yet he had heard of instances when drugs were planted by the D.S. if they had some reason to bear you a grudge. He wondered if it was true of the anti-terror lot. Adam sat with his head in his hands and elbows on knees, feeling dreadful. He felt sure it was the worst headache he had ever had in his life and was sincerely regretting that he had drunk too much the night before. He wanted so much to lie down. Since he had been forced to sit up, he had been feeling increasingly nauseous. Suddenly he stood and groaned 'gotta puke,' as he lurched forwards and staggered towards the bathroom. The policeman who he had previously thrown up on was in his path and just managed to step to the side thereby averting a repeat of the experience.

'Watch him, Evans,' ordered leather jacket, 'we don't know if he's putting it on or not – we don't want him flushing anything else do we?' With a look of distaste, the man reluctantly did as he was bid, although the sound that followed demonstrated the authenticity of Adam's condition.

The female officer came out of the bedroom and looked at leather jacket. 'Nothing there sarge,' she reported impassively. The other two had now ceased their rummaging as well, also with no results. The detective raised his thin eyebrows and then frowned, obviously disappointed. Throughout the entire time of the search, the tall man with the tweed coat had stood motionless and silent at the window as if engrossed in some goings-on in the street below. Now he spoke for the first time, but still without turning.

'The settee and armchair, Detective Sergeant Andrews,' he said impassively, 'and Mr MacKay's pockets.'

'Up you get, you two,' instructed Lynn and Nick's minder and the female officer guided them to the fireplace where they stood dejectedly and with reproachful looks, like two teenagers unjustly castigated by authoritarian parents. The sound of the toilet flushing was followed by the sight of a bedraggled-looking Adam, who then had his pockets searched by his escort. The other two officers proceeded to remove cushions from the furniture and to cautiously slide their hands into the crevices. Apart from a button, a few coins and a lot of gritty fluff their search proved fruitless and Adam's pockets yielded merely his tobacco, rolling papers, a cigarette lighter, a crumpled tissue, his door key, library card and eighty-seven pence.

'I told you you wouldn't find nothing!' reasserted Lynn crossly, 'and you've made a right mess too, you scumbags!' Nick wondered if the hormones of pregnancy were responsible for her crabbiness – she was usually the level-headed one regardless of the situation, while he ranted and railed.

'Careful missy,' warned Andrews, 'there's only so much shit we'll take from you before we *make sure* we find something, if you get my drift, so you'd better button you lip, alright?'

'You...' she started, but Nick stopped her.

'Leave it Lynn,' he advised firmly, half raising a hand as she struggled to control her temper, but his eyes betrayed the fact that he too was very annoyed.

The man in the coat finally turned from the window, but looked at no one. He walked towards the door, eyes forwards, as if he were alone in the room.

'Bring Mr MacKay in for questioning will you sergeant,' he said simply and strolled out of the flat.

'But...' Adam started to protest weakly.

'Now, now, Mr MacKay,' admonished the detective, 'I advise you to accept our invitation gracefully. It will be better for all of us, but especially for you. You see, if I have to arrest you, then under the Prevention of Terrorism Act 2008 we are authorized to hold you for up to fourteen days without charge and believe me, our surveillance has revealed that we have sufficient and justifiable suspicions for that eventuality.'

'Don't worry, Adam,' said Nick resolutely, 'we'll be on your case. We'll contact Liberty. They won't be able to keep you long – he's bluffing, they've got fuck all on you mate.'

Reluctantly, Adam allowed Evans to shepherd him from the room, the other officers following in silence and Andrews bringing up the rear voicing a sarcastic, 'have a nice day,' as he disappeared through the door.

'Fuck!' uttered Nick, hitting the wall.

'Bastards!' declared Lynn vehemently.

They looked at each other for a moment before sighing heavily and then hugged in silence. A minute later Lynn moved away slowly and sank into a chair. 'Poor Adam,' she said dejectedly, 'I don't know how they got it into their heads that he's got anything to do with terrorists and stuff. That's so weird.'

'Yeah,' agreed Nick, 'he's a peacenik if ever there was one. I'll see if I can find the number for Liberty in the phone book and see if they can help.'

'I 'spose I'd better start tidying up too,' said Lynn without enthusiasm, 'I'll see if they broke anything that matters. I'll start in the kitchen.'

'Then we'll go down the station,' said Nick, 'and hassle those fuckers until they let Adam go.'

'You bet.'

#

The working day finished at 4.30 on Friday afternoon at Fantasy Furniture. Rhona always felt that nobody was going to do anything useful in the last hour before a weekend, so there was no point being there. "Poet's day" Rory called it: 'Piss Off Early, Tomorrow's Saturday,' he piped up every week without fail, but the others didn't mind the repetition because he was such a genial character. Charlie had left in a hurry, eager to start preparations for his trip, having been given permission for his requested time off.

Rowan was the only one denied the early finish. She had to stay for an extra hour to tidy up so the workshop was clean and clear for the next working week. She usually met her best friend Jenny afterwards at the "Organic Planet" café in town to exchange their week's news. She didn't mind being the only one left working on a Friday; in fact she rather enjoyed having the place to herself. She was using the powerful industrial extractor and vacuum cleaner, nicknamed "Marvin" by the staff to suck up all the chippings and sawdust from around the workbenches. Due to the noise of the machine she was listening to her MP3 player "to take the groan out of the drone" as she put it, today's selection was her own "System of a Down" playlist. Consequently she didn't hear the door to the workshop open and close, but she gradually became aware of an unwelcome and disagreeable presence. She turned slowly and with a sense of dread to see Grant watching her steadily and stonily. The fresh dressing on his injured nose was a conspicuous patch of white that remained motionless whilst the rest of his face twisted as he smiled humourlessly through his gum chewing.

'Forgot my jacket,' he announced impassively, showing no sign of looking for it. Rowan sensed a sinister undercurrent in his manner and bearing. She could tell his thoughts were not on his jacket, but on her, with his all-too-familiar leer and cocksure posture. Immediately she knew that he had hostile intentions, so with a sudden surge of dread she turned nervously and quickly fled towards the storeroom wheeling Marvin behind her as a protective shield.

'What's the matter darlin'?' he crooned, a lopsided grin distorting his face as he swiftly followed. 'Don't you like me? Come on now – I only want to be *friendly*. How about a kiss love? You know you'll like it!'

She could tell he was drunk and realised with a growing sense of terror that he had become both emboldened and careless with the effects of alcohol. She managed to summon up enough courage to face him and speak. 'Go away!' she ordered indignantly, but seeing it made no difference she became more desperate and pleaded, 'leave me alone!' She sounded weak and whiney and her fear almost overwhelmed her as Grant got closer, but fuelled by her panic, she pushed the extractor in his direction as hard as she could and dashed into the storeroom. She had misjudged the speed of his reactions, not quite managing to slam the door before he got his foot between it and the frame, having nimbly dodged the machine. She pushed hard against it but with his greater strength he managed to force his way through easily. She retreated across the small room and Grant closed the door before slowly approaching. He spat out his gum.

'Come on now, you know you're gagging for it, you little gothic tease,' he whispered hoarsely, 'what's under that boiler suit, eh? I bet it's tight black leather, eh? All nice and hot and sweaty. Let's have a look shall we?'

Rowan's back was now against the wall and her heart was pounding painfully in her chest. A cold, tight fear gripped her, constricting her lungs and causing her breath to become shallow and ragged. All memories from her self-defence classes had abandoned her, so she felt utterly helpless and completely vulnerable. She managed to force a tiny voice to whimper feebly from her knotted throat. 'Please leave me alone,' she begged piteously.

'Well, let me see...' he responded, rubbing his chin, '...your eyes are wide, your face is flushed and you're panting – I reckon you're getting turned on here....I know I am.' He looked her up and down. 'Take them off,' he said, indicating her overalls.

Paralysed with fear, Rowan found herself incapable of movement. She couldn't summon the impetus to either flee or fight, or even to scream, her adrenalin seemingly spent on her racing heart. She merely stood against the wall, rigid and trembling.

'I see I'm going to have to help you,' said Grant, reaching his hand towards the poppers. Finding a moment of strength, she slapped his hand away and started to move, but he was too quick and managed to pin her back with his hands on her shoulders.

'Oh, you've got some spirit after all,' he observed casually moving his face closer to hers to kiss her. She could smell his fusty sweat, the beer and cigarettes on his breath. She quickly turned her face away in revulsion, almost gagging on the combination of odours. He started to kiss and lick her neck and ear, his rough stubble scratching her sensitive skin. Revolted by the feel of his wet tongue, she grunted and squirmed in disgust. Twisting her head, she struggled in his grip, but he just laughed and then pulled his face away to stare menacingly into her eyes. Engrossed by his desire, he let go of her arms to rip open the front of her boiler suit. He grabbed her breasts, one in each hand and started kneading them roughly, pinching her nipples hard through her bra. The intense pain caused anger and indignation to course through her, reviving her survival instincts. Now her hands were free she started hitting him around the head.

'Bitch!' he shouted, grabbing her arms again. Not so easily subdued in her fury, she brought her knee up with all the strength she could gather. He doubled over with a loud groan, holding his stomach. Realising she had missed her target, she nevertheless tried to bolt for the door. She was jerked to a stop as Grant grabbed her collar and wrenched her overalls down over her shoulders, trapping her arms. With one hand knotted in her clothes at her back, he turned her quickly round and glowered at her, raising his fist. Without further thought she head butted his nose. With a cry of pain, he released her to bring his hands to his face. She dashed towards the door again, but somehow, probably numbed by the alcohol, he managed to recover quickly enough to grab her wrist and twist it to force her arm up behind her back. He rammed her forwards so hard against the wall that it knocked the air from her lungs and split the skin on her temple. She gasped and tried to wrench herself away, but he pressed the full weight of his body against her back, so she merely struggled ineffectually in her attempt to escape. She knew that he was now controlled only by his animal impulses and that he wouldn't stop until he had satisfied them fully. He put his mouth next to her ear and, breathing heavily, grunted, 'I'm going to fuck you *so* hard you little slut, your cunt'll be sore for a week. You've been baiting me ever since I got here, with your tight little arse and page three tits. Now I'll show you what it's like to have a *real* man inside you.'

Repulsed by his intentions and by his hot, moist, stale breath on her neck, she struggled more fiercely, drawing strength from her increasing rage. Suddenly he spun her round and punched her hard in the side of her face. She heard her cheekbone crack and, stunned by the force of the blow, became dizzily aware of flying across the room as if in slow motion. She hit the floor like a falling tree. After a second of numb shock her head exploded in agony and her mind reeled sickeningly. She tried to stir weakly, but her body was limp and inert as if the impact had driven out her capacity to move. The pain intensified further until her whole being wanted to scream, but her voice had disappeared too. Then abruptly, she felt all of her physical senses cease. Even though she was still looking from her own eyes she felt completely separated from her body. She watched as if in a trance, detached and unable to resist, while Grant crouched over her like a predator with its quarry. Blood had oozed through the bandage on his nose and merging with the sweat on his lip it dripped slowly onto her clothes. He grabbed the front of her boiler suit with both hands and as he tugged it down off of her arms and then from her legs, her seemingly lifeless body flopped like a rag doll. The reprieve from her bodily suffering was short lived however. As he ripped off her flimsy top, her head bounced on the floor and all bodily feeling suddenly rushed back Her emotions also returned in full force. The pain was unbearable, but caused by someone else, instead of being self inflicted, it incensed her - but she *knew* pain. She had utilised it in the past, so she focussed on it and took control of it, as she had done before, riding it and using it to focus her anger. Her loathing for him erupted with a force she had never felt before completely displacing all traces of fear. She *would not* allow this to happen! But her body refused cooperate or to respond in any way, feeling weak and useless from her struggles against his superior strength and the maltreatment it had already received. He reached underneath her back to unfasten her bra, thrusting his face in her cleavage to nuzzle at her breasts, his slimy tongue revoltingly wet and his unshaven chin like a rasp scraping her soft tender skin, but in his increasing frenzy he was unable to unhook the clasp, so he turned his attention to the button of her jeans. His eyes were bulging dementedly and he seemed totally overcome by his all-consuming lust. She had put up with his taunting and leering for too long and now he was subjecting her to the worst kind of abuse. He was an abhorrent, hideous maggot and she *could not* allow him to do this.

All at once Rowan's mind became sharp and clear and she tried to summon up all her reserves of strength. Gritting her teeth and grimacing she concentrated on the hate and the bitterness and the hostility she had been suppressing months. She felt it stirring like an agitated wasp's nest. She had driven it deep inside herself, burying it beneath a thick layer of self-harm, but now it was finally released and came bursting through, disgorging like septic pus from an inflamed and suppurating wound. Panting excitedly, Grant unzipped her fly and grabbed the top of her jeans. She felt herself fill with an intoxicating, exhilarating power. He had succeeded in yanking her jeans and underpants to her ankles, freeing one foot and was now fumbling with his belt buckle as he kneeled between her legs. The invigorating, turbulent energy boiled up and swelled within her until she could no longer contain it, so she focused on his detestable face. He unfastened his trousers and leaned forward. At that point she lost control, unable to contain the build-up of force as it exploded in a frenzy of hysterical wrath.

Die you bastard, die! she thought, with such an intense animosity that it felt like her head was being torn apart. In that instant, her brain and sight filled with an overwhelmingly bright, white light as a searing flare of malevolence burst like a laser from her mind. Suddenly Grant shot upright, went rigid and stopped breathing. His mouth gaped stupidly and his eyes glazed over. Silently he toppled backwards, fell heavily against the door and his last breath sighed out of his lungs like the sound of a punctured airbed.

#

After eight hours in an empty cell Adam was beginning to feel an improvement in his condition. He had accepted a plastic cup of water, then lay down on the bed and slept. The duty officer opened the door, offering him more water, which he gladly accepted. The man then led him wordlessly to a stark interview room where he was left alone to sit in a cold plastic chair one side of a grey Formica-topped table. Now that his faculties were beginning to return, he was feeling both depressed and somewhat confused about the events of earlier that day. What had appeared to be a drugs bust, turned out to be an anti-terror raid and this left Adam completely bewildered. How on earth could they suspect him or his friends of any terrorist activity? His brain still hurt, so he rested his elbows on the table and put his head in his hands. He wasn't worried about his situation – he knew that they had nothing on him, but he was pissed off at the infringement to his liberty and by the fact that he was totally powerless and at their mercy until they saw fit to release him. Where were they anyway? All he wanted to do was answer their questions so he could go home and crash out in his own bed. His circumstances were made to feel worse by his hangover; there was no denying it. He felt like shit. Why had he drunk so much? Then he slowly recalled the revelations of the night before and a surge of shock welled up in him, as if he was again hearing the news for the first time. Lynn was pregnant! She was giving up dope and drink! Not only that but Nick was doing the same. They were moving away too. Basically his two only friends in the world were turning his world upside down. *How could they do this to me?* he thought. He then quickly realised that he was being utterly self-centred and inconsiderate. Nick and Lynn had every reason to be blissful. At a moment of great joy in their life they had made decisions to enhance their happiness and now he was secretly castigating them for it. *Wow, I never realised I was such a bastard,* he thought, *I'm just jealous, selfish, self-absorbed, thoughtless and mean.* He recognised that his inappropriate infatuation with Lynn had clouded his reason and his tendency to dwell on his own petty troubles had completely distracted him from the path of wisdom. Intellectually, he had imagined that he held high ideals of universal goodwill in a kind of Buddhist-cum-New Age-cum-Taoist-cum-humanist melting pot of the philosophies that appealed to him. With a depth of comprehension that belied his predicament he understood at last that the time had come to walk his talk and to actually live his life in the way that he believed everyone should. He should let go of petty grievances, worldly desires and self-obsessive behaviour and embrace the way of altruism, compassion and service. Maybe this is why he had spent most of his adult life in discontent – he had been ignoring his true destiny.

The door opened, interrupting his thoughts and he looked up to see Constable Evans enter followed by the man who had been wearing the tweed overcoat when the flat was raided that morning. Having dispensed with the coat his suit was revealed, which bizarrely was the same strange shade of grey as his hair. His jaded expression bespoke a world-weary character, with just a few scant but irritating years to endure until the yearned-for relief of retirement. To Adam he brought to mind the commonly used clichéd character of detective fiction.

He remained on his feet. 'I am Detective Inspector Gordon,' he said flatly by way of introduction, 'and there are a few questions we would like you to help us with Mr Mackay.'

'Can I get a coffee and some paracetamol please?' asked Adam politely.

'Coffee we can do,' said Gordon, nodding to Evans, 'but we are not authorised to supply medication.'

'What, even though you're the D.S.?' joked Adam feebly.

D.I. Gordon did not smile. 'We are *not* the drug squad Mr Mackay,' he said levelly,' If you could remember the details of the events this morning, you would recall that I am with the Special Branch.'

'Oh yeah, I forgot.' A puzzled frown creased his pasty brow. 'So, how come you think I've got anything to do with terrorism? What was that raid all about?'

'We were searching for evidence,' came the reply.

Adam was beginning to feel exasperated, 'I haven't got a clue what you're talking about. When are you going to tell me what's going on?' he demanded impatiently.

'I'll leave that to my colleagues from the Security Services,' said Gordon wearily, looking at his watch.

At that moment two men in dark suits entered, accompanied by Evans bearing Adam's coffee in a cardboard cup. One of the men was aged about thirty with broad shoulders and a blonde army-style crew cut, whilst the other was in his forties with short black hair and of a slighter build. The expressions they bore were both cold and aloof. Evans placed Adam's drink on the table in front of him, glanced nervously at the newcomers and left briskly.

Detective Inspector Gordon spoke impassively. 'He's all yours gentlemen,' he said and walked unhurriedly from the room, closing the door quietly behind him.

Adam sipped his coffee, slightly apprehensive at the appearance of these two "military types". What was the "Security Service" anyway, he wondered. Was it MI5 or MI6? Was it more like James Bond or John le Carre? The older man sat opposite him and placed a file on the table. The blonde man moved to the other's shoulder standing like a soldier at ease, maintaining an icy glare on his pale and frozen face. The first opened a file of printed pages and placed his hands flat on the table as he made a show of perusing the first page. Adam tried to read the tiny print upside down, but his head was still hazy and he found himself painfully craning his neck, so he gave up.

The man looked up, his face unreadable and spoke in a level and reasonable tone, 'We'd like you to cooperate fully with us Mr Mackay and then we can release you promptly.'

'Who are you people?' demanded Adam, his headache souring his mood, 'What is this, the bloody Matrix or something? Are you Agent Smith? What's with the dark suits and all the mystery?'

'Now Mr Mackay, there is no need to get excited,' said the man calmly, 'I am Agent Cameron. If you could just answer the questions, we can get this over with and then we can all go home.'

Adam sighed as he resigned himself to accepting this. 'O.K. fire away,' he said.

'When did you last see Professor Thomas Oakley?'

Adam's stomach tightened. That was the last thing he expected to hear. What could Tom Oakley have done? He certainly looked and sounded incredibly nervous when he'd seen him the other day. Adam still felt a strong sense of loyalty to the professor, which combined with his natural inclination to be unhelpful when confronted by figures of authority, led him to conceal the truth. He wasn't sure if he managed to hide his reaction or his feelings, so feigned an expression of mild surprise and bemusement.

'Gosh, I haven't heard that name for a while,' he said, which he believed was not in the strict sense of the word an actual lie, 'he was my old archaeology professor when I was at university. Is he still alive? What's the old bugger been up to?'

'Just answer the question please Mr Mackay,' said his interviewer wearily, 'when did you last see him?'

Adam frowned and pursed his lips, then looked at the wall and scratched his head as if trying to remember. 'Oh, er it must be about ten years or so, I guess.'

'Really?' said Cameron sceptically.

'Yeah, I reckon it must be about that,' Adam asserted more positively.

'So, in that case could you tell me who it was you were seen chasing through the streets on Wednesday at approximately eleven a.m.?

'Ah,' said Adam, '…er.' His eyes darted about as he tried to think quickly. 'I, um, saw him take a purse out of an old lady's bag, so I gave chase.'

'Really?'

'Yes, really.' Adam knew he was unconvincing, yet couldn't help but keep up the charade, not knowing what else to do.

'Oakley has been under continual surveillance for the last week. You were *seen* Mr Mackay.'

'Was that really the prof? I didn't recognise him after all these years.'

His questioner gave a heavy sigh. 'You are not a very convincing liar and believe me, I've met quite a few. Please do me, yourself and everyone else a favour Mr Mackay and *never* consider a career in the theatre. Your acting skills are truly pathetic and if you keep up this pretence, I shall become rather annoyed.' He paused, glanced briefly at his colleague and then stared fixedly at Adam. His dark eyes showed an intensity betraying the impatience that was still not apparent in the tone of his voice.

'Are you threatening me?' asked Adam. 'You can't do that.'

'Perhaps you don't fully appreciate the seriousness of your situation,' he continued evenly, 'under the Prevention of Terrorism Act, we are empowered to detain you without charge for up to fourteen days. Now if you would rather avoid that outcome, I suggest you cooperate fully with our enquiries.'

With growing unease, Adam realised that he was trapped. He had thought they didn't have anything with which to implicate him so he had sustained a somewhat flippant attitude to his situation. The reality he now faced was beginning to fill him with fear. The thought of being held in detention was terrifying to him and the pain in his head had eroded his resolve.

'O.K., I'm sorry,' he relented, 'but I don't have anything to do with terrorism. I'm a peace campaigner, I deplore violence in all its forms!'

'Any kind of subversive activity implicates you as far as I'm concerned and associating with the prime suspect in an act of terror consolidates my view, especially when you make an effort to conceal your involvement.' Cameron's demeanour was becoming increasingly stern as he spoke. 'Now if you can't be more forthcoming it will not go well for you.'

'But I haven't associated with any terror suspects,' pleaded Adam, 'Nick and Lynn are the only people I know…you don't suspect them do you?'

'Only by their connection to you Mr Mackay.'

'But…'

'Now let me get to the point. It seems that I'm going to have to spell it out for you. Two weeks ago, there was an attack on the School of Humanities at Southampton University where there was a conference and exhibition of Sumerian artefacts. An explosive device was employed to cause extensive damage to the property and to priceless, irreplaceable exhibits therein.'

Adam still didn't see how he was connected with any of this. 'I saw that on the news,' he said, 'no one was hurt were they?'

'Luckily not. The attack was at night and the security guard was given a two minute warning.'

'Didn't they get a call from some Muslim extremists claiming responsibility?' asked Adam, not seeing where this was going, 'something about sacred relics they reckon were stolen from their country?'

'We suspect the call to have been a hoax. It made no sense, why would they destroy the relics they held sacred?' It was a rhetorical question, but the next one required an answer. 'Where were you on the evening of twentieth of April Mr Mackay?' snapped Cameron.

Adam's heart leapt at the sudden directness of the enquiry. 'Oh, er…I don't know, I don't do much that's memorable and I never know what the date is - I don't need to. I was probably at home or at Nick's – that's where I usually am in the evenings.'

Cameron looked unconvinced. 'Hmm. I shall return to my earlier question: when did you last see Professor Oakley?'

Adam realised there was no point in trying to conceal the truth. He was scared enough now, just to comply and get this nightmare over with. 'O.K. I did see him on Wednesday,' he conceded, 'but *that* was the first time I had seen him in ten years. It was a complete surprise to see him after so long, especially in Pompey. So I went to talk to him and he ran away, so I chased him because I didn't understand why he was running – I thought he must have mistaken me for someone else. Anyway, what's he got to do with all of this?'

'He is our chief suspect for the bombing.'

'No way!' exclaimed Adam.

'We have a considerable amount of CCTV footage, although the suspect was hooded which makes positive identification difficult.

However, the phone call giving the warning was traced to a mobile phone registered in his name. The only reason we haven't arrested him was so that we could follow him and see if he led us to any accomplices. That was how you became implicated. Unfortunately, he somehow gave our operatives the slip after your encounter.'

'Bloody hell, he did look a bit shifty when I saw him. I wondered why he ran away. I never would have thought it of him. I knew him quite well when I was at university. That was why I ran after him – I hadn't seen him since and then suddenly there he was in the supermarket. I couldn't understand why he panicked. I thought it might be something to do with his research, you know? He got his career ruined, had death threats and got his place done over. They nicked his computer and beat him up and everything, so he must have been on to something.'

'You may be disappointed to hear that your conspiracy theories have no grounds in reality,' commented Cameron. He was beginning to look bored again and continued dispassionately, 'Professor Oakley has long been an alcoholic and a compulsive gambler, the one habit fuelling the other. The incidents to which you refer were more likely to have been related to the non-payment of debts from "unofficial" sources. Needless to say, he would not have divulged to you or anyone else the true nature of his troubles for the shame and stigmatism attached to such activities.'

Adam was shocked. 'Blimey, I knew he liked a drink, but I never knew he was an alcoholic.' He thought back to the times he spent as a volunteer on archaeological digs. There was always a crowd of students gathered in the evenings for a few beers in one of the "portakabins" or marquees, more often than not accompanied by Tom, but Adam had not noticed him drinking any more than anyone else. Then again, he couldn't remember ever seeing him drunk either, which either spoke of self-limiting behaviour or the higher levels of tolerance gained by a hardened drinker. Suddenly a thought occurred to him.

'Hang on a minute,' he said, 'if Oakley knew that his assailants were loan sharks or whatever, how come he bombed the exhibition?'

'Decades of alcohol abuse take their toll on the mind, said Cameron. 'There is no doubt that he has become quite deranged in recent years and virtually lost all grip on reality. We have seen his medical records.'

'Poor guy,' said Adam quietly.

'He may be unfortunate Mr Mackay, but nevertheless, quite possibly guilty of a very serious crime. Do you know where he is now?

Is there anywhere you can think of that he might be hiding or running to?'

'No, sorry,' he replied truthfully.

'Is there anything else you can tell me which might shed light on this case?'

He shook his head.

Cameron stood, gathered his papers and left the room without another word.

Adam looked at the stony-faced subordinate. 'Can I go now?' he asked.

The man's eyes shifted to Adam's face, although every other part of his body remained immobile giving the impression of a sinister exhibit in a waxwork museum.

'No,' he replied simply in a deep voice and returned his gaze to some unknown blank spot on the far wall.

Adam still couldn't believe that the Prof was capable of the bombing. He used to *care* so much about even the tiniest fragment of any artefact as if they held some sacred significance to him personally. In a way, they did, Adam supposed. Archaeology was Tom's religion and the awe with which he held any of the finds was tantamount to worship. Maybe the guy was framed. Could it be that he was still in trouble with undesirable characters, due to unpaid loans, who having failed to locate him had resorted to extreme methods so that the police would find him instead? For a few minutes, Adam's thoughts spiralled in confusion until his headache throbbed once more. *God, I'm hungry,* he realised suddenly. He had completely emptied his stomach that morning so now that he no longer felt nauseous his appetite had returned with a vengeance. As he realised this he began to feel weak with hunger.

'Can I have something to eat?' he asked his guard. This initiated the same response as his previous request, so he sighed miserably, crossed his arms and sulked, feeling quite sorry for himself.

Five minutes later, Cameron returned with Constable Evans in tow.

'Well, it seems that there is no implicating evidence at your flat – in fact all indications seem to point to the fact that you are just a sad loser - so we are going to release you for now. Please do not attempt to leave the city until further notice in case we need you to help us with our enquiries again. Thank you for your cooperation. P.C. Evans will show you out'

#

Jenny sat alone, hunched forwards at a table in the "Organic Planet" cafe, sipping an apple juice and flicking through the latest copy of "Vegan Futures" magazine. Her bleached hair with scarlet and purple streaks hung like frayed curtains obscuring her features. Wearing purple Dr. Marten boots, black tights and a short red dress under a long, dark blue cardigan knitted by her grandmother, she had given up on her attempts to look cool and fashionable more than a year previously, accepting that it was unrealistic given her build and shape. Now she dressed for a combination of comfort and self-expression, which whilst it may not have resulted in less ridicule from those of her peers who had more spite than heart, made her feel better about herself nonetheless. Besides, she had almost entirely convinced herself the she no longer really cared what they thought, having reached the conclusion that their opinion was unworthy of consideration. Above the gentle buzz of conversation she could hear the unmistakeable and stirring voice of Michael Stipe from R.E.M. She lifted her round, freckled face to glance once more at the clock on the wall. Rowan was now thirty-five minutes late. Ever conscious of her appetite, Jenny wondered whether or not to order her meal. Next to the placemat her dormant phone waited expectantly for an explanatory text. She guessed that Rowan must have had overtime or something, although that had never happened before. She drummed her fingers impatiently on the varnished wood, beginning to get annoyed. Rowan was her best friend, in fact one of her only friends, so she considered that she was at least entitled to a message to account for her tardiness. She tried to be more accommodating. She too had been a bit of a loner, an outcast because of being slightly overweight, clumsy and unstylish. When Rowan had befriended her a couple of years previously and accepted her the way she was, she felt so pleased that she was initially more tolerant of the girl's sometimes strange behaviour. She sighed and as she put her glass to her mouth to drain her drink, the stud in her lip chinked on the rim. At least it was no longer painful. She wondered how Ro's new piercing was doing. Last time she had seen her, it had got infected and looked very sore. She tried to revive her interest in the magazine but failed. She found it hard to believe that Rowan was so thoughtless as to not send a text when she knew that Jenny was waiting.

Jim, the café's genial proprietor, started clearing an adjacent table that had been recently vacated. Bent willingly to his task, his wiry frame moved in time with the music as he hummed along to the tune.

He was clean-shaven, had blond dreadlocks tied into loose a ponytail whilst working and wore a clean green apron, sporting the establishment's logo, over his combat trousers and blue "ban the bomb" t-shirt.

'Where's Rowan today then?' he enquired, familiar as he was with the habits of his regular customers. 'Not still working surely? She doesn't do overtime does she?'

'I don't know,' said Jenny crossly, 'she's late though. She should have been here ages ago and I'm starving. She hasn't even sent me a text.'

'Have you tried phoning her? Maybe her phone's broken or run out of charge,' he suggested helpfully.

' 'spose it could be,' she admitted grudgingly, 'I could try calling her, but I don't see why I should.'

'Fair enough....but if you want to know what's going on...'

'Okay, you're right, I'll give it a go.' She did so but there was no answer and after a few rings the message service cut in. She sighed heavily and looked at the clock again.

'Do you want another drink while you're waiting?' asked Jim having finished the wipe down.

'No thanks. Actually, I think I'll wander down to the workshop and see what she's up to. I might be able to hurry her up.' She stood reluctantly and put her phone in her pocket. 'Can I leave my bag here?' she asked indicating her small rucksack, which bulged with folders and heavy books from college.

'Sure, no problem,' he said, 'I'll just put it behind the counter for you.'

When Jenny reached the premises of "Fantasy Furniture" she saw a flashy-looking blue car parked outside and guessed that Rhona must be helping out one of the other staff. The windows showed her that the lights were on inside so she opened the door and stepped over the threshold, but seeing no one in the main workroom called out, 'Rowan! Are you there?' Receiving no answer, she crossed to the entrance of the "lizard lounge" and peered in. It was unoccupied. Next she tried the finishing room but here the lights were off. *That's odd,* she thought, *the workshop's not locked and the lights are on – there must be someone here.* It was only when she tried the office that she noticed

Rowan's bag. Then she thought she heard a faint shuffling noise from the adjacent storeroom.

'Ro?' she called nervously as she approached the door. When there was no response, her concern deepened. She cautiously turned the handle and pushed the door, but there seemed to be something against it on the inside, preventing it from opening. There was a faint whimpering noise and some incoherent murmuring. 'Rowan, let me in!' she called urgently, pushing harder, 'What's the matter?' The heavy obstruction shifted slightly as she shoved with more force, until there was enough of a gap to put her head through. Rowan was huddled in a corner, only half clothed, curled into a ball and rocking backwards and forwards.

'Oh my God! What's happened?' asked Jenny as she squeezed her body into the room with difficulty. She quickly stepped towards Rowan, but tripped over the obstacle that had been blocking the door so that she stumbled to her friend's side. She was so concerned with Rowan's welfare that she didn't think to look back. She gently parted Rowan's hair with her fingers and suddenly saw her bloody and bruised face.

'Oh my God!' she said again in horror. Tears sprang into her eyes as she realised how badly her friend was hurt. 'Oh Ro, oh shit…. I'll call an ambulance.' As she fumbled in her pocket for her phone Rowan whispered indistinctly.

'What? What did you say Ro? I didn't hear you,' prompted Jenny softly.

'I killed him,' Rowan repeated hoarsely, 'I killed him, I killed him.' She started to whine and moan and then broke into sobs, but still repeating the same words over and over.

An icy realisation crawled into Jenny's heart and clenched. She slowly turned her head and for the first time saw Grant's body. His face was turned towards them so that she could see the blood that had oozed from his nose and ears to form a sticky pool beneath his head. His lifeless eyes were frozen wide open, staring blankly and horribly at the world he had left. She gasped in shock and involuntarily inhaled so deeply that her breathing stopped. After a few seconds her heart was pounding so strongly that she exhaled with a moaning howl of dread. She bit her hand and stared transfixed with fright, until Rowans' litany penetrated her senses. She fought back her rising hysteria and set her mind on taking deep, even breaths, trying to calm herself sufficiently to cope with the demands of the situation.

'Oh God, Rowan! Oh no! Did he…,' She stopped unable to articulate her question.

Her friend shook her head. 'I stopped him... I killed him, I killed him...'

'Well, the fucking bastard deserved it if you ask me' Jenny said vehemently. 'Don't worry, Ro,' she added reassuringly, switching on to "coping" mode, 'it's all over now. I'm here. I'll look after you.' She realised she was gripping her phone so tightly she could have crushed it, so she relaxed her grip. 'God, your face is really swollen, he must have totally whacked you. Here, let's get your jeans back on shall we and I'll call an ambulance.'

'Rhona,' said Rowan weakly, 'call Rhona.'

Jenny phoned for an ambulance, called Rhona and then put a comforting arm around her friend and sat shaking uncontrollably whilst hoping that help would come soon.

CHAPTER SEVEN.

Nick and Lynn were waiting in the reception area when Adam was released. They each hugged him warmly and he enjoyed the comfort it gave him.

'Bastards took their time didn't they?' said Nick by way of greeting.

'Shh!' admonished Lynn, noticing the stern glare that his comment had drawn from the duty officer. 'Anyway,' she continued, 'more importantly, how are you Adam? Are you alright?'

'Well, apart from a splitting headache, I'm bloody starving,' he replied. 'I could eat a horse!'

'That won't be necessary, mate,' Nick informed him with a grin, holding up a carrier bag, 'we've brought some sandwiches. I'm not surprised you're hungry though after the amount you puked – what a waste of all that lovely grub.'

'Yeah, sorry about that,' said Adam shamefacedly, 'but I can tell you I really appreciated it at the time.' They walked to Adam's flat, arriving as the streetlights came on and he'd just gobbled the last of the food. 'God, what a day,' he mumbled through his mouthful as he lifted his key to the lock, 'I'm glad to be home. That's funny…'

'What?' asked Nick.

'Could have sworn I'd locked the door, but it looks like I just pulled it to…ah well.' He shrugged and pushed the door open. They walked into the tiny entrance hall and hung up their jackets. 'I'm still famished,' he said, 'but I think there's not much in the cupboards at the moment. Shall I ring for pizzas or something?'

'Sounds good to me,' agreed Nick.

Lynn opened the door to the bed-sitting room and gasped, 'Oh my God!'

'What?' asked Adam, edging past her. 'Holly shit! The bastards....' he muttered, 'the complete and utter bastards.' He sighed heavily and seemed to deflate in the process.

Nick followed them in. 'What a bunch of cunts!' he blurted fiercely.

They moved into the middle of the room and looked around them at the mess. The place had been well and truly ransacked. Adam's books and clothes were strewn across the floor and furniture. All the cupboard doors hung open, as did those drawers that hadn't been upturned onto the carpet. He collapsed into an armchair, put his head in his hands and made groaning noises. 'I really could have done without this,' he complained, 'why is this happening to me?'

'What is it with these guys?' fumed Nick, 'they have absolutely no fucking respect for anyone or anything. The sooner we get our arses out of this city the better, I say. And you're coming too, Ad – you don't have a choice – we can't leave you on your own in fucking Babylon, man - not when there are wank-stains like these guys around.'

'Come on Adam,' urged Lynn and pulled him to his feet. She put her arm around his shoulders and gave him a squeeze, 'we'll help you get tidied up, yeah? It won't take long with the three of us.'

He rose half-heartedly and looked around dejectedly, scratching his head, uncertain of where to begin. It seemed like such a monumental task. Lynn gave him another hug of encouragement.

'You start on the clothes, yeah?' she proposed, 'and me and Nick'll like, do the books and stuff?'

They started picking up items at random, attempting to establish their original locations. This was going to take a long time.

'I know what,' chirped Nick, 'let's put on some shit-kicking music, shall we? That'll put us in the mood.'

'Good plan,' agreed Lynn, 'what d'you reckon Ad?'

'Er, yeah, O.K.' he consented unenthusiastically, 'you can choose.'

Lynn went over to the stereo and perused the adjacent shelf of CDs.

'Ah ha, this is the one,' she stated eagerly, 'no-one kicks shit like the Chilis –let's get red hot!'

Lynn's assertion proved to be correct. The beats of "Blood Sugar Sex Magick" combined with her good cheer soon got the men in the mood for the clear-up and before long all three had wholeheartedly embraced the task, embellishing it with dance moves as they worked.

One and a half hours later they all sat cradling cups of tea, job done.

'It's amazing nothing was broken,' stated Nick, 'those anti-terror fuckers are a law unto themselves. Though, having said that, the D.S. probably would've done the same.'

'Just a couple of bent paperbacks,' agreed Lynn, 'pretty lucky really.'

'Yeah, could've been a lot worse,' said Adam. 'What about your place? Any damage?'

'Well apart from the door...only to Nick's pride,' commented Lynn wryly with a slight smile and a sideways glance at her partner. Nick chose to act deaf to the comment.

None of them had even considered that putting in a complaint was an option. They had been part of the soft drug sub-culture long enough to have learned how the system *really* operated at street level when you were on the "wrong side of the fence".

'I wonder what they were looking for?' pondered Nick.

'D.I.Y. bomb kit or something, I guess,' ventured Adam, 'or something to link me to Tom Oakley at any rate.'

'God, isn't that totally crazy though,' Lynn surmised, 'your old prof tied up in a bombing an' all. And what is he, like sixty or something?'

'Yeah, at least. Though I still can't really see him doing anything like that, despite what the pigs said. I knew him quite well before and he never seemed the type...I can't imagine he would have changed that much, not even in ten years.'

'Well, you never can tell,' commented Lynn, 'it's amazing sometimes what people do under duress – who knows what he's been through?'

'Well, I don't know about you guys,' interjected Nick, 'but I'm ravenous, let's ring for those fucking pizza's before I flake out!' The others agreed. 'Tell, you what Adam,' he added, 'while we're waiting, how about I pop down the "offie" and get some beers in, eh?'

'Oh, no way Nick,' said Adam categorically, shaking his head, 'after last night I don't think I could face another drink yet – my headache's only just gone.'

'Oh yeah mate, sorry, I forgot you've got a delicate constitution. But hey, I reckon I'll leave it out too – I don't want to be the only one drinking and it's time I started cutting down anyway, you know, in solidarity with the marvellous mum-to-be and all that.' He grinned and gently patted Lynn's belly. She smiled back with adoring eyes, which moistened at his words. Nick leant over and kissed her tenderly.

'Oh God,' commented Adam with a sigh, 'now I'm going to have to put up with you two lovebirds turning all gooey! I'm going to skin up...'

#

There was a vast soundless emptiness, an immensity of absolute nothingness. Rowan's consciousness stirred feebly in the immeasurable void and as she gradually became dimly aware of her own existence, she began to perceive the silence and the endless space. It was not the quiet of peace nor the spaciousness of freedom, but more of a bleak, unending absence of time and matter in which she drifted as an insubstantial, insignificant speck of solitary perception. She felt a growing sense of hopelessness and despair, floating impotently as the only entity in the perpetual, noiseless gulf. She was simultaneously lost and trapped, stranded and isolated in an infinite yet smothering vacuum. Although she had no memory of recent events she was certain that everything and everyone she knew had gone and she was left alone, bereft and forsaken, irrelevant in eternity. Panic gripped her heart, although she had no awareness of a body, no corporal presence, nor any physical sensations that she could identify. If she could remember how she came to be here, she might be able to find her way back. But there was no way of getting her bearings, there were no directions in this featureless existence, it all looked the same; although she couldn't actually "see" at all. Perhaps if she tried to picture the people she cared about, a connection might be established with the real world. She thought about Rhona, Jenny, Charlie and Bess, but she was unable even to conjure up their images. Desperately she strove to search out, to find anyone, anything, anywhere in this unceasing desolation. But there was nothing. She tried to call out, but she had no voice. She was completely and utterly lost. *Is this the end?* She wondered. *Am I dead? Will it stay like this forever or is this just a "waiting room" before the final stage?* She wasn't ready to die. She felt her life was only just beginning. Surely her future was not going to be so quickly snatched away from her? Wretched and forlorn, she abandoned her hope with her aborted attempt to reach beyond the eternal chasm and surrendered herself to the unwelcome numbness of oblivion.

#

When dinner was ready, Charlie called Bess in from the garden where she had been picking dandelions for wine making.

'Shall I open a bottle of plonk?' he offered when she entered the kitchen. Even dressed in her baggy old gardening clothes she looked sexy to him.

'Mm, yes please,' she replied enthusiastically, 'what have we got left?'

Charlie examined the bottles in the larder. 'Er, rhubarb... blackcurrant... plum... dandelion...gooseberry...'

'Dandelion,' she interrupted, 'seems appropriate today.'

He opened the bottle and filled their glasses whilst she hung up her jacket and washed her hands. They hugged lovingly before sitting down to eat.

'Here's to the weekend!' proposed Bess lifting her drink.

Charlie chinked her glass and took a sip. He smacked his lips. 'I still reckon this was our best wine from last year,' he observed.

'It is very nice,' she allowed, 'but I think that the gorse flower just has the edge.'

They started eating and discussed the possible places on Skye where they could park up their camper van. It was only two hours drive to the bridge, so they would have plenty of time to reach the right spot.

The phone rang. Charlie sighed and started to rise saying, 'why do people always ring at dinner time?' It was true. Invariably, no matter what time they sat down to eat, be it six o'clock or nine, someone would call.

Bess held up her hand. 'Leave it for the answer-phone,' she suggested, 'whoever it is can wait. It'll probably be double glazing or a "free" energy audit.'

'No, I've got a funny feeling we should get this...' he said, sensing a significance in the call, albeit not apparent in any difference to the ring tone.

'Alright, but I'll go – you cooked the dinner after all.'

She walked through to the office and picked up the phone.

Charlie waited uneasily whilst he listened to Bess' responses, his anxiety growing with each one.

'What?...When?....Oh Jesus.....How is she?....Can we visit?....OK...' There was a longer pause. 'Oh fuck....bloody hell....but how?...' Bess listened quietly for a minute before commenting further. 'Shit. What did they say...? Uh huh...do you want us to come round...? Do you need any help....? Right, well give her our love....yes we'll ring Sunday. Bye.'

Charlie looked at Bess when she re-entered the room. She was deathly pale with an expression of shock on her face.

'Something's happened to Rowan,' he said. 'What is it? What's happened?'

Bess looked even more astonished at this. 'How did you know?' she said.

'I don't know, I just knew. Tell me what happened. How is she?'

'She's in hospital with a broken cheekbone,' she said slowly, 'Grant tried to rape her.'

'What? The bastard, I'll kill him...'

'He's dead,' she interrupted.

'Dead?' He asked incredulously.

Bess nodded.

'How?'

'Apparently, he just keeled over in the attempt.'

'Bloody hell.... Well, good riddance I say - that saves me having throttle him.' Although intellectually and in his heart Charlie was a pacifist opposed to the death penalty, he was finding that at the moment, for the first time, he was glad that someone was dead. However, he was too concerned with Rowan's welfare to consider the moral implications. 'And how's Rowan? Apart from the broken cheekbone I mean. I guess he must have hit her? Can we see her?'

'She's unconscious and still in shock and at some point they'll have to operate to put a plate in her face. We can't go in for a couple of days at least. He punched her pretty hard....'

'Bastard! I hope he suffered.' Charlie was experiencing unprecedented levels of hatred. He had never felt like this before. His usual outlook was one of tolerance, understanding and forgiveness. Injustice and the strong subjugating or abusing those weaker than themselves, had always angered him to some degree, but in this case his affection for Rowan as a kind of surrogate daughter had aroused intense and unfamiliar feelings. He had always disliked Grant, but until now would not have wished him dead.

'Apparently not,' said Bess, 'it seems he just dropped dead in an instant. They're still waiting for the autopsy, but they reckon it must have been a heart attack or something.'

'Poor Rowan...' muttered Charlie, starting to feel teary, now that his surge of shock and hatred of Grant had subsided a little. Their forgotten meal grew cool as they sat in silence for a couple of minutes, unable to form any words while the distressing news sunk in. They had both become very close to Rowan in the last few years; Bess as Rhona's best friend, Charlie as a workmate and both of them on many social occasions. They had watched her grow from a secretive pre-teen to a delightful, though at times unfathomable, young woman and they had come to love her dearly.

'You said that you knew that something had happened to her,' Bess reminded him.

'Oh...er...aye well it was just a kind of feeling really,' Charlie said hesitantly, 'just when you were on the phone, I couldn't hear who you were talking about, but I somehow guessed who it was...' He was beginning to realise that it was more than just a feeling. He *had* been certain it was Rowan, but he didn't know how. He felt a little uncomfortable with the idea but didn't dwell on it as his concerns for her well-being were his predominant thoughts. He toyed with what was left on his plate, unable to revive his appetite.

'Do you still want to go to Skye?' asked Bess.

'Shouldn't we be here for Rhona? You know, moral support and all that?'

'She says no. She's going to be staying in Inverness till Rowan's out of hospital so I expect she'll be by her bedside most of the time.'

'What about their cat?'

'Neighbour.'

He thought for a moment, then let out sigh. 'Well I can't say I'm really in the mood for a holiday....but if we can't visit her for a couple of days we might as well go, I suppose. It won't be the same, but if we stay at home we'll just be moping about feeling kind of useless.'

#

A light warm breeze caressed his wet hair. Close by, a beach of white sand skirted by gently swaying palm trees was gleaming in the sun. Adam was joyously happy. He was swimming naked in a warm ocean with the woman he loved. His companion gave him a mischievous look, dived beneath the crystal clear water and then tugged playfully at his foot. She surfaced laughing and her eyes, the same colour as the bright sky above, were sparkling magically in the sunlight. He smiled and lunged towards her so that she squealed delightedly and fled toward the shore. He gave chase, pursuing her red head as it bobbed amongst the splashes from her flailing arms. He caught up just as she emerged from the water and he pulled her into a tight embrace.

They kissed passionately and sank onto the warm sand. He could smell and taste the sea salt as they caressed. The balmy sea breeze gently tickled his skin. It couldn't get better than this.

An incongruous tapping noise intruded into Adam's head. He looked up and glanced around quickly but there was no one else on the beach. He gazed back into the adoring eyes of his sexy, pixie-faced lover and his heart melted. He kissed her tenderly all over her face but as he closed his eyes and nuzzled her neck, the tapping returned, this time more persistently. He opened his eyes but it had become dark and the air stale. He was alone in his bed with his face buried in the pillow. Feeling disoriented and a little dizzy he turned onto his back and stared at the ceiling that dimly reflected the sickly orange glow of the streetlights outside his grubby window. His feeling of bliss fled as the dream diminished in his mind, driven away by the increasingly insistent rapping.

He was devastated – it *couldn't* be gone. He felt unable to cope with the prospect of losing the best thing that had ever happened to him. Closing his eyes he desperately tried to grasp the last vestiges of his utopian vision. He wanted to go back to that place, that time, to regain the euphoria of that carefree experience, to maintain it forever, to stay there and never come back. His efforts were futile. It sounded like a huge bird was pecking at the glass of his windowpane, as if some irresistible morsel laid just the other side. Feeling a combination of dejection, frustration and disappointment, Adam groaned in self-pity. He slowly and reluctantly sat up, peered at the clock next to his bed that displayed the numerals 4:17a.m. in red lights and then squinted in the direction of the irritating noise. There was an indistinct silhouette just outside resembling the head and shoulders of a complete and utter bastard as far as he was concerned. As a result of Adam's movement, the visitor stopped tapping and started to wave the outline of a hand. Adam groaned. He really enjoyed his sleep and the comfort of his bed and didn't like being disturbed from it under normal circumstances, but whoever this caller was had better have a bloody good reason for so heartlessly demolishing his ultimate fantasy. He approached the window to see the anxious features of Tom Oakley, who was frantically indicating that Adam should admit him to the flat. He did so grudgingly, feeling a vestige of the affection he once held for his mentor and not a little curiosity at his unexpected reappearance. The professor hurried in, looking around apprehensively with wild eyes as if he feared that an armed assailant could lunge from an unforeseen direction at any time. The wire-rimmed spectacles that perched crookedly low on the bridge of his nose appeared to have been hastily repaired with tape. His thinning grey hair was dishevelled and greasy, obviously neither washed nor combed for many days.

'What's going on?' demanded Adam impatiently, turning on the light and shutting the door, 'it's the middle of the night....'

Oakley was extremely agitated. 'You've got to help me Adam!' he pleaded. 'They're after me. My life is in danger. Hide me. Help me get out of the city. Anything, but don't let them kill me.' In his flustered condition he seemed unable to speak in anything but short sentences as if imagining that longer ones might be used to entrap him. Adam was still struggling to come to terms with the contrast between his feelings from the tantalising taste of paradise in the best dream he had ever had and the bleak reality of a night in a grotty flat in a grimy city with an overwrought madman ranting in his face.

'Just tell me what's going on,' he pleaded. 'What have you done? What about that bombing in Southampton? I *really* don't want to have anything to do with that kind of shit.'

'It wasn't me!' squealed the professor, 'I was framed!'

'Would that be anything to do with your gambling debts and the alcoholism?' asked Adam. He was not feeling particularly sympathetic to his old teacher at the moment, given the circumstances and the information that he had recently acquired.

'None of that's true!' claimed Oakley with a maniacal grimace. 'It's all part of their plot....' A thought suddenly struck him. 'How did you know about that?' he asked.

'Police,' said Adam. 'They burst into my mates' flat where I was staying and hauled me in for questioning because I'd been seen talking to you.'

'Oh my goodness, it's worse than I thought. That means they're probably watching. You wouldn't believe what I've discovered. Incredible stuff. And they're going to kill me to stop me telling.'

'The police won't kill you!' exclaimed Adam. 'They might put you behind bars, or in the loony bin, but they're not going to do you in.'

'You don't understand!' insisted the professor, 'they're just puppets. They don't know what's going on! They'll hand me over to the *others*. I burnt their house...their box...and I know things... Is there a back way out? Quickly!'

'This is a basement flat, but you might be able to crawl up into the garden if I unscrew the grille in the bathroom. I'll get the screw driver.' Adam had decided that if there was some way he could get rid of Thomas Oakley, he would. He no longer cared whether or not the man was telling the truth – he was babbling, crazy and made no sense. Whatever he'd done, Adam couldn't help him. He just wanted Oakley out of his flat, out of his hair and out of his life. If he could just get time to think long enough to puzzle through the strange events of the last few days, he was sure he would be able to cope a bit better, but he wasn't being given a chance. Just when he thought he was going to get some rest and assimilate these experiences, some other weird stuff would happen and confuse him even more. He started rummaging in a drawer looking for the long unused screwdriver.

'Are they safe?' asked the professor with desperation in his voice, his manic eyes darting from side to side.

'Who?' responded Adam confusedly, but there was no time for explanations. A loud thump and the sound of splintering wood heralded the arrival of the police as they burst through the front door. Suddenly the room was full of uniformed officers. Adam found himself inadvertently nudged into an armchair by the jostling melee as two constables seized the professor and frog-marched him from the premises, his frenzied protests receding into the distance. The last words he heard were: 'Hide them away Adam! Keep them safe!' He wondered to whom Oakley could be referring. What could he do to keep anyone hidden or safe? Suddenly a penny dropped and Adam's jogged memory revealed a long forgotten guilty secret. However, he had no time to dwell on it. The room remained occupied by four policemen who stood scanning the corners suspiciously as if expecting more villains to be concealed in the shadows, but to his bemusement they ignored Adam completely. Detective Inspector Gordon entered slowly and glanced around like a prospective buyer sizing up a property. His eyes finally came to rest on Adam with a look reminiscent of a reproachful father who is reluctantly preparing to reprimand his wayward offspring.

'Well, Mr Mackay. I thought we might see each other again,' he stated levelly. He slowly turned towards the window and frowned at it as if it was an autocue and he was short-sighted. 'What was Professor Oakley doing here?' he asked.

'Er…he wanted help, to hide or escape or whatever, but he took me by surprise – I was asleep,' Adam said. 'I hadn't seen or heard of him since that day at the supermarket. Come to think of it, I don't know how he knew where I live.'

'Incredible as it may seem, I believe you,' granted Gordon, 'but don't leave town – we might need to question you further.'

'He said someone was trying to kill him,' said Adam, 'and something about burning down a house.....'

'Just the ravings of a madman I'm afraid. I expect that when we finally apprehend him and this comes to trial he will be declared criminally insane and he'll be put into the hands of er....professionals.'

With that he turned and walked towards the door, followed swiftly by the four other officers. Coming to his senses, Adam hurried after them.

'Was it your lot who searched and wrecked my flat?' he demanded, suddenly realising he was annoyed. They either didn't hear or chose to ignore him as they trooped out without slackening their pace.

'What about my door?' he called. He received neither an answer nor a backward glance. 'Bastard wank stains,' he muttered. Despondently, he wedged the door shut with one of the fragments from its frame and traipsed into the kitchen to make a cup of tea.

Cradling the hot mug in his hands he sat slumped at the table trying to take on board the seemingly accelerating chain of events that were disrupting his life. The recurring dreams in the ancient city were disturbing enough, especially as they seemed to be shared by Charlie and now this business with the police and the professor.... he wondered if there could be a connection. The only one he could think of was the fact that the city resembled one in a book that he had acquired when studying with Oakley, but that was pretty tenuous. Now there were stirrings of remorse over an act of past negligence that had been buried unthought of for years... He was finding it difficult to focus and started pacing the room. There was just no making sense of it all. He wished that life could be simpler, that he had no worries, that he could steer his own course unimpeded, that he had a soul mate with whom he could share his troubles...

Then he recollected the wonderful dream he'd been so maddeningly awakened from. He yearned to be back there in the arms of that gorgeous woman in paradise with no anxieties, no concerns in the world. He wondered whether she really existed. She seemed so familiar, but he had no memory of encountering her previously either in dreams or in real life. He felt he would never forget her face or the touch of her lips or the exhilarating thrill he felt in her company. At least it was a fantasy he could hold to replace the guilt-ridden yearnings he had for Lynn. Now that she was pregnant, he knew (as he always had) that he had to eradicate his secret lust. Although he had formerly convinced himself that he had tried before and that it was not achievable, he was now determined to strive towards that goal. He would use the vision of the woman in his dream to replace any images of Lynn in his mind, a kind of "fantasy replacement therapy" he thought.

Feeling a little more at ease, he decided to go back to bed, resolving to start the next day with a new frame of mind. Before laying down he realised he had to make his flat safe but he was unable to secure his broken door and imagined that opportunist burglars or itinerant squatters might enter and take advantage of the situation, so consequently, his sleep was fitful at best and crowded with disturbing images of Professor Oakley screaming as he rattled the bars to his cell, alternating with visions of cities being destroyed by tsunamis, volcanoes and earthquakes. Each time he woke he tried to visualise the face of the impish lover from his dream to calm his mental turmoil, but found that her image was becoming increasingly indistinct and frustratingly he could no longer quite recall her exact likeness.

#

There was something there. It was a slight stimulus, a faint undertone on the edge of her diminished awareness; a subtle impression of a feeling that Rowan could recognise. Floating in the directionless, colourless void she reached out desperately, trying to expand her consciousness to locate and discover that tenuous spark; anything that had a form in this barren, eternal vacuity. She felt a fuzzy indistinct recognition some element of existence. Concentrating harder she found its source. Turning her attention to the only thing that she was aware of outside her own being, she managed to identify what it was. It was pain. Her mind lurched frantically towards it and seized the familiar sensation as a drowning sailor might seize a lifebuoy. It was not pleasant, but it was something she could relate to and much preferable to the interminable emptiness. It gave her a focus and it was one she had utilized many times before. Now she knew she was still alive. With a concerted effort she directed her full attention to making the contact, striving towards the source. Fighting the massive weight of unrelenting nothingness that saturated her soul, dragging her down and hindering her attempt, she determinedly hauled herself against the tide. It was as if she were slowly ascending from a deep, dark place burdened by a heavy load. All at once Rowan felt like she had emerged into the air from beneath the surface of a cold, fathomless ocean and she gulped greedily for breath. She became aware of her body, the origin of the pain and dived into it, wildly seeking sensations. With a jolt, as if she had dropped from a great height, she felt all of her physical senses in one intense moment. The sudden shock caused her to open her eyes abruptly and gasp. Blinking in the dazzling white light she was wrenched back into a reality saturated with pain. She cried out briefly as the all-consuming agony reached a peak but then it rapidly subsided like a breaking wave to become a diffuse but throbbing ache throughout her body. There remained however an excruciating pounding on the left side of her face that felt like a massive swelling about to burst with accumulated pressure. Trying to move, she felt too weak and only managed to stir slightly. Her hands felt restrained. As her sight adjusted to the light she realised that her left eye was only half open. She was lying on her back and above her she could see bare white ceiling and a bright, rapidly flickering fluorescent tube. Her mind felt slow and foggy as if heavily drugged. Lowering her gaze she saw that Rhona and Jenny were sitting either side of the bed, each holding a hand. An enormous surge of relief coursed through her. She was not alone, not lost, not forsaken in an everlasting unknown. She had returned from limbo to a world where there were people whom she loved and who loved her. She managed a brief smile but then, overcome by pain and a flood of emotions, stinging tears welled out of her eyes and steamed down her face to soak the pillow. She tried to speak but only managed a weak groan. Rhona squeezed her hand and smiled, her own tears flowing freely.

'Welcome back,' she said.

#

The mountain range ahead sported massive peaks hooded with sun-brightened snow that reached astonishing heights in their apparent defiance of the Earth's gravity. Charlie was walking slowly through an unknown landscape. Beyond the ridge, dark clouds languished, seeming unable to rise to such an impossible altitude and thereby conceding to the matchless blue above. Charlie's attention, however, was more focussed on his immediate surroundings. The ground was soft and soaking wet, abundant with the prolific growth of unfamiliar marsh plants. Fascinated as he always was by the wonders of nature, he stooped to more closely examine the leaf shapes and delicate flowers that blanketed the area. There was a fragrant, yet earthy aroma and before his eyes a tiny green beetle waved its antennae as if sampling the smell for itself. He was in awe of the beauty around him and felt privileged to be able to witness it. A deep joy filled his heart as he looked around and enraptured, he moved slowly on. A few minutes later he paused at a wide pool of bubbling mud that resembled molten, simmering chocolate but resisted the temptation to dip his finger in for a taste and smiled at the thought. As he continued on his way the ground gradually became drier, small bushes and herby undergrowth replacing the wetland vegetation, which in turn were superseded by deciduous woodland. Respectfully admiring the stately presence of the tall trees he felt at one with nature and at peace with himself, as if he had achieved a level of spiritual perception only available to those who had gained an understanding of their place in the universe. As he proceeded the forest thickened until he saw light between the tree trunks ahead. Heading towards it, his excitement rose anticipating an even greater sight awaiting him further on. Suddenly, Charlie emerged from the trees to find himself at the top of a steep slope overlooking a large crater that looked as if five acres of forest had been plucked from the earth by a giant hand. What was in the basin below was even more astounding. He stood motionless, dumbfounded by the implausible and wonderful sight. The entire hollow was crowded with tall dark green edifices, three times his height and spaced seemingly at random two to four metres apart. Each monolith appeared to be uniquely and extensively eroded, yet with glossy undulating surfaces reminiscent of ancient but highly polished tombstones. They stood like a host of sculptures shrouded in satin covers, awaiting the unveiling ceremony that would reveal their true forms. Although the sun had risen above the trees and shone brightly onto the scene, the stones seemed to cast no shadows because the rock from which they appeared to grow was of the same emerald hue.

All at once the exhilaration that had stopped him in his tracks now prompted Charlie's advance and using the prolific growth of creepers and vines, he scrambled over the edge and clambered down to the crater floor to investigate this wonderful congregation. Approaching the first stone cautiously and reverentially he gazed up towards its apex as if expecting a face to appear. He stopped an arm's length away, unwilling to risk contact with such an outlandish object. As close as this it appeared that the structure was in fact an intricate mosaic of countless tiny pieces, interlocking geometrical shapes fitted together so accurately that no gaps were visible where hair-thin lines indicated the joints. The blemish-free surface was so smooth and glossy that Charlie could see reflections of the sky, the trees, the other stones and himself. He thought he had seen something like this before, but couldn't recall where. He felt irresistibly drawn to touch the stone, yet simultaneously hesitant and humble as if unworthy of such a privilege. He briefly glanced over his shoulder, half expecting an admonishing figure of authority to prevent this irreverent act and then tentatively reached out with a trembling hand. As the tips of his fingers made contact he was surprised to feel warmth from the mirror-like surface – he had expected the coldness of hard rock. He thought he heard the sound of distant conversation and guiltily dropped his hand to look around. The muttering disappeared and seeing no one around he touched the stone once more. Again he heard indistinct speech, but this time it was slightly louder. It sounded like the murmurings of an immense and expectant crowd. Confused, Charlie broke contact and glanced about but the talking stopped. *Could the sounds be coming from the stone?.* The thought made him uneasy, but he had to confirm it. This time, as soon as his skin touched the surface he could hear the voices but they were even more clearly audible. He reached out with his other hand and its contact increased the volume further. He strained to discern a single voice or recognisable words, but despite his attempt the speech remained infuriatingly indistinct. There were too many speaking at once in what sounded like a foreign and unfamiliar language. He tried putting his ear to the stone but it just seemed to add more volume and more confusion. He listened harder and gradually made out a single familiar female voice tentatively calling his name.

'Charlie?' it repeated, louder this time. A tap on his shoulder suddenly alarmed him and he spun around with his heart in his mouth to see Bess with a quizzical look on her face.

'Jesus!' he gasped pressing his hand to his chest to subdue the amplified beating, 'you scared the shit out of me!'

'Sorry,' she said, 'I kept calling your name, but you didn't seem to hear me.'

'No, I was listening to the voices in the stone.'

'Voices?'

'Aye, when you touch it...'

'You've touched them?'

'Only this one.'

'I was too scared.'

'It's like there's hundreds of people in there, but I can't make out what any one person is saying. Do you want to try it?'

'Um...okay....' she replied uncertainly, looking from him to the stone. She reached out slowly, biting her lower lip. As her fingertips touched the polished surface she jerked her arm away with a sudden intake of breath.

'Are you okay?' asked Charlie.

'Yes, fine,' she replied, 'it was just a surprise, that's all.'

She tried again, more confident this time and closed her eyes, using the palms of both hands to make contact. Charlie watched her in silence for a couple of minutes, trying to discern a reaction on her expressionless face.

'Bess?' he ventured, 'do you hear anything?'

She opened her eyes and let her arms fall to her sides.

'It's amazing,' she said, 'what do you think it is?'

'I haven't a clue,' he replied, shaking his head, 'but since I came to this place I've had an incredible sense of well being.'

'Me too,' she agreed, 'shall we explore?'

They wandered slowly between the obelisks for a while as if appreciating the finest works in a world-class art gallery.

'Whoever made these must have had knowledge and skills way beyond our technology,' proposed Charlie, 'how could they have cut and fit so many tiny pieces of stone so accurately? It's incredible.'

'Maybe they're natural?' suggested Bess. But Charlie shook his head unconvinced. 'And the rock must be *so* hard,' she added. 'The polished surface is just amazing. What is it onyx or jade or something?'

'Could be...'

Each stone was different from its neighbours although they all appeared to flow seamlessly into the ground, which was constituted from the same dark green rock.

'How old do you think they are?' Bess asked, 'and do you think they started out like this or were they worn down from rectangular shapes over the ages?'

'I couldn't begin to guess,' admitted Charlie, 'the rock is so hard, I can't imagine how anyone could work it, let alone how long it would take for them to get worn into these shapes by the elements. It's awesome.'

'Look over there,' said Bess, 'there's someone else.' She pointed into the distance between the stones to the other side of the basin. There was a dark haired young woman teetering uneasily back from one of the monoliths.

'It looks like she's been a bit overwhelmed by the voices,' observed Charlie.

The stranger shook her head as if to clear it.

Suddenly the ground trembled and the earth emitted a deep rumbling noise. Their mood immediately changed from a state of wonder and curiosity to one of fear.

'Earthquake!' exclaimed Charlie.

They looked around in panic as the earth heaved beneath their feet, unsure in which direction they should flee. As he fell Charlie woke, his pulse racing, but the movement didn't stop. It took him a moment to realise that he was in bed in the camper van and it was rocking side to side, buffeted by a strong wind. He looked at Bess in the dim light of the dawn and saw her eyes pop open to dart frantically about in apprehension.

'It's okay' he reassured her, 'just the wind.'

They looked at each other and both knew instantly that they had shared the same dream.

'Did you....' muttered Bess.

'Yes,' replied Charlie.

'But how...?'

'I don't know, but it's pretty bloody scary.'

'And a bit wonderful and exciting too.'

'Aye.' He paused. 'And preferable to those nightmares too.'

#

The policewoman looked at Rowan sympathetically from where she stood at the foot of the girl's bed. She had a daughter of a similar age, so her own feelings were genuinely affected. Rowan was propped up in her hospital bed with Rhona seated on her left, holding her hand and Jenny on her right. She was lucky to get a private room. Normally there would not have been one available for this kind of injury, but given the nature of the associated trauma, the medical staff had made an exception. After two days she was able to respond to simple questions but she was still dazed by painkillers, concussion and in a state of shock. Feeling emotionally numb and strangely detached, it was as if she had left part of her inner core in that dreadful fathomless, dismal place. In fact, she didn't really feel like herself at all. She felt like a helpless observer, as if she was watching the scene on a television and she didn't feel capable of fully engaging with the characters or the plot. She thought that maybe she had lost one of her senses, which appeared to make the world and the people who populated it in some way indistinct as if smothered in cotton wool. She could hear everything that was spoken, but couldn't fully understand it – some of the meaning was somehow missing. She had never before realised how much of her comprehension of speech was sustained by her mind's ability to discern the thoughts and feelings behind it. Was this how most people related to each other? If that was the case, it was no wonder that there were so many communication problems between them, if all they had to rely on were words. She hoped the loss of her abilities was only temporary.

'There is no doubt that you had just cause in defending yourself,' the police officer said reassuringly, 'but I doubt very much that you killed Mr. Skinner. There will have to be an autopsy of course, but at first glance, the doctor said that apart from a slight bruise to his temple and the unhealed broken nose there's no sign of any injury that could have caused his death. It was probably a heart attack or something. We'll need to speak to you again in a few days, to get an official statement. But that can wait until you're out of here and you feel a bit better. Any questions before I head back to the station?'

Rowan shook her head slowly but regretted it immediately as she felt the jig-sawed pieces of her cheekbone scraping against each other. The woman turned her gaze to Rhona and raised her eyebrows, using the gesture to repeat the question.

'Will you need to come to the workshop again?' asked Rhona, 'you know, to check the crime scene or whatever? Or to interview any of my staff?'

'I don't think that will be necessary, Miss Flemming,' the sergeant replied, 'we've got your statement and Miss Ross's here and I'm sure that once we've got the result of the post mortem, that will be the matter closed.' She smiled at Rowan, nodded and left the room.

Jenny and Rhona returned their attention to the invalid between them. Their combined looks made her self-conscious and feeling like withdrawing further, uncomfortable with the scrutiny. Under the burden of her increasing sense of guilt, she wanted to shrink into a corner unnoticed. Although she knew she had acted in self-defence and she despised Grant, she didn't want to kill him, well not quickly anyway. No, she didn't want to be *responsible* for killing him was closer to the truth. She was appalled to recognize that she really did want him dead after what he had attempted, because if she hadn't stopped him he would have succeeded. That outcome was even more appalling to contemplate. She was also struggling with the realisation that she could unleash such a terrible power. She could never have imagined that her mind possessed the strength to wield her abilities in such an awful way and never wanted to again. She had lost control. Her emotions had become so intense that her thoughts seemed to have been taken over by this unmanageable force. It was a frightening prospect if every time she got really angry her mind could erupt with deadly intensity. Could she unintentionally hurt her friends or family or any other innocent bystander? She really did not want to have to face that eventuality.

'I killed him,' she muttered.

'But you heard the policewoman,' protested Jenny, 'you couldn't have. A couple of feeble slaps around the head wouldn't kill anyone.'

'No, I know that,' said Rowan mumbled impatiently. In addition to trying to talk without moving her mouth, her voice was slurred by her swollen tongue and inflamed lips. She suddenly felt excessively irritated with her friend. 'I killed him…with my *mind*,' she muttered.

'Don't be daft Ro, you can't kill people with your mind,' said Rhona gently, but uneasily.

'But I *can*,' she persisted, 'or rather, *I did*.' Although she could hardly move her jaw and any attempt at speech hurt terribly, she was annoyed at being called daft, so she continued slowly, forcing each word out through the pain and her immobile mouth with all her effort. 'I was just thinking…"*die you bastard, die*"…while I was….hating him with my entire being….and then suddenly there was like…this surge of power…and a kind of searing white light…and he just like…keeled over.'

'It's just a coincidence, Ro,' asserted Jenny softly, 'you had quite a blow to your head. I expect it was spinning and you were like totally dazed and stuff. Anyway, like the doctor said, he probably just a heart attack or something.'

Rowan became more annoyed. Why wouldn't they listen? Why didn't they believe her? 'Look, you don't understand, you morons,' she insisted angrily, 'I know I did it!' Her whole head had begun to throb now, which didn't help her mood. The other two exchanged worried glances.

'Come on Rowan, you've had a nasty shock,' said Rhona squeezing her hand, 'something really horrible happened to you and you're bound to feel confused for a while.'

'Rhona, I am….*not* confused,' she claimed, feeling exasperated. This conversation was also becoming very tiring, but she felt she had to convince them, to make them appreciate what she was going through. 'Look, I'm bloody telepathic alright!' she blurted, 'I can read people's minds….and now I've just found out I can kill people….and I don't like it….and I'm bloody well scared!' Her attempts at talking aggravated her injuries causing her so much pain she almost fainted. She hadn't meant it to be like this. She had envisaged sitting alone with Rhona in the kitchen or in the conservatory with a cup of tea and calmly explaining the whole lot as if it was no big thing, but now she'd murdered someone and blabbed out her secret and it had all gone wrong and she was in no fit state to talk about it properly. She burst into tears, feeling miserable and frustrated, her emotional numbness now replaced with aggravation and despair. Then fatigue swept over her and she was too exhausted to even think any more.

Rhona looked at Jenny again. They both wore worried expressions. She looked back at her niece and tried to be patient. This ordeal had obviously had a profound effect on Rowan, but after the shock had worn off and a period of recovery in peace at home, she would get back to normal. Rhona had also called Rosalind in Milan, who had promised to come on the "next available flight", so she hoped the girl's mother would have a calming influence, although she couldn't be certain of that.

'Okay, okay,' said Rhona appeasingly, 'we'll talk about it later, when you've calmed down and rested. You mustn't upset yourself any longer. I know you've been through something truly awful, but don't worry - I'll take good care of you.'

'Me too,' added Jenny with feeling.

#

The heavy rain had finally stopped and remarkably, within twenty minutes the clouds had completely disappeared, leaving the wet rocks glistening in the sun. With crystal clear visibility manifesting from the previously clogged air, the west coast of Ross-shire immodestly flaunted its showy peaks. Bess and Charlie sat on their jackets at the base of The Old Man of Storr, grateful for the respite in the conditions. Although they had remained dry inside their weatherproof clothing, the walk up from the car park had become a drudge in the relentless downpour. The sunshine was warm and pleasing on their faces as they admired the view.

'That dream the other night,' ventured Charlie.

'Yes?'

'Do you think that was a real place?'

'I don't know, probably not,' replied Bess, 'I think if there were really any stones like that around they would have announced it wouldn't they? Unless it was in some really obscure and remote jungle wilderness where no one had found it yet. And anyway, whoever heard of talking stones?'

'Well, there are legends…' murmured Charlie, scratching his beard thoughtfully, 'and it might have been a real place but in a different time…'

Bess showed slight surprise. 'So, you're coming round to the ancestral memories theory are you?'

'I don't know what to believe any more,' he replied quietly, 'but I'm glad it wasn't another one of those disaster dreams again or anything to do with that damn box.'

They sat in silence for a few minutes. Charlie had been concerned about Rowan but when they wanted to phone Rhona earlier, they couldn't get a signal. He supposed it might be easier from this altitude and decided to make another attempt.

'Shall I try calling Rhona again?' suggested Bess, 'We might get a better reception up here.'

'I was just thinking that myself,' said Charlie smiling and passed her the phone that he had already grasped with his hand in his pocket. They were no longer surprised at these little coincidences of thought that had been occurring with increasing frequency over their many years together, but they still pleased him.

After the call, Bess brought Charlie up to date.

'She should be out of hospital in a couple of days,' she told him, 'once they've operated to put a plate in her cheek – they're just waiting for the swelling to die down. Apparently, if it wasn't for the concussion and the emotional trauma of what happened they would have sent her home to wait. It's amazing how quickly they turf people out these days…shortage of beds I suppose…. Understandably there's a lot of bruising, but she'll make a complete recovery in a few weeks and there shouldn't be any noticeable scars.'

'Apart from the self inflicted ones,' he commented.

'What?'

'You know, all the piercings.'

'Oh, right. Well she's probably going to lose the ones in her left eyebrow,' said Bess, 'they had to take the studs out because of the swelling, so the holes might grow over before she can replace them.'

'There's something else, isn't there?' probed Charlie.

Bess nodded. 'Rhona says that Rowan's claiming to be telepathic and insisting that she killed Grant with her mental powers.'

'What? Wow, that's a bit crazy. I don't know about telepathy, but I do know you can't kill someone with your mind, otherwise people would be dropping like flies.'

'It seems she's convinced that she can. Rhona reckons the shock and maybe the blow to the head must have unhinged her a bit.'

'I'm not surprised. Poor girl. When can we see her?'

'As soon as she's home probably,' Bess told him, 'but we're to ring first to see if she's up to visitors.'

CHAPTER EIGHT.

There were seventy-two steps from ground level to the fourth floor in Raigmore Hospital in Inverness. Rhona had counted them. She rejected the elevator as a possible mode of transport, not through fear or claustrophobia but as unnecessary for her personally. She was physically fit, so she had no need to use the lift – she would leave it free for those less able than herself. A little extra exercise was welcome when one ran one's own business and found that time was at a premium. The elevator was no quicker by the time you had waited for one to come along and anyway she found the stuffy atmosphere and lurching motion made her feel slightly nauseous. Climbing the stairway also gave Rhona time to think. She was still a little worried about Rowan's assertion that she had killed Grant with her mind. She didn't believe it for one minute, but if her niece did, it might be difficult and time consuming to undo the psychological harm. It was going to be hard enough anyway for the girl to overcome the trauma of the attack without the added complication of her self-blame. She would seek the advice of the NHS counselling service for help in formulating an appropriate emotional healing programme. That is if such a service still existed amongst all the cuts she thought wryly.

As Rhona passed the desk on the surgical recovery ward, the duty nurse caught her attention.

'Oh, Miss Fleming,' she called, 'Mr. Adeyemi asked if he could see you when you next came in.'

'Is he free now?' asked Rhona. She was keen to see the consultant, not just about Rowan's mental state, but also to ask about her physical recuperation.

'Yes, you can go right in.'

Rhona was astonished. She had heard that even with an appointment you could be kept waiting for up to an hour. She knocked and entered the surgeon's office where, smiling amicably, he bade her sit in the chair opposite him at the desk. The room was swelteringly hot, as if Mr. Adeyemi were trying to emulate the climate of his country of birth in microcosm. Although he was very happy to live and work in Scotland, given the political tensions and social injustice prevalent in his native land, he had never managed to become accustomed to the lower temperatures, even after five years of residence.

'I imagine you would like a little more detail about your niece's recovery,' he suggested cordially, steepling his fingers.

'Yes please,' Rhona replied.

'Well, as you know the cheekbone was depressed and would not have stayed in position if we merely lifted it back into place, so we'll have to insert a titanium plate. This involves making an incision close to the outside end of Rowan's eyebrow, which is why we had to remove the stud, and another inside the mouth through the gum above the back teeth. These stitches will dissolve in about a fortnight, but the others will need to be removed in a week or so – just see the nurse at your local medical practice. Rowan will experience some pain in the first few days, for which she can take painkillers as required and the bruising will gradually diminish over the next two or three weeks. We have an information sheet with more details.' He paused passing her the leaflet and then removed his spectacles to clean them.

'What about food?' asked Rhona, 'she won't be able to chew will she?'

'No, not for a few days, maybe a week,' he replied, replacing his glasses, 'she will have to survive on soup, porridge, smoothies and maybe a little consolatory ice cream.' He smiled briefly. 'She should gently rinse her mouth with warm salty water after eating to remove any food debris.'

'And how about her mental state?' Rhona enquired, 'she seems a little...um...'

'A certain amount of shock is inevitable when someone has been physically assaulted, 'Mr. Adeyemi informed her, 'and it is also quite likely that she will suffer a degree of post traumatic stress...'

'And how will that manifest?' interjected Rhona, thinking that this may be the cause of her niece's claim to have killed Grant, 'What are the symptoms?'

'PTSD can take many forms,' the surgeon told her, 'including flashbacks, nightmares, denial....problems with concentration or sleeping, feelings of guilt, irritability or outbursts of anger....'

Rhona interrupted again. 'These guilt feelings – could they make her think she was responsible for her attacker's death?'

Adeyemi pursed his lips, 'Possibly...is that what she's claiming?'

Rhona nodded.

'Hmm, interesting,' he commented quietly with a strange expression on his face. He removed his spectacles again to inspect them and clean them with unnecessary fastidiousness, as if thinking deeply about what he should or should not say next.

Rhona regarded him dubiously. She felt that there was something he wasn't telling her. She waited a moment but he remained silent, his eyes lowered to his task. It was uncomfortably hot in the room, but Rhona could tell that the consultant was ill at ease for another reason.

'There's something else isn't there,' she demanded, becoming impatient. The worry over Rowan's attack and recovery were beginning to make her tetchy.

He put his glasses back on and pushed the bridge of them slowly and firmly into place with his middle finger before meeting her gaze. He regarded her with intensity in his dark moist eyes and then steepled his fingers again whilst biting his lower lip.

'Yes, there is, Miss Fleming,' he admitted, in such a way as to suggest to her that he held some privileged information usually only made available to the medical elite. He cleared his throat as if to relieve the discomfort of divulging the truth.

'Normally, this information would be withheld due to the constraints of patient confidentiality,' he said, 'but as your niece is not quite eighteen and you *are* her legal guardian, I think I should share the facts with you…. In these circumstances I am permitted to make a discretionary decision.' His reluctance to do so was obvious, but Rhona was unsure if this was due to his sense of superiority, supposed legal restrictions or whether he was uncomfortable in a "client facing" role. She wondered what on earth this information could be and edged anxiously to the front of her seat.

'When the nurses removed Rowan's clothing prior to the physical examination,' he continued levelly, 'they found a number of small but significant scars on her upper arms and inner thighs, like tiny burn marks inflicted by perhaps hot needles or incense sticks…' He left his disclosure hanging in the air, seeming to await Rhona's reaction.

She was shocked and gaped wordlessly for a moment before blurting, 'Surely you don't think I….'

'No, of course not!' he said hastily.

'Then who…. Oh my God! Do you think she was being tortured?' she gasped, horrified at the thought. 'But how could anyone….how could she keep that a secret?' Her mind had not yet seen the obvious answer. 'Who could have done that to her?' she demanded as if the doctor possessed the identity of the perpetrator. 'Did Grant do that before...'

He sighed heavily and rolled his eyes. 'The wounds were *self-inflicted*, Miss Fleming,' he said.

'Jesus Christ!' she exclaimed. It only took a moment before the implications flooded rapidly into her reeling mind. Not only had Rowan kept this secret from her, Rhona was also responsible her niece's welfare and had obviously been failing in her duties as a guardian. She suddenly felt a mixture of guilt, hurt and anger. After more than a decade of care, she must have gone seriously wrong if she had been unable to gain Rowan's trust, but Rhona felt she had always been so loving and really believed that they were close enough to share confidences. How could Rowan have got so desperate without disclosing her troubles?

Mr Adeyemi's voice startled her when he interrupted her thoughts. 'I would recommend counselling for the PTSD as soon as Rowan is well enough, he said, 'and possibly psychiatric help for the self-harm. Of course the first step should be for you to talk to her, but I believe that professional guidance is essential at this stage. There are support groups for this kind of thing too...'

'Do you know how long it's been going on?' she asked him, 'I mean, can you tell from the scars....'

'It's difficult to tell exactly, but certainly some of the injuries are quite recent and others have long since healed, so I imagine she has been at it for quite some time.'

Rhona left his office in a state of bewilderment and confusion. She walked unsteadily to the waiting room where she sat in a daze, feeling unable to face Rowan immediately. She tried taking deep breaths to calm herself and collect her thoughts. She was accustomed to confronting and resolving issues as they arose in her business but she knew that in this case it would be better to wait at least until Rowan had recovered from the initial shock of her ordeal or possibly longer depending upon the degree of post traumatic symptoms. She made an effort to put all of that aside and steeled herself to create a façade of what would normally be expected under present circumstances.

\#

The camper van slowly splashed through the puddles on the track leading to "The Haven", rocking side to side like a waddling hippopotamus. Charlie enjoyed taking trips away and visiting other places but he *loved* coming home. Although his problems had not been resolved by this break, he felt a little more at ease and had decided just to take each day as it came. He found that talking things through with Bess always helped - she was such a good listener. Charlie was more of a thinker, but that didn't mean that he was necessarily able to unravel his thoughts into a comprehensible whole, in fact he often found that the more he thought the more confused he became. Their cottage came into view with its surrounding trees and garden and he felt, as he always did at such times, that warm, comforting glow that accompanies reconnection with the familiar. Bess said, 'I'll phone Rhona when we get in and see how Rowan is. We might be able to pop over later.'

'You won't need to phone her,' Charlie said, 'her car's there – look.'

The roof of Rhona's V.W. Beetle was just visible. Its red shiny dome rose cheekily above the dry-stone wall, globs of water from the recent shower clinging to the glossy surface like limpets.

'She must be waiting for us,' said Bess.

'But how did she know when we'd be back….she didn't phone did she?'

'No, but she knew we'd be home sometime this afternoon.'

They pulled in next to Rhona's car. She had been sitting on her coat at the picnic table waiting for them but stood when she saw them coming, her features betraying her distressed state of mind. Her abundant halo of flame-coloured frizzy hair had half escaped from its restraints adding a slightly deranged edge to her appearance.

'Is everything O.K.?' asked Bess hopping quickly out of the camper to hug her friend. 'How's Rowan? Is she home yet?'

'No, she's not home yet,' replied Rhona, 'and yes she's O.K., kind of….but not O.K.' She seemed unusually flustered, both her level of worry and her lack of sleep were evident in the extra lines on her brow and the bags beneath her eyes.

Charlie looked from her to Bess and back again. 'What do you mean?' he asked, a little confused. Rhona wrung her hands and uncharacteristically avoided direct eye contact, her gaze switching nervously from left to right and then to the ground. Charlie had seen her like this only once before, when she first told him about the casket job, and wondered what could be wrong, as surely something must be. She was always so full of confidence and self-assurance, knowing exactly what to do and when, quick at decision-making and problem solving.

'I wanted to talk to you before you saw Rowan,' she said, again glancing side to side awkwardly before finally looking up and then speaking in short, quick bursts as if releasing built up pressure in carefully controlled doses. 'It's not just her claims of telepathy that worry me.... it seems she's been self harming...I don't know how long for.... the nurses found the scars...she's been burning herself with joss sticks...I can't believe she could get so screwed up and not talk to me.... how could she not trust me?'

It was obvious to Charlie that Rhona was distressed and deeply hurt that her niece had kept such a big secret from her. He stood awkwardly, shocked and discomforted by the news, not knowing what to do or say.

'I thought we were really close, you know, more like sisters than Aunt and niece,' continued Rhona in despair, seemingly angry with both herself and Rowan, 'and now I find she's got this huge skeleton in her cupboard she's hidden from me for God knows how long. What did I do wrong? I really tried to give her a secure and happy home...but for her to do this! She must have been miserable! But she hid it so well – I feel like a bloody fool – how could I have been so blind?'

Bess put a hand on her shoulder. 'Come on Rhona,' she said, 'it's not your fault. Let's go in and have a cup of tea.' She led her friend slowly towards the house, Charlie trailing and somewhat baffled by the whole situation. Maybe all of Rowan's piercings were another manifestation of the self-harm, he thought, but he was mystified by the inner workings of the mind, more so by those of women and especially that of a teenage one. When they reached the kitchen, Bess gently guided Rhona to a chair, but as she sat she burst into tears.

'This is all too much,' she said squeezing words out of her constricted throat between the sobs, 'first the person I love most in the world....is beaten up and nearly raped by a man I employed.....who she'd already told me she was worried about....and then it seems she was so unhappy in the life I'd helped create for her....that she felt she had to resort to secretly hurting herself...' Finally she could speak no more so Bess sat next to her, took her in her arms and allowed her to cry freely on her shoulder. She signalled to Charlie with her eyes that he should make the tea. He was happy to oblige and let her to do the comforting – she was much better at it than he was. Nevertheless, he had a lot of sympathy for Rhona, feeling very fond of his friend and employer.

'None of this is your fault Rhona,' Bess assured her, 'you did everything you could. You provided Rowan with a safe, secure and loving home and it's obvious to everyone that you care for her deeply. And I know that she loves you too – she thinks the world of you. No, if anyone's to blame it's that sister of yours, for abandoning her daughter and dumping her on you to pursue her own shallow, selfish lifestyle. I'm sure the divorce and then rejection by her mother must be the root cause of this self-harming. Separation anxiety....abandonment issues...it's a well known fact that children blame themselves in situations like that.'

Rhona had stopped crying and was wiping her eyes with her sleeve as she spoke. 'But why didn't she speak to me? I really thought we had such a good relationship, you know, able to share anything. For her to resort to self harm just seems so desperate – like a last resort almost, or the last thing before suicide anyway.'

Bess handed her a tissue. 'No, I think that's completely different. They say that suicide attempts are like a cry for help, so people generally hear about them, but this was a secret. No, I think that she probably thought that there must have been something wrong with her....that it was her fault her parents split up and that Rosalind left. Maybe she felt that she deserved to be punished or something and never told you because she felt ashamed of what she was doing.'

'Maybe...,' Rhona conceded doubtfully.

Charlie listened and thought whilst busying himself with kettle, cups and teapot. He wasn't sure how useful it was to examine causes. He was a practical man and liked fixing things, problems included. 'I think that perhaps we should work out where to go from here,' he said, 'I don't know if apportioning blame and scrutinizing the past is particularly useful. Let's just try to help Ro from where she is now, because it sure sounds like she could do with a lot of help.' He gave the women their tea. 'There's probably some specialist self-harm organisation that would offer good support and some post-trauma counselling – you know, professional stuff.'

'She's going to need *us* too,' added Bess, 'the people you love and who love you are really important in helping through tough times.'

'You're right,' said Rhona, 'but we have to be careful not to smother her – that could make her back off and retreat inside herself. When you're feeling vulnerable you don't want to be overwhelmed with attention. Rowan's experiences are so extreme I think we need to adopt a softly softly approach.'

'When does she get out of hospital?' asked Charlie.

'Tomorrow evening after the doctor's been round.'

'Do you want us to be there?' offered Bess.

'Thanks, but best not to straight away. I expect she'll just need rest and quiet to start with. Ring me the next morning and see how she is – maybe you could come round for dinner.'

#

The ticking of the clock and the sound of an occasional car driving slowly by in the street outside the window were the only sounds to be heard in the room. Adam had spent most of the day sitting and pondering everything that had happened, trying to turn it over in his mind and make some sense of it. He was so tired and confused, having had so little sleep, that his thoughts circled dementedly like a cloud of gnats on a hot summer's day. Attempting to develop some kind of order from such chaos was as difficult as trying to follow just one of those insects in their seething throng. He had had a disturbing dream, shared by his brother and painted by Lynn. Then he'd seen a picture of the city from his dreams in an old book from University. Then he'd seen his Professor from University in the supermarket after a gap of ten years and the guy had run away terrified and when he caught up with him he seemed to have pretty much lost the plot. Then there was the bust and arrest at Nick and Lynn's followed by the interrogation and the revelation that Oakley was somehow implicated in a bombing. He got home to find his flat ransacked. The Prof came tapping on his window in the middle of the night jabbering utter nonsense, followed by the police who then dragged him off. On top of that he found out his best friends are having a baby and moving to the North of Scotland. *And* he suddenly remembered, he was soon going to Poland on holiday. With all the strange and traumatic events going on, he'd completely forgotten about the prospect of his first trip abroad. In the present context he felt his enthusiasm for it had waned somewhat. Still, he supposed that it would at least help him to take his mind off things, provided that is, that his life didn't continue in such an unwelcomingly over-eventful manner. He decided to phone his brother again to tell him about finding the identity of their dream city and talk over the other developments. Maybe other things had happened to him too. He looked at the clock and seeing that it was six-thirty, judged that Charlie may have returned from work by now. However, even though his brother was at home, he seemed unwilling to chat much. Apparently his boss' niece had been attacked and was in hospital. Charlie seemed quite upset about it and finished the call quite quickly, leaving Adam feeling dissatisfied and restive.

By mid-evening, it was warm, humid and sticky. Adam decided to have a long walk and then visit his friends. To him, the air felt like a hot wet blanket weighing him down as he trudged the streets to Old Portsmouth. He stood outside "The Still and West" public house, smoking a cigarette and looking across the water to Gosport, his musings momentarily diverted by the way the lights twinkled on the ruffled surface of the sea. A large ferry cut effortlessly through the waves carrying its cargo of channel crossing travellers. He turned away, following the seafront along the fortified walls, past the square and round towers, finally reaching Southsea Castle before cutting back across the common. By the time he got to Lynn & Nick's flat, his breath laboured to find enough oxygen from the sultry atmosphere and his next roll-up, slightly dampened, tasted like an old musty dishcloth. Lynn answered the door wearing only skimpy shorts and a low cut vest with no bra. Adam's heart skipped a beat as his desire stirred involuntarily. He struggled not to gawp at her chest, apprehensive of discovery, but as usual she seemed unaware of the effect she was having on him. His guilt ran deep, not just because Lynn was living with Nick but also because he regarded himself as a feminist sympathiser and believed that women should not be regarded as sex objects. He suffered a turmoil of internal angst when these feelings came unbidden from somewhere in the depths of his being and he felt powerless to control them.

'God, it's so hot ain't it?' she was saying, apparently oblivious of his thoughts, as she fanned herself with her hand, panting heavily and causing her chest to heave temptingly in front of his treacherous eyes, 'I can hardly breathe, you know? It's so weird for it to be like this so early in the year – and it changed so quickly an' all.' She led the way into the flat, leaving Adam to close the door.

'Nick's in bed,' she continued, 'he's been puking half the day and dozing the rest.'

'Wow, I thought it was you who was supposed to get morning sickness!'

'Yeah well, I'm not complaining. But it's funny though – last night he didn't sleep well, he was kind of feverish you know and sort of…uneasy, yeah? He kept like tossing and turning and whenever he did nod off he was muttering about being scared and unhappy and stuff but when I woke him up he totally couldn't remember anything but said he felt inexplicably sad. I've never known him like this before.'

Adam frowned, 'hmm...maybe he's got a tummy bug or something.'

'Yeah, maybe. Cup of tea?'

'Thanks,' he replied. As Lynn sauntered out he slumped lethargically into the sofa and looked out through the open window at the streetlights, which seemed hazy in the thick air. 'Oh Wow!' he breathed suddenly, 'Lynn!'

'What?' she said, coming back from the kitchen.

'The other day when Nick was round looking at those dream books, he looked up some dreams he'd been having....and now they've all come true: getting busted, fear, depression and illness. It was all there...bloody hell, that's *really* spooky.'

Lynn sat slowly in the armchair opposite. 'Are you sure?' she asked, 'I mean, you know what he's like, he's always having a laugh. Don't you think he could have been having you on, you know winding you up?'

'But the stuff he read out hadn't happened then! He couldn't have known what was going to happen...' Adam paused leaning his elbow on the arm of the settee and scratching his head distractedly, '...though I suppose it could be that reading those books planted the thoughts in his mind, like a kind of subliminal message or something...'

'No, I don't think so,' said Lynn, shaking her head, 'just think about it, right. In the last few weeks, I've like, suddenly become driven to do loads of paintings inspired by my dreams, *you've* been having recurring dreams about some disaster in this ancient city that I've unwittingly painted and you said was more like a memory *and* you've discovered a picture of it ruined in one of your books *and* your brother's been having the same dream...' She had started talking slowly, but built up speed, as if each point made were another gearshift, '...and then there's this professor bloke who like, appears out of nowhere after ten years who gave you the book with the picture in it and now this stuff with Nick! There's just way too many coincidences, yeah? I reckon something's going on, like I don't know - some kind of major shift in human events caused by a....like a...planetary alignment or something, yeah?' She paused for breath. 'I'll make the tea,' she added, as if this could be the only possible option from this point. She rose hurriedly and strode from the room.

'Yeah, maybe...' Adam muttered as she left, his mind reeling. He resisted his habitual reaction to stress, which was to roll a joint, knowing that Lynn would not partake, and tried to breathe deeply and evenly despite the humidity. He thought he probably couldn't cope with inhaling the smoke anyway in such a thick atmosphere. He had previously experienced inexplicable events in his life and had always liked to imagine that there were cosmic forces at work but he was never able to substantiate these beliefs, so had remained not entirely convinced. He had a idealistic notion that influences such as destiny and fate were complicit with serendipity and happenstance in weaving a complex tapestry of reality across time, space and dimensions, but in such a way that there were clues left for devoted acolytes, which when contemplated would lead in tiny steps towards a greater understanding of "life, the universe and everything". Now he could see no other possible explanation. There were just too many bizarre happenings to be explained away by the convenient use of the word "coincidence". He wondered which of the heavenly bodies, or other powerful agencies might be influencing their lives and if they were, then surely they would be affecting lots of other people too. He would have asked his other friends if he had any.

Lynn reappeared with the drinks.

'Have you or your family or other friends had any other strange goings on?' Adam asked her, 'only I just wondered if this was some kind of major planetary happening, then it would be affecting others too, right?'

She thought for a moment. 'I dunno....I don't think so...only my mum really. When I phoned her to tell her I was pregnant, she said she already knew. But that didn't seem unusual to me cos stuff like that's always happening in my family.'

'Well, it sounds pretty amazing to me,' said Adam, 'especially as she's in Turkey...'

'Don't be daft,' she said smiling, 'distance doesn't make any difference to stuff like that.'

'It doesn't? Why not?'

'I dunno, I'm no scientist. It's something to do with quantum physics, yeah? You know, like a butterfly flaps its wing and a quark or something spins on the other side of the universe?' She dismissed further details with a wave of her hand. 'Anyway, last night I had another dream that made me want to paint it.'

'Oh,' said Adam. A moment later he realised he had yet to relate to Lynn the events of night before, so he proceeded to do so. She sat in silence and listened in rapt attention.

'What a crazy guy,' she commented when he'd finished. 'More tea?' she added brightly, 'oh and I'll remember the biccies this time!'

The thought then occurred to Adam that there might be something on the Internet to explain the increase in unusual events. He knew quite a few "alternative" websites that posted up to date astrological interpretation and others that specialised in monitoring strange phenomena from around the world. He suggested to Lynn that they try searching the web for some ideas. She turned on the computer and cleared the empty cups while it booted up. Adam sat eagerly at the keyboard, ready to type in the first site. By the time she had returned with the drinks, he was already scanning the text on the screen, searching for relevant information. Lynn had to lean across him to place his cup on the desk causing a quiver in his stomach as he got a delicious view of her cleavage where her smooth skin was moistened by sweat. She licked her lips and blew a damp lock of hair that was hanging over her mouth. He almost gasped at the proximity of her nipples pushing out the thin cotton of her vest and trembled at the sweet smell of her perspiration. A secret thrill trembled in his core as he imagined just reaching out…No, no, *no!* He mustn't look! He knew it was wrong but it was the most arousing and exquisite torture. He turned and pretended to look out of the window to hide his face as he bit his hand to both calm and distract himself. He couldn't go on like this. He would have to go home, have a cold shower and meditate or seek therapy or something - anything to overcome his depraved thoughts. It went totally against the whole of his moral and ethical principles regarding women and friendship but it seemed to be getting worse. It was as if the more adversity appeared in his life, the more perverse and traitorous his urges became. *I'm a victim of my own testosterone,* he thought. He suddenly remembered the woman in his dreams, so he tried to conjure up an image of her to replace the centre-fold of Lynn in his mind's eye, but he couldn't remember what she looked like.

'Here Adam, look at this,' said Lynn having pulled up a chair and taken control of the mouse. With an enormous effort he returned his attention to the screen, thankful for the diversion. The computer was logged on to his favourite astrology site, "Astromancy for the 21st century".

Lynn was pointing at a section of the text so he started reading it aloud, ' "The Grand Cross is one of the most significant astrological alignments ever seen in history and represents the entelechy of humankind…..," what's that? Do you know what "entelechy" means?'

'Er, yeah I think so,' she replied, 'it means like, the fulfilment of purpose and realisation of potential as related to our guiding principles or essential nature. Something like that anyway.'

'Cool,' Adam remarked sincerely, nodding. He was often both surprised and impressed by the extent of Lynn's knowledge but tended to forget about it until the next time it was demonstrated. 'And there's more too,' he continued, 'listen to this: "The Jupiter-Uranus alignment combined with the culmination of the Saturn-Uranus opposition series imply a transcendent death-rebirth cycle on an intense and dramatic scale. The timeless struggle of old against new, the schism between two parallel but contradictory evolutionary paths will culminate in a harmonious renewal of a higher consciousness." ' He paused and whistled quietly. "Sounds like pretty powerful stuff, eh?'

'Yeah, and look at this bit – it looks like some *very* hectic stuff might happen too.' Lynn pointed to the bottom of the page. There was a prediction that through periods of transformation in human psychic evolution there were often episodes of huge conflict, extremes becoming more polarised and confronting one another in a major fashion, often manifesting as social strife, revolution and war, before the realisation that the only way forwards was to work on reconciling differences and uniting in a common cause. It was indicated that this really is a tremendously momentous period because four out of the five planets are forming a T-square alignment echoing the 1960's in respect of far-reaching comprehensive and radical reconstruction leading to a more empathic perception and a more appropriate social paradigm. A phase of consciousness-raising would inspire a healthy scepticism, making the public more aware of how they had been manipulated and controlled. The advice was that people had to let go of outdated beliefs and habits in favour of new modes of experience thus creating more liberated socio-political dynamics better able to serve a larger percentage of humanity. Adam had noticed another section that he didn't read out, implying that the T-square formation involving the moon suggested an emotional tension related to confrontations between the sexes, in particular men's issues about women. Well, as far as he was concerned that was certainly manifesting itself in his life at the moment. He scrolled further down the page, then back up again.

'Wow, that all sounds pretty far out...but I can't see anything about dreams,' he murmured.

'Try a different site, yeah?' Lynn suggested. He went back to the search page and navigated his way through various alternatives. Finally he found something.

'Here we go,' he said, 'there's a link to something about personal implications of the "Grand Cross". Let's see...ah-ha, they reckon that Neptune in Aquarius might have quite a significant effect on people's dreams. It says, "On an individual level people can expect an increase in the power and frequency of dreams and visions" '

'That must be it then,' asserted Lynn, 'so it must be happening to more people than us, yeah? I'm going to ask everyone from now on and see if I can find anyone else.'

'Nick is not going to believe this!' commented Adam, 'But he's going to have to – the evidence is undeniable, especially now it's happened to him! Bugger me! Something really far out is really actually happening!'

'Oh my God, Ad, look at this!' urged Lynn, ' "The rise in consciousness energies will also lead to an increase in telepathic experiences and the resurgence of ancestral or past-life memories!"'

'Bloody hell!' Adam was very excited by this confirmation of his suspicions. He wheeled his chair back and shook his head slowly in wonderment. They were both silent for a minute, each trying to assimilate these mind-boggling revelations into their own versions of reality.

'Whoaa...' said Adam slowly, 'have you heard about the Mayan Calendar and their prophecy about the end of the world?

' 'Course, December twenty-first 2012 innit?' Lynn replied. 'But it's not the end of the world though is it?'

'Yeah, that's right, absolutely!' He continued earnestly, 'it's just a transition to a new equilibrium....a new level.....a new balance, like it says here. Maybe this is the start of the process and the Mayans were right. They've just been misrepresented as far as the Armageddon scenario goes.' He looked aside at Lynn, enthused by New Age zeal but saw that she was frowning. She stood up and started slowly pacing the room with a worried look on her face.

'I don't know Adam,' she stared uncertainly, 'I would *so* like to think that the world was set to change and that people was going to have like a total shift in consciousness or something...but look what happened in the sixties and seventies, yeah? It was supposed to be a dawning of a New Age and all that, the Age of Aquarius, right? And there was like the "Summer of Love" and Woodstock and everything but it all got distorted and turned into student riots and the Vietnam War and everyone went commercial and made "Glam Rock" or got angry and violent and became skinheads or punks. Then came Ronald Raygun and Margaret-fucking-Thatcher and cruise missiles and the Falklands and then New-Thatcher-Labour with Phoney-Two-Faced-Blair and Dubbya Fuckwit Bush and the invasion of Iraq and the "War on Terror", as if you can have such a thing, and now there's climate change and fracking and global recession, they're drilling the shit out of the Arctic and the fucking Tories are back in and there's riots and no-one gives a shit and the whole bloody human race seems hell bent on self destruction!'

Adam gaped as Lynn's tirade became more passionate, watched bemused as she finally collapsed into an armchair and tears started pouring down her face. He moved closer and crouched on the floor beside her with genuine concern reflected in his face.

'Blimey, Lynn, it's not like you to be so negative.' He held her hand and gave it a squeeze. 'To be honest,' he added, 'it's usually me.' It was also unlike Lynn to cry. He thought perhaps he'd only seen her in tears once or twice before.

She snivelled, wiping her eyes and cheeks with the back of her hand. 'Maybe it's something to do with being preggers and bringing an innocent and like totally helpless little new life into the world. You know, you start thinking about, like the future and everything for your children and that, and how they're going to like, totally inherit the mess we're making of it now.' More tears welled from her eyes. A sudden wave of sympathy and care overcame Adam. He rose and sat on the arm of her chair to give her a comforting hug. By now, his lustful thoughts were subdued by his heartfelt and more appropriate compassion for a friend in distress. She sobbed quietly against his side whilst he tried to console her.

'I know what you mean,' he said, 'but think of all the people all over the Earth who working really hard to make the world a better place. Like in "Positive News" - that's always full of uplifting stories of hope and courage and positive change.'

'I know,' she said reaching for the tissue box on the coffee table. She blew her nose and smiled at him. 'You're right of course, Adam. This being up the spout *so* messes with my head with all the different hormones and stuff, you know? The slightest thing seems to set me off now.'

Adam nodded knowingly, despite not actually comprehending anything about the emotional aspects of pregnancy. 'Besides,' he said, 'isn't the dawn of a New Age supposed to be about fifty years long anyway, seeing as the whole thing is about two thousand years? I reckon it's going to an exciting time for a new life to grow and a new person to develop, even if reaching a harmonic balance means a bit of upheaval first.' He paused and looked at the bedroom door. 'Talking of upheaval, I'd better see how Nick's getting on.' Having ascertained that his friend was comfortable and not suffering greatly, Adam accepted

Lynn's assurances that she was okay too. He headed off through the door and had descended several steps of the staircase when Lynn called after him.

'By the way Adam,' she said with a wry smile, 'I think it's time you got yourself a girlfriend!' She winked knowingly and shut the door.

#

The sun warmed Rhona's face as she sat in the conservatory on one of the cushioned cane armchairs, eyes shut yet still seeing an orange glow through her lids. One open window admitted the swishing rustle of young leaves from the breeze-tickled birch trees in the garden and a blackbird sang melodiously from a ceanothus bush. She appeared to be both relaxed and content but her thoughts remained in a fraught and anxious state after a restless and sleepless night. Rowan had gone straight to bed as soon as they had got home from the hospital the previous evening and was still there. Both the police and the consultant had advised counselling, but Rhona didn't raise the subject with Rowan, believing that her niece needed to at least recover from the worst of her shock before the mental wounds were probed. The drive back from the hospital had been a little awkward. Rhona was attempting to focus on her role as the loving and supportive guardian, but was preoccupied by the worry, betrayal and remorse she felt about Rowan's psychological state, about her secrets and about her own responsibility for the presence of Grant in her workshop and in their lives.

Following her unconsciousness, all of Rowan's senses had gradually returned so she knew the state of her aunts' emotions but felt completely exhausted both mentally and physically. Her own fragile state left no room for efforts to appease, despite her unwavering love for and steadfast loyalty to Rhona. She knew that sometime soon she would have to explain everything, but she needed to try to understand herself first, why she had chosen self-harm rather than confide and what the true causes might have been. It was going to be a difficult process, but unavoidable now that it was known what she had been doing. She wasn't sure how she could get Rhona to believe in her telepathy, but it was such a vital ingredient of the whole interconnected complex tangle of her psyche that it could not be ignored. Just now however her wits were too befuddled by drugs, the fatigue of enduring the pain and the mixture of guilt, horror and remorse at having taken a human life with the power of her mind. She slept late, partly because it had taken her so long to get to sleep propped up on a mountain of pillows so her face wouldn't press against them and also because her body was demanding the extra downtime for healing. It was not a restful sleep though, her dreams plagued by visions of Grant's contorted features as he pressed himself against her. By the time she emerged Jenny had been waiting impatiently for over an hour to see how her best friend was. Twice Rhona had quietly eased open the bedroom door to check on her patient, but seeing her sleeping peacefully and breathing regularly she did not disturb her. Jenny couldn't disguise her look of repulsion when she saw Rowan's face. Since seeing her only yesterday in the hospital, the increase in bruising and swelling was extraordinary. Her left cheek was puffed up and discoloured blue, black and yellow whilst her eye was bloodshot and almost closed by the swollen purple inflammation. Even her right cheek was a little yellowed and her right eye dark-rimmed.

'Oh my God Ro!' exclaimed Jenny in dismay, 'your face looks like a baboon's arse!'

'Thanks a lot Jenny. That's just what I need,' came the somewhat terse reply. Rowan winced at the pain of moving her mouth to talk, then continued more quietly and with less movement as if in a poor attempt at ventriloquism, 'and yes, I have looked in the mirror.' She had woken with a pulsing, aching face after a night for the pain killers to wear off and was feeling somewhat grumpy and sorry for herself. She had not been able to recognise herself in her own reflection. She had transformed into a hideous monster with a deformed and discoloured face. Not that she ever imagined she was a real looker, but she would certainly be glad when she had returned to normal.

'Sorry, it was the shock,' said Jenny. 'How are you? I mean, how do you feel?'

'Well, apart from a throbbing head ache and a face that feels like it's been trampled by elephants, just kind of numb really.' She was finding that talking without moving her mouth was quite difficult.

'Do you want something to eat love?' asked Rhona tenderly.

'I don't know if I can chew actually,' Rowan replied gingerly investigating the inside of her mouth with her tongue. 'I've got that incision where they put the plate in,' she continued in a slurred voice, 'that's pretty sore and I don't think I can move my jaw much, or put pressure on it. Maybe I'll just try a cup of tea.'

'Of course, I wasn't thinking. What about porridge, do you think you could manage that?'

'Hmm, even that's probably a bit chewy – just some tea first. With a straw,' mumbled Rowan wearily as she sagged into an armchair sighing. 'Maybe you could pop to the shop later and get some like, Ready Brek or something?'

'Okay, sure. Right, I'll go and make some tea and I'll get you a cold compress too.'

Rhona put her hand on Rowan's shoulder and squeezed gently, her face almost oozing with compassion and love, then went to the kitchen. She was being uncharacteristically motherly. As long as Rowan could remember, her aunt had always encouraged her to fend for herself whenever possible. Even when she was ill, Rhona would use a no-nonsense approach when giving her care, never making a fuss but behaving more like a professional nurse with a detached pragmatic manner. This time, however, was much more serious and Rowan knew that Rhona had been very scared and felt partially responsible for what had happened. Having employed Grant and then belittled and dismissed Rowan's concerns as exaggeration, she felt a degree of blame for what had happened and was finding her guilt difficult to cope with. She desperately wanted to apologise but dreaded Rowan's judgement, having suddenly realised how dependent she was on her affection.

Jenny sat quietly and ill at ease, eyeing Rowan nervously. Having so far lived a fairly sheltered life in this comparatively safe backwater, an incident such as that just experienced by her friend was so far outside her experience she didn't know what to say or do. She retreated behind her customary social inadequacy, even though Rowan was one of the few people she usually felt comfortable with. Tongue tied and self-conscious, she was relieved when Rhona returned with the tea and the pack for her niece's face. As the woman fussed about with clearing a space amongst the letters and magazines on the table whilst trying to place the tray on it, her fragile state was apparent in her furtive movements and nervous chatter. Once she was no longer occupied, she stood awkwardly for a moment before saying, 'right, I'll nip to the shop then,' before turning to leave the room.

'Wait!' called Rowan and then sighed wearily. She couldn't hold back any longer. Although she had hoped to postpone the conversation until she felt better she knew how much Rhona was suffering and had to clear the air. Perhaps her own recovery would be aided by getting everything off her chest, but first she had to offer some solace to the one she loved most.

'It's not your fault, Rhona,' she stated categorically, 'What Grant did - I don't blame *you* at all.'

Rhona turned slowly to face her, somewhat taken aback at being pre-empted in sharing her anguish. How could Rowan have known that she blamed herself for the assault?

'I'm *so* sorry,' she gasped desperately. 'If I hadn't employed him, or if I'd listened to you, taken you more seriously when you told me what he was like, this wouldn't have happened!' Unbidden tears were welling from her eyes as she struggled with her emotions.

'I told you, it's *alright*,' asserted Rowan as emphatically as she could without opening her mouth too far. She stood and went over to hug Rhona. 'I said it's not your fault.'

Her aunt was now sobbing into her shoulder as she rubbed her back and gently rocked her from side to side. Jenny felt embarrassed to witness this display of raw emotions and vulnerability in a woman who had previously seemed so strong. She looked out of the window at a small group of swaying tulips and pretended not be present.

'I'm really *really* sorry,' muttered Rhona through her tears.

'You are not to blame for what happened,' repeated Rowan, her own eyes now watering too, 'you couldn't have known what he was going to do. I don't blame you alright? I *love* you.'

This prompted more sobbing from Rhona who after a moment managed, 'I love you too.'

'I know…I know.'

A minute later, Rhona slowly broke the embrace and dried her eyes, then smiled weakly. 'I made your sweatshirt wet,' she said softly indicating the damp patch on Rowan's shoulder and wiping her face with her sleeve.

'That's ok, it needed washing anyway,' came the response, 'how about that cup of tea – I think we could all use one don't you?' Rhona nodded mutely and Rowan also glanced at Jenny making sure she caught her eye so that she didn't feel left out.

'I'll do it!' her friend volunteered over-eagerly, glad of something to do and sitting them down, she served them dutifully from the tray.

After Rowan's breakfast – she had just managed a large cool and soothing smoothie through a straw – the three women sat quietly enjoying the sun's heat but unsure of what to say or how to start saying it. Jenny still felt uneasy, but wanted to stay with her friend and offer her comfort yet didn't know how, while the other two both knew that there was more to discus but that it needed to be a long and deep conversation that neither of them really felt ready to cope with and in any case, it would have to be in private. Nevertheless, the warm rays of spring sunshine flooding through the glass in combination with the birdsong from the haven-like garden eventually lifted their spirits. It felt like a calm and peaceful sanctuary.

Rowan was the first to break the silence, preferring to be in control of the dialogue initially, so that she could steer the discourse away from the issues surrounding her self-harming, especially as Jenny was still unaware of that particular aspect of the situation and she wanted to keep it that way.

'There's something I need to explain...' she began. Suddenly she cried out in surprise as she felt a stinging, buzzing tingle in her face. Then Jenny's phone rang. Rowan stared incredulously as her friend answered to tell her mother when she would be home. 'Oh shit, I hope that's not going to happen every time someone's phone rings,' she muttered.

'What?' asked Rhona.

'The plate in my face just totally reacted to the phone signal – it was horrible – like an electric shock or something.'

'They didn't tell us about that,' Rhona commented, 'hopefully it will wear off...'

'Anyway, as I was saying,' continued Rowan, determined to get this over with. She looked from one to the other, uncertain with whom to make eye contact. She decided on Jenny, perceiving that she might be the most deeply affected by what she had to say. 'I know this is might be difficult for you to like, accept and understand,' she continued slowly and quietly, knowing that this was going to be challenging, 'but I really *am* telepathic.' She paused while Jenny and Rhona exchanged a dubious glance. 'Look, I know you think this is just like a shock thing, right?' she continued, 'Or cos I got my head bashed, but it *isn't*. It's something I've kept quiet for a long time, but now all this has happened I've decided I've got to tell you.'

Both of the others looked uncomfortable, but Rhona's thought's were less certain than Jenny's, the latter believing that Rowan was unhinged, even if only temporarily.

'Ro, can't you leave it till you feel better?' suggested her friend, 'and think about, like, if this is *really* what you want to be saying.' She shifted awkwardly in her seat and looked at Rhona again, hoping for support, but receiving none as the older woman sat motionless and expressionless, her unreadable eyes fixed upon her niece.

'No Jen,' persisted Rowan in a calm but firm voice, 'I've decided that I like, *definitely* want to talk about it now. I know it sounds like, totally crazy and stuff, but you'll have to bear with me because I *so* need to share it with you both, the two most important people in my life. I know it's like really difficult to believe, but I want you to believe me…so I'm prepared to prove it to you OK?'

'OK, if you insist,' muttered Jenny reluctantly, casting her eyes upwards and sighing audibly. Rhona remained silent, watching Rowan's face closely.

'Right,' said Rowan, looking at her friend, 'I want you to think about what's in your bag – everything you can remember, OK?'

Jenny shut her eyes and thought. 'OK,' she said thirty seconds later, 'now what?'

'I'm going to tell you everything that's in your bag, right? Or leastways everything that you could remember….well, there's the obvious stuff that I know you always have anyway like memo pad and pen and student card, keys, purse and phone and stuff…then there's things that you only *sometimes* have that I'd have half a chance of guessing like tampons, reading glasses, your book "American Gods" which I know you know I know anyway, but there's some other stuff too…..a letter from your uncle in Australia….' Rowan had been watching and waiting for a reaction and this is where it came.

'But how…' Jenny started, looking perplexed and a little worried, but Rowan interrupted and smiled but then winced as this hurt her injured face.

'Ow! Shit!' she said quickly then, '…and you got me a present!'

Jenny put her hand to her open mouth, shocked and again looking to Rhona for help.

'It's a bar of fair-trade organic chocolate with nuts and raisins,' continued Rowan, 'thanks, but I'll have to save it – can't chew.' She pointed to her swollen cheek and then held out her hand.

Her friend reached slowly into her bag and pulled out the chocolate that was exactly as described. She looked at it briefly then at Rowan's face before slowly handing it over without a word.

'Thanks!' said Rowan again.

'You looked!' asserted Jenny. 'You must have somehow managed to peek in my bag.'

'How could I? I haven't been left alone with it have I?'

Rhona looked on in silence, wondering if the two girls might have had a chance to plan this as a joke, to fool her into believing the impossible only to reveal the truth later and laugh at her gullibility. They might have spoken on the phone earlier, before Rowan got up and before Jenny came round…. but then Jenny had arrived a long time before Rowan appeared…although that could have also been part of the plan….

'You *could* have guessed though,' said Jenny uncertainly, 'like, I mean, it *is* your favourite chocolate and you know me well enough to know that it's the sort of thing I *would* get you…..'

'And the letter?' asked Rowan, 'in which your Uncle Dave tells you that he's getting divorced and coming back to Scotland?'

Her friend's jaw dropped once more. 'No, you could *not* have known that,' she admitted quietly, her face showing her increased levels of unease as she shot another quick look at Rhona who remained impassive in her seat. Jenny seemed about to speak again but could not quite formulate what she wanted to say.

Rowan continued. 'Now you're wondering if I've always been reading your thoughts and found out anything I shouldn't - like your embarrassing secrets and stuff.' Jenny suddenly looked worried, her eyes darting side to side and Rowan realised she might have been going too fast for her sensitive friend's delicate constitution. 'But I *so* haven't,' she added hastily, trying to reassure her, 'well mostly not anyway - not on like purpose or anything. It's like I can choose to use it or not and most of the time I don't cos it's way too weird seeing inside people's heads. I can't help picking up on random emotions – I'm quite sensitive to them, but I haven't been delving into like, your innermost secrets and stuff, honest.'

Jenny was becoming more upset, seemingly unreceptive to the attempt at dispelling her fears. 'But why didn't you say anything before?' she said, 'I'm supposed to be your best friend aren't I? You totally could have told *me*! Why didn't you tell me?'

'I'm sorry, Jen, I know I should've, but I didn't want you to have to worry about hiding your thoughts from me. I thought that if you knew, then you wouldn't be able to relax in my company and that would affect our friendship.'

Jenny was now becoming annoyed. 'Too right it would! Well it seems like I can't keep any secrets from you, but you've been keeping them from me. How am I supposed to feel? How can I trust you?'

'Don't be like that, Jen,' pleaded Rowan, 'please understand it wasn't because I wanted to keep things from you. It's not like that. I just wanted to be like…I mean to have a *normal* friendship with you.'

'But it wasn't though was it,' snapped Jenny angrily, standing up, 'and I don't know if I *want* to be around you any more with you like, probing my mind and stuff!' She turned and walked over to the door.

'But I don't, Jen, that's what I'm saying,' said Rowan in exasperation. Her friend glanced over her shoulder, then opened the door and stepped outside. 'Please don't go!' she implored, but Jenny slammed the door and hurried away, confused and scared and angry.

Rowan sat heavily in her chair and sulked. 'Shit! That didn't go very well.' She sighed then looked up at Rhona's sympathetic face. 'This mind-reading isn't all it's cracked up to be.'

Her aunt finally spoke. 'How long have you been able to do it?' she asked quietly.

'As long as I can remember.'

'How could I not have noticed? You've been with me since you were six years old – surely I would have noticed...' Rhona seemed almost to be talking to herself and cast her mind back searching for clues. Then she slowly shook her head, looking puzzled.

'By that age I'd already discovered that it could get me into trouble, so I learnt to keep it secret. How do you think Mum found out about Dad's affair? In my innocence, I didn't realise that she didn't know what I knew. For years afterwards I blamed myself for their break-up. And you saw how upset Jen was. That's just what I was afraid of – scaring off the people I care about.' Having said that, the reality of her friend's distraught reaction and flight hit home. The fact that her closest companion had shunned her finally registered and she began crying softly. Her quiet sobs seemed to Rhona to be all the more heart-rending. She took her hand and squeezed it gently. 'She'll be back,' she stated confidently, 'It's just the shock, you know. It's hard to believe, let alone understand and accept. And she's frightened too. Sometimes people try to cope with fear by getting cross. Don't worry, give her a day or two and she'll come round, you'll see.'

'Yeah, you're probably right, thanks.' Rowan dried her eyes carefully with her sleeves trying to avoid pressing on her bruised face. 'You don't seem so upset at me keeping it a secret all these years. You seem to understand.'

'Well, I'm a bit older and wiser than Jenny, but I have to admit it's still a bit of a shock and will take some getting used to. As to the implications on our past....I'm not sure it's worth dwelling on that. I think I'll have to come to terms with the situation as it is now, accept it and move on and well, hopefully we can move on together.' Rhona squeezed her hand again, reassuringly, then stood saying, 'I'd better clear the breakfast things.'

'Wait,' said Rowan. 'Now you're wondering if I really did kill Grant....' Rhona turned to face her realising that her mind had been read. 'Sorry, I couldn't help it that time,' she added, 'it's all the emotions and stuff.'

'Then I guess there's no use me denying it is there?' said Rhona with a slight smile, 'But I didn't want to ask you about it when you were still upset.'

'I know.'

'Of course you do,' said Rhona, shaking her head. 'This is going to take some getting used to.'

'Right, okay. Yes, I really *did* kill Grant, like I said,' Rowan began, starting slowly but then speeding up as she spoke as if it might somehow diminish the impact of her words, 'but I didn't mean to....or rather I did at the time....but I didn't like, know that I could....otherwise I wouldn't have. You know me, I'm a Vegan. I wouldn't hurt a fly, not even the lowest and crudest form of life, i.e. Grant. It just sort of happened. He hit me like, really hard, like totally flattened me and I was completely helpless on the floor and I knew he was going to rape me and I was so scared but then like, my fear totally turned into hate and anger and suddenly I felt so angry, like I've never felt angry before, like a total *fury* and at that moment I just like, wanted him to die and then my anger kind of focussed into like this beam of light like a laser or something and I suddenly felt really powerful but like, *really full* of power so that I couldn't hold it all in and then WHAM!' She paused for breath rather than dramatic effect and then continued more slowly, 'It happened. It shot out of me. He looked like, really surprised. He just totally froze. Then he slowly fell over backwards. Dead.'

Rhona tried to speak, but Rowan carried on. 'Now I'm just so scared that it might happen again,' she said quietly, 'because I don't know if I could stop it and I don't want to like hurt anybody else. I don't want to be a killer...'

'But it was such extreme circumstances,' said Rhona, 'You'd been viciously beaten and Grant was going to rape you – that's not going to happen again...'

'Maybe, but I don't *know* that.'

'Can you do anything else I should know about?' asked Rhona, trying to change tack slightly, '....like, er...moving inanimate objects or anything....?'

'A bit. I've moved stuff a couple of times, but it's not really as fun as it sounds and you've got to be so careful cos you never know who's looking or what might happen that you haven't thought of. Like once at school, some totally spotty nerdy kid sent me a love note so I like, moved his chair when he went to sit down. Trouble was he fell awkwardly and broke his wrist. I felt awful.'

Rhona heaved a sigh, forgetting that her thoughts might be noticed.

'You're upset because I didn't tell you,' stated Rowan, 'and you thought we were close enough in our relationship to share everything and you were right...almost. And I'm sorry, but I felt so ashamed of it – like it was a curse – that's what mum thought, though she didn't really say it out loud. She didn't need to. I totally blamed myself for my parents break-up because I told mum about dad's affair and he never wanted to see me again after that and then mum was always away on business so I felt like she was rejecting me, so I've just mostly tried to suppress it, you know?'

'And that led to the self-harming?'

Rowan exhaled noisily. She knew that she would have to talk about this. She also knew that Rhona, whilst trying not to reproach her, felt annoyed and hurt that she could reach such depths of despair without sharing her feelings.

'That was one of the reasons,' she began, 'but it's like, more complicated than that. I totally coped to start with after dad left and then mum, because I had you and *you've* done nothing wrong, you've been wonderful, I couldn't have hoped for like, a better guardian and companion or a more loving home and stuff. But as I got older and thought more about it, I began to really believe the divorce was totally my fault and blamed on me so I'd been rejected. Then at school the other kids knew I was like, different in some way, though they didn't know how and I *felt* different too, like I didn't fit in and stuff, but that was OK to start with too cos I felt like kind of special. I managed to avoid a lot of trouble cos I totally knew what they were thinking and stuff and when I was young it could sometimes be fun, like a game or something, but once I got to High School the taunts and everything got like, crueller you know? You wouldn't believe how horrible pre-pubescent teens can be, especially the girls. Then with all the like, emotional turmoil of adolescence, I started to care more what they thought and stuff but I didn't know what to do with my feelings...'

'You should have told me...' interrupted Rhona tearfully, 'I would have understood.'

'But I loved you too much – I *so* did not want to burden you with it. You were trying to single-handedly start a business – a tough job for a woman in the traditionally man's world of woodwork, especially in the Highlands – and I already knew and understood how much you had sacrificed to bring me up, how it so messed up your chances of a social life and proper relationships and stuff, just like you were a single mum – there was no-one to like, support *you* emotionally.'

At this Rhona felt a twinge of guilt at those feelings that she'd had.

'So anyway, that's when it started,' continued Rowan, 'and I didn't want you to think I was mad or like, attention seeking or anything and I *so* could not face getting sent to some shrink or something and having to like, "face my inner demons" and stuff. In a way it was just easier to hurt myself. It seemed like a way of coping with all the feelings of like, confusion and distress and guilt and everything.' She paused to exhale and moisten her lips before resuming. She was unaccustomed to talking so much and even though her face ached from the injury she felt she had to carry on regardless, to get it all said in one go, so that it was out there and she didn't have to hold back any longer. The more she spoke, the more relieved she felt to finally get it all out into the open. She began to feel lighter, not just in her mood but physically, as if her words had some mass that she was able to shed like ballast discarded from a hot air balloon enabling it to float higher up into the sky.

'But...'

'No, please let me finish – now I've got going I have to like, say it all. It started with pinching myself when I was little and though the pain was distracting it wasn't quite enough so I tried banging my head on the wall which was better, but a couple of times I broke the skin and bled and I didn't want to like, arouse suspicion or anything, so then I started biting my arm. It was like I was a pressure cooker and the pain was a safety valve and I found that when I like, burnt holes in myself I was totally releasing the emotional pressure, like it was a way out for all those pent up feelings. Without it I felt like I was going to explode, you know? It was also like a replacement thing, like the physical pain was easier to cope with and more controllable than the emotional stuff. As I got older, I did like, make a couple of friends – other "outcasts" who also self-harmed, who felt isolated and different and rejected and stuff - like me....though in other ways and I never let on about why I was different, and we totally helped each other, we weren't alone any more, it was us against them. We could like, talk to each other and like support each other and stuff, like a little self-help group or something, so gradually I felt I didn't need to do it anymore.

Eventually I gave it up and I hadn't done it for a couple of years until Grant turned up.'

Rhona grimaced. 'You *did* talk to me about that too!' she said remorsefully feeling another pang of guilt, 'I should have taken you more seriously.'

'Yeah, but you couldn't like, read his mind like I could. You gave him the benefit of the doubt and stuff cos you're a like, totally decent human being.'

'But I should have given *you* the benefit of the doubt...'

'But you didn't know *I* could read his mind either. You just thought I was oversensitive and needed a bit of toughening up and harden myself in the world of men.'

Rhona bit her lip and furrowed her brow, still feeling some degree of blame.

'Look don't worry,' Rowan reassured her, 'It's over. I won't do it again. Now that Grant's dead and I've totally spilled the beans, I won't need it any more. I know that now I'll be able to talk to you about *anything* instead of bottling it up and like, hurting myself. No more secrets, I promise.'

'The doctor was recommending counselling,' Rhona ventured, 'not just for the self-harm, but also for the trauma, you know? There are special people in rape crisis....'

'But how could I get like, effective therapy if I couldn't tell them the whole story? Without the telepathy none of it makes any sense,' Rowan paused and her eyes smiled, even if her mouth couldn't, 'anyway, I've got you and you are the best thing that ever happened to me...'

'You too,' said Rhona as they stood and hugged tearfully.

Rowan groaned. 'I've done too much talking,' she stated, 'I'm going to take drugs and lie down.'

Just then the phone rang.

'It's Charlie,' stated Rowan as her aunt moved to answer it.

'So you can do that too!' she remarked before lifting the receiver and saying, 'Hello Charlie.' She listened for a few seconds and then said to Rowan, 'they want to visit tomorrow. Will you feel up to it?' Receiving a nod she confirmed the response on the phone and invited them to come for an early dinner.

CHAPTER NINE.

Time stopped. In the airless, parching heat Adam's throat and lungs tightened so that he felt unable to draw breath. Hot pulsing flushes rose through his body and his heart thumped so hard in his chest that he felt like it might burst through his ribcage. The pressure throbbed in his ears and neck and his legs began to tremble and weaken. His stomach constricted into a tight knot of anguish. His life was in tatters, ripped apart by one brief comment from a dearly beloved friend. From the moment the door shut he had become paralysed in an agonising torment of mortification and humiliation. He had already been punishing himself through the guilt he felt over his desire for Lynn, but now she had discovered his secret, he didn't know if he would ever be able to face her again. How did she know? He thought that he was well practiced at concealing his lustful glances, but his attempts to conceal them on this occasion had obviously failed. Was it possible she had noticed before and not spoken of it? He knew that he should have stopped himself, controlled his urges and mastered his weakness, but now he was going to pay the price for his inadequacies. He remained rooted to the spot on the iron platform that served as a landing between the top two flights of the staircase, staring unseeing at the familiar brightly painted doorway above with a futile yearning to go back in time, to undo what he had done. But it was too late. Eventually his body could no longer maintain the levels of tension that it had been mirroring from his tortured mind and he sagged, his back slowly sliding down the rusty railings until he sat on the dry, hard, scorching metal.

Another terrible thought suddenly occurred to him: what if Lynn told Nick? If Adam didn't return, which of course he couldn't due to his excessive levels of embarrassment, she would have to tell him. He had ruined his relationship with his only friends. His wretchedness and misery were now complete. He gasped as a flood of hot tears gushed from his stinging eyes and all at once he had to escape. He jumped up and fled down the remaining steps creating a rapid, cacophonous arpeggio of ringing notes, as if from an ill-tuned xylophone, which reverberated from the high brick walls of the overgrown garden, startling a recumbent cat. He ran all the way home, as if his flight could somehow help him leave his emotions behind but they clung to him like briars and he was hopelessly entangled in their thorns. Bursting through the door and slamming it behind him, he flung himself on his bed, wheezing from the exertion. As his panting subsided he realised that he would have to face and suffer the torture he had brought upon himself. There was no thought of a brighter future. He wallowed in self-indulgent remorse over his shattered friendship and didn't even consider allowing his former companions the capacity for forgiveness, because he knew that his transgression was unforgivable. He could no longer contemplate accompanying them, neither to Poland for the holiday, nor to Scotland when they downshifted to raise their nuclear family in a private and unreachable hideaway, a sanctuary for their elitist love where he would be considered both unwelcome and unworthy.

After an hour filled with a mixture of self-pity and self-loathing, the sustained levels of stress had left him exhausted, desolate and numb. He rose unhurriedly from the bed and shuffled dejectedly to the kitchen, like a toy robot with depleted batteries, where he put the kettle on for tea.

#

Despite the drizzle, Charlie and Bess used their tandem to reach Rhona's on Thursday afternoon. In fact, the only things that ever prevented them from using their bikes for journeys of less than ten miles were strong wind, ice or snow. They even had a trailer to take for their weekly shopping. They arrived with dripping cagoules and wet legs. It is easier to dry one's legs with a towel than to try to dry leggings for a return journey and besides, except in the most extreme cold, legs get too hot in anything but cycling shorts anyway. They found Rhona in the kitchen organising the meal. They hugged their greetings and then helped themselves to glasses of water before accepting the wine.

'How's Rowan?' they asked simultaneously.

'Not bad considering,' replied their host, 'but she's a bit hesitant about coming down just now – she wanted me to speak to you first.'

'Of course,' said Bess as they sat at the table, 'she's been through a lot.'

Charlie noticed even more of a change in Rhona's demeanour than had occurred during his weekend away. She was looking twice as tired and dispirited; the additional creases furrowing her brow spoke of anxiety and confusion; her eyes, usually so bright and vivid, had lost their characteristic intensity and seemed to languish moistly in reddened hollows. 'And how are *you*?' he asked with concern.

'Me? Oh, I don't know...' she replied hesitantly, '...bearing up I suppose. I've been worried about Rowan obviously and I've had a lot to think about, but I'm not the one who was beaten and nearly raped and thinks she's killed someone.' Charlie reached across and squeezed her hand. 'Anyway,' she continued, 'the first thing is that Rowan's a bit self-conscious about her appearance. She wanted me to warn you first because she finds the reaction a little difficult to cope with. Basically, Grant must have *really* whacked her pretty hard to break her cheekbone and her face has come up like a putrefying pumpkin – it looks bloody awful.'

'I know I shouldn't feel this way,' admitted Bess, 'you know, I've always been an advocate of peace, tolerance and understanding but now that something's happened to someone I care about...' she shook her head, '...to tell the truth, I'm glad the bastard's dead.'

'Yes, me too I think...,' Rhona confessed, 'but that's another thing – Rowan still insists that she killed him and although we all think he deserved it, to have actually done it is an entirely different thing. She's finding that particularly difficult to come to terms with.'

'You don't believe it though do you?' asked Charlie incredulously, 'I mean, she may be under the delusion that she's responsible, but that's just the shock and the trauma and probably some kind of coping mechanism. It was just a coincidence after all...'

'Well, she's pretty much proved her telepathy to me,' she answered slowly, 'and I wouldn't have believed that a couple of days ago. I don't know, I don't want to believe she's capable of such a thing, but I feel like my framework of what's possible and what's not and what's real and what's not is getting a bit shaky – what with all that stuff about the casket and the dreams and now this....I don't know what to think.'

'She's *proved* her telepathy to you?'

Rhona nodded and explained what had happened.

'Wow, that sounds pretty conclusive I suppose...' muttered Bess.

Charlie exhaled and shook his head. He found himself in a numb state of mind where he could no longer assimilate any more extraordinary phenomena. He felt he ought to now just accept whatever anyone told him and maybe try to get his head around it later....should the opportunity arise.

'Yeah well telepathy's one thing,' said Bess quietly, 'but...*mind murder* or whatever she thinks it is – that's something else again. Unless she's done it before that is?'

'No. She says it's the first time and it has deeply shocked her. She said she's never even tried to hurt anyone before – nor even wanted to. I think for now it's probably best not to dispute it – believe me I've tried, but she's adamant. She just needs our support, okay?'

'Okay,' said Bess.

'Sure,' agreed Charlie, although he wondered that if Rowan *was* able to read his thoughts then she would also detect his scepticism regarding her powers to harm others. He did speculate, nevertheless, whether his disbelief was an attempt to avoid consideration of that which he had previously deemed impossible. If his certainties were continually challenged and found to be *un*certain, then he was not sure how he would face a world in which there were no fundamental principles upon which he could rely, no structure to reality to provide him with a secure reference.

Rhona had started busying herself around the kitchen, putting the finishing touches to the lunch when a quiet voice came from the doorway.

'Hi,' said Rowan meekly.

Charlie looked up and couldn't suppress his reaction to the sight of her battered face. It looked appalling and he supposed very painful.

'Holy shit!' he exclaimed involuntarily, followed quickly by, 'oh, sorry...'

Bess stood and embraced her gently, being careful to avoid her injuries. Charlie rose too, but then hesitated awkwardly, wondering if rape victims became wary of all physical contact with men.

'It's O.K. Charlie,' Rowan assured him and walked over to hug him too.

'How are you feeling?' he asked.

'Still in shock, I think,' she said through her narrowed mouth, as she plonked herself dejectedly in a chair, 'and I'm *so totally* miffed with this face. It hurts like fuck *all the time* and it like, tingles sometimes like pins and needles, especially when a mobile rings – I've had to turn mine off - and I can't even eat properly.'

'Didn't they give you pain killers?' asked Bess.

'Yeah, but I can't take the strong ones except at night 'cos they like, totally mess my head up and the others don't do much. Still, it'll get better eventually.' She paused and held her face briefly with her eyes closed as if talking had aggravated her damaged tissues. 'Anyway,' she continued, 'I have to admit, I'm more worried about people's reactions to what I did, you know, what they're going to think about me being like, a killer and stuff.'

'But no-one else need know,' Charlie said, 'I mean you're not going to go round telling everyone are you?'

'No way. Just you two, Rhona and Jenny… except I've already totally frightened *her* away and pissed her off.'

'It's probably just the shock,' Bess reassured her, 'she'll come back soon, once she's thought about it for a bit.'

'That's what Rhona said,' commented Rowan glumly, 'you're probably right. But she's supposed to be like, my best friend and I *so* needed her support yesterday and it hurt me when she ran off.'

'Of course,' said Bess, 'but we won't. We'll stick with you, won't we Charlie.' He nodded.

'Yeah, I know, thanks. But I know you're not convinced that I like, killed Grant and stuff, none of you, and I'm worried that when you like, finally realise that I did, *you* might get totally scared off too.'

'Not a chance,' stated Charlie firmly. 'It was self defence after all, but regardless of that I would stand by you even if you stabbed him in the back after what he did. He was a complete and utter bastard who deserved to be tortured to death! *Very, very slowly….*'

'*Charlie!* That's a bit extreme,' Bess admonished him.

He shrugged. 'Yeah, well….'

'Thanks for your support Charlie,' interrupted Rowan, 'but I still don't like the fact that I did it. Actually, as far as I know I've never even like, *hurt* anybody before, so it'll take some getting used to.'

'Food's ready,' announced Rhona, 'do you want to go through to the conservatory or eat in here?'

'Here's fine,' replied Bess, 'It's raining anyway.'

The others agreed and they began serving themselves and eating in thoughtful silence, though Rowan had to make do with just the soup.

Charlie's mind wandered back to his dreams and the ones he shared with Adam and Bess. He realised that he hadn't updated Rhona on those he had more recently experienced and wondered if now was an appropriate time and whether or not they should discuss this subject in front of Rowan. He looked up from his plate and watched her seemingly preoccupied with gingerly sipping from her spoon. At that moment a thought occurred to him.

'Do you ever get weird dreams, Rowan?' he asked in unison with Bess. They both gaped at each other and said, 'stop doing that!'

Rowan just smiled slightly but Rhona looked bewildered. 'Hey you two, that's pretty uncanny,' she said, 'does it happen often? Is it your new party trick?'

'It's definitely happening more often,' replied Bess, as Charlie made a conscious effort to try to hold his tongue. 'It started gradually with just getting a feeling for what the other one was thinking, then we kept finding that things we said were just being thought of by the other and now we've both had and been in the same dream together.'

'Back to my question to Rowan,' said Charlie, 'Do you get weird dreams?'

'Totally,' she replied simply with a nod.

'O.K., what about when....er, how shall I put this...does stuff ever seem to kind of cross over from dreams into real life and vice versa?'

'Yep, all the time.'

'Oh.' He thought for a moment. 'So you don't think it's odd when that happens?'

'It's like, totally *normal* for me.'

'Oh. Right.'

'Actually, I've like only recently realised that it isn't like, normal for everyone else.'

Charlie was finding this a bit laborious, but continued nonetheless. 'So, do you know what it means or why or how it happens?'

'Never really thought about it much.'

'Oh. Erm, okay...' He glanced at Rhona and then back to Rowan. 'I guess you must know, even if Rhona hasn't told you, about this new job and the dreams we've both had about it?'

'Yeah, well I was like, totally picking up on something from you the other day when I was working with you, especially after you'd been into Rhona's office and seen the pictures and stuff...' she winced having opened her mouth too far as she spoke more, so continued a little more carefully. 'Then when she had her dream I was getting really strong signals, but it's not very clear or detailed or anything cos usually it's enough to like, deal with my own thoughts, let alone everyone else's, so unless I concentrate it's all a bit vague and we haven't like, spoken about it cos until all this stuff happened with Grant I was totally happy to keep my secret and since then we haven't had a chance. Until now, that is.'

'So what do you think,' asked Rhona, 'about our dreams and their connection this job?'

Rowan looked a little apprehensive, as if she were an inexperienced apprentice being asked by a master craftsman what she thought would be the best approach to a particularly complex task.

'Well, I don't like, know all the details, but I do know how it felt.' She looked from Rhona to Charlie to Bess and then continued unhurriedly. 'See it's like....I can't totally read people's minds exactly, unless I try *really* hard, it's more like super-enhanced empathy. I can pick up emotions and intentions and stuff, so I kind of interpret people's thoughts, but the stronger the emotions or intentions, the more I get of actual thoughts.' She stopped briefly as if gathering her own. 'So anyway,' she continued, 'as far as that job goes, I say trust your feelings. If it doesn't feel right, don't do it. I don't even *know* if those old guys in Rhona's dream were like, real or not but they *felt* real to me and I didn't like them and I kind of felt like they were, you know, like totally up to something creepy and if they *are* real and they can like, get inside your head and stuff, then I don't think you should have anything to do with them.'

They sat quietly for a few moments contemplating this and its implications. Charlie had never heard Rowan talk so much at once, even though he had worked with her for the last fifteen months, and all that in spite of her pummelled face. Now it seems there was an awful lot he had not known about her. He had been mistaking her reticence for timidity and introversion. He couldn't imagine how their lives could ever be the same again after this and although the future was uncertain he felt that something was underway that would change them even more.

'Do you know how we can stop them interfering with our thoughts and dreams?' he asked hopefully.

'Not really...' she admitted, shrugging.

'Oh,' said Charlie, disappointed. No one talked again for a minute so he asked another question. 'Do you think that they can...do anything else to us...er, you know, punish us in any way if I don't make the box?' He was thinking that if Rowan's mind could kill, could theirs too?

'I don't know, Charlie....maybe.'

The room went quiet again for a while.

'There's something else we have to tell you,' said Bess breaking the silence, 'as if we haven't already got enough on our minds.' She looked from Rowan to Rhona, feeling perhaps that the former wouldn't require eye contact if she had mind contact. 'When we were on Skye, we shared an identical dream – we were both in it and we both remember it as if it were something we had actually experienced in real life.' She described the experience in detail, concluding with, 'and the stones seemed to be full of voices – hundreds of them, sort of murmuring in the background....'

'Co-ool,' said Rowan, clearly impressed.

Bess continued, 'but that's not all. Last night when Charlie was watching the news something incredible happened...'

Rhona merely raised her eyebrows, indicating her curiosity, but Rowan's face lit up in eager anticipation, like a small child about to be told a fairy tale. Bess looked at Charlie and indicated that he should relate his experience to them.

He rarely bought a newspaper or watched the news on the television. Not only did the media appear to him to concentrate on, or even *revel in*, bad news, it also seemed to be padded out with so much speculation, had such little substance and was repeated so often that he marvelled at how so many significant domestic and world events could be ignored. No matter how many months had elapsed since he last tuned in there were always the perpetual elements: a politician's infidelity or embezzlement; more civilian casualties in the latest war; job losses; youth crime, especially with drugs, knives or guns involved; a so-called "celebrity" getting married, divorced or going into rehabilitation; a raped and/or murdered child or student or O.A.P. with the injuries described at length and in great detail; something about football managers, coaches or players, but rarely the matches; elections in the United States for President or Presidential candidates which seemed to involve almost continual rolling campaigns for one or the other and increasingly, reports of what was happening in the latest reality television programmes. The whole thing simultaneously bored and exasperated him. Charlie wanted to hear what was going on in the world, on issues that really mattered. His preferred source of information was the internet, where there were several "alternative news" websites and also a weekly magazine to which he subscribed entitled "Positive Planet". This recently launched publication, that Adam had told him about, was a spin off from a digital radio station of the same name and was rapidly gaining in popularity. It focused on extraordinary things that ordinary people all over the world were doing to improve their lives and the lives of others. It was very uplifting to read, having the opposite effect to that of the mainstream media that concentrated disproportionately on negative news often presented as if it were the latest episode of a soap opera. He knew how his own mind and outlook were affected by this bias, which is why he chose to focus differently. The majority of the Earth's population with access to the mainstream sources, which was now in fact most of them, had their attitudes and opinions shaped by this unbalanced emphasis. He sometimes wondered if his paranoid brother was right that this was a deliberate policy. He could easily believe that the world's most powerful people, who of course owned and controlled both the media and the governments, had a vested interest in creating and maintaining a culture of distraction and fear. Frightened people are easier to control and if offered small but tempting material gains, dreams of massive rewards for the few ("It could be you!") and trivial "entertainment" as diverting fodder, they will continue to trudge through the unfulfilling mire of their lives as the easiest option available to them. Thus they served the invisible and anonymous puppeteers to the grave as subjugated units of production and consumption, unaware of the contributions they had made to their masters. Charlie usually stopped himself getting too deeply embroiled in conspiracy theories though, because he realised it just led to more negative thinking and paranoia. Anyway, what could he do about it? He was of the opinion that if more people concentrated more frequently on being nice to each other and resisted attempts to manipulate each other's thoughts, then the world would become a much better place. In his small way, replicated by millions of others across the globe he hoped, he tried to do just that.

Despite this, on Monday night, Charlie was tempted to catch up on the latest BBC bulletin or at least watch the main points, so while Bess washed the dishes in the kitchen he reclined on the sofa and switched on the television. He also felt a need to divert his attention from dwelling on the increasing overlap between his dreams and reality. No matter how hard he tried to puzzle it out he had come no closer to an understanding. He also wanted to distract himself from worrying about Rowan's state of health in the aftermath of her trauma. Her condition was outside his control. He would be seeing her in a couple of days anyway and phoning Rhona for an update before that. As he sat on the settee Nimbus immediately sought the comfort of his lap and then quickly settled, purring loudly as Charlie absent-mindedly scratched behind his ears.

The initial headlines had included a mention of a remarkable archaeological discovery in southern Chile so, his interest roused he continued watching to find out more. After about twenty minutes of the main stories, which Charlie found rather depressing, the item was finally included in the programme.

'Following the devastating floods in Southern Chile last month,' started the newsreader, 'geologists surveying the region have made a startling discovery. What appears to be some kind of ancient temple has been uncovered when the floodwaters that washed down the mountainsides eroded the deep topsoil in an area of forested foothills near the Andes.' The picture switched to an aerial view shot from a helicopter as it approached a clearing of about two hectares. The announcer continued in a voiceover. 'The finding has baffled the country's scientists due to the level of sophistication they say would have been required to erect the construction.' The camera zoomed in to show numerous large dark green stones in a shallow depression, some still half buried in the earth, but enough revealed for Charlie to receive a shock of recognition.

'Bess!' he shouted, 'Come here, quickly!' She joined him in seconds, hastened by the urgency in his tone, gasped and stood open-mouthed as she saw the image on the screen in front of them as revealed by the helicopter circling over the scene. The view changed to show the site from the ground level film crew, where a team of people were examining the stones.

'State archaeologists from the University of Santiago were sent by the Chilean government to investigate the site after the geologists who discovered it claimed that it must have been buried in silt for at least twenty thousand years and that the stone monoliths were not natural but man-made structures.'

'Oh my God!' Bess managed to gasp eventually and then sat hastily in an armchair with her eyes glued to the screen.

'Initially the archaeologists asserted,' continued the report, 'that the level of technology needed to fashion these strange sculpted stones is so advanced that they could not be as old as the geologists allege. However, they now admit to being completely baffled by the find, as it appears that the skills and equipment required to create these artefacts have yet to be acquired even here in the twenty-first century.'

There was no doubt that this was where Charlie and Bess had been in their dream.

'What is being described by those on the ground as an extensive sacred site of international significance, consists of at least two hundred highly polished standing stones each intricately pieced together from segments of hard dark green crystal cut with such accuracy that no gap can be seen between them. Our Southern America correspondent, Peter Wainwright is at the site talking to the head honcho.'

The leader of the expedition, a balding middle-aged man was singled out for interview by an out of shot reporter. 'Professor Carlos Fernandez, head of the Department of Ancient Studies at Santiago University, just how significant do you see this find in relation to the established view of history?'

'It is very significant indeed,' answered Fernandez animatedly, waving his hands as if to further emphasise the level of importance, 'In fact it turns on the head so much of what we thought before. To begin with I did not believe the geologists' claims as to the age of the site, but now I have myself examined it, the evidence I see. I cannot deny it, even though we had previously dated the oldest known civilisation to about three thousand years B.C. But a finding of such artefacts at over twenty thousand years old and in such numbers is unprecedented and becomes a discovery of international significance. I have been authorised by the Chilean government to invite the world's most respected archaeologists, anthropologists and geologists to join a team to study at the site and to undertake further excavations to reveal the full extent of what we here have.'

The camera now panned around to show the correspondent standing holding a microphone with the green stones in the background cordoned off with striped plastic tape. 'Academics of international renown are being requested to examine the evidence for themselves to help verify the date of the site, but so far most of those who have expressed an opinion have been fairly dismissive of the claims.'

Back in the studio, the guest was Professor Hugh W. Rawlinson from Cambridge University. 'I have seen some of the footage, studied the photographs and scrutinised the findings of their tests,' he said shaking his head, 'but I can only conclude that this must be some kind of elaborate hoax, perhaps even a publicity stunt to help boost their ailing tourist industry. These claims are absolutely preposterous.'

The studio interviewer looked up at a screen showing the image of Carlos Fernandez. 'What do you say to that Professor Fernandez?' he asked.

'Unfortunately this the kind of scepticism we are meeting everywhere,' replied the Chilean sadly, 'but I can understand because this is just so incredible to find, earth-shattering in fact because it contradicts everything that has been postulated by ancient historians for the last one hundred years. But I appeal to the sceptics to try to be open-minded instead of stuck in their old ways and I can only repeat my invitation to come and see this for themselves and then there can be no doubts. They should prepare themselves to be amazed. This is an opportunity of a life time for anyone in this field.'

'Well, Professor Rawlinson, there you have it,' stated the presenter, 'you have a challenge. Can you turn down the chance to examine the evidence first hand?'

'Of course I can turn it down,' he replied haughtily, 'I have more important things to do than waste my time gallivanting to the other side of the world to refute bogus claims! If I did that every time some crackpot postulated some outlandish theory, I'd *never* get any work done.'

'Well Peter, what do you make of it?'

Wainwright stood next to a stone twice his height but facing the camera, his unkempt hair stirring dramatically in the morning breeze. His weight was on one leg as he attempted to strike a pose contrived to appear as intrepid as possible. 'Well David, I'm no expert,' he stated as he reached out to gently touch the smooth face of the edifice, 'but I can certainly tell you that standing here I feel I am part of something momentous.' The camera zoomed in for a close up of the surface. 'You can see how each stone is like an intricate mosaic which the geologists say could not have formed naturally. Whenever this was made and whoever made it, there's no doubt in my mind that it was created using very sophisticated skill and technology. These are no ordinary rocks and I'm sure this conundrum will keep the boffins busy for quite some time.'

Charlie switched off the television and looked at Bess. They simultaneously took a deep breath and exhaled.

'Bloody....hell,' muttered Charlie slowly, shaking his head, 'and I didn't think things could get any weirder.'

'Did you notice,' asked Bess quietly, 'how some of the stones were still half-buried in silt? They hadn't been totally uncovered.'

'Aye...so?'

'Well in our dream, there was no silt at all – everything was exposed...or not yet covered.'

'And?'

'That means that what we saw...where we were...was over twenty thousand years ago....*or in the future.*'

'Ah.' Charlie scratched his head and frowned. 'I don't know if I can handle this,' he said.

'We have to Charlie, no matter how hard you try, you can't run away from your dreams.'

There seemed to be an increasing number of occasions recently when he wished he could do just that. The more he attempted to make sense of it all, the more difficult it became to understand and he was just getting more and more confused. All the same, Bess was right, he couldn't escape what was going on but neither could he comprehend it, which made the situation all that more difficult to cope with. He knew he should just accept what was happening and go with the flow…"like a dead fish…" said a little voice in his head, but trying to fight it or trying to fathom it out was so tiring.

'Oh my god!' Bess' exclamation startled him from his thoughts.

'What is it?' he asked, looking around in alarm as if expecting a new threat to have emerged.

'That stone you found a few weeks ago, the one from the beach, you know the dark green one.'

'Oh yeah, I'd forgotten about that. What about it?'

'It's like the ones in the dream! Only smaller.'

'You reckon?'

'Yes! Have another look.'

He went upstairs and picked up the stone from the table by his bed. Bess was right. It was the same hard glossy emerald green material, seemingly made up from small, irregular shapes fused together in such a way that there were no gaps, not even hairline cracks. As he studied the rock, he absent-mindedly stroked the smooth surface, enjoying the sheeny sensation beneath his fingertips. Suddenly his skin began to tingle where it made contact and it felt like the object was buzzing with tiny vibrations in his hand. Then he heard voices and got a flash of an image in his mind, causing him to cry out in alarm and release the stone so that it dropped with a thump onto the carpeted floor.

Bess appeared in moments. 'What happened?'

He looked up, still in shock. 'It vibrated….' he said quietly, 'and then I heard voices….and then I saw something…just a quick flash….a girl in a yellow robe….being sacrificed!'

Charlie had finished relating their experience, but they now all sat in silence for a minute, lost in thought. Rhona was wide-eyed and open-mouthed. Rowan seemed pensive. He looked at the girl and asked, 'have you experienced anything like that before? Do you know what it means?'

She shook her head slowly saying, 'Look, just because I can like, do a bit of mind reading and stuff doesn't mean I'm a world authority on the paranormal all of a sudden.' To Charlie she looked sulky for a moment, as if the injustice of other people's expectations was an emotional burden too far. 'No, wait a minute,' she added suddenly, 'I *do* remember something. I read it somewhere in a magazine...about certain types of quartz having like, a memory for electrical impulses or something, but nobody understands it and there's this crystal skull that's like, really ancient and they totally don't know how it could have been made because they couldn't do it now and it's kind of like, all made out of one piece but got a moving jaw and stuff and I'm sure they said something about it having weird energy or something...'

'So maybe that stone has got something to do with your dreams...,' murmured Rhona. 'Is that when they started – when you found it on the beach, took it home and put it by your bed?'

'Er, I don't know...maybe...' Charlie pondered. He couldn't remember exactly when he'd found it nor when the dreams started, but it was possible. He looked at Bess who shrugged, as unsure as he was.

'Someone's coming,' announced Rhona.

Charlie looked at her in astonishment. 'How do you know?' he asked, 'Are you becoming telepathic too?'

She laughed. 'No Charlie,' she replied levelly, 'I just saw a shape pass by the window.'

'It's Jenny!' declared Rowan happily, jumping up from her seat. She rushed from the room to let her in the door. After reconciliatory hugs the two friends went upstairs to Rowan's room to talk whilst the others cleared the dishes.

'Do you really think it's the stone that triggered all this?' Bess asked them. 'First Charlie's dreams and then ours. And how does it all tie in with that casket? You've both had dreams about that too. How can that be connected to the stone?'

'Well,' said Charlie, 'maybe one of the stones I saw put in the casket's lid with the other gems in my dreams are like the one I found on the beach...but I'm tempted to chuck it away and find out if it makes any difference. There we were quite merrily pootling along with our lives and then suddenly the world's turned upside down. I for one could do without it. I can understand dreaming about something *after* it's happened or after you've seen it, but when it happens the other way round it freaks me out. What worries me most is the blurring of the edges, the crossover from dreams into real life.'

'What worries me most,' said Rhona, 'is that I've been living with a telepath for twelve years and didn't know it!'

#

Over the next few days Adam descended into a pit of depression unparalleled in his experience so far. Deprived of his self-dignity he didn't wash or change his clothes and only ate what he needed, nibbling on biscuits and dry cereal to stave off the cravings of an appetite diminished by chain-smoking roll-ups and morose brooding. His shabby curtains remained drawn and the windows closed despite the heat so that the air his flat became stuffy, its atmosphere as oppressive and melancholy as his mood. His radio and television remained inactive and he neglected to play anything on his compact disc player as he sat in a lonely, miserable silence. His phone rang once, but he turned it off immediately, even though he saw it was a call from Lynn, unable and unwilling to face communication with anybody, especially not her. His shame was all-engrossing.

During this period he slept fitfully regardless of the time of day or night, completely losing track of the passage of time, but not caring. He had numerous strange and disturbing dreams, most of which he forgot on waking. Several times he saw himself spying on Lynn as she showered or undressed, only to be discovered and roughly ejected from the flat by a furious Nick shouting, 'And never show your fuck-ugly face here again, you little shit!' In other dreams he felt he had been charged with an important mission, yet each time he failed to complete it. In one such as this, which stuck in his mind for long after, so powerful was its impact, he carried a leather bag of heavy stones that he knew were to play a vital part of a momentous ceremony. He had been given the task of delivering them to their destination, but unarmed and clad only in a loincloth, he had to pass through an unknown forest populated by hostile tribes and dangerous wild animals. He spent the entire dream in a state of perpetual terror as he hurried anxiously yet as quietly as he could through the undergrowth and between the trees. A crashing sound in the undergrowth to his right signalled the approach of a gigantic bear that reared on its hind legs to get a better look at the quarry it had scented crouching in the bushes. Adam panicked and fled but soon realised he was too slow to outrun the enormous creature, so he dropped his heavy burden and climbed a tree as fast and as high as he could. The bear roared in frustration as its prey escaped, knowing it was too bulky to pull its own weight up the trunk in pursuit. Adam cowered in the upper branches until the beast, having circled the tree a few times, got bored and wandered away in search of an easier meal. He was about to return to the ground when he heard voices in the forest drawing nearer. A band of a dozen or so fierce-looking face-painted warriors, bearing spears, bows and arrows, were coming through the trees and getting closer. In his fear and trepidation he gripped his branch tighter as if in some way this might make him less visible, but the men did not look up. Their eyes and those of the tracker at the head of the group were on the ground and he realised in horror that they were following his trail. One of his pursuers called out to the others and pointed as he noticed Adam's discarded load. As the bag was seized and the contents examined amongst whoops of triumph, he felt an acute pang of dismay, suddenly aware that he had failed in his sacred duty. So great was his distress that he let out an involuntary groan of anguish, feeling his inadequacy to the core of his being. He immediately regretted the utterance as the tribesmen abruptly stopped their celebrations and looked up, malevolent grins widening on their savage faces as they spotted him trapped above their heads. He shifted uncomfortably but had nowhere to go. The men all set arrows in their bows and got ready to fire. Panic gripped him and he squirmed in a futile attempt to get more of his body behind the branch, but his movement caused it to creak ominously. Suddenly there was a loud cracking noise, the branch separated from the trunk and he plummeted with it towards the ground and the surprised men below. He woke the moment before he hit the ground to find himself overheated in bed, his heart thumping rapidly and his breath gasping from him in short bursts.

Ten minutes later, sipping a cup of tea he considered the meaning of the dream. He wondered if it could be a manifestation of his general feelings of failure and unworthiness or whether it might be an ancestral memory or past life experience. He now regretted returning the dream books to the library, but in their absence his mind was pulled back to his current dilemma. Eventually, as he sat slumped forlornly on the bed, a solution presented itself to him as an uncomfortable idea emerging from his tortured mind like a maggot from an apple. He tried to ignore it to start with, but like the princess with the pea beneath her mattress, in the end it drove him to distraction and he had to face it. The thought was telling him he should leave Portsmouth and start afresh somewhere else, move to a new city as he had done several times before. He had no friends and therefore no life left for him here. The prospect of starting over was not an attractive one, yet he could see no alternative. Before long he found himself once more almost paralysed with sorrow. He didn't want to move away. He wanted to stay here and be on good terms with his friends, but he had destroyed that friendship beyond repair and his punishment, although he judged that he deserved worse, was self-imposed exile. Although he thought he had cried himself out, he wept again, whilst biting on his hand, with quiet, dry sobs and moans of self-loathing until he drifted into sleep once more.

He found himself on the same tropical beach where he had first encountered his petite, ginger haired lover. Happily together again, they ran hand in hand along the shoreline giggling in delight. They swam and chased each other and laughed in joyful abandon. Their paradise was not just of the earth but also of the soul as they were totally secure, trusting and blissful in their mutual adoration. When he woke, he desperately wished he hadn't. If only the dream were true! Why couldn't his real life be like that? The contrast between the two was so extreme that he plunged again into a dark whirlpool of misery, unable to resist the inexorable pull of the vortex. Drowning in melancholy, he moaned aloud like a forlorn child aching for comfort. After a time he fell silent, an empty, numb shell, incapable of feeling anything. He slowly rose and shambled aimlessly around the room, like an inmate who had been too long incarcerated in an institution, until he found himself facing the bookcase. His gaze wandered with no purpose over its contents until they came to rest on one volume in particular. The conspicuous and eye-catching bright yellow spine bore the title "Facing Depression – a Buddhist Perspective". Several times over the years, Adam had bought books on personal development with good intentions, only to give them a cursory skim before placing them on the shelf to be studied on an unspecified future occasion. Invariably he soon forgot of their existence so they remained overlooked and untouched like treasures obscured by grime. As he reached out to take the book down, he was startled by a sudden knock at the door. He paused with his arm outstretched, motionless and momentarily uncomprehending this noisy invasion of his muffled enclave. The thumping was repeated, louder this time and seemingly more insistent. He dropped his arm and turned slowly, his brain dull-witted by lethargy. He began to move towards the door, but then froze as his visitor began rapping persistently on the window.

'Adam! It's me, Nick,' called the familiar voice, 'I know you're in there mate. What the fuck are you doing? Come on, open up! Don't be a tosser, I just want to talk to you.'

Adam remained immobile. He did not feel able to either face or talk to Nick. What if his former friend wanted to thump him? He could not imagine what he could say to him either, other than to crawl on the ground like the worthless and contemptible worm that he was and plead for forgiveness, but he knew he could not muster the strength even for that. His friend knocked and called out twice more before abandoning his attempt. His parting words were, 'Look mate, I know what this is about, but you've got to get over it. You're forgiven right? Don't take it so seriously. Come round soon, yeah?'

Well, that was easy for Nick to say, he thought. They may have forgiven him, but how could he ever forgive himself and how could he stop himself from drooling over Lynn again like a Sun-reading, ape-brained yobbo deprived of his daily page three titillation? He sighed and sat heavily on the bed. It was no good, he realised. He would have to face them at some point. The thought of a lonesome future without his only friends was not one he relished. Sure, he could possibly make new friends eventually, but he had always found the process to be a painful chore and it was highly likely that he would never find such good companions again. So many people were totally stressed out and screwed up these days (*like me*, he thought ironically), carrying their emotional baggage like a parasitic monkey clutched to their back sucking out their spirit, playing mind games and taking advantage of those with weaker.....monkeys.

Adam shook his head and smiled humourlessly at his tendency to spin off into far-fetched and ridiculous little fantasies. He sat for a while trying to clear his thoughts. Not having smoked dope for a few days he found this a little easier than usual. He knew he had to change. In fact he had known it for some time. He recognised that he had a tendency towards paranoia, self-indulgent and obsessive behaviour, and that he had several times in the past resolved to work on his personal, emotional and spiritual development. He acknowledged that he was weak willed, having failed in all his previous attempts at self-improvement. Nevertheless, he now felt, in a remarkably sudden reversal of mood that he was ready to try again. He knew that this time would be different because he had a powerful incentive. He was determined to rebuild his friendship and in so doing would strive to be a better person. Maybe he had to go through this catastrophe in order to find the motivation. He would be reborn like a phoenix rising from the ashes, or like a caterpillar pupating he would re-emerge metamorphosed as a magnificent butterfly. At that moment he imagined a bipolar comic-book character, "Crumbling Will" and "Will Power" being the two sides of his personality. He had been living like Crumbling Will, but from now on he would aspire to be more akin to Will Power and build up his emotional, spiritual and mental strength through a disciplined programme of self-analysis, yoga, meditation and abstinence. He had suspected for some time that a decade and a half of cannabis smoking had had an effect on his emotional stability, yet had repeatedly rejected the notion rather than face the fear of change. He had enjoyed getting stoned *so much* that he did it more and more until it became an integral part of his life and his normal state of being. He had believed it kept him laid-back, insulated against the harsher aspects of this crazy world. It had opened his mind to a different method of thinking, superior in some way to the mundane concerns and thoughts of the "straight" members of society. He was part of an enlightened sub-culture with its outlook founded on two well-established precepts: "A mind blown is a mind shown" and "Don't let the bastards grind you down". He now understood that for the last fifteen years his lifestyle had been based on falsehood. Up until this moment he would never have admitted such a thing, not even to himself, regardless of what he knew in his heart to be true. Long-term dope smoking, like any habitual drug or alcohol use, was merely a coping strategy for post industrial civilization, where the norm was just to submit to the role of a unit of assembly and utilization of resources, a tool of a global capitalist system, a puppet controlled by the unwitting servants of multinational mega-corporations using the media to promote greed and fear as a carrot and stick to manipulate the thoughts and behaviour of the masses, blowing them along as soulless husks in a spiritual desert. Adam knew there was another way, a get-out clause. The philosophies and spiritual outlook of the east had for thousands of years espoused methods designed to lead to inner calm and contentment no matter what the circumstances. Taoist and Buddhist wisdom instructed novices to cultivate mindfulness, whatever that was, to gain insights on the path to enlightenment. He remembered that humility and compassion were advocated in these teachings, but he couldn't recall what else, nor the methods by which such characteristics were to be attained. He returned to his bookshelf and pulled out the friendly-looking yellow book to start out on a new adventure. His work began now!

CHAPTER TEN.

The sound of early evening birdsong, carried by a warm breeze, flooded through the open window from the trees and densely planted shrubs in the spring-flushed garden below. The black, star-spangled curtains, stirred slightly by the draught, swayed in and out causing their shadows to stir on the carpet. Unconscious of this, Rowan sat on her bed nervously nibbling at her fingernails. Unsatisfied with this she stood and paced the room for a few seconds before stopping in front of the hi-fi. She rummaged through her cds in frustration until eventually she found one that she thought would appease her mood, or perhaps distract her from it. She selected "Puzzle" by Biffy Clyro and turned up the volume. She preferred loud music from large speakers to the headset on the mp3 player, not just to save her hearing but also because the music seemed somehow bigger and more satisfying when it filled the room. She was beginning to wish that she had gone to work to take her mind off what lay ahead, but it was out of the question as long as she was still slightly befuddled by the painkillers.

She hadn't seen her mother for well over a year. Rosalind usually returned for the winter festivities, but last year she had postponed her annual homecoming at the last minute claiming that she "simply had to" attend a Christmas party in Milan where she would have an invaluable opportunity to network with all the "right people" in the fashion world. Following this, her flight back was cancelled due to unprecedented levels of snow at Heathrow airport and by the time it had thawed a week later she was already back at work.

'One just can't afford to take *any* time off if you want to make it in this business,' she had said when she phoned, 'It's all *very* cut-throat darling, horrid really, but it's the only way to succeed in the rag trade.' By way of compensation she had sent a ridiculous dress, "as seen on the Paris catwalks" and designed by one of her fashionista cronies, showing how little she knew her daughter. To Rowan, who hated "girly" clothing with a vengeance, the concoction of flaps and straps in scarlet satin was a monstrosity – she wouldn't be seen dead in it. It seemed to have been devised to barely cover only those parts of the body which if revealed on the street would get her arrested. Despite being backless, the garment reached to the floor at the heel with a fine fishnet train, whilst the front exposed the thighs to crotch level, left the midriff bare and contrived to lift the breasts and enhance the cleavage with as little fabric as possible. She didn't even bother to try it on but merely stowed it in the wardrobe with all the other unworn offerings, which hung neglected and despised in equal measure.

Fear of her mother's discovery of this forsaken hoard was not however the reason for Rowan's trepidation. She knew that Rosalind had detected something of her psychic abilities in the past and had made it abundantly clear that it was a characteristic she should eradicate from her mind or at least bury so deep within her that it was irretrievable. Whilst Rhona had promised not to reveal this aspect of her recent trauma, Rowan feared that her mother would somehow manage to divine the information from them. In the past she had demonstrated an uncanny ability to "read between the lines" in any given situation and Rowan had found it very difficult over the years to keep secrets from her. Consequently, she felt she had an additional reason to worry. If Rosalind discovered that she had been self harming, her reaction would be neither sympathetic nor supportive. She knew that her mother, like Rhona, considered herself to be a strong, independent woman and she expected no less from her daughter, once even claiming that her absence was another part of the process of training to become a self-sufficient adult. Rosalind despised weakness and would judge Rowan's behaviour as such, viewing with contempt and scorn what she would see as self-indulgence and self-pity. Her fiery temper ('it's the Italian in me,' she had said, with deliberate innuendo) and sharp tongue often generated vitriolic tirades that could hurt much more than mere physical pain, with the power to leave her daughter overwrought and sobbing uncontrollably. This would result in a rapid reversal of her mother's mood accompanied by an ebullient apology and over-sincere declaration of love, which given the preceding verbal abuse did little to comfort her. Somehow Rosalind always seemed to engineer these episodes to coincide with when Rhona was out, so that when Rowan recounted the incidents to her aunt she felt that she was being regarded as being prone to exaggeration. Of course she loved her mother, but she yearned for an easier, less nerve-racking and more stable relationship;

one not of prolonged absences punctuated by brief visits dominated by extremes of emotional manipulation.

Rowan detected that Rosalind was just a couple of minutes away from her arrival, so she steeled herself and went down stairs to greet her.

'Mum's coming,' she told Rhona who was engrossed with installing new design software on the computer. She looked up, surprised for a moment before remembering that she needn't be.

'Right, I'll just get this uploaded,' she said, 'why don't you put the kettle on.'

The visit was not at all how Rowan had feared or imagined. After the initial shock of seeing her daughter's swollen and discoloured face, Rosalind tendered her affectionate greetings, which seemed uncharacteristically authentic, followed by subdued but heart-felt sympathy and commiseration. Nevertheless her genuine concern could not conceal an undertone of disquiet of a slightly different nature. Rowan perceived a fundamental change in her, despite her mother being one of those rare people whose mind she normally found unreadable. There was something in her demeanour, something implied by a slight yet significant chink in her usual supercilious, unshakeable bearing; an atypical carelessness in the application of her makeup and the arrangement of her hair. She seemed circumspect and distracted, eyes darting around the room as if she imagined that some adversary might at any moment emerge from behind the furniture. The change was so evident that even Rhona noticed it and by mid-evening she felt compelled to question her sister.

'It's the dreams,' disclosed Rosalind hesitantly, wringing her hands, 'since I phoned you about that first one, there have been others....nearly every night.' She shifted uncomfortably in her seat. 'Have you had any more?' she asked looking at Rhona who shook her head in silence. 'Maybe that's why I'm getting them then,' she continued, 'with us being twins...maybe my resistance is lower because of my stressful lifestyle. It's not as easy as you think you know. I put on a brave face, pretend, even to myself that I'm having the time of my life but sometimes I think, it's all held together by a weak fabric of willpower alone and that the slightest extra burden might rip my world apart....and that's what's happening now.' Rowan was taken aback, not just at the substance of her mother's admission but by her unusual candour. Rosalind continued, 'It's those loathsome old men. Every time I fall asleep, I'm afraid I'm going to find them there again, invading my mind. I've dreamt I'm on an old sailing ship, in an ancient city, on a beach...it doesn't matter where I am they always seem to appear and try to intimidate me, always insisting that I make that damned casket, threatening me, saying they'll scar and disfigure my face and body, cause accelerated aging or torture me in unspeakable ways.....' She was becoming more distraught, until she found herself unable to remain seated any longer and rose to pace restlessly. 'Why me?' she pleaded, her voice becoming shrill as she became increasingly hysterical. 'Why am *I* getting these dreams, when they're supposed to be *yours!* It's you who's responsible for this....this....bloody box thing. Why don't they leave me alone! *I* can't do anything! Why don't you just make the damn thing and be done with it so I can get on with my life? Then I might get some peace...I need my sleep you know! I've got a business to run and there's a high profile fashion show in Rome next month and I'm supposed to be running the marketing strategy. How can I communicate sensibly with journalists and editors and deal effectively with media reps when I can't sleep and my mind is.....*contaminated* by hideous geriatrics. You've got to make it stop Rhona – this is all your fault!'

Rhona was stunned and incredulous. 'How can it possibly be *my* fault?' she demanded indignantly. 'You're hundreds of miles away in bloody Italy! You can't blame me for your dreams!' The frustration and anxiety of the last few days found an outlet in anger at the injustice of the accusation and as a habitual defensive response to a verbal attack from her sister. All at once it was as if they were teenagers again, fighting over what to watch on television or clothes or boys or bathroom time. 'It's not my fault that you've run away from your responsibilities as a mother and adopted some stupid, hollow, superficial existence based on vanity and narcissism. You always were *so* self-centred. Everything had to revolve around you didn't it, Miss "Centre-of-the-Bloody-Universe"!'

Rowan had never seen Rhona like this before and she didn't like it. She hated scenes. She didn't understand how people who loved each other could be so spiteful and antagonistic. She had seen couples whose love had turned to hate, boys fight their best friends and parents harshly scold or even strike their own children, all through a lack of communication and understanding.

'Now you listen to me,' her mother was saying, 'you have no right to pass judgement on me and my life, Miss....Goody-Two-Shoes!

You've always been so high and mighty, claiming to be so perfect whilst behind my back you slept with my boyfriends....'

'That only happened once!'

'Stop it! Stop it! I can't stand this!' shouted Rowan followed by 'Ow!' as the effort hurt her face, causing tears to leak from her eyes. 'Shit!' she added, putting her hand to her cheek, 'It's bleeding again.'

The older women fell silent and Rhona handed her a tissue, so she could spit out the blood.

Rowan breathed out heavily. 'It was me alright? I wanted to save Rhona the stress and worry, so I've been blocking her dreams, or at least the ones from those old guys anyway. But I didn't know they would get diverted to you, I didn't think about *where* they would go, I didn't know they would go *anywhere*. I'm sorry.'

Rosalind looked aghast at her daughter. It was as if Rowan had just admitted to the most disgusting crime imaginable. She clasped at her throat as if she could barely breathe and rasped out a few unintelligible syllables before fainting.

Blue smoke curled up from the joss stick as Rowan stared at its glowing tip. The fumes seemed to waver in time to the beat of the Black Stone Cherry song that rang around the room. Rosalind had gone again, although it was only the next morning. Before rushing off to catch her fight back to Italy, she had behaved normally, as if nothing had happened. Despite a subdued heart-to-heart after she had recovered from her faint the night before Rosalind, it seemed, was still unable to discuss anything related to the extended mind. She and Rhona had apologised to each other, both promising to try to be more considerate and understanding in the future, but when Rowan tentatively tried to raise the subject of the dreams, her mother quickly cut her off claiming fatigue and went straight to bed.

'Thanks for trying to protect me,' Rhona had said squeezing her hand, 'but it might be better now if you lift your "dream blockade", for the sake of my sister if nothing else.'

It was so exasperating that Rosalind would not face the truth. How could she be so stubborn? Rowan was beginning to suspect that the reason she was so resistant to the idea of psychic abilities was that she too possessed them but perhaps out of fear wouldn't or couldn't admit it, even to herself. She blew on the ember in front of her watching it glow brighter as the smoke fled in the air stream. She felt abandoned once more by an inadequate mother whose answer to every problem was to run away. She had been beaten and nearly raped and her mother's awkward, hasty visit was not enough. *Why didn't she stay and comfort me and support me like a good mother should?* wondered Rowan. *What is wrong with me that she should repeatedly reject my needs?* She pulled off her top and blew on the incense again. Maybe she would go back to the right arm this time. She had always favoured the left in the past, being right handed. She looked at the pale soft skin, blemished only by faded scars, trying to choose the right spot. The burning point hovered over her arm. She waited. She wondered about Rosalind. Maybe she deserved her sympathy rather than distain. Rowan tried to imagine what it would be like to be her mother. She couldn't. She looked at the joss stick again then moved it away and extinguished it in the ashtray. She didn't want to hurt herself any more. She had been hurt too much. Causing herself more harm had never solved her problems and never would, she realised. It didn't make her feel better. It was simply a temporary diversion, one kind of pain to replace another, not a reduction in suffering at all. She poked aimlessly at the frayed corner of a poster, shivered slightly and then replaced her sweatshirt. Although she had too much going on in her mind and just wanted it all to stop - Grant's attack, the manifestation of her own frightening power, all the weird dreams people were having, her mother - she decided to find another way of distracting herself so went in search of a good book.

When Rhona returned from work, she told Rowan that the police had come to the workshop to deliver the result of the autopsy.

'It seems he had a massive brain haemorrhage,' she said.

Rowan said nothing, but sat biting her lip and looking at the table.

'The doctor said that when you tried to defend yourself,' Rhona continued, 'it wasn't even with sufficient force to cause any bruising, so there's no way the impact could have caused a blood vessel to burst in his brain. As far as he's concerned, with Grant's heavy drinking, heavy smoking and unhealthy diet, it could have happened any time and was probably triggered by an increase in blood pressure due to his state of heightened excitement.' She walked around the table and put her hand on Rowan's shoulder. 'Anyway, you won't be bothered by the police again.'

'I *know* it was me,' insisted Rowan quietly.

'Yes I know and I have to admit I'm beginning to believe you too,' conceded Rhona, 'but no one else needs to know okay? Charlie and Bess won't mention it, neither will Jenny. Regardless of that, the guys at work are all behind you anyway and Flora said if she had her way she would dish out the death sentence to people like that, after a slow castration with a blunt instrument. So even if she knew, she'd support you.'

'At least mum didn't find out,' added Rowan, 'I *so* could not have handled that on top of everything else. She would have totally freaked.'

'I know, but she's gone now. Shall I cook the tea? What do you want? Can you chew yet?'

'It's OK, I'll cook tonight.'

'Are you sure?'

'Yeah. You've been working and I've like, had the day off and stuff after all. But I want to try to come to work tomorrow. It's so boring at home on my own all day and the telly's total shit.'

'What about those diclofenac tablets, they make you drowsy don't they? You won't be able to operate machinery or use sharp tools.'

'There must be something I can do – anything to avoid this cabin fever.'

'Okay, but you'll have to take it easy.'

It was Rhona's scream that woke her in the early hours. Rowan felt like she had only just fallen asleep, but she leapt out of bed and rushed into her aunt's room. Rhona was sitting bolt upright, her unrestrained hair a wild mane, eyes wide with fright and tears running down her face.

Her niece held her softly and muttered, 'It's okay it was just a dream. You're awake now…it's all over.' It was a reversal of the roles they had filled when she was a child. 'Do you want to talk about it?' she added.

'Um, I don't know if I should….,' muttered Rhona, sniffing and wiping her face on her sheet.

'Well, you know you can't hide it from me, remember?' said Rowan, 'so you might as well tell it in your own words.'

'Ah, okay….I was standing…in front of an archway…,' she began haltingly, trying to grasp at the rapidly fleeing details, staring down at the bedspread, '…a huge stone entrance to a city or a temple or something and there were strange carvings of weird faces and figures, sort of South American looking…Incan or Mayan or I don't know, one of those. Anyway, through the arch I saw two people approaching. It was that weird old guy who brought the plans in and he was dragging you along by a rope tied around your wrists.' She paused and looked briefly up at Rowan and then away again before continuing. 'He stopped under the archway and wrapped the rope round and round you before tying it in a tight knot. Then he said, "this is all your fault," and pulled out a huge knife. I couldn't move. I was just rooted to the spot. I wanted to run and help you but I couldn't.....I just couldn't move.' She paused for a second time, tears flowing once more. 'And then... and then....he grabbed your hair.....and....pulled your head back and...' She stopped completely, unable to continue as she broke into sobs.

Rowan held her again, stroking her hair and whispering words of comfort.

'If anything should happen to you because of this...' murmured Rhona when she could speak again.

'It won't,' Rowan reassured her, 'it was just a dream, okay?'

'But couldn't it have been sent by those weirdoes to put the frighteners on me?

'I suppose...maybe...but they wouldn't actually do anything like that would they? I mean, it's just a coffin really isn't it? It's not like a gilded wooden box with a few rocks stuck on top is really going to like *actually* resurrect anyone.'

The next morning Rowan's face was throbbing so much she had to increase the dosage of her medication. This was an indication of her level of discomfort – she usually rejected conventional medicines as "synthetic toxins that totally mess with your body".

'I thought it was supposed to get better not worse,' she complained, 'I hardly slept a wink last night.'

'Well, that was partly my fault wasn't it?' said Rhona.

'Not really,' responded Rowan wearily, 'it didn't make a lot of difference with it hurting so much.'

'You had better stay at home then,' Rhona suggested, 'there's no point you coming to work if you're tired and miserable.'

Rowan agreed and went back to bed without delay. Eating her breakfast and driving to the workshop alone gave Rhona plenty of time to dwell on her dream but that soon changed when she arrived at Fantasy Furniture to hear the phone ringing in the office. Rushing in and answering it just in time she heard Flora's voice, a little distressed.

'I know I've had all my holiday for this year,' she said, 'what with our trip tae Canada and everything, but can I stay at hame the day?

My Angus has taken bad and I want tae take care o' him. I cannae bear to think o' him all alone when he's so poorly. If he needs anything I'd like tae be there tae help.'

'Of course, Flora,' said Rhona, thinking *oh no, there are invoices to draw up and the customer database needing updated urgently,* 'you stay at home where you're needed.' She groaned inwardly at the extra workload. She was supposed to be designing a bedroom suite in order to make a bid for a lucrative contract to furnish six rooms in an exclusive five star hotel. She would have to take some work home this evening. Normally she would have stayed in the office but felt she ought to be there for Rowan if needed. Sighing she turned on the computer and thought that at least being busy would take her mind off all the complicated and bizarre happenings of recent days.

Thirty minutes later as she sat at the PC laboriously and unwillingly preparing invoices, the machine crashed.

'Fuck, fuck, fuck, fuck, FUCK!' she said pounding the desk with each word.

There was a knock at the door. Feeling slightly embarrassed, more for the thought of being caught losing her cool than for swearing she said, 'Come in,' expecting one of her staff. A tall broad-shouldered, stern-looking woman of about sixty years old and dressed entirely in black, marched into the room and glared down at her with flinty grey eyes.

'Miss Flemming?' she demanded haughtily.

'Yes.' Rhona nodded cautiously, feeling wary of the stranger's attitude. She really didn't want any more problems right now. *What could this woman want?* She wondered as she stood slowly.

'I'm Mrs. Skinner. Grant's mother.'

'Oh, right. You'd better sit down,' said Rhona indicating a chair, but the visitor remained standing. She was definitely not prepared for this unforeseen circumstance, but couldn't understand why she suddenly felt so guarded. Maybe it was because she was reminded of her boarding-school head mistress whose extreme methods of intimidation had left Rhona feeling uneasy in the company of any woman of that age who presented herself as a figure of authority. 'This is a little um....unexpected,' she added nervously.

'And *I* wasn't expecting my son's death either!' declared Mrs. Skinner severely, as if she believed that Rhona was somehow responsible.

'Er, no, neither were we,' Rhona muttered lamely as she walked behind her desk where she felt safer and realising that it was a defensive manoeuvre. 'Please take a seat, won't you?'

'I would rather stand,' the woman stated. Her arrogant and hostile manner was beginning to irritate. She guessed that as Mrs Skinner was grieving for her son, she could be excused a certain amount, but in her current mood she felt she couldn't put up with much of it before she lost her patience and possibly also her temper.

'Suit yourself,' she said simply, 'what can I do for you?'

'The police inform me,' she began frostily, 'that you had *dismissed* Grant on the day before his death.'

'That's right,' Rhona replied levelly, 'on the grounds of sexual harassment.'

'And that this *person* who accused him, *also* claimed that he was trying to seduce her when he died.'

'It's called "attempted rape" Mrs Skinner and there were witnesses to his previous behaviour prior to his dismissal. He *groped* my niece in full view of the rest of the staff! What exactly is your point?' God, this woman had a nerve!

'I was aware that my Grant felt unwelcome here from the first week of his employment and I believe that the workforce, egged on by this *girl*,' she spat the word out as if it scalded her tongue, 'who seemed to have it in for him from the very start, undertook a regular programme of rumour and intimidation designed to force his resignation. When that didn't work, realising he was made of sterner stuff, they resorted to entrapment and an assault that resulted in his broken nose. So my *point,* as you put it Miss Flemming, is that my son has been wronged, his reputation tarnished by false allegations and that the brutal assault made on him by this girl may have led to the haemorrhage that caused his death.'

For a moment Rhona was speechless. She couldn't believe what she was hearing. It seemed obvious that the woman's mind had been seriously warped by her grief and turned her into a raving nutter.

'I can assure you that that was definitely not the case,' she stated categorically, trying to remain calm, 'and whilst I regret that you have had to suffer the loss of your son, his behaviour had been totally unacceptable and had he *not* died he would have been facing criminal proceedings.'

'I know my son,' seethed Mrs Skinner, 'and I know that he would *never* have behaved that way. I intend to have the circumstances fully investigated and clear Grant's name. I know how your *incestuous*

Highland communities always do everything they can to protect their own – I've seen "The Wicker Man" you know - but I won't put up with it!' The woman was becoming increasingly agitated whilst Rhona sat incredulously watching her rant. She had no idea what to do or say when faced with such ludicrous accusations. She was about to call to the guys in the workshop to help her eject this neurotic unhinged lunatic when she started spouting off again.

'Just because you are related to this little *slut*,' she fumed, almost choking on last word, 'it doesn't mean you can hide and protect her forever. I'll get to the bottom of this – you mark my words.'

Rhona stood, now totally outraged. It had gone too far. 'Now you listen to me, you stuck up, poison, rancid-hearted harpy,' she began, bristling indignantly, but Mrs Skinner had turned on her heel and stormed from the room without looking back. Rhona went after her to finish her own tirade, so as not to be left frustrated, but when she got to the door her adversary was already exiting at the other side of the workshop, the men staring after her.

'Bitch!' called Rhona, seething. 'God, the nerve of that woman!' Her staff turned their heads from the swinging door to look at her in surprise. It was very rare for their boss to lose her temper or raise her voice.

'What was all that about?' asked Dougie.

Rhona sagged against the doorframe. 'Don't ask,' she replied shaking her head. She slammed the door in exasperation at not having had her say, angrily strode around the office insulting her antagonist in her absence and finally sat behind her desk with her head in her hands. This was going to be really bad for Rowan when she found out and she knew that she wouldn't be able to hide it from her.

#

The streets were inundated by the relentless downpour. Adam felt the first incursion of moisture as it penetrated as far as his shoulders, soaking through the inadequate protection afforded by his over-worn coat, which hung sodden and heavy from his bony frame like a urine drenched nappy long overdue its change. He was practicing mindfulness, attempting to be "in the moment" and increasing his awareness of his mind and body. This enabled him to notice the tension he held in his shoulders and when he realised that this would neither keep him drier nor make the coat lighter, he deliberately relaxed them, feeling an immediate improvement. Next he became conscious of his feet squelching in the cheap synthetic trainers, like frogs wrapped loosely in plastic bags. He released his clenched toes and slackened his ankles thereby putting a spring in his step that he had not experienced for many years. He marvelled at how such simple techniques could make so much difference to his mood and physical well-being. It even seemed as if he was using his energy more efficiently and anticipated a reduction in the fatigue he would normally expect to follow this brisk walk. Suddenly he realised that his shoulders had tightened again, so returned his focus there, only to find that in doing so he had abandoned attending to his feet. This was proving a little more difficult than he had imagined it would be and hoped that it would become easier with practice.

His mind returned to his purpose. He had resolved to face Nick and Lynn to say sorry for his unseemly behaviour and to promise them that he could and would change. Despite his newly acquired esoteric knowledge and outlook, it was not without great trepidation that he approached their flat. However, he had decided that despite his fear, he would go ahead. He was both nervous and embarrassed in advance, although through his faith in their friendship he hoped and trusted that they would be inclined to forgive him. He attempted to picture the scene. Would they stare at him in stony silence, keeping him on the doorstep until he'd made his apology and begged for their forgiveness? Would Nick thump him? He didn't think so. He tried to concentrate on what he was intending to say and how he was going to say it. He had practiced it in his mind before leaving home, going over his plan half a dozen times, visualising not just every step of the process but also its successful outcome. He also knew he was going to have to remain totally attentive to where his eyes wandered and to discipline his mind not to indulge in lustful thoughts. This would be easier now that it was cooler and hopefully Lynn would be wearing more clothes.

The heat wave had broken quite suddenly that morning. The clear blue skies were rapidly obscured by surging dark clouds, which appeared over the rooftops like a horde of angry giants. They voiced their rage in bellows of roaring thunder that reverberated between the buildings causing loose casements to judder in their frames. The first flash of lightening was like a missile strike accompanied by a thump so loud and deep that it seemed to resonate in the bones. Adam had been prostrate on his unmade bed where he presented an image, if there had been another present to witness it, of such unconstrained and haphazard disarray that it could almost have been contrived by a desperate and talentless artist determined to be worthy of consideration for the Turner

Prize. He looked up from his book, startled by the noise and rose to walk over to the window, stretching his limbs that had become stiff from immobility. He licked the fingers of his right hand and rubbed at the glass to create a smeary circle slightly less grimy than the rest of the pane to enable easier observation of the weather outside. He recoiled in alarm as another explosion of light and sound shook the world, then stood a moment in awe at the power of the natural world before he realised that it had become quite dark. He flicked the light switch but nothing happened, so he shrugged, threw his book on the bed and returned to the window to watch the spectacle. A new sound emerged to add its voice to the storm's chorus. An onslaught of fat raindrops plummeted in huge globs to splatter the city's concrete skin, smacking it with millions of vigorous slaps as if in punishment for its incalculable crimes against nature. The resulting noise was like an enthusiastically applauding multitude gratified to see such transgressions atoned for. As he watched the pavement getting washed clean by the deluge, Adam wondered if his own soul could be similarly cleansed. Would the book he was reading and the wisdom proffered within its pages flush away the detritus clogging his aura's pathways?

All too quickly he found himself at the foot of the steps leading up to his friends' flat. He hesitated, reluctant now to face his forthcoming ordeal. He tried to look up, as if the sight of his path might ease his passage, but was obliged to turn his face down again due to the force of the downpour. He took a deep breath, tried to relax his shoulders once more and slowly began his ascent. His feet felt like lumps of heavy, claggy mud sticking to the steps and adding to the pull of gravity. Before long he was climbing the last flight to the door and trying to compose himself, although he knew he was merely procrastinating and that no further preparation would make any difference now. He was still several steps from the top when the door suddenly swung open and Lynn stood facing him.

#

Rowan was indeed more than a little perturbed by the news of Mrs Skinner's appearance, but the next day returned to work regardless. Under normal circumstances she would have revelled in the chance to spend some extra time at home, getting up late, listening to music, sketching, writing poetry, watching movies and surfing the net. However, these were not normal circumstances. She found it impossible to concentrate on any of her usual leisure activities. The chronic ache in her face continued and it often felt numb or tingly from the nerve damage, but it was the mental turmoil that disturbed her most. The image of Grant's ghastly face, frozen in shock at the moment of his death, was deeply embedded in her memory. She was already feeling extremely uncomfortable with the concept that her mind had the power to kill before Grant's mother had appeared on the scene. Although she may have wished for him to be hurt, even maimed, and certainly to be punished, to suffer for what he had done and for what he had attempted to do, she would not have wanted him killed, especially by not by herself. It was not that she felt truly responsible as such. She knew it wasn't exactly a conscious decision, but an action brought about by extreme fear and by both emotional and physical trauma. Nevertheless she felt guilty and hypocritical for having compromised her own principles. A new wave of hate for Grant surprised her – she now despised him anew for making her kill him. Thus her thoughts spiralled in confusion as her turbulent and conflicting feelings fluctuated. She hoped that at least back in the workshop her mind would be preoccupied with concentrating on the tasks in hand. The first hurdle, however, was to face the crew she worked with. She disliked being the centre of attention at the best of times and although she knew that the guys genuinely liked her, being the focus of their sympathy and kindness would embarrass her hugely.

In the event, most of the workforce was actually very good in their treatment of her. They seemed to understand her feelings better than she'd given them credit for. She still received an enthusiastic welcome and kind expressions of concern, but within minutes everyone had settled into a fairly typical day. However Rowan had not been prepared for the Flora's reaction. She was the one member of staff she was least acquainted with, never having had the occasion to work alongside her. When Flora entered the workshop at five to ten she rushed anxiously over to Rowan. She wailed in dismay at the sight of the girl's face.

'Och, you poor wee thing!' the elderly secretary exclaimed in consternation although she was a good head shorter than the teenager, 'you must have suffered terribly! Does it still hurt much? It must do! Let me have a look at you. Shouldn't you still be at home?' While Flora fussed around her, Rowan cringed inwardly but didn't wish to offend the well-meaning woman, knowing that her sentiments were genuine.

'I'm fine Flora, really,' she reassured her, 'it looks worse than it is. And I'd much rather be at work than rattling around on my own at home.'

'If you say so, dear,' said Flora, unconvinced, 'but it was a terrible thing that happened to you.' She shook her head and then added vehemently, 'if that monster hadnae upped and died, I would have killed him mysel'. I don't care what the law says, people like him should get nae mercy. Maybe the good Lord intervened to save one of his innocent children. It's just as well or I'd have become a sinner too, having to join Lucifer himsel' down in the fires of hell for taking the life o' one of his ane folk.'

Rowan fidgeted uneasily, finding it difficult to believe that the character in front of her could actually exist. Witnessing her niece's discomfort, Rhona called Flora from the office doorway, saving the girl from further embarrassment. Rowan breathed a sigh of relief and gratefully returned to her work.

During the next week, things seemed to gradually get back to relative normality. Work continued as usual and nobody mentioned Grant at all. At "Fantasy Furniture" it was as if he had never existed. The police however, did visit the house early on Friday evening. Rhona showed the two officers, one male and one female, into the lounge and called Rowan to join them. They had met them both before during the last few days and Rhona was impressed by their courtesy, tact and professionalism. The woman brought them up to date. It transpired that Mrs Skinner's insistence on further investigation had backfired. It had been discovered that Grant's references had been faked by his brothers and that he had left Berkshire soon after two fifteen year old girls had alleged that he had propositioned them after stalking them after school for two weeks. The neighbourhood constabulary had still been investigating the case and appealing for witnesses when he had suddenly disappeared. It seemed that, although they denied it at the time, only his family knew of his whereabouts. The local police authority was now considering whether or not to bring charges of withholding evidence and attempting to pervert the course of justice. Despite this, Mrs Skinner was still expounding her outrageous opinions and recruiting an expensive law firm to represent the whole family. They didn't say so, but Rowan could tell that the police officers suspected the family's money was not honestly gained. Before they left they reassured her that, in the doctor's opinion, neither her punch on Grant's nose nor her other attempts at self defence could possibly have resulted in his brain haemorrhage and regardless of Mrs Skinner's demands, they considered the matter closed.

Rhona didn't quiz Rowan any further about her telepathy, although it was continually on her mind. She hoped that her niece would gradually be more forthcoming as time passed, especially as she no doubt knew her aunt's mind, but for now she had decided that it was best not to pry. Jenny on the other hand had become an enthusiastic inquisitor once she had overcome her initial shock and uneasiness. She took every opportunity to question her friend about her abilities. To start with Rowan was reluctant to divulge too much information, but the restoration of Jenny's trust and her eager perseverance eventually persuaded Rowan to open up. Jenny was genuinely fascinated by the answers she received and eagerly anticipated each new disclosure. For her part Rowan was feeling buoyed up and liberated by the release of finally being able to share what she'd kept secret for so long, thankful that her friend was not going to hate her for it.

#

The smile of welcome on Lynn's face as she stood aside to let him in was to Adam like a personal blessing from the Pope to a devout Catholic. The knot in his chest unravelled so that his heart beat freely once more and his lungs were released from constriction. He hadn't realised how much tension he had been holding until he had let it go.

'Good to see you, Adam,' she said cheerily, 'come on in and get dry.' Thankfully she was wearing a baggy tracksuit.

'Er...,' he said as he stepped over the threshold. She shut the door behind him. 'Were you just going out?' he asked, a little bemused. She shook her head. 'But you just opened the door and I hadn't knocked....'

'Yeah, I just kind of got a feeling you were there, you know?' He didn't. Disconcerted, he followed her meekly into the lounge where a recording of Transglobal Underground was filling the room with the beat of dub fusion music. Nick was kneeling in the middle of the floor on an island of spread-out newspaper surrounded by a dismantled chainsaw. Although he wore latex gloves to keep his hands clean, he had managed to smear his arms up to his elbows in grease and a black smudge darkened one side of his nose.

'Alright mate?' he said cheerfully, as Lynn went to put the kettle on, but then noticing Adam's expression added, 'don't look so worried, I won't use it on you. I'm fixing it for Harry The Tree.'

'Right. No. I was just thrown a bit by Lynn guessing that I was at the door you know?'

'Oh that. Yeah it's weird isn't it?' commented Nick lightly, 'she's always been a bit psychic, you know, doing stuff like that, but it's happening a lot more since she got up the pole. Maybe it's Mother Nature's heightened awareness or something.' He turned his attention back to cleaning engine parts, leaving Adam to muse on his usually cynical friend's acceptance of the extraordinary.

'Skin up will you, Adam?' Nick requested nodding towards the tin on the coffee table, 'Only I can't manage it at the moment,' he added holding up his greasy latex gloves.

Adam complied hesitantly, still unsettled by Lynn's premonition while at the same time remembering her revelation that she painted her dreams, one of which resembled a scene from his. *I mustn't get distracted* he thought, feeling like he needed to get his apology underway, but also wondering whether or not he really wanted to get stoned again, having so recently resolved to work on his spiritual growth. He remained silent and pensive, rolling the smoke whilst Lynn made the tea, wanting to speak to them both at the same time. He lit up without inhaling and then passed the joint to Nick, who with his hands occupied, puffed away whilst keeping it in his mouth – a skill that Adam had never been able to acquire, finding that the smoke always spiralled up into his eyes and nose.

Lynn returned with the drinks, so wasting no more time and wishing to get it off his chest, Adam stuttered with his eyes averted, 'Look, I'm really sorry about....you know...I...um..'

'Don't worry about it Adam,' interrupted Lynn, 'I know what guys are like.'

'Yeah but, I really shouldn't...'

'Like I said, get yourself a girlfriend, yeah?'

Adam sighed. 'Well that isn't so easy done as said, so until I do, I wanted you to know it won't happen again, I'm ashamed of myself you know?' He looked at Nick. 'And I'm sorry to you too. I mean Lynn's your...'

'Yeah, yeah, whatever. Don't take it all so seriously,' said his friend waving a hand dismissively and starting to reconstruct the chainsaw as he spoke. 'Look *I* know how sexy Lynn is so I can't really blame you for gawping right? Just don't get obsessed OK?'

'Yeah but...'

'Like she said, you need a woman of your own. But don't worry, we'll help you find one.'

'Yeah but...'

'Forget it mate. Here, shut the fuck up and smoke this.' Nick held up the joint delicately gripped between two oily latex-clad fingertips. Adam hesitated. He wanted to say that he'd given up, but…..*Oh well* he thought, taking the reefer, *just now and again won't hurt and this one's a celebration.* He was massively relieved that his friend's had forgiven him so readily, though in his heart he had known that they would. He reflected on how stupid he had been to get so screwed up over it and cause himself so much mental suffering. His book had something to say about that he remembered. He inhaled the familiar and comforting fumes and felt mellower. Following his new path was going to be like being reborn. He was going to have to be watchful, observe when he fell into old habitual thought patterns and in recognising them, overcome them as minor obstacles on the road of self development. Lynn's voice interrupted his thoughts.

'I'm getting like, so totally excited about our holiday,' she enthused brightly, 'only two weeks to go! I've been looking at the guidebooks yeah? I got two to get a balanced view and there's so much to see and do! You know, there's castles and medieval villages, forests and mountains and that. It's going to be *great!*'

'I'm planning on doing some bird watching an' all,' added Nick, tightening nuts on the engine in front of him, rebuilding the chainsaw with the dexterity and proficiency of an experienced soldier reassembling his rifle. 'You know how I love the birds of prey,' he continued merrily, 'Well I'm hoping to see a Black Kite, maybe even a Lesser Spotted Eagle and if I'm incredibly lucky,' he paused meaningfully, 'a Saker.'

'What's that?' asked Adam.

'It's a kind of falcon, about the size of a buzzard, but pretty rare and not usually found in Western Europe.'

'Cool.' Now that he had emerged from his despair, Adam was also beginning to anticipate the trip. Slightly stoned he visualised the expected sights as listed by Lynn and attributed to them romantic notions of rural idyll, social collectives of noble peasants, proud to be living their simple lives, fulfilled despite the hard physical demands. He pictured himself spending a day on a farm, lending a hand for no reward other than a plain but hearty meal served by a plump ruddy-faced woman wearing a headscarf.

He was jolted from his fantasy by the puttering noise of Nick yanking on the starting cord of the chainsaw. After two more pulls, the machine roared hideously into life as he revved its throttle. He chuckled with demonic glee from a cloud of black fumes like an incubus released from a smoky abyss. 'Ha ha! Far fucking out!' he yelled above the din, 'I've fixed the bastard!'

#

Two weeks had passed since Grant's death and a spell of warm dry weather was cheering everyone's spirits. More buds were bursting into leaf on the awakening trees, the geese had mostly departed for their nesting grounds further north and east and the swallows had finally returned to the Highlands. Charlie delighted in the first sightings of the year when these charming little birds graced the skies once more. Their excitable chittering as they sat on the telephone wires, their rapid yet graceful aerobatics and what they signified – that spring had truly arrived – all this made his heart sing. It also meant he could use his beloved bicycle more often too. Although he was no "fair weather cyclist" he found it too hazardous to ride on icy roads and too arduous in the frequent high winds of winter to cycle the five miles to town and work a full day. He didn't understand people who drove to work and then spent an hour exercising in the gym. Why not cycle, run or walk to the workplace, thus maintaining a minimum level of fitness whilst simultaneously reducing damage to the environment and saving money on fuel and sports centre fees? Charlie also valued the extra thinking time available to the rural cyclist-commuter. It required much less concentration than driving and the increased duration of the journey allowed him the freedom to ponder the interesting convolutions and idiosyncratic episodes of life's long road. He was feeling more relaxed than he had for a long time. The dreams seemed to have eased off or at least they came less often and were less distinct; Rowan was settling back into work and thankfully they had heard no more from their sinister and anonymous would-be clients. They had also had an email from Luke, who was finding his work very rewarding and was enjoying the company of both the locals and the other volunteers.

Wheeling smoothly into the yard, he parked his bike in the usual place and took his habitual perusal of the surrounding trees. The air was full of the sound of birdsong and the gentle breeze carried the faint aroma of Balsam Poplar. *Fantastic*, he thought, *I'm really so lucky to be working here.* He was also delighted to have a wonderful wife and a lovely home to share with her. He was glad to see the back of those disturbing dreams too and frankly, their significance and impact had already diminished appreciably. He guessed that he had merely experienced a few weeks of random turmoil but now, infused with the full vigour of spring's vitality, he was feeling pretty good. Cheerfully, he entered the building and started his work for the day.

Just before lunch Rhona called him into her office.

'What's up?' he asked noting the unease in her expression.

'Shut the door Charlie,' she bade him. He did so.

'I've just had a phone call from that weird old man,' she told him.

'What, not the box guy?' His heart sank.

'Yep, that's the one. His name is Nasaru apparently,'

'Damn, I thought we'd heard the last of him.'

'You wish,' Rhona sighed.

'So what did he say?'

'He said that time is running out and that if we don't start work on the casket soon we'll miss the deadline, which apparently would be the most catastrophic of outcomes as far as his masters were concerned.' She paused and bit her lip. Charlie shook his head in dismay. He really did not want to deal with this.

'Hadn't you already told them that we weren't doing it?' he asked.

'I couldn't, they hadn't left any contact details, so I told him just now on the phone. But he wasn't having any of it. He completely lost his rag. He said that they had originally expected us to do it without question and then the dreams were supposed to have persuaded us to take the job. Now that it seems that because that didn't work they would have to resort to "more serious measures" to make sure we complied with their demands.'

'What? What kind of measures?' Charlie was becoming infuriated by the audacity of these people.

'He didn't say but it definitely sounded like a threat.'

'This is getting out of hand. We should call the police.'

'That's what I told him,' said Rhona. 'He said that it would be a bad idea so I told him to bloody well get stuffed. Anyway I wanted to talk to you before I called them. I don't think we should mention the dreams, they'll think we're crackpots.'

'No need,' said Charlie, 'they're not relevant. This is a straightforward case of someone making a threat. I know we don't know who or where they are, but at least if we've reported it, then if they do anything it'll be part of the evidence against them.'

Rhona sat thoughtfully for a minute.

'Actually Charlie, if you take out the dreams what are we left with? A guy who seems a bit weird and a call saying that they would "take measures" – that could just mean that they would write a nasty letter. If it wasn't for the dreams, we wouldn't be so worried by all this and wouldn't have considered phoning the police.'

'Hmm, I see what you mean.'

'Let's talk to Bess about it,' suggested Rhona, 'she always seems to see sense.'

'Aye, good plan. Do you want to come round this evening?'

'No,' she said firmly, 'I want to go now and I want you to come too. Let's just deal with it. We'll have a head to head, the three of us.'

As they pulled up at Charlie's house, he said, 'she'll be outside on a day like this, probably in the herb plot.'

Rhona followed him through the gate into the garden. A half-empty mug sat on a rustic table next to a paperback. They glanced around the immediate vicinity, but saw no one.

'She must have nipped inside,' said Charlie. He popped his head and shoulders through the open top half of the kitchen stable-door.

'Bess?' he called. He entered the house and called again, listening for a response. Receiving none he went back outside. 'She must be out here somewhere.'

'Yes, it's a big garden,' agreed Rhona, 'let's have a look.'

Ten minutes later, having searched all three acres, calling her name, they concluded that Bess must have gone for a walk, probably to the beach. They decided to have coffee while they waited. Rhona sat at the garden table and picked up the book for a closer inspection. Charlie went inside and put the kettle on. It was only then that he noticed the overturned side table and the fallen pot plant. He frowned, confused. Although neither of them were keen on housework, it was unlike Bess to leave a mess like that neglected for long.

'Rhona,' he called, 'come and see this.'

She hastened in and surveyed the scene. 'Maybe the cat did it?' she suggested, 'you know, after Bess went out.'

'Aye, maybe…,' he said doubtfully, 'but Nimbus is usually pretty laid back. I suppose…'

At that moment the phone rang. Charlie crossed the room and picked up the receiver.

'Mr MacKay?' enquired a man's voice.

'Yes.'

'Good. You may have noticed the absence of your wife by now…'

'What? Yes. Who are you? What's going on? Where is she?' demanded Charlie, a little perplexed.

'There's no need to worry, Mr MacKay, she is er...safe with us. Unharmed, I can assure you,' came the reply in a self-satisfied tone. The hesitancy in the voice suggested an unfamiliarity with telephone use rather than lack of confidence or uncertainty of purpose.

'Where is she?' Charlie demanded again, becoming both frightened and angry, 'and who the hell are you? What do you want?'

'Surely you must realise, Mr Mackay, that you compelled us into er....taking this action by your refusal to...follow our instructions. Your reluctance to um, cooperate left us little choice.'

'What?' he said, but then it suddenly dawned on him. 'Do you mean the casket? But what's that got to do with Bess?'

'It is your...emotional attachment to her that will provide the um, incentive for you to undertake our assignment. She is quite safe and well cared for. We are not er...uncivilised....just a little impatient. She will be restored to you unharmed as soon as we have collected the er, completed article.'

'But that'll be weeks away!' exclaimed Charlie in alarm, beginning to feel panic rising in his chest. 'You can't just kidnap someone and keep them prisoner for weeks just to get a job done! It's just a fucking box for Christ's sake! Are you mad?'

'Far from it,' came the response. 'Resolute and determined certainly...perhaps obstinate too and, er, unfortunately for all concerned, increasingly desperate. But definitely not mad.'

'Well if you're that desperate, you can do me a deal,' fumed Charlie, 'I'll make your stupid box, but not until you return my wife!'

'Mr MacKay, the um, "box" as you call it is not in any way stupid and you are in no position to er, negotiate, as it were. We thought you would have understood our situation from the messages we sent you and Miss Flemming.'

'Messages? You mean the drawings?'

'No, no. Oh, this is becoming tedious.' The formerly calm voice started to betray some impatience. 'I suppose you would have called them dreams. Anyway, I really must insist you start work right away. Do not try to contact the police or you may never see your wife again.'

'But..' The caller hung up leaving Charlie to lower the receiver and gape at it in disbelief. He slowly replaced the receiver and looked desperately at Rhona. Fear and anguish clenched at his guts. 'What am I going to do?' he gasped. 'They've got Bess.....I don't know what to do!'

PART 2

CHAPTER ELEVEN.

The courtyard glowed dazzlingly in the bright spring afternoon, the whitewashed walls throwing the light generously onto the freshly blooming flowerbeds as if it had an inexhaustible supply. The windows of the castle reflected the blue sky so clearly that it seemed to be contained within its rooms. The birdsong filling the air from the surrounding trees and the buzzing of insects visiting the blossom gave voice to Mother Nature's seasonal excitement.

Oblivious to all of this the two fair-haired sisters embraced tightly, tearfully and at great length, neither wanting to let go. Their pale lemon robes, echoing the colour of the joyful Mayfest sunshine, did nothing to cheer their hearts.

'Come now girls,' sung the kindly matron, 'you'll see each other again next year.' She squeezed their shoulders affectionately. 'The time will fly by!' she added brightly, before retiring to a discrete distance to allow them to finish their farewells.

To Sonilla however, thirteen moons apart was unthinkable after spending their whole lives so far together. But as Lendi had now come of age, having recently celebrated her eighteenth birthday, her time had come to meet "The Ancestors", the privilege and duty of all of "The Select". Sonilla knew that she was lucky that only one year separated her from her sibling, so she would follow then, but she couldn't imagine how she was going to get through it without the continual companionship of a loving sister. They had never parted company before, except during lessons, so they had always been there for each other - *always.*

They broke apart briefly to dry their eyes and look into each other's faces.

'You'll be fine,' Lendi assured her whilst, as the eldest of the two, trying to maintain her own composure although she knew she

225

could not hide her feelings from Sonilla. Then, in their final embrace, she whispered, "At least you have Andor."

That was true, thought Sonilla, Andor was a real comfort – more than that, he was a soul-strengthening, sea-deep, river rush of passion. Yes, of course she'd be fine - she had Andor, but only for the next six months before he too went to serve the ancient ones. Then she would *really* feel alone. She tried not to think about it – there was nothing she could do to alter the facts. Anyway, this was her sister's departure and she had to bid her farewell. Lendi stepped back, turned and walked slowly towards The Ancestors' Gate to join the small cluster of other nervously waiting acolytes. As she moved her silver-threaded white silk cape rippled in the warm spring breeze, her long straight blonde hair swayed gently side to side, emulating the motion of her hips, and the low heels of her bright red boots alternately flashed from beneath the hem of her yellow robe. She paused briefly to glance back, an excited but apprehensive sparkle in her striking opaline eyes and smiled as she waved goodbye.

'I love you!' she called.

Sonilla smiled and waved back. 'Me too! See you next year!' She almost choked on her words. 'Good luck!'

She watched, biting her lip in an unsuccessful attempt to hold back more tears, as the two regal guardians, robed in gold-edged blue linen, escorted the group through the gate, shutting it and locking it behind them.

Lendi was gone.

The matron turned quietly away and re-entered the castle, leaving Sonilla standing alone, motionless, her stinging eyes fixed on the closed gate, almost as if she expected Lendi to return to wait with her through the next annual cycle until it was her turn to serve, so they could go away together. But she knew it would not be so – none of The Select ever came back after going to meet The Ancestors.

That morning, as Sonilla had stood fretfully gazing from the narrow turret window, she barely noticed the stunning scenery stretching to the horizon. Beyond the sturdy perimeter walls, which enclosed their forty-acre self-sufficient enclave, the trees proliferated in a rippling swathe extending across the rumpled hills into the hazy distance. The mountains to the south were the only other things overlooking the expansive forest, their lofty snow-clad ridges yellow-hued in the early sunshine. In the room she had shared with Lendi for the last two years, since their promotion from the bustling dormitory as privileged seniors, Sonilla nervously bit her nails, apprehensive of the forthcoming separation. Her sister had been called at dawn for the ceremonial purification rites – the last requirement of an accomplished disciple. They had lain awake most of the night, unwilling to waste their last hours together, sharing memories of their years of education and training.

It was at the age of twelve that the children were tested for the level of their abilities to see if they were worthy of being amongst "The Select". Their psychological profile was studied, together with the history of their aptitude and attitude to learning since arriving at the foundation at the age of six. Finally, but most importantly, they had to show the most advanced psychic and telepathic skills. Sonilla had been disquieted by the news that Lendi had been chosen to receive the special training and spent a year on tenterhooks fearful that she might not be able to join her. When her turn came she was ecstatic to discover that she too had passed. Despite being sworn to secrecy, Lendi had already told her of the first lesson given to the newly segregated about what it meant to be among The Select and what special training was given. Thus Ur Oltans' words to the group of excited pre-teens came as no surprise to Sonilla after she herself had been chosen.

'Now children,' he called over the clamour of voices as he entered the classroom, 'I'd like to welcome you to your first class as newly chosen acolytes.'

He cleared his throat and stroked his short brown beard as he took his place facing the centre of the semi-circle of eager, bright faces, then pushed his spectacles up to the bridge of his nose with the little finger of his left hand. His green robes with yellow braiding denoted his rank as "first-guider", a position he had enjoyed for the past five years.

'As you know,' he continued enthusiastically, 'you have been selected for a special reason to receive advanced training because of your superior abilities. At the age of eighteen, when you have completed your instruction you will go to serve with The Ancestors. You will know that from now on your lessons will be separate from the other students, although you will still work together in your domestic and gardening duties and of course eat, play and socialise with the rest.'

He paused to clear his throat, stroke his beard and adjust his spectacles again, habits that the youngsters would find more amusing with familiarity.

'The first and most important rule is that you must not divulge any information about your lessons to any of the other students. There is a very good reason for this, namely that if any of those who have not had special training in these advanced skills are to attempt them, they could cause harm to themselves or others.'

An over-excited, fidgety pupil shot his hand in the air, bursting with curiosity.

'Excuse me Ur Oltan,' he blurted, unable to contain his considerable eagerness within his bantam-sized frame, 'what does it mean, "to serve The Ancestors" and who are they and where are they and what do they do?'

Oltan raised his eyebrows and a hand simultaneously, gazing at the boy in mild but good-natured reproach.

'Please contain yourself, Damus,' he requested calmly with a gentle smile, 'I *was* just coming to that and I must inform you that all the information you require will be divulged at a rate that we judge you will be able to assimilate it and at a time that we consider appropriate. If you will allow me to continue uninterrupted, I will take any unanswered questions at the end of the lesson.'

Once more he stopped, this time looking at the ceiling. He coughed gently, caressed his chin and toyed with his glasses. Then returning his gaze to the class, continued, 'Now, going to meet The Ancestors at the end of your training involves leaving the foundation by the Ancestors Gate in the company of two guardians who will lead you to the departure point in the forest from where you make your journey to the dwellings of the ancients. Once with the wise elders you will require the special skills that you are now to be taught to serve them in their work and, therefore, benefit all of humanity. After many years of service and further tutelage you will eventually acquire enough knowledge and wisdom to be able to join their ranks and attain the same status as them...'

At the end of the lesson, the pupils had a lot of new information to contemplate. When Oltan asked if there were any questions only Damus raised his hand.

'What happens to the others Ur, the ones who aren't chosen?' he asked, 'I know they leave the foundation, but I don't know where they go.'

'Ah yes, the others,' began the tutor, 'they too have special training and duties to perform, otherwise they wouldn't have been brought here for their education in the first place. They go on to learn more about the outside world, where they join societies of ordinary citizens and help do the Ancestor's work, such as influencing and improving the Earth's cultures, businesses and governments, identifying future pupils for this and our other foundations, assisting with adults who have slipped through the net or are just awakening to their abilities....something that is happening more and more as we approach the "Resurgence".'

'What's that?' asked Damus before anyone else had the chance.

Ur Oltan smiled and stroked his beard. 'I'm afraid that is too big a question for just now but we shall be devoting an entire lesson to it next week.'

'What about the "outside world"?' persisted the boy, 'What's it like? Have you been there? Will we see it?'

Their guide listened patiently, attentive and sympathetic to the needs of a curious and thirsty young mind.

'Well, again I do not have time just now to give you detailed answers, but I will in the future. For now I shall tell you this.' He pushed his glasses up again and cleared his throat. 'I have been there as part of my training and I did work there on behalf of the ancestors for a number of years. There are areas of forest and nature such as surrounds us here, but most people live in large collections of dwellings called "towns" and "cities" where they lead very busy and stressful lives. They try to cope with this by alternately stimulating and dulling their senses with distractions and/or substances of various kinds thus disabling their latent psychic potential and generally shortening their lives. This is why The Select are kept separate, to protect them from these misled and self-abusive societies. You are so super-sensitive to the unguarded thoughts of the mind-blind that until you are fully trained you would be completely overwhelmed and unable to cope with the telepathic over-stimulation in that environment.'

The next morning, the assignment rota had put the young sisters on poultry duty for the first spring lunar. They fed the chickens, released them into the orchard, collected the eggs and once a week were required to clean out and replace the litter in the huts. Sonilla loved the work, especially at this time of year when there were several clutches of chicks, so fluffy and cute and easy to pick up and stroke with a careful finger. The day dawned so sunny and warm they rose early and were able to spend extra time in the enclosure before their lessons. Lendi was gently petting a tiny hatchling that she had cupped in her hand.

'Oh, they're so light and fragile,' she commented.

'And *so* sweet,' added Sonilla, gathering up one in each hand and smiling happily.

After a few minutes of fondling their precious charges, they carefully released them and watched cheerfully as they hurried to rejoin their nest mates with the protectively clucking hens. Just then the big red cockerel that was perched prominently on a water butt, suddenly crowed, loudly declaring his presence and stature. The girls giggled at its puffed up self-importance in the context of Lendi's recent sex education class that she had eagerly discussed with Sonilla afterwards. They strolled unhurriedly to the chicken sheds to collect the eggs, visiting each nest box in turn to gather the day's bounty into their baskets.

'Wow, this one's still warm!' announced Lendi in wonder, 'feel it!'

Sonilla did as she was bid, smiled and then placed the egg in her basket.

'Lendi?' she said.

'Um?' replied her sister dreamily.

'There's something I've been meaning to ask you.'

'What's that?'

'Well, you know how we've both been chosen?' she started, projecting her feelings simultaneously, 'You know that means that we'll get separated for a whole year when you're eighteen and you go to meet the ancestors? Well, I'm going to be stuck here all alone...'

'Don't worry Soni, it won't be so bad. I'll miss you too, but you'll have other friends here. We'll be grown up by then and it won't seem such a big thing. Anyway, Thu Mayla told me that as you get older time goes quicker so a year won't seem so long.'

'Maybe...but she's over *eighty*, so it's different for her. I can't bear the thought of us being parted for thirteen whole lunars!'

'It's because you've only just heard,' Lendi reassured her, 'it came as a shock to me to start with too, but it's years away yet, so I'm sure you'll get used to the idea and it won't seem so bad then.' However, feeling that Sonilla was not entirely reassured she tried to distract her. 'Come on, I'll race you back to the kitchen!'

'But we might break the eggs...' Sonilla said weakly but then scampered reluctantly after her sister who had just darted out of the shed.

Reminiscing on the night before the departure of The Select, the happy memories were tinged with the sorrow of their coming separation.

'It has been sad to see our friends get sent off to that strange world,' sighed Lendi from her bed, 'knowing the kind of world they are entering…but it was their destiny…just as I face mine tomorrow and as you will face yours in thirteen lunars.'

Sonilla nodded silently, remembering the many goodbyes over the years and dreading the one to come the next day. It did not seem any easier now that she was older than she thought it was going to be when she had been twelve. She did not want this last shared night together to end. The bond she had with her sister could not be replaced by anyone else. She got up and climbed into Lendi's bed, facing her and sharing the pillow. She hadn't done this since she was eight years old but she needed the physical closeness tonight.

'Do you remember Thu Mayla?' asked Lendi, suddenly smiling, 'she was so funny!'

Sonilla grinned too. 'Wasn't she just! I don't know how she was ever allowed to teach voice music – she was half deaf and couldn't sing in tune to save her life! When she tried to demonstrate the chants her monotonous droning just gave me the giggles so badly I could hardly sing the repeats.' She paused in the memory then added, 'she was sweet though, really kind. I do miss her.'

'Me too,' agreed Lendi, 'everybody loved her. When she finally finished with her body, her life's tribute celebration was so joyful and heartfelt, I still tingle when I think of it.'

'I bet you won't miss "Clammy" Kellar though,' said Sonilla, 'he gives me the creeps, the way he tries to undress you with his eyes and he thinks we don't notice!' She shuddered at the thought.

'And what eyes!' added Lendi, 'they're like snakes eggs in moles holes!' Sonilla laughed at the picture in her mind as her sister continued. 'I complained about him to En Nergal once after I felt his thought's fingers groping me, but he said I must have imagined it and that he had "complete faith in Ur Kellar's integrity". I know Nergal's the overseer, but I reckon Clammy's got some power over him.'

Sonilla pulled a face. 'Urgh! How can you leave me with him!' she said in disgust.

'You're well able to look after yourself,' responded Lendi, 'and at least there's Ur Etlu, he's a dish! Now you won't have to compete with me for his affections.'

'You know he's not my type - I only have eyes for Andor.'

'It's more than eyes you've got for Andor! Since you two started your weekly assignations you've been drinking and breathing him too!' Lendi pretended to be scandalised. Sonilla grinned. 'You will be careful, won't you,' cautioned Lendi seriously, 'After your joinings your aural glow is so obvious I don't know how you've not been caught. You know that we "Selected" are supposed to be virgins...'

'Well I think it's a stupid rule. If anything, loving sex has made us even more spiritual – it's a wonderful, pure, transcendent thing...'

'But if you get caught you might not be allowed to join me with the ancestors.'

'Don't worry, I will *never* let that happen. We've worked very hard on our mind-wall defences,' Sonilla informed her, 'I doubt if even a thought probe by En Nergal would be able to penetrate. You see, we've not just learned some very useful things in this place, we've devised some clever techniques of our own and we just don't let on how good we are.'

Finally they agreed to try to get some sleep. Lendi had to rise at daybreak and she didn't want to face the most important day of her life so far torpid and dopey.

At the tower window the next morning, Sonilla had been roused from these recollections by a gentle tapping. The matron, Thu Molla squinted around the side of the door with myopic eyes.

'It's time dear,' she offered gently before retreating back into the stairwell. Sonilla followed slowly down the spiral steps to the corridor below and thence to the senior's dining room for the farewell breakfast. She sat opposite Lendi and between Andor and Damus at the long refectory table.

'You look stunning!' she told her sister, noticing the ceremonial cape over her lemon-coloured robe and Lendi's radiant face, 'I can't believe you only had two hours sleep.'

'Thanks,' replied Lendi, smiling affectionately, 'I don't think I've been so clean in all my life. Thu Ahatu almost scrubbed me raw, and then massaged me with sweet oils. I feel amazing!'

'Nervous?'

'Oh, yes, but excited too! I've been preparing for this for so long, but I still don't really know exactly what to expect.'

Three sharp raps from the high table brought a hush to the room. The farewell breakfast, held twice a year to coincide with The Selecteds' leave-taking, was attended only by the teaching staff and the senior students, who now all turned their attention obediently to En Nergal as he prepared to make his customary speech. Beneath his shiny bald head his eyebrows, in contrast, were like thick black bushy bears perched precariously above his ashen, rodent-like eyes. These lurked like spiders in dark close-set tunnels either side of his long, hooked nose from the bottom of which deep creases ran to the edges of his narrow, lipless mouth. Although his features conjured up visions of pure evil in some of the children's minds, he had proved to be a gentle mannered and completely benign, if a little patronising, overseer of the foundation for the last ten years.

'Students and colleagues,' he intoned in a sombre voice, 'we are gathered here this morning to bid a fond farewell to our beloved and gifted youngsters who, having reached the age of eighteen and having completed their studies here, are going to join The Ancestors, to serve them, to learn from them and eventually to become one of them and with them oversee the transition of the human race to the wise and just society being recreated in the great awakening of the impending Resurgence....'

Sonilla's mind drifted from the familiar liturgy as she tried to imagine what was in store for her sister. Although they had repeatedly been told in general terms what their duties would be and what their ultimate purpose was, the details were vague and insubstantial, like getting an impression of what was happening inside a castle by looking at the walls from a distance. She guessed that none of their guides would really know what it was like because none of them had actually been to meet the ancestors themselves, otherwise they wouldn't be here teaching. Still, it made her feel uneasy on Lendi's behalf.

'Aren't you girls eating?' chirped Damus noticing their untouched plates and still as artless and energetic as he had been as a twelve year old.

'Not hungry,' muttered the sisters in unison, the appetites of both diminished by the effects of nervous anticipation. They knew they still had hours of ceremonies, songs and games ahead to mark this significant occasion, but neither could bring themselves to eat.

Throughout the day, Sonilla accompanied Lendi everywhere, listening to the words of congratulation from staff and the wishes of luck from fellow students. Finally, feeling suffocated by the attention and a surfeit of platitudes they managed to escape for ten minutes to a quiet corner of the garden. With only an hour to go before they parted, Sonilla became tearful. Lendi put a comforting arm around her shoulders.

'Come on Soni,' she urged, 'we're supposed to be celebrating. After all it's a privilege not a punishment.'

'I know, Len, I'm sorry,' said Sonilla, 'I'm just being selfish. I didn't mean to spoil your special day.'

'You're not spoiling it. I'm going to miss you too - terribly. But the time will soon pass, you'll see.'

'I bet you're glad to finally be wearing your new boots,' Sonilla ventured brightly, trying to lift the mood. The Select were permitted to craft themselves one special item to take on their journey with the stipulation that it must be functional. Lendi's boots, which she had painstakingly hand made from shiny red leather, were her pride and joy. She had managed to make them both practical and attractive and was very excited to be wearing them now she had changed for her departure.

Suddenly Thu Molla appeared from behind a rose bush.

'Ah, there you are!' she said, 'come on girls, the whole school is waiting – it's the final sing-song.'

Now it was all over and Sonilla hadn't stirred since the gateway shut. She stood numb and statue-like, paralysed by dejection. Watching the indifferent door with her unseeing eyes finally empty of tears and raw from too much crying, she knew there was no hope of Lendi's return, but still could not turn away. Nobody disturbed her in the deserted courtyard, respecting her grief and knowing she needed this time alone. As the sun sank, the soft low light diffusing through the slowly swaying branches seemed to highlight the emptiness of the garden. The birds' lazy evening melodies struck her as particularly melancholy. The colourful flowers gradually became subdued and drab as the light faded. Eventually, in the twilight, the first doleful tears returned, trickling down her waxen cheeks, slowly to start with but then welling up again as she sank to the floor sobbing quietly. The matron returned and helping her to her feet, gently guided her back inside.

#

The chords from Newton Faulkner's guitar, accompanied by his distinctive voice, filled the lizard lounge where Rowan sat alone chewing on a sandwich and thoughtfully stirring her tea with a pencil. The others were outside enjoying the sunshine, seated shirtless on the picnic benches that had been thoughtfully provided by Rhona for the purpose. Despite the puss that still slowly seeped from her nostrils and the remains of bruising and swelling, she now felt that she had come to terms with what had happened a couple of weeks ago and could more or less get on with her life. She knew it would be different now that Jenny, Rhona, Bess and Charlie knew her secret, but different only with them.

With everyone else it would be the same. Work would be the same. She was alone now for two reasons. Firstly she was not a big fan of the sunshine. She found it too hot to sit in and she certainly wasn't going to take any clothes off in front of the men. Anyway she didn't want her pale skin to get scorched by ultraviolet rays, even though she had attempted to burn it herself in the past when she mistakenly thought that a tan was a desirable attribute. The second reason for being by herself was that she had come to appreciate such times as an opportunity to let her guard down and relax without having to block or filter out the unwelcome shenanigans in the minds of others.

Today, however, she was contemplating the reasons why Rhona and Charlie had left the workshop a few minutes earlier to go and speak to Bess. She had gathered the nature of the phone call this morning and felt concerned at the message it contained. She was also a bit miffed that she hadn't been included. Since her revelation she felt that she was now part of a team with them and would be party to any discussions about dreams or strange happenings. She resented being treated like a child – she was nearly eighteen after all and with her special skills she felt that she really had something to offer. She had felt uneasy about the casket job ever since it first came in, but now she was detecting a growing sense of menace associated with it. Her awareness was more attuned to those important to her, but she was still a little hazy from a distance. She had felt uncomfortable earlier and she thought she had perceived a feeling of distress or a sense of danger from Bess, but it was a very vague impression and she couldn't be sure. There was a…*wrongness* in the air was the only way she could describe it.

Suddenly she stopped eating. There was a powerful sensation of alarm and upset from Rhona and Charlie and she knew for sure that something was seriously amiss. Abandoning the remnants of her lunch she dashed out of the workshop and grabbed Charlie's bike. Her basking workmates looked on in bewilderment as without a word she hurtled past them, out of the yard and pedalled furiously down the road.

CHAPTER TWELVE.

The car wound its way uphill revealing ever more of the stunning scenery. During the last three days of their leisurely tour, the flat, intensively farmed monotony had gradually, almost imperceptibly transformed into a quaint rural landscape of small farms, woods and pretty villages. This undulating idyll had risen to become the forested foothills of the imposing mountains ahead. As Lynn drove them competently along the snaking road, Adam surveyed the sights that had been enriched by being bathed in the hazy sunshine. Thankfully the hire car had come fitted with a decent CD player and having brought some music with them, their experience was being enhanced by the huge sound of "Black Holes and Revelations" by Muse at high volume.

'The music's got to be big enough to match the scenery, right?' asserted Nick when Lynn pleaded for something a little more laid back.

'Yeah, but I've got to concentrate on driving on the wrong side up all these wiggly roads with no safety barriers,' she countered.

'You must have got the hang of it by now,' Nick persisted, feeling a little cranky through nicotine withdrawal, although he did turn the volume down a little, 'but if you can't handle it, let me take over.'

'O.K., I think I will,' she responded thankfully, 'just as soon as I can find somewhere to pull over. They don't seem to have many viewpoints or anything here do they? I would *so* like a chance to clock this landscape properly an' all.'

Adam was thoroughly enjoying himself. He had finally relaxed after three days in this strange country. He had survived his first ever flight and had let go of the need for the security of familiar sights and surroundings. On the other hand, anticipating the air travel had caused him significant trepidation. Such was his flustered state that when leaving his flat he forgot his phone and passport. Luckily, he had only walked twenty metres before remembering the latter, although he did not discover his lack of phone until he thought to text Charlie at the airport. He shrugged and decided he could do without for the holiday. Besides he had more serious worries on his mind. He knew that thousands of plane flights operated successfully each day all over the world and that accidents were rare, but they *did* happen occasionally and when they did, you hardly stood a chance. It was difficult to believe that something as large and heavy as an aeroplane could be held aloft by the laws of physics alone. He wasn't entirely sure he could trust Bernoulli's principle to resist and overcome the overwhelming and irresistible force of gravity. After all, there was a whole planet down there trying to pull you down. In order to face this challenge he decided it was probably best to try not to think about it and resolved to swallow a few grams of hash to mellow him out. He was easily dissuaded from trying to take any dope in his pockets or luggage after Lynn cast doubts on the Polish authority's tolerance of drugs and the comfort of their prisons. Besides, Nick had decided to use the holiday as an opportunity to completely give up smoking all together and Adam didn't want to be the only one stoned on the holiday. A wee nugget inside him for the flight was just to calm his nerves. However, the one aspect he had overlooked was the difficulty in judging the correct dose and the exaggeration of his paranoia. Reaching the airport with a larger than necessary lump of oily black resin dissolving in his stomach, entering his bloodstream and washing through his brain, he began to suspect that the customs officers at both ends of the flight might feel inclined to pick him out as a likely miscreant and x-ray his gut to uncover his crime. In preparation for the ordeal and in an attempt to make himself look less conspicuous, he had brushed and tied back his hair, shaved off his stubble and dressed in the "straightest" clothes he could find in his local charity shop. The final effect was, however, somewhat different to the one he'd anticipated.

'Jesus Adam, you look like a fucking pimp!' Nick had exclaimed when he saw him and laughed uproariously.

'Don't be cruel!' admonished Lynn, 'anyway, I think he looks quite smart...' Adam smiled. '...but maybe just a little creepy,' she added with a giggle. His smiled vanished instantly. The last thing he wanted was to look "creepy".

'Only kidding, Adam, really,' she said hurriedly, seeing the look on his face.

He did feel uncomfortable though. The last time he'd dressed smartly was when his mother insisted upon it for the first of his university interviews. He was appalled to discover that he was one of the few to do so and avoided talking to the other interviewees, not wanting them to think he was the type of person to dress like that, nor that he had done so at his mother's requirement.

On this occasion he couldn't be sure whether or not it was his attire that spared him the strip search and dreaded rubber glove intrusion. Even though his eyes were half closed and bloodshot, with Lynn virtually having to lead him by the hand through the confusing and alien environment of the airport terminal, the customs officers hardly gave him a second glance, either at Heathrow or Krakow. Their focus was more on the fear of the potential threat posed by terrorists than by the possibility of passengers carrying a small lump of cannabis. Adam's only previous trip abroad was by ferry to France as a student when he was singled out, strip-searched and had the contents of his rucksack examined and spread over a large table. Even though nothing was found, they abandoned him to repack his bag himself.

Thanks to Adam's stupefied senses the flight proved to be fairly painless, despite his fears. Once the aircraft started taxiing along the runway he gave up scrutinising his fellow passengers for potential suicide bombers, distracted as he was by a growing sense of uncertainty as to the airworthiness of the plane. Nevertheless, through the almost all-consuming terror he did feel exhilarated by the adrenalin rush of take-off, particularly as on Nick's insistence they were seated towards the back so that as it left the ground they experienced a sudden drop in altitude, the tail plunging towards the runway as the nose lifted for the surging ascent. As they levelled off he began to calm down. By now he was so stoned that he became distracted from his fear by the view from the window. He gaped in wonder at the diminishing world below, which shrank rapidly from model village scale to that of an ant city before disappearing completely as the plane entered the clouds.

'Are you alright Adam?' asked Lynn from the adjacent seat. He couldn't take his eyes off the swirling mist outside as it roiled and rushed past the window but managed to register the enquiry as a minor disturbance on the edge of his awareness.

'What? Oh yeah...sure...er fine,' he mumbled dreamily, 'I'm totally getting into these clouds, you know, they're really far out.' A moment later they emerged into dazzling sunshine.

'Wow!' he exclaimed loudly, oblivious to the other traveller's stares. He saw a seemingly infinite field of purest white fluffy cotton wool radiant beneath a bright sky of an impossible yet perfect shade of blue. Once he became accustomed to the unprecedented levels of awe, Adam just gazed imbecilically out of the window with a slight inane smile on his face. Nick and Lynn, satisfied that he was in no immediate need of care, ordered cups of tea and started a game of cards. Nick said he needed to be constantly distracted from his craving for tobacco, in spite of the nicotine patches, otherwise he might start chewing the seats. A little later when a gap in the clouds revealed the shimmering ocean, Adam giggled idiotically and said, 'hey, look at the tiny little ship!' pointing to a minute speck below.

Having survived the flight in a semi euphoric daze, Adam was however petrified when it came to landing. After all this was when the seemingly insubstantial but nonetheless heavy shell of much too thin metal hurtled towards the earth at tremendous speed. To his amazement and great relief, this episode passed without catastrophe. The final ordeal was to run the gauntlet of the Polish customs, which to him were still associated with the repression of the former Soviet regime. Having overcome this, he was beginning to feel the dense, dull numbness of the brain that followed the high after ingesting hashish. His beleaguered mind became confounded by the impact of the unfamiliar. Bewildered and sheep-like, he followed his friends through the maze of corridors, escalators and signs in a strange language, surrounded by crowds of people uttering gobble-de-gook. He grew very tired and his legs turned into heavy, stiff tree trunks so that he trudged wearily behind Nick and Lynn like a zombie until they finally reached their hire car. Once ensconced on the rear seat, he curled up, slept and did not stir until the last of Krakow's grimy suburbs and industrial zones were behind them. They were so desperate to flee the urban environment that they had rejected the opportunity to view the city's historic architecture.

Adam sat up and rubbed his puffy eyes. 'I need a pee,' he said. 'Me too,' added Nick. Lynn turned off the main road and pulled over in a lay-by so they could stretch their legs. She was the only one who had bothered to learn any Polish, having taken evening classes for the last six months, so she was the one who had organised the car hire. Her admirable attempt to speak the language delighted the agent who was used to visitors like Nick who expected those abroad to speak English.

'Well, it's the universal language isn't it?' he had piped up when he was nagged by Lynn to join her when she started her classes.

'Global, you mean,' she'd commented sullenly.

'Whatever,' he'd shrugged, 'I was never any good at school anyway. Still, one of us understanding it should be enough – we're only going for a couple of weeks after all.'

Adam, of course, had only had one month's notice of the trip and although he was in Nick's words "a brainy sod", he claimed his head wasn't in the right space for learning such a difficult language at the moment being "a bit screwed up with all these crazy dreams and stuff". Lynn didn't really mind though, she just liked to wind them up and felt that it gave her a certain authority over "the boys" who she found fairly biddable in most circumstances anyway.

As they stretched their limbs and breathed in the fresh air, they studied their surroundings.

'Well it doesn't look much different to England here,' Nick commented.

'You wait till we get into the country though,' said Lynn, 'I bet all the little farms and villages look different and the forests and mountains and castles and that, yeah?'

'Yeah,' agreed Adam who, still in a fairly dazed state, was even more economical with his words than usual.

They climbed back into the car and Nick took the wheel.

'Alright, let's head for the hills!' he exclaimed.

All three whooped with excitement and Nick accelerated back onto the road leading east.

It wasn't until the Muse CD had almost reached the final track that Lynn found somewhere to stop. She had taken over from Nick when they reached the hills so he could scrutinise the sky for bird life.

'At last!' she said with relief, 'they could do with a few more lay-bys in this country,' and pulled over at a magnificent viewpoint. They piled out, left the doors open and Nick reached back in to turn up the volume on the stereo. Revelling in both the scenery and the music, the companions stood with arms outstretched like three high divers preparing to leap. After the soaring introduction, they started singing along to the chorus of "Knights of Cydonia" at the tops of their voices.

They bellowed out the first line in a remarkably accurate imitation of the band. Lynn jumped onto the bonnet of the car and spread her arms spread wide again. As they sung the next line Nick climbed nimbly onto the roof and took up the same pose. With the third line Adam joined Lynn on the bonnet. The fourth line they yelled even louder, though still in passable harmony. After the chorus was repeated, all three leapt to the ground in unison and started head-banging as the pummelling chords stirred them with pounding energy. They followed this with virtuoso air-guitar and dancing in wild abandon accompanied by yells of delight until the track ended and they collapsed panting and laughing on the grass verge.

'Woohoo!' exclaimed Adam, 'I've never had so much fun! Thanks for bringing me guys - this is brilliant!'

'No worries mate,' said Nick warmly, his broad smile aimed at the bright blue sky, 'it's good to have you along.'

'Let's have a look at the map,' suggested Lynn after she had caught her breath, 'see if we can spot somewhere to camp tonight, yeah?'

A little sightseeing had slowed their journey but so far, unable to find any suitable free spots near the road, they had been obliged to use official campsites where Adam hadn't managed to sleep very well. To him it seemed that some families let their children stay up too late, gleefully squealing their delight at the privilege before they became over-tired and grizzly. Some fighting and screaming then usually ensued followed by parents shouting and then noisy protests as the youngsters were sent to bed at midnight or beyond. Other parents whose routine was structured around a relaxed and childfree evening put their offspring to bed much earlier. However this meant that the high-pitched demands of infants requiring breakfast started at the crack of dawn. The short hours of night thus available for sleep were further disrupted by barking dogs. Every time someone wandered from their tent or caravan to the toilet block, the yelping and yapping of a canine cacophony heralded their progress. Adam usually didn't mind dogs, but he hated barking, especially when he was trying to sleep, so locating a wild camping spot now that they were in a more remote area was very high on the agenda.

#

Bess gradually regained consciousness, becoming aware of a thumping headache and a tight, sore throat. She groaned in pain, slowly opened her eyes and with bleary vision noticed that she was in unfamiliar surroundings. It was a bare stark room illuminated only by a thin slot of a window high up on one of the sterile grey walls. There was a damp, clinical smell as if old mouldy surfaces had just been scrubbed and disinfected. She was lying on her back on a hard narrow bunk, which was the only thing in the room apart from her and a single unlit light bulb dangling from the ceiling. The door looked heavy and strong, possibly painted steel plate from the look of the bolt heads around its perimeter. *How did I get here?* she wondered, her wits befuddled and her mind suffused with pain. She knew it wasn't a dream. Shaking her head in a futile attempt to clear her thoughts, she winced having caused her head to throb all the more. Her memory seemed blank, so she attempted a few deep, calming breaths whilst remaining motionless. Slowly she began to recall pieces of that morning's events.

She had been sitting in the sun in the garden sipping camomile tea. Charlie was at work. There was birdsong. It was peaceful, yet she felt troubled. She had a book. She had tried reading, but her mind kept returning to the mysterious dreams that they had had. Charlie seemed to have put them out of his mind, but Bess felt a nagging uncertainty about their meaning and significance. Adam's thoughts confused her further, Mandisa hadn't really been much help as far as she could make out and Rhona seemed just as mystified. And what was the connection between the stone Charlie found and those uncovered in Chile? Bess also felt that they hadn't heard the last of the commission to make the sarcophagus or whatever it was. She kept her worries to herself though, because she was so relieved to see Charlie in a better frame of mind.

The rumble of an approaching vehicle interrupted her thoughts. She stood and walked to the garden gate to greet the visitors as a large black people-carrier drew to a halt, its tinted windows reflecting the blue sky and obscuring the occupants. She didn't recognise the car so waited patiently for the callers to emerge. Her first thought was that it would be prospective clients from a local hotel or restaurant who had come to hear of her business. Both front doors opened simultaneously. From the driver's side, nearest to her, a large thick-necked man climbed out unhurriedly as if his bulk somehow slowed the passage of time. He wore mirror-lensed sunglasses and a black suit so that he almost matched the vehicle's appearance and shape. On the other side an older, thin stick of a man appeared, unfolding awkwardly in such a way as to suggest that it was unnatural for his long body to be bent. He too was dressed in black, but wore clear spectacles with a bowler hat to shade his eyes. Bess thought he closely resembled the man whom Rhona had described. His thick-bridged, parallel-sided nose and small, intense, closely-set shifty eyes gave him the appearance of an emaciated blunt-beaked eagle eager for its next meal. The two men did not look particularly friendly but she hid her misgivings and said, 'Good morning,' managing to affect a casual smile, 'how can I help you?'

The man-mountain remained silent and expressionless as if awaiting further instructions so she turned her gaze to the older man who seemed to have glided closer without her noticing. Despite herself she couldn't help stepping back from the gate as he approached and put his hand on it - this guy gave her the creeps!

He addressed her in a dry impassionate rasp, 'Mrs MacKay?'

'Who wants to know,' she responded guardedly, becoming a little apprehensive as the larger man also began edging slowly forwards.

'I'm representing the interests of my employers,' the first man croaked, 'might I come in to discuss the matter with you?'

'You still haven't told me who you or your employers are,' she countered, feigning self-assurance, 'and anyway, it's not convenient at the moment.'

He started opening the gate saying, 'I'm afraid I really must insist.'

Bess backed away further as both men unhurriedly entered the garden. She was now becoming quite scared as it came to be more obvious that their intent was not an amiable one. Slowly retreating towards the kitchen's open door she blurted foolishly, 'I don't know who you are but if you don't leave now I'm going to call the police!'

They continued their advance so she span and dashed inside. The heavyset man suddenly displayed a velocity seemingly inconsistent with one of his size. He reached the door just as she slammed it shut and whilst she was fumbling hastily with the lock he pushed through it with ease so that she overbalanced, knocking over a small table bearing a pot plant as she fell awkwardly to the hard flagstone floor. Before she had a chance to recover he had a huge hand squeezing at her throat. Instinctively she struggled in his grip but this just resulted in him tightening his hand as she floundered. She blindly drove her knee upwards with all her strength and heard him grunt in pain releasing his grip as he rolled off her. As she lay enfeebled and gasping for breath, unable to rise, he recovered sufficiently to clamp a damp rag over her face soaked in a soporific liquid. Her flailing became weaker and ineffectual as her deep gulping breaths ensured a rapid absorption of the anaesthetic. Just before she lost consciousness she heard a voice as if from the bottom of a well say, 'I told you to be gentle, you fool!'

The headache, sore throat and disorientation she felt were now explained. She gently rubbed her neck muscles, which were becoming increasingly tender. The memory of that thug's hand around her throat scared her. If she hadn't kneed him in the groin he may have killed her, she felt so weak under his grip. But then she realised that he'd given her chloroform, so murder was not on his mind. She became aware of other pains. It felt like her hip, shoulder and the back of her head had struck the floor quite heavily and were now bruised. She tentatively eased herself into a seated position and held her pounding head in her hands, elbows on her knees. Now she seemed to ache all over. Allowing a couple of minutes to adjust to the vertical, she then rose slowly and unsteadily to her feet with one hand on the wall to balance herself. She started moving different parts of her body in turn to check for possible damage. Assured that nothing was broken or badly hurt she carefully attempted to take a few steps. She staggered a little and then returned to the bed feeling dizzy, still partially under the influence of the sedative.

Bess began to wonder why she had been abducted and who her captors were. What did they want? As her faculties gradually returned so her fear and confusion began to grow. Was it something to do with those clients of Rhona's? Surely the box couldn't be *that* important. Unless it really was a rejuvenation device. But then what could she do about it? After ten minutes of useless speculation she felt sufficiently recovered to feel anger and indignation. The lousy rotten scumbags! What did it matter what their motivations were? They had no right to treat her like this! She stood up, suddenly furious and marched determinedly to the door, pounded on it and shouted, 'Oi! Let me out, you bastards!' Her fists were ineffectual on the slab of metal, frustratingly unable to produce any satisfactory volume, so she stopped and, realising that she had instead succeeded in exacerbating the thumping in her head, slowly subsided onto the mattress and closed her eyes. She started trying to relax both her mind and body by closing her eyes, breathing calmly and deeply, then releasing the tension in her muscles by starting with her toes and working upwards.

She must have dozed off because when she opened her eyes again, the slot of light from the outside world had dimmed considerably. Suddenly the light bulb flared into full brightness, dazzling her sleep-weakened eyes so she covered them with her arm. A clattering, clunking sound came from the door as it was being unlocked. Squinting, Bess looked over as it swung silently inwards on stout, well-oiled hinges. The gaunt matchstick man who had come to her house earlier stood stiffly in the opening.

'What do you want?' Bess demanded crossly, 'Why am I here?'

Only the lips on the man's expressionless face moved as he spoke. 'Follow me please Mrs Mackay,' he instructed, 'I shall take you to my masters. They will inform you of the circumstances of your detention.' He turned and moved away from the entrance out of sight as if he just expected her to follow meekly. Bess remained seated on the bunk, thinking, trying to digest her predicament. She heard the man's voice call back to her in a bored world-weary tone. 'If you wish to learn more, you must accompany me.'

Bess stood carefully, then discovering herself to be more steady on her feet and clearer in her mind than earlier, she reluctantly trailed after him, realising that she had little choice in the matter. Her cell was on one side at the end of a passage with three other similar doors. The place looked old but recently refurbished and she could smell fresh paint. She followed her guide round a corner and then up some concrete steps to what she supposed was the ground floor of the building. They emerged into a wider corridor, richly carpeted and with the bottom half of the walls lined in figured quarter-sawn oak. Dark green velvet curtains concealed the windows at the end and solid panelled doors framed with heavy moulded architraves interrupted the walls at regular intervals. There were no sounds other than their softened footsteps and the air held a slightly damp, unlived-in mustiness.

'What's your name?' she asked the stiff back of her minder, merely for the sake of injecting some life into this empty feeling edifice through which they moved. He stopped, half turned and glanced back over his shoulder with one eyebrow raised as if it alone was surprised at the question. It was the first expression she had seen on his face. 'You do not need to know,' he stated simply as he turned away and continued walking.

'But what do I call you? She persisted, trying to irritate him or at least provoke some kind of human reaction. She slowed her pace.

'You do not have to call me anything,' he repeated, but then after a brief pause added, 'but if you *must* refer to me by name, I suppose you could use Nasaru.'

'That's unusual,' she said lightly, hoping that by engaging him in conversation, he may become distracted and drop his guard. However, he merely muttered, 'Is it?' atonally, without turning.

Having dropped a few metres behind, she seized her opportunity and dashing behind the nearest curtains, tried to unlatch the window. His voice wheezed through the cloth, too close for him to have walked there already.

'There is no point in trying to escape.' The slight exasperation in his tone betrayed the first hint of emotion in his voice so far. 'It is quite *literally* impossible,' he added.

Certainly the catch seemed to be jammed. Bess couldn't budge it so she gave up on her attempt and emerged sheepishly from behind the drapes. Nasaru's face seemed strangely both deadpan and smug at the same time. Again he turned and led the way. She traipsed unenthusiastically behind him until they reached a large high-ceilinged entrance hall where the carpet gave way to slabs of polished green and white marble. A magnificent mahogany staircase rose and then divided from a landing below a stained glass window depicting a coat of arms, to sweep up in two curved flights to an ornate gallery above. A huge chandelier hung in the middle, adding to the space a sense of opulence and ostentation. The walls were dominated by four large portraits of pasty-faced pompous looking old men glaring from dark indistinct backgrounds. Opposite the stairway, a pair of massive grandiose doors stood slightly ajar, showing a pencil-thin slice of twilight from the outside.

Without stopping to think, Bess made a dash for freedom and plunged towards the tempting aperture. Grabbing the polished brass handle she wrenched the door open and darted through. A wide tier of curved steps extended to a gravel driveway, beyond which an elegant fountain dominated the extensive manicured lawn. She fled down the steps but as she neared the bottom she felt herself slowing down instead of accelerating though not through any lack of effort. It seemed as if she was trying to move through rapidly congealing porridge until as her feet touched the gravel she could advance no further. She struggled to force herself on but became exhausted in the attempt.

'I told you that escape was impossible,' Nasaru pronounced from the entrance, sounding more like a world-weary teacher castigating a recalcitrant child. Stunned and confused, fear gripped her heart and she felt a suffocating panic rising from within her. Desperately she tried once more to free herself but her efforts were futile. She felt like she was flailing against a strong and unyielding net but she could see nothing blocking her way. To avoid completely losing control of her emotions she tried to calm herself by taking a few deep breaths and then focused her mind on transforming her fear into anger. She turned to face him.

'Let me go!' she shouted. Nasaru sighed wearily.

'That is not in my power to control,' he asserted levelly. 'Now if you will just come with me you can meet their lordships who summoned you and discover the reason for your confinement.' He turned and went back inside.

Bess was damned if she was going to submit quietly to being kidnapped and then "summoned" by anyone for any reason, though at the moment it seemed she had no choice but to follow him. She seethed as she stomped after him, with little exertion required heading in this direction.

'What just happened?' she demanded, 'What was that? Why couldn't I get away?'

'Please be patient, Mrs MacKay,' said Nasaru in a bored tone of voice, continuing to lead the way through the house.

Finally they reached a door that the servant opened and then stood aside for her to enter. She marched boldly through, scowling and ready to berate those responsible for her captivity. Taken aback by the heat and the stifling atmosphere, her eyes swept a room furnished in the manner of a Victorian gentleman's study, yet also full of shelves cluttered with unidentifiable artefacts and relics. Then she located the objects of her displeasure. Two strange looking men were installed in shiny leather-upholstered armchairs either side of a blazing fire. Bess stared in amazement at the pair of almost identical figures. They were virtually bald-headed but with long, white, wiry beards suspended beneath ancient, shrivelled faces of flaking ashen skin like dry, wrinkled parchment. Dressed in loose, rumpled black suits, their diminutive forms resembled little more than emaciated albino monkeys whose weight was so insubstantial that they hardly dented the cushioned seats. Only their eyes differed, one pair a pallid grey, the other pasty green. Taken aback by the bizarre sight, Bess momentarily lost her resolve, thereby losing the opportunity to speak first.

The man on the left with the green eyes spoke in a strong deep voice, if a little breathy, belied by his fragile appearance and delicate frame.

'Allow me to apologise for the method in which you were conveyed here,' he pronounced clearly in an unrecognisable accent, 'this is not our usual way of issuing invitations.'

'Invitation!' The word erupted out of Bess' throat in an un-sought-for squeal. 'That wasn't an invitation,' she asserted indignantly as she regained control of her voice, 'it was a bloody kidnap! You send some bloody great brutish gorilla to assault me, drug me and capture me, then you lock me in a prison, have some kind of force-field to stop me escaping and now I find I've been abducted by two of the seven bloody dwarfs! Excuse me if I think your apology sounds a little insincere.'

Now the other man spoke, his grey eyes watery and pale, but his voice equally strong if slightly higher pitched. 'The man in question was indeed a little over-enthusiastic and somewhat overstepped the mark, but has now been...um, "let go", I suppose you might say,' but his intonation implied something more sinister than mere dismissal.

Bess shuddered inwardly and felt a little of her fear return. 'Why didn't you just ask me come if you wanted to see me?' she asked impatiently, 'and where am I anyway? And who the hell are you and what do you want?'

The first man spoke again. 'One question at a time please,' he said holding up a hand as if to fend them off and *she* was the unreasonable party. 'We didn't invite you *formally* because we didn't have time,' he explained. 'We needed you here immediately, but thought it unlikely that you would drop everything to visit total strangers at a moment's notice.'

'Too bloody right,' said Bess.

'As to your second question,' said Grey-eyes, 'I'm afraid we cannot tell you where you are at this moment in time.'

'And as to who we are,' added the other, 'I can tell you that I am Belum Asar...'

'...and I am Belum Ki...'

'...but you can drop the "Belum" if you wish..'

'...it is merely a formality. "Mr" or "Lord" will suffice,' said Ki generously.

Bess looked back and forth between them whilst they took turns in speaking as if they shared the same mind. She was having trouble assimilating the strangeness of her circumstances and merely gawped at them incredulously, suddenly feeling dizzy and unsteady on her feet.

'Nasaru,' called Asar to the impassionate attendant waiting silently by the doorway. 'Bring Mrs MacKay a seat,' he instructed.

'Yes master,' the servant replied with a brief nod. He wheeled a leather executive chair from the desk to just behind where Bess was standing and she sank into it immediately. Her anger gave way to fear again as her incomprehension overwhelmed her and she stammered as she tried to frame her question.

'How, er...what am I...what do...why do you want to see me? What do you want with me?' she asked.

'Ah, yes...,' started Asar, but Ki continued, '...it's quite simple really. We just need you so that we can persuade your husband to accept the commission he's been asked to undertake...'

'You mean that stupid box thing?' interrupted Bess, 'is that who you are?'

'The "box" as you call it is in no way stupid, Mrs MacKay,' said Asar sternly, 'it is of utmost importance to us...'

'...which is why,' continued Ki, 'we have taken such extreme measures. We are civilised men, as you can see and we do not normally resort to adopting coercive behaviour...'

'So you kidnap *me* because you want Charlie to do something?' asked Bess in disbelief. She felt her anger growing again and with it she seemed to regain some strength. 'Why don't you just speak to him?'

The two men exchanged glances and then Asar spoke. 'We thought it more likely that he could be persuaded if you...'

'Well you were wrong,' she said standing up, incensed at their audacity. 'You can bloody well get stuffed!' she shouted, 'Why should I help you after the way you've treated me? If you're so "*civilised*" you should know that a more *civil* approach is more likely to produce a reasonable response. You will have to find someone else to make your box. I'm leaving now."

She stormed across the room towards the door, hoping that if she feigned courage and self-assurance, they would let her go. However as she grasped the handle she unexpectedly found herself rooted to the spot. The sensation was not like the one she had experienced earlier when she had tried to escape down the steps and felt that it was too much effort to fight the restraining force. This time it was if she had forgotten how to make herself move. It suddenly seemed so difficult to understand. Her mind had become aware that there were numerous intricate processes required to put her body into motion and it was all far beyond her understanding. There were so many nerves that needed to be triggered in the correct sequence, every muscle that had to be stimulated in order to animate the complicated assemblage of bones and tissues in her body. Then she heard Belum Ki's voice penetrate her mind's baffling conundrum.

'Escape really is quite impossible,' he insisted calmly, 'it would be much better for all concerned if you would cooperate.'

All at once Bess felt herself released from her confusion, able to move again without having to work out how to do so but she felt completely defeated so she returned to her seat meekly and started whimpering, scared and completely overcome by her ordeal. The see-sawing of her emotions had left her exhausted but after a minute she managed to mutter quietly, 'What happened then? At the door. What did you do? Did you do that?'

The elderly twins again exchanged glances before turning back to her. Almost immediately she noticed herself becoming calmer. Her pulse slowed, she felt comforted and less afraid. *Could these men be controlling my emotions?* she wondered.

Asar spoke carefully, as if unsure of the effect his words might have. 'My brother and I have...er...certain abilities.' He paused and for once Ki did not continue for him. 'I suppose you would call them "psychic powers"...?' He looked quizzically at Bess to see if she understood. She tried to process this snippet of information, as if by defining it, it would become more acceptable.

'You mean telepathy, telekinesis, extra-sensory perception....that kind of thing?' she ventured.

'Yes, something like that,' confirmed Ki.

Bess thought about Rowan's recent revelations, but considered it best not to mention it. 'But...I've never heard of anybody who could control someone else like that,' she said softly. Her fear had subsided a little but she was still very disconcerted. 'It's hard to believe... to accept,' she added.

'We understand that that would be the case,' said Asar, 'there are very few of us with such strength and ability and we are usually very reluctant to employ these skills in the presence of the...um, *unlearned.*'

'But these are portentous times that call for decisive action,' added Ki.

'Which is why,' continued his brother, 'we shall have to ask you to telephone your husband to inform him that you shall be our guest for the duration of his task...'

'...to ensure his cooperation.'

Bess looked up in despair. 'But that could be weeks! *Months* even! You can't keep me that long!'

'Don't worry,' Ki reassured her, 'you shall have more comfortable accommodation and we shall see that you want for nothing.'

'Except my freedom,' said Bess icily.

'Ah. Yes, quite,' admitted Asar reluctantly.

'And you still haven't told me what all this is about. Why is the casket so important to you?'

'But your husband told you about his dream...,' stated Ki categorically.

'And Miss Mackay told you about hers...' added Asar.

Bess gaped, still refusing to accept the obvious despite the other unbelievable things that had been happening. 'You don't seriously expect me to believe that this box thing can rejuvenate your bodies...?'

'What you choose to believe is of no consequence to us,' said Ki disdainfully.

'But...' Bess stopped herself in exasperation but then thought of another question. 'How come the dreams stopped for a couple of weeks? We thought you'd given up or gone away...'

'Ah yes, for a while our attention was required elsewhere....' said Ki.

'...to arrange an er...insurance policy...,' added his brother vaguely. 'Now, if you will excuse us, Nasaru will show you to slightly more comfortable accommodation.'

The two men turned their heads away to gaze into the fire and Bess felt herself dismissed. Although still angry and scared she complied meekly, rising slowly and then allowing their servant to lead her from the room.

#

The moonlight cut through the gap in the curtains creating a sharp bright sliver on the bare wall as if a knife had slashed through the stone to reveal some source of brilliance on the other side. Sonilla was restless and whilst she might have been inclined to blame the brightness for her inability to sleep she knew that it was not really the cause. In the hours since her sister had left, she so desperately missed Lendi that her thoughts were dominated by despondency. She couldn't bear to be without her sister. All her years of training were of little help. Intellectually she knew that attachment to something or someone you love was self-harming dependency and enslavement of the object of your affection. She had been taught how to let go of transient desires and supposed emotional needs, to put into perspective her own wants when compared to the greater good. But her sentiments were without reason and all of the tools of rationality she had learned to make second nature failed miserably in this, her first real crisis of the heart. She could not hang around for a year before seeing Lendi again; they were inseparable. The wait would be an agonising torment that she was not prepared to "get used to" as she had been advised. Then, earlier this evening she felt she had lost contact with her sister. That was completely unexpected. She had always felt Lendi's presence even when they weren't together. She had never imagined that with increasing distance between them, that bond would disappear. But also she had felt a sudden and intense shock. She had sensed acute distress associated with her sister, but as her panic rose, the feeling stopped abruptly and she felt all connection vanish. At that moment she decided that she would follow her sister. The consequences of such action she could not imagine, but it was the only course of action she could contemplate. She did not question her chances of success in tracing Lendi; she just knew she had to do it. Her rendezvous with Andor was in thirty minutes so she would ask for his help...she would *need* his help.

They routinely met to make love in the laundry every Friday at midnight, a time they knew that the guides would be engaged in their weekly liturgies. It was incredible that, despite the celibacy rule, the students were trusted to keep to their beds at night, although their psycho-sensitive carers easily detected most of their subversive thoughts because the guilt attached to them acted as a telepathic beacon. Nevertheless, as the most advanced of the acolytes, Sonilla and Andor had learned for themselves how to suppress these signals and in any case felt no guilt about meeting surreptitiously to engage in the physical aspect of their love.

As Sonilla crept quietly into the washroom she sensed that Andor was already there, waiting for her. Although the room was dark they slipped into each other's embrace with well-practiced and unerring ease, sharing all of the senses of their bodies and extended minds. On this occasion, Sonilla's uncharacteristically rapacious onslaught alerted Andor to her desperate state of mind; he felt the trauma of her parting from Lendi. It was almost as if she thought she could make up for the separation or even forget about it in a more intense experience, even if it was only a temporary outlet for her frustration. Although he suspected that there was a danger in adopting this form of behaviour as a coping mechanism in the longer term, he knew that it was what Sonilla needed before she could calmly discus her feelings. He swiftly overcame his initial surprise and was drawn willingly into the indulgence by his own increasing arousal.

Later, as they lay on the heap of cool off-white linen sheets, nuzzled in a close, comforting embrace, satiated with a tingling after-glow and breathing heavily, Sonilla finally felt able to share her thoughts. Customarily, they spoke rather than projected on these occasions to minimise the risk of detection.

'Andor, I'd like you to help me follow Lendi.'

'What? You must be joking!' He propped himself on one elbow and looked at her. 'You know that's impossible,' he added.

'Why? Just because no-one's done it before, doesn't mean it can't be done.'

'But you'll ruin everything! All these years of preparation…you won't be able to join the ancestors if you break the rules and then you'll never see Lendi again.'

'How do you know that? The guardians subject us to so many rules that are ridiculous and unnecessary just to make their own lives easier. They can't all be essential to remain one of The Select. You must be able to tell how desolate I feel without her – it's like half of me is missing.'

Sonilla was gripping his hands tightly, eyes wet with tears and although he felt his heart wrenched by the prospect, he knew he had to try to dissuade her.

'But we can't....we're not old enough to meet the Ancestors, Soni,' he pleaded. 'Even if we could find them, they wouldn't let us in.'

'Well that's what we're told, but we don't know it's true. Even En Nergal has admitted to us seniors that we were sometimes deliberately misled as juniors "for our own safety" or because we were judged "too young to understand".' She sat up, pulling her nightdress around her shoulders as her sweat cooled on her body. 'You'll be gone too in six months time and then I'll really be alone. I know I won't be able to cope with that.'

'Of course you will,' he said, trying a reassuring tone, 'you're the best student in the school – you out-perform everyone in all the psycho-mental tasks and tests.'

'Only because you and Lendi are around,' she countered, 'on my own, I don't know what I would do. My emotions are more vulnerable. I *need* to do this Andor, you know I do. *Please* help me. I am going to follow Lendi and try to find her. I want you to come with me because I don't want to leave you either. You know how much I love you and you know how much I love Lendi too, so you must see there is no other way.'

Andor was feeling he was losing the argument because it was being fought on emotional rather than logical issues. But the thought of what Sonilla was proposing was terrifying. He began dressing as he spoke.

'But what if we get lost, can't find any trace and then can't find our way back? What if we find them but are turned away? What if they won't let us back in? We might be banished to the outside forever.'

' "What if?" "What if?" ' she mimicked, 'you're scared aren't you?'

'Of course I'm scared! We could be severely punished and might lose out on our chance of a wonderful future forever.'

'Look, the only kind of wonderful future I can imagine is one with both you and Lendi in it. If what we are told is true, the Ancestors are the most benevolent and understanding beings on earth who put a high value on love and compassion. They won't punish us – they'll probably congratulate us for our perseverance and tenacity, for overcoming our qualms, for our loyalty...for not letting fear but *love* rule our actions. After all, we've been told we are the most advanced the school has ever seen, they won't want to lose us over a piffling issue such as going on a little night-time adventure.'

'I don't know....' Andor was uncomfortably aware that he had nothing else to say.

'Oh *please* Andor, *please*,' Sonilla begged desperately, 'do it out of love for me if nothing else.'

Andor sighed heavily, knowing he was beaten. 'O.K.' he said.

Sonilla hugged him and kissed him repeatedly saying 'thank you, thank you, thank you,' over and over again.

Andor pulled back and held her at arm's length, looking into her eyes. 'There's something else isn't there?' he said, 'there's something you're not telling me....'

'Yes, OK, to be honest there is,' she confessed. Hesitantly, she told him about her experience just after sunset when she could no longer feel Lendi.

'Why didn't you tell me that before?' Andor asked.

'I don't know,' she admitted, 'I guess I thought you would think I was imagining it – you know "projecting my fears to create a false interpretation of reality" as Ur Kellar puts it.'

'Come on, I know you better than that. And I know your abilities too. If you felt something it was because there was something to feel. But don't worry, I'm sure we'll find Lendi and everything will be fine – we've just got to make sure, right? When do we leave?'

'Tonight,' she said simply.

'What? Hadn't we better formulate a plan?'

'What's to plan? Climb the wall, follow Lendi. Simple. Besides, there's no time; we have to go before they get too far...before the trail fades too much. Get your coat and meet me back here – and remember to keep your mind screens up. The guardians will be finished soon and they'll be out on night patrol.'

#

'What am I going to do?' fretted Charlie in anguish, tears streaming down his face and beside himself with worry. 'I can't go to the police in case they hurt Bess, but if I agree to make the casket, it will take weeks and I can't bear to have her imprisoned for that long and then there's no guarantee they'll let her go even then. Not only that, but they also seem to somehow know what we've been doing and saying – this guy even knew about your dream!'

Rhona sat opposite him at the kitchen table trying to control her own anxiety so that they weren't both falling to pieces.

'Maybe they've got the office bugged,' she suggested, 'possibly your house too...and my car...?'

'But why would they go to such lengths just to get some stupid box made?' asked Charlie, drying his eyes.

'Is it possible there could be some truth in the dream?'

'Don't be daft, how could lying in a coffin make you younger?'

'How can people get into your dreams? How can you share dreams with others? How was Rowan able to kill Grant with her mind?'

Ignoring Rhona he got up and started pacing the floor. 'I *should* go to the police,' he continued more to himself than to her, 'that's what they always say you should do, but if they find out they might do something to Bess and I can't risk that.'

Rhona could think of nothing else to say as he continued to pace the room. Her mind was struggling with the same dilemma and it seemed that the only course of action open to them at the moment was to acquiesce to the kidnappers' demands until a better idea or some new development indicated otherwise.

A scuffling sound outside was followed by Rowan bursting in through the door.

'What's going on? Where's Bess?' she asked breathlessly, looking from one to the other as they looked at her in surprise. 'What's happened to Bess? Fuck! She's been kidnapped! Oh my God! What are we going to do....phone the police...no, make the box...no...shit, what are we going to do...?'

'What are you doing here?' demanded her bewildered aunt interrupting her rapid babbling, 'how did you know....oh.' She nodded her belated realisation.

'We don't know what to do,' stated Charlie. His shock, fear and grief were now levelling out into a kind of numb ache in his soul. He no longer felt able to think. He just wanted to curl up in a ball, go to sleep and wake to find Bess in his arms, returned to their home safe and unharmed. His life meant nothing without her.

'I can help,' said Rowan before suddenly sitting down and cradling her face muttering, 'Ow, shit!' as she was overwhelmed by intense throbbing pain from the over-exertion of the cycle ride. In her alarm she had forgotten the surgeon's warning not to undertake any vigorous exercise for two or three weeks, especially as it was something she tended to avoid anyway.

'Oh aye, really?' said Charlie sarcastically, without thinking. He quickly caught himself and apologised, 'Sorry Ro,' he said, 'I'm not at my best. How?'

'I can sort of pick up on residual emotions and stuff, like for a while after they've happened,' she muttered, 'and with people I know the feelings are stronger – I can sort of feel a kind of trace of energy…like a psychic trail or something…'

Charlie tried to understand in a context he could relate to. 'O.K., so it's a bit like a hawk can see the U.V. reflected from rodent's urine…' he said.

'Er…I guess so, maybe….whatever,' she said hesitantly.

'OK, do it,' said Charlie.

'Alright, be quiet a minute, I have to like, totally concentrate and stuff…'

Rowan closed her eyes and wrinkled her brow in concentration. After a minute's silence, she opened her eyes again.

'She must have been drugged or something,' she said slowly, 'she gets kind of faint and fuzzy near the door….let's go outside.'

They followed her in to the afternoon sun where she focussed again, this time holding her head in her hands. 'Two guys took her away in a car,' she said, 'if we get in yours Rhona, we might be able to follow them.'

They climbed in, Rowan in the passenger seat and Charlie in the back.

'Hang on,' said Rhona, 'if these people can pick up our thoughts like you can and like they seem to have done so far, aren't they going to know we're coming?'

'Oh right. Yeah, well they would, but I can kind of block my thoughts from others and maybe yours too as long as you're close to me.'

'You can?' asked Charlie, still surprised at the continuing revelations from his youthful workmate.

'Yeah, well there's a few telepaths out there,' she told him, 'and what with having to suppress it or be shunned by society, most of them…us…are pretty wacko, so I've learned how to like, protect myself ? It's better if they don't know about me, believe me.'

'Right, enough of the interview,' said Rhona impatiently, 'which way?'

'Well, it's pretty faint….but I reckon it's left.'

After twenty minutes of decreasing certainty and diminishing daylight, Rowan reluctantly admitted to having lost the trail.

'Sorry Charlie,' she said meekly.

'Don't worry, Ro – you tried and I'm grateful for that,' he said and squeezed her shoulder reassuringly.

'I'll try again tomorrow,' she promised.

When they got back to Charlie's house he asked if they would stay. He said that he would miss Bess all the more if he was alone and wreck himself with worry. At least some company would distract him and perhaps prevent him from drowning his fears in too much homemade wine.

#

Bess was crouching in thick dark woodland, attempting to mollify a huddled group of frightened children. Other women comforted more youngsters in clusters nearby with whispered reassurances. In the evening sky through the trees to her left she could see thick black smoke highlighted by the pulsing orange glow of flames. A tall proud looking woman approached, her dark green hooded robe smudged with soot and blood. Bess knew her to be an elder and looked up to her in anticipation of further instructions.

'I believe we have gathered all the surviving children,' the woman stated grimly, 'but it's not safe here. We must flee immediately. I know you are hurt but try to carry one of the injured youngsters if you can.'

Bess then noticed the pain in her left arm and looked down to see a torn and bloodied cloth tied around her biceps. Observing the children she noticed a small girl, no more than three years old, leaning back against a tree trunk her eyes glazed and her head lolling to one side. A trickle of blood oozed slowly from a swelling wound on her temple. Bess gently picked the girl up and winced as her own arm twinged in protest. Herding the rest of the group she joined the other women and children as they hurried quietly through the trees. The youngsters didn't need to be hushed; they knew that their lives depended on their silence. Soon they came to a rocky cove with a stony beach where small waves, given shape by the light of a waning moon, lapped softly on the shore. A large wooden boat with a tall central mast sat a stone's throw away, rocking gently on the water, waiting with a compliment of eight oarswomen. Another stood at the tiller and an elderly priestess at the bow. In different circumstances it could have appeared to be a serene and mystical sight, which would normally have evoked a sense of reverence and awe. Now, with fear in the hearts of the refugees, it offered hope of salvation from their trauma. They had to wade through the shallows and pass the children up to the crew and then clamber over the bulwarks themselves, aided by the pull of the rower's strong arms.

Including the crew they were sixty in all, crammed onto a deck built to accommodate half that number but before they had a chance to settle the priestess captain gave the signal to weigh anchor and the oarswomen began to row. Once they were beyond the cove, Bess looked back and made out the tallest of the city's towers above the trees a mile away. As she watched she saw it lean slightly and then topple into the flames below. It was at that moment that it finally dawned on her that their exile was to be permanent. The beautiful city where she had grown up, had her children and hoped to have grandchildren was now completely destroyed by the madness. Those few who had survived, who had warned of the disaster to come and had prepared as best they could for it, were now fugitives with an unknown and insecure future; adrift not just literally but also in their souls and psyches, their way of life and civilisation devastated in their complacency and by the failure of their collective consciousness to cope with unprecedented circumstances. Bess knew that she was amongst the fortunate to have escaped the insanity and the destruction and felt that there had been a change in history of global proportions, that nothing would ever be the same again, but she couldn't quite remember what it was. The harder she tried to remember, the more tenuous the past became until she couldn't recall what had happened before she had entered the woods. Suddenly she was overcome by fatigue and her surroundings began to dim. She closed her eyes, allowed her body to relax, let her mind rest and drifted into the comfort of nothingness.

She woke feeling well rested and comfortable. As her awareness increased she came to realise that she was in an unfamiliar bed; soft and warm but smelling of someone else's washing powder. She was dressed in a t-shirt and knickers but couldn't recollect removing the rest of her clothing. After a moment of further disorientation, she remembered when and where she was, simultaneously despondent at her circumstances and puzzled by her dream. Intrigued, she pondered its content and then was hit by a powerful sense of déjà vu. It felt so real it was more like a memory than a dream. Hadn't it actually happened to her once? She pulled up her sleeve to inspect her arm, but saw no sign of an injury, not even a scar. No, it couldn't have happened; it didn't fit anywhere into her life's story so far. *This* life's story. She wondered then if it was perhaps a glimpse at a previous life's experience. She had always had an open mind regarding the possibility of reincarnation and she had read that some people claimed to have "regressed" and reconnected with past incarnations.

Climbing out of the bed, Bess walked over to one of the windows and opened the heavy velvet curtains. In contrast to the day before, it was overcast and drizzly outside. The view gave her no clue as to her whereabouts. Beyond a wide paved terrace, a short broad flight of stone steps led to a close-trimmed lawn, which stretched about a hundred metres to the shrubby border of a wood. She pulled back the drapes on the other window to let more of the grey light into the room and looked around her. It was the largest bedroom she had seen. It was furnished and decorated in Queen Anne style, but she couldn't tell if the furniture was reproduction or not. She suspected that it was genuine. There was the "low post" bed in which she had awoken, a large chest of drawers, a dressing table with an oval mirror in an ornate frame, a desk with an upright chair and an armchair upholstered with a bright red and orange floral motif. Three walls were coloured a pastel shade of yellow, like watery custard, unbroken by any paintings; the fourth, containing the door was panelled in quarter-sawn oak, darkened by age and glossy from the unfortunate use of too much varnish. A large and exquisite Persian rug with intricate purple, green and rust patterns dominated the centre of the room. Bess couldn't help herself. She stood on it in her bare feet and wriggled her toes on the tightly woven pile, then still bare legged, knelt on the softness and with her fingers, stroked its pure silk surface in wonder. She had never encountered such luxury except on an occasional visit to a stately home open to the public where one was never allowed to touch anything. Feeling a little chilly, she hugged herself and searched for the rest of her clothing, but couldn't find it anywhere. She stood to investigate a door, opposite to the panelled wall, which she found led into an en suite bathroom, fitted out from a later period in history when plumbing had become a little more advanced.

Suddenly realising her bladder was bursting, she pulled down her knickers and sat with relief on the toilet, appreciating the warmth of the wooden seat compared to the usual thigh-chilling plastic. Looking through the doorway to the bedroom, she didn't imagine that it was usually occupied by anyone. It was clean but it had that vacant, slightly dusty sterile air of a guest room rarely used, neglected despite the lavish nature of its décor and fittings and without the imprint of any personal touches that would hint at the occupant's personality.

Without warning the bedroom door swung inwards. Bess instinctively squealed and stood, tugging her panties hastily up her legs. Nasaru wheeled in a tea trolley bearing food and drink.

'Breakfast ma'am,' he declared.

'God, don't you ever knock?' Bess shouted angrily standing in the entrance to the bathroom, 'I was on the sodding toilet!'

'Knock what?' he responded quizzically with naive puzzlement apparent on his pallid features.

'On the door of course! You know…to make your presence known.'

'Surely you become aware of my presence when I enter the room?' he retorted dryly.

'Of course I do,' replied Bess indignantly, 'but it's only good manners to give some kind of warning before bursting into the room!'

'Is it?' he enquired, but didn't wait for an answer. 'I was unaware of this custom, being as I am more familiar with my presence being detected in advance of my arrival.'

'Well I can't do that!' she snapped. Why did this man annoy her so much? There was something about his inscrutability and impenetrable demeanour that she found infuriating. She couldn't accept that he felt no emotions, even if he didn't show them. 'Don't you ever get "normal" people come here?'

'No ma'am,' he replied, seemingly unmoved by her outburst, 'we don't usually have visitors.'

'Well, I'm not a "visitor", I'm a bloody prisoner,' she railed indignantly, 'and I would appreciate it if you knocked before entering. Jesus, I was on the loo anyway and I could have been naked or…something'

Nasaru raised an eyebrow slightly. 'At this time of day?' he asked rhetorically with a disapproving look that rendered her speechless. 'I have to say that the thought had not occurred to me,' he added impassively, 'and regardless of that I am indifferent to your state of dress or undress.'

Infuriated by his nonchalance, she slammed the bathroom door to block him out and tried to calm herself in an attempt to regain some dignity. When she pulled it open again, he was just leaving.

'Wait a minute,' she said. 'What happened to my clothes?'

'They are being laundered,' he informed her, pausing to look back over his shoulder, 'and they shall be returned when they are dry.'

'Well I'm going to need more than that anyway,' she told him. 'You see I didn't have a chance to pack before I came,' she added in a voice heavily laced with sarcasm whilst smiling sweetly.

'I'll see what I can do,' he responded stony faced.

'And I want to phone my husband,' she continued, 'to tell him I'm O.K. – he'll be worried about me.'

'Belum Asar has already done so,' he informed her. 'He has also been told what is required of him.'

'But can't I speak to him?' she asked, trying not to seem as desperate as she felt.

'Not at the moment I'm afraid. It will be his reward once he has started on the project.'

Bess sighed, disappointed, and began to feel a little tearful. She fought back the urge to cry, not willing to show any weakness to this loathsome flunkey. She didn't want to give him the satisfaction of seeing her waver; not that he was necessarily capable of expressing satisfaction. She was beginning to think that he was actually incapable of feeling any emotion at all.

'Just get me some clothes then will you?' she demanded, 'And quickly, I'm getting cold,'

He nodded, turned slowly and departed, shutting the door behind him.

Bess sighed heavily and moved to the window to consider her options for escape. It was only then that she remembered how she'd been stopped before; that suffocating, sickening immobility that had been inflicted upon her. 'Bastards!' she exclaimed and sat dejectedly on the bed. Before long she became aware of a cinnamon aroma and realised that she was ravenous. Moving to the trolley she lifted a stainless steel dome to reveal a bowl of steaming spiced porridge. Next to it were two slices of wholemeal toast, a jar of raspberry jam and a pot of green tea: her favourite breakfast. Briefly she wondered how they knew before she recalled her captors' apparent ability to read minds. Putting the uncomfortable notion aside she wheeled the trolley over to the desk and tucked in.

She had just finished when there was a gentle tap at the door, followed by a brief pause before Nasaru appeared with a blue soft looking woollen bathrobe draped over his arm. Her mood had not really improved with eating, so although she was grateful for the extra layer, she was damned if she was going to show it.

'This is all we could come up with for the moment,' he said proffering the garment in her direction, 'but we shall purchase something more appropriate shortly.' When she didn't move he hung it on the back of the armchair moved to the trolley and began wheeling away the remnants of her breakfast.

'I need some clean underwear too,' she stated evenly.

'Of course,' he said. 'It shall be arranged.'

'And some socks and slippers. My feet are cold.'

He nodded wordlessly.

She was getting weary of maintaining a churlish mood. It was not in her nature and even though she was still annoyed, frustrated and scared, she decided it might be more pleasant for herself if she was more amenable. Additionally, she may be able to get some information out of the man if she could let go of or at least hide her feelings of hostility.

'Thanks' she said, indicating the robe and then tried adopting a conversational tone. 'Does anyone else live here?' she asked, 'or is it just you and the two old guys?'

'At the moment, it is just the three of us ma'am.'

'You must have your work cut out for you then, looking after a place this size?'

'Indeed,' he agreed, 'although most of the rooms are not used.'

'What about your accent? Where are you from?' she asked.

'You wouldn't know it,' he said dismissively.

'Try me,' she countered, 'I've travelled a lot you know.'

'I really must go,' he said hurriedly and pushed the trolley through the open doorway.

'One more thing.'

'Yes?' he said, but this time showing definite signs of impatience.

'Can I have some books or magazines?' she asked, 'I'll go out of my mind with boredom stuck in here with nothing to do.'

'You may go to the library,' he conceded and gave her directions, warning her not to enter any of the other rooms nor make another attempt to escape. With that he left accompanied by the squeaking of the wheels on the trolley.

Bess stared at the door. She was still afraid and she missed Charlie. She knew he would be worried about her and she began fretting over how he would cope with that worry. She just wanted to hold him and tell him she was all right. She wanted *him* to hold *her* in *his* arms and tell *her* everything was all right. At that point she gave up holding her feelings back and crumpled sobbing onto the bed.

CHAPTER THIRTEEN.

Escape was not so easy as Sonilla had anticipated. Creeping through the corridors she had come across a second year boy in his long nightshirt making his way to the toilet. He was startled from his dreaminess when he saw her.

'Oh, hi Sonilla,' he chirped happily.

'Hush Aiken,' she whispered urgently with a finger to her lips, 'we don't want to wake anybody.'

He then became curious when he noticed her outdoor clothing. 'Where are you going?' he asked quietly with a look of puzzlement on his face and his head tipped slightly to one side.

'Err..couldn't sleep,' she answered quickly, 'just going for a walk.'

He seemed satisfied with this and continued on his way. Sonilla stole hastily back to the laundry to meet Andor. Together, they crept to the door into the courtyard, opened it a crack and peered out. The moon in its third quarter dimly illuminated the flagstones and reflected from the whitewashed walls, just as the sun had done earlier, but less intensely and with a soft bluish glow. With the night-time breeze, silhouettes of honesty flowers and the tall leafy shoots of monkshood swished gently in the borders.

'There shouldn't be anyone patrolling yet,' whispered Andor, 'there's always a bit of a party after the rituals on a Friday night – they really let their guard down.'

Nevertheless, they had agreed to keep mind-silent to reduce the risk of detection. Sonilla began to ease the door open a little more when she suddenly jerked back into the shadows.

'There's someone there!' she rasped. Her heart started beating hard in her chest and her throat tightened in panic. Realising that they had not yet broken the rules nor been caught she calmed down and giggled nervously, then bit her lip to silence herself. Andor remained serious, peeked through the gap and saw a robed figure walking back towards the shrine. He watched as the guide entered the building and then waited a moment.

'Come on,' he urged and slipped out into the garden followed closely by Sonilla. They crept in the shadows from bush to bush until they reached a thick growth of ivy that clung to the wall by the "Ancestors Gate".

'You first,' said Andor.

Hasty in her nervous state, Sonilla began scrambling up the vine before testing its strength. Parts of it began coming away from the wall and as she clutched wildly at the stems in alarm, some of those snapped and came free. She just managed to get both hands over the top of the wall and started to push herself up with her right foot. The branch supporting her weight cracked and her knee bashed into the rough stonework. She grunted, stifling a curse, and then hauled herself up to straddle the top.

'You next,' she called softly from her perch, holding her throbbing knee, 'but be careful, the ivy's loose.'

Andor briefly studied the branches and then cautiously mounted the creeper. Although slightly heavier than her, he tested each hand and foothold before trusting his weight to it and successfully reached the summit. 'It's a long way down,' he cautioned, 'peering through the darkness to survey the undergrowth below. We'll have to jump, but I can't see the bottom through all the plants.'

'We'll be fine,' said Sonilla confidently, 'just bend your knees when you land to absorb the impact.'

Andor jumped, thudding into the ground below and rolling to soften the impact. 'Ow! Nettles!' he hissed, 'Hang on a minute I'll try to clear them a bit.' He stamped to flatten an area for Sonilla's landing, then stood back. As her feet struck the ground, her weakened knee gave way, she fell sideways and her face brushed the nettles. With a sharp inhalation she recoiled and leapt to her feet holding her face and swearing under her breath.

'Are you alright?' asked Andor with concern, rushing to her side.

'I think so,' she replied, 'just my knee's a bit sore where I bashed it on the wall and now I've stung my face. Are there any dock leaves?'

'I can't see – it's too dark. But here, let me help.'

'No, don't worry, I'll survive,' she said, smiling and grimacing simultaneously, 'come on, we'd better get going.'

Favouring her left leg she limped quickly along the path, only just discernible in the murky gloom beneath the trees. They hurried along through the wood, the worn trail showing slightly darker than the leaves of the undergrowth, unsure what to expect ahead of them. The sense of adventure combined with the knowledge that they had transgressed filled them with a mixture of excitement and dread, but Sonilla's over-riding concern was for Lendi. Never before had she been outside mind-reach of her and she was finding the emptiness where her sister belonged close to unbearable.

Concealed in the shadows, Thu Salamu witnessed the two miscreants scale the perimeter wall; watched as Sonilla slipped, hurting her knee and observed them disappear over the wall into the darkness beyond. She had divined their intentions. Her skills were much greater than they or anyone else suspected, including En Nergal. The runaways' feeble attempts to shield their immature minds were no barrier to her greater perceptive powers. She wouldn't stop them, but was determined to follow at a discreet distance, undetected but continuing to monitor their movements. Half a minute after they had dropped into the woods, she moved swiftly to the gate, unlocked it and passed through. Securing it behind her, she secreted the key safely in a deep pocket and engaged in her stealthy pursuit.

#

Charlie slept despite his worries about Bess. He had lain awake for at least two hours before exhaustion overcame him. He dreamed he was gilding the carved sarcophagus he had been asked to make, but it was in a different time and place. The other craftsmen in the simple workshop had oriental features and were dressed in outlandish clothing. He then realised that he was too and paused to examine his own garments, feeling suddenly out of place. He noticed that his hands were unfamiliar too, smaller and with a yellowish-brown hue.

'Back to work Ishida!' commanded his overseer severely, noticing his momentary inactivity, 'You must concentrate – the quality of this work is of vital importance!'

Charlie carefully lifted the next sheet of gold leaf with tweezers and brush, but stopped midway to his work piece, becoming aware of an unfamiliar sound and feeling a sudden sense of foreboding. He heard a deep distant roaring that was growing almost imperceptibly louder. Within a few moments all of the craftsmen had stopped work, looking uncertainly at each other and towards the window, mystified as to the source of the noise and becoming increasingly uneasy as it intensified to become a thunderous din accompanied by a rapidly deepening vibration. Fearing an earthquake, the other men fled their shack through the open door. Charlie hurried to the unglazed window to gape in the direction of the rumbling. Beyond the low wood and stone buildings of this shabby costal town was an impossibly high wall of moving water. Within seconds it had demolished the settlement and hurtled towards the workshop pushing before it a rolling barrage of masonry and roof beams, trees, people and livestock. Charlie stood transfixed, too petrified to move yet also aware of the futility of any action and in a moment the wave slammed into the building, engulfing him in darkness.

He woke with a jolt and a cry of alarm. He slowly regained his breath and shook his head to clear his mind as his pounding heartbeat slowed. *Well,* he thought, *that was a strange variation on the recurring theme.* He rose and sat on the edge of the bed sighing as the heaviness reawakened in his chest; Bess' absence was an aching gap that filled him with despair.

There was a gentle tapping at the bedroom door.

'Are you alright Charlie?' called Rhona's voice softly, with an edge of concern, 'I heard a yell.'

'Aye, I'm fine thanks,' he replied, 'just a dream.'

'Shall I make some tea?' she offered.

'Yeah, sure, great,' he managed, still a little dazed by his shock, 'I'll be down in a minute.'

By the time he reached the kitchen, Rhona was pouring freshly boiled water into the teapot. She looked up and noticed his dishevelled appearance.

'So, what was this dream about?' she ventured.

'Well...same subject, different setting this time,' he said thoughtfully, 'I was Japanese or something, gilding that same damn box, but it was.....I don't know, hundreds of years ago and there was this incredible roaring noise and then we got hit by a massive tidal wave......that's when woke up.'

'That was no dream,' observed Rowan shuffling sleepily into the kitchen clad only in a knee-length black t-shirt emblazoned with "WHAT?" in large white letters.

'What?' asked Charlie, 'What do you mean? Of course it was a dream – I mean, I'm not wet am I?'

'No, I mean it's a *memory*,' stated the girl tiredly, ruffling her tousled hair, 'you know, from like a previous life or something.'

Rhona looked up from pouring the tea. 'How do you know that?' she asked with a puzzled frown.

Rowan seemed a little embarrassed. 'I just kind of know,' she muttered sheepishly, 'I can tell the difference...' She grimaced at their bewildered expressions. '...I can't explain it,' she finished lamely.

'So, another of your "gifts",' persisted her aunt, 'is to be able to see into other people's dreams *and* memories?'

Rowan nodded mutely. She still wasn't accustomed to their discomfort at her newly revealed true nature. She saw these aspects of herself as her normal state, not as "gifts" or "skills" or "abilities", although she recognised that with outside pressure they could become a curse, hence her reticence and unwillingness to admit to too much too soon. She sighed and traipsed over to the worktop where she busied herself with making toast, taking a little pleasure from the thought that her mouth was just about healed enough for her to indulge in her favourite snack.

Charlie was too overburdened to attempt comprehension. With his overriding and dominant thoughts of worry concerning Bess' fate, his brain now seemed cloaked in a filter of numb acceptance of any other new information that came his way. He merely sat at the kitchen table, dazed, and sipped his tea.

Rhona broke the silence a minute later. 'So, Rowan,' she tried, in a matter-of-fact tone, 'do you feel up to having another go at searching for Bess? Seeing if you can pick anything up?'

'Yeah, sure, I'll try,' she replied through a mouthful of toast.

'How about it Charlie?' she asked looking at him, 'shall we try the power of Rowan's mind for a couple of hours and if we have no joy then we'll phone the police, okay?'

There was no response for a full minute. Rhona wondered if Charlie had heard her or not. She was about to repeat herself when he looked up suddenly and spoke.

'No,' he said quietly.

The others exchanged a glance but then he continued in a hollow, despondent voice.

'I want to phone the police first. I can't believe that the kidnappers can read our minds or know what we're doing. We'll use Rowan's mobile – that won't be tapped – get this reported and *then* we'll try looking again.' He shook his head. 'I should have phoned straight away and not been intimidated – the sooner it's reported, the sooner the police can act. They always say not to give in to kidnapper's demands - let the experts handle it.'

'Whatever you say Charlie,' Rhona concurred, recognising that in his stricken state it was his right to make these decisions. She squeezed his shoulder affectionately and nodded to Rowan to get her phone.

#

The library was a spacious but dim room, the daylight from its one bay window seemingly absorbed by the thousands of dark-spined books that filled the shelves covering the entire surface of the walls from floor to ceiling. Bess entered slowly, shutting the door softly behind her as if she feared she might wake these dusty tomes. Approaching the books almost reverentially, she reached out a tentative finger and gently stroked one of the leather-bound volumes. She looked around with the sense of awe of one witnessing the discovery of a hoard of historic relics. In the centre of the room there was a large dark polished table of some antiquity surrounded by six well-worn chairs upholstered in red leather. Under the window a huge heavy sofa squatted like a half-deflated elephant behind a low oval table. She returned her attention to the books, perusing the nearest shelves to see what titles were ranked there. She was familiar with the usual collections of classics and obscure oddities that generally filled the libraries of stately homes, so she was not surprised to see works by Dickens, Shakespeare, Sir Walter Scott, Kipling and others nestled between sections of poetry and drama. Then she noticed an alcove containing something more unusual. The publications here showed a greater range of sizes, appeared to have been bound by hand, with less care and seemed to be of variable age, some ancient and others quite recent. They mostly covered the subjects of archaeology and ancient history, but the bottom two shelves bore works relating to psychology, parapsychology, dreams, telepathy, telekinesis and other studies of the mind. One title in particular drew her attention, so she pulled it from its place and re-read the words on the front cover where the gilt lettering spelled out "The Great Forgetting – 'The Shift' and the Loss of Telepathy". Intrigued, she took it to the settee to browse its contents by the light of the window.

After two hours of growing astonishment Bess' mind had reached saturation point. The information she had discovered was so astounding that she was now sitting staring at nothing trying to make sense of it all. How could this knowledge not be known in the wider world? Was this the only library that contained such extraordinary revelations? Her worldview had been so shaken that she was temporarily distracted from her predicament. With the book still open on her lap, Bess tried to order her thoughts. Like Charlie, she knew that people emotionally close to each other occasionally "clicked" and that "crowd mentality" could affect an individual's behaviour so that they might act in a way that was completely out of character. However, what the author of this book proposed was a much more progressive hypothesis. In fact, he was actually claiming his information to be historical truth. He claimed that tens of thousands of years ago, prehistoric humans had developed extensive telepathic and psychic abilities, a group of senses termed the "Supra-mind", which enabled them to live in harmony with each other and their environment. Following a global catastrophe, he asserted, the trauma caused by the extensive devastation and suffering virtually obliterated these skills, effectively turning back humanity's evolutionary clock by millennia. The writer went on to describe how the development of advances in agriculture and technology to all intents and purposes actually stifled the "re-evolution" of the mind in all but a few isolated groups. There were still a handful of tribal peoples who retained a vestige of these skills. Most notably, some of the aborigines of Australia who could navigate huge tracts of wilderness using chanted maps called "songlines" and using a mental state accessed through the "dreamtime" could communicate with their ancestors and be connected to many places and times simultaneously. The Bushmen of the Kalahari also astounded anthropologists with their seemingly psychic skills. They also had an uncanny knack of accurately predicting visits by other tribes or families. Additionally the author suggested that all humans should still have these skills sitting dormant in their brains because they were not lost through natural selection where unfavourable characteristics were bred out of the gene-pool. Thus the DNA of everyone alive today should still retain the code to build these abilities into the mind and all that was needed was the right stimuli and the correct training in their use. The potential to re-learn was in us all.

At this point, Bess had stopped reading. Fascinated by these ideas she sat gazing into space and considering the possibilities. It could be that this book was written by just another crackpot. But what if it were true? What would the world be like if everyone became telepathic? Of course it could never happen; so few would accept that it was even feasible and wouldn't even try. She guessed that it could only be entered into willingly. But if it was to come about, she imagined that initially it might cause global chaos as people learned to cope with a deluge of other's thoughts but eventually, surely honesty would have to prevail as people realised that they could no longer hide their emotions and intentions. On a more personal level it could do wonders for unrequited love....or perhaps not if these feelings were not reciprocated, but it might make it easier for individuals to find and keep partners. Then again, it could cause more relationships to end if it became apparent how often one's partner secretly appraised and desired others around them. Alternatively the whole process may come to pass more gradually, if it was to be an evolutionary development.

Bess shook her head and castigated herself for such frivolous thoughts in her present dire circumstances – after all she had been kidnapped. However, she felt powerless to do anything about it at the moment so, she thought philosophically, she might as well make the most of her situation. Turning her attention back to the book, she flicked to the last few pages and noticed the bibliography. Included in the list was a guide entitled "Teach Yourself Telepathy – A Beginner's Guide". Intrigued, she felt compelled to return to the shelves to see if this was included in the collection. She was thrilled to find it on the next shelf down and took it eagerly back to the sofa.

The preparation exercises seemed to start quite simply and were similar in a way to those she used for starting meditation – concentration on the breath, clearing the mind of unnecessary thoughts and focussing the mind. All this was familiar to her so came quite easily. After reading lesson one she decided to have a go. This was just a listening task where one had to learn to open one's senses to detect the thoughts of those in your vicinity. If it worked, she hoped it might even give her an insight into the motives of her captors. Following the instructions in the first lesson, Bess' questing mind tentatively reached out into the unknown. Perceiving nothing she tried a little harder, striving to discern some hint of someone else's psyche, but only became more aware of the gentle pattering of rain on the window panes. She realised that she was becoming frustrated and that this might interfere with the process, so she brought her attention back to her breathing and tried to let go of her expectations. Wryly, she thought that she didn't actually have any expectations – she didn't *really* believe that this could work, so why even bother?

Suddenly she sensed someone else in the room and quickly opened her eyes in alarm. There was no one there, but for a few moments her heart beat more rapidly. She had definitely felt that she was being watched, she *knew* she was being watched, but apart from her the library was empty. With a strangely novel certainty born from newly stimulated areas of her brain she had no doubt that someone somewhere had been alert to her attempt. This was both worrying and enthralling, but she was not the sort to let fear get in her way. She decided to try again.

This time, when she thought she felt another's presence, she ventured towards it, as instructed, but discovered some kind of obstacle. Annoyed, but not discouraged, she persevered in focussing her effort. Finding what seemed to be an impenetrable barrier, she made herself try harder, pushing against the obstruction with all the strength she could muster. Abruptly she felt an unexpected shock as if someone had struck her mind with a powerful force. Alien thoughts entered her brain overwhelming her own like a flash flood hitting a placid stream. There were no words, but she was in no doubt as to the meaning of the message imparted to her. A frighteningly potent incursion from a mocking, patronising intruder informed her that her pathetic efforts were futile and any further attempts at spying would be severely punished. With the communication came an irrefutable conviction of its truth, so that Bess immediately felt humbled and ashamed, like a guilty child caught in an act of disobedience who was then humiliated by an unkind teacher by being made to confess in front of the whole class. She opened her eyes to escape but the thoughts were replaced with pain. She sat shaking and hugging herself, sweating despite feeling cold, nauseous with her head spinning and her heart pounding. After a few minutes, feeling slightly calmer but no less perturbed, she staggered from the library and made her way back to her room. Once there she sat on the bed, willing the headache away and attempting to steady herself with deep regular breaths.

Now back in control of her thoughts she guessed that the feelings associated with the message she had received had been projected into her simultaneously – they were not her own feelings at all. With a sense of horror and amazement she realised that her abductors had not only the power to overcome her mind and body but they were also able to manipulate her emotions. Beneath the dread she felt anger and revulsion at how her mind had been violated. Her adversaries could block their own thoughts from her intrusion, so perhaps she could learn to do the same. The significance of this in relation to a telepathic world only increased her fascination. If thoughts could be hidden then human relationships would be no better than now, although if one could attach emotions to telepathic messages understanding could be increased. Misinterpreted motives must often become a barrier to clear communication. Pondering these ramifications rekindled her curiosity to the extent that she resolved to return to the library later to discover more, although this time she would not dabble in personal experimentation. At least not yet. She walked over to the window and examined the grounds and their setting, wondering where she was. The plain well kept lawns and neatly trimmed hedges bordered by woodland gave no clues. The tall trees and drizzly air obscured the distance and blocked any potential landmarks from view. She wondered again how Charlie was and felt her heart tighten as she ached to see him. Perhaps the instruction book in the library could help her send her thoughts to him. She knew he would be worried sick and hoped that he had some company or support to help him cope. She was not concerned for herself, despite her experiences so far. She sensed that although her kidnappers were determined and possibly desperate, fanatical even, they were nevertheless not malicious of intent.

Without warning, the bedroom door swung inwards and as Bess spun around she saw Nasaru entering with a laden tea-trolley.

'I asked you to knock!' she reminded him crossly, startled by his sudden and unannounced appearance.

'As you can see, Mrs. MacKay,' he stated impassively, 'my hands are otherwise engaged.'

Bess tried to think of a suitable remark, but he spoke again.

'Luncheon is served,' he said loftily and with that ceremonious announcement he turned and left, disallowing her any further comment.

#

After twenty minutes of following the moonlit trail in silence and nervous excitement, Andor began to perceive Sonilla's growing sense of unease. He had been feeling it too but was unable to discern its cause. He stopped and turned to face her.

What do you think it is? he asked wordlessly.

I'm not sure, came Sonilla's reply. She squinted around through the dark trees surrounding them. *But something's not right,* she added, *I feel other people's fear in the atmosphere.*

They both concentrated, eye's closed to concentrate their attention.

Some felt dread, some felt excitement....it's confusing, they agreed.

'Well, I guess the acolytes would have been nervous,' suggested Andor hesitantly, 'walking into an unknown future.....meeting the ancestors...'

'No, it was more than that,' Sonilla asserted, now whispering out loud and feeling more fearful by the moment, 'I can sense real terror.' She glanced around with a look of consternation in her eyes. 'Something's *wrong* Andor, very wrong....something to do with Lendi.....I can't find her....it's like her thought's just...' she paused, shaking her head as if it would change what she was feeling and then looked at him in alarm, '....stopped....her thought's just stopped! *All* of their thoughts just stopped!'

'But how...?' muttered Andor uncertainly, then with a sudden realisation, he knew that she was right but couldn't fathom it. He stopped himself from thinking the unthinkable – there must be some other explanation. 'Maybe she's just asleep...,' he ventured.

Abruptly, Sonilla dashed past him along the path further into the woods, heedless of her injured knee and with panic rising in her chest. Andor followed hurriedly, not willing to believe that any harm could have come to Lendi. He tried to force those thoughts from his mind, replace them with a voice of reason that explained that somehow, once with the ancestors, one's mind becomes cloaked for the sake of secrecy. Yes. Surely that must be it. He tried to convey this to Sonilla, but in her state of heightened anxiety, she could not be reached. They soon noticed the smell of burning wood mixed with a different, more acrid smoke and discerned a haze of fumes drifting through the trees, glowing eerily where it was struck by moonbeams.

Sonilla lurched to a halt at the edge of a wide glade, a slight depression of about an acre, and Andor stopped beside her, both of them panting for breath. Near the centre of the space was a heap of smouldering embers left behind from a huge bonfire, with the unburned ends of a few logs protruding from the edges, issuing wisps of pale smoke. Andor guessed that there must have been some kind of ceremony here, perhaps to celebrate the young votaries' recruitment by the Ancestors, but scanning the area he saw that there was nobody in sight now; the clearing was deserted.

Sonilla edged her way down the bank and moved slowly towards the remains of the fire and although she had recovered from her sprint, she was nonetheless still breathing deeply, her heart thumping. A knot of trepidation was constricting her throat and she felt her pulse pounding in her temples like two extra hearts. As she gradually approached the glowing ashes, her breath slowed and shallowed until an aching tightness almost immobilised her lungs. Andor, reaching her side thought that she had stopped breathing altogether and found himself compelled to hold his own breath as his foreboding grew. In the dim light he saw a slight reflection from a shiny red object just outside the circle of embers, which seemed to have partially escaped incineration, although a trace of smoke curled up from one side. He stooped to get a better look at the item and picked it up to examine it. It was the front half of a boot. He regarded it with a frown. A red boot....

Suddenly Sonilla let out a gasp of dismay. It was one of Lendi's.

*But why would anyone burn her boot...*he wondered. Then as the unthinkable dawned on him he noticed Sonilla's gasp and horror-struck expression, so looked in the direction of her gaze. Peering into the ashes, he realised with a jolt of revulsion and unspeakable terror that not all of the charred sticks were wooden. There were the remains of human bones including a half buried skull, one eye socket pulsing with a deep red flickering glow. He sank to his knees and his throat finally released a strangled, croaking whimper as he was overcome by Lendi's abominable plight. Becoming hysterical, Sonilla screamed over and over again, recoiling from the sight. As she retreated she tripped backwards over a branch and hit the ground heavily where she lay and howled in anguish. Suddenly she scrabbled frantically to her feet and fled into the woods, continuing to wail piteously as she ran.

#

After two hours of driving in ever-widening circles, all three were ready to give up the search. The police had told them to stay by the phone in case the kidnappers tried to call, but Charlie was too restless. He tried phoning Adam but there was no answer and then Rowan offered to try her luck at tracing Bess from the car.

'I'm sorry, it's no good,' said Rowan dejectedly, 'I can't seem to pick anything up. Well not Bess anyway – there's like, plenty of farmers out there, whose thoughts I'd rather not hear.'

'Don't worry,' said Charlie, 'but thanks for trying, I really appreciate it. The police might come up with something – they seemed very supportive down at the station.'

'Right,' agreed Rhona who was driving, 'let's head back. They might be trying to get in touch with us.' She didn't sound convinced. As she pulled over to reverse into a farm track to turn around, Rowan gave a sudden cry.

'Oh! Wait! I've got something!' she said excitedly.

'What?' asked Charlie quickly, 'have you found Bess?'

'Yeah, well I felt her at least,' she replied with a slight smile, 'it's like she was reaching out or something – trying to contact us. I totally didn't know she could do that! Not many people can. It's gone now but I felt where it came from...carry on down that road, it was quite close I think.'

Rhona drove on, whilst they all glanced from side to side, trying to spot a building amongst the surrounding fields and trees.

'Can you still feel her?' asked Charlie.

'No, it's weird, it's like she was suddenly blocked or something, but I've got a kind of trace on her so I think we're O.K.'

'What do you mean blocked?' he said with concern. 'Is she alright? Not hurt or anything?'

'No, she's fine. It was just like a stronger mind...shut a door or something.'

A minute later Rowan pointed to an area of woodland about half a mile away.

'That's it! Over there,' she announced, 'in those trees. That's where she is.'

Another two hundred metres along the road Rhona pulled into an entrance on the left. A formidable pair of heavy wrought iron gates filled the only opening they could see in a two metre high wall topped with shards of broken glass that appeared to encircle the grounds of the extensive property within. There was a small, deserted looking gatehouse just inside, but no other buildings visible. A driveway disappeared into the trees beyond.

'We're being watched,' cautioned Rowan.

'Where? I don't see anyone,' said Charlie, scrutinising their surroundings.

'No, you won't. I mean we've being detected, like with someone's mind...just kind of *noticing* us – I can feel it.'

'Do they know who we are? Are they reading our minds?' asked Rhona.

'I don't think so. It's a kind of low-level sensing – like a sort of early warning system. Let's get away from the gates and they'll probably ignore us...hopefully.'

Once they were parked in a field entrance half a mile away they tried to formulate a plan.

'We could phone the police again now,' suggested Rhona, 'they'd be here in no time.'

'Or a rescue attempt,' proposed Rowan, 'we could...'

'It's too risky,' interrupted Charlie, 'we don't know how to break into places. You saw those gates and that glass-topped wall. Even if we did get in, they'll almost certainly have guards or weapons or both and they might hurt Bess by the time we find her – it's probably a huge mansion in there.'

'Same if the pigs, sorry the police, tried it,' pressed Rowan, 'but I reckon I could do it.'

'What? Not on your own surely?' demanded Rhona, 'It's way too dangerous.'

'But they'll sense your presence as well,' protested Charlie, 'we can't risk anything happening to Bess. Or to you. Can't we just let the professionals deal with it?'

'*They* don't have any experience of telepathy though do they?' countered Rowan.

'Well no,' admitted Charlie reluctantly, 'but Rhona's right, it's too dangerous.'

'Could be,' the girl agreed, 'but I think I've got a good chance.' She looked at them both from the back seat and persevered. 'Look, if you two rattle the gates or something, you know, like cause a distraction, I can climb over the wall, home in on Bess and totally sneak her out while they're like, still focussed on you guys.'

'Maybe...but how could you manage that bloody great wall anyway?'

'Look, just 'cos I'm a bit of a Goth, doesn't mean I've just crept out of a coffin,' she declared earnestly. 'I'm like, totally fit you know. I used to be athletics champion at school and I still cycle a lot. Anyway, I saw some trees close to the outside of the wall in that field over there and I can like, use those low branches to help me get over, especially if I take the foot mats out of the car to put over the glass.'

'But...' started Rhona, thinking that her niece had somewhat exaggerated her levels of activity.

'*And* I reckon I can shield my mind – I've had years of practice,' Rowan continued relentlessly. 'They're complacent, I can feel it. They totally won't expect anyone to like, even *try* to slip through their defences and I'm pretty sure they don't know about *me*.'

When she saw the others exchange a glance she knew she would get her way.

'O.K.' Charlie relented after a moment's thought. Rhona reluctantly agreed but insisted that they wait until dark so that Rowan was at least not seen by any physical eyes.

It seemed like a long wait. They had driven a little further away just to make sure that they escaped discovery and sat nervously and impatiently anticipating sundown. When at last it came, they left the car under a tree by a thick hedge and split up – Rowan making her way across the fields to the trees by the perimeter wall whilst Charlie and Rhona headed for the main entrance. Reaching the gates, they hesitated feeling edgy and tense, both filled with the misgivings of those committed to a course of action they were doubtful of in the first place, but it was too late to change.

Unsure exactly how to proceed, Charlie reached out slowly and tried the handle on the gates.

'Locked, of course,' he observed evenly.

'Well,' said Rhona taking a deep breath, 'let's give them a shake...yes, let's do that - we're supposed to be making a diversion here, after all.'

The decrepit twins exchanged thoughts with an effortlessness born of centuries of experience, though they still found it agreeable to use speech on a regular basis. Although these bodies were reaching the end of their useful life, it was still prudent to exercise different muscles from time to time and most physical sensations were still pleasing to those who clung so greedily to the corporeal form.

'Tedious,' commented Asar wearily.

Ki nodded, then added, 'It is hard to believe that these paltry mortals are actually trying to enter the grounds to attempt a rescue.'

'Rattling the gates like monkeys in a cage....'

'...except that they are on the outside!' They both let forth dry, rasping chuckles.

'Yes, laughable, yet wearisome all the same.'

'Indeed brother. We grow weaker every day...'

'I suppose we should deal with it.'

'Let's send Nasaru - he can give them a scare.'

'He can tell them to give up or we will have to harm the woman.'

'Yes, he can take the dogs too, to add emphasis to our communiqué.'

'Ah yes, the dogs will be hungry...'

After lunch, Bess returned to the library, drawn to the book of telepathic instruction. Following her earlier experience, she did not intend to undertake any practice, but just read through the exercises in order, determined to attempt them at some point in the future. She was disturbed mid-afternoon by Nasaru bringing her an unasked for but gratefully received cup of green tea. On this occasion he even remembered to knock. She was struggling to understand her captors. They seemed determined, possibly even ruthless in the pursuit of their aims yet at the same time, apart from the means of her abduction, remarkably civilised between threats. She decided not to dwell on it and focused instead on the compelling book in front of her. After her drink she took a break from reading to do some yoga. Her body was unaccustomed to such inactivity so she really needed to stretch. It felt good and not only invigorated her body but refreshed her mind too. Returning to the book she was both pleased and excited to discover that the next section covered methods of shielding and protecting one's mind from unwelcome scrutiny so, fascinated, she eagerly immersed herself in the details. She was so engrossed by her reading that she was somewhat taken aback when Nasaru returned declaring that it was time for dinner.

'You are cordially invited to dine with you hosts this evening,' he stated importantly.

Bess hesitated. Should she accept? It would be intriguing to discover more about her strange custodians and they had been treating her reasonably well......Then she remembered the method of her capture, the intrusive mind probe and the fact that she was after all being held against her will and used as a cruel bargaining chip to coerce the man she loved.

'Tell them to sod off!' she snapped crossly, 'They can't kidnap me and then expect me to be civil towards them!'

'As you wish,' said Nasaru coldly, raising his left eyebrow, seemingly his only facial expression, 'I shall inform my masters of your decision and serve you in your own room presently.' He wheeled and marched from the room as if deeply affronted and personally insulted by her rejection of this conciliatory gesture.

Bess felt that finally getting the man ruffled was a minor victory – seeing that crack in his demeanour momentarily eased her powerlessness. She was not vindictive in nature, but being abducted and held captive had provided both an opportunity and a catalyst for her to act out of character. She had never before encountered such a situation, so it was a blank canvas upon which her disposition could play. She was so accustomed to being in control of her own life that this incarceration, this removal of her freedom, had thrown her into uncertainty and dread. Her customary fortitude and resolve had been severely eroded in the context of her helplessness. At least when making her own choices she had a rough idea of what some of the consequences might be and if unforeseen circumstances arose she still had options open to select a suitable course of action. Now that she had no choice but to submit to the whims of these eccentric, powerful men she was eager to seize this chance to offend them and rile their servant, even if she would normally view it as petty and spiteful. Nevertheless, when she gave it any thought, her future prospects still filled her with trepidation and fear. She had no idea what these people were really capable of but she suspected that the fate dealt out to the heavy-handed lackey had probably been somewhat terminal in nature.

Back in her room she became calmer, unable to sustain the levels of stress held in her anger, indignation and fear. She deigned not to notice as Nasaru wheeled in the food trolley, staying at the window to stare at the overcast and darkening sky. Despite herself she couldn't help feeling slightly guilty when he lifted the covers from the dishes and she noticed out of the corner of her eye an exquisite selection of gourmet vegetarian fare. As soon as he left she tucked in avidly, finding herself inexplicably ravenous despite her inactivity. The incongruity of her treatment confused her. She found it difficult to comprehend the behaviour of her captors and still doubted the stated reason for the casket's construction. It was impossible to believe that it could truly rejuvenate the elderly.

Later, after Nasaru had wordlessly removed the trolley, Bess returned her attention to the book that she had brought back to her room from the library. After a few minutes her studies were distracted by a tenuous yet niggling feeling that there was something she had forgotten or somebody she should be looking for. She felt drawn to the window and noticing the darkness outside, she started to draw the curtains. Her heart leapt into her throat at the sudden appearance of a white face popping into view outside the glass. All at once she was shaken from her fright as she recognised that it was Rowan clinging to the windowsill displaying a timid grin. Bess hurriedly slid open the casement and helped the girl clamber into the room.

'Hi Bess,' Rowan chirped brightly as she gave her a quick hug.

Bess was both pleased and appalled simultaneously. 'What are you doing here?' she gasped.

'Rescue,' answered the girl simply, 'come on there's some thick vine thing out here, we can totally climb down.'

'But the defences....the force...'

'It's gone,' Rowan interrupted, 'I think they're weakening and can't keep it up all the time. Anyway, they probably reckoned that you wouldn't like, try to escape again once you believed there was a barrier to stop you. It'll be fine, trust me. Come on.'

Bess hesitated just long enough to grab her book and put it in her pocket before hitching up her robe and following her rescuer out of the window and down the ivy.

After five minutes of creating a commotion at the gates, Charlie and Rhona were beginning to tire of their efforts and wondered if they were even being noticed.

'I could try to climb them,' suggested Charlie peering upwards.

'What about the spikes?' asked Rhona with concern, 'they look really sharp.'

'Don't worry,' he answered, 'I'm not going over, just acting up a bit.'

'Okay...'

He found his first foothold and started to pull himself up.

'Hang on Charlie,' warned Rhona, 'I think I can see someone coming.'

He hopped down and squinted through the bars of the gate, scrutinising the darkness.

'You're right,' he said as he perceived a tall shadowy form slowly approaching from the gloom in the distance. As the figure neared it became clear that it was preceded by a pack of six snarling Rottweilers, straining at their leashes and seemingly eager to reach the intruders before their master.

'I'm very glad of the gate now,' commented Charlie drily.

'Too right,' agreed Rhona, eyes fixed on the slavering sharp toothed jaws.

As they approached, the dogs became more excited, growling and barking with increased enthusiasm. A sweat broke out on Charlie's skin, his heart fluttering as he tried to control his fear. He had never been a huge fan of dogs, having been attacked by his aunt's German Shepherd when he was a child, so it was all he could do to stop himself from running away as fast as he could. Nevertheless, he held his ground, hopeful that the gates would remain shut.

Once the human figure was within ten metres of the entrance, Rhona recognised him.

'You!' she exclaimed, 'I knew you'd have something to do with this!'

'Indeed,' stated Nasaru neutrally.

'Who the hell is he?' asked Charlie.

'He's the guy who came into the office with the drawings,' replied Rhona.

'Let my wife go you bastard!' Charlie demanded angrily, finally faced with a target for his pent up rage. He grabbed the bars and scowled at the man, but leapt back quickly as the dogs lunged toward him.

'You know what you have to do to enable that to happen,' stated Nasaru categorically. 'Now, I suggest that you leave before I open the gates and allow my eager companions to investigate your presence. As you can see they are most anxious to meet you.'

As he lifted a large key to the lock they backed away slightly.

'We could just call the police, now that we know where you are,' warned Rachel hesitantly.

'That would be *extremely* inadvisable,' cautioned Nasaru sternly, with the tone of a court judge cautioning a wayward youth. 'My masters would be forced to take more....uncongenial action, which I am sure you *and* Mrs. MacKay would rather avoid. The um...constabulary would be ineffective but their involvement would irritate their lordships. Do not underestimate their power or their desperation. Make the casket as soon as possible and all will be well.' He put the key in the lock and began to turn it. 'Still here?' he asked.

'Okay, okay, we're going,' said Rhona as she and Charlie turned and walked quickly away, hoping that they had done enough to distract the overseers within.

'Shit,' gasped Charlie, as the sound of the dogs' frenzied barking receded, 'I've never been so scared in my life.'

'Me neither,' said Rhona. 'God, I hope Rowan and Bess are alright. I hope we managed to divert their attention long enough.'

Charlie's anxiety on Bess's behalf had reached a maximum. He now regretted their pathetic attempts and agonised over what effect it may have had. What had they been thinking? They had no chance against these ruthless villains. The only way he could prevent himself from curling up in a ball and sobbing pitifully was to keep walking, faster and faster, and hope desperately that Bess and Rowan had escaped and were waiting for them back at the car.

As they approached in the darkness, he couldn't see anyone waiting there and started whispering, 'where are they....where are they....where the hell are they,' over and over until they were within five meters of where the car skulked in the shadows. Suddenly a side door flew open and Bess burst out. She flung herself into Charlie's arms and they clung to each other in a fierce embrace, both sobbing with relief whilst repeating each other's names over and over. As they started frantically smothering one another with kisses, they were quickly interrupted by Rhona and Rowan tugging insistently on their arms.

'*Come on,*' they pleaded insistently.

'They'll be after us soon,' urged Rowan, 'I can't block them out for long.'

They piled hastily into the car and Rhona drove off at great speed.

'Where are we going?' she asked, 'we can't hide can we? They'll be able to find us anywhere.'

'To the police station,' suggested Charlie, 'now that Bess is free - thanks to Rowan,' here he leant forwards and planted a kiss on her cheek, 'they can offer us protection. If those guys turn up, they can just arrest them on the spot.'

Staring into the flames of the blazing coal fire in the hearth, Belum Asar and Belum Ki were looking feeble and weary. They exchanged thoughts as they slowly stroked their beards.

'*The network has only provided us with one vessel,*' thought Asar, '*they said the demand is too high at the moment and the supply of suitable candidates...somewhat limited.*'

'*But we know,*' added Ki, '*that they have their own, more sinister uses for the young, pure and gifted.*'

'*Nevertheless, it makes it all the more important to get the casket completed.*'

'*We shall have to send them a stronger message, to persuade them to undertake the task as soon as possible...we are getting weaker by the day...*'

'*Should we harm the woman? Send a body part perhaps? These simple people are so stubborn and obstinate that I feel they may only respond if we send a more serious and obvious signal of our intentions.*'

'Yes, but perhaps just a finger to start with – we are not barbarians after all – and maybe a more powerful incursion into their dreams....'

'....yes, we could plant an auto-suggestive coercion impulse...'

'....so they feel compelled to obey...'

'Wait!' interrupted Asar, *'Nasaru is coming, something is wrong!'*

Their servant entered the room but didn't need to speak as they saw in his mind how he had gone to check their captive after the encounter at the gate only to discover her gone.

'How could this be?' gasped Ki aloud, looking aghast at his twin.

'They must have a psychic accomplice...' muttered Asar.

'...who affected a rescue under our noses whilst we were distracted...'

'How could we have been so stupid?'

'We have become complacent brother.'

'And a little weaker.... the time is nearing.'

'But surely we should have detected the mind of the rescuer?'

'Unless whoever it was has reached an advanced stage of training....'

'But we are unaware of anyone like that around here...'

'Surely we would have felt them before....'

'....unless they are stronger than us......'

'No! That cannot be. There are so few of us left. It would have been noticed by the Network....they would have told us...'

'We had better contact them....'

'...to let them know....'

'....or to discover if they already knew...'

'Meanwhile...Nasaru,' said Asar, 'contact our local agents to put the frighteners on these miscreants – just intimidation mind you, no *serious* injuries....yet. And recapture the hostage, maybe even take this psychic one as an extra vessel, as an insurance policy....'

'Yes, in fact brother, that is a brilliant idea,' commented Ki, knotting and unknotting his fingers in a moment of excitement, 'we do not need the network to supply another vessel – we can take another ourselves and then there will be one for each of us should they be required.'

'And we shall concentrate on some psychic retribution,' added Asar icily, 'we cannot let them get away with this.'

CHAPTER FOURTEEN.

Andor followed as quickly as he could, trying to keep up as Sonilla ran crashing blindly through the dark wood, oblivious to her damaged knee, heedless of the branches and brambles that caught and scratched at her clothes, hair and skin. Eventually she tripped and slammed headlong into the forest floor. She gasped, winded, and then fought for breath until a long and wretched moan issued from deep inside her, followed by crying so intense it convulsed her body with a continual shuddering. She scarcely noticed as Andor lay down beside her and wrapped her in his arms. There was nothing he could say. Desolation suffused every part of her body and mind. She felt she couldn't cry hard enough to fully express or expunge her wretchedness and grief. She opened her soul and tried to force her misery out from every fibre of her spirit, but still there was no end to her anguish and despair.

After a time her sobs gradually subsided into whimpers as her entire being depleted itself of energy, until at last she lay still and finally slept, totally exhausted and encircled by her lover's arms. Andor remained alert, horrified by the experience and dumbfounded by the significance of what they had witnessed. So, this is what it meant to "meet the Ancestors". To be put to death and burned to ashes. All the training, the honing of the mind and the will, the discipline and the skills cultivated, were for nothing. He found this incomprehensible in the context of their teachings, which had compassion and service to others at their heart. Yet there was the evidence, in a gruesome, smouldering mound of embers in a clearing.

Since early childhood, they had been fed such enthralling stories about joining the old ones and how they would live with them in wondrous, bright cities and be part of helping to bring a new age of enlightenment to the world through the re-evolution of human consciousness. Now it seemed to involve brutality and death....but they would be unable to help from beyond the grave. It had always been emphasised that violence was an unacceptable form of behaviour for *anyone*. The death of the body was seen as a stage on a path, your awareness a form of energy that would reunite with the one mind until a new body needed it. He tried to recall the lesson from one year ago, but it had been on the morning after he and Sonilla had first made love and he had been too distracted by his feelings of joy and ecstasy. Ur Rammel had been explaining how the essence of sentience survived the transition between states of being, but memory was a function of the organic brain, so in effect it was lost by consciousness between incarnations until one reached the highest levels of transcendence and learned how to imprint this information in the energy field. At this point the persona became an "Ancestor" and when they reincarnated all memories were retained so that the wisdom of the ancients could be taught and passed on until the day when the few had become the multitude who would lead the utopian transformation of The Resurgence. In a few, rare cases enough traces of the DNA of the pre-Shift wisdom could come together in the same individual through coincidences of genetics and breeding to advance an untrained mind to a higher stage. If these were found at a young enough age they could be guided and selected to be chosen to work with the Ancestors, whilst others remained anonymous often unaware of the latent abilities they held. No one knew how many of the latter there were, but the suspicion was that the closer humankind came to the dawn of the next age, the more there would be and the more obvious it would become. The younger Andor's mind had now wandered to the much more interesting recollections of Sonilla's soft smooth skin, the smell of her hair, the intensity of the emotions, the sensations of their physical joining....

A sudden jolt shot through his mind, bringing him back to the present, where he lay uncomfortably on the hard, damp, twig strewn ground in the misty chill of dawn. He realised he must have dropped off to sleep and in his exhausted state let his defences down because the probe he had felt was somebody searching for them. Imagining the fate that may await them after the discovery that they had made, he realised they would have to move swiftly. He quickly recreated his mind's defences and gently shook Sonilla awake. Her mind seemed numb and vacant.

'Come on,' he whispered, 'they're searching for us, we've got to go.'

Reluctantly she allowed herself to be dragged to her feet and led stumbling passively through the undergrowth. Andor didn't know how far away their pursuers were, but he felt sure he had been detected when he had let his guard down. Sonilla was in a trance, seemingly anaesthetized to all sensation, both physical and mental, but submissively she permitted him to take her hand and guide her, limping slightly, through the forest.

The rising sun and the exercise of walking soon warmed the damp chill from his bones as he followed a deer path downhill. Sonilla remained silent, unreadable and docile, but Andor found some inner strength to continue, knowing that one of them must remain steadfast, although not having been outside the castle grounds since he arrived at the age of six he had no idea where he was leading them nor what to do when they got there. He just knew that they had to get as far as they could as rapidly as possible and avoid those who sought them so that they would not share the fate that had befallen Lendi. He had no doubt that having escaped and witnessed what they did, their punishment would be severe. The lies they had been told covered up an appalling truth that the foundation would want suppressed at all costs. The students had been told very little of the outside world, apart from warnings of the dangers it held for the untrained, but Andor liked to think that most of the people out here would be of good enough will to offer them help or shelter.

Sonilla felt remote and detached from Andor and her surroundings. She had exhausted her emotions to the point of total depletion but still teetered on the edge of a pit of grief, misery and fear, which she held off with a fragile screen of deadening exhaustion. She was vaguely aware of Andor and the forest, but as a distant and dispassionate observer. To consciously engage with her emotions or reality would have precipitated a realisation of the recent horrors that she didn't have the strength to face. She yielded compliantly to being escorted by Andor but she would have been equally indifferent if he had laid her on the ground or dragged her through a stream. She continued only because he pulled her hand and urged her on, but if he'd let go and walked away she would have stopped, impassive and sunk to the ground.

As the day wore on it became clear that the forest through which they were fleeing was immense and it could be a long time before they encountered anyone else. By mid afternoon, Andor was ravenous but could see nothing on or amongst the trees that he could recognise as food. There had been spring greens in the foundation's gardens, hen's eggs, fresh goats' milk, stored grain and nuts but he could see nothing resembling any of these. They quenched their thirst at a stream; Sonilla was still passive and dumb but she drank all the same. He knew that she must also be tired and hungry. They would have to stop soon and find somewhere to rest and shelter overnight. He had detected no further hint of any pursuers, so believing his defensive walls to have been effective he deemed it safe to do so. Although he realised that they had no choice either, their exhaustion would stop them regardless. He dared to hope that the search had been abandoned, but did not allow himself the complacency of believing it. Wearily cresting the next rise, Andor smelled a hint of wood smoke in the air. This could mean habitation of some sort and hopefully food. Eager with hunger he checked the direction of the breeze and followed the scent down the slope. Sonilla resisted, making faint noises of distress. Realising that the smell had reminded her of their awful discovery, he spent a few moments sending her pacifying thoughts and softly reassuring her before gently urging her onwards.

Soon the trees thinned and eventually yielded to an area of small neat fields with a mixture of various crops and livestock. Just beyond was the source of the smoke, an aged timber farmhouse with a weathered grey shingle roof huddled against a copse with an untidy cluster of ramshackle wooden outbuildings scattered around it as if they had been shaken off like clods of soil from the roots of an unearthed plant. They skirted the fences, keeping to the edge of the woods and gradually made their way towards the homestead, but as they approached the yard a large white hound began barking, suddenly aware of their presence. Andor stopped, unsure whether or not to proceed. In his limited experience of the world, he had never before encountered a dog. Just then a middle-aged, weatherworn woman emerged from the house to investigate, a look of mild curiosity on her ruddy features. When she saw them standing uncertainly by the gate, she hushed the dog and with a wiry arm that emerged from the short sleeve of her dress like an overlong turtle's neck, beckoned them to approach. Cautiously Andor led Sonilla towards the house. The woman's greeting was strange, 'Dzień dobry', to him some meaningless utterance followed by, from the intonation, what sounded like a question, but totally unintelligible. This had not been amongst the languages he had been taught, so Andor was perplexed. Why hadn't they been educated in the language of the country around them? He guessed that it was so that they couldn't communicate effectively if they chanced to escape. It had been explained to the students that communication through the mind involved two levels of meaning. One involved the language that the person was thinking in and the other was on an emotional plane that imparted the intention and associated feelings, thus allowing a deeper level of understanding than speech alone. Thus, even if he could not understand fully, he could reach the woman's mind and discern an amiable intention, a kindness in her heart and an offer of hospitality. He advanced slowly, smiling a greeting and said 'Good evening, do you have any food?' The woman was taken aback and seemed also not to understand his speech, so he mimed eating to communicate their needs. She smiled as his meaning dawned on her and indicated that they should wait on a rustic wooden bench by the door. As they sat completely exhausted on the rough-sawn plank she disappeared back inside the house. The seat was placed to catch the setting sun, so the wall behind them was warm to lean on. The dog approached silently, wagging its tail, head lowered and Andor regarded it with curiosity. The only other animals he had come across were the ducks, chickens and goats at the school, although he had seen pictures of a wide range of creatures. The minds of the poultry were primitive; the goats had some intelligence but were strange, whereas this dog displayed a more emotional disposition. It accepted them as friends now that its owner had welcomed them and derived pleasure from Andor's touch when he stroked its head.

The woman reappeared with some bread, cheese and dried fruit on a wooden platter, which she handed to Andor before sitting next to him. He managed to induce Sonilla to take some food and start eating it before hungrily devouring his own share. Whilst they ate their host gabbled her strange words, 'Uwielbiam tu siadać i obserwować zachód słońca.....' which Andor discerned to be amiable small talk. When they had finished she poured them glasses of water from an earthenware jug, nattering the whole time.

Suddenly the dog barked and ran to greet a burly man in his mid-fifties. His weather creased face showed surprise at the presence of visitors, although as he approached to greet them he smiled amicably and said, 'Witajcie nieznajomi. Rzadko się zdarza, aby ktoś tu zawitał w dzisiejszych czasach.' Andor nodded and smiled mutely so the farmer looked to his wife who seemed to be explaining what little she knew. He looked back to the young couple in their soiled and torn robes with a quizzical expression and then shrugged and bade them enter the house. The doorway led straight into a low-ceilinged kitchen warmed by an old range and with a large pine table in the centre. Their hosts sat them down and produced a bottle and some small glasses, chatting to each other and their guests. Looking at the display of framed photographs on the dresser and the quantity of empty seats around the table, Andor deduced that the couple had raised a large family here. Their slight air of sadness and the eagerness of their welcome indicated that they now lived alone and were disheartened by the emptiness of their home. The farmer poured them each a measure of clear liquid from the bottle and raised his own drink in a toast. Andor swallowed a mouthful before realising the potency of the fiery liquid. He gasped and spluttered as it burned his throat, much to the amusement of his hosts who had downed their own shots in a single gulp. He easily managed to stop Sonilla before she drank her own as she seemed to still require inducing to commence any action. Alcohol was unknown to the young people of his school, so he was shocked by the impact of the liquor. As soon as his mouth and throat had recovered his head began to swim, his thoughts became fuzzy and he felt very sleepy as his fatigue caught up with him.

Becoming aware of his state, their hostess poured him some water and mimed sleep. Andor nodded gratefully and gulped the whole glassful as she disappeared from the room to return a moment later with two old but clean woollen blankets. Lifting his hand in thanks to the farmer, he helped Sonilla to her feet and escorted her from the room following the woman back outside. She guided them to a barn, opened the door and pointed towards a wooden ladder that led to the hayloft before bidding them 'Kolorowych snów' and closing the door behind them. Andor's attention was momentarily sidetracked by the machine that occupied the space in front of them. It had wheels, as did the barrows and carts that he was familiar with at the castle, but the two at the rear, behind the seat, were enormous whilst those at the front were much smaller. The painted metal contraption between seemed to have only a seat to carry a single person, with a wheel to hold on to and an enormous mechanism in front of that, yet no visible way to carry anything else. He reached out to stroke the cold, hard, smooth green surface of the body, which bore glass lamps at the front, and then touched the deeply ridged back wheels marvelling at their strange texture. Despite his mystification and curiosity, the unpleasant sharp greasy smell emanating from the device combined with his tiredness forced him to move on towards their sleeping place.

He helped Sonilla up the ladder and settled her gently in the dry, sweet-scented hay. His concern was growing at her vacant expression and now he considered they were temporarily safe he decided to try to get through to her. As he whispered her name he tentatively probed her mind but found she was still walled off from him. He was unaccustomed to dealing with grief, both his own and that of others but nevertheless sensed that he would have to tread carefully. He knew that her pain would have to be faced, experienced and accepted before she could come to terms with it and move on, but it would take time and patience. He would stay by her and support her. He felt that their love for each other would help them both through the process. He spoke again, gently calling her name. Getting no reaction, he repeated it slightly louder, over and over again until he perceived a slight flicker in her eyes. Then he carefully ventured to touch her mind again.

In the desolate grey fog of her numbed psyche, Sonilla gradually became conscious of an insistent stimulus, patiently encouraging a response. She fought against the force that was trying to drag her through the barriers, reluctant to contend with further pain, but she was too weak; it took too much energy to maintain her defences. Her awareness returned in harsh waves, like layers of skin peeled off to expose the raw nerves beneath. Suddenly, she saw Lendi before her, her chest ripped open with a massive gaping wound, exposing a mess of flesh, ribs and blood. A hooded figure triumphantly held her still beating heart high in the air before her still convulsing body was thrown on to the huge fire by two others in blue cowled robes. Sonilla screamed. Every cell in her body screamed, every part of her mind. The sum of all her anguish erupted with the full force of her unconstrained emotions. Andor had fallen back in alarm, but now he cradled and rocked her as she sobbed and moaned unremittingly.

A minute later, the barn door below flew open as the farmer and his wife ran in to investigate. Their unintelligible questions subsided as they shone a bright torch up and saw the young couple. Andor made gestures of appeasement as Sonilla continued to cling to him, continually weeping. Looking suspiciously around the dark barn as if for malevolent intruders, the farmer finally retreated, frowning and muttering under his breath, followed closely by his flustered-looking wife who peered back guardedly over her shoulder as she left.

Utterly heartbroken, Sonilla cried herself to sleep in Andor's arms. He knew that, although unsettling, this was part of the process she must undergo, so he resolved to keep control of his own emotions in order that he could give her all the support she needed.

There were clattering and scraping noises below which pulled them from their sleep in the first light of dawn. Andor crawled to the edge of the hayloft and peered down to see the farmer attending to his wheeled machine.

'Good morning,' said Andor blearily.

The man looked up and raised a hand distractedly as he returned his attention to his task. A moment later he looked back and, adopting an enquiring expression, indicated past Andor, voicing the query, 'jak się miewa twoja żona?' in his strange language. The young man discerned his meaning and beckoned to Sonilla.

'Sit up,' he said gently, 'show him you are alright.'

Slowly, she half rose from the hay and gave a cursory wave to the man below. He smiled and seemingly satisfied, he returned to his tinkering while humming tunelessly under his breath. His sounds were accompanied by the peppering of steady rain on the shingled roof.

'How do you feel,' asked Andor, still judging it best to use spoken words to minimise their risk of discovery, although he could easily tell without telepathy that the bout of hysteria in the night had released a blockage that would now enable her to at least begin to function in some way.

She looked at him briefly with a doleful expression that pained him to see, and then dropped her eyes. 'Devastated,' she said simply, 'heartbroken, dismal, wretched.....' she continued mournfully, her eyes brimming with tears once more. He reached out and took her hand, squeezing it gently. At least she was communicating now, he thought thankfully.

'I just can't believe that Lendi is gone.....and in such a horrible way.' In short, gasping phrases she described her vision of her sister's murder as Andor listened with growing horror. Suddenly he found that could no longer suppress his own feelings. It was as if, now that Sonilla had allowed herself to articulate her emotions he could let go of his strained grip on his anchor and flow in the river of grief that had been tugging at him too. For five minutes they cried in each other's arms before Andor took a deep breath and wiped his face with the sleeve of his robe. Sonilla followed suit.

'It is difficult to believe that this could be the fate of the "Select",' muttered Andor hoarsely, 'All the training....the years of guidance in what seemed to be a loving environment.....I just don't understand.' Sonilla nodded mutely and they sat in silence for a while.

'My knee hurts,' she observed, as if only just noticing it for the first time and pulled up the hem of her robe to expose the swollen and bruised joint.

'You walked a long way on it when it should have been rested,' Andor remarked. He had elected to specialise in the healing arts as part of his education, so now concentrated his attention on the injury. He laid his hands on her knee and tried to discern the extent of the damage. The techniques he had learned enabled him to channel and boost the body's own curative processes, directing its influence at the targeted area and facilitating a much-accelerated response to the tissue repair process. 'Close your eyes and concentrate on your breath,' he instructed her as he did the same. 'Now visualise streams of energy coming from the sky entering your crown chakra and the flow of energy coming from the earth entering your root chakra. See this energy as a glowing pink light focussing on your knee, soothing the inflammation, reducing the swelling and repairing the damaged tissues.'

After several minutes, they both opened their eyes simultaneously. 'Thanks, that's much better,' said Sonilla with a weak smile. As they became aware once more of the noises below them, the farmer opened the large barn doors thus causing a protracted jarring creak, accompanied by a gradual increase in light. A few seconds of shuffling feet was followed by a sudden whirring whine that echoed around the building, a mechanical croak and then a loud throbbing, rattling roar. The noise rose in volume and pitch as they scrambled to the edge of the platform to witness the farmer riding the strange carriage out through the barn's opening and into the morning light. A dark grey cloud had erupted spluttering from a vertical pipe on the contraption leaving a trail of noxious gasses poisoning the air. Gagging and coughing, the young couple scrambled hastily down the rickety ladder and staggered outside gasping for fresh air. Although sheets of chill rain soaked them in seconds, still they stood watching as the machine ambled away across the field until its chugging was swallowed by the sound of the deluge. Andor became aware of the farmer's wife observing them from the door of the house. Strangely, she seemed amused by their plight yet he sensed that she meant them no harm. Beckoning them to follow she disappeared within. Entering the kitchen, they saw two plates heaped with generous portions of scrambled eggs and thin slices of cooked meat; glasses of fresh milk stood alongside and a pile of buttered homemade bread graced the centre of the table. As the woman took their robes to dry by the range, which radiated comforting warmth, they sat in their damp undergarments shivering and feeling slightly embarrassed. They ate hungrily, grateful for the hearty breakfast whilst the woman bustled around the room busying herself with the morning's tasks. When they had finished eating, they helped clear and wash the dishes.

Keen to get further from any potential pursuit, Andor began taking their clothes down. They were still wet and filthy. The woman came over and inspected them critically, shaking her head and saying, 'powinniście wyrzucić te stare rzeczy!' before disappearing up the steep staircase that rose from the corner of the room.

'I think she's finding us something else to wear,' commented Andor standing next to Sonilla, where with their backs to the stove, their underwear steamed in the heat.

'I'll be thankful for that,' she remarked crossing her arms over her breasts, attempting to warm them beneath the clammy linen vest. 'Those clothes are not well suited to travel,' she added poking the moist robes where they now sagged heavily on the back of a kitchen chair.

Their hostess returned with an armful of garments, evidently gleaned from the leavings of her now departed offspring. Handing them each a selection, which included dry underclothes, she bade them go upstairs to change in privacy.

Five minutes later they returned feeling more comfortable in simple, practical country garb of cotton, linen and wool. The colours had long faded, but the cloth still had plenty of serviceable use.

Since they arrived, Andor had sensed that the woman bore some chronic pain in the hunched shoulders of her sinewy frame, which she stoically endured through each of her long days, so he felt moved to help ease her suffering. He gestured towards a chair, implying that she should sit at the table, but she seemed confused and merely frowned, shrugging her shoulders. He repeated his signal and she complied uncertainly as Sonilla gently guided her into a seat whilst sending calming thoughts to relax her and then sat opposite, managing to smile some reassurance in spite of her devastated soul. Andor placed his hands on their hostess' shoulders, shut his eyes and extended his awareness. Two minutes later the lines of tension eased out of the woman's face and a euphoric smile appeared. She opened her eyes and got slowly to her feet with an expression of radiant glee transforming her features. Overcome with gratitude, she grasped Andor's hands and kissed them repeatedly, and then danced around the table the kitchen table, laughing like a child. They were a little taken aback by her reaction, accustomed as they were to tension relieving techniques and endorphin stimulus in daily use at the foundation.

Eager to be on their way they made ready to depart, bowing their gratitude for the kind hospitality, but the woman held up her hand to stop them, muttering, 'czekajcie, czekajcie!' then hastily dashed out of the room, returning a moment later carrying two oilskin coats and a well worn canvas knapsack. Evidently Andor's attentions had stimulated even more goodwill than they had already received because she hurried to the larder and proceeded to pack the bag with provisions. When she could no longer cram in any more, she handed it over and bade them farewell, kissing them affectionately on both cheeks. They walked from the farm hand in hand down the muddy wheel-rutted track accompanied by the friendly dog that seemed inured to the relentless downpour. Looking back they saw the woman standing in her doorway and waved one final time. As they reached the edge of the forest, the dog sat and watched as they receded from view following the curve of the trail into the trees.

#

The carriage clock ticked on the mantelpiece and the cat purred contentedly on the rug in front of the woodstove, but they were virtually unaware of either. Charlie and Bess sat cuddled together on the sofa in their small cosy living room where they clung to each other like koalas determined never to be parted again. Rhona and Rowan sat quietly in nearby armchairs slowly sipping comforting mugs of cocoa, exhausted both mentally and physically but glad to be safe.

The police, whilst sympathetic, did not deem it necessary to provide them with sanctuary at the station. They did send a squad car to investigate the mansion where Bess was held captive, but when they couldn't find it from the directions provided, they offered two night duty officers could keep watch outside the cottage and then asked that the next day they could be shown the way.

'I think we need to do more to like, protect ourselves and stuff,' suggested Rowan, breaking the silence, 'I don't want to like, worry you or anything but the police will *so* not be able to match a full on psychic assault, which is what we should totally expect from these guys I reckon.'

'What do you suggest?' asked Rhona.

'Well, they'll probably attack when we're at our most vulnerable, like when we're asleep or something. So we should take it turns to stay awake and try and like, block them you know and if we feel anything weird, wake the others. Actually it's probably best to do it in pairs.'

'You'll have to teach us,' said Charlie simply, 'we don't know how to do any of that stuff.'

'Yeah well, I wouldn't have a clue where to start if it wasn't for that book that Bess nicked...'

'*Liberated*,' interjected Bess with mock indignation.

'Whatever...anyway I don't know how much use it'll be but we've got to try.'

'We don't have much choice do we?' said Charlie.

'Nope.'

'Let's hope that tomorrow when we show them that house the police will be able to lock the bastards up and we'll be left in peace,' said Rhona.

'Well there's no guarantee that locking them up will help,' observed Bess doubtfully, 'with minds as powerful as theirs.' She had now disentangled herself from Charlie, though continued to hold his hand. 'How about it Rowan?' she asked, looking at the young woman, 'If it was you, do you think you could pick the locks with your mind? Slip past the guards unnoticed?'

'Dunno,' she replied dully. The happiness after the success of the rescue seemed to have been short-lived as they came to realise that they wouldn't be completely safe until their adversaries were securely incarcerated. She also could still not shake off the feelings of dread that kept resurfacing with the knowledge she had unintentionally killed and this stark truth stifled any desire to explore her abilities further.

'Why don't you have a go?' proposed Charlie, 'just to see if it can be done.'

'Um, I don't think I really want to, you know?' she replied, feeling discomfited by both the request *and* her wish to refuse it. 'It kind of opens up unknown territory and stuff and I don't really know if I'm like ready to go there yet...'

'Actually Ro, it might help *us* understand our enemies a bit more,' ventured Rhona, 'you know to see what they're capable of, what we might have to face if the police don't catch them...'

'If the police don't catch them we're fucked....'

'Rowan!' Her aunt was not so shocked at the language as the attitude. She believed that in dire circumstances one needed to keep a positive attitude to maintain morale.

'Well, we are,' asserted her niece stubbornly, 'what hope have we got of fighting off those powerful like, *warlock* guys?'

'We *do* have some hope Ro,' Bess assured her, 'Don't forget you just rescued me from under their noses!'

'I may have like, totally slipped through their net while their guard was down,' countered Rowan, 'but I don't reckon we'd stand a chance of doing anything like that again now they know there's someone amongst us with some metal powers and stuff.'

'You're probably stronger than you think are,' maintained Bess, 'and I've a suspicion that they are weakening. Remember what this casket is to them - the longer they don't have it the weaker they get. Please just indulge our curiosity by trying to open my petty cash box and then we'll try out some of those exercises in the book. What do you say?'

Rowan heaved a sigh and looked around at the others. She realised that she was probably their only hope. If she could help them learn the basics they might be able to protect themselves if they managed to present a united front.

'Okay,' she said wearily.

Charlie left the room and returned with a small metal box. 'It's just got the petty cash in it from Bess' yoga class,' he said, 'it's just a simple lock I expect.'

He handed it to Rowan who took it gingerly, as if she expected it to suddenly spring open like a jack-in-the-box. She tried the lid to check that it was locked, but it wouldn't open. 'Okay, here goes,' she said uncertainly. Closing her eyes, she concentrated on focusing her awareness on the locking mechanism. Her first perceptions came slowly but gradually resolved themselves into something sharp, oily and hard.....an arrangement of levers and springs....yes, it was quite simple really.....she just had to shift a couple of small components to release the mechanism. She concentrated her will on moving first one and then the other....there was a clicking noise. She opened her eyes and handed the box back to Charlie. He took it and lifted the lid.

'Wow!' he said, stunned despite the increasing evidence of psychic phenomena he had witnessed recently. 'That's pretty impressive.'

'Well, I'm not sure about that,' she said modestly, 'but it does mean that if I can do it, so can they.'

'That's amazing Rowan,' commented Bess, 'the things you could do....'

Rhona looked at her niece in wonder. 'Does Roz know any of this?' she asked.

'Yeah probably, sort of, but she totally won't admit it or anything,' said Rowan sullenly, reminded of an old irritation, 'whenever I've tried she's always like refused to talk about it? She's just scared really, you know, afraid of what *she* could do....' She looked at the floor.

Rhona was startled, 'What? Rosalind?' The look of astonishment on her face showed that she had no idea that her sister was capable such things.

'She can't do anything though,' continued Rowan quietly, "cos she's like, totally suppressed it for so long and denies it anyway...but I reckon I got most of it from my dad anyway.'

'Martin? Psychic?' blurted Rhona, shocked once again. After a brief pause Rowan nodded and a look of understanding dawned on Rhona's face.

'Oh my God!' she gasped in realisation, 'that would explain a lot.... he must have known Rosalind had a bloke in Milan...that's why he went off with Alison!'

'Yes, *alright*,' said Rowan cringing, 'that's enough of my sordid family history for now. Let's get on with teaching you guys how to like, totally fight off a brain bashing and stuff, shall we?'

'Right,' agreed Rhona levelly, 'Bess, it's time to get out that book.'

After Charlie and Bess had gone to bed, Rhona and Rowan sat together in awkward silence. Sitting half reclined with her legs curled up, Rhona was trying to absorb the impact of the continuing revelations. Her niece, who had shared her home, been her almost constant companion for the last twelve years could read her thoughts, move things with her mind and had even killed someone, albeit unintentionally, just by thinking it. She was wondering what secret or private thoughts she may have unwittingly shared and whether or not she should be embarrassed or worried by that. She looked up. Rowan bit her lower lip feeling guilty at keeping her secret for so long from the one person in the world who was closest to her. So much seemed to have happened since Nasaru had entered Rhona's office just a few weeks ago that there hadn't been time to absorb it and the events of the last forty-eight hours had strained their fraught nerves still further. Rowan felt that she was the one who should break the silence, being somewhat at an advantage in her ability to discern the thoughts of her aunt.

'I'm sorry,' she began simply, but as she took a breath to continue, Rhona interjected.

'What for?' she asked, lost in her own deliberations.

'You know, the telepathy and stuff....' muttered Rowan weakly.

'Don't be,' her aunt responded. 'Don't be sorry for what you are... *who* you are.'

'No, I'm not. I meant I'm sorry for like, keeping it a secret and stuff. I know that must be hurtful. But mum always made me feel so totally ashamed of it, as if it was like a curse or something? If ever she caught an inkling she was like, "Devil child, stop that! It's evil!" and often as not she'd smack me too.'

'Well, if you can read my mind, you'll know that there's no need to apologise,' Rhona affirmed. 'I was just feeling embarrassed in case I'd ever had any weird private thoughts....or the times I've had a guy stay over...and guilty because of the self harming and I know there have been times that I've had negative thoughts about you and I don't want you to think badly about me or to think that I think badly about you....' as she continued tears welled up in her eyes and began trickling down her cheeks, '...because you're the person I most love in the whole world and I couldn't bear to lose you just because you thought that I thought that...oh, I don't know..' She put her face in her hands as if by hiding it she could conceal her discomposure. This uncharacteristic display of emotion didn't surprise Rowan as much as it would anyone else who was acquainted with Rhona, because *no one* knew her aunt as Rowan did. She was well aware that part of the reason Rhona usually appeared to be so level headed was an attempt to provide a steady, supportive framework for her niece's upbringing, but she also knew that it wasn't easy to always be the strong one and regretted now that she hadn't made it easier for her. She went over to join her aunt on the settee and took her in her arms.

'Don't worry, I'm still here aren't I?' she said reassuringly as Rhona hugged her back. 'You haven't scared me off yet. And anyway, it's not like I can read every thought you ever have. It's not like that. Usually, I try to like, totally screen myself because just having my own crazy thoughts is enough for my poor brain to handle without having to deal with other peoples' too – I'd go completely loopy. And I *so* appreciate like, everything you've done for me and stuff, bringing me up as your own while mum's been gallivanting off across Europe getting rich and getting laid while you do all the hard work. It's always been you who stayed and I totally know what you've sacrificed to be there for me. You have *so* been like my rock – someone strong to cling to through the storms of like, all my emotions and stuff. It is *so* not easy being telepathic with no one to guide you, but over the years I've taught myself to like, control it thanks to the stable home you've provided. I've not been scrutinising your private thoughts or anything though, so you don't have to worry about that. But I can totally sense emotions and stuff so I know that you love me and I love you too – like nobody else in the world...' Her voice broke here as she joined Rhona in weeping and they cuddled in silence for a while, comforting each other.

'I haven't cried like this in years,' murmured Rhona in a soft voice, muffled by Rowan's shoulder.

'But you needed to though.'

They began sniffing, the tears causing their noses to run. Simultaneously, they broke the embrace and reached for the box of tissues on the table. They both giggled girlishly, now completely at ease with each other.

'See, you're telepathic too!' declared Rowan, smiling. Rhona blew her nose quietly, mindful of their friends sleeping in the room above but Rowan just had to wipe hers, suddenly remembering the doctor's advice against blowing it for a few weeks. She frowned at what had appeared in the tissue. Was there no end to the seepage of puss?

'That's not telepathy though is it?' said Rhona, 'It often happens that when two people are close to each other they have the same thoughts sometimes – look at Bess and Charlie, they do it all the time.'

'But that *is* a kind of telepathy,' asserted Rowan. 'How else could it happen except by thought transference? The minds are totally linked in some way and they're more likely to be the closer they are to each other, like emotionally, and the longer they've been close too.'

'Of course.... you're right!' agreed Rhona with sudden realisation. 'I'd forgotten about me and Roz – being twins it happens to us a lot when we're together and even sometimes when we're apart, but I'm so used to it that it just seems normal. I've never given it a second thought.'

'But it is normal! Don't you see – all humans have some kind of telepathic ability, some more than others, it's just that they totally don't realise it or accept it because it doesn't like, fit into their belief system. In the twenty first century everyone's minds are like, so caught up in recession and telly and celebrities and stuff and anyway those kind of ideas are totally relegated into the realm of wacko New Age hippie claptrap.'

'Hang on a minute,' said Rhona thoughtfully, 'How come Rosalind's so gifted, even if she's stifled it, whereas I'm not? Wouldn't we both be similar in that, being identical in everything else?'

'Well, your personalities are *so* definitely not identical!' stated Rowan categorically. 'And you probably *are* just as gifted but never really had the chance to like, realise it or trigger it or explore or anything.'

'So are you saying that I could learn to do what you do?'

'Totally.'

Rhona looked astonished and shook her head slowly. 'I don't know if I'd want to though.... not after what you've told me...'

'It's a mixed blessing, right enough.'

Rhona thought a little longer. 'What about these dreams then?' she asked. 'First Charlie, then Bess, then me and Roz..... is that something to do with telepathy? And why's it happening now? Have you had any weird dreams?'

'Like I said before, I *always* get weird dreams,' replied Rowan wryly, 'I totally thought everyone did. But as to why you lot are getting them now, I can only like guess that it's got something to do with those old guys and their weird box and stuff? I never knew people could like, influence other people's dreams, but if *they* can do it....'

'But who are those guys anyway? Did your....*brainwaves* pick up anything about them?'

'Not really, except they seem to be like really powerful. If they can make a force around that house that Bess couldn't get through....'

'But you got through and got her out from right under their noses. Does that mean you're really powerful too?'

'I don't know....I don't think so....I mean, you and Charlie were like distracting them and stuff....and they've got complacent and weak. They just couldn't imagine that anybody would be able to like sneak past their defences, so they didn't even look. But I don't reckon they'll be fooled so easily again. I've got this like, uneasy feeling that they might try something else....I can totally sense a kind of like, *desperation* or something.'

Rhona agreed. 'Yes, that's what I felt in my dream too. What do you think they'll do? What do you think they *can* do? What do you think *we* should do?'

'I'm not sure,' replied Rowan nervously, 'but I don't reckon those two policemen outside will be very effective in like, stopping them or anything....'

\#

As they walked, the rain diminished to form a light misty drizzle, though the trees still shed heavy droplets concentrated from the moist atmosphere. Apart from the soft pattering of the water on the needle-covered ground, the forest was eerily silent, despite it being spring. The air was heavy with the sappy tang of pine and musty earth. Sonilla now seemed more able to engage in conversation, but still Andor began hesitantly, sensitive to the nature of her present temperament.

'It seems that people in the outside world can be very kind,' he said slowly, 'that couple were really generous.'

'Yes,' agreed Sonilla quietly.

'We will need to think about what to do next, where to go,' he ventured, 'and we still need to keep our thoughts guarded, in case we are still being pursued.'

'I am finding it difficult to think of....the future,' she told him in a faltering voice, 'I am still in shock....I just can't....' She took a deep breath before continuing. 'Do you think we would have been noticed, back at the clearing, when we....' She had to stop, biting her bottom lip, as if saying again might make it worse.

'Probably,' he replied evenly, 'We were both so stunned....and horrified, that we must have let our guard down. Later in the forest I'm sure I felt a questing mind.....and they must have noticed our absence too by now. I don't know how long they will follow. The wrongness of what they are doing....they may go to great lengths to keep it hidden from the outside world. We may be safer amongst the unguarded minds of the common people - their uncontrolled thoughts may shield us - so we should probably find a settlement of some kind.' He paused, trying to consider what options may be open to them in an unfamiliar society, but could not see through the uncertainties. 'But I'm not sure what we'll do after that. What do you think?'

'Oh, I don't know Andor,' she responded dejectedly, 'I just can't imagine life without Lendi....it's like a part of my soul has been ripped out.' Once more, her breath caught and her eyes flooded with tears. Andor took her hand in his and squeezed it sympathetically but knew it would give little comfort. He could think of things to say, things he had been taught about the psychology of loss, grief and bereavement and the recovery from them, but it was too early for those things and he felt disinclined to offer useless platitudes.

'Let's just take one day at a time,' he said and they walked on in silence, hand in hand.

They saw no one else all day although they passed several small farms and a forester's cottage that sat away from the dirt road, each served by their own private tracks. The woodland gradually thinned and became increasingly patchy as it was supplanted by more agricultural incursions. Finally, exhausted from their prolonged brisk pace the runaways took shelter in an old stone barn. They were becoming chilled by their dampening clothes, the donated waterproofs succumbing to the deficiencies of age. There were no other buildings nearby so they judged it a relatively safe place to stay for the night. The heavy, rotting doors seemed almost rooted to the ground, hanging crookedly from corroded hinges. Nevertheless, they managed to squeeze their slim young frames through the gap between them to gain entry to the surprisingly dry interior. They could just make out a few broken farm implements slouching against the back wall, a crooked heap of rusting paint tins and several worn tyres of various sizes. A rough wooden ladder led to a hayloft above so Andor climbed up to assess its suitability as a sleeping place. There was still a pile of hay remaining on the platform and even a discarded blanket, possibly abandoned by a previous wayfarer. They strung up a rope, which they had found amongst the discarded detritus below, stripped off their wet clothes and hung them up to dry. Using the blanket to alleviate the worst of the scratchiness, they made themselves a nest on and beneath the hay. Huddled together for warmth and comfort, they ate some of their supplies.

'This stuff is really itchy,' complained Andor between mouthfuls, referring to the stalks poking at his naked skin through the threadbare wrap, 'I don't know if I can sleep like this.' He wriggled and squirmed, trying to get more comfortable.

'Ow! Mind your elbows!' hissed Sonilla, crossing her arms to protect her breasts from his bony limbs. 'Anyway, you can use your mind to over-ride the nerve stimuli – you know, like we learned in fourth year.'

'Oh yes, I had forgotten about that – it's so long since I've been uncomfortable. I hope our clothes are dry by the morning.'

'I hope it has stopped raining by then, otherwise we'll just get wet all over again.'

'Well, at least it's warm and dry in here. Let's get some sleep.'

They woke to the sound of tweeting and fluttering wings. On a rafter in the roof above, a swallow's nest brimmed with yellow gaping mouths competing for the serving of insects being delivered in the beak of the parent bird. Relieved of its compact bundle, the diligent provider sped off to catch the next helping. Andor yawned and rubbed his eyes. Feeling slightly cold, his sleep had been fitful and he kept waking up from unsettling dreams of being chased through the forest. He stretched and then reached out to feel their clothes. Although no longer soaking, they were still damp so it was with a certain reluctance that they dragged the clammy, clinging material over their warm dry skin.

'We'll warm up once we get moving,' stated Andor confidently after a hasty breakfast, 'At least it has stopped raining now.'

In fact, once they noticed the low beams of the bright morning sun piercing the gaps in the barn's rickety doors, their spirits lifted considerably. Emerging into the bright warm morning, they had to pause and squint momentarily to allow their eyes to adjust to the dazzling light.

All at once they became aware of several hooded figures spread out in a wide semicircle in front of them, blocking all routes of escape. Behind the group were two glossy black vehicles, doors open as if hastily alighted. Sensing immediate danger adrenaline rushed into their systems and they turned to dash back into their shelter. Abruptly, they were compelled to stop, seized by the powerful force of their pursuers' unified minds. Caught unawares by a combined attack their inadequate defences were unable to protect them and they slumped helplessly to the ground as they involuntarily relinquished control of their bodies. En Nergal's thoughts pierced their awareness with a harsh reprimand, castigating them for their foolhardy behaviour. They would have to be taken back to the castle and kept in confinement until it was their own time to meet the Ancestors. Sonilla's mind reeled in terror as she realised the implications of the message but then anger surged through her as she recalled that these were the people responsible for Lendi's unspeakable fate. Focussing her rage and reaching out to link minds with Andor she battered furiously at the power constraining her. He added his own efforts to the fight, but their attempts were ineffectual. Their juvenile skills whilst advanced for their age, were undisciplined by the surge of raw emotions and proved no match for the combined might of seven masters.

En Nergal's voice once more filled their minds.

You are wasting your efforts, he asserted as the group moved forwards gradually to encircle them, *you do not have a hope with your puny struggling.*

The truth of the statement could not be disputed so the young couple abandoned their efforts and yielded compliantly. Exhausted and enfeebled, they allowed themselves to be lifted to their feet and shuffled docilely to one of the awaiting vehicles, utterly dejected. As Sonilla sat next to Andor in the back of the car, the doors were slammed and locked. Andor felt the stirring of his earliest memory...of a similar experience when he was a small child...something about the feel of the seats...the acrid smell. The strangeness of the unfamiliar technology barely penetrated Sonilla's subdued perception although she was dimly aware of the peculiar and intense odour of off-gassing from the new vinyl covering the seats. Unexpectedly, her sense of smell seemed to become supersensitive, filling her awareness and almost overwhelming her. She rapidly became nauseous and dizzy and then began to panic as she realised she was trapped in a sealed chamber with the airborne toxins. She frantically scrabbled at the door, searching for the opening mechanism and then started pounding on the window, becoming hysterical. Suddenly, she screamed as a searing arrow of white-hot fire pierced her head and then everything went black as she lost consciousness.

CHAPTER FIFTEEN.

It was bitterly cold and tiny grains of dust-like snow were needled into his face by the harsh icy wind. Unprepared for the rapidly changing climate, his clothes offered inadequate protection against the increasingly severe conditions. He stood on a long curving pier built of finely wrought white stone, which stood in stark contrast to the dark choppy sea that slapped noisily at the walls and matched the colour of the iron grey sky. Inshore, huge rocky mountains encased in snow and ice loomed like the shattered ruins of a crashed moon.

Charlie was supervising the loading of an ornate jewelled and gilded casket by two men whose inappropriate footwear was slipping on the frozen surface. Urging greater care in the handling of the precious load, he led them to the heavy wooden dockside crane where a lifting cradle had been prepared. Several large ships were moored in the harbour, sleek handsome sailing vessels with tall masts, each with a pair of huge outriggers and all being loaded with crates, bundles and barrels. Many hundreds of people were gathering at the waterfront, streaming from the nearby city, milling in confusion as they prepared to board the ships in a mass evacuation. The graceful pinnacles of the capital would soon look down upon frozen canals, empty squares, dead gardens and a deserted landscape. The colourful cloaks of the emigrants appeared muted, eclipsed by the grim sky, the drifting snow and their apprehensive expressions. Charlie could sense the shared regret and great sadness with which the residents were leaving their land, their fear of an uncertain future, but they knew it had to be so. The climate had cooled so much that the crops would no longer grow. Incredibly they had escaped most of the immediate and catastrophic effects of The Shift, as their continent was the furthest from the impact, losing only a quarter of the population but since then the summers had got shorter and cooler as the winters longer, colder and darker. The astronomers told them that their land was still moving even further south and there was no option left but to evacuate. The people were uneasy, nervous of the change, the journey and what may yet come to pass. They felt unhappy at the division of their community between different settlements but at the same time resolute and united in their purpose, determined to succeed despite the odds.

'Careful with that!' he cautioned as the bearers tried unsteadily to load their burden into the lifting cradle. 'The Belums will be needing it soon. As he spoke he looked up and saw the elderly twins watching from the ship's rail and his heart leapt into his mouth in unwarranted fright, the brothers being well known for their benevolence. But then he noticed their intense glares, which seemed filled with uncharacteristic malice. As their eyes bored into him pain grew in his head until it became so unbearable that it felt as if his brain would rupture. He screamed and sat bolt upright in bed. Although his head still hurt he had stopped screaming, but could still hear it piercing his mind. He held his head in his hands as he disentangled himself from the dream. The screaming continued. It was Bess. He shook her awake and she broke into sobs, holding her head and moaning.

'Oh God!' she cried, 'It hurts so much, oh God, oh God!'

The door burst open and Rowan rushed in with Rhona on her heels. Rowan held Bess' head between her hands for a few moments until she quietened and then did the same for Charlie. At her touch, he felt his pain rapidly dissipate, leaving him panting and sweaty.

'Thanks,' he gasped. 'What was that? How did you stop it?'

'That was an attack by those old guys,' she told him, 'and it's like just a case of giving the right signals to the nerves you know – both to cause it and to cure it.'

'Bastards,' muttered Bess looking shaken. 'Is there any way we can prevent...'

Just then they heard a crash of breaking glass followed by a whoosh and a roaring noise gradually increasing in volume. The accompanying crackle of flames soon alerted them to the fire. Bess and Charlie leapt naked from the bed, donned hastily grabbed dressing gowns and they all rushed downstairs to see smoke and flames erupting from the lounge.

Rhona stopped aghast. 'We were just in there!' she yelled in alarm. Ever practical yet thoughtless in her haste, she leant in towards the blaze, grabbed the door and slammed it shut. Bess & Rowan frantically patted her now flaming hair, their speedy action extinguishing it in seconds.

'Quick, let's get out,' pleaded Charlie urgently, pushing them before him, 'there's nothing we can do!'

They ran out of the house into the front garden where they were confronted by four burly men holding baseball bats. The thugs moved slowly forwards but then suddenly stopped and collapsed lifelessly to the ground. Charlie, Bess and Rhona all looked horror-struck at Rowan who had her hands raised in front of her, palms forwards.

'They're not dead!' she blurted hastily. 'I wouldn't do that again! They're just like, *stunned*, you know? I just sort of did it....kind of without thinking, but I knew it wouldn't kill them though, honestly!' She looked at them beseechingly, begging them to believe her. 'I wouldn't.....'

'It's alright, I believe you...,' Rhona started.

'Yeah, well it might not last long,' Rowan added hurriedly, 'we'd better get out of here.'

'Wait!' cried Bess, 'Water for Rhona's head, quick!' She dragged her friend to the garden tap and made her kneel whilst she splashed her still-smoking hair with cold water. 'It will stop your scalp blistering!' she stressed as Rhona complained.

'But my scalp didn't get burnt!' she insisted, 'Just my hair. I'm fine, let's go!'

Although baffled and shocked, the situation demanded action, so the others followed to her Beetle. In the police car parked next to it Bess could see the two officers slumped forwards.

'Are they...'

'No, just unconscious,' Rowan assured them. 'And it wasn't me! It was those thugs. Come on, let's go, we can phone the fire brigade and ambulance from the car.'

They piled in and Rhona started the engine. Just before slamming the door, Rowan paused and stared intently at the ruffians' car. There was a sudden bang as one of the tyres burst.

'That should slow them down a bit,' she said.

They sped out on to the road as Bess dialled 999.

'You seem to be getting a bit, er...accustomed to this aren't you?' said Charlie turning in his seat to regard Rowan thoughtfully.

'What, the dangerous lifestyle?'

'No all the psychic stuff – you're doing it more and more. Is there anything you can't do?'

'Yes, of course. It's just that I don't need to like hide it from you guys anymore and the totally desperate circumstances kind of call for it, you know? And I'm still learning – *I* don't even know everything I can ....'

'Where are we going?' interrupted Rhona.

'Back to the police station I guess,' said Charlie looking back at his burning home. 'They'll have to shelter us now.'

'Look, about those guys back there,' said Rowan, 'I didn't know I could do that and I didn't like doing it either – I just sort of panicked 'cos there didn't seem to be anything else we could do. We couldn't just stand there and get clubbed could we? I know it's like, really scary for you to see and to know I can do it, but it's *so* scary for me too. It seems I've got more power and stuff than I realised and I am totally going to have to learn to like, control it....'

'Don't worry, Ro,' said Bess, 'we know you were just trying to protect us back there, well succeeding actually, and we appreciate it. And you helped me escape, which I'm really grateful for too. As you said, the circumstances have become desperate and call for desperate measures....we none of us know what to do.'

Twenty minutes later they reached the police station, where the duty officer recognised them from the day before.

'I'm surprised to see you lot,' he greeted them sternly with a humourless grimace, 'after all the trouble you've put us to.'

'What?' said Bess, as taken aback as the others. 'What do you mean?'

'Ah, you're the "kidnapped" one aren't you madam? The one your friends "rescued" from the non-existent house in the middle of nowhere that took up four hours our officers' valuable time to not find.' He rocked back on his heels and seemed rather pleased at their discomfort. Before they had a chance to respond, he continued. 'Then you assault the two officers we sent to "guard" you, rendering them senseless and then torched your own house, putting them in further danger...not to mention leaving the scene of the crime...'

'This is outrageous!' protested Charlie indignantly. 'You can't be serious, we...'

'I suppose you're going to tell me that those alleged "kidnappers" attacked your home?' said the man raising a sceptical eyebrow.

'Well yes actually,' said Bess stonily, 'they threw a petrol bomb through the window and when we tried to escape there were four huge thugs confronting us with baseball bats.'

'And you....disarmed them?' the sergeant suggested dubiously.

'Yes, Rowan here...' indicated Charlie before he realised what he was saying and then seeing the man's appraisal of the teenager, stammered to a halt and cleared his throat uncertainly. 'Hang on,' he added suspiciously, 'how do you know what just happened? We came straight here.'

'One of our patrol cars happened to be in the area. They were alerted by the ambulance after you called *them*. When they arrived there was no sign of anyone else but two dazed and confused constables with splitting headaches.'

The four companions stood nonplussed, unsure how to make their story more plausible.

'There must have been footprints,' ventured Rhona hopefully. 'Four heavy men must have left footprints and tyre tracks from their car.'

'Well, apart from the fact that it's pitch black at this ungodly hour,' said the sergeant, seeming to blame them for the time of night and adding the darkness to their list of offences, 'there has been an ambulance, paramedics, a fire engine, a fire crew and another police vehicle at the scene. There is a lot of water, lots of footprints and lots of tyre tracks...'

'Oh,' said Charlie.

'You see, so far we've only got your word to go on,' said the officer as if this was highly questionable.

'But why would we want to burn our own house down?' asked Bess in exasperation. 'It's ridiculous.'

'Insurance?' he suggested.

'What?' exclaimed Charlie becoming increasingly irate. 'That's stupid, it doesn't make sense at all. The insurance would only be enough to buy another house – why would we do that?'

'Well, it was an *old* house wasn't it?' posed the man knowingly, raising his eyebrows, 'probably had a leaky roof...bit of subsidence, damp, rotten windows... too costly to repair?'

'Look, can we see someone else?' Rhona put forward, trying to control herself. Inside she felt like slapping him. 'Shouldn't we be talking to your superior officer - a detective or something?'

'All gone home I'm afraid,' he said haughtily and obviously relishing in their frustration, 'just a skeleton staff at this hour. I suggest you spend what little is left of the night in our um.....*guest* rooms. I'm sure that in the morning my *superiors* will be eager to interview you at great length.'

#

As she slowly regained consciousness, so the throbbing of Sonilla's head magnified, exacerbated by the lurching of the world into which she was waking. She opened her eyes but immediately had to squint, dazzled by the sun flashing between the trees as the car sped through the forest on the uneven road. The noises of the engine, the rumbling of the tyres on the rough surface and the air rushing through the open windows seemed to fill the parts of her mind not already hurting. She sat up slowly, disoriented by the movement and the saturation of her senses. She noticed Andor next to her, his face blanched by pain as he too rose gingerly into an upright position.

'Sorry about that,' said a familiar voice from the driver's seat, 'I had to knock everyone out in order to rescue you. If I'd warned you to shield yourselves, the others would also have been alerted. The pain will soon subside.'

Sonilla gawped stupidly at Thu Salamu, totally bewildered. So much had happened in the last two days that she felt unable to fathom this continuing kaleidoscope of experiences. Andor found his voice first.

'What's happening?' he asked in a weak voice. 'Where are the others?....Wait...are you helping us?... Why?'

'Right now,' she replied evenly, 'we are fleeing those who would do you harm. The others, hopefully, should be at least an hour behind us if they were similarly affected by my strike and they will be even further behind once they run out of fuel, which should be fairly soon as I managed to siphon most of it out of their tank....' The two young fugitives looked at each other in confusion, failing to understand the additional details for their pursuers' delay. 'As to why I'm helping you,' continued Salamu matter-of-factly, 'the quick answer is that I disapprove of what they are and have been doing to The Select and to the foundation they have infiltrated. The full story is much more complicated and will have to wait. For now, if you will just sit back and try to relax I've got to concentrate on driving on this awful road. And keep your minds closed and quiet too.'

For the next hour they sat silently holding hands and glad that the open windows let in enough fresh air to eliminate the worst of the dreadful odours of the car's interior. The unfamiliar surroundings passed by so rapidly that they remained in a condition of detached neutrality, feeling relatively safe for the first time since their escape, yet overwhelmed by all that had happened. The extensively forested hills seemed unbroken for many miles, but as the landscape settled into more gentle undulations they glimpsed an occasional homestead or hamlet surrounded by small fields.

Eventually their former teacher pulled over announcing that it would now be safe to stop briefly to stretch their cramped limbs. They stepped out of the vehicle on unsteady legs, gratefully inhaling the fresh air and thankful to be standing in the spring's gentle sunshine. As they had become more accustomed to the strangeness of their means of transport, so the recent events had risen once more to the front of their thoughts. They were still in a deep state of emotional shock, but had reached the point where they needed to start to understand. Everything they had been taught had been thrown into doubt; their entire world had changed irreversibly and the people who were responsible for their upbringing, guidance and emotional support seemed now to have been planning to do them harm.

Thu Salamu discerned their discomfort and fragile state of mind and sought to reassure them. 'Don't worry,' she said, 'I'll look after you now. There is a safe place I can take you.'

'Please tell us what's happening,' begged Sonilla, looking at her desperately, 'They killed Lendi instead of sending her to the ancestors and now we're being chased into an unknown world by people who taught us about love and trust.'

'Do not believe that your carers knew what was going on,' she urged, 'All but En Nergal and his inner circle were genuine in their guidance and teachings, unaware of the true purpose of what he and his accomplices outside the foundation were doing.'

'True purpose?' asked Andor huskily, 'What do you mean?'

'Well, you were certainly all being groomed to meet the Ancestors, just as has long been the way,' Salamu told them grimly, 'but unfortunately control of the foundation fell into the hands of En Nergal ten years ago. He has been extremely clever and devious at keeping his activities hidden, but we have recently discovered that he is a leading member of a nefarious and powerful faction of misguided fanatics, calling themselves "The Everlords", also known as "The Network" who are convinced that the best way to send trained acolytes to join the Ancestors is to literally dispatch them to the realm of the departed, in some imagined netherworld from which they can bestow favour on their living followers.'

Tears were streaming down Sonilla's face again, struck by another aspect of her sister's awful demise. 'But what about Lendi?' she implored desperately, 'What has happened to her soul? Did they send her spirit somewhere dreadful? Has she wasted her life? And where are the Ancestors? Are they just dead souls? Why can't they do anything to stop it? Do they even exist?'

Andor put his arms around her, even though he knew it would offer little comfort and she wept against his shoulder, inconsolable. Nothing could bring Lendi back and the cruel way in which her life ended only made it worse. He too wanted answers.

'Well?' he said dourly, 'Can you answer any of this?'

'Yes, but it's neither quick nor easy,' replied Thu Salamu hesitantly, 'and it will take some time, so I think we had best get back in the car and move on. I'll explain as well as I can whilst we travel.' They did as she said and were soon moving quickly through another area of dense forest. 'I'll need to put this all into context, so excuse me if I cover old ground,' she began. 'As you know, tens of thousands of years ago much of the human race reached amazing heights of intellectual, psychic and telepathic achievement. Following The Shift, the immense loss of life, suffering and deprivation drove people to desperate measures just to stay alive. The elders who endured tried in vain to reach all the pockets of refugees and survivors to calm and guide them, but they were too few in number for such a task. Eventually they gathered as many as they could who still retained the ancient knowledge and built underground cities on each continent in which to live and work towards the re-evolution of enlightened human consciousness. It was from these small beginnings that the global network of foundations were engendered, to reach and train as many as possible to join the descendants of the "Ancestors" of this civilisation and help in the mission. This much you probably know. Unfortunately however, at the time of The Shift, the levels of trauma were such that many were driven insane, their minds warped by the collective suffering. Others were reduced to little more than apes in their behaviour and abilities. It was at this time that some, although they had retained their intelligence and psychic skills, were overwhelmed by their experiences and became unhinged in a tortuous psychosis that led them down an iniquitous path. They discovered that by using their powers they could control and dominate the people of the earth, primarily the inlanders who had not evolved so far, with fear, guilt and greed. Thus whilst one group strived to recreate the utopian civilization of former times, so the other sought to create disorder by instigating the spread of myths, legends and religions which divided and distracted the human race, leading to mistrust, unrest and war as they strove for dominance. Over the millennia, the lust for power fragmented the movement into squabbling factions leaving the chaos which reigns to this day.'

'But what about the Ancestors now?' asked Andor.

'And what about Lendi?' persisted Sonilla, 'will her consciousness survive?'

'Her spirit energy form will endure,' Thu Salamu assured her, 'and will be reincarnated into a new body at some point. It is possible, but unlikely, that she will retain any memory of this life. Certainly some of the most advanced individuals can do this, which is who the "Ancestors" are who are alive today – those who have managed to keep memories, personality and skills though the many incarnations since before the Shift. They are the keepers of the ancient wisdom. There are tools and techniques to facilitate this of course and in ancient times it was universally practiced by all. You, as The Select will learn these methods from the elders and thus start on the same road yourselves. You will also help in identifying other potential adepts in the outside population – to recruit young acolytes and to help those too old to attend the foundations but willing to be trained in the arts of the extended mind.'

'But didn't the Ancestors notice that The Select weren't reaching them?' enquired Andor.

'Yours is not the only foundation, Andor,' Samalu told him, 'there are many more scattered around the world, so it took some time before suspicions were aroused. I was sent to infiltrate your foundation to discover if our fears were true. However, the reality was even worse than we imagined. I only learned of the sacrifices when I followed you to the clearing. We had thought that the novices may have been used as vessels, which is bad enough, but never did we envision such a terrible crime.'

Andor noticed Sonilla shiver at this and took her hand. 'Who are the "we" of whom you speak?' he asked, 'are you one of the Ancestors?'

'Not yet in this lifetime, but I was one of The Select thirty years ago and I will unite with an Ancestor when the time is right. I serve them and our common purpose. Now that I have rescued you, I can take you to where you should have been going once you reached the age of growth, as long as we can outrun these villains - which I feel confident we can. Then I shall have to report what I have discovered so that we can reclaim your foundation for...'

'But where *are* the Ancestors, where are we going?' persisted Andor, wanting to know everything now that there was someone to ask. 'And what are these..."vessels"?'

'Well it's....' she began, but she didn't have a chance to finish because at that moment another vehicle came hurtling around the bend on the wrong side of the road. Thu Salamu swerved to avoid a collision, but the other car clipped the rear wing and sent them spinning out of control. They hit a tree broadside and were slammed against their doors.

#

'Coffee?' asked the young officer amicably, poking his head into the cell. 'Or would you prefer tea?'

After too few of hours of inadequate sleep, it took Charlie several seconds to regain the power of speech and several more to remember where he was. His brain felt clogged with cotton wool, but shaking his head didn't help. He squinted and then rubbed his eyes. He regarded the uniformed youth blankly and wondered how long the police had been recruiting such young lads to their ranks.

'Have you got anything herbal?' he heard Bess ask, 'I don't take caffeine.'

'Sorry ma'am,' the constable replied sheepishly, 'we're a bit wee to have all the trimmings at this station.'

'Just hot water then,' she mumbled.

'Coffee please,' said Rhona.

'Me too,' managed Charlie and Rowan together.

They were given their drinks in the interview room together with a passable breakfast, a carry-out from the café next-door. They sat morosely eating in silence, still dazed from the events of the night before. Charlie and Bess were desperate to get home, yet dreading the extent of the damage to their home. They had dedicated two years of hard work to renovating the cottage and spent the next ten lovingly embellishing it. Rhona was devastated at the scorching of her hair; she had been growing it for more than four years. The quarter of it that remained was frazzled and uneven.

'Ah there you are,' said a middle-aged officer as he strode confidently the room. He sounded to Charlie almost as if he suspected them of hiding. 'Inspector MacGregor sorry to keep you waiting the lads are just back from your house having had a better look around now that it's light and it seems that they discovered four baseball bats trodden into the mire that was once your lawn impossible to get fingerprints I'm afraid too much mud and water but there was also a fragment of tyre and a short section of tracks showing the passage of a vehicle driving with one bare wheel rim...' The man spoke without pausing for breath, as if he wanted to say as much as he could as quickly as possible before any chance of interruption. '..so it seems we have to give some credence to your story and that I must apologise for Sergeant Hendry's accusatory attitude last night he does get a little um *enthusiastic* at times but I *do* have a few questions for you if you don't mind just to help with our investigations you understand but it won't take long and I will have to ask you to stay in the area for the next few days in case we need to fill in any details...'

The structure of The Haven was not as badly damaged as they had feared. Rhona's swift thinking at shutting the door had contained the blaze significantly and luckily the fire engine was quick to arrive. Nevertheless, the living room was badly affected, the smoke damage was extensive and the stench of wet ashes and charred wood, combined with the floods of darkened water made the house uninhabitable for quite some time to come. They spent a few hours trying to clear up the worst of it until exhaustion and despondency drove them to give up and decamp to Rhona's place.

Their mood was subdued. Rowan had finally decided to reply to Jenny's text messages that had been enquiring as to where she'd disappeared to the last couple of days and why wasn't she answering. However, she just sat staring at the little screen not knowing what to say. Leaning on the kitchen table with both elbows, Rhona tugged gently at the scorched, uneven and ragged locks that remained of her once proud head of hair, her eyes fixed unseeing on the wall opposite. Bess had her head resting on Charlie's shoulder and he had his arm around her. Both looked careworn and tired. Finally Rowan just sent a brief message apologising for the lack of contact but telling her friend she was okay, just tired.

'What are we going to now?' Rowan asked the others quietly, looking up from her phone. She knew that they didn't have the answers in their heads, but she wanted them to think about it and stop dwelling on their misfortunes. Her question elicited a collective sigh from the other three, who all shrugged, shook their heads and pursed their lips as if their minds were one. She felt she had to do something to lift their moods. That or to just go out for a long walk on her own, but it didn't feel right to leave them.

'I know, let me cut your hair!' she suggested brightly, smiling at her aunt.

A look of dismay took hold of Rhona's features and she recoiled slightly as if she had been threatened. Then she relaxed and gave a wry smile as she realised the ridiculousness of her situation.

'Don't worry,' Rowan assured her, 'I can hardly make it much worse can I? Anyway, it will like give me something to do while you lot sit around sulking.'

Half an hour later Rhona surveyed herself critically in the mirror, unsure as to whether or not she approved of the "new look".

'I think it suits you,' said Bess, 'it's more balanced you know. Before you had more hair than head....now you look kind of...well, *sophisticated* I'd say.'

'Really?' asked Rhona doubtfully.

'Aye,' said Charlie, 'Bess is right. You *do* suit short hair. It will be a hell of a lot easier to look after too.'

Rowan was pleased with herself. 'Do you think I could start a new career as a hair-dresser then?' she asked jokingly.

'Well, I think I'll withhold judgement on that,' commented Rhona, 'but thanks anyway. It certainly looks better than when you started.'

They spent what was left of the evening practicing some more of the exercises from Bess' book with tentative guidance from Rowan. The women seemed to make a little progress, but Charlie couldn't get anywhere with it and became increasingly frustrated.

'Am I just thick or am I missing something here?' he asked in exasperation. 'How come you two can "sense" something and I'm just getting a headache.'

'Maybe you're trying too hard Charlie,' Rowan suggested, 'or it might be just like tuning in to the right frequency or something....like a radio or a T.V.'

They decided to call it a night and head off to bed, fairly sure that they would be safe now that they had successfully survived the attack they had been expecting.

Rowan browsed idly, half-heartedly perusing the scores of hats in the gloomy shop. It resembled a Victorian milliner's, with a counter and shelves of dark polished wood, but the goods on display were inconsistent with the period. Amongst the baffling array of headgear were multicoloured plastic designs, elaborate structures of thin-coiled metal and fragile looking glass tiaras. Absorbed by the curious nature of the shop's merchandise, she was startled when the salesman suddenly emerged from behind the curtain that concealed the back room. He was dressed in a grey suit and though elderly he stood upright, tall and bony, with soulless eyes seeming bulbous, magnified as they were by the thick lenses perched on his small thin nose.

'Can I be of assistance young lady?' he rasped in a papery voice that seemed to carry ancient dust from arid lungs. She was unaccustomed to being addressed as a "young lady", especially given her appearance and wondered if he was being sarcastic. Although his tortoise-like face was smiling, Rowan suddenly felt uneasy, imagining she sensed an undercurrent of malevolence behind his courteous manner. His mind was unreadable and she couldn't perceive any trace of emotion from him at all.

'No, I'm fine,' she declared hastily, wanting to be rid of him. 'Just looking,' she added as she turned away and moved quickly towards a display of feathery headdresses.

'Of course miss,' he allowed obsequiously, 'please take as long as you like.' Nonetheless, as she continued to browse he hovered three steps behind her causing her to feel somewhat edgy. She decided to leave, but as she turned found him blocking her way, holding out a strangely shaped helmet. It was made from a pale grey-brown material, the surface of which was both super-smooth and completely non-reflective, like a matt metal alloy. It was shaped to cover the whole head apart from the nose and mouth, but including the eyes.

'I think this is what you were looking for,' he stated gravely.

'I er..., no it's not. I don't want anything,' she said trying to sidestep the man. 'I'd like to go now please.'

'Just try this on first would you?' he suggested, proffering the helmet and moving to block her path, 'I think you'll find it functions very effectively. It really is for the best you know.'

Despite the mistrust she felt for the man Rowan was intrigued by the phrase "it functions very well" when applied to headgear. That momentary pause was enough. As she hesitated the man lifted the helmet and she found herself unexpectedly incapable of movement. He placed it over her head and clipped a chin clasp into place. All at once she felt claustrophobic, as if her senses were being constricted or squeezed somehow into a smaller space. Panic gripped her with the sudden sightlessness and she grasped the bottom of the helmet, trying unsuccessfully to tug it off. She pulled frantically at the fastening, but to no effect. Although she could breathe she felt almost asphyxiated, as if her encased brain was the organ allocated respiration. She gradually became dizzy and weaker, her struggles diminishing until she crumpled to the floor as the strength drained from her legs. Somebody tied her hands behind her back and she tried to protest, but found that her voice was weak. Her captor taped her mouth so that she could only breathe through her nose. Panting from the exertion of her fruitless struggle, her breathing became more laboured as fear tightened her throat and she became scared that she might suffocate if she could gulp air into her mouth soon. She was pulled roughly to her feet, lifted over a shoulder and carried down some steps. She was put back on her feet once again, man-handled out of the building and, she guessed by what she could hear through her muffled ears, into a van. A growing dread chilled her to the core, as it dawned on her that her dream had now blended seamlessly into reality. She reached out with her mind in an attempt to make sense of what was happening. There was nothing. Alarmed, she frantically strived to extend her awareness once more, but all she could detect were the blank walls trapping her mind. Fear was making her heart beat faster and heavier in her chest, seeming to increase the pressure with each pulse. She tried to calm down, to think clearly, to breathe more slowly and evenly. Somehow the helmet had suppressed the mental powers that were normally so much a part of her life. She felt blinded and isolated from the world, her neural receptors stifled. As she began to sink into the misery of her despair, her physical senses began to impinge on her consciousness, although she couldn't be sure exactly when she stopped dreaming and when real life rematerialized. She became dimly aware of the smell and touch of her surroundings, the roughness of the rope tied tightly around her wrists, the cold metal of the van floor on which she lay and the renewed pain where the helmet touched her incompletely healed face. Suddenly she heard the rumble of the engine starting and felt the vibrations as the vehicle began to move. She remained prone on the hard surface and surrendered helplessly to her fate.

After half an hour of discomfort in the juddering vehicle, Rowan was feeling feeble and decidedly queasy. Deprived of most of her senses she was particularly susceptible to the effects of the unpredictable motion. Worried that the nausea would cause her to vomit, she imagined choking on it as it filled her nose and she breathed it back in. Just when she thought she might sick, the van came to a brief halt and then continued more slowly, crunching along a gravel surface. Before long it shuddered to stop and the engine was turned off. The back doors opened and she heard the shuffling feet of her captors. She was pulled upright and the tape was ripped from her mouth.

'What's going on?' she demanded weakly, her anger lending no strength to her voice. 'Let me go you bastards!'

'Rowan?' said a woman's voice nearby. 'They got you too.'

'Bess!' exclaimed the girl, 'I thought I was on my own. Are you okay?'

'Slightly bruised and carsick, but not bad. You?'

'Same but they've put a helmet on me – it's closed off my mind.'

'Me too….but I thought I was dreaming.'

A gruff voice interrupted them.

'Come on you two,' it said and they felt themselves handled firmly out of the van.

Rowan's legs had become numb during the journey so she immediately started sinking to the ground, but strong hands under her arms pulled her upright again until she found the sensation and strength return. She could just discern dim light from the bottom edge of the helmet.

'And they put one of these on you too?' she asked Bess.

'Yes, I guess they thought my mind needed blocking too.'

Powerless to resist, they allowed themselves to be led up some steps and into a building.

'I think we're back at the mansion,' Bess observed quietly, 'it smells the same anyway.'

They were led through passages and down a staircase to a room where their bindings were untied before they were abandoned behind a locked door.

'At least they cut our ropes,' said Bess, rubbing her chaffed wrists in relief.

Rowan felt her way to a bed, sat heavily on it and held her helmeted head in her hands.

'I don't know how I'm going to cope with this,' she droned gloomily. 'I've never had my mind totally cut off from the world before. It's kind of like losing a sense or something….it *is* losing a sense, one I've always had. No, it's two senses actually with my eyes covered as well.'

'Let me see if I can get it off for you,' suggested Bess.

'I've tried, it's useless.'

'Well at least let me have a go,' she persisted, 'it might be easier for someone else.'

Five minutes later she had to admit defeat. 'Sorry Ro, you were right. I can't do it. I guess it would be stupid of them to use something that we could remove.'

Miserable and helpless, they resigned themselves to their circumstances.

CHAPTER SIXTEEN.

Nick was enjoying the empty roads through the forest, taking full advantage of the fact that he wouldn't have to pay for the wear and tear on the hire car.

'You will if you dent it,' Adam pointed out. 'We paid a deposit remember?'

'Slow *down* Nick!' pleaded Lynn with more than a trace of irritation in her tone. 'There might be someone coming round one of these bends.'

'I don't think that's very likely,' he countered, jovially dismissing her concern, 'we haven't seen a single vehicle since we turned off the main road two hours ago.' He was finding that the faster and more recklessly he drove, the less he felt the need for a cigarette; the excitement and the adrenaline it produced seemed to be a temporary, though adequate substitute that diminished his irritability.

'Come on Nick, ease up mate,' requested Adam whiningly, 'I'm getting carsick with all this lurching around corners and stuff. You don't want puke down your neck do you?'

'Okay, Killjoys, just one last bend.' As Nick wrenched the wheel over to the right, their vehicle careered around the curve on the wrong side of the road, the rear end snaking out of control.

'Jesus!' he exclaimed as he suddenly saw another car fast approaching from the other direction. The two drivers swerved to avoid each other. Nick slammed on the brakes and the wheels locked sending them skidding with a screech of tyres into the rear wing of the other vehicle. The car skidded round and shuddered to a halt facing the opposite direction.

Nick was gripping the wheel tightly, knuckles and face white, taking quick panting breaths as some extra adrenaline coursed through his veins.

'Everyone okay?' asked Lynn.

'We are, but I don't know about them,' said Adam gravely, indicating the other car where it lay bent against a tree just off the road.

'Oh, shit...,' sighed Nick heavily.

'You fucking idiot!' Lynn berated him. 'I told you to slow down. Oh god, we'd better go and check...'

She opened the door and started climbing out. 'Come on then!' she snapped brusquely. They all hurried over to the other vehicle, hearts pounding with apprehension. With shaking hands Adam and Nick each opened a door on the undamaged side.

'You alright?' asked Adam noticing the three occupants within. They were all conscious but looked shaken.

'Anyone hurt?' asked Nick fretfully, 'I'm really sorry....'

'I'm alright I think,' said the woman who had been driving. She turned to look at the passengers behind her. 'How about you two?'

'I'm okay, a little bruised perhaps,' said the young man, 'Sonilla?'

The young woman's face was white. She was sitting on the side of the vehicle that had impacted with the tree. As she opened her mouth to speak, a whimper of pain escaped. She screwed up her eyes and gritted her teeth. 'My arm...' she managed weakly, 'I think it's broken.'

'She is also in shock,' her companion observed. He leaned across to inspect her injury, but her arm was between her body and the door. 'Let's get her out of here and comfortable,' he suggested earnestly.

He carefully helped her from the car aided by Lynn who joined in with a confidence gained from regularly updating her first aid skills. They lowered Sonilla next to a tree and leant her against the trunk as the others gathered round in an anxious cluster. Adam felt very concerned but also a bit useless. He had no idea what to do in such situations, not that he'd ever before been in circumstances such as these. He noticed that the young couple were wearing old well-worn clothes that looked like they had been home made on a farm and the older woman wore a robe and a cloak as if from the middle ages.

'Let me have a look, I'm a qualified first-aider,' Lynn informed them. 'I can make a splint and a support bandage.'

'Thank you but that won't be necessary,' said the driver, 'Andor is well schooled in the healing arts. Let us give him some room.' Adam didn't recognise her strange accent, but it didn't sound Polish to him.

They obediently stood back as Andor placed his hands on Sonilla's arm.

'I don't think you'll be driving anywhere in that,' commented Lynn regretfully, indicating the wrecked car. 'Can we take you somewhere? Obviously the insurance on the hire car will cover your damages – it was all Nick's fault, driving like a complete tosser.' She gave him a filthy look and he averted his eyes, shamefacedly muttering apologies.

'Sonilla and Andor must get moving soon,' said the woman indicating the young couple, 'You will need to get them away from her as quickly as possible.'

'To a doctor? A hospital?' Lynn enquired. 'Where's the nearest town?'

'No. They must leave the country,' she replied evenly, 'they are being hunted by a criminal gang.'

'What about the police? Can't they go to the authorities?' proposed Nick.

'They have no identification, the "establishment" would not help,' replied the older woman, 'they would be of little use anyway.'

'But how are they going to get out of the country?' enquired Adam quietly, a little confused and still shaking from the shock of the accident.

'You will have to take them while I delay their pursuers,' she informed them simply.

'Whoa now! Hang on a minute,' said Nick, 'I know the accident was my fault and everything but...'

'There is no time to explain,' she interrupted, 'but you have no choice. Just bear in mind that this is a serious responsibility. Up until three days ago these young people had led a very sheltered life in a secluded institution with medieval technology. They have little knowledge or experience of the modern world. Now they are fleeing for their lives from desperate and ruthless killers.'

The gravity and perilousness of the circumstances that they were being told of added fear to the after-shock from the crash.

Adam was gob-smacked. 'Bloody hell,' he muttered, an awful dread growing in the pit of his stomach.

'Right, where do you want us to take them?' asked Lynn. Nick and Adam looked at her incredulously and then at each other. She seemed the least affected by the emotional impact of the accident and its consequences. Her tone suggested that she knew that there was a job to do and they just had to get on and do it without making a fuss. Although he had known her for five years now, Adam had not seen this side of her before; he admired her self control and resolve in this troublesome situation.

'I will give you an address in Amsterdam where Andor and Sonilla will be safe,' said the older woman. 'I'll meet them there as soon as I can.'

'Amsterdam!' exclaimed Nick in astonishment, shocked into forgetting his remorse. 'Fuck me, that must be getting on for a thousand miles! You *must* be kidding, surely. We've got to take this car back to Krakow.'

'Nick!' growled Lynn angrily. She had never been so cross with him and he was beginning to stretch her patience to the limit. He opened his mouth to speak again but her warning look silenced him. 'Just remember, this was totally, utterly and completely *all your fault*, yeah?' she scolded tartly and then turned back to the stranger. 'Of course we'll do it,' she said.

'Bloody hell,' commented Adam again. *Somehow*, he thought numbly, *I've lost command of my own life again.*

'But they could be on the run from the law,' protested Nick in a moaning voice. 'How do we know she's telling the truth? We could be aiding and abetting terrorists or something...'

Lynn rounded on him and fixed him with a steely glare. 'Look into your *fucking* heart Nick,' she said frostily, '*if* you still have one.'

He cringed visibly, seeming to shrink before her gaze and it was obvious that he had surrendered, although he remained silent, looking sheepishly at the ground like a schoolboy caught red handed in some forbidden and shameful act. Adam had never seen Lynn so angry before or Nick so humiliated and ashamed. He guessed that the impact of the accident was affecting them all differently. He felt the discomfort of everybody else's emotions and stood uncertainly to one side, awkward, embarrassed and indecisive. The situation was completely out of his control and he was certainly not going to make any suggestions. The easiest option was going to be just to do what he was told, probably by Lynn.

'It should only take you two or three days if you take short rests and share the driving,' the woman told them.

Andor helped Sonilla to her feet. She was looking much better and to Adam's surprise there was no improvised splint or sling on her arm.

'How are you?' Lynn asked her caringly, 'is your arm alright...I thought it was broken...'

'I am much improved thank you.' She replied softly. 'It was broken, but Andor fixed it. There will just be a little bruising.'

'But how...' began Lynn but she was interrupted.

'There is no time,' the older woman cut in, 'you must get moving immediately. There will be plenty of opportunity for explanations in the car – you have a long journey ahead of you.' She took a notebook from her pocket and quickly scribbled an address in it. She tore out the page and handed it to Lynn. Then she took out an envelope stuffed with money and handed over a fistful of notes. 'For the petrol,' she explained. They stood uncertainly for a moment. 'Go *now*,' she insisted urgently.

'But how will you stop these dangerous criminals on your own?' asked Lynn as they started towards the car.

'Don't worry, I'll be fine,' she answered, 'see you in Amsterdam.'

'But what if…?'

'Go!'

As Adam climbed into the back seat with their new passengers he looked back at her. Why did she seem familiar? He couldn't believe that he had met her before yet he had a niggling feeling that he recognised her from somewhere.

Nick sat in the front passenger seat with a hangdog expression, staring glumly at the road as Lynn drove in stony silence, still seething at his unwillingness to help after his stupidity that had led to the car crash. Adam decided to try to ease the atmosphere by engaging the newcomers in conversation.

'So, er…what's this weird school you went to?' he ventured hesitantly, 'some sort of Luddite thing is it? And how come you speak English, not Polish?'

'The foundation is one of many, established to train and guide the Select,' Andor told him, 'We do not break machines but have found that most modern technology represses the mind's abilities making people psychically lazy. We are taught several languages but it has only recently become apparent why the local one was omitted – so that if we escaped we could not communicate with the locals.'

'And who are these "Select"?'

'Those chosen to meet the Ancestors, with whom we will work towards the reawakening of the collective unconscious of human kind, what we call "The Resurgence". '

'Blimey,' commented Adam, 'that's a tall order.' After a moment he asked, 'how come you guys were "Select"'.

'We have certain abilities which have been lost by most of the human race over many millennia.'

'What kind of abilities?'

'Those of the extended mind – psychic skills, such as telepathy and telekinesis.'

'Far out...'

Nick turned round to face the other passengers and join in the conversation, but with a sulky and doubtful look on his face. 'What? You're telling us you can read our minds?' he asked sceptically, 'you're having us on, right?'

'On the contrary,' responded Andor patiently, 'most telepaths do not lie because untruths are too easily detected.'

'Yeah, well you would say that wouldn't you?' he commented dubiously, 'especially when you know we're not.'

'Leave off will you Nick,' pleaded Lynn wearily, 'you're becoming a right pain. I don't know what's got into you today. Just because you're like, too proud to admit your mistake and apologise...'

'It is okay Lynn,' interjected Andor good-naturedly, 'Nick believes that if we can read his mind then we may judge him harshly for the crash about which he feels more remorse than he is prepared to disclose, but a mixture of pride, self-doubt and fear are distorting his perspective.'

'I'm not scared!' asserted Nick, 'fear of what?'

'Fear that your belief system is being challenged. If you have to accept the existence of the higher senses of the extended mind then your long held down-to-earth "what you see is what you get" philosophy is called into question and you will find that you have no reference point in an unfamiliar reality.'

'Hah, that's just fucking psychobabble, that is,' Nick scoffed, but fell silent and thoughtful as he gradually came to realise that Andor was correct in his evaluation. This meant that either Andor was a very clever analyst or that he actually *could* see into his head. If this guy really was able to read his mind then he would have to be careful what he thought.....but how could he control that? Surely his thoughts came unbidden...they weren't in his conscious control were they?

'Don't worry Nick,' Andor reassured him amiably, 'we do not judge you. Do not feel that you have to guard your thoughts. We have no desire or intention to probe your mind and besides, you will find that with practice you can regulate and choose your thoughts – they *are* within your control.'

'Wow, this is amazing!' remarked Adam, 'I've read all about stuff like this – I always knew existed, but I've never met anyone who can do it!' During the revelations of this conversation he had temporarily forgotten that they had been told a violent gang was pursuing their passengers. He was so excited that his mind was filling with the ramifications of this newly confirmed knowledge.

'You will be further surprised to learn,' continued Andor, 'that in fact all people have these abilities dormant as a potential within them and with the correct training they can learn how to use them. Most never realise it, yet there are also a few who discover that they are born with these gifts and to varying degrees either teach themselves or suppress it, depending upon their disposition. Some of those with an inborn capacity are discovered, offered guidance in one of the foundations and if they excel they may become one of the Select.'

'You're saying, right,' interjected Lynn, briefly glancing in the mirror, 'that we can all learn to read minds, yeah?'

'Yes.'

'Wow,' commented Adam again. 'So this is why you were at that special school.' Andor nodded.

'How come you had to run away then?' continued Adam his head suddenly filling with questions, 'and who are these criminals who are after you and why are they out to get you anyway? And why haven't you got I.D.?'

'We have just learned from Thu Salamu that our foundation is now in the control of a misguided faction who have very different ideas about how it should run. Their motives are self-serving and entirely sinister.'

Lynn suddenly gasped as if punched in the stomach. 'Something totally bad happened didn't it?' she ventured uneasily. 'Something really terrible...something to do with Sonilla....that's why she's so quiet, yeah?'

'You are very perceptive Lynn,' he stated, 'I believe you may have an awakening psyche. You are right, something terrible has happened.' Haltingly, he told them the story of their last three days. He was unused to communicating without some projection of his feelings, so he continued to include that aspect, hoping that the strangers would detect some of it. When he recounted the discovery of Lendi's shoe, his voice broke with emotion but after a brief pause he swallowed it back and continued. Sonilla sobbed quietly throughout his account. When he had finished, the other three remained silent, appalled by what they had heard. All of them, even Nick, had tears running down their cheeks.

None of them had ever encountered anyone who had suffered so diabolically.

'Oh my god...' gasped Lynn finally.

Nick swallowed, wiped his eyes and then exhaled heavily. 'And so, when you were running for your lives...' he said hoarsely, '...and after all you've been through...I forced you off the road when I was being a complete and utter wanker. Fuck me, I am *so* sorry, I am so fucking sorry...*really*. Jesus, I am such a fucking useless cunt.' He buried his face in his hands.

'Oh Nick...' said Lynn softly.

Andor reached forwards and squeezed his shoulder. 'Well, you are helping us now,' he said, 'and for that we are grateful. The past cannot be undone.'

They travelled in silence for a while, gazing out of the window at the slowly changing, unknown landscape. Sonilla was still hurting deeply from her grief. She could not imagine how the pain would ever lessen. It was as if acid had eaten a hole through her heart, burning deeply into her soul, just as Lendi's body had burned away to her bones. She could feel nothing else but despair and was still only dimly aware of her surroundings. The unfamiliar sights they were passing had little impact on her, despite the fact that until three days ago she had not been outside the castle since she first arrived as a small child, nor seen any indication of any technology beyond that of the Middle Ages. She had known that she was to be parted from her sister for one year and she had accepted that she had to bear that, but now she knew that she would never see her again....it was a future she could not imagine. How could it be that someone could just *not exist* anymore, except in the memories of those who knew her? That someone could be snatched away without warning, with no time for proper farewells or preparation for this change of state of reality. Sonilla had been taught about death at the foundation, but it had always seemed like an abstract concept, except for when Thu Mayla died but she was incredibly old. She had never envisaged that it could happen to someone young, someone close to her, someone important to her, someone she loved so much that when she was taken away she could not abide the pain. She withdrew once more into a shell made from her sorrow and heartache.

'Man, you guys are really caught up in some heavy shit,' observed Nick, now taking a turn at driving. Despite his reservations, Lynn persuaded him to get back behind the wheel. She thought it was important not to leave it too long before driving again, otherwise it could take quite some time to regain his confidence. 'This teacher woman...Fu Samalu?' he asked, 'Is she really going to be able to fight off those bastards on her own? I mean, how many did you say there were? Six? Seven?'

'Thu Salamu. She is highly skilled,' replied Andor, 'but I doubt she can do much more than delay them. For how long I do not know, especially now that they are aware of her sympathies. I can't seek her mind without broadcasting our presence. We will just have to hope she succeeds for long enough for them to lose our trail. She will also be calling for aid but I do not know how long it will take to come.'

'But you can't keep running for ever, right?' said Lynn turning to look at him. 'Won't they find you eventually?'

'I expect we will be taken to one of the hidden cities of the Ancestors. I believe that is where Salamu will lead us after we meet again. I expect that we will be safe there.'

'Let's hope so,' said Adam. After a few seconds pause he looked at Andor and asked, 'What did you do back there, when we crashed? You know, to Sonilla's arm...it was broken right? Is that some kind of magic power you've got?'

'Not magic, no,' he replied candidly. 'Such a thing does not exist. Just because something is beyond your understanding, it does not mean that it is magic or divine intervention or any of the other mystic explanations that humans have dreamed up. It has not all been explained yet in a way that most people can understand and it may not have been proved within the narrow confines of the methods preferred by your modern scientists, but that does not mean it is unfounded. It is merely the application of techniques that manipulate, supplement, amplify and intensify some of the forces of nature. It is quite simply pure science; as is telepathy, telekinesis and the other aspects of the extended mind.' Andor paused but despite his youth spoke with the authoritative tone of an expert warming to his subject. 'Take Sonilla's fracture for example; first there is tissue damage and bleeding at the site of the fracture, then death of bone for a few millimetres back from the fracture line. This is followed by an acute inflammatory reaction with proliferation of cells under the periosteum, which is the fibrous covering over the bone. Following this is callus formation: the cell population changes to osteoblasts, cells that make bone, and osteoclasts, cells that absorb bone; the dead bone is mopped up and there is the appearance of woven bone. Then there is consolidation: lamellar bone, strong and permanent, replaces woven bone, weak and disorganised but forms quickly and the fracture is solidly united....'

'Whoa, hold on there mate,' interrupted Nick, 'you are going *way* too fast for me! I've read a lot of text books in my time, but I don't know your jargon and I usually go at my own pace you know?'

'I'm sorry Nick,' said Andor, 'I am used to learning by different methods. Usually this information is passed from mind to mind without the use of words, but your mind has not yet awakened so I had to speak it out loud.'

'Well, fuck it, you might as well carry on now – some of it might sink in – you never know.'

'Alright. The final part of the process is remodelling: the crude 'weld' is reshaped by a continuous process of alternating bone resorption and formation until it resembles the normal structure. These actions are controlled by a number of chemical enzymes that either promote or inhibit the activity of the bone remodelling cells, controlling the rate at which bone is made, destroyed or changed in shape. I merely used my own energies as a force to accelerate the production of these enzymes within Sonilla's body, thereby speeding up the healing process significantly.'

Adam was staring at him open mouthed. 'Er...*merely*?' he managed.

'Yes, once one has mastered the techniques and understands the application, it is not so difficult. Remember, I have had advanced training in the healing arts.'

'And you have to know all that technical stuff to make it work?' asked Adam.

'No, not really,' continued Andor earnestly. 'It can be done intuitively and anyone can learn the techniques with the correct training, although some, like myself, have more aptitude than others. It is just a case of using one's own energy field to manipulate another's, but I like to study the processes to understand the context in which I am working.'

Nick gave a low whistle. 'Jeez, you are totally fucking with my reality man,' he said, looking back over his shoulder. 'I can't deny what I've seen and felt today, but it ain't easy to take on board.'

'I think you'd better concentrate on driving, Nick,' advised Lynn, 'that's the reality you need to totally focus on right now, yeah?'

Nick ignored her saying, 'how come you know all this stuff when you know nothing about modern technology? Why did they teach that in this "foundation" of yours?'

'They focussed on what was most important to us,' Andor replied, 'and all of that was possible without the use or knowledge of modern technology. If anything the distraction caused by the influence of these things would have been detrimental to the training and expanding of our mental faculties.'

Lynn turned to ask Andor a question that had been on her own mind. 'You said earlier that you thought I might have an "awakening psyche", yeah? What does that mean? That I'm going to be telepathic too?'

Andor smiled. 'Yes, I believe so,' he told her. 'Although in most people these senses remain almost entirely dormant, in a few cases, such as yours, they can be awakened more easily or may even start to manifest without intervention.'

'Yeah! She's one of those!' exclaimed Adam excitedly. 'She has dreams about stuff that hasn't happened yet and paints it and can paint stuff from other people's dreams too....' Then another thought suddenly occurred to him, transforming his excitement into awe. 'Bloody hell.....' he said softly, 'Lynn, that picture you did of those two blonde women in the courtyard..... could that have been Sonilla and her sister? You said they were saying goodbye...'

Lynn glanced at Sonilla briefly. 'Oh my god...,' she gasped breathlessly, 'it *was* you!' She described the painting and the feelings she had associated with it; how she had felt that there was a great love between them and a terrible sadness at the parting. As she spoke, her throat became tighter as she experienced the emotions once again, but this time even more intensely because of what she now knew of Lendi. Tears welled from her eyes and flooded down her cheeks as she shared in Sonilla's despair. Sonilla was crying too, but reached out and tightly squeezed her hand. Lynn suddenly felt a strange mixture of appreciation, companionship and feminine affinity of a moment shared and bonded, which was both comforting and poignant at the same time.

Whilst sympathetic, Adam felt the need to divert his attention from the raw feelings that seemed to fill the car. He cleared his throat. 'So, what's this work you are going to do with the Ancestors then?' he asked Andor. 'Tell us about this "Resurgence" thing.'

'We are to be working towards helping the human race regain the higher level of consciousness they had attained before The Shift,' he replied.

'What shift?' Adam enquired. It seemed the more he heard, the more puzzled he became.

'The Shift that brought about the "Great Forgetting", the "Lessening".

'Er... the lessening of what?'

'Ah, I see now that you don't have any knowledge of history relating to that period. I shall have to explain that first.' He paused and closed his eyes briefly as if to access an internal file. 'Thirty thousand years ago the greatest civilisation ever to exist had reached the pinnacle of intellectual, cultural and psychic achievement. A global society of coastal cities were linked by maritime routes established by millennia of nautical excellence. The senses of the extended psyche were accepted as the normal state of the human mind....'

'Hang on,' interrupted Adam in wonder, 'are you talking about Atlantis?'

'The place you refer to as Atlantis was one of the cities, yes, but it was called "Ehursagkalamma" in the ancient tongue.'

Adam's thoughts were in turmoil; he was so full of questions he didn't know which one to ask first. For years he had been researching the evidence that such a place had existed, believing and wanting it to be true. 'This...er, Ayhusglamma or whatever, so did it really sink then? Is that what this "Shift" was?'

'No, not exactly, but most of the cities were destroyed by tsunamis or inundated by rising sea levels. Ehursagkalamma was buried in ice.'

'What? How? Was it in Antarctica then?'

'It wasn't then, but it is now, not far from the South Pole.'

'Are you talking about Earth crust displacement theory? I read about that once. Is that the "Shift"?'

'Exactly, Adam, but it is not a theory.'

'What's that? What's "Earth crust displacement"?' asked Lynn.

'It is the Earth's thin skin of crust,' explained Andor, 'sliding over the interior as if it is the detached peel of an orange, but moving almost as one piece.'

Unlike Adam, Lynn had never heard of this process and the concept astounded her. 'And the Earth can do that?' she asked.

'Sometimes, but not often. Only in extreme circumstances. The last time it happened it was caused by the impact of an asteroid. It hit the Earth at a very low angle with such an incredible force and at such a tremendous speed that it caused the Earth's crust to shift over one hundred miles on impact and then over one thousand more in the following years as a series of smaller meteors struck and before the affect dissipated.'

'And that's what shifted Atlantis to the South Pole...,' concluded Adam.

'It did a lot more than that,' continued Andor. 'The asteroid may have only glanced off the surface before continuing into space, but it was so large that it also put a wobble in the Earth's spin and ravaged the atmosphere. There were earthquakes, new volcanoes, splits in the Earth's crust, giant tsunamis, total disruption of the climate due to all the dust and water vapour created and complete rearrangement of the wind patterns and ocean currents. Incredibly, Atlantis survived the onslaught of the seas but was moved closer to the pole so gradually became engulfed by snow and ice.'

'Bugger me,' commented Nick, 'that's totally fucking mind-blowing. I had no idea there'd been such a huge catastrophe. But you said there were other cities, right? What about them? How come no one ever found any ruins?'

'Because all of the cities were on the coast. They were either destroyed by tsunamis or submerged as sea levels rose up to one hundred metres when the old ice caps melted. The new ones took millennia to form.'

'Some of those old cities *have* been found,' said Adam, 'though the establishment denies it. They've found ruins in the sea off Japan and one off of India and another one in the Caribbean I think, but being underwater, they're really difficult to study or survey and they're covered in coral and weed and stuff. Most archaeologists are blind to anything that challenges the existing theories too much. The hint of any existence of civilisation before Sumeria and they all go into a flap. So they see these sunken cities that have to be like, over ten thousand years old, right, and they say they're just weird rock formations or if it's too obviously buildings and stuff, they say they must've got submerged by later earthquakes or whatever. Most scientists don't believe in Earth crust displacement either and 'cos there's no funding it doesn't get properly looked into.'

'I'm not surprised,' observed Nick, 'it sounds pretty wacky to me an' all. It seems a bit too *convenient* that all the evidence is virtually unreachable....'

'To us it is history....incontrovertible fact,' stated Andor. 'The ancestors still retain those memories. It set back the evolution of human consciousness thousands of years.'

'How's that then?' asked Lynn. 'Surely the survivors were telepathic or whatever, yeah?'

'It is true that some retained their skills, but most suffered terribly. There is a method whereby psychics can join minds to become "one". Sometimes it is for social pleasure, sometimes for mutual support. At the time of The Shift many thousands in each city joined with the many thousands in others to become "one" in an attempt to divert the path of the asteroid. It was the greatest empathic unification ever, consisting of fifty million minds, but even then they did not have the power to stave off disaster. When millions perished, the intensity of the shared suffering and trauma destroyed or damaged the minds of millions more. In the ensuing chaos, the weakened remnants of the once great civilisation suffered a series of further catastrophes with the impacts of the additional meteors and the after affects of the first. The survivors were separated into small groups of desperate refugees who eventually either tried to start new communities or joined with tribal "inlanders" all over the world. The advanced civilisation and the development of the extended mind had been accelerated in costal peoples because of the diet rich in marine foods, so that by the time of The Shift there were huge differences between them and the "inlanders". There are myths that endure to this day of gods visiting the Earth and bestowing gifts or using magic, unexplained leaps in human development or achievement long-ago, the sudden rise of civilisations; all of this was the result of the refugees joining ancient, more primitive peoples and travelling the world over many centuries trying to accelerate human re-evolution. They were responsible for introducing acupuncture to the East, the pyramids to Egypt, the Nazca lines in Peru, Stonehenge and much much more. Ever since those times, those few who retained all of their faculties, who we call the Ancestors, have been trying to retrain minds, to rekindle those latent skills, which potentially almost everyone has, to prepare for.....'

'I'm sorry to be the voice of doubt again mate,' said Nick reluctantly, interrupting Andor's flow, 'but are you trying to tell us that these guys have been alive for over ten thousand years? I mean, I might just be able to get my head around the mind reading thing up to a point, given a bit more proof, but immortality? Nah, that's complete and utter bollocks.'

'Nick!' warned Lynn sternly.

'Well....'

'It's okay, Nick, you are right,' said Andor. 'I did not explain myself very well. I have never before had to relate this to someone so ignora....I mean someone on the "outside". When an Ancestor's body expires, all of his or her memories can be passed on to another, who then becomes an Ancestor and so on. "The Select" are chosen as the most suitable for this purpose. This way accumulated wisdom can be passed on to future generations.'

'So, in a way,' Adam surmised, 'because one of these ancestors can live on in another body and then another they do kind of live forever.'

'Not exactly. The living body retains its own personality and consciousness, but absorbs the memories and wisdom…it becomes like a library in the mind. The most recent psyches are the most significant, gradually losing their individuality over time, but the living person is at the centre of a united community like……like a queen bee in a hive'

'So how do they go souping-up the minds of the masses then?' asked Nick.

'Some of their work is identifying people, children in particular, who already have these abilities and making sure that they get the right training – usually by attending one of the foundations. The Ancestors can also project their thoughts at a distance to help awaken minds in their sleep, when there is least resistance. Gradually more and more people will have dreams related to events in real life and ancestral memories, an increase in remote vision and what we call "minor telepathies". Every day a greater number of individuals are born with a more heightened potential. Over the millennia since The Shift the genetic code that enables easier use of psychic skills has been spread so widely throughout the world that for the last few centuries it has been re-combining and strengthening in more and more of the population.'

'Like what's happened to me,' said Lynn quietly as the implication slowly dawned on her, 'with my dreams and paintings, yeah?'

'Yeah!' agreed Adam earnestly, 'And my dreams and my brother's too…'

'It has been predicted that once enough people have reached the right levels of skill, a sort of *critical mass*,' continued Andor, 'it will automatically lead to more and more "awakenings" and then a huge transformation in human consciousness.'

'The "Hundredth Monkey" syndrome…,' whispered Adam.

'This will be the dawn of a new age of enlightenment. It is what we call "The Resurgence".'

Adam was thrilled about what he was hearing. He had read so much and thought so deeply about what had been foretold of the coming era that the confirmation of his beliefs was for him the equivalent of a Catholic seeing a weeping Madonna.

'This is *really* far out!' he proclaimed delightedly. 'The New Age!'

'Ha! Here we go into the realms of fantasy again!' scoffed Nick. Just when he was beginning to believe certain elements of Andor's "story", such as the parts that had affected him, it was veering back into whacko land.

'Actually Nick,' Andor told him calmly, 'Adam is close to the truth, but it is just one of the various interpretations of what is certain to come. In fact the fragmentation of humanity caused by the shift and the co-mingling of the ancients with the inland tribes eventually gave rise to all of the world's religions and belief systems.'

'Like the Tower of Babel in the Bible...' said Adam, '...and Noah's Ark and those South American stories of white faced gods with beards bringing peace and bestowing gifts...'

'Yes, all these myths have their origins in truth,' confirmed Andor, 'but they have been reinterpreted so many times by so many people, a lot of whom had self-serving motives and over such a long period that their accuracy has been lost. At the core of most of the major religions however, is the message of love, peace and understanding. Unfortunately this is the part generally ignored. Most often, changes in doctrine and scriptures have been made by those in power in order to maintain or gain control of the populace using fear or unrealistic promises of rewards in the afterlife.'

'This is getting like one of your conspiracy theories Adam,' said Nick.

'But it is true,' Andor maintained. 'Just because some conspiracy theories are incorrect it does not mean they all are. There are many cases of those who have abused the ancient knowledge to further their personal status, power or control leading to terrible atrocities. Mao Zedong and Robert Mugabe are two notable examples in recent history, but many world leaders have been and continue to be affected, even if subconsciously.'

'So if these bad guys are in control, how's this utopian age ever going to come about?' asked Nick.

'As I said before, there is a cumulative effect over time,' Andor replied. 'There are many more good people than bad, so once they are more in control of their own minds they will not be so easily manipulated and will refuse to be dominated. This will lead to more peaceful revolutions, such as those in Eastern Europe in 1989.'

Nick considered this. 'So it's not going to happen in a hurry then,' he said.

'On the contrary, the process is accelerating. The most accurate remaining prediction is that of the Mayan calendar. The Mayan civilisation grew from a colony of refugees who joined the people of Yucatan after the shift. Gradually they attained great levels of culture, skill and sophistication which remained until their conquest by the Spanish.'

'December the twenty-first 2012!' blurted Adam. 'That's when they said the world would end!'

'Again, another slightly imprecise interpretation. They were not predicting "the end of the world", but the end of an age and therefore the beginning of another. From their advanced knowledge of genetics and mathematics they calculated the projected rate of population growth, forecast the rate at which the human race would reawaken and extrapolated the statistics to forecast the date by which universal consciousness would be gained.'

'So it will be around the twenty-first December 2012?'

'Most probably not Adam. Whilst they were great mathematicians and scientists, the accuracy of their prediction has been affected by too many variables, such as the rate of population growth, the random nature of recombining genetic characteristics, deviations in the Earth's orbit and spin and many other factors. Nevertheless, they did account for much of this in their calculations so they may have been as close as ten years to the actual date of the tipping point.'

'It could be any time soon then?'

'It could be.'

Adam considered this for a few moments and his thoughts began exploring new directions of enquiry.

'What about all the other unexplained phenomena,' he began eagerly, 'like ghosts and aliens and the Bermuda Triangle and weird seemingly impossible things that happen...'

'Unexplained phenomena are just that,' said Andor matter-of-factly, 'if they were impossible, they wouldn't happen. If the explanation eludes us, it is because it is currently beyond our understanding or we do not have all of the information....or we are not asking the right questions. Sometimes perceptions are clouded or corrupted by cultural, religious, scientific or societal conditioning or prejudices.'

'Oh,' said Adam in disappointment. That was not what he wanted to hear and he now wished he hadn't asked. Nevertheless, he had heard a lot of other exciting things that required processing on top of the craziness of recent events, so he stared out the window and lapsed into a thoughtful silence for a while.

As they approached the German border with Lynn taking another turn at the wheel, Adam yawned widely. Having donated his tent to Sonilla and Andor he spent an uncomfortable night attempting to sleep in the car. His brain felt fuzzy with fatigue and, despite his yoga workout at dawn, his body still ached from the hours of being cramped. He began to feel apprehensive about facing the border guards and was regretting the front seat position he had requested as a result of carsickness. He knew he was a magnet for suspicion. He didn't know why but invariably whenever he encountered a situation that required him to be inconspicuous and discreet, his demeanour would betray his inner turmoil of paranoia. His eyes would dart shiftily from side to side and he would acquire a nervous stutter. Sometimes he wondered if he had been born with a guilty conscience. He suddenly had a terrible feeling of foreboding – perhaps he was beginning to become more psychic too. Carrying passengers with no identity, they could get into a lot of trouble. He felt he had to air his fears to the others.

'Guys, I don't want to seem too paranoid or anything,' he began, 'but I'm a bit worried about this border crossing. I mean Andor and Sonilla don't have passports do they? What if we get stopped?'

'Don't worry mate,' said Nick from behind him, 'they stopped doing border checks a few years back. Everyone's all matey in the EU now.'

Sure enough, Adam's fears appeared to be groundless; the kiosks at the crossing point were long unused and deserted so they sailed through without having to slow their speed much at all.

Travelling across the flat monotonous terrain of Northern Germany was extremely tedious. Nick and Lynn now took turns in driving and snoozing so that they could travel virtually non-stop to their destination. The others dozed fitfully and were grateful for the infrequent stretch breaks when they came. They gazed drowsily out of the windows, feeling subdued and speaking little; the relentless drone of the car's engine and the incessant vibration of the vehicle seemed to numb the mind into submission. They stopped at a service station in the early hours of the morning, all needing to spend a short time away from the claustrophobic confines of the noisy, reverberating vehicle. After a double espresso coffee to prepare him for his next stint behind the wheel, Nick's curiosity had been rekindled.

'These bad guys,' he began, looking at Andor across the table, 'what's going on there then? I mean, you know, what's their game...what are they after? Why have they gone over to the "dark side"? If this New Age is so amazing, why don't they want to be part of it?'

'Even before The Shift damaged so many minds,' Andor told him, 'there had always been a small percentage whose ethics had become debased so that they craved only selfish pleasures. For many centuries there had been trade with the less sophisticated inlanders, who viewed the coastal people with fear and awe. Unfortunately a few of the ancients misused their advantage to exploit them, using them as slaves for sex or mundane work. Some even went to live amongst them and took over rule of their villages, enjoying the thrill of power and control. The oppressors initiated the belief amongst the natives that they were divine and due special privileges. There have been such people ever since; usually the positions of power were passed to subsequent generations or were taken by force by those with greater strengths or deviousness. In a handful of cases it was rumoured that some had managed to devise a way to regenerate their bodies many times, but of that there is no evidence. As to what the aims of our pursuers are and the reasons for their seizing control of the foundation, we shall have to ask Thu Salamu.'

#

The tick of the clock echoed hollowly around the otherwise quiet kitchen. In other circumstances some may have considered the room, bathed in the lambent glow of the morning sunlight, to be a realm of tranquillity. The two figures sat motionless and silent at the scrubbed pine table, their postures symptomatic of defeat and sheer hopelessness. Rhona's vivid hair, now displaying the newly acquired short and spiky style, seemed inappropriately cheery and playful given the recent turn of events. A few glistening drops shone on the tabletop where the slow rivulets of tears that streaked over her cheeks from her reddened eyes had fallen to the surface. Her failure to prevent Rowan's abduction gnawed at her conscience and this, combined with her worry at both her niece's and Bess' fate, consumed her thoughts and feelings in an agonising tangle of fraught emotions. Charlie had his head in his hands, his dark ruffled hair sprouting from between his fingers, with a feeling of helplessness like a lead casing around his heart. His life seemed to him to have become a living nightmare in which he knew he had no choice but to become an unwilling servant to those who had imprisoned his wife, a mere puppet coerced by the threats to do their bidding.

When they woke to find the others gone earlier that morning, there was a hand-written note on the kitchen table explaining the situation. Should the casket not be completed satisfactorily and on time, Bess would be killed and Rowan's fate was to become a "vessel". What the kidnappers meant by this was not clear but it sounded ominous and the tone of the letter undoubtedly menacing. They again ignored the warning not to call the police, but when Charlie picked up the phone the line was dead. They both tried their mobiles, but neither could get a signal. After the initial panic, rage and exasperation they became utterly miserable and dejected.

'Well,' said Charlie eventually, 'I'd better get on with it then.'

Rhona merely nodded and stared vacantly out of the window as he slowly stood, as if stiff from age and inactivity. He picked up his jacket and left for the workshop.

CHAPTER SEVENTEEN.

The overcast sky glowed sombrely with the ghostly candescence of the city's streetlights flushing the solid, leaden clouds. Arriving in the outskirts of Amsterdam at twilight Adam had mixed feelings. He had always wanted to visit this conurbation of cannabis cafes, bicycles, trams and canals, but his anticipation had been tempered by the fear of the unknown danger from their young companions' pursuers and the profound, overwhelming fatigue brought on by their interminable, incessant travelling. He had never spent so long in a car and was dreading the return journey, which would have to start the following day in order to meet their deadline to get the hire car back. There would be no time to sample the delights he had so long looked forward to. There was also no guarantee that they would even get a bed at the address they sought. He also felt a pang of regret at the thought of having to bid farewell to their newfound friends. Spending three days in a car with someone was a good way to discover whether you we going to like or loathe them. Adam had grown fond of the strange couple; even Sonilla had become a little more communicative in the last day, though she was still very much subdued by her grief. He had learnt more of their sheltered medieval lifestyle, their version of history, the civilisation of their ancestors and the skills that they had been "guided" in. They did not regard their learning to have been the result of teaching or training. It seemed that youngsters were encouraged to explore and focus upon the subjects they felt drawn to or were naturally gifted in. The foundation appeared to operate in an atmosphere of love, with a unity of purpose towards the common goals of improving themselves and when they were ready, integration into the wider world where they could help others. It was difficult to believe that such a place could fall foul of the distorted influence of a malevolent faction. They must be very clever to have been able to seize control without revealing their intent.

They stopped at a petrol station to buy a street map and then Adam attempted to navigate as Lynn patiently followed his directions.

After two hours searching, three wrong turns and twice falling foul of one-way systems, they finally drew up outside the address Thu Salamu had given them. It was a flat above a bookshop in a tree-lined road laid with tram rails. The trees swayed in the breeze casting distorted, dancing shadows on the dark pavement. They could not see any lights on in the apartment, just the reflection of streetlights in the windows making them look like vacant orange eyes, soulless in the gaunt flat face of the building.

'I do not think anyone is there,' said Andor dully, his tone belying his state of exhaustion. 'I cannot detect any sign of human life within the building.'

'Well, now we're here we might as well ring the bell, eh?' proposed Nick. He got out of the car and went over to the door. Feeling conspicuous in the empty street, he looked up and down before pressing the button, making him appear shifty. He pulled his jacket collar up to protect his neck from the cool, damp gusts that rippled the canal. He stood uneasily, moving his weight from one foot to the other as the draught wafted his unruly hair.

Lynn wound down the window. 'Let's go Nick,' she requested uneasily. 'They aren't in and something doesn't feel right. He climbed back into the car and Lynn pulled off quickly. 'Andor feels it too,' she told him. 'We think someone else got here first....' She glanced nervously in the mirrors as she drove. 'I don't think we're being followed though.'

'What do you mean, "someone else got there first"?' asked Nick gravely, looking over his shoulder through the back window. 'You reckon the contact's been done in?'

'That or kidnapped,' she said.

'Where are we going to go now?' asked Adam.

'I don't know,' Lynn replied, 'I just want to get away from there.'

'Well we can't just keep driving,' he said. 'We have to go somewhere.'

'There's always my old mate Spud,' Nick said after a moment's thought. 'He lives on a barge. He said I was always welcome to visit.'

'Do you have his address though?' asked Lynn.

'No, but I went there once....it was about five or six years ago but I reckon I could find it again. Gis the map Adam. Pull over under a street lamp will you Lynn.'

As Nick scrutinised the map Lynn probed him further. 'Has he got room for five extra people?' she asked, 'and will he welcome us lot turning up without any warning? I mean, it's a bit of a cheek isn't it?'

'Don't worry, it'll be fine. It's a huge boat as far as I remember, though I have to say I did spend the whole time out of my tree. But anyway, he's totally cool, he'll be fine – you can't phase old Spud.' Tracing his finger over some time- and drug-misted pathways, he muttered under his breath as if uncertainly reciting a half remembered poem from his childhood. 'There it is!' he exclaimed suddenly, 'Far out! I knew I'd find it – Prinsengracht. If we drive along there I'll definitely recognise the boat – if it's still there that is. Anyway, it's only just round the corner - let's go.'

'What are we going to do about meeting Thu Salamu?' asked Adam. 'She's not going to know where we are is she?'

'We'll just have to come back in the morning and try again, yeah?' suggested Lynn. 'If it's a no show then we'll have to do a re-think, right?'

Nick's memory was surprisingly accurate. Despite a couple of minutes of confusion due to the repainting of his friend's vessel, he correctly identified the barge at its mooring near a bridge. Lynn parked the car and they all climbed gratefully from its cramped confines, stretching their long bent, aching limbs. Adam's shoulders scrunched as he tried to roll the tension out of them. In this quiet part of the city the rustling of the leaves and the gentle lap of water against boat side eclipsed the distant sound of traffic. A motorcycle accelerating noisily on the other side of the canal briefly shattered the peace and set a dog to barking. The barge was long and low, its bulk evoking an image of a beached whale in Adam's mind. In the darkness they could make out a clutter of curios and found objects adorning the decks and roof, interspersed with planters bulging with flowers. They boarded the vessel and Nick rapped firmly on the door. There was the sound of scrabbling from within as if objects were being hastily moved and then the silence of someone listening. Nick tapped again.

'Spud?' he called softly. 'You in there?'

'Who's that?' came a gruff voice from inside.

'It's me, Nick.'

There was a pause. 'Nick who?'

'Nick Barton. C'mon Spud mate, open up.'

'Nick?'

'Yeah man, fucking *Nick!*' He rolled his eyes skywards. 'Come on mate, let us in.'

'Nick? Nick Barton? Buddha's balls!'

There was the rattling sound of bolts being drawn and then the door swung inwards to reveal a round, sweat-shined, unshaven face smiling in happy astonishment. His features bore a sallow complexion, untidily framed by dark lank shoulder length curls, starting to grey at their thinning roots.

'Well bugger me backwards with a barge pole! 'Allo mate,' he enthused, 'Bloody hell, good to see you man. Haven't heard for…God, I don't know…ages.' Noticing the others behind his friend he added, 'Christ, you've got a whole bleedin' posse with you! You'd better come in.' He stood back to admit them and then peered suspiciously outside, as if to make certain that they weren't being watched, before securing and locking the door. He was wearing a patchwork waistcoat over a blue collarless shirt that bulged over the belt of a pair of baggy faded jeans.

Adam inspected the interior of the boat with admiration and a certain degree of envy. If he were to choose a home from all of those he'd entered in his life so far, this would be the one. The space was lined with well-crafted cupboards, the pine clad walls and ceiling glowing warmly in the lamplight. The floor was covered in thick, colourful Persian rugs and at the far end the galley boasted a wood-burning stove that radiated heat into the area. Knick-knacks and works of craft littered every shelf or hung from ceiling hooks. The artwork filling every vertical surface that remained and the Indian hangings used as curtains completed the vision of a bohemian haven. A well-worn but lovingly polished table graced the centre of the surprisingly spacious room, its surface littered with paperwork. Sitting adjacent to a dirty ashtray a chipped and stained mug announced "I ♥ Weed" above a sunflower face between cartoon images of Bill and Ben the Flowerpot Men.

Spud rubbed his hands together and grinned as if expecting a special treat. He urged them to sit and make themselves at home whilst he put the kettle on. Nick made the introductions and his friend shook hands with them each in turn, repeating their names as if to commit them to memory. His eyes were red and slightly swollen but emanated a peaceful benevolence such as Adam had never seen before but could have imagined seeing on the face of a stoned Dalai Lama.

'Cor blimey - bloody Nick, eh? Well sew my socks to a dog's ear! What a surprise man, you turning up on the doorstep after all these years!' he said, shaking his head as he clattered mugs and a teapot onto a tray. He removed the lid from a biscuit tin and peered inside as if its contents were a mystery to him. 'Far out, Hobnobs,' he muttered quietly and tipped some on to a plate. He poured the boiling water into the teapot and brought the refreshments over to the table.

'So, how's it going? How the devil are you man? What are you lot doing here then?' he asked, but continued talking without waiting for the answer. 'You know I ain't dealing any more Nick? The scene just got too heavy, you know man, with people cutting the dope with all kinds of shit and gangs with guns wanting to control the market...really *really* hectic, know what I mean? Too much for an old hippie like me anyway. I run a veggie café now, bought with my ill-gotten gains, he he he. But I'm all legit now see - here's me cooking the books.' He indicated the disarray between them on the table's surface.

'Yeah, cool,' said Nick. 'But I'm not looking for blow anyway. We just need somewhere to crash for the night. There's no answer at the address we were given so we had nowhere to go and it was a good excuse to look up an old mate, right?'

'You don't need an excuse, Nick mate,' said Spud amicably, 'you should know you're always welcome.' His expression changed to one of feigned reproach. 'Here, you weren't going to visit the city without calling in were you? After all these years...'

'Well, it's kind of complicated, right?' said Nick feeling a little embarrassed. 'We're on a kind of mercy mission for Andor and Sonilla here and we've got to get the hire car back....'

'Sounds interesting, tell me more,' urged his friend, pouring the tea, 'and what's with these young 'uns in their peasant getup?'

'Well, it's a long story Spud and I don't know if you want to get involved...it's a bit, er, dodgy you know?'

'Oh, I see. International man of mystery eh?' He tapped the side of his nose with a finger with the air of one well versed in clandestine activities. 'Ask no questions and you'll tell me no lies right? No worries, man. As well you know, I too have been embroiled in a fair share of sticky situations in the past. Only too happy to help.' He took a brightly painted tobacco tin from his waistcoat pocket, opened it and started rolling a joint. 'As luck would have it,' he continued, 'there's a flat above my café that's between tenants right? Sort of...awaiting redecoration, you know? You're welcome to stay there if you like - it'd be a bit cramped here on this old tub with five extra bods, know what I mean? There's plenty of room at the flat and it's fully furnished – two double bedrooms and a big sofa for your mate Adam. I can't feed you though, I'm afraid. Living on my own I don't keep much food about the place, see, especially as I don't have a fridge – not enough power on the boat, right?'

'Don't worry, we'll get a carry-out,' said Nick. 'That's brilliant about the flat though, thanks a lot man.'

'No problem, Nick me old mate,' said Spud smiling. He lit the joint, inhaled deeply, held it in for a few seconds and then exhaled noisily. 'Man, that's the stuff,' he said and took another drag. 'I'll pop in in the morning when I open up the café and you can come down for slap-up brekkie – my treat.'

Sonilla and Andor couldn't hide the look of distaste on their faces as the thick, choking fumes filled the air.

'Oh, non-smokers eh?' noted Spud. 'Sorry an' all that, but it's my pad you know?'

The young couple left the cabin coughing to wait on deck in the fresh air.

Whilst they drank their tea Nick and Spud began catching up on how their lives were now, but when their host offered the joint, only Adam accepted.

'Man, times *have* changed!' he commented. 'You never used to turn down a smoke Nick. Can't take the pace, eh?'

'Something like that,' replied Nick awkwardly. 'I'll explain tomorrow. I think we'd better go now though. We're knackered and starving.'

Spud got them the key and showed them on the map where to go.

By the time they arrived at the address of Spud's café via a take away, it had started raining. Despite this, Lynn was pleasantly surprised at both the building and the district in which it was situated. From the impression she had formed from meeting Nick's old friend she had expected a ramshackle establishment in a rundown part of the city. However, the eighteen-century façade graced a terrace of other, similar shop fronts on a wide pavement opposite a leafy park in a very picturesque neighbourhood. A sign above the coffee house window named the enterprise as "Café Relaxo".

'Well, Spud's done alright for himself hasn't he?' observed Nick. 'Nice place.'

A door to the side admitted them to a small hall with an electricity meter where Nick was able to switch on the mains as instructed by their host. A single low wattage bulb, which dangled forlornly from a long frayed wire, inadequately illuminated the steep uncarpeted staircase.

'I liked the outside better,' commented Lynn bluntly.

'Yeah well, beggars can't be choosers right?' said Nick. 'Up here I guess,' he added leading the way upstairs. At the top of the flight was a plywood door with a large puncture in the thin surface showing its cardboard "egg box" filling. A second key allowed them entry to the flat. After the grandiose exterior façade, the interior of the building was a disappointment. Although it retained many of its original features, such as panelled doors, moulded skirting boards and ornate plaster cornices, the paint was peeling and the corners of almost every sheet of wallpaper had curled away from the damp walls as if in distaste. It also felt cold.

Lynn shivered and hugged herself. 'It's a bit grim isn't it?' she remarked. 'And chilly.'

'I've slept in worse,' admitted Adam.

'Yeah, me too,' Nick agreed, 'and at least we're out of the car and out of the rain. It'll be good to sleep in a bed again. Right, let's find the heating and then eat this grub – I'm bloody famished.' He set off to search out the boiler according to Spud's directions.

Lynn became aware of a light flickering on and off, so followed its source to discover Andor in the kitchen playing with a switch. Both he and Sonilla were staring in wonder at the bulb.

'We had no idea that people had harnessed energy in such a way,' he muttered quietly. 'I wonder why we were kept using candles and oil lamps all this time.'

He left the light on and began exploring the room.

Sonilla ran her fingers over the melamine worktop. 'What a strange surface,' she stated. Then she quickly crossed the room, suddenly having noticed the refrigerator. 'What's this?' she asked.

'That's a fridge Soni,' Lynn told her, 'we use it to keep food cold, yeah?'

Sonilla opened the door to the dark interior, which apart from the shelves was empty and smelled musty. She slowly put her hand inside. 'It doesn't seem very cold in there,' she observed.

Lynn smiled indulgently. 'It's not switched on yet,' she informed her. 'It runs on electricity, like the lights, yeah?' She followed its cable back to a socket and flicked the switch. The light came on inside as the appliance hummed into life. 'It takes a little while to warm up..er I mean cool down.' She said as she shut the door.

'Amazing,' commented Sonilla softly.

'Right, heating's on guys!' declared Nick as he entered the room. 'Where's that grub? I reckon the science lesson can wait til the morning, right?'

The thin, ragged curtains did little to block the tawdry glow from the streetlights outside. Despite this and the persistent splatter of raindrops on the windows, Adam felt reasonably content to be lying in his sleeping bag, motionless and outstretched on the soft surface of the sofa. The heating system had finally taken the edge off the damp, chilly atmosphere in the flat. The last three days of constant travel had left him feeling physically shaken to the core from the constant vibration and the discomfort of being squeezed in with four other bodies had made him ache all over. He extended his limbs gratefully and breathed deeply, but his mind wouldn't let him sleep.

After their meal, the two couples had found serviceable duvets in a cupboard and made their way up to the bedrooms on the next floor. When they were all together Adam felt a little like the odd one out, being single. He enjoyed his privacy, his own thoughts and the freedom do as he chose, but he sorely missed other aspects of being in a relationship. Sex was certainly one of them, but "making love" was incomparable. At its best his time with Julia had been amongst the happiest days of his life. To be so intimate with another person, both physically and emotionally had done wonderful things for his disposition, temperament and self-confidence. It was so enriching to share experiences with someone you loved, to laugh and cry together, to be in awe of a sunset or beautiful scenery holding hands in silent companionship. When she left him, he had been devastated. His world and his soul had seemed torn apart. Lynn once told him that she thought he had a tendency to dwell too deeply and for too long on his problems, that he should learn to let go of the past. 'There's no point crying over spilt milk,' she had told him, 'but you can learn from your mistakes and then move on, yeah?' Well, he thought that he had "got over" Julia now, but the pain of their parting had discouraged him from trying any more. He was afraid of being hurt again. Bonding that closely with someone had left him too vulnerable, yet he was disinclined to have a superficial relationship. He tried to tell himself that it was because he didn't want to hurt someone else if *they* got too involved, but in his heart he knew he was only trying to protect himself. The problem was, he could not control his sex drive and when testosterone reared its ugly head he found himself drooling over Lynn. The unacceptability of this was without question, so he had again resolved to make more effort and to be more courageous in his romantic endeavours after this vacation. And what a memorable holiday it was proving to be! He contemplated the events of the past few days. Despite the change of plans and their escape across three countries he had found it quite exhilarating. Scary too, but somehow it was easier to be scared in the company of friends. Maybe he was getting better at facing his fears. He was also delighted to have confirmed that telepathy really did exist and that there were ancient advanced civilisations just as Professor Oakley had postulated. He wished Tom was here now. The information Andor had shared with him over the past few days was totally amazing and would take a long time to absorb. The most exciting parts for Adam were that there *really was* the coming of a new age of human consciousness and the fact that Andor had told him that with guidance, he too could learn telepathic skills. That would be totally amazing. He would *love* that.

It seemed that Lynn already had some skill in that area. He had known about the connection between her remote vision dreams and her paintings, but Andor reckoned she was beginning to be able to pick up thoughts too. Since she had noticed his gawping that hot day a few weeks ago Adam had been trying really hard to control his lustful inclinations. It was even more important now, if she could start to read his mind.

'Cor, that was great,' muttered Lynn contentedly, stroking Nicks hair. 'I've really missed sex the last few days, cooped up in a car like that with a load of other people.' Her black hair was stuck to her forehead with sweat and she'd thrown the bedding aside to cool down. The heating system in the flat was proving to be very effective and she was wishing now that they had turned it off when they came to bed.

'Yeah...,' Nick agreed without opening his eyes. 'I thought I was too tired, but somehow you managed to tap into my hidden reserves. Absence makes the knob grow fonder....or longer...'

'Oh, *very* romantic,' commented Lynn with a smile. 'Though there's going to be more absences when my bump gets too big and then when the sprog first pops out, I might get ripped up a bit and be sore for a while, you know?'

'Ah yes, the post-natal drought – I've heard about that. Well if you can put up with pregnancy and childbirth, I can put up with a bit of abstinence. I'll tell you right, even though I admit it *is* a bit scary, I'm really looking forward to being a dad, you know? And I'm so glad that you're the mum an' all. A baby born out of love has got to be really cool, right? This kid's going to be fucking amazing.'

'You bet,' agreed Lynn placing a hand on the slight swell of her belly. With her other hand she wafted the edge of the duvet to create a cooling draught. 'Bloody hell, it's hot in here,' she said.

'I'll turn the heating off,' offered Nick then pulled on his boxer shorts and tiptoed away to do so. A minute later he returned to her side and said, 'I guess we'll have to get back on the road before lunch tomorrow to get the car back in time and get our flights. I hope there's someone at that address for those kids or that Salamu turns up. I'd hate to abandon them here, but I don't know what else we could do.'

Lynn propped herself up on her elbow to regard him seriously. 'We should make sure they're okay though before we go, yeah?' she said. 'We can't just leave them, they'd be hopeless. They're not "kids" but they haven't a clue about the real world. Maybe Spud could let them stay here for a bit if they're stuck…'

'Yeah, I don't see why not. But let's see what happens tomorrow first, you know? We might not have to think about it if someone turns up.' Nick paused to reclaim the duvet now that he and the room were beginning to cool. 'But whatever happens, we'll make sure they're okay before we go, no matter how long it takes, right? If we're going to be late, we'll phone the car place and if we miss our flight, we'll get on the next one, alright? They're a nice couple regardless of all their crazy stories. I'm glad we met them, though it's a shame it meant crashing their car.'

'Yeah, I know what you mean,' said Lynn as she snuggled further down in the bedding. 'But there's no excuse for driving like that,' she added sternly, 'you were lucky no one got more badly hurt.'

'I know, I know, I'm sorry. I just meant that it's been good meeting them and we wouldn't have done if that hadn't happened, right? That's all.'

'Yeah, I'm going to miss them.'

'Well we can give them you're mobile number and when they escape and get safe and everything's calmed down, they can get in touch, right? Even if we've moved.'

'Good plan. Now let's stop nattering and get some sleep, yeah?'

In the dim radiance entering the curtainless room from the city outside, the gentle hiss of rain offered a fitting backdrop to their whispers. Sonilla lay with her head on Andor's shoulder and her left hand resting on his chest as it rose and fell slowly with his breath.

'I'm sorry I've been so distant these last few days, Andor,' she murmured softly. 'I've just felt so….empty….and *depleted* since….since…' Her voice faltered, but she managed to swallow, sighed and then continued, '…you know. Lendi has been such a big part of my life, *all* of my life. She was like a twin to me. No, more than a twin…we were linked so closely I can't describe it. I don't know what I'm going to do without her.' A single sob escaped from her throat, releasing a trickle tears. 'It's like I've lost a part of myself…not my body, but my *soul*.'

'I know,' said Andor, pulling her closer. His own tears dribbled down his cheeks. It was still too soon for either of them to have overcome their shock and sadness. The rawness of their anguish would take much longer to heal. 'I feel it too…we are so close that I share your emotions almost as if they are my own. And I also grieve for her on my own behalf, she was like a sister to me. It is always a tragedy when one so young is lost to the world, but especially so to those closest to them. But Lendi would have wanted us to carry on….to help stop this happening to others…to help make a better world for everyone.'

'You're right Andor, I know it….but in my heart…oh, it just *hurts so much*,' she said tearfully.

'I know, I know,' he said, and then just held her silently, trying to send comfort with his thoughts. After a few minutes she stopped crying and he said, 'I love you Soni, don't ever forget that. I'll help you through this in any way I can.'

'I love you too Andor, you know that. Thank you for being here for me, it really helps.' She kissed him tenderly. 'But I'm not ready to make love yet though,' she added, 'I'm still just too upset.'

'I know and it's fine,' he responded. 'Not until you're ready. Let's get some sleep now, we're both exhausted. It's been such a hard few days.'

The traffic rumbling and swishing over the wet road outside sounded like a procession of water-skiers towed by a flotilla of motorboats. Adam groaned and slowly sat up, rubbing his crusty eyelids. He had slept deeply, but his body ached from lying on the lumpy, sagging sofa. He stood and stretched, yawning widely and then walked over to the window to draw back the curtains. As he yanked them open on their squeaky rails he saw that the downpour continued unabated, creating a trembling grey screen that partially obscured the view. In addition to the cars, the street below was fairly busy with pedestrians and bicycles. Walkers hurried along hunkered beneath umbrellas or bent headed like the cyclists in hooded rain jackets with shoulders hunched as if this would keep them drier.

'Morning Adam,' came Lynn's cheery voice from behind him, 'sleep okay?'

He turned to see her standing in the doorway, not seeming fully awake and smiling dippily.

'Yeah, fine thanks,' he replied, returning her smile. 'You?'

'Yeah, great. I slept like a slab.'

'A slab?' repeated Adam, puzzled. 'Er, like a log but colder?'

'No silly, like a paving slab. A log's never completely inert, you know – beetles and stuff crawling about under the bark, yeah? But a concrete slab – solid, totally unmoving – dead to the world, yeah? And it was *so good* to sleep in a bed again.'

'Yeah, absolutely,' agreed Adam, wishing that he had too.

'I'll stick the kettle on, yeah?' she said merrily and then skipped away towards the kitchen.

Adam heard the sound of a key in the front door. It clicked open and then closed again. Footsteps clumped steadily up the stairs and then Spud's portly figure emerged up onto the landing.

'Mornin' all,' he said brightly, 'lovely day!' He took off his sodden cagoule, wiped his dripping face with both sleeves and then coughed noisily, the sound of phlegm struggling against its ejection from his tarry lungs. 'Ah tea!' he managed as he turned his attention to the sound of the kettle heating in the kitchen. Adam followed and saw Sonilla treading softly down the stairs barefoot followed closely by Andor.

'Everyone up except Nick, eh?' observed Spud wryly. 'No change there then, hah! You all sleep okay? No bedbugs, fleas, rats...?'

'No, it was great thanks,' said Adam, 'it was good to lay on something soft.'

'As the actress said to the bishop, eh? Ha ha,' joked Spud, 'or was it the other way round?' He turned to Sonilla and Andor. 'What about you two? Everything alright?'

'Thank you, yes we slept very well,' Sonilla replied gratefully. 'The bed was very comfortable and we were untroubled by vermin.'

A short loud laugh burst from Spud's throat setting off another bout of coughing. 'That's priceless girl,' he said to Sonilla's deadpan expression. '"Untroubled by vermin!" That's classic that is! Very good, very good.' He looked momentarily thrown by her bewildered look, then cleared his throat and suggested, 'comfy chairs?'

They filtered into the lounge and Spud plonked himself heavily in one of the armchairs by the window. Adam thought that the way he sprawled with his arms and legs splayed made him look like an overweight starfish. However, he seemed a very relaxed character with an easy manner that made him instantly likeable.

'How do have your tea Spud?' Lynn called from the kitchen.

'Coo and two please love,' came the reply. He peered out of the grubby window. 'Cor, Pan's pisser, this rain's a pain, isn't it?' he commented. 'It hardly stopped all week.' They all nodded mutely in agreement. 'Here's the man!' he added as Nick emerged bleary-eyed from the landing, scratching his head.

'Hiya Spud,' he said, 'How're you doing?'

'Not bad, not bad, better than most, eh?' his friend replied. 'Listen, how about you lot coming down to the café for breakfast, eh? On the house – anything you like. I felt bad about leaving you to go hungry last night.'

'You are very kind,' said Andor earnestly.

'Not at all, not at all,' he said dismissively with a wave of his hand.

Lynn appeared with a tray full of steaming mugs, which she distributed to a round of thanks.

'Are you going to rent this flat out again Spud?' she asked.

'Yeah, come the next autumn term,' he replied. 'I usually rent to students see, they're not too fussy, so I don't have to tart the place up too much - though I admit, at the moment it could do with a lick of paint, but there's plenty of time for that. I've got all summer – I'll do it meself once the weather's a bit warmer...and drier.'

After their tea, Spud led them downstairs and showed them round to the front entrance of the café, which he unlocked, standing to one side as they filed in. He locked the door behind them.

'I don't normally open up 'til eleven,' he explained. 'If you want to serve breakfast in this city you have to start at seven in the morning to catch all the workers. Man! Sod that for a game of soldiers! Buggered if I'm getting up that early! No need to bust a gut, eh?' He patted his stomach, smiling. He led them between a maze of well-worn tables, surrounded by a mixture of mismatched upholstered, wickerwork and bare wooden dining chairs, and then through an area in the middle of the café graced with settees, armchairs and dark, low coffee tables. Although the furniture was well used it wasn't dilapidated. The thick, soft, dark green carpet, the slightly faded velvet curtains, the delicate pastel pink walls adorned with modern paintings and several framed posters of rock concerts from the nineteen-seventies, all combined to produce a relaxed, homely atmosphere.

'Nice place,' remarked Nick as their host showed them to a large dining table near the back of the establishment.

'Yeah, thanks,' said Spud. 'Here, take a pew and I'll get the lads to rustle something up. It's all veggie mind, so I hope there's no hunger crazed meat addicts amongst you, eh?' He grinned widely.

'Anything would be great,' said Adam, 'I'm famished. I could eat a horse.'

'I just *said* there was no meat though didn't I, man, eh?' chuckled Spud and disappeared through a pair of swinging doors in to the kitchen. As they seated themselves around the table, music emerged from hidden loudspeakers.

'Daby Touré!' enthused Adam. 'I love African music and this guy always sound so happy. It's really uplifting stuff.'

Lynn was admiring some of the paintings. 'Do you like art?' she asked Sonilla. She had decided that she wanted to try to engage her new friend in more conversation before they parted. Hopefully it would help her to reconnect with the world and begin the process of overcoming her grief.

'Yes, I do,' the young woman replied, nodding. 'At the foundation we were encouraged in all aspects of creativity and imagination, but painting was my favourite activity, especially using bright colours.'

'Me too,' agreed Lynn eagerly, 'and I like using bold strokes of the brush too, no messing, you know? Not too much thinking either, just letting it flow without the mind getting in the way, yeah?'

'Andor is the opposite,' Sonilla told her, 'he likes to work in minute detail. He has amazing patience and his work is incredible.'

'But you will produce ten pictures to each of mine,' contributed Andor, 'I am very slow. What amazes me about your work is how you manage to capture the essence of your subject so efficiently. There is great skill in that.'

They talked about art for a few minutes. Adam and Nick listened politely, but neither of them felt they had any abilities in that direction. Shortly Spud returned with a pot of coffee and another of tea, followed by a thin young man in his early twenties with short, spiky ginger hair. He wore tight black drainpipe jeans and a smart blue shirt under his stripy apron and carried a tray bearing cups with a jug of milk.

'This here's Hank,' indicated Spud. 'Him and Vince are going to cook us up some grub.'

'Hi,' said Hank with a nervous smile. They all said 'Hi' back and thanked him as he handed out the mugs and put the jug on the table before hastening back to the kitchen.

'Bit shy that one,' Spud told them, 'Heart of gold though. Good chef too.' He poured the coffees whilst Adam poured the teas.

'So,' continued Spud settling back into his chair at one end of the table, 'what brings you motley crew together then? And why Amsterdam? It doesn't seem to me to be a *planned* adventure anyways. I'm most curious about you two.' He wiggled his finger at Andor and Sonilla regarding them with a crooked smile. 'You've got funny ways about you, like….I don't know…and you look like Medieval serfs from the middle ages or something.'

Andor hesitated, uncertain how to start. 'Well, we have recently left a kind of special school…' he began.

'What, you mean like a loony bin?' sniggered Spud before hastily adding, 'oops, sorry, only joking, only joking. So, what then, a monastery or convent or some other religious cult, eh?'

'Not exactly,' replied Andor, 'but we were rather isolated from the outside world.'

'So, how did you hook up with this bunch of reprobates then?' Spud nodded towards the others. It was obvious he was keen to hear a good story, but at the same time couldn't stop his curiosity from interrupting with questions.

'Er….I do not believe that they are immoral people,' Andor remarked frowning slightly. 'We had an accident,' he added, 'a car crash…'

'It was all Nick's fault,' interjected Lynn, wanting to help Andor with the telling of the tale, 'he was driving like a maniac.'

'Well, yes, I admit it,' agreed Nick. 'It was just one of those stupid moments, you know?' Spud nodded, sipping his coffee. 'Anyway, as it was all my fault,' continued Nick, 'we decided to help them out and give them a lift to their, er, destination…'

'Right, right,' said Spud, nodding some more. 'Fair enough. So where was this crash then?'

Adam, Nick and Lynn exchanged glances, realising how strange the answer would sound.

'What? Where?' asked Spud, seeing their hesitancy.

'Near the Tatra Mountains,' Lynn told him, 'South East Poland. We were on holiday in Poland.'

Spud's mouth dropped open in amazement and he gawped at each of them in turn.

'Poland!' he spluttered in astonishment. They nodded slowly. 'Krishna's crap, you *are* the good Samaritans! Jesus, that must be, what, over a thousand kilometres to the Tatras!' He shook his head in disbelief.

'As the crow flies maybe,' said Nick, 'even more by road.'

'Blimey, how long did that take you? Four, five days?'

'Three actually,' said Lynn. 'To start with the roads were pretty slow, you know, all hilly and bendy, yeah? But we didn't even stop for one night, just to like, get a break, or anything – just took it in turns to drive or sleep.'

'Well send my knickers to a laundry on Mars.....you don't say,' commented Spud, smiling. He was enjoying the advent of a quirky tale interrupting his life. He was quite contented with his lot, settled into a comfortable life and routine after his years on the edge of criminality, but nonetheless took pleasure in a little change now and again, or at least hearing of it from others. 'So, what about you Adam? How'd you get mixed up in this? Did they pick you up hitching?'

'No, I came on holiday with Nick and Lynn,' he answered, 'I live in Portsmouth too. I've known them for years.'

'Well, they've given you quite an adventure haven't they? I don't suppose you were expecting a little diversion to Tulip land, eh?'

'No, but it's been kind of exciting, I suppose. And I've enjoyed meeting Sonilla and Andor too.'

The kitchen door opened to admit Hank, closely followed by Vince, a short, dark-haired, wiry man with bare, hairy arms, moist red eyes and a placid expression. They each carried three plates, two expertly balanced on their right arms, and they placed one apiece in front of the diners.

'Da da!' sang Spud as if he had waved a magic wand to produce the food. On each plate were two fried eggs, two vegetarian sausages, potato croquettes, baked beans, fried bread, grilled tomatoes and fried mushrooms. It smelled delicious.

'Tuck in,' bade their host as he himself started to eat and they did not hesitate to do so.

A few minutes later, their hunger sated, they sat back in their chairs to enjoy the sensation of fullness. Spud pulled his tin from his pocket and rolled a joint while Nick brought him up to date on his life with Lynn in England.

'Wow, congratulations!' beamed Spud to the news of Lynn's pregnancy. 'Ho ho, that's the slippery slope to responsibility mind, know what I mean? But no, really, that's far out. I always wanted kids myself, man, but never managed to keep hold of a woman for long enough, you know?' He looked slightly wistful for a moment before coming back to himself. 'So, when's it due, eh?' he enquired of Lynn. 'You feeling alright with it? Morning sickness or anything?'

'October. And I'm feeling great,' she replied with a huge smile. It was obvious that she was currently relishing the prospect of becoming a mother.

'Cool. And you look good too,' he observed, his head nodding. 'Picture of health and all that. What is it they say? Booming? Blooming? Blossoming? Whatever - you know what I mean. You're a lucky man, Nick my friend, a lucky man indeed.' He held up the spliff. 'Anyone?' he offered. To Spud's bemusement Nick declined again, although Adam accepted gladly.

'We're moving to Scotland before the birth though, yeah?' Lynn informed him. 'Don't want to bring a kid up in Pompey. It's become a shit-hole over the last few years, you know? So we're going to where the air is clean, the crime is low and the living is good.'

'What, Glasgow then?' he mocked gently.

'Don't be daft,' she responded.

'Only kidding,' he placated unnecessarily.

'It's the Highlands for us!' declared Nick fervently. Spud could see that his old friend was relishing both the new challenge of fatherhood and the venture into unknown territory.

'Well bash my daddy with a custard flan!' he commented. 'Man, that's a big move. I never thought I'd see the day when Nick Barton became a country bumpkin. My, my.' He shook his head in disbelief before continuing. 'So, you like rain and midges then, eh?' he suggested.

'No mate,' replied Nick, 'on the East coast it's much drier and hardly any midges either.'

'Cold though, eh?'

'Fuck me, Spud. Ever thought of working for the Scottish tourist board? It's only cold in the winter and it'll be nice to see a bit of proper snow. But it's one of the sunniest areas of Britain, right? And it hardly gets dark in the middle of summer, you know? Anyway, what with global warming and the seasons all fucked up like they are these days we'll probably be growing peaches in a few years.'

'You doing that "good life" thing then? Back to the land and all that. What do they call it..."downsizing"?'

'You bet,' said Nick enthusiastically, 'I'm really looking forward to growing fruit and veg, right? We'll get a poly tunnel, few chickens, you know? "Living off the fat of the land".'

'We grow food at the foundation,' interjected Andor, 'and we had chickens and goats too. Most of what we ate, we grew ourselves.'

Sonilla surprised them all by contributing at this point. She had been so quiet since they all met that any utterance by her was unexpected. 'I used to enjoy tending the hens,' she said meekly with her eyes staring down into her tea as if she could see her memories played out there. 'They could be so funny sometimes and the little chicks were so sweet.' Adam thought he saw a slight hint of a smile at the corner of her mouth and a trace of life in her lacklustre eyes. It was a very subtle change, but the reminiscing seemed to be producing the first expressions on her face that were not born out of despair. 'The cockerel was so full of himself too,' she continued softly as if talking to herself. 'He would strut up and down, all self-important, as if he owned the world. Then, if he found a tasty morsel, he would have a special cluck that brought the hens running to share it with him. My sister and I used to collect the eggs together. Sometimes Lendi would...' She stopped suddenly as her voice caught in her throat and her eyes filled with tears. She covered her face with her hands. 'Sorry,' she managed to mumble through a sob, 'I can't...' Andor pulled her close and sniffling quietly she buried her face in his shoulder.

Spud was taken aback by Sonilla's behaviour and looked quizzically from Nick to Lynn, then back again, noticing the sympathy in their expressions.

'Her sister was killed last week,' Lynn informed him in a hushed voice.

'Oh, Jesus, I'm really sorry Sonilla,' he said sincerely, the shock clearly visible on his face, but she did not respond.

'You were not to know,' said Andor simply.

'Wow, that's really heavy,' commented Spud with a deep sigh and then proceeded to gaze into his mug, swirling the dregs of his tea.

The young woman's grief had been eating at Adam's spirit since they had teamed up. His sympathy was of little use to her. He could only imagine how it felt to lose such a cherished sibling. Of course he would be devastated if Charlie died, but he hadn't seen him for several years and they had had little contact in that time, so undoubtedly his own sorrow would not be as deep as Sonilla's. Nevertheless, he was beginning to weary of the impact her melancholy was having on the mood of his holiday and guiltily, he was looking forward to saying goodbye so he no longer had to share in her bereavement. He thought less of himself that his compassion was finite, especially as he liked his new friends, but he couldn't help how he felt. It was not as if he had any control over his emotions – they were just something that happened in response to his circumstances weren't they? He took another deep lungful of smoke and held it for a few seconds before passing the joint back to Spud, feeling comfortably numbed.

After a couple of minutes of sober silence, Lynn spoke up. 'Well, we'd better make tracks, yeah?' she suggested. 'These guys need to meet their friend and we've got a long drive ahead of us.'

Nick nodded mutely and Adam said, 'Yeah, thanks for everything Spud, it's been good to meet you.'

'No problem mate,' he responded. 'Good to meet all of you too. And great to see you again Nick. Any time you're in this neck of the woods you're always welcome, you know? And the rest of you too. Mi casa es su casa.'

When they went up to retrieve their bags from the flat, Lynn suggested that young fugitives should change their outfits to look less conspicuous. Andor was taller than Adam but shorter than Nick, so he had to make do with clothes from the larger man. Sonilla was only slightly smaller than Lynn.

'I'm getting bigger all the time, yeah?' said the latter, 'so these won't fit me much longer anyway.' She laid a few things on the bed for Sonilla to choose from. 'I ain't got any bras though,' she added, 'I don't know if you wear 'em?'

'What's a bra?' asked the girl innocently.

'Ah-ha, a woman after my own heart!' said Lynn, smiling. 'It's something that modern women strap themselves into to stop their boobs swinging about, you know? And maybe to try and hide the fact that they've got nipples and stop blokes gawping at their chests – but you'll never stop that! Anyway, I can't stand the bloody things – all sweaty and constricting. No, I'm all for keeping them free myself.'

They trooped back downstairs to return the key to Spud and then bade their final farewells. The rain had eased to become a fine but continual drizzle, driven into their faces by a strong breeze and they traipsed unenthusiastically along the wet pavement with their heads bowed, all but Adam reluctant to hasten the division of their small party. Lynn in particular felt that on their journey over the last few days, she had forged a very strong bond with their newfound friends and was not looking forward to their separation. Andor was a mine of astounding information offering a completely contradictory version of human history, an in-depth knowledge of the workings of the human body and an enticing glimpse into the potential of the extended mind. Sonilla had been almost completely withdrawn, yet Lynn felt an inexplicable and formidable emotional connection with the girl that filled her with both awe and wonder. The empathy she had experienced with the young woman's grief had affected her deeply but the exhilaration she felt from this newfound budding *psychic* relationship was adding an entirely unexpected and extraordinary dimension to her life and her perceptions. Furthermore, she was beginning to discern those first tiny stirrings of a living being inside that are such an exciting landmark in pregnancy. At only fifteen weeks, the slightly twitchy fluttering sensations gently tickling inside her belly were the earliest indications of her baby's movements. However, even beyond and above this physical manifestation, was her awareness of the quickening of the infant's mind. She could detect a tiny, pure spark of consciousness, which although distinguishable from her own, was nonetheless intimately linked and inseparably intertwined. This filled her heart and spirit with an electrifying, invigorating euphoria beyond any joy or ecstasy she had ever experienced or imagined in her life before, with or without drugs. Adam's voice interrupted her thoughts. She knew how he was feeling and she didn't judge him for it, but would not let it affect her own frame of mind.

'So, Andor, er, have you thought about what you're going to do after you've met up with your contact?' he asked.

'Not really,' replied Andor, walking hand in hand with Sonilla. 'We have not lived outside the foundation since we were small children and don't know much about how to manage in the outside world. I was rather hoping that Thu Salamu would return to guide us and that we would still be able to join the Ancestors in their work.'

They arrived at the car and Lynn unlocked the doors before seating herself behind the wheel. Nick stowed their bags and sat next to her in the front, the others squeezing onto the back seat. As he fastened his seat belt Nick asked, 'Do you remember the way?' and reached for the street map on the dashboard.

'Of course I do,' answered Lynn loftily, 'you know I've got a photographic memory.'

'Oh yeah, sorry,' he mumbled, 'I forgot.'

'Everyone strapped in, yeah?' enquired Lynn, checking her rear view mirror as she started the engine. Indicating and pulling out into a gap in the traffic, she drove them back to the address Salamu had given them. When they arrived at the correct street, they discovered that all the parking spaces were taken. It was a road lined with cafés and boutiques and despite the dreary weather it was bustling with the brolly-bearing public.

'Busy isn't it?' posed Nick unnecessarily. 'We'll have to try round the corner.'

As they drove slowly past the door, Adam noticed two dark suited men hunkering under a large black umbrella. 'Look, there's a couple of dodgy looking blokes hanging about outside,' he observed.

They all looked.

'Do you recognise them?' asked Nick. 'Can you read their minds?'

'No, maybe it has nothing to do with us,' Andor replied, 'and it's too busy to determine what they are thinking, although I can tell they are bored.'

'Well, I reckon we should approach with caution, yeah?' suggested Lynn. Eventually they had to park in a quieter street two blocks away. When they emerged from the car, the rain had finally ceased.

'Thank fuck for that,' commented Nick, 'I thought it was never going to stop.'

They made their way back to the street where the contact's apartment was but Adam stopped them with a hand gesture while he peered nervously around the corner like an amateurish spy who had learnt his trade from watching B movies on afternoon television.

'They've gone,' he declared with relief, visibly relaxing. 'Maybe they were nothing to do with you guys.'

'Okay, let's go,' prompted Nick, 'and hope that there's some bugger at home today.'

They stood in a restless huddle on the sidewalk and while Adam scrutinised the street for suspicious characters, Lynn rang the bell. Nick stepped back a few feet and looked up at the windows above.

'The curtains are still shut,' he observed. 'I reckon they're still not here, you know?'

Lynn rang the bell again.

Two minutes later Adam said, 'what are we going to do now?'

'Why don't we try again later?' proposed Lynn. 'Look, let's go and wait in that café over there and we can keep an eye on the front door, yeah?' she pointed to an establishment on the opposite side of the road that offered an ideal view of the flat. They crossed the road and filtered in through the narrow doorway. The air was thick with pungent fumes, which Andor and Sonilla found unbearable. Lynn was also finding that her tolerance of smoke had diminished more and more as her pregnancy progressed, despite only having stopped a matter of weeks previously. They decided to sit in the courtyard garden so they edged through the haze and out the back door. They would take turns in checking on the apartment. A sullen, hollow-eyed young waitress with a slight bony frame, like that of a fragile unfledged nestling, dried the seats for them before scurrying away without speaking or making eye contact.

'Blimey, she was cheerful,' remarked Adam wryly.

'She has many worries in her life,' Andor told him gravely. 'Her vulnerability left her mind wide open to me. She has an eating disorder and her father is terminally ill in hospital. She sat at his bedside the whole of last night.'

'Oh,' said Adam contritely, 'I can see this mind reading would be useful to the socially inadequate such as myself.' He sometimes felt that his lack of insight into the feelings of those around him was becoming a bit of a curse. His long-held view of himself as a sensitive, selfless, gentle guy was gradually being replaced with an increasing awareness of his inconsiderate, egocentric, judgemental and self-serving aspects that he had denied for so long.

'Don't give yourself a hard time Adam,' advised Lynn, 'just remember not to judge people by appearances, right? Or by a single incident – there's always a back story, yeah?'

Finally, the sun's rays had begun to penetrate the thinning clouds and they sat enjoying the brightness and warmth. The waitress returned to take their order and Adam tried to project sympathy and goodwill towards her. He wasn't under the impression that it would do her any good, but it had to be better than his former disparagement. He resolved to give her a generous tip and told himself it wasn't just to buy an easier conscience. Sonilla turned to him and fixed him with a searching gaze. Disconcertingly, he felt like she was seeing further into him than his face, as if her eyes could read an x-ray of his mind.

'Why do you and all those other people in there, fill your lungs with burning smoke?' she asked, nodding towards the interior. 'I could hardly breathe in there...and I felt that even those of them that are fairly content with their lives are still willing to poison themselves in an effort to dull their minds and their senses. Surely it is better to face life's inconveniences and challenges, then contemplate the solutions and one's self improvement with a clear mind? Why would one opt for making these choices with impaired judgement?'

Adam squirmed uncomfortably and scratched his head, frowning. 'Er...' was all he could manage as he considered the lack of reasonable and logical answers to her enquiry. He knew that there were psychological and socio-economic factors that could explain some of it, but he couldn't begin to structure his thoughts in a way that would enable him to articulate any clarification of their behaviour.

Lynn tried to rescue him. 'Well, it's kind of difficult to explain, you know?' she began. 'I've given up now I'm preggers 'cos I don't want to like, harm the baby or nothing, but when I smoked it was just a way of life and I got used to it I suppose and when I started, when I was young you know, even though we were told as kids it was harmful, we didn't really care because it was about being cool and stuff, yeah?'

Andor looked at her quizzically. 'So, you are saying that doing something harmful to yourself gained you merit amongst your peers?'

'Well yeah, sort of. It was about seeming tough and strong and stuff I suppose, like a form of defence, but also a kind of casual indifference, you know? A rebellion against an authority that demands respect without like even earning it or deserving it. And because it didn't do any immediate harm, the decades in the future when it might just seemed so distant, yeah? It's like when you're young, you just can't imagine that you're ever going to get old, you know? And then of course, before you know it you're hooked and the thought of giving it up is worse than the possibility of some bad health in the future. And you say to yourself, "Oh yeah, I'll like, totally give up one day soon" but you never do because you enjoy it so much. And then dope smoking's something else again.....' She trailed off as the waitress returned with their drinks and their chosen selection of pastries. Lynn, who had ordered two, never one to have observed social niceties, wasted no time in tucking in ravenously.

'But you gave up for your baby,' stated Sonilla. 'A mother's instinct to protect her child can be a very powerful force.' She turned to Nick. 'And you gave up smoking to support Lynn – an admirable testament to the strength of the love you feel for her. And you,' she said facing Adam again, 'you don't want to give up tobacco, but you feel you should because your friend's have and you know it is a poison that does you physical harm. You also suspect that your long term use of cannabis may do psychological harm and is the cause of, or has a strong influence on, your paranoia...but you still enjoy having your wits dulled as a way of cushioning you from difficulties, the feeling of mild euphoria, relaxation and even the satisfying sensation of the hot smoke in your lungs. You face a dilemma, but to avoid thinking about it, you stupefy yourself all the more.'

'Er, yeah...' muttered Adam awkwardly, feeling a little self conscious and embarrassed, 'I guess that just about sums it up.' He shifted in his seat as a physical manifestation of the discomfort he was feeling in his mind. How could this young woman so disconcertingly not only probe his thoughts but also come up with a concise and unsettlingly accurate analysis of his psyche? He sighed and looked at the table, unsure whether or not he should say anything else.

'How long shall we give it before going back, do you think?' asked Nick of the group, rescuing Adam from his unease, 'About an hour?'

'Yeah, probably,' agreed Lynn.

The others nodded their agreement.

'I'll go and buy a paper,' offered Adam, keen to divert his attention from the uncomfortable introspection unwittingly triggered by Sonilla. 'It might help pass the time I suppose,' he added, 'I think they'll have English ones here.'

Five minutes later he returned breathing heavily, his face pale and a look of panic in his eyes. 'We're in trouble,' he panted and dropped a newspaper on the table so they could all see the front page. Under the headline "Studenten Ontvoerd!" there were photographs of Andor and Sonilla.

'Holy fucking shit!' exclaimed Nick, to be immediately hushed by Lynn who tipped her head in the direction of another table in the courtyard now occupied by a smart middle-aged couple who were regarding them suspiciously. Luckily, the two fugitives had their backs to the strangers, so it was more likely that it was Nick's exclamation that had caught their attention and the group's dishevelled appearance that had gained their disapproval.

'What does is say?' whispered Lynn.

'I couldn't find an English paper, but the picture says enough,' said Adam in hushed tones, giving the couple a sidelong glance. 'Anyway, I asked the bloke in the shop and he said the headline said "Students kidnapped" and then it goes on to say how they were snatched in Poland by a criminal gang from England who are now on the run in the Netherlands. We are supposed to be armed and dangerous and asking for a ransom of five million Euros.'

'Oh man, this is all we need,' rasped Nick putting his head in his hands.

'Let's get out of here,' suggested Lynn quietly. 'Maybe we can like hole up in Spud's flat til we work out what to do, yeah?'

They hastily left the café, trying not to behave too conspicuously, Sonilla at the last moment snatching up the newspaper and stuffing it inside her jacket. They decided to try their supposed "safe house" once more. It didn't seem to be being watched but Sonilla and Andor stayed alert as Lynn rang the bell to the flat. There was still no answer so they headed back towards where they had left the car.

As they approached the junction to the street where they had parked, Sonilla stopped and held up her hand, indicating that the others should do likewise. She looked at Andor, who nodded slowly.

'There's something wrong,' he informed them levelly. 'The car has been discovered.'

Nick carefully chanced a peek around the corner but quickly withdrew his head.

'Fucking hell!' he blurted, 'the car's surrounded by fucking pigs!'

Lynn hushed him urgently, putting her finger to her lips with an exasperated look on her face.

'I saw at least three squad cars, lights flashing,' he gasped, 'and it's crawling with coppers clearing the street.' He looked terrified. 'What the fuck are we going to do now?'

'Get the hell out of here.' proposed Lynn.

Suddenly a deep, deafening boom thumped through their chests. Adam staggered and belatedly covered his throbbing ears. He turned to look back at the junction where the sound of shattering and falling glass was followed by a slowly roiling wall of smoke, dust and debris. He stood frozen for a moment, stunned by the physical shock, before the implication of what had just occurred grew in his consciousness.

'Oh my God, no!' Lynn gasped putting her hands to her mouth. They looked at each other in horror. Adam felt a knot in his throat as tears welled up in his eyes. He had never before been so close to such a disaster. The thought of the police officers who had been surrounding the car and anyone else who hadn't got clear and what must have happened to them, was too much for him to bear. He was jolted by Sonilla lurching into him, letting out a mournful groan. As she collapsed lifelessly in his arms he instinctively grabbed her and lowered her gently to the wet pavement. Andor slumped against the wall and crumpled to the floor, breathing heavily, eyes closed and a grimace contorting his features. Lynn rushed to his side.

'There is...death,' he muttered weakly, then winced and clutched his abdomen, 'and...much pain...'

'They can *feel* it too!' said Lynn, looking up at Nick who was standing shocked and bewildered, scratching his head. 'Come on!' she added insistently, 'we've got to get them moving and get out of here!'

Nick shook himself and went over to help her lift Andor to his feet while Adam gently patted Sonilla's cheek in an attempt to rouse her. He could hear cries of pain and urgent shouts from people in the next street. Others rushed past them towards the scene to see if they could help.

Andor slowly opened his eyes. 'It's okay,' he said, 'I've managed to screen it out now. When one is caught unawares it can be quite a shock. I've never felt such pain before.....nor been so close to violent death...'

He rose and joined Adam who was crouched supporting the still dazed Sonilla with an arm around her shoulders. Andor placed his hands either side of her head and calmed his breathing, looking intently into her face. Her eyes flickered open and he removed his hands. She shook her head as though ridding herself of an internal irritation and allowed Andor to help her stand.

'Those poor men....' She murmured tremulously, tears trickling down her cheeks. They were all quietly weeping now as the appalling depth of the tragedy reached their emotional awareness. To be so close to and witness such a horrendous and gruesome incident made it so much more traumatic than hearing about it on the news. Dazed and frightened, they slowly began moving away from the scene. Finally Nick spoke, having remained uncharacteristically silent since the explosion.

'That could've been us,' he stated dully, too stunned to swear. 'But who could've done that? And why? Whoever is after you two is very, very scary and very, very bad.'

Nobody responded but Adam started shaking uncontrollably. The shock and fear plunged to his core and he suddenly felt nauseous. Lurching to the gutter he fell to his hands and knees and vomited. Before he had a chance to recover Nick, as white faced as his friend, had him on his feet and moving. They quietly made their way through the back streets in a state of disbelief, urged on by Lynn, who of them all seemed to have regained the most composure. An hour later, they were approaching Spud's café.

'I think we should use the back door, yeah?' Lynn suggested. 'God knows who is watching what or where at the moment.'

They crept through the gate from the alley and gathered with the rubbish bins in the small yard at the back, concealed by the six-foot high walls. Nick peered through the half-open door into the steamy kitchen where a Dutch radio station blasted out "I Can't Get No Satisfaction" by the Rolling Stones. Just inside, Hank was loading the dishwasher and singing along in a loud, tuneless voice.

'Pst! Oi, Hank!' called Nick. The young man raised his flushed, freckly face and smiled expectantly, eyebrows raised.

'Go and get Spud will you mate? Cheers,' said Nick.

His friend appeared a couple of minutes later, looking slightly bemused.

'What's going on?' he enquired half smiling. 'What you skulking around back there for?'

Nick looked both uncomfortable and scared.

'Er..., Spud mate, can we hole up in the flat for a few hours?' he requested, 'Something's happened that means...er, we need to discuss a...change of plan.'

'Yeah, 'course you can man,' said Spud, picking up on the seriousness of his friend's demeanour, 'but you've got to tell me what's happening – I know when something heavy's going down. I'll just get you the key.'

'Er, it's probably best if we don't use the front door,' confessed Nick, 'we um, don't really want to be seen...'

'Oh, like that is it? What have you gone and done?' Spud sighed and shook his head, 'Come on, you can go up the fire escape.'

He indicated a metal ladder fixed to the wall that led up to a window on the first floor.

'I'll go round through the front door and open her up,' he added.

As Adam, the last to ascend, clambered through into the kitchen of the flat, Spud crossed his arms and leaned back against the worktop.

'Right,' he said grimly, 'let's have it then. If you're caught up in some heavy shit and you want my help, you're going to have to tell me *everything*.'

'Buddha's ball bag!' commented Spud after he'd heard their story. They had so far omitted any mention of telepathy, considering that it might be adding too much for him to handle at this time. 'You really *are* up shit creek,' he continued solemnly. 'I heard about the explosion on the radio, but I never would have guessed it was anything to do with you lot.' He slowly shook his head and signed heavily. 'Man, this is very, *very* heavy.'

'What did they say?' asked Lynn.

'Two police killed, four seriously wounded,' he told them grimly, 'and countless other minor injuries amongst passersby. They said they were investigating a suspicious vehicle – supposedly a rental car reportedly used by kidnappers in Poland – when they were tipped off that it might contain a bomb. They had just started trying to clear the street when it went off. They reckon it's probably some terrorist group, though no one's claimed responsibility yet and they want to find and question the English couple who hired the car but they think they might have been killed or held hostage by the terrorists...or they *are* the terrorists.'

'So they *have* linked it to the "kidnapped" students then?' asked Nick. 'Have you seen the paper?'

'Yep and nope,' replied his friend.

Sonilla pulled out the newspaper from her jacket and handed it over.

'We don't know exactly what it says,' Lynn told him, 'but it doesn't look good.'

Holding the paper in one hand Spud pursed his lips, scratched his head and squinted at the page. He scanned the text for a few moments before looking up.

'Well, it says here that these guys are son and daughter of a British diplomat stationed in Poland and they were kidnapped from some posh school by an armed gang who are supposed to have fled to Holland and are demanding a huge ransom for their safe return.'

'But that's not right,' asserted Sonilla, frowning and looking perplexed. 'Why do they print untruths?'

'I see you've got a lot to learn about the world darlin',' commented Spud levelly, '...especially the media.'

'They must've been fed the story by your enemies,' decided Adam.

Spud looked around the room at the others, one by one. 'So, what are you going to do then? You are well and truly in deep do-do - but you can't hide here forever. You need a plan.'

The response was merely a round of shaken heads and sighs.

'Tell you what,' he proposed, 'I've got to go back to work for a couple of hours. I'll come back later – give you time to think about it. If there's any way I can help that doesn't involve getting banged up or killed, I'll be happy to oblige.' He squeezed Nick's shoulder, turned and left them to it, shaking his head as he went.

CHAPTER EIGHTEEN.

The hatch on the cell door scraped open and the evening meals were pushed through onto the shelf inside before it was slammed shut again. In the weeks of their imprisonment the women had given up on any attempts at engaging Nasaru in conversation, not because of the man's reticence, but due to their increasing resentment at the fact of their incarceration, the deprivation of their sight by the helmets and the cramped, uncomfortable conditions in which they were being kept. After their capture, Bess was expecting to return to the fairly luxurious surroundings she had "enjoyed" previously, but on enquiring as to when this would happen she was informed that due to her earlier escape "their lordships" had considered it judicious to resort to more secure accommodation. They had to endure the degrading experience of using a bucket as a toilet that was only collected for emptying once a day and they weren't even given any washing facilities.

On their first day Bess began to detect a distant noise, just on the edge of her hearing. When she alerted Rowan to it, she listened too. They came to distinguish it as the sound of a girl or young woman crying. Trying to discern which direction it was coming from, they crept slowly and silently around their cell. Bess stopped at the wall opposite her bunk and putting her ear against it, heard the sobbing more clearly. She guessed that there must be another captive in the adjacent room. They attempted to devise a system of knocks to communicate with the wretched girl. They had tried calling first, but either she didn't hear or chose not to respond and although to begin with tapping on the wall seemed to stop her crying she still didn't answer. Presumably the knocks meant nothing if they had not previously agreed a code for the signals. Over the next few days they often heard sobbing in the neighbouring cell, although it gradually decreased in frequency.

It was extremely difficult to sustain any kind of upbeat mood in the cool, stale chamber, blinded and with ears muffled by the tough head coverings. They had begun by swapping life-stories in ever-increasing detail, sharing their thoughts and feelings about loving and living in a rapidly changing world and in the process they forged a bond between them that could last a lifetime, though what length that might now be was uncertain. They soon ran out of word games they could maintain an interest in and as time passed, they gradually spoke less, their depression deepening at the interminable boredom of the seemingly endless, unchanging days. Although Bess was finding it difficult, Rowan was the worst affected by the helmets that they had been unable to remove since their capture. The stifling of her extended mind was such a crippling blow to her spirits that she would sometimes spend days in melancholic silence, no more than grunting in reply to Bess' most persistent entreaties. The girl felt as if she had been deprived of most of her senses, living a half-life as a sub-human in a perpetual nightmare. After two weeks of incarceration she began self-harming again, knowing that Bess couldn't see her. Without the use of her psychic powers she felt driven to compensate for the sensory deprivation by finding a way to intensify one of her remaining faculties – to create a physical substitute - so resorted to one with which she was familiar – pain. She took to biting the tender inside of her forearms, using more force each time, until she eventually drew blood. A week later, these self-inflicted wounds covered her arms, some scabbed over, others infected due to the unhygienic conditions until all she had to do to revive almost unbearable agony was to pull back her sleeves and scrape her arms down the rough concrete walls.

On this day when the food came, Rowan didn't move to take her plate. Bess started eating, but soon noticed that her companion did not.

'Food's here Ro,' she said, 'get it while it's hot.'

'Not hungry,' the girl muttered weakly.

'Why, what's up? Aren't you well?' Bess moved over to Rowan's bunk and reached out her hand to find the young woman's neck. 'Jesus Ro, you're burning up!' she gasped, 'you've got a raging fever...how long have you been like this?'

'Dunno,' her friend replied quietly.

Bess fetched some water and gently lifted Rowan's head, trying to feel where her mouth was to avoid tipping the liquid over her chest and neck. Rowan drank thirstily and then coughed weakly, choking slightly on the last mouthful.

'You need medical attention,' asserted the older woman, 'I'm going to call for help.' Rowan did not object.

'Nasaru!' Bess shouted at the door, 'we need a doctor! Rowan's really ill!'

There was no answer. She continued calling for some time, but still no one came.

#

The bed lurched sickeningly and Adam groaned, slowly opening his sticky, bleary eyes. He pulled himself up with difficulty until he knelt on the bunk and, grasping the edges of the porthole, peered out through the bespattered glass at the churning chaos of huge white-topped, granite coloured waves seething between him and the indistinct horizon. Hearing a spluttering retch behind him, he turned to see Nick sitting on the edge of another bunk with his head bowed over a bucket held between his knees. Lynn had her arm around his shoulders and stroked his matted hair. Adam couldn't speak. He just needed to follow his own body's urgent need for fresh air. Although the cabin was relatively spacious and comfortable, he found that the air became stale and stifling after six people had spent the last few hours sleeping in it, or at least attempting to do so. Clambering from his mattress he tottered wordless towards the door, arms outstretched to keep his balance as the floor lurched unpredictably beneath his feet. Out on deck, he quickly staggered to the gunwale, grasped it firmly with both hands and breathed deeply.

'Keep eyes to horizon,' instructed a thick-accented voice behind him, 'it help you have…how you say…point of reference, yes?'

Adam turned his head to see an amiable smile on the swarthy weather-beaten features of a burly sailor whose name he'd forgotten since the hasty introductions to the multiracial crew late the previous night.

'Thanks,' was all he could manage before taking the advice, though after five minutes he had rallied sufficiently to allow himself to glance around the yacht. The wind buffeted his hair, blowing it across his face. He puffed it from his mouth and then raked it away from his eyes with one hand while still gripping the rail with the other. The ninety-foot vessel was elegant, stylish and classy. It seemed to ride the choppy sea with exuberance, like a spirited thoroughbred horse given its rein. All but the foresail were furled because of the strength of the wind, but beneath the hum of the rigging and the ceaseless pinging of the lines against the masts Adam could hear the deep growl of a diesel engine helping to propel the boat. He looked to the stern and saw Andor and Sonilla sitting on a bench with Thu Salamu. She had suddenly and unexpectedly reappeared the previous night, just when it looked as if they had run out of options.

They had been attempting to devise some kind of strategy as they sat around the kitchen table in Spud's flat, but had soon fallen into silence, their spirits growing heavier as the horror of the bombing sank deeper into their minds. Adam, Lynn and Nick were staring at the scratched and dented wooden surface as if they might find an answer to their dilemma. Sonilla and Andor held hands and stared expressionlessly into the distance out of the window. Nick summarised their position admirably.

'We are well and truly fucked!' he concluded morosely. 'We're being chased by a bunch of evil mind-bending cunts *and* fucking Interpol for Christ's sake, for kidnapping some rich bastard's teenage kids...and on top of that, not only are we wanted for car theft, we're also suspected of fucking terrorism and the murder of a load of Dutch coppers.' He paused to take a breath and shake his head before adding, 'And you know what? Somehow I just can't see them believing our story either.' He stood and started agitatedly pacing the floor, a grim frown creasing his brow. He seemed imbued with desperation, fear and sadness. 'I'm soon to become a dad,' he continued sullenly, 'and the poor little bastard's going to be born to parents spending the rest of their lives in the fucking nick. I *so* wanted to be a good dad too. Now I'm going to be worse than fucking useless....shit!' He banged his fist on the table and sat heavily with a heartfelt sigh. Lynn put her arm around his shoulders, her dark, cheerless eyes moist with imminent tears.

'Don't worry babe,' she pleaded, 'we'll totally figure something out, yeah?' but her words lacked conviction.

Adam also felt at the end of his tether. Despite the many emotional upheavals in his adult life, this was by far the worst. He just felt so powerless; it all just kind of *happened* to them without them having any choice in the matter and then it all spiralled out of control. He didn't think that getting back to England would be any help, but that's what he wanted. If he was going to go to prison for the rest of his life, he would rather it was a British one. But how could they get there? All the ferries and airports would certainly be watched.

'I know,' he said aloud as the thought came to him, 'maybe we could get a boat back to England – you know, just go to the docks and ask around some of the private yachts – there's bound to be someone.'

'Come on Adam,' said Nick disparagingly, 'even if we could find someone daft enough and with enough space for five fugitives, we'd have to pay a fortune for the privilege – we're fucking very high risk cargo now, you know?'

'There could just be three of you,' said Sonilla calmly. 'You do not need to take us.'

'What? No way can we abandon you now!' protested Lynn. 'You'll get nabbed for sure!'

'No, really, it's fine,' said Andor. 'We can look after ourselves now. You have done enough and we are extremely thankful for your help. If you had not got involved with us, you would not be caught up in these circumstances.'

'Here...I know what you're up to,' claimed Lynn. Her mouth widened and her mouth dropped open as the realisation came to her. She pointed across the table. 'I just totally picked up on your thoughts or something...or, no...like your intentions or whatever. You know that if you stay behind you'll get caught and though the police will still be after us, them people who're after *you* won't be, which'll give us more of a chance – it's a self-sacrifice, martyr thing isn't it? You would do it to give us more of a chance.'

Everyone in the room stared at her. Adam looked from Lynn to the young couple and could tell from their expressions that she was right but that they hadn't expected her to figure it out.

'Bloody hell Lynn...' he said slowly, '...are you getting more telepathic?'

'Well...a bit maybe,' she replied hesitantly, 'you know...just gradually...I think I've been like *sensing* stuff more...'

'It's true,' confirmed Andor, 'we had noticed an increase in Lynn's psychic awareness. That is often how it happens. She is....'

A sudden noise at the window startled them, and they all looked over to see Spud sliding open the casement. He clambered awkwardly over the sill causing Adam to wonder why he hadn't used the door – after all it was not Spud who was the fugitive. The man straightened himself, breathing heavily from his exertions. In addition to being a heavy smoker and overweight he was obviously unaccustomed to physical exercise.

'Right, here's the plan,' he declared without preamble, 'I know this guy with a boat – sets sail for good old Blighty tomorrow before dawn. With a bit of luck, I should be able to get you lot on board.'

'Won't he expect a payment?' asked Lynn, 'I mean like five extra passengers on the run from the law is a bit of a risk isn't it?'

'What we don't tell him, he won't know,' stated Spud simply. 'Anyway, he owes me big time.... and er, his um...cargo is already "high risk", if you know what I mean, so you lot won't make much difference.'

'Why? What's he up to?' asked Adam suspiciously, immediately imagining the worst kind of international criminal. 'What kind of bloke are you trying to get us mixed up with?'

'Probably best if you don't know mate,' Spud replied candidly.

Adam discerned that Sonilla and Andor had more than an inkling by the way they exchanged glances, but they remained silent. He looked over to Lynn and saw the fear in her eyes before she quickly averted them. In another situation he may have been more disgruntled by this feeling of missing out on something, but at the moment he wasn't sure if it was a blessing or not.

'Anyway,' continued Spud, 'beggars can't be choosers right? Do you want to get out of here or not?'

Spud's dubious acquaintance was not as willing as their friend had led them to believe and certainly not as cooperative as he had obviously expected. They had waited until almost midnight before climbing out of the window and piling into Spud's beloved old VW camper van behind the back yard of the café. Ten minutes later they clambered out of the vehicle into a thick and fetid atmosphere amongst the hulking grubby-looking warehouses that seemed to sulk moodily by the docks. Their friend had decided to park between the buildings so that his van wasn't seen near the yacht, 'just in case...' he had muttered. The air was motionless and humid, reeking from a putrid cocktail of rotting seaweed, diesel and fish. The sky was as dark as it ever gets in a city, heavily laden as it was with thick black clouds, but with a sickly glow from reflected streetlights. Adam caught his breath and looked around. He recognised that he had a tendency towards paranoia, but still couldn't help feeling that someone or something malevolent lurked in the shadows. They followed Spud between the buildings and along the wharf in the direction of the marina.

'I phoned and told him we were coming,' Spud whispered as they trod their way along the floating jetty towards the gangplank, 'so he'll be expecting us. He's not the kind of bloke you want to surprise really...I'll just need to fill him in on some details, but let me do the talking alright? He's a right crafty geezer this one.'

The reflections of the dim lights surrounding the harbour swayed languidly in the inky water. The boats crowding the moorings were each twinned in the distorted, shimmering mirror, where they appeared like anguished ghosts trapped behind malformed glass. At this hour and at this distance from the busier parts of the city, the silence of the still night was broken only by the faint creak of straining ropes and the almost inaudible caress of the of the sea on the smooth hulls.

'This is it,' Spud informed them as they approached his acquaintance's vessel.

'Fuck me,' uttered Nick, 'this bloke must be loaded! A boat like that, what is it...a hundred feet long.... must have cost millions!'

'Yep, about ten of them I reckon,' his friend responded, 'but keep your voice down mate – we should be trying to be low profile right?'

Adam looked in awe at the luxury "super yacht" before them. His worst fears regarding the nature of the owner's business could only be reinforced by such an ostentatious display of wealth. He had imagined that the character they were to meet might be involved in people trafficking, drug smuggling or gun running, but now he was convinced that he must be participating in *all* of these activities, if not more.

'It's a bit conspicuous though isn't it?' Lynn remarked in hushed tones, 'I mean, if you're like doing dodgy deals and smuggling and stuff, you'd think that you'd want to be like a bit less obvious about it, yeah?'

'Yeah, but he's got a good cover, see,' Spud whispered back, 'he owns a mining company with mines in several East European countries – he's stinking rich anyway.'

Adam was about to ask why this bloke needed to be involved in criminal activities when he so obviously did not need the money, but just then they heard footsteps approaching on deck. They were scrutinised and then allowed on board by a burly but amiable Irishman whose thick-set figure led them into a lavish stateroom where they found their potential saviour awaiting them. Juris Asaras, an impeccably dressed but grizzled Latvian of middle years, sat reclined on a leather sofa with his arm around the shoulders of a young, elegant and voluptuous blonde who was smoking a gold filtered, blue cocktail Sobrane in an ivory cigarette holder. On the teak coffee table before them sat a tumbler, a half empty bottle of single malt whisky and a silver cigarette case, presumably containing more of the coloured Russian cigarettes. With a slight gesture of his hand Asaras dismissed his companion who obediently disappeared into a cabin without a word. He greeted Spud affably, calling him "my old friend" and the others politely, bidding them settle in the plush seating. His accent was thick, but his English fluent and as sophisticated as his clothing. He glanced briefly at them all when introduced but his gaze lingered on Andor and Sonilla for a few more seconds as if he suspected that there was something a little unusual about them.

Spud briefly explained their dilemma, giving as little information as possible and asked the Latvian if he would be so kind as to offer his friends passage across the North Sea.

'Well, I *do* have spare bunks on this trip,' admitted Asaras, 'but you must understand that due to the high level of risk involved, the service will not come so cheaply.'

'Oh, but it's not *that* high a risk...' Spud started, but Asaras cut him off.

'I *do* read the papers you know,' he stated sternly, his steely grey eyes narrowing slightly, 'and I resent that, considering our long association, you have started this meeting by attempting to conceal the true nature of your "friends" circumstances and character.'

'Oh but the papers got it wrong!' the café owner blurted, gesticulating with his pudgy hands 'they're not who they say they are and they've not done all that stuff either.'

'Nevertheless,' Asaras continued unmoved, 'the mere fact that they are suspected of and wanted for such things is enough to justify a substantial fee. Remember, I am the one who is to be inconvenienced here. I was anticipating a quiet and trouble-free crossing without the burden of additional and bothersome cargo.'

'Ah well, you see Juris,' said Spud cockily, 'none of us have got much in the way of funds at the moment and the situation being somewhat urgent, so to speak, I didn't want to mention it...but I thought it might be time I could possibly call in an old favour. You remember that time I...'

'Of course I remember,' snapped Asaras briskly, sitting forward in his couch and clearly angered by the presumption, 'I do not need to be reminded of the *special* debt I owe you – that is a matter of personal honour – but this is a *business* proposition incomparable and irrelevant to those past circumstances.' He sat back and glared hard at Spud who seemed, after his futile attempt at misplaced bravado, to visibly wither under the more assertive man's gaze. 'Let me be quite clear about this,' the Latvian continued, 'I keep those two parts of my life completely separate *at all times* – no exceptions.'

'But...'

'No buts! I regret that you have felt it necessary to remind me, but I assure you that I had not forgotten my obligation and as soon as I have fulfilled it, I will be happy if our paths do not again cross.'

Adam's heart sank as he watched Spud slump back slowly shaking his head and sighing heavily – defeated. What were they going to do now? He thought for a moment that they could steal a boat, but then as far as he was aware, none of them knew how to sail. He was guessing that it was probably time to leave, so he started getting out of his seat, but Juris Asaras hadn't finished.

'I am not a cruel man you know, but operating my organisation incurs many overheads,' he told them, addressing the whole group, much calmer now. 'In order to be successful, each undertaking must also be costed in proportion to the risks involved. For a service such as you require I would charge normally five hundred thousand Euros each, but as a gesture of goodwill, because you say they are "innocent", and in view of the fact that I am making the crossing already, I could consider accepting one million for the group of five. Hope you understand that this is a *very* generous discount.'

The companions looked at each other, their hopes dashed.

Spud shook his head and sighed again. 'It may be so in your eyes Juris, but we just don't have that kind of money,' he muttered despondently.

Asaras was adamant. 'Then I am sorry, I am not in a position to help you.' As they stood to go he added, 'I wish you luck nonetheless,' but it sounded hollow and insincere.

The hapless group shuffled dejectedly down the gangplank. A light drizzle had started to fall, dampening their hair and clothes to match their spirits. During their short time aboard the yacht the darkness seemed to Adam to have deepened and the atmosphere thickened as if the sound, light and air and been sucked out. They ambled wordlessly and listlessly back to the Volkswagen where it seemed to have furtively sidled deeper into the shadow of the warehouse, as if fearful of some hidden menace of the night.

'Sorry folks, I really am,' muttered Spud quietly as they gathered in a huddle by the van, 'Man, I really thought he would have helped, you know, considering the enormous favour he owes me.'

'Don't worry about it mate, you did all you could,' Nick assured him. 'Anyway, what did you do for him that he's so much in your debt?'

His friend looked uncomfortable and stuffed his hands in his jacket pockets. 'Well, it's a bit complicated and embarrassing really,' Spud said, 'but basically...I saved his life.'

'Wow man!' commented Nick, 'he really *does* owe you – big time.'

'Yeah, well...actually, it was nothing heroic,' Spud admitted modestly, 'I kind of saved him by accident really, you know? And he's always kind of resented it too, cos he feels he owes me and *really* does not like being in debt to *anyone*. Anyway, it's a long story best left for another time.'

'So what do we do now?' said Adam in an unintentionally whiney voice. 'We're on the run in a foreign country, we can't hide here forever, we won't be able to work and we'll run out of money.'

'We'll just have to find another way back,' said Lynn, determined not to give up hope. As a future mother she felt she had even more reason to remain safe and free. 'Maybe we could get like, false passports or something...'

'Yeah but...' began Adam, but Andor interrupted him.

'Wait!' he said, raising a hand to silence them. Both he and Sonilla peered into the night towards the dimly lit road. They all gazed in the same direction, but it was silent and still except for the fine drizzle, highlighted by the glow as it floated down past the streetlights like sifted flour.

'Well, I can't see or hear *anything*,' commented Nick after a few moments.

'I can,' said Lynn softly.

At that moment, Adam heard the far-away murmur of a car travelling at speed and then saw the tiny moving glimmer of headlights in the distance. They stood in silence as the sound gradually increased and the lights grew closer. They watched as the vehicle turned off the main road with a screech of wheels and approached the dockyard.

'Er, do you think maybe we should hide or something?' ventured Adam growing uneasy, 'You know in case it's the police or those bad guys...'

'No. Do not be afraid,' Andor said smiling, 'it is a friend.'

The car, a red sporty looking convertible two-door Mazda, sped directly to where they stood and stopped abruptly next to the camper van. The driver, invisible in the dark interior behind the headlights glare, cut the engine, opened the door and climbed out.

'Salamu!' gasped Adam.

She faced Andor and in a brief moment something seemed to pass between them.

'Well, fuck my old boots! How did you find us here?' exclaimed Nick, before realising his dimness. He smiled and said, 'Oh yeah.'

They all greeted the former teacher warmly but she curtailed their enquiries saying, 'we have no time to lose!' Turning back to her car, she opened the passenger door and reached in to retrieve a leather brief case. She opened it to show them that it was packed full of bank notes and said, 'come on, we've got a boat to catch.' Then she held out the car keys, offering them to Spud. 'Have fun,' she said with a smile. He took them slowly and wordlessly, looking at them as if he had never seen such things before. He looked at the car and then at his friends, bewildered and gawping from one person to another.

'But how...what the...who...?' he stuttered.

'No time to explain mate,' said Nick giving him a quick hug, 'it would blow your fucking mind! I know it's blown mine! But thanks for all your help. Hopefully one day you'll get the whole story.'

'We'll write,' promised Lynn, kissing him on the cheek.

With that they all hastened to follow Thu Salamu with smiles, thanks and a final wave, leaving Spud staring after them open-mouthed, bemused and alone in the rain.

A group of quietly wheeling gulls followed the yacht, rising, falling and gliding above the turbulent wake, graceful and silent in their flight, pale against the sea, or darker when silhouetted against the pallid grey sky. The murky grey-green water was only slightly choppy but rocked the sleek craft with a significant swell. Adam wondered whether a cigarette would be advisable. He certainly craved one, but was unsure how it would affect his nausea. He glanced towards where the others were sitting and then Andor beckoned for him to join them. He walked unsteadily across the deck and sat next to Salamu on the bench.

'You guys not seasick then?' he asked of the trio.

'No,' replied Sonilla, 'to a certain extent we can control some physical processes.'

'Lucky you!' he commented, then remembered the seaman's advice and fixed his gaze on the shifting horizon again.

Thu Salamu addressed him. 'I understand that you have a brother in the Highlands of Scotland.' He nodded. 'We will have to stay with him on our way north,' she continued, 'there is a safe haven on Orkney where we can gain sanctuary. No one will be able to find you there.'

'Okay, but how are we supposed to get there from Eyemouth?' he asked. 'I expect our pictures will have been in the British papers by now *and* on the telly.'

'I can hire a vehicle,' she said matter-of-factly, 'you can remain inconspicuous within it. We can break our journey in less inhabited areas.'

'What about the bad guys?' Adam continued pessimistically, 'Presumably they're still following us? And I guess it was them who blew up the car right?'

'Yes, they wanted to make sure that there was a higher likelihood of you getting apprehended. I was successful in slowing them quite considerably but they have agents within the authorities of many European law enforcement bureaus and they do not want any surviving witnesses to the secret of their operations at the foundation in Poland - and that includes me. But do not worry, we have allies too and I am certain that they will succeed in delaying our pursuers further. They will certainly have trouble tracing us across the ocean – the energy patterns in large bodies of water create too much disruption to the field - and by the time we get to Orkney our trail should be undetectable. At the moment they are unaware of the refuge there, so they won't be looking in that direction. However, if they should somehow manage to discover us, they would not be able to enter – the defences are impenetrable, even to them.'

It wasn't just Salamu's words that reassured Adam; she also seemed to project a wave of calmness that soothed his emotions and quietened his thoughts, almost as if he had just smoked a joint of some really smooth Moroccan hash. He smiled at himself, remembering Sonilla's evaluation of his toking habit. He had known she was right, but at the time the fear of change in his way of life and the loss of his emotional and psychological prop was too much to contemplate. Since then, despite all that had been happening, he had been considering her words and their implication in some depth. He used dope not only as a recreational enhancement but also as solace, a comforter in times of stress; in fact there was hardly any situation in his life where he wouldn't consider approaching it under the influence of cannabis. However, he was now coming to acknowledge what he had known but refused to admit for some time: that being a stoner, combined with his addiction to tobacco, he wasn't really in charge of his life, but was actually letting himself be controlled by these substances. Over the years he had managed to convince himself that he couldn't fully enjoy music, food, films, sex, the countryside, reading or even the company of others without being stoned. He had used it as his ally in times of adversity; not that he actually believed that it solved anything, but it certainly enabled him to care less or at least help him stick his head in the sand and avoid confronting difficulties. On the rare occasions when he had been unable to obtain his narcotic of choice, straight tobacco – always roll-ups - served as a temporary, though inferior, surrogate. Now, here was this strange woman who seemed able to emanate some kind of soothing energy, replacing any need for his usual sedative. There was obviously more to this telepathy than just reading minds. He wished he had come across it in less perilous circumstances, so that there would be more room in his brain to contemplate and assimilate these revelations. Just how many of these "superminds" were out there, he wondered, mixing with the regular folk and influencing their lives for good or ill, unknown to their subjects.

'What happened to the contact in Amsterdam?' he asked, suddenly remembering the absence of an answer at their supposed safe house.

A look of pain momentarily creased Salamu's eyes. 'Unfortunately he was captured,' she said sadly. 'We don't know how he was identified and found, but it is a terrible loss. He was a good man and a good friend.'

'Oh, sorry to hear that,' said Adam, sensing that her distress was greater than she was showing. 'So are they going to kill him or torture him or something?'

'No...but his fate could be worse...' she said, almost choking on the phrase, '...he may be forced to become a *vessel*.'

'A what?' asked Adam, thinking that it didn't *sound* like a particularly dire fate.

'A "vessel" is used by those who wish to prolong their time as an individual consciousness by stealing, invading and occupying another's body when their own reaches the end of its natural lifespan.' Salamu paused, struggling to describe such misfortune when it applied to a friend. Adam reached out and squeezed her hand in a genuine but rather inadequate attempt to offer consolation. She gave him a slight smile of appreciation, realising his intentions. 'The victim's mind is overwhelmed,' she continued slowly, 'and subdued by the aggressor, but not destroyed – it is doomed to a helpless existence trapped in the depths of the psyche, deprived of physical senses and where it is conscious of nothing but its own existence, fate and impotence. Thus, when one body is worn out, the occupier can colonise another. In this way an individual can survive as a single ego indefinitely – a kind of immortality of the psyche.'

'Bugger me...,' remarked Adam in astonishment, '...everlasting life!' He found the concept difficult to grasp, unable to imagine how someone could relocate their entire consciousness from one body to another. He had always believed that the mind was generated by the brain – or at least inseparable from it until death, apart from maybe brief excursions of "astral travelling". He presumed that the abandoned body would perish after transference and he could see how anyone would be tempted by the prospect of being able to live forever, but to do so by stealing the body of someone else...it was horrifying really, a kind of human parasitism.

'This is of course completely different to the relationship between "The Select" and the Ancestors,' Thu Salamu asserted. 'In that case the "host" retains their own individual consciousness and ego, merely adding the accumulated knowledge, wisdom and experience of the ancients to their mind's memory bank. They are willing participants and the dying elders are happy to let go of their "selves" for the good of all.'

Adam couldn't tear his mind away from the terrifying thought of being possessed by another's psyche.

'There is a problem with the practice of vessel appropriation though,' continued the teacher grimly, 'it is not without its side effects. The vessel's mind requires a large amount of effort to suppress, especially if they have great skills – although these are the most often sought after because the brain retains a "skill memory" that adds to the aggressor's power. The mental stamina required to keep the host's intellect in check involves tremendous strain that disrupts the occupier's mind's energy patterns to such an extent that it causes some permanent distortion and damage manifesting as a form of insanity. It is a cumulative effect, so the more vessels a coloniser has acquired, the greater the derangement and corruption. Some of the transgressors have been practicing this travesty since The Shift, so not only are they incredibly psychotic, they are also powerful and extremely dangerous. There have been unfortunate times when some of these villains have reached positions of authority and managed, through their powers, to influence enough weaker minds to perpetrate great atrocities. Hitler, Stalin and Genghis Khan are some notable examples.'

'Is there nothing that can be done to stop them?' Adam was flabbergasted by the thought of the combination of such power with evil and insanity.

'Very little,' Salamu admitted unhappily, 'we do our best to deprive them of talented vessels, but there are many that we don't manage to identify or reach in time...and the promise of an extended lifetime attracts a lot of devotees.'

'Can you kill them?'

'They *can* be killed of course,' she responded, 'but we, that is who you might call "the good guys", remain totally opposed to the death sentence or in fact violence of any kind. We even hesitate to coerce or influence anyone except in the most extreme circumstances. The most we can do, if we manage to capture one is to helmet them and keep them as involuntary, but well cared for guests until their body expires.'

'Er...what's this "helmet" thing?' asked Adam; he was beginning to tire of all the things he was discovering he did not know.

'Sorry. It is a device made from *Sepsudannum*, a synthetic material which was discovered to block all forms of energy waves. Its use was banned for millennia – it was considered as inhuman and abusive to deprive someone of their extended mind – but eventually and in desperation, its use was reluctantly approved for this purpose alone. However the "Everlords", as they call themselves, also use it when capturing their vessels.'

'Bloody hell, this is scary stuff,' commented Adam, 'worse than all the conspiracy theories I've believed in the past.'

'Don't worry,' she assured him, 'there are more of us than there are of them, and the closer we approach The Resurgence, the faster our numbers grow.'

A terrifying thought suddenly occurred to Adam. 'Shit! What about Spud?' he asked, fixing her with a desperate gaze, 'won't they find him and torture him or turn *him* into a "vessel" or something?' He had grown to like the genial middle-aged hippie in the short time he had been in Amsterdam and he couldn't bear the thought of anything happening to him.

'No. There is no need to be overly concerned,' she said soothingly, 'he is not a suitable candidate to become a vessel and anyway, we have more people there now and they will be watching over him – even if the Everlords manage to link him with you he will be well protected.'

He sat quietly for a few moments but then another thought occurred to him. 'The first time I saw you,' he said 'I thought I recognised you but I couldn't think where from. Then, on the journey to Amsterdam I remembered. I saw you in a dream. It was long ago in an ancient place...how could you have been there?'

'It is possible that somehow your dreams have become tied up with your ancestral memories,' she replied slowly, as if thinking whilst she spoke. 'When you are sleeping, doors open in your mind that may normally be suppressed by everyday concerns. It seems feasible that someone in my line may have met with one of your predecessors in ancient times. Physical resemblances can also recur....' She paused and gave him a strange look as if noticing something about him for the first time. 'Tell me about the dream,' she said.

He did so, explaining that there was more than one and that Charlie shared the experience to some extent. She listened intently throughout, but offered no comments even when he had finished.

'So... what do you think then?' he asked.

'I believe that you and your brother have tapped into some ancestral memories,' she began, 'and that the telepathic link between you is stronger than you have realised given your degree of estrangement over the years.'

'And the casket thing with the old guy in it...?'

'It is another, though less iniquitous, method by which a lifespan can be extended,' she explained. 'Whilst the psyche remains within the same body, there is a great deal of...force required to rejuvenate the body. It carries similar but less severe risks to vessel use. Nothing can be gained without some cost.'

'And what about Charlie being asked to make one of these?'

'I admit that is a worry...' Salamu paused and frowned at her hands where they lay tightly clasped in her lap. 'It can only mean that someone powerful, perhaps one of the ancients or one of the Everlords is living near him and desires an extension to their life. I shall have to ask him more when we meet.'

'Blimey, I've got a lot to think about,' Adam said. He rose slowly and walked back to the gunwale where he stood looking down at the turbulent wake, trying to make sense of it all. After five minutes he gave up and went back to the cabin to roll a cigarette out of reach of the sea spray.

The rolling, breaking waves crashed and frothed at the shoreline and then sucked noisily at the steeply banked shingle as they receded. Although there was now little wind, the swell had created white-topped surf as it approached the coast. The travelling companions sat leaning against the warm sea wall at the top of the beach, and like lizards turned their faces towards to heat of the midday sun, eyes closed against the glare. Thu Salamu had headed into town to rent a minibus and buy food for the next stage of their journey, advising them to remain inconspicuous.

Juris Asaras had previously arranged a rendezvous with a small fishing boat about a mile from the coast where he transferred his other cargo, but the vessel's captain was unwilling to take an additional burden on board. Consequently, the Latvian had reluctantly come in to Eyemouth harbour and forced the fugitives to hastily disembark on the quay without even tying up. The proficient crew had the yacht moving off within seconds and as soon as it was clear of the harbour it sped off at full throttle. Realising that a group of strangers so hurriedly dumped at the wharf would be a probable source of suspicion, the friends had quickly moved away until they found a spot where they could wait out of view of potentially wary locals.

'Fuck that for a game of soldiers,' grumbled Nick. 'That is the first *and last* time I'm *ever* going on a fucking boat – for *any* reason!'

Adam had yet to inform his friend that they were actually on their way to Orkney, which would necessitate a ferry crossing. He judged that now was perhaps not the best time to impart the news, hoping that a more opportune moment would occur and that someone else would do it. Nick had suffered the worst from the seasickness and not having eaten for the duration of the two-day crossing, had also complained of "visions" and voices in his head, which Adam had guessed must be caused by the lack of food.

'I don't know about that...,' Lynn had voiced doubtfully when she had shared a quiet moment with Adam on deck, 'he seems to have like, I don't know exactly, a *troubled spirit* or something, yeah? I don't think it's like, just him being delirious and stuff. I noticed even before we got on the boat he was gradually becoming uncharacteristically quiet and sort of thoughtful and that, which just isn't like him you know? Anyway, he always used to go sailing a lot when he was younger and boasted of his "sea legs" and tough constitution.'

Salamu had appeared behind them. 'Although Nick is not yet consciously aware of it,' she told them, 'he is "awakening" too, but his persona's scepticism and innate opposition means that his mind and body are fighting it. The conflict is manifesting as physical disorder. I believe the visions and voices are the thoughts of others.'

Well, thought Adam now, as he watched the churning rollers whilst making himself a "rollie", *Nick is already back to relative normality after only an hour ashore. Maybe it was just seasickness.*

'Jesus, I'm starving,' his friend was saying impatiently, 'I hope that woman gets back with some food soon. I could even eat a Big fucking Mac I'm that hungry!'

To take his companion's mind off of his appetite, Adam distracted him by summarising what he'd been told by Salamu on the sea crossing. Nick listened with only the occasional "tut" until Adam had finished.

'Nah, sorry mate, I don't buy it meself,' commented Nick doubtfully. 'Okay, I'll grant you that there might be something in this mind-reading lark – I can't deny the evidence put in front of me after all, but all this Atlantis stuff and some big "Resurgence" thing and being possessed by fucking devils – I mean it's all a bit *biblical* isn't it?'

Adam didn't bother arguing. He had on many occasions in the past attempted to discuss with Nick some of the more esoteric and mystical issues facing humanity, but by so doing had always encountered his friend's more stubborn side. As for himself, despite their dire straits, he was becoming more and more excited by the prospect of investigating the powers of the mind and the possibility that at this so-called "safe haven" he might meet other telepaths and psychics who could help him to train his own faculties in order to enhance his personal latent skills. He envisioned something akin to Tolkien's Rivendell, where elegant and dignified elf-like figures glided in flowing robes along airy corridors between graceful vaulted halls where they discussed matters of great magnitude and significance with sages and soothsayers. He pictured himself accepted as a respected member of the community, consulted on issues pertinent to the times, welcomed to the feasts and celebrations that were incorporated into the calendar to ensure that the focus of the society did not become too sombre. His daydream was disturbed by the sound of a vehicle parking above them. It was their escort returning with the transport and shopping.

'Ha-ha! Far fucking out! Food at last!' blurted Nick happily, leaping to his feet. 'Me first!'

'You'd better get in,' said Salamu grimly and when they had done so, she showed them a copy of a daily newspaper. Beneath the headline 'Terrorist Kidnappers Could Be Brits!' were photographs of Sonilla, Andor, Nick, Lynn and Adam. The story followed the same line as the Dutch media.

'Where the fuck did they get photos of us?' gasped Nick indignantly.

'Passport records of course,' said Lynn. 'You have to send them a spare with your application, yeah? So they must like, keep them on file you know?'

'So, as I said before,' insisted Salamu, 'until we reach our destination, you will need to remain inconspicuous – we will have to stop only in uninhabited areas.'

As the older woman drove, Lynn handed out the food and they began eating unenthusiastically and in sober silence, their appetites somewhat diminished by this reminder that they were no longer in complete control of their own destinies.

#

On the mantelpiece the George III bracket clock clunked noisily as it slowly measured the passing seconds. It continued unaffected by the mood of the room's occupant, just as it had done almost non-stop for the last two hundred years. Likewise the bulky desk of a similar age, its waxed mahogany surface divided into a striking contrast of light and shade by the bright sunshine pouring through the tall window in the castle's wall, remained sunk heavily into the thick woollen carpet in the same position it had occupied since it was first brought into this office.

En Nergal sat behind it and he was angry. He was very, very angry. Not only had his attempts to follow and recapture the runaways been thwarted by Thu Salamu, but his agents had failed to detonate the car bomb when the targets were in the vehicle. Now they had disappeared and his people could find no trace of them. The last place they were known to have been was with a cafe owner in Amsterdam who now had physical protection provided by his adversaries and whose thoughts, according to his team, were a virtually impenetrable and cloudy muddle due to the amount of cannabis he smoked. Even his influence within the Netherland's law enforcement and intelligence agencies had proved fruitless. He struck the desk top in frustration with fists as clenched as his enraged features. It seemed that he would now have to go and pick up the trail himself. He was reluctant to leave the foundation, but as one of the most powerful of the European Everlord's, he felt he could trust no one else's abilities to fulfil the task. Although there was some likelihood that Salamu had alerted the Ancestors to his takeover, he believed that the forces he had gathered at the school since the acolytes' escape would be more than strong enough to withstand an attack from the so-called "Peaceful Warriors", especially now that they were alerted to the threat. They would not be taken unawares again.

To pick up the trail he would need more specifics and although torture was to his mind the quickest and most satisfying way of acquiring it from obstinate individuals, En Nergal recognised that the surreptitious bodyguards minding this "Spud" character could complicate the situation. No, there was another method - the oldest and most effective way of acquiring information that had the advantage of leaving the victim unaware that they had been deceived - and he already had the perfect operative in the field.

CHAPTER NINETEEN.

It was late when Charlie left the workshop. He didn't know what time it was – he hadn't even bothered to look; it was no longer relevant. He worked until he could work no more, slept the minimum he could survive on and then worked again. After four weeks of intricate fretwork and painstakingly detailed carving, the casket was ready for gilding. Tomorrow he could apply the size and start the laying on of gold leaf. Then, all that remained was the burnishing. Hopefully it would be finished within a week and then he could get Bess back. For the last month he had worked doggedly and relentlessly, despite the misery and desolation of living without the woman he loved and the constant torment of his anxiety regarding her well-being. He ate and slept little, barely sparing any time for personal hygiene and slowly becoming more like a zombie as the fatigue and torment eroded his spirit. He was a man possessed; consumed by his desperation to see Bess free again, haunted by his worry for her and crazed by the unremitting toil he had to endure, trapped in continual purgatory. Only once in that month did he have a day off. The previous Saturday evening Rhona had discovered him asleep, slumped over the workbench. She managed to convince him that by taking some rest he would be able to achieve more without the risk of creating extra work by making a stupid mistake or injuring himself due to complete exhaustion. Since his house had been fire damaged, the importance of which had paled into insignificance under the present circumstances, he had continued staying with Rhona. Despite her own concern at not only Bess's abduction but also her niece's plight, she was managing to cook simple meals for them both and force Charlie to eat some. In fact, she realised it was probably this – having to keep Charlie going - that enabled her to face each morning herself.

They had both been compelled to return to work by the circumstances. Charlie because the only way he could see to free Bess and Rowan was by fulfilling the kidnappers' requirements and Rhona because she had a business to run with clients and employees relying on her. They decided it was best not to tell the staff that the two women had been abducted. Rhona told them that Rowan was suffering from post-traumatic stress following her assault and attempted rape so she had gone to stay with her mother in Milan, but Charlie didn't need to concoct a story because Bess rarely came to the workshop anyway. Thus they tried to behave as normally as possible whilst at work, but nevertheless the strain showed more as time passed. Charlie's unresponsive and morose demeanour they put down to the fact that his home had been ruined – they had been told it was an accident – and that he was doing so much overtime to meet a tight schedule, although they were unaware of how early he was starting and how late he was finishing. They sometimes saw him shuffling into or out of the old storeroom, but these sightings were becoming less frequent. The boss, they thought, had been deeply affected by Grant's attack on her niece and was understandably taking time to get over it. The mood at "Fantasy Furniture" had infected the entire workforce and the men would now often carry out their tasks in silence – even lunch breaks in the "Lizard Lounge" were subdued with neither Rhona nor Charlie joining the others.

Jenny came to see Rhona at home one evening. She was both worried and annoyed that she couldn't seem to get Rowan on her phone and that her supposed best friend wasn't even answering texts or email messages. Rhona concocted a story on the spot about her niece losing her phone and forgetting her webmail passwords, but that she had heard from her sister that Rowan was alright and responding well to the buzz of Italian city life and culture. Rhona saw the dubious look on Jenny's face. This certainly didn't sound like the sort of thing Rowan would have said, but it was too late to undo the lie so she braved it out for the few minutes it took for Jenny to leave.

Now, even with the end of the project so close and the hope of soon being reunited with Bess, only a slight lift to Charlie's spirits was able to penetrate the numbing fatigue. He climbed wearily into the driver's seat of his car and shut the door; working such long hours meant that he had abandoned his beloved bicycle as his usual method of transport – it now sat neglected in his shed, gathering spider webs. For what seemed like a moment he rested his head on the steering wheel but then suddenly jerked awake realising that he had nodded off, though he didn't know for how long. He started the engine and drove back to Rhona's house in a daze, oblivious to the candescent golden glow on the skyline on this clear northern summer night.

#

Although it was ten in the evening, the sun was still above the horizon and it cast an amber glow onto the oak door. The heavy iron knocker cast into the shape of a fist would save him from bruising his own knuckles on the dense, thick timber. Adam hesitated and looked over his shoulder to the others where they still sat in the vehicle. Having discovered his brother's house vacant and locked up, with smoke marks above a boarded up window, he was apprehensive about what he was going to discover next. Luckily a passing dog-walker had told them where Charlie was staying, but had moved on without mentioning Bess. They had found Rhona's house easily and now Adam stood nervously on the doorstep. He knew that the only way to find out was to knock, but he was always reluctant to encounter more distress, feeling inadequate as a sympathising ear. He never knew what to say. "I'm sorry" wasn't really true, after all it wasn't his fault and "it will be alright" was often just a meaningless platitude. Aware that his companions were watching him, he raised his hand but before he could lift the knocker, the door swung inwards. Seemingly the occupant had seen his approach. The face of the woman inside momentarily stupefied him. Her quizzical expression was tinged with anxiety and fatigue, yet he found her elfin features and her bewitching sapphire eyes so alluring that he momentarily lost the ability to speak. As he stood gormlessly on the doorstep with his mouth hanging open, she decided to talk.

'Yes, can I help you?' she prompted, wondering if she had met this odd, bedraggled character somewhere before. There was something strangely familiar about him.

As soon as she spoke, it dawned on Adam who this woman was – the short spiky red hair, the small, cute, slightly upturned nose, those *amazingly* blue eyes…and despite the concern seemingly etched in her brow he knew that she was the fairy-faced lover in his dreams. He felt his face flush hot with embarrassment but despite his surprise he was just able to collect himself enough to stammer a few words.

'Oh, er hi…' he managed, forcing an uneasy smile in an attempt to dispel any suspicions she may harbour regarding his purpose, '…um, sorry to bother you…I'm Adam, Charlie's brother and er…his house is locked up....and I was told that he…er…might be here?' He felt remarkably self-conscious, he was trembling nervously and his pulse was racing but he couldn't stop himself from gazing into those mesmerising eyes; even though she was deeply troubled they still held an enchanting sparkle that captivated his attention.

'Oh, *right*, I thought I recognised you,' she said finally smiling a little and for a euphoric split second Adam's mind leapt to the conclusion that she had seen *him* in *her* dreams too. 'I saw a photo of you when Bess was showing me the family albums,' she continued, causing his heart to drop in disappointment, 'I'm Rhona, Charlie's friend and employer.' She held out her hand and he shook it awkwardly. 'He's still at work, believe it not, but you can come in and wait if you like.'

She stood back to let him enter, but he remained where he was waving his arm vaguely in the direction of the minibus parked behind him.

'Er, well...I mean...there's actually a lot of me...um, us,' he said falteringly.

Rhona peered past him, shading her eyes. She hadn't noticed the occupants of the vehicle previously as the bright, low sunset was behind it. She made out an indeterminate number of faces, but despite recent occurrences felt a sense of trust.

'Okay, well you had better *all* come in then,' she said. She watched as Adam beckoned and the others climbed out of the vehicle, stretching their limbs in a way characteristic of those who had been too long cramped together on an extensive road trip. He waited just outside the door as his strange companions filed past in the direction indicated by Rhona nodding a greeting or muttering hellos. Finally he entered and she shut the door behind him.

'I'll put the kettle on,' she said, 'and then you can tell me what this is all about.'

'I'll help,' he volunteered eagerly, trailing after Rhona towards the kitchen and feeling that he just wanted to stay close by her. He had never felt like this before; even when he first became attracted to Lynn, he had not been so strongly affected. Now that he had met Rhona, it was as if he had suddenly found a part of his heart and soul that had been missing all his life, like he had found a peg to fit the hole he had been previously unaware of. In just one short moment the bliss he felt lifted his spirits higher than the narcotics he had habitually used for this purpose. Whilst the kettle was heating the water, Rhona collected mugs and biscuits on a tray and prepared the teapot. Adam stood awkwardly and uselessly to one side following her every move as she glided gracefully around the kitchen, until she asked him to put sugar in a bowl and gather some teaspoons from the drawer. He began an attempt at explaining how such a large company of strangers had suddenly appeared on her doorstep, but realised that quite a lengthy explanation would be necessary, which he found himself incapable of instigating, distracted as he was by what he came to realise was "love at first sight". He understood now that what he had felt for Lynn had been a combination of a schoolboy-like crush, obsessive lust for her voluptuous figure and an infatuation born of an almost worshipful awe of her beauty worthy of a venerated goddess. To this had been added the slowly growing love of friendship and the virtually unbearable frustration of her status as "forbidden fruit". With the soul searching he had done since he inadvertently revealed his shameful desires to his friend he had come to recognise that he had been emotionally crippled for some time. The feelings he was having now were entirely different - he was completely smitten. He knew virtually nothing about this woman but already felt that he recognised her as his soul mate. He soon ran out of words and, like a car running out of fuel, faltered to a stop.

Rhona for her part was aware of his gaze on her but realised that she didn't actually mind. She would usually resent the assumption by some men that she was fair game for their ogling eyes, but for reasons she couldn't fathom she felt curiously comfortable in the presence of this strange, dishevelled little man. Although a bit scrawny, he was also quite cute in an offbeat, tousled kind of way that she found rather engaging. She realised that at the moment his appeal may be similar to that of a wet puppy rescued from a bramble patch, but reckoned he would clean up nicely and intuited a gentleness and sensitivity in his nature that was kind of attractive. Her experiences of men to date could be separated into two groups. On the one hand there were those whose sturdy frame and good looks stimulated an almost entirely instinctive and physical response in her as if based on a primitive and animal drive to procreate and preserve the continuity of the species. However, although some of them could be good in the sack, they generally seemed to have the personalities of alpha males wanting the role of leader and protector. Well, Rhona certainly didn't want to be led and never felt the need for protection. The other type of men she had been involved with had much more empathic natures, often very sensitive, caring and discerning, but if they didn't end up being manipulative using "passive-aggressive" emotional blackmail, they were somehow a little too deferential and, she had to admit, kind of wimpy really. Neither kind fulfilled her expectations for the qualities she hoped to find in a potential long-term partner and of course it was too soon to say whether or not this guy did either. In fact her first assumption was that he might fall into the second camp, but realised that for some reason she didn't care. She then wondered why she was even thinking like this when she had only met him ten minutes ago and didn't really know him from ....well, Adam.

She let him carry the tray to the lounge where the others were waiting. After he introduced his travelling companions, they all pieced together their stories as briefly as possible to explain their situation to her. She then outlined her own circumstances, starting with Nasaru's visit to the workshop. Seated next to her on the sofa Adam felt the depth of her distress about the abduction of two people so close to her. He suddenly realised that he was holding her hand but he didn't release it because she was also tightly grasping his.

Thu Salamu baulked at the news that the elderly twins were threatening to use Rowan as a "vessel" and felt compelled to explain the full meaning to the girl's aunt. She then proposed that they should rescue the captives. Rhona made an anguished protest. Her distress regarding her niece's safety overrode any reassurances the others could offer. Adam thought she would crush his hand in her grip.

When he arrived Charlie was taken aback by the presence of an extra vehicle in the driveway. Rhona hadn't mentioned that she was expecting company, so he guessed that the visitors were unanticipated. Despite the lateness of the hour, the downstairs lights were still on and as he approached the house he heard voices through the curtained windows.

When he entered the living room it seemed to be thronging with strangers. He stood dazed for a moment, found Rhona's face looking distraught, and then recognised the slight, bearded guy sitting next to her *holding her hand!*

'Hey Charlie!' called Adam, leaping to his feet. He hardly had time to register his brother's presence before being gripped in an enthusiastic hug. 'Good to see you bro!' declared Adam before adopting a more sober tone to say, 'really sorry to hear about Bess though.' As he was released, Charlie found his voice.

'What are you doing here,' he asked, shaking his head in bewilderment, 'and who are all these people? I mean it's good to see you too, but what a time to turn up unannounced....' He was feeling somewhat overwhelmed and in no state to deal with any visitors, not even his long not seen brother. 'And how did you get *here* anyway...I mean to Rhona's house?'

'You'd better sit down Charlie,' his friend and employer bade him, 'it's a long story and I'll let your brother do the introductions. His friends have offered to help, but I'm really not sure....I'll make you a quick sandwich and a cuppa.'

Adam presented his comrades and then briefly summarised his recent adventures. 'Anyway,' he concluded, 'because Sonilla, Andor and Salamu are powerful telepaths, they reckon they can overcome those old guys and their minions and rescue the girls.'

'Well, I don't want to put a dampener on your enthusiasm,' countered Charlie, 'not that I'm ungrateful or anything, I appreciate the thought, but it's just....well, I just *really* don't want to risk anything happening to Bess. I mean, I've nearly finished the casket now and once they've got that they'll let her go anyway.' It was easy to see that his spirit had been broken by the anxiety and emotional turmoil of the last few weeks, but there was now a need for urgency. Rhona re-entered with his refreshments, although he had no appetite.

'There is something you don't know Charlie, Rhona,' Salamu said levelly, 'The Belums have miscalculated the time they have remaining. Since I arrived I have probed their energy field and concluded that they may have as little of two days left in these bodies. They get weaker by the day and I believe it is only a matter of hours before they realise it. At that point they will immediately possess the "vessels" they hold captive – an irreversible process. We cannot allow that to happen. If we can prevent innocent parties from coming to harm, which we *can*, it is our duty to do so. Don't worry, we are almost certain of our success and we shall see that no harm comes to Bess or Rowan – but we must act now.'

Although he didn't like the sound of "*almost*" certain, Charlie finally relented. Rhona's nerves so dominated her that she couldn't even answer and had no choice but to listen to their plan.

#

The relaxing groove of Oliver Shanti's album "Seven Times Seven" mingled with the floating, coiling marijuana fumes in the post-coital bliss of the gently rocking narrow-boat as Spud passed the spliff to his bedmate. He could hardly believe his luck. Whilst he was not one to pursue women solely to satisfy his sexual desires, he was only human and couldn't deny his needs. At his age, with increasing girth and, he believed, failing looks, he wasn't usually that fussy about appearances when it came to seeking out female companions, otherwise his occasional liaisons would be even less frequent. However, this time was a remarkable exception.

That afternoon one of the most beautiful young women he had seen in years came into the cafe asking for him. He emerged from the kitchen to behold someone that to him appeared to be an example of a perfect female human being. She had long, naturally wavy brunette hair and Marilyn Munroe's body. Her angelic face portrayed an innocent vulnerability that nevertheless bore a warm endearing smile and kind ginger-brown eyes. Dressed simply and casually in a low-cut top and short denim skirt, she looked to be in her early thirties, but without the slightest suggestion of any telltale lines on her face. Unable to control his eyes as they followed a route from her face to her sandaled feet via her breasts and her shapely legs then back again, he cleared his throat in an attempt to disperse his slightly awkward embarrassment and asked what she wanted.

She said she was Nick's sister Tamara, 'You can call me Tammy,' she added sweetly, and she was trying to find her brother to give him news of a shared inheritance from a distant, recently deceased relative. Whilst Spud thought he could vaguely remember Nick mentioning a sister at some point in the past and although he was instantly smitten with the gorgeous apparition before him, he wasn't born yesterday so considering his knowledge of recent events decided to play it cautiously until he could be certain that Tammy was who she claimed to be. He led her to an empty table in a quiet corner.

'I can't help, I'm afraid,' he lied, 'I haven't seen him in ages.'

The look of disappointment on her face almost broke his resolve but he asked why she thought Nick might have come here.

'He texted me on his way,' she answered. 'We always keep in touch see, we always have, being so close and all.' She looked very concerned as she continued. 'He must have changed his mind then...but it was only a week or so ago. What could have happened to him?'

'I expect he's alright love,' Spud said as convincingly as he could, 'you know, if he's on holiday, change of plan...maybe his phone's out of charge or something...'

Tamara didn't seem entirely reassured, but appeared accept his word for the moment. She said she would stick around for a couple of days to see if Nick turned up or in case she received a message from him. She added that she knew no one else in the city and wondered if he would mind showing her around after he had finished work. Unable to resist the offer to spend more time with such an attractive woman, he quickly and eagerly agreed. After all, he now had a nice little sports car he could impress her with. The weather had improved considerably, so they could cruise around the city with the top open and the wind in their hair...

Later, whilst showing her the sights, it became apparent that they had a lot of interests in common and they got along remarkably well. She seemed genuinely interested in what he had to say, shared his views on politics and their tastes in music, art, literature and lifestyle seemed to add to their compatibility.

Well as they say, he mused, thinking back on the evening, they found themselves back at the boat, one thing led to another and overcome by mutual attraction, the inevitable followed. Several times! He smiled again, bathing in the joy of the moment. Whilst physically exhausted he felt more alive than he had done in years, even though it was gone three in the morning. Tamara turned to him and kissed his ear, sliding her hand over his chest and then tracing little circles there with her fingertip.

'I'm actually really worried about Nick, you know Spudling?' She spoke hesitantly as if not really wanting to bother him with her fears, but feeling too anxious to hold back. There were tears forming in her eyes as she spoke. 'I mean, he said he was coming to see you and then didn't and now he's not answering his phone. Anything could have happened, right? Do you think I should go and tell the police or maybe check on the hospitals to see if he's had an accident or something?'

Spud was quiet for a moment before turning his head to look at her face. The sight of her tear-filled eyes seeped into his soft heart and broke his resolve. In any case, he thought, she seems pretty genuine after all we've shared in the last few hours.

'Well actually love, I did see him,' he admitted. 'I'm sorry...'

''What?' She sat bolt upright, surprise and annoyance clouding her features. 'Why didn't you tell me before? Where is he? Is he alright? What's going on?'

Spud swiftly tried to placate her, not wanting to scupper their relationship at this early stage. 'I'm sorry, I'm sorry,' he blurted desperately, 'it's just that he said there were people after him, or people after the people he was with at least, so I had to be sure you were who you said you were, you know...so...'

'So you seduced me?' Tammy clutched the sheets to her chest as if this could undo what he had done to her. The look of hurt, reproach and indignation on her face tore at his innards. Frantically he tried to think of some way to mollify her, to reassure her that he was not the kind of guy to take advantage.

'No love, no it was never like that!' he insisted propping himself up on an elbow. 'Buddha's balls, I would do a thing like that. Before I knew who you were I'd fallen for you and then when we spent those hours together today....you know, I've got genuine feelings...'

Tamara interrupted him. Although less irate, her manner was still grave. 'Who's after him?' she demanded anxiously. 'What's he gone and done now? He's always been reckless...is he in danger from these people?'

Spud briefly explained what he could remember of what he had learned of Nick's predicament, finishing with the escape on the yacht over the North Sea. Tammy listened carefully, chewing her bottom lip.

'Oh God, I hope he's alright...,' she muttered quietly.

He took hold of her hand and squeezed it reassuringly. 'I'm sure he'll be okay,' he said. 'After all, no one will be able to follow a boat like that, even if they knew he was on it – which I doubt. I mean how could they? There was nobody around at the docks that night.'

Her eyes met his and showed that she seemed to have stopped feeling resentful now. She squeezed his hand back, then gently pulled hers away and slowly got out of bed. Despite the serious turn of the conversation he couldn't help but admire her luscious body once more as she stood up and stretched.

'I'm going back to the hotel,' she said as she glanced around for her discarded clothing.

'You don't have to go,' he told her. 'You can stay if you like...'

She reached down and stroked his cheek. 'I know, I would like to Spudling.' He loved that she had given him a pet name. It made him feel that this relationship would develop into more than just a one night stand. 'I've had a really nice time,' she continued whilst getting dressed, 'but I want to leave as early as possible in the morning and get back to England, see if I can't catch up with Nick somehow. I've got to get a bit of kip, you know? If I stay here I might be tempted to...well...' She left the thought hanging there as she pulled her clothes on. She was so sexy that watching her get dressed was almost as arousing as when she removed her clothing earlier.

'You'll come back though,' he said hopefully, 'I mean, I'll see you again won't I? I'd like to see you again...'

She leaned over and kissed him warmly on the lips. 'You bet,' she said with an affectionate smile. 'I'll come back to Amsterdam as soon as I can. I've really enjoyed being with you. I'll ring too, as soon as I know anything about Nick.'

Tamara's hand was already on the door latch when Spud suddenly realised he hadn't given her his phone number. 'Hold on!' he called as he leapt naked from the bed. He rushed over to the table and scribbled on a scrap of paper. 'Text me...or call me...anytime,' he stammered handing it to her.

'I will,' she said winking coyly. 'So long, lover boy.'

As she descended the gang plank she glanced back over her shoulder and raised a hand to wiggle her fingers at his reddened, smiling face where it peeked through the gap of the almost closed door. When she heard it shut, "Tammy" screwed up the contact details and tossed them into the canal. She wouldn't need to see him again.

#

'*There's another disturbance at the gate,*' thought Asar irritably.

'*It's that Flemming person again,*' added Ki, '*how can she be so stupid?*'

'*And she's persuaded some other fools to accompany her.*'

'*Has she forgotten that we have hostages....*'

'Nasaru! Take the dogs to the gate to scare them off....'

'And threaten them with the gun too....'

'If necessary fire over their heads and if they persist...'

'Shoot them...'

'And feed them to the dogs...'

'Then kill the Mackay woman...'

'And prepare the Vessels for transference – we can't wait any longer.'

As Nasaru nodded and left to do his masters' bidding, they turned their gaze back to the ever-burning coal fire.

'*We grow weak brother...*'

'*We have already waited too long, we should have used the vessels earlier...*' remarked Asar with a pang of regret.

'*But we are not monsters,*' Ki reminded him, '*our mercy and our ethical principles stayed our hand....*'

'*And the occupation process is not without discomfort to ourselves.*'

'*Nevertheless, we have avoided resorting to this for many life spans.*'

Asar leaned slowly over the side of his chair to reach a small, dry log that he threw onto the coals. A small flurry of sparks fled up the chimney as flames eagerly embraced the fuel. He rubbed his hands together slowly and then held them out to the heat.

'*I have to admit though,*' confessed Ki, '*the thought of possessing the body of a young, vibrant woman is quite....arousing. I can anticipate a great deal of physical pleasure will be available to us.*'

'*Yes, it is now seeming like quite a thrilling prospect...it is fortuitous that we managed to acquire the additional vessel.*'

They dwelt in their anticipation for a few moments, both wearing slight, dreamy smiles.

Asar broke the mood as his thoughts were disturbed by the troublemakers at the gate.

'*Before the transfer, let us send a final psychic shock to those miscreants out there – just to put them in their place.*'

'*Yes, they deserve to be taught a lesson. In any case we need to release our anger to prepare ourselves for the possession, so we might as well put it to good use...*'

At this time of year it didn't get completely dark, even in the early hours of the morning, particularly when the sky was free of clouds and moonlit like it was tonight. Nonetheless, Adam heard the dogs before he saw them. They sounded distinctly unfriendly as their barks grew louder and closer. This impression was confirmed as the animals burst from the woods bordering the drive. They rushed at the gate, growling viciously, leaving no doubt that they were ready and eager to rip flesh from bone as soon as they were able.

'Woo, it's the Hounds of the Baskervilles!' exclaimed Nick, feigning terror whilst managing to control his real fear secure in the knowledge that high, locked gates protected him from attack.

'Poor things are half starved,' observed Lynn sadly.

'Well, I for one am glad that those "poor things" are on the other side of the gates,' commented Adam wryly.

'They won't be for much longer,' rasped Nasaru appearing suddenly from the shadows and levelling a shotgun at Rhona's chest. 'Now, Miss Fleming, I suggest that you and your three *brave* friends make your way home before I am forced to take more persuasive, extremely painful and possibly *terminal* action.'

Rhona didn't move but her gaze hardened as she glowered at him, narrowing her eyes, their intense blue seeming to turn to ice and able to pierce him as if they too were a weapon. Regarding her now it looked to Adam, from her bearing, that she took the man's appearance and threats as a personal affront from a loathsome shit whom she would not waste bog roll on. He wondered if she was as fearless as she seemed or whether she was just a good actor. He admired her ability to remain, or at least *seem* to remain calm with an instrument of death pointing straight at her. Adam was absolutely terrified. He had always done his best to avoid confrontation wherever and whenever possible. He even got a bit shaky on the rare occasions when he found himself drawn into an argument, especially when tempers flared. The involvement of a firearm took it to another level. Frozen to the spot, he found his lungs had tightened so much that he could hardly breathe, as if he had been winded by a blow to the chest. His mouth was dry, he couldn't swallow, he felt hot and sweaty and his heart fluttered like a moth trapped in a jar.

'Come on Frankenstein, give it a rest,' Nick scoffed, also seeming a lot braver than Adam felt, 'your hollow threats are wasted on us. You know that you can't just set the fucking dogs on us and shoot us when we *just happen* to be pausing for a breather outside the grounds on the *public* highway whilst on our moonlit walk.'

'Well *sir*,' said Nasaru in a grating voice that revealed he was able to feel at least one emotion – that of severe annoyance, 'should they ever find what's left of your bloodied corpses after these hungry hounds are finished with you, they will discover the remains of four trespassers who were unfortunate enough to encounter the guard dogs when they tried to break into the house.'

Rhona opened a carrier bag and threw some pieces of raw meat through the railings towards the snarling beasts. Their distraction was merely momentary however as they guzzled the scraps in seconds.

'Now, you really are trying my patience,' said Nasaru asserted, releasing the safety mechanism on his gun, 'your pathetic attempt at calming these creatures is to no avail. They are, as your soon-to-be-much-less-attractive companion so rightly pointed out, quite literally half starved and their mood is perpetually hostile due to the pain from the open wounds we cultivate on the back of their necks.'

'You cruel bastard,' said Lynn, seething. She had long been an advocate of animal welfare and viewed with hatred anyone who deliberately inflicted suffering.

'How come they don't attack you then?' asked Adam, trying to prolong the distraction.

'My masters' powers have granted me protection from their feeble canine minds,' he answered, 'but now I think, since you have given them a starter, it is time for their main course.' He cradled the shotgun under his arm while he pulled a bunch of keys from his pocket and placed the largest in the lock of the gate.

At that moment a wall of pain slammed into the four friends, accompanied by a gut-wrenching fear that shattered their resolve. They staggered from the force and were left gasping for air. They looked at each other uncertainly.

'Er, okay, you win,' said Rhona hastily, 'we'll go.'

Nasaru shouldered the weapon as he raised his eyebrows and smiled humourlessly. 'I have to admit,' he said, 'I'm a little disappointed that you have seen sense. I was beginning to relish the thought of your untimely and *grisly* termination.'

They began to back away slowly, not yet willing to lose sight of the potential danger. Adam was so scared that he was shaking uncontrollably and felt he was not far from soiling his underwear. It was all he could do to stop himself from turning tail and running away at great speed. Suddenly their adversary frowned in disbelief, then gasped in horror and looked back at the house.

'No!' he shouted, a look of deep shock and distress claiming his ancient features. He quickly looked down at the dogs, threw the gun aside and started running. Adam watched aghast, helpless to prevent the inevitable as Nasaru shambled away in a doomed attempt to escape. They were spared the gruesome sight of his demise by the fact that the old servant had reached the bushes by the time the pack caught up with him. However, his cries as he was eaten alive were to haunt Adam's dreams for some time to come.

'What the fuck happened there?' exclaimed Nick. Horror-struck, the others just shook their heads in bewilderment.

Nasaru was already dead when the sedative from Rhona's doped offerings took effect, the dogs tottering a short distance away before collapsing one by one into a stupor. The sleeping pills she had once been prescribed but had refused to take had finally come in useful. The key was still in the lock, so Nick put his arm through the railings, turned it and pushed the gates open. Adam still hadn't budged – he was frozen to the spot by the shock of what he had witnessed, but finally Rhona tugging at his sleeve prompted him to stir and he followed his friends towards the house.

Meanwhile, Salamu, Charlie, Sonilla and Andor had scaled the wall behind the mansion, secure in the knowledge that the aged twins were both becoming weaker and had been distracted by the activities at the gate. As they crossed the threshold through the back door Salamu paused and held up her hand for them to stop.

'That's odd,' she whispered, 'I can only perceive the minds of the two Belums.' Andor nodded wordlessly.

Charlie tried to force himself not leap to the worse conclusion possible. 'Maybe they're holding Bess and Rowan somewhere else,' he suggested hopefully, 'you know, to make rescue more difficult.'

'Perhaps,' said the teacher noncommittally. 'Let us find out. The old ones are upstairs.'

Charlie's nerves threatened to get the better of him; he was feeling flushed and his pulse was racing so fast his temples were throbbing, even though they had been moving slowly and the air in the house was cool. The fear of what they may discover also played on his mind. He couldn't bear to think about what may have happened to Bess if the psychics couldn't detect her, but his thoughts defied him nonetheless. *Has our rescue attempt been noticed?* he wondered, *and have they already harmed the hostages?* He followed, trying not to panic.

As they moved past the former servants quarters, Sonilla trailed behind. She thought she felt something very faint...*couldn't the others feel it?* she wondered. They seemed to be totally focused on their goal, but she hadn't felt focused for weeks now, not since her world had been torn apart and her life changed forever. While she hung back, the others moved on, even Andor seeming oblivious to her hesitation. She watched them disappear through a doorway ahead and she almost followed but she was now feeling an irresistible urge compelling her to divert into a side passage. She took one step towards it, paused for a second to glance after the others but then chose to follow her own instincts and stole into the corridor.

Charlie followed up the wide staircase and along a creaking passageway until Salamu and Andor stopped at a dark wax-polished door indistinguishable to him from the others they had passed. Salamu turned the large brass knob, pushed open the door and entered the room.

'You!' exclaimed Asar and Ki in unison when they saw the woman.

'How did we not know?' gasped Asar.

'We grow weak my brother....,' uttered Ki.

Charlie recognised them from his dreams, but he could see that they were even more wizened than he remembered. It was almost as if the aging process had accelerated and with each day that passed they diminished in size like slowly drying apples withering unplucked on a naked winter branch.

'You must help us....' Asar pleaded pathetically, 'we have overstretched ourselves and we are about to expire...'

'We have vessels ready...' said his twin in an equally feeble voice.

'That is wrong! I cannot allow such an atrocity to take place,' snapped Salamu angrily. They visibly cringed at her tone, pitiful now in their weakness and desperation. 'For generations,' she added, 'you have abused and defied the laws of nature by artificially prolonging your warped, self-indulgent egos.' She unshouldered her bag as she spoke and then continued, her voice calmer but still icy. 'However, I do have some echo stones - not out of any feelings of mercy for you, but in the hope that some of the ancient wisdom you have acquired over the millennia has survived the corruption of your evil minds and may be of some benefit to others.'

'But we shall lose our.....*selves*,' murmured Asar as he and his brother held out their hands beseechingly.

'Tough shit, scumbags,' responded Salamu coldly as she placed the smooth glossy stones in their hands, 'you've already misused your skills too much. Your time is *over*.'

Charlie recognised the stones – they were almost exactly like the one he had found on the beach, the one he had put by the side of his bed, of the same substance as the huge monoliths they had found in Chile and that in the dream he shared with Bess had seemed full of whispering voices. The distraction was only momentary however.

'Where's Bess?' he demanded urgently. The old men did not answer. He watched in horror as the ancient dwarf-like figures weakly clutched the stones to their chests, closed their watery eyes and exhaled their last dry breath.

Andor suddenly perked up his head as if he had heard something. 'This way,' he said and dashed from the room.

There was a flight of unlit bare concrete steps descending into the gloom. Sonilla stopped and peered into the shadows. She took a deep breath and make an effort to reach out and explore ahead with her perceptive field. Concentrating hard she tried to focus her awareness on the faint traces of whatever it was that had attracted her here. A stirring of consciousness? Yes, there was definitely someone down there but strangely they seemed totally devoid of detectable thoughts and emotions. Either that or the person concerned was blocking her, but it didn't feel like that. Nor did she think that they were unconscious. It was almost as if their mind was *empty*. She was also unsure whether or not this person would be friend or foe.

Curious but wary, she cautiously moved down the steps into the dark, listening intently, but all she could hear was the quiet tread of her feet and the sound of her own breathing. At the bottom she could just make out that a corridor led to the left and right, but the weak light from behind her didn't penetrate far enough to discern what lay in either direction. Drawn by her intuition, she turned right and putting her hand on the wall was relieved to feel a light switch. She flicked it down, the sharp click echoing around the cold concrete surfaces like two small stones tapped sharply together. The switch activated a buzzing, flickering fluorescent light that emitted a weak, pale, sputtering glow as its current tried to pulse along the length of the failing tube. Walking slowly along the narrow unpainted passageway she saw two heavy wooden doors in the wall on her right. She found a small key hanging on a hook outside the first and taking it down, regarded it curiously. Looking back to the door she noticed that although it was securely bolted on the outside, it had no lock, so she replaced the key on its hook. She stood uncertainly for a moment, unsure whether or not it was safe to proceed, then listened at the door. She heard a faint scuffle.

'Hello?' she called softly. A moment later came a response.

'Hello?' came a woman's voice, muffled by the thick metal of the door. 'Can you help us? Can you let us out? Please!'

Sonilla slid back the two heavy steel bolts and pushed open the door. Inside she saw two women, one standing and the other prone on a thin mattress. The bulb within the cell was unlit but from the light coming in behind her she could see why – the eyes of both occupants were completely covered by the thin grey helmets that encased their heads, leaving only their mouths and noses free. She had heard of this appalling practice in her history lessons, but was taught it had been outlawed long ago. This explained why she had been unable to pick up the captives' thoughts. Suddenly she knew who they were.

'Who are you?' The standing woman asked tentatively. 'Do you work for....*them*?'

'No, I'm here to help,' she replied quickly, moving into the room, 'I'm Sonilla. You must be Bess and Rowan.'

'Yes, can you get these helmets off? *Please*,' pleaded Bess, 'and Rowan needs help, I think she's really ill.'

Sonilla flicked the switch just inside the door and then realised what the key was for. She retrieved it but when she tried to unlock Bess' helmet, discovered that it was also secured by a "psychic lock", which although mechanical in nature, could not be released by any key. Focusing her awareness she analysed the device, deduced its workings and unfastened the catch. The woman tugged it off and threw it to the floor. Then squinted her eyes shut against the unaccustomed light. Sonilla turned towards Rowan but stopped in horror when she saw the girl's arms. They were swollen and inflamed with suppuration, puss oozing from the septic wounds. Fighting back the urge to retch, she crouched next to the bed, then unlocked and removed the young woman's helmet.

'You are right,' she said to Bess gravely, 'your friend is very sick. The wounds on her arms are seriously infected and I think it has poisoned her bloodstream. But do not worry, my companion Andor will help.'

'Her *arms*.....?' muttered Bess still unable to see.

Rowan groaned, the release from the helmet having briefly stimulated her mind from the torpor of her fever.

'Next door...,' she mumbled weakly.

Sonilla looked at Bess. 'What does she mean?' she asked.

'There's someone else held prisoner in the next cell,' Bess told her, 'we don't know who, but she cries a lot.'

'I shall free her,' stated Sonilla simply, 'the others will be here soon.' She stood and hurried from the room.

Bess tried opening her eyes again but found the unaccustomed light too harsh so she felt her way to the switch and turned it off to give her sight a more gradual reintroduction. She scratched at her scalp to discover that her hair had been reduced to no more than a tight felted mat against her skull. She went back to Rowan's side, where she had been spending most of her time recently and, peering closely, strained to see what Sonilla had been referring to. She recoiled involuntarily. Even with her vision only partially restored she could see the severity of the contamination. How could she have not noticed? All the time she had sat and held her friend's hand she was only inches from the putrefaction. She had discerned that Rowan's hands were *slightly* swollen but had considered it just another aspect of the fever. Now she knew why the girl had become so afflicted. She could just make out the darkened half-moon lesions of the bite marks and realised how they came to be there.

'Oh God Ro, what have you done to yourself?' she uttered sadly and stroked the young woman's hot, moist brow. Despite this, in the few moments since the removal of the helmet Bess felt a rapid easing in the heaviness of her spirit. The enormous relief she felt over her rescue, coming so suddenly and unexpectedly, prompted a surge in her emotional state almost too intense to cope with. It was as if all of the feelings she had been deprived of by the head covering were now flooding in at once like a tidal wave of conflicting emotions. She gasped as the effect coursed through her and tears poured from her eyes.

Sonilla opened the next door along the corridor. Behind it was a small room no different to the first. She flicked on the light switch and saw a female figure on the bed, helmeted like the others had been. The captive stirred seemingly woken by Sonilla's entrance and seemed confused.

'What's that? Who's there?' she muttered blearily, 'It can't be time for breakfast already.'

Sonilla recognised the voice immediately and almost collapsed with the shock.

'Lendi!' she cried, 'I thought you were dead!'

'Sonilla!' gasped her sister in elated surprise.

Sonilla rushed over, fumbled to unlock the helmet and then threw it aside. As soon as she saw Lendi's face her tears flooded out from an overpowering combination of emotions. Engulfing her beloved sister in a tight embrace she broke into uncontrollable sobs. She wailed out all the needless pain she had suffered in recent weeks whilst at once soaring on the overwhelming euphoria of the un-hoped for reunion.

'It's okay, I'm fine,' comforted Lendi, also crying with tears of relief and happiness. Sonilla was not only unable to speak, but also too overwrought to share thoughts, being completely overcome by her feelings. They hugged in silence, Lendi rocking her younger sister gently from side to side trying to emanate calm and reassurance from her so recently liberated mind. Despite her own extended trauma and now this sudden joy, she felt able to keep her own exhilaration under control with Sonilla as a priority for her care, though she still wept with delight at being back in the presence of her sibling.

Andor appeared at the door and wordlessly gathered them both in a firm hug. He gradually and tenderly helped them balance the intensity of their feelings until, as soon as Sonilla felt able to think, she let Andor know about Rowan's condition. He rushed into the next room where Charlie and Bess were hugging and crying and Rhona knelt distraught by Rowan's side, tears streaming down her face and looking in dismay at the state of her niece's injuries. He gently moved her aside saying, 'I can help,' and then crouched next to her by the bed. He laid his hands on Rowan's head and remained motionless.

'What are you doing?' Rhona asked him uncertainly through her tears as the young sisters entered the cell.

'It's okay,' Sonilla reassured her, 'Andor has trained in the promotion of healing.' Feeling Rhona's confusion she tried to clarify her meaning. 'He can rechannel the body's resources to help accelerate the curative processes,' she said, 'Rowan will now make a speedy recovery.'

As she spoke, the patient's eyes flickered open and Rhona gently took her hand, oblivious to the crowd accumulating behind her.

'Ro? Can you hear me?' she asked her niece tearfully, 'you're being rescued.'

'Cool…,' said Rowan quietly, then gave her aunt a slight but mischievous smile and added in a weak croaky voice, 'about fucking time too…'

CHAPTER TWENTY.

There were now eleven in the company gathered in Rhona's living room, all of them having recently congregated at the house for rest, refreshments and respite - needing to wind down from their collective experiences. Mugs of freshly made steaming tea, coffee and herbal infusions cluttered the low table in the centre of the room. Charlie looked around at all the faces and the mixture of expressions they held. Bess was next to him on the couch, holding his hand and looking beautiful to him despite her matted hair and the extra lines that her trauma had etched on her face. For someone held captive for so long it can take a fair time for them to come to terms with their release, a period of adjustment is necessary as they reacquaint themselves with freedom and their normal life. In this case though, Charlie thought, he was not yet sure what normal was going to be. It had been a dreadful few weeks and he was glad it was all over, but he couldn't help feeling that their lives were never going to be the same again. However, the most important thing to him was that he had Bess back. When she was by his side Charlie felt that he could cope with pretty much anything and, despite his complete exhaustion, if she needed his support he could find resources of inner strength.

Before they left the mansion Bess had insisted that she needed to see the bodies of her captors, as a form of "closure" she explained. In their armchairs either side of the fire, which although down to the last few embers had more life in it than its former devotees, the corpses of Belum Asar and Belum Ki looked like empty, dehydrated husks. Their faces, whilst colourless and lifeless like bleached fragile leaves desiccated by winter winds, nevertheless retained expressions of sad resignation to their fate. Bess regarded their harmless remains through squinted eyes that had still not readjusted to daylight with a curious lack of emotion. She could no longer be angry at these pathetic twisted creatures despite all that they had done. Neither was she sorry to see them dead. The ancient lords had already indulged themselves in an obscene quantity of unnatural life spans and deserved far less. Salamu walked over and prised the echo stones from the stiff bony fingers of

410

one and then the other brother and without speaking, dropped them into her bag before adding the large gems on the mantelpiece. In the short time since then Charlie and Bess hadn't spoken much, both just overjoyed to be reunited, their joint ordeal now over. Time would allow details to be forthcoming.

Back in Rhona's lounge, Charlie glanced over at Adam. He wasn't sure how well he really knew his brother any more. Their adult lives had been separated by distance and become somewhat disconnected by a gradual drifting of changing lifestyles. Despite Charlie's early attempts to stay in touch, Adam had not reciprocated and he had eventually pretty much given up trying except for sending birthday and Christmas cards when he had an address to send them to. Maybe there would be a chance to catch up now, thought Charlie, but was not yet sure how long Adam was going to stick around. His last visit, several years ago was fairly fleeting. He had been uncommunicative and moody with a haunted look in his eyes. Now his brother looked no better, possibly due to the events of the last couple of weeks, but Charlie couldn't help wondering if Adam now always looked like this. He had also seemed the worst affected by the sight of Nasaru's grizzly carcass. As they were leaving the grounds of the mansion they had walked past the bloody, ragged heap by the bushes near the driveway and his brother's eyes seemed drawn to it by a kind of morbid fascination. However, as the true horror of the sight sank in Adam became truly shocked and he hurried on. The dogs, sprawled on the grass by the remains, somewhat mollified by their feast and still subdued by the drugged meat, regarded them warily as they passed. Salamu suggested they lock the gate behind themselves. Allowing the animals to roam free would not be wise.

Now Adam's eyes were fixed on Rhona with a look of adoration reminiscent of a pilgrim looking for the first time on a rare and hallowed shrine. Charlie had to admit that his boss was certainly pretty, though he had never been attracted to her, and now that he had got used to it, he thought that short hair quite suited her. He was aware of, and mystified by, what appeared to be a budding romance between her and his brother. From what he knew of her choice of men in the past, Adam could hardly be more different. At the moment though, all of Rhona's attention was given to Rowan. Never one to make a fuss over her niece, having brought her up in the "school of hard knocks", she was now doting over her niece like a mother hen and trying to gently untangle her intertwisted greasy hair. The girl was sitting on the floor at Rhona's feet but near the three other young people. Her face had the look of one suffering from battle fatigue, but her dark hollow eyes were intent on examining her sores whilst she gently explored the skin of her arms with her fingers, seemingly fascinated by the experience.

'Leave it alone,' chided Rhona softly, 'poking will only make it worse.'

Rowan didn't look up but stopped touching the scars. 'I can't believe how quickly it's healing,' she said in quiet awe. 'It's amazing.' She had needed help to stand when she finally rose from her bunk in the cell. Careful not to touch her wounds, Rhona and Andor each supported her under her armpits as she tottered from the cell. Gradually gaining strength, she was walking unaided by the time they reached the end of the drive, albeit slowly and with guidance as she was still half-blinded by the light. As the fever left her brain, her disorientation subsided and she began regaining her wider range of senses. Trapped in the helmet had felt like she was encased in thick black glass and its removal was like the glass being suddenly shattered. The companions paused as Salamu locked the gate. Bess and Charlie tightly embraced once more in desperate happiness. This precipitated another spell of jubilant hugging and tears of joy between Andor, Sonilla and Lendi, who simultaneously shared their thoughts and feelings with each other. Rowan physically staggered as she felt it too. She had never before encountered such an intensity of collective emotion spilling unrestrained from anyone. Thu Salamu quickly supported her, radiating calm and reassurance. As her disorientation rapidly subsided she felt a sense of both amazement and happiness in the growing realisation that here were others who were possessed of an extrasensory state. Until now she had felt that she was virtually alone in having these capabilities, living with a persistent feeling of isolation at the root of her being. Now and again she had discerned that an occasional individual she passed in the street unconsciously manifested some semblance of psychic skills, some even knew it but suppressed it or attempted to keep it hidden, but nothing like this. She felt herself becoming engrossed in her sense of wonder at the possibilities she imagined might be associated with deeper telepathic relationships. Oblivious to her surroundings she recklessly plunged into the group's bond. Almost immediately she lost control, became detached from herself and began drowning in the vast ocean of experience. Just as suddenly she felt herself wrenched out and made aware of her physical senses again, reeling with the shock of it.

'Careful,' Salamu cautioned, 'you must also remain mindful of the exterior world or you could become lost. Although you are highly skilled you will need guidance for these new experiences.'

Charlie had been appalled by Rowan's state when they found her. Over the several years he and Bess had known Rhona he had grown to love her niece in a way almost like a daughter but also as a friend, especially since working more closely with her during her apprenticeship. Furthermore, he felt quite protective towards her, so the girl's ordeals over the last few weeks from Grant's assault to her incarceration had quite deeply affected him, causing him much worry on her behalf. He was pleased now to see her recovering unnaturally quickly and in the company of others close to her in age. Having been forced to accept, from the irrefutable evidence before him, that Rowan was indeed telepathic he was not so surprised as he might have been by the appearance of more people with similar skills. It was strange though, to see a group of them together in silence and with blank yet serene expressions on their faces, presumably communicating in ways beyond his understanding or experience.

Lendi had shared her story with the rest of the group when they first returned to the house. When the newly come-of-age acolytes had been led to the clearing they were unaware that anything was amiss. Their guides' thoughts were closed to them, which they put down to the fact that their elders liked to generate an air of mystery regarding their activities and as they had not been told exactly what to expect, they suspected nothing. As they reached the clearing, Lendi was pleased to see a large fire burning at its centre. Many of the ceremonies and celebrations they had experienced at the foundation had involved the building of a fire and everyone enjoyed the sight of the spluttering, swirling flames dancing riotously in the night. The Select gathered in a line on one side of the blaze, feeling the heat on their faces and hands. Without warning Lendi felt herself roughly grabbed from behind by a pair of strong arms. As she flailed and kicked, one of her boots flew from her foot and landed at the edge of the fire. Screaming in fear and protest she was dragged to one side, forcibly bound and gagged. Held tightly by two unseen figures, yet finding herself unable to close her eyes, she was forced to watch in horror as her companions were stripped of their clothes and brutally murdered. One at a time they had their chests gashed open, their hearts ripped out and their bodies thrown onto the fire amid choruses of increasingly frenzied chanting from their hooded captors. It was made clear to Lendi that she escaped the same fate only because someone required a living body as a vessel and her superior psychic abilities meant that she was the most suited for the purpose. Then she was helmeted and underwent the torment of a seemingly never-ending journey until she was locked in the cell at the Belums' mansion. It is no wonder she wept for so long, thought Charlie, after such a harrowing experience.

'Why would they do that?' asked Bess, breaking the shocked silence that followed Lendi's account, 'I mean, with the sacrifices...what did they hope to achieve?'

'Their minds have been corrupted by the repeated use of vessels over many millennia,' Salamu answered. 'Some now believe that they can buy favours from the spirits of the ancestors by sacrificing virgins to them. Moreover, the excessive use of echo stones, which they have sought out and hoarded since The Shift warped their minds, curses them with a penchant for cruelty and malice, which they also use to increase their power and gain support amongst their followers.' For a moment there was a break in her mask of composure. 'It sickens me that they persevere in such abhorrent practices,' she spat vehemently, 'and it takes all my self-control not to mete out the same treatment to them.' She inhaled deeply and then slowly let her breath flow out. Calm once more she added, 'the way of peace is the most noble and just, but not always the easiest.'

Thu Salamu, with her exotic name and authoritative bearing was still an enigma to Charlie. There had been so little time for explanations since they had all come together, that he felt he hadn't had a chance to comprehend who and what she was. He knew that she and whoever she represented abhorred the unspeakable behaviour of these so-called "Everlords" and that they were doing their best to terminate their barbaric deeds. Just exactly how they were going to go about this whilst following "the way of peace" remained a mystery to him. She had now composed herself and sat with an air of serenity like a genial guru patiently waiting for a class of initiates to settle before imparting wisdom.

In the few short hours of their company, Charlie deemed Nick and Lynn to be the most down to earth of the strangers. Lynn, despite fleeing half way across Europe, was showing a radiant glow of health and joy characteristic of some women in early pregnancy - that is, those who were lucky enough to escape morning sickness. She also seemed to be fairly emotionally stable; a confident, plucky, self-assured yet compassionate woman who took no nonsense and candidly spoke her mind. Nick seemed to have a similar temperament but even though Charlie hardly knew him, he could tell the man was being uncharacteristically quiet; there was an uneasy look in his eyes despite his attempts to put on a brave face. He had some deeply troubling thoughts but was reluctant to share them. Charlie had gathered that Adam and his friends were on the run and would have to go into hiding in a safe haven that Salamu knew of. Perhaps it was this that Nick was concerned about. It seemed quite likely that being a "wanted man" and having to abandon his home and former life was at the root of his anxiety. Rather him than me, thought Charlie, at least I can go back to my job and hopefully, once the insurance has paid out for the repairs, go back to my home.

When they returned to Rhona's house Lynn had stared hard at Bess and Charlie, unnerving him somewhat, but then she suddenly exclaimed and explained herself.

'Oh my God! I *knew* I recognised you two!' she declared. 'I saw you in a dream I had!'

'Really?' said Bess. 'When? What was it about?'

'It was a few weeks ago now, yeah? There were all these like, massive green stones....' Lynn began.

'In a huge depression in the jungle?' interrupted Charlie.

She nodded mutely.

'We both had that dream too,' Bess told her.

'No way!' gasped Lynn, 'That's like *totally* amazing!'

'Actually, I think we weren't *having* the same dream,' corrected Charlie, 'I think we were *in* the same dream. We saw you too, well we saw someone and I guess it was you.'

'But how is that even possible when we don't even know each other then?' asked Lynn, 'I mean I know that some of my dreams have been true or linked to reality and stuff, yeah? But what was my connection to you guys?'

'Remember, you saw Sonilla and Lendi too....' Adam chipped in, 'like in that painting you showed me.....'

'Prevision has not yet been fully explained,' Andor told them. 'One theory is that time is not linear, but pan-dimensional and omnipresent, so that somewhere everything that has passed is happening now and all possible futures are played out continuously and that some individuals are receptive to the echoes from these scenarios. However, I am not certain we shall ever know for sure.'

The room fell silent for a few moments as the friends tried to comprehend this outlandish notion.

'But now there are more pressing matters that need to be spoken of,' said Salamu interrupting their deliberations, 'and urgent action that needs to be taken. I know that everyone has been under great stress, but I'm afraid that we cannot pause for long. There is still a faction who mean us harm and we must continue to make good our escape. Whilst it is but a remote possibility, our recent activities may just have alerted our enemies to our presence, if not confirmed our identities, but in any case it will not be long before the network becomes aware of the Belums' fate and seeks to find those responsible.' She paused and looked Charlie straight in the eyes with an expression of apology and regret. 'Unfortunately, by your involvement with us,' she continued glancing briefly in turn at Bess, Rhona and Rowan, '*and* the incidents involving the Belums, you too will have to accompany us.'

'What?' said Charlie in panic and disbelief, 'but *we* haven't done anything to them....why should they want *us*? And we won't tell them anything – they won't get a word out of me. We'll deny all knowledge....We just want to get back to normal....*please.*' Somehow, Charlie knew that they were to be given no choice but he didn't feel able to face a future of such uncertainty.

'I'm sorry Charlie,...all of you,' said Salamu softly, 'but you would not be able to hide your thoughts from these people – they would probe your mind heedless of any harm it might do you and when they discover what has happened to their associates, even though they may have been rivals at times, they will be seeking revenge. While these dissidents are all too egotistical and power hungry to form a cohesive movement, they do collaborate to a certain extent with those who share their anarchistic obsessions and would see an attack on their confederates as an attack on them all. The "Everlords" are merciless and sadistic subversives - you would not wish to meet them, especially when retribution is their intention. The Belums were kittens in comparison.'

'Just how long do you suggest we hide for?' Bess asked, dispirited and disappointed, all she wanted to do was stop and be safe and secure in her own familiar and comforting environment.

'Until it is safe,' replied Salamu, 'that is all I can say.'

'But what about my garden and my business...and my yoga group?' she protested. 'Who will look after it all? I've got loyal students who love coming to class every week, clients relying on my products...there's a polytunnel to water, harvesting and drying of herbs....'

'I'm sorry Bess, but for the immediate future your lives are in danger. Your safety is more important. You will have to cancel some things and make alternative arrangements for others.'

Her heart sank and she looked hopelessly at Charlie. With a kind and loving look in his eyes he took her hand and said, 'I know love, I don't want to go either...but we'll have each other – that's the most important thing - and I trust Salamu – we'll be alright.'

'You don't know that!' she snapped as frustration and anger surfaced from her fear and confusion. She pulled her hand away and stood up. 'How can you give in to these people so easily? We only just met them today....how do you know we can trust them?'

'Well they helped rescue you, didn't they?' Charlie reminded her, trying to remain calm. He recognised that it had been an exceptionally traumatic and emotional time for both of them and they were exhausted. It would be too easy to fall into an argument fraught with their raw feelings. Even so, he also knew that when Bess was getting upset it was very difficult to reason with her. Usually he would wait for her to calm down before attempting to win her round with his logic, but on this occasion there was not enough time. 'If these guys hadn't come along, you might have been dead by now...or possessed by one of those old loonies. You've seen how desperate the Belums were. They tried to burn our house down, they kidnapped three people, they were even prepared to kill if they thought necessary – if their pals are more evil than them we could be in even more danger.'

Bess sat down again and burst into tears. 'But I don't want to go...,' she muttered through her sobs, '...I don't want all this to have happened...I can't cope with it...I want to go back to normal. I just want to go home...'

Charlie cuddled her, stroking her head gently with one hand. He didn't know what else to say, so he said nothing. He just wanted to go to sleep and when he woke to find out it was all simply a dream, like in the stories he so loved as a child. But it was not to be.

'You all need to get some sleep,' said Salamu, 'but I fear you shall have to do so on the road. I do not know if we have been detected. It is best we keep moving until we reach safety.' Everyone in the room turned to look at her as she spoke, except Bess whose face remained hidden on Charlie's shoulder. 'We will all be completely safe once we are within Atargatis,' their guide assured them. 'I will have to ask you to turn off your mobile phones. When we get there we can relay your messages through an untraceable system and you will also be able to send and receive emails. You will be well provided for and you will want for nothing....'

'Except our home....,' commented Charlie glumly with a sigh.

'I know Charlie, but for a short while at least, you will have to make a new home.'

#

News of the Belums' death reached en Nergal as his private jet approached Edinburgh airport. The whisky tumbler shattered in his grip as his shock was replaced by cold intense fury such as he had not felt for centuries. Although he would not have described the twin brothers as his friends, he had shared several millennia with them as they prolonged their lives with the rejuvenation caskets, just as he had extended his own using vessels. An assault on any of the members of the Network was to be dealt with swiftly and mercilessly. He would consult with his allies and summon them to his aid. The strongest possible message must be sent to their enemies. It would not be long before they would either have to submit to the Everlords' greater might or be destroyed.

As the plane began its descent, he began pondering his next incarnation. He imagined that within a handful of years he would have tired of this body and would once more crave the feeling of possessing a new corporeal form. He relished the feeling of surging into a fresh young healthy body, trapping, subduing and dominating the previous psyche as he took control; it gave him a huge sense of satisfaction and a renewal of his confidence in his own powers. The Belums had claimed their weak willed resistance to this path was for ethical reasons, but he knew that emotional co-dependency filled them with the fear that separation from their twinned bodies would somehow sever their conjoined minds. Now their reluctance had resulted in their deaths. Had they sourced and used their vessels sooner they would have survived. Nonetheless, the brothers' culpability in their own demise did not absolve those who in the end were truly responsible. The dithering fools who failed to fashion a casket in time and the interfering miscreants who rescued the vessels would have to be punished. The Everlords could not allow anyone to get the better of them. They must be seen to maintain a state of invincibility. The so-called "Ancestors" and their minions had been growing in both strength and numbers in the last few decades and it was time they were reminded that they had ruthless adversaries. These upstarts must die. He had no idea where they were heading, but it was imperative that he reach them before they secreted themselves in one of the Ancestors' safe havens. He had traced them to Scotland and now had pinpointed some more recent activity. It would not be long before they made some other mistake and his prey were located, yet he knew he could not defeat them alone and he needed help quickly. The other Everlords would be sympathetic but were routinely slow to respond to calls for assistance. Most preferred to indulge themselves in pampered lives of selfish pleasures and could be reluctant to prise themselves away from luxury. He was usually disinclined to use mercenaries; they were surprisingly susceptible to their emotions but their weak minds were so conditioned into accepting orders that they were easily manipulated and he had to admit that there were some circumstances when swift and ruthless action, although potentially messy, had to be taken to affect the desired out come. Now was such a time.

The aircraft landed and En Nergal approached the cockpit to speak with the pilot. With the news of the Belums' deaths he decided to head north as soon as possible. Unfortunately there would be a delay for refuelling and for the necessary clearances to be secured for takeoff but it would still be quicker to fly to Inverness than drive from here. En route he could consolidate his information with that of his operatives in the area.

#

'So, where are we going exactly?' asked Nick. The minibus was winding its way along the coast on the A9 north towards the ambience of the predawn light as it emerged from the short night's sunset. Rhona was taking a turn at the wheel; the tarmac, glinting in the headlights, was wet from a recent shower of rain and the vehicle's windows had steamed up with condensation from the muggy humidity and the combined breath of eleven people. Charlie and Bess were dozing, leaning against each other, as were Sonilla and Lendi. Adam kept finding himself nodding off, his head getting heavier and lolling onto his chest, but each time they hit a bump in the road he jerked awake with a crick in his neck.

'Are we going to stop somewhere for a kip soon?' added Nick. Since the rescue they hadn't stopped to rest except for a quick breather at Rhona's before hitting the road again, having raided the cupboards for supplies. The last time he had slept was on the boat and that wasn't exactly restful as he had to wake so often to puke. 'I can't sleep lurching around and squashed in to this tin can,' he complained. Lynn knew why he was so disgruntled. So much had happened that he hadn't had the chance to ask all the questions he wanted and besides, with so many people in the group there was hardly a chance to get a word in edgeways especially with the reunions: brother to brother, sister to sister, husband and wife and aunt to niece. Adam hadn't been much company either since he'd been mooning over Rhona, although she was glad to see this development at least. For Nick though, Lynn knew, there was good reason for his usual cheery temperament to be eroded; the combination of fatigue, the relentless travelling since the car crash in Poland, the feeling of being hunted, the burden on his rational ideology of the new and strange revelations relating to the extended mind and ancient civilisations – it had all taken its toll. Now he was just scared, tired, confused, irritable and *powerless*. He was so accustomed to being in control of his own destiny that he felt imprisoned by lack of choice and bound by the uncertainty of their circumstances.

His questions were directed at Salamu because she seemed to be in charge, as pretty much the only one who really knew what was going on and as their unelected leader who considered herself their "guide" to a safer future. Up till now, as far as Nick knew, they had only been told that they were going to some kind of "haven". He couldn't imagine the nature of such a place if it could add eleven more people to its occupants and keep them hidden from their supposedly ruthless and powerful pursuers.

'It is better if you do not know,' she informed him turning her head from her position in the front passenger seat to look at him as she spoke, 'we are still subject to a pursuit, not just physically, but psychically – the "Everlords" will be scanning for all our thoughts and whilst I am able to offer us all a background level of protection, you are not yet trained in how to resist a full mind-probe if they locate us. As for stopping, I'm afraid all we can do is have a break to stretch our legs. If you need to sleep, Andor can help you with that.

'Oh no!' protested Nick immediately, holding up his hands as if to fend off an attack, 'I'm not having anyone fucking about with *my* head.'

'You want to sleep don't you?' she countered.

'Yeah but...'

'Go on Nick, don't be scared,' Lynn urged him.

'I'm not scared!' he blurted, 'I'm just...'

'Scared?'

'It will be alright,' Andor assured him, 'no harm will come to you.'

It was the thought that Lynn might think him afraid that caused him to relent. Grudgingly he nodded at Andor. 'Okay mate, do you stuff,' he said.

'Close your eyes and try to relax,' Andor instructed. He put his hands on Nick's head with his thumbs resting lightly on his eyelids. 'I'm just going to redirect your thought patterns to bypass your resistance, but it will be easier if you offer no opposition.'

Despite his misgivings Nick had grown to trust the young refugee, having spent so much time with him in the last week and having been through a great deal together, so he consciously relaxed the tension in his muscles and started to breathe deeply an evenly. In seconds he was asleep.

They stopped at dawn to stretch their legs but Nick remained dead to the world. It felt slightly chilly now but the air was completely still. An amber radiance blushed the north-eastern horizon, a sharp line separating it from the dark gunmetal hue of the strangely waveless sea. The scattered clouds became edged with a scarlet tinge that gradually spread and brightened to infuse their dusty grey with an ochre wash. A bright gold speck rapidly became an intense yellow sliver as the sun pushed its way up out of the ocean. The sky grew brighter, becoming more vividly coloured with pink, peach, bronze and apricot tones vying for brilliance in a heavenly beauty pageant. The friends stood scattered along the roadside in silent awe for a while, appreciating the rare and sublime spectacle.

Charlie and Bess were holding hands. He turned and hugged her once more as he had done numerous times in the scant hours since their reunion. She smiled and hugged him back with equal fervour. She too had missed him terribly during their separation. He was so happy to be back with her that for the moment at least he didn't care where they were going or what they were doing. He now accepted his fate, as long as he was never again parted from his life-long lover. They released each other to watch the sky again. Charlie felt the weight of the stone in his jacket pocket, but chose not to touch it. After they had left Rhona's, he and Bess were taken home for a five-minute stop just to see if there were any "essentials" they might need that had escaped fire damage in their home. Scooping up an armful of clothing, another pair of shoes and a couple of unread books in the bedroom, he noticed the dark green stone on his bedside table. After a moment's hesitation, he grabbed that too, but in the short instant it took him to thrust it into his pocket a dramatic vision flashed through his mind. In that single second he saw Bess wearing a crown wrought of golden filigree and dressed in a luxurious red velvet cloak embroidered with elaborate designs in gold thread. But the thing that made his heart leap was the sight of her climbing into and lying down in a gilded casket just like the one he had been making for Asar and Ki. He hadn't told her yet, wanting time to discuss it with her alone and had avoided touching the stone again since. He also wanted to ask Salamu more about its mysterious properties, why so many of his dreams included the casket and what was the link between them. He was hoping that there would be plenty of time for this once they had reached their destination.

Rhona and Adam were spending every spare moment talking quietly. They seemed to be totally at ease together, often making each other laugh and engrossed in their conversations, the whole time with attentive and admiring eyes. They were side by side now in joint appreciation of the view. Adam noticed Rhona hug herself and rub her arms at the chilliness of the air having neglected to extricate her coat from the luggage pile. In a moment of bravery, but not without some trepidation, he slowly and gently put his arm around her shoulders. To his surprise and delight she leaned into him and put her arm around his waist. A thrill of elation tingled up his spine and he squeezed her a little tighter.

Rowan was leaning with her back against the side of the minibus, in the company of Andor, Lendi and Sonilla. She cared even less than Charlie of their destination. She had finally found friends who she could *fully* relate to, not because they were her own age but because they shared her abilities. Their exchange of thoughts and feelings had enabled them to bond quickly. For the first time in her life she felt understood and completely accepted for who she was. She was no longer the odd one out, the freak, the misfit. The recent events – the assault, the attempted rape and her abduction – seemed to pale into insignificant memories now that she had her first truly intimate friends. She had been close to Jenny and still cared for her, but she had no idea how superficial their friendship had been until this moment. She hoped that Jenny would be okay now that she was out of the picture for the indefinite future. She was a nice girl who deserved more friends. She guiltily wondered if she should contact her now that she was free from her captors, but Salamu had told them that their phones might be detected by these "Everlords" or their agents and so forbade their use. Anyway it might be best if Jenny still thought she was in Italy with her mother rather than have to try to explain her current circumstances.

With sweeping gestures of her hands, Lynn was telling Salamu about her paintings and dreams and more detail of how they related to Lendi and Sonilla, Charlie and Bess. Their guide informed her that it was an aspect of her awakening consciousness that had been simmering for some while, but was now growing more rapidly. As time progressed and she spent longer in the company of telepaths, so her own skills developed further. Lynn had recognised that she was registering more snippets of the messages, or "impressions" as Salamu called them, that were travelling between the others. It was like tuning a radio into a foreign station whilst attempting to learn the language being broadcast. She had also been practicing the projection of her own thoughts at the telepaths and discovered that surprisingly, they were also being received by Bess, even though *her* mind remained a blank to Lynn. Salamu had warned her off further experimentation until they were out of reach of their pursuers.

Everyone felt the guide's wordless signal that it was time to move on and they slowly clambered back into the vehicle. An hour later they had arrived at the Scrabster ferry terminal. While Salamu went to purchase tickets from her seemingly endless budget, Nick woke, yawned and said, 'Blimey, I slept well,' before looking blearily out of the window. He looked confused at the sight of the lines of cars and the proximity of the harbour.

'What's happening...where are we?' he asked Lynn in a groggy voice.

'We're going over to Orkney,' she told him lightly.

'What?' he exclaimed, a feeling of panic obliterating all traces of sleepiness. 'No way am I getting on another fucking boat! That was the worst experience I've ever had in my life and I'm not going to repeat it!'

'Don't worry love,' Lynn said tenderly, retaining her deep affection for him despite his recent grouchiness. 'It's only a short crossing,' she continued patiently, 'one hour, tops.'

'Besides, you don't really have a choice mate,' Adam informed him blithely, 'we're on the run remember?' He was beginning to feel a little tetchy towards his friend, who now seemed to whinge a little too often, but tried to mask it behind a jocular tone; it was not in his nature to openly air his petty grievances with those close to him.

Nick knew they were right, but still felt bewildered by the inexplicable changes to himself and those around him and vulnerable not being in control of his own destiny. Lynn looked at him intently and he met her eyes. She took his head in her hands and pulled it gently towards her. She kissed him deeply but he felt much more than the physical pressure on his lips. He felt that she was imbued with a serenity of spirit that transferred comfort and reassurance with such loving intensity that he was elevated and liberated from the well of despair he had gradually sink into.

'Wow! How did you do that?' he asked, pleased, amazed and troubled in equal measure.

'Dunno,' she replied nonchalantly, 'just thought I'd give it a go.'

Suddenly Nick looked queasy and made a rush for the door just as Salamu returned with the ferry tickets. He just managed to reach a low concrete wall by the waiting area before he threw up over it.

'Oh no!' cried Lynn guiltily. 'Did I do that to him?'

'No Lynn, it was not your doing,' Salamu reassured her. 'Remember what I said before. His denial and resistance to the phenomena he is witnessing are causing the inconsistencies in his mind to manifest in his body. He is also blocking his *own* development, which I suspect has been trying to break out for some weeks now. The longer he opposes the change, the more unwell he will become and the more intense his transformation will be. He is fighting his own telepathic awakening.' Lynn looked anxious at the prospect of Nick's "intense transformation" so Salamu added, 'but don't worry, we will be there to help him through his crisis and no real harm will come to him – he is just unintentionally teaching himself a hard lesson.'

Discovering that it was to be at least thirty minutes before they could board the ferry, Rowan decided to use the toilet in the terminal. Sitting in the cubicle, now that she was a little more distant from the others, she felt a sudden yearning to contact Jenny. It did not seem fair that the girl had been parted from her best friend. Rowan knew she had no one else and was probably both lonely and desperate to hear from her. The feeling of guilt at her neglectful behaviour in that moment outweighed Salamu's warning of a potential risk. Surely, she thought, just one short text would be okay?

As if acquiescing to Nick's fears the ferry journey seemed to be as easy as could have been imagined, although due to a last minute "technical fault" the departure was delayed by an hour. The waters of the Pentland Firth were uncommonly tranquil. A rare combination of the stillness of a tide on the turn, a sea without a swell and not even a hint of a breeze, created the calmest crossing anyone on board could remember. The railings were lined with passengers enjoying the warm weather and marvelling at the flat glassy surface, broken only by the ship's wake, that showed almost perfect reflections of the pale morning sun, the pastel blue sky scattered with cumulus and the gliding sea birds. Watching a gannet that was escorting their boat, Adam couldn't remember the last time he felt this relaxed and contented. He was literally sailing into an uncertain future, but he felt that it did not worry him. He glanced over to where Rhona stood with Charlie and Bess a few metres away, his heart fluttering with exhilaration and anticipation at the sight of her. He already knew that there was something between them; they had held hands, stood arm in arm and chatted easily. *And* she was gorgeous. He didn't even attempt to comprehend how it was that she had appeared in his dreams before he met her – it was just part of this amazing new beginning, this new adventure. Any future involving Rhona was going to be wonderful. Out of habit, Adam absent-mindedly put his hands in his jacket pockets and felt his tobacco. He automatically pulled it out to start rolling a cigarette. He stopped, looking down at the plastic pouch and suddenly becoming conscious of what he was doing. Of the eleven people in the group, he was the only one who remained a smoker. He knew that Rhona didn't like it. The notion occurred to him that, for the first time in his life, he *really wanted* to give up the habit and strangely, the thought no longer terrified him. Not only that, but he actually *believed* he could do it too. The idea was a little unsettling of course; it would herald a big change in his daily life. He had always known that he *shouldn't* smoke and that he *ought* to stop, but he had never really *wanted* to until now. Regardless of the health issues related to inhaling the hot, toxic fumes and tar-laden particulates, the addiction held him like a slave, except that unlike a slave he had the choice of freedom. He could liberate himself with a conscious decision and all that he would have to endure would be a short period of craving and discomfort. Somehow, at this point in time, the prospect did not fill him with dread but rather appeared as more of an exciting challenge on his path of personal development. A little firmness of purpose and strength of will, when appropriately applied, would boost his self-confidence and could thereby enhance his ability to deal with a whole range of new experiences. After all, if Nick and Lynn had managed to kick the habit, albeit on Nick's part with a certain amount of anguish and agitation, he was sure he could too. Adam turned from the railing and, spotting a litterbin nearby, crossed the deck to reach it with a determined stride. With unwavering resolution he flung his tobacco into the aperture and immediately experienced a sense of both release and relief as he broke the bonds of dependency that had shackled his mind and body to the odious substance. He knew he had made an irreversible decision and felt an unfamiliar pride in this newfound strength of will. Pleased with himself he looked up and saw that Rhona was walking towards him, smiling. Their eyes met and he stood transfixed as she moved closer. Happily entranced by her beguiling blue irises, he was unconscious of the fact that he had now been captured by another, albeit benign influence. She didn't stop until their bodies gently touched.

'For the sweeter breath and strength of character,' she whispered, 'here's your reward.' She reached one hand behind his back, the other around his neck and pulled him into the most exquisite kiss he had ever experienced.

Charlie observed his boss and his brother with a mixture of surprise, amusement and delight. He nudged Bess and nodded in their direction.

'I would never have predicted that,' he said, 'Adam just doesn't seem like Rhona's type.'

'I know,' agreed Bess smiling, 'it's totally out of character too – I've never known her come on to anyone in that way before.'

'They both seem to be enjoying it though.'

'Yes, it's kind of sweet isn't it? Good luck to them, I say.'

Nick approached grinning and in a much improved mood. 'Who'd have thought it, eh?' he said, referring not to Adam and Rhona who he hadn't noticed yet, but to what he considered as his newfound sea legs. 'I was dreading getting on a fucking boat again after my last time, but this is a doddle.'

'I think we're pretty lucky,' commented Charlie, 'a crossing like this is almost unheard of. It's *so* still.'

'The calm before the storm maybe?' joked Nick, 'though in our case it's more like the calm *after* the fucking storm considering all the shit we've been through, right?'

'Dolphins!' someone called excitedly from the starboard rail. As passengers rushed over there was a chorus of thrilled cries and a frenzy of enthusiastic, if hurried, photograph taking.

The three of them went to join their friends near the crowd of eager onlookers. No more than twenty metres from the ferry a large pod of dark grey-blue shapes disturbed the calm waters. At least two dozen of the animals cut through the reflected sky, matching the speed of the vessel; their glossy backs, topped by rigid dorsal fins, arched gracefully as they broke the surface. Suddenly one of them shot from the sea to perform an acrobatic vault, delighting its appreciative audience. Its behaviour was soon emulated by another from the group. For several more minutes the dolphins treated them to further displays of exuberant antics before slowly moving off to the east.

The eleven companions gathered in an enthusiastic cluster to share their glee.

'That was fucking amazing!' raved Nick.

'Yeah, totally!' agreed Lynn, 'I've never seen dolphins before!'

'Me neither,' said Adam, eyes wide from the wonder.

Bess and Charlie had made occasional trips to Channonry Point on the Black Isle to spot dolphins from the shore, but had not previously seen them so close.

Rowan cleared her throat uncertainly. 'I could like…um…totally *feel* them. Er,…kind of…,' she mumbled self-consciously.

'Of course. You would be open to their thought patterns with your psychic skills,' confirmed Salamu encouragingly, 'What did you feel?'

Charlie was astounded by this concept and along with the others gave Rowan his rapt attention.

'Um, well it's kind of difficult to put into like words and stuff,' she began haltingly. 'I could like feel a sense of their kind of uninhibited freedom and exuberance and. ..it was all like intense, raw emotion, but not in a like primitive way or anything, more like a kind of totally *alien* intelligence I guess. It was weird. I sort of knew that animals had like feelings and stuff, but I could never have imagined the *depth* of it and how it was like their whole essence.'

'Wow! That is so cool,' commented Adam, 'does this mean that you guys,' he indicated the other telepaths, 'can actually *talk* to the animals?'

'Whoa…Doctor fucking *Doolittle*,' muttered Nick under his breath, not without a hint of sarcasm.

'Not in any way that you could understand,' Salamu informed them evenly, 'I could probably make them aware of my intentions or my needs, but their thought processes are so different from humans, that they wouldn't understand our reasoning and logic. That is not how they reach their decisions. They are creatures of action who mostly live very much in the moment, so they receive stimuli and act according to the nature of their senses – they have full use of all seven.'

'*Seven?*' queried Charlie. 'What are the other two?'

'One is a combination of instinct and intuition,' she said, 'most humans still possess this to some degree but generally don't know it or admit it, and the other is that of the extended mind which includes telepathy and the other psychic processes. Some divide these further and identify up to five more.'

'Far out,' remarked Adam, nodding sagely.

'Oh, here we go, story time again,' remarked Nick with a quiet chuckle.

Lynn gave him a withering look but didn't say anything. She found it hard to believe he was still being so stubborn and unwilling to amend his worldview. She loved him a great deal and could only hope that he would come round eventually.

Twenty minutes later they were passing close to the soaring, weather-beaten face of Hoy, its sheer cliffs looking as if they plunged right to the bottom of the sea. The numerous horizontal striations seemed to be more clearly defined because of the sunlight and contrasted markedly with the dark vertical shadows where the deep clefts slashed the rock face. A tall, crooked stack – the Old Man of Hoy – stood aloof, separated from the cliffs by a wide chasm as if having broken free to start marching across the ocean on a proud and solitary adventure. Once more, this sight instigated a flurry of activity involving the pointing of fingers and digital cameras from the passengers crowding at the rails.

Once beyond the cliffs, the ship navigated Hoy Sound, the strait between the island and mainland Orkney, past the tiny isle of Graemsay and into Stromness harbour. The waterfront was crowded with small fishing boats that were being heckled by wheeling gulls. Charlie wondered why they were not all working out at sea on a day as calm as this, though he had to admit he was completely ignorant of the normal practices of the fishing industry. Stromness, in Charlie's opinion, looked as if its buildings had been thrown into a tumbled heap against the hillside by the colossal waves of an unusually powerful storm. The haphazard clutter was nonetheless quite attractive but more in the style of Lowry than Constable. The town had a friendly look to it, with people and cars bustling between the crowded buildings. He wondered if it was a Saturday, but had completely lost track of the days of the week recently and then supposed that it was now probably the beginning of the tourist season. The settlement, judging by its architecture, seemed to have been built mostly in the eighteenth and nineteenth centuries, although he knew that these islands had been settled since Neolithic times. A large and unsightly modern edifice frowned sternly over the town like a colonising power passing judgement on the primitive locals, though its vast expanse of glass reflected the more handsome buildings as if to claim their good looks for itself. Charlie had nothing against new buildings in principle, having seen a few that were quite pleasing to the eye, but he never understood how such incongruous structures were allowed through the planning process where they did nothing but spoil the sight of a historic setting.

As the ferry inched carefully towards the quay, the intercom crackled into life and the passengers were requested to make their way either to the vehicle deck or, for those on foot, to the appropriate exits. Just as he turned away from the view of the town, Charlie noticed something from the corner of his eye. Two police vehicles, a van and a car, were approaching the landing stage, their blue lights flashing insistently. For a moment he considered it strange that their sirens weren't blaring but this thought was almost immediately obliterated by the upsurge of panic corkscrewing through his body. He suddenly realised that someone on board must have recognised them from the photos in the newspapers or on television and called the police from the boat. His companions were already passing through the door from the deck to the interior of the vessel, oblivious to this alarming development. He rushed after them and gestured urgently to gather them in a huddle at one side of the lounge. He whispered the news to them, glancing nervously at the other folk moving slowly by.

'Don't worry,' Salamu bade them calmly, 'with a little help from Lendi, Sonilla and Andor, I will be able to influence the thoughts of the police officers. Even if they stop and search our vehicle, they will fail to recognise any of us. You could help too – just imagine yourselves as indistinguishable from anyone else. Trust me and remain composed.'

Regardless of what he had witnessed in the last few weeks, Adam was still not wholly convinced. As he sat waiting nervously in his seat next to Rhona he held tightly to her hand once more. His fear caused his body to flush with heat and sweat started to trickle down his back. His heart pounded against his ribs like an angry ape trying to beat its way out of a cage and despite the tightness gripping his chest like a barrel hoop, he felt it might burst at any minute. Glancing around uneasily, he could tell that Charlie and Nick were similarly fraught and fidgety, but the women seemed surprisingly calm, at least on the surface. He wondered if they were perhaps more attuned to the soothing influence of Salamu's neural signals or just more trusting of her abilities to obscure their identities. Their minibus started moving slowly forward, driven by their enigmatic guide, following the line of cars in front of them. They emerged into the dazzling brightness of the late morning sunshine and continued down the ramp at a snail's pace. As soon as they could see ahead it became clear that the police had created a chicane from their two vehicles and were scrutinising the occupants of every car from both sides as the queue crept past them. When their turn came, Adam willed himself to remain impassive, although it took all his effort not to scream and make a run for it. He could not remember a time when he had so much adrenaline pumping through his veins. Even when he had been detained after the raid on Lynn's flat, he'd had such a bad hangover that his physiology was dominated by trying to overcome a moderate case of alcohol poisoning - his adrenaline hadn't stood a chance. One officer was standing in front, impeding their progress, while four others were scrutinising them through the windows. The most senior looking, a stern-faced character of about fifty, muttered a few words to his closest companion and then moved to the driver's window.

'I'm sorry madam,' he growled, not sounding in the least bit apologetic, 'we shall have to enter your vehicle as we can't properly see the occupants in the middle seats.'

In Adam's awareness time slowed to an agonising pace, like a snail struggling through treacle. Why was it that when bad or scary stuff was happening it seemed to take so much longer than the good stuff? One of the policemen grabbed the handle of the side door and slid it open. He was dour faced, stocky and freckled youth with short ginger hair and thick, bushy eyebrows who to Adam, had the look of an Appalachian backwoodsman in need of a victim upon whom to deliver his testosterone-fuelled frustrations through unspeakable acts of cruelty and perversion. He eased the front half of his body through the gap and leaned in to squint at their faces. Adam had stopped breathing and was shaking uncontrollably.

'What's wrong with him?' enquired the officer in a surprisingly squeaky voice.

'Oh, er….fever,' muttered Rhona and placed a hand on Adam's sweaty brow as if to confirm her diagnosis.

The constable merely nodded and then took some photographs from his top pocket. He glanced at each image and then scrutinised every one of the vehicle's occupants in turn, apparently determined to undertake his duties and responsibilities diligently. Finally, he replaced the pictures and smiled. His face was transformed into that of a young man so cute that Rhona could imagine the island's aunts and grannies queuing up to bake him cakes.

'Thank you for your cooperation,' he said cheerfully, 'and enjoy your holiday. I hope the weather stays good for you. Bye just now.' He shut the door and they were waved through.

'Holy fucking shit on sticks!' exclaimed Nick, laughing with relief as they drove on. 'Phewie! That was a close call, I nearly crapped myself!'

'Talking of which, I *really* need the bog,' blurted Adam, the trepidation and fear having had the customary effect on his digestive system, 'I'm turtle-necking here!' Salamu pulled in to the harbour car park where there was a public toilet. He leapt out and ran into the gents where with great relief he discharged the churning contents of his gut.

The friends' mood was now quite buoyant after their narrow escape and they filled the minibus with light-hearted chat. After a brief drive they were to make another short ferry crossing to the brooding hulk that was Hoy. Nick hooted at the irony when given the news. Now that he considered himself acclimatised to sea travel, this piffling stretch of water held no fear for him. The Orkney mainland, aside from being windswept and dreary seemed remarkably tame. This was not surprising though, considering it had been deforested centuries ago and relentlessly farmed (or "agri-vated" thought Charlie wryly) right to the edge of the shoreline wherever possible. With barely a tree in sight, wire fences and power lines criss-crossed the bleak landscape, occasionally augmented by a dry-stone wall. This stark, austere backdrop was littered with a scattering of houses, like dice flung haphazardly by the gods onto an uneven green carpet. There were older stone-built farms and croft-style cottages, some quaint, some tatty, some dilapidated ruins; others were smart incongruous bungalows reflecting the latter day desire for the comfort of all mod cons in a hermetically sealed environment, immune from the ravages of the elements and out of touch with nature apart from the picture windows installed for the views. The coast and its beaches were nevertheless mostly quite pretty and the sky was also to Charlie's liking, extensive and open, giving him the sense of liberty to which he was accustomed. Looking across to Hoy he sensed a wilder land, its sturdy heights implying a resistance to cultivation and a scantier population. Adam bemoaned the fact that they were not given time to investigate the world famous archaeological sites this island boasted; he particularly wanted to visit Skara Brae, the acclaimed Neolithic village and the Ring of Brodga, a particularly impressive stone circle. Salamu told him that the latter, and indeed all such monuments were attempts by ancient people to recreate some of what had become lost to them since The Shift.

Once across the Sound of Hoy they took a small single-track road towards Rackwick that followed a valley between the hills. After about three miles they turned left onto a gravel track that wound up onto higher ground ahead. Their progress slowed as Salamu attempted to avoid the potholes. They had not driven far when Rowan thought she heard a rhythmical pulsing. She strained to extend her senses to determine what it was. She felt a sense of anxiety creep into her.

'Can anybody else hear that "whumping" noise?' she asked. Before there was a chance to answer, the sound intensified and a shadow fell over them.

'What the hell?' exclaimed Charlie. Suddenly a helicopter appeared in front of them, hovering over the track fifty metres ahead. It was so low that Salamu, uttering a low curse, was forced to stop the vehicle as small stones flew up to ping off the windscreen. The aircraft landed on the gravel amid a swirl of dust, sweeping the surrounding area of loose twigs of heather.

Rowan's feeling of dread grew and as she watched the door on one side of the helicopter flew open. A group of eight soldiers armed with rifles poured out and formed a semicircle, aiming their guns at the minibus. Above the noise of the engine and the rotors she heard their commander bark, "Get out of the vehicle with your hands up. Now!' The aircraft's engine was cut and the rotors began to slow.

'What do we do, Salamu?' asked Andor.

'We do what he says,' she replied levelly.

'How the fuck did they find us *here*!' snapped Nick angrily. He had thought they were safe now, so close to this "haven" of Salamu's.

Rowan suddenly remembered the text she had sent to Jenny from the ferry terminal and her conscience shrank with remorse. How could she have been so stupid? She was about to own up, trying to coin an apology that didn't sound too lame, when Lendi spoke.

'How they found us does not matter now,' she stated simply.

Rowan realised that her new friend had perceived her intention and saved her the embarrassment of confessing. Even in these dire circumstances she felt increased affection for her. Following her companions as they emerged nervously from the vehicle she tried to read the minds of the troops in front of them. Despite her trepidation, she felt determined to find a way to overcome this obstacle. It was her fault that they had been traced so it was her responsibility to get them out of this fix. They had come so close to safety, that she couldn't bear the prospect of being captured again, of being "helmeted" again, to undergo the indignity and humiliation, the powerlessness of imprisonment. But her greatest fear was the possibility of becoming a "vessel"; to have one's mind subjugated and possessed by another was beyond anything she wanted to contemplate. She would rather die...or even kill again, to avoid such a fate. In the brief moments she had, the only thoughts Rowan was able to detect from the squad were a mixture of the excitement of being engaged in a mission combined with disappointment at the perceived inadequacies of their opponents. The scruffy and motley crew the mercenaries were now faced with seemed to be no threat to anyone. A black-clad figure alighted nimbly from the helicopter and sauntered over to take up a position in front of his forces. He grinned demonically and rubbed his hands together with maniacal glee.

" En Nergal!" exclaimed Salamu.

'Ha! What a sorry sight you make!' he exclaimed with delight. 'You cannot oppose either the strength of my mind or the firepower of my men here.'

Rowan felt her legs weaken as waves of malevolent force emanated from the man. Suddenly unsteady on her feet she reached for Lendi's arm and her new friend helped support her. Salamu slowly raised a hand as if to placate her adversary and Rowan felt an immediate easing of Nergal's power.

'Ah, Salamu...,' he said with a slightly amused and patronising tone. 'So good to see you again. You would have been a great and powerful ally if you had not been so emotionally weak. But your compassion and misguided morals have become your limitations. You are no match for the powers I have built in myself. He raised a hand towards Salamu and as he started to slowly curl his fingers, she gasped and fell to her knees.

'Stop!' shouted Rowan. 'You can't do this, you bastard!' He dropped his hand, bemused and regarded her with curiosity, as if she was a puppy in a litter of kittens. Salamu rose unsteadily to her feet, breathing heavily.

'What's this,' he remarked pompously, maintaining his supercilious smile, 'a lamb that thinks it's a lion? You should beware, little one. You have no idea of the powers I possess. I could turn your puny mind into pulp with less than a click of my fingers.' He help up a hand as if about to demonstrate. His conceited, overconfident and condescending manner triggered a fiery rage in Rowan's spirit. Finding a level of courage and recklessness surging irrationally through her fear she blurted, 'And you have no idea of the powers I possess, you arrogant shit!' She yelled and ran at him, throwing all her anger and the full force of her mind behind a mental and physical attack.

'No Rowan!' called Rhona, but it was too late. As she reached him, En Nergal punched the girl in the throat and she fell choking to the ground. Charlie made to rush forwards, but Bess grabbed his arm.

'The soldiers Charlie!' she warned him. The gunmen still stood in a semicircle, weapons poised, motionless and awaiting instructions.

'*Everyone hold hands.*' Bess heard Salamu's voice enter her thoughts. '*Together we can join our minds and resist him. We are stronger if we become "one".*'

The companions all reached out and formed their own arc opposite their foes. Bess felt her fingers tingle with energy from both Charlie's and Andor's hands.

'I wouldn't do that if I were you!' The icy menace had now returned to En Nergal's voice. He had crouched next to Rowan and lifted her head between his hands. 'You know I could kill her with a single thought.'

Rhona let go of Lynn and Adam's hands to hold her own gripped in front of her as if in prayer. 'No, please don't,' she implored him tearfully, falling to her knees. She had already come too close to losing her niece and could not abide the thought of further harm befalling her. Rowan looked up suddenly and met her aunt's eyes. She smiled mischievously. Rhona despaired at this sudden display of foolhardiness and could not imagine what her niece hoped to achieve. Fear for the girl's safety gripped her thoughts, overwhelming every other consideration.

Rowan had in some way managed to find a stillness within. Somehow her fear had disappeared and she had discovered a calmer undercurrent where her mind could swim undetected beneath the powerful mass of En Nergal's domination. She surreptitiously reached out to the awareness of the mercenaries, trying to find a weakness. All she found however was a barrier of well trained, disciplined minds, unquestioning of the authority in the command structure. Years of military life and dedication to combat training had stifled their decision making as individuals when on active duty.

Meanwhile Lynn had decided to attempt a similar approach. Although her mind was still in the early stages of awakening to the possibilities ranged before it, she was finding it came naturally to her, as if she had learned psychic techniques as a child but neglected to use them since. Although the troops were completely under the control of their leader, the captain retained the independence necessary for his role. As a mercenary he was loyal to the contract, but only up to a point. Lynn could sense his doubts so she attempted to encourage and stimulate them. Unfortunately her lack of experience left her intentions exposed. She felt the sudden impact of a malign assault and crumpled to the floor. Nick immediately crouched beside her to check her condition but before he even had a chance to vent his anger, En Nergal spoke again.

'I've had enough of this!' he shouted. 'Captain! Kill them all! Tell your men to fire at will.'

There was a brief pause, as if time stood still for a moment. In that long second they all believed they were about to die. Lynn didn't want to die. She was soon to become a mother and no one was going to kill her unborn child. She focussed on the captain once more.

One side of En Nergal's head exploded in a spray of skull bone and tissue as a loud crack ripped through the air. He remained motionless for a moment, his remaining eye wide with shock, before releasing Rowan and toppling over. Rhona looked with horror at her niece. For a moment she thought Rowan had killed again, but then she saw the captain of the mercenaries lower his rifle. The others followed suit and then visibly relaxed.

'We didn't get into this to kill unarmed civilians,' stated the officer matter-of-factly. 'There's no honour, excitement or glory if you are not facing a worthy opponent. Now I don't care who thinks who is "good" or "bad", but I don't like unfairness, nor the strong crushing the weak.' It was quite clear that he considered this group to be the latter. 'Whilst I don't particularly like hippies, I take no pleasure in killing them. We'll take the body and chuck it in the sea. Come on men.'

Two of the soldiers dragged Nergal's body to the helicopter and within half a minute it had risen above the friends and started moving towards the coast.

Rowan rose to her feet, rubbing her throat.

'Are you okay?' asked Rhona.

Rowan nodded. 'For a moment there, you totally thought I killed him, didn't you?'

Her aunt shifted her weight uncomfortably. She didn't like having had the thought, no matter how fleetingly, but she couldn't deny it.

'I'm sorry Ro, I....'

'Don't worry,' said Rowan, taking her hand. 'I might have done, if I could have....I don't even know myself any more. Hopefully I'll get some training soon and I'll be able to like, control it and stuff.'

Rhona hugged her and led her over to join the others who were still standing in various states of shock. This latest encounter had left them all deeply shaken but also strangely numb, as if there was a limit to how much the human mind could continue to react to unexpected, adverse conditions and strange phenomena. Lendi took Rowan's hands in hers and their eyes met.

'I'm so glad you're alright,' she said.

'Me too,' agreed Rowan with a half smile before giving her a hug.

Salamu seemed the least affected by the ordeal and gently encouraged them all to get back in the minibus. She placed a hand on Lynn's arm and gave her a look that indicated she knew what she had done but also contained both admiration and approval. Adam was so traumatised he clung to Rhona as if one of them would float away if left unattended. He knew it was supposed to be off-putting to a woman if you seemed too desperate, but in his current state....well he *did* feel desperate. Not desperate for a woman, but desperate to feel safe again. He had had enough of danger and just wanted it all to stop. Then he could get on with thinking about how to have a proper relationship. Luckily, Rhona didn't seem to mind and held him with equal force. In fact she felt much the same as him, although with the additional distress of concern for her niece's wellbeing.

Bess stopped as they reached the vehicle. 'Hang on,' she said, 'now that evil bastard's dead can't we just go home? I mean, we're not in danger any more are we?'

'You forget Bess,' Salamu said gently, 'that En Nergal was just one of the Everlords. If you remained at large, the others would find you. If anything, the danger is even more severe. Nergal was much more closely tied to the Network than the Belums ever were and his death will be seen as an extreme provocation. I'm sorry, but we must continue as planned.'

The companions clambered into the minibus in silence. Although they had escaped unharmed, the adrenaline released into their blood by the recent threat was still flowing through their veins. Salamu sat behind the wheel and drove on. Lynn sat quietly holding Nick's hand with mixed feelings. She wasn't sure if she should take blame or credit for any influence she may or may not have had over the captain's mind. The extreme circumstances had led her to feel glad that their adversary was dead but it was not without a twinge of guilt. Killing, or being responsible for it, did not sit comfortably in her conscience. She did not want to imagine that this could become part of her life in the future.

They followed the track over the barren boggy moor until, just before they reached the south west coast of the island, they came to a checkpoint in a high fence that stretched away for five hundred meters in both directions before turning to meet the cliffs another half kilometre ahead. A large sign at the entrance declared that the establishment beyond, a sprawling amalgamation of concrete, steel and glass, seeming to Charlie to be copied from a five-year-old's Lego model, was called "The Institute for Geodynamic and Pelagic Research". A large radar rotated on top of a mast that rose from a small control tower on the wide flat roof. The two security guards glanced for a moment at Salamu and nodded, then briefly studied the occupants of the minibus through the windows, their impassive faces revealing to Charlie nothing of their mood or thoughts. Suddenly they smiled and without a word opened the barrier to let them through.

There was a pulsing, throbbing noise of a motor and Charlie looked up through the window to the right and saw a small helicopter approaching.

'Oh shit!' he said.

'It's alright, it's one of ours,' Salamu assured him.

He watched as it descended and circled the building ahead, finally coming to land on a helipad nearby. Their guide drove them to the car park in front of the complex that contained surprisingly few cars for the size of the place. Slowly, they all extricated themselves from the minibus, stretched and shook their limbs.

'Most of the people here are resident,' answered Salamu to Charlie's unspoken question, 'land transport is rarely needed, so vehicles are owned and shared by everyone.'

'Not by the institute?' he asked.

'There isn't really an "institute" as such,' she told him, 'that is a front to satisfy the inquisitive, although some research *is* carried out for our own purposes. We are more of a community. All will become clear in due course.'

Charlie looked at the faces of those nearest to him. Bess, Rhona and Adam all shrugged, as mystified as he was. He turned to the others. The youngest four in the company stood in silence, ostensibly calm and serene. No doubt, he thought, they probably know what's going on. Rowan's face though did reveal a hint of excitement and anticipation. Behind her Lynn's features held a similar expression, but Nick, by her side, looked sick again and oblivious to his surroundings. Salamu bade them grab their bags and follow as she led them towards the building ahead. At the main entrance there were CCTV cameras and another security guard who smiled benignly and nodded as they passed. Inside it was cool, but the air smelled fresh. They were led along a wide empty corridor with a grey tiled floor, reminiscent of utilitarian public buildings the world over. Windows and doors to either side showed sparingly staffed offices and laboratories. At the end they came to the steel doors of an elevator.

'Must be up,' asserted Nick, 'cos we're on the ground floor.'

Salamu shook her head and pressed the "down" button that he had not noticed before.

'Ah,' he said, his look of nausea now replaced by a little anxiety, 'I'm not that keen on the underground.'

There was a "ping" and the doors slid open. Lynn took his hand and led him in, followed by the others. The doors closed again and they began the descent. It seemed a long way down to Charlie, but there was no indication that they had passed any other levels; no little lit-up numbers measured their progress. Finally the lift stopped and after a long second the doors opened to reveal the most unexpected sight he could possibly have imagined. His initial reaction was one of utter astonishment. He stumbled out onto a wide balcony, beyond which the view before him was of a city so surreal and yet so beautiful that it resembled a Roger Dean progressive rock album cover from the 1970s. Circular and conical spires in a range of heights rose like carved stalagmites from between a vast formation of dome-like structures spread out below. The towers were joined by delicate arching walkways of impossible spans seemingly without adequate structural support. Creeping vines, shrubs and trees grew between, up and over the buildings giving the impression that this subterranean metropolis had somehow risen through a previously existing forest. The entire city was contained within an immense cavern of unfeasible dimensions, yet it was not dark. Charlie stood dumbfounded, for a while oblivious to his companions, as he noticed ever more detail and he became increasingly overwhelmed by the implausibility and wonder of what he saw.

Adam was similarly affected, but also experienced a rush of elation so powerful that he felt dizzy and had to steady himself by grabbing hold of Rhona's shoulder.

'Welcome to Atargatis,' proclaimed Salamu grandly, 'beautiful isn't it?'

'I knew it!' gasped Adam with a look of blissful wonderment on his face, 'you guys *are* aliens! Holy shit! This is *so* amazing.'

'We may seem strange to you Adam,' she responded, 'but we *are* from this planet. We are ordinary humans. We may have acquired extraordinary abilities, but they are available to all who wish to master them.'

Nick, who had been frozen to the spot since the elevator doors opened, groaned and crumpled to the floor in a faint. Lynn rushed to his side and cradled his head in her hands.

'Don't worry,' said Salamu kindly, 'he will get help here. His resistance will dissipate and his condition will improve rapidly once he accepts what is happening to him. I sense he will undergo a dramatic awakening, but he will delight in his new condition.'

As Nick slowly regained his faculties, Adam went over to help Lynn get him to his feet. Charlie glanced at Bess, wondering how she was handling this and judging by the look on her face guessed that she was in the same state of incredulous awe as he was. Rowan was standing near Sonilla and Andor, hand in hand with Lendi and with a radiant smile on her face. He had never seen her look so cheerful and he was glad for her. The poor girl had been through so much. He took a deep breath, trying to adjust to this new reality. His feelings were somewhat mixed. Whilst relieved to be in a place of safety, he still felt like he had no control over his life and had no idea what he was going to do next, what to expect next, nor how long they were going to have to remain here. Ever since he found that stone on the beach, the weight of which he now became newly aware of in his pocket, his previously stable existence and concept of reality had been gradually unravelling up until this moment. It didn't seem as if that process was about to stop. Despite the marvel of the revelation before him he felt totally helpless, clueless and a little scared. Nevertheless he was so grateful to have Bess by his side that for now at least he felt comforted and able to accept his situation. This acceptance diminished his fear and he experienced a wave of pleasure just to be in the moment. He actually felt physically lighter. He turned to Bess and he knew, looking at her face that she felt the same. As they embraced the love surged through them stronger than ever before, like a force emanating from the earth beneath their feet, channelled through their bodies and upwards into space. He swayed dizzily with the sensation and wondered if this place was enhancing or exaggerating their experience. He had loved Bess so much and for so long that this increased intensity in his emotions was another surprise –

he hadn't realised it would be possible to love her even more than he had before.

Rowan was happier than she had ever previously felt in her whole life. The bond that had grown between her, Lendi, Sonilla and Andor, with the shared affinity of their common abilities, was more than she could have hoped for, more than she believed possible. It was both exciting and comforting. At last she had the security and confidence to use her mind freely and companions with whom she could safely share it. As soon as she saw the city, Rowan knew she would feel at home here. She sensed an ambience of goodwill generated by a population united in mutual compassion and with a common purpose. Holding Lendi's hand and sharing her thoughts openly, she realised there was a love growing between the two of them that would develop into a relationship much more intimate than ordinary friendship. Her heart and spirit delighted in the prospect.

Now that Nick was able to support himself and she was less distracted by his condition, Lynn's hands went to her mouth in shock as she suddenly recognised the scene.

'Oh my god.... it's another one of my paintings!' she said. 'From a dream....just like the others.'

'As I said before, your skills in pre-vision are remarkably well advanced for one with no training,' Salamu told her. 'There will be ample opportunity here for you to develop them further.'

Adam was impressed too, but also glad now that he did not find this to be another reason to worship her. He felt free of his infatuation for his friend and realised again that it had been just another addictive fixation he had clung to in the self-inflicted torment of his confused and troubled mind. He knew though that his release from this anguish was not temporary. He really felt that he had overcome a huge obstacle in his personality traits and he had not just replaced Lynn with Rhona as an object of mindless adoration. This time, he was quite certain, it was true love and in the context of his budding personal growth, it promised to be a genuinely fulfilling relationship.

'What is this place?' asked Charlie. 'How did it get here? I mean.... there's nothing holding up the roof - it should cave in, surely.'

'What you see before you,' Salamu replied, 'is the result of highly skilled feats of engineering combined with advanced science and assisted by the powers of the mind. These methods have been developed, refined and perfected over millennia. It is one of the rediscovered cities from ancient times. Due to their costal locations very few of the early settlements survived inundation, but gradually, over the last few centuries we have managed to find twelve and build ten more. As we approach the Resurgence the Ancestors, the acolytes, such as these three here, and the newly awakened, are gradually repopulating them all. Atargatis is the most recently restored to us, though there is still much work to do with less than half the buildings yet habitable. The original inhabitants had unwisely fled in terror of earthquakes, only to be swept away by a tsunami. A few hundred refugees briefly repopulated it after the shift, but they were so traumatised that between them they were unable to revive the necessary skills required for the city's effective survival. Their descendants became the builders of the Neolithic settlements on these islands and the memories of this place lost to myth and legend.' She turned and indicated a descending stairway to the right that curved down the wall of the cavern to the ground below. 'Come,' she said, 'we are tired and hungry. There is food and there are beds waiting. You can all sleep and eat. Then there will be the opportunity for more answers and a tour of the city. After your rest you will be better able to relate to and assimilate these new experiences and revelations.'

CHAPTER TWENTY-ONE.

An intriguing smell greeted Adam's nostrils when he stirred. It was emanating from the soft pillow under his head and had the crisp, clear aroma of freshly laundered linen but without the chemical perfumes of modern cleaning products. It was somehow more pleasing...more *refreshing*. He woke abruptly, not through any kind of shock or stimulus but more like he had been "switched on" or activated in some way. He felt remarkably well rested and alert. Usually he found it really difficult to rouse himself in the mornings. Despite many hours of deep slumber, he would still feel tired and curl back under the covers seeking further oblivion. This was much better. He wondered how long he'd slept for. He couldn't even remember dreaming. Then he suddenly realised with newfound glee that he was not alone and happily recalled the previous day.

They had been shown their beds not long after midday and at that point, so tired that no other possibility entered their minds, Adam and Rhona had gone to separate rooms. They were accommodated in one of the dome-shaped structures that contained eight bedrooms arranged about a central circular space. Lit from above by a round skylight this room seemed to function as a communal kitchen, dining area and lounge for the occupants. By early evening the companions, somewhat rested, had all gathered at the large central table, now five couples sitting with their partners, sharing their thoughts and feelings. Salamu arrived accompanied by a young man called Silas, tall and pale with a cheery disposition, who swiftly proceeded to create for them a feast of seafood, vegetables, leaves and fruit.

With gentle coaxing from Lynn, Nick began to relax and surrender to this unfamiliar world. Refreshed by sleep and fortified by food he seemed more like his old self, if a little subdued owing to his shaken confidence, but better able to respond to the ambience of his surroundings.

Once they had finished eating, Salamu offered to answer more of their queries.

'Where did you get all the food?' asked Bess, 'it's fantastic and so fresh. Surely this can't all be grown on Orkney – it's too windswept and cold.'

'Apart from the seafood, which is caught in the surrounding waters,' replied Salamu, 'it is all grown here in the city. We have a comprehensive system of light tunnels and mirrors to collect, reflect, direct and concentrate daylight. We also store the energy of the sun in "light batteries" for use in the winter when the day length is short. I will show you tomorrow when I give you the full guided tour of your new home.'

'Er, new home?' said Nick coolly, 'that sounds a bit um... *permanent* to me. I thought we were just going to lie low for a bit while the dust settled, you know, have a bit of a holiday and then get back to normal. I don't remember agreeing to stay here, living like some bat in a fucking cave. I mean, it's *underground* for Christ's sake, it's not natural.'

'I'm sorry Nick, but you have to remember your circumstances. Due to your unfortunate adventures in Poland and Amsterdam, you are now a wanted man – an internationally sought-after criminal with an overwhelming weight of circumstantial evidence against you. Eventually, when the "dust has settled", as you put it, you will be able to start a new life with a new identity.' Salamu paused for the import of her words to register before continuing. 'Add to that your guilt by association with the "runaways" and your knowledge of the whereabouts of Atargatis and you will find yourself as a prime target for the attentions of the "Everlords". They could easily extract all the information they require from you, but would also relish the opportunity to inflict great pain in retaliation for your involvement. You saw what lengths En Nergal went to and he was by no means the most powerful of his kind. In due course, once you have received full training and gained adequate proficiency in the methods necessary to protect your mind, you will be able to venture out once more.'

'And how long will that take?' asked Nick glumly.

'About two years.'

There was a stunned silence as Rhona, Bess, Nick, Lynn exchanged incredulous glances, followed by a sudden clamour of objection which Salamu silenced by raising her hands.

Before she had a chance to speak, Nick piped up. 'I am not staying here two fucking years,' he protested, 'whatever you say.'

'Nick, your stubbornness is becoming a little wearing. I'm afraid you have no alternative.'

'You mean we are prisoners?' he said indignantly.

'If you choose to see it that way, then regrettably, yes.'

'Come on Nick mate,' put in Adam, 'we're wanted for car theft, kidnap and terrorism. What did you expect?'

'He's right love,' said Lynn softly, as ever more willing and able to adapt, 'you have to admit, whether you like it or not, we are *all* gradually becoming telepathic in one way or another and here we can really be helped with that. Anyway, this is a totally safe place for our baby to be born, yeah? It'll be just like we planned but with a lot more help and support and stuff and with like real friends.'

He felt his will to remain antagonistic slipping away as he adjusted his thoughts. Just because he didn't like being told what to do, didn't mean they were wrong. 'I guess you're right,' he acknowledged reluctantly.

'Can we contact friends and family?' asked Charlie, concerned about his son Luke and his aging parents.

'You will be able to send messages,' Salamu assured him, 'but without revealing your location.'

'I've got a business to run,' murmured Rhona quietly, as if she had only just remembered, 'I've got staff who rely on me for their wages...'

'If you can devise a method of delegating, from a distance, all the necessary tasks required for it to continue, could it function without your presence?'

Rhona shook her head and sighed heavily.

'I'll help,' offered Charlie, 'I'm sure we could work something out – the guys are pretty sussed on the whole and Flora as good as runs the office single-handed.'

'But what are we going to tell them? I mean....*two years!*'

'I'm not sure...I expect we'll think of something..'

'But there's the designing and pricing....'

'I reckon Rory could do that if you we're able to help him from a "virtual" office.' He glanced up at Salamu, who nodded to confirm that this was a possibility.

Rhona looked doubtful but said no more, after all what choice did she have?

Nick sounded sulky, like a child who had had his dream day out taken away as punishment. 'But we were going to start a new life in a croft with our new baby and grow veg and stuff...' he muttered.

'You can start that here,' Salamu assured him, 'and then, when you are ready, continue on that path in the outside world.'

There was a minute's silence whilst they each contemplated the future.

Bess finally spoke of her own concerns, which had been slowly infiltrating her mind now that she had rested, though she already knew she was stymied.

'I've got a business to run too,' she protested weakly, 'and there's no one else there who can run it for me, I don't have any staff...my customers are going to be left in the lurch. You deceived us! You deliberately didn't tell us the length of our...*incarceration* so that we would agree to come!'

'I am truly sorry, Bess,' said Salamu earnestly, 'but I knew you would not come otherwise.'

'But my herbs will get overgrown with weeds....everything in the polytunnel will die if it's not watered. I'll lose all of my clients......and what about my yoga class? They're going to be left without an instructor.... I've got a responsibility to them. All those weeks shut in a cell and now I'm a prisoner again.' After the emotional turmoil and disrupted life of the last few weeks, the temporary calm she had tried to keep in her composure was beginning to disintegrate.

'I understand your worries, believe me,' stated Salamu, 'but all of those people will cope with what is, after all, just inconvenient. I am more concerned about Atargatis remaining concealed from the Everlords for as long as possible *and* about all of you remaining unharmed.' She reached across and squeezed Bess' hand - her first gesture of affection so far. Bess felt a wave of reassurance emanating towards her and rapidly felt soothed by it. 'Wait until you see the gardens here Bess,' added Salamu smiling. 'You will find your heart there and will no longer feel a captive, I'm sure. And when it is safe for you to go back home, I am feel you will be able to restart both your business and your yoga class.'

She looked around the group, as if inviting further comments.

'You've mentioned some kind of "Resurgence",' said Adam, quickly grasping this opportunity to satisfy his curiosity, 'can you tell us more about that? Andor said it's like a shift in human consciousness or something isn't it?'

She seemed relieved to have the opportunity to talk of something else.

'Indeed,' she said, 'there will come a time in the near future when enough people will have awakened to their mental abilities for there to be a leap in psychic awareness worldwide. For some it will happen more quickly than for others. I have heard it said that it can be like opening curtains to let the sun in. The room fills with light revealing all that is within it but taking up no more space than before. For those who undergo a slower transformation it is more like gradually learning a new language. After a period of adjustment and transition the human race will once more become a global confederation of cooperative communities.'

'*This is the dawning of the Age of Aquarius,*' sang Adam quietly with a widening smile.

'Something like that,' she agreed.

'This "period of adjustment" sounds a bit ominous,' observed Charlie. 'I imagine that they might be some people who don't like the changes and might cause trouble.'

'Yes, that will unquestionably be the case,' admitted Salamu, 'those who benefited greatest from the old world order will be the most resistant. Often it will be those in positions of power – governments, the military, multi-national corporations, financial institutions, some of the very wealthy. They will cling on greedily and fearfully, which will inevitably lead to further and more extreme oppression and violence before peace is finally established. Also some with very strong religious convictions will either interpret the changes in their own way or lash out at scapegoats if they are unable to reconcile the changes with their doctrine.'

'Sounds like one of the Armageddon myths,' said Adam, 'or that Nostradamus prophecy of the end of the world...'

'All of these predictions stem from the original estimates, but due to countless natural variables such as irregularities in the Earth's spin and orbit, mistakes in translation and transcription, the prejudices and preconceived notions of the writers, coupled with the corrupt influence of those in control of the reproduction and redistribution of the knowledge, they suffer from numerous inaccuracies. Unfortunately, a lot of those who consider themselves as devout believe every word to be the truth. In any event, due to the very nature of the process it will be, as I said before, a period of transition not a single date, but there is no doubt that eventually the new balance will be one of harmony and empathic coexistence – people living in harmony with each other and nature.'

Adam looked at Rhona and squeezed her hand, hoping that she too was excited by the prospect of the enlightened utopia to come. Meeting his eyes, Rhona came to a sudden realisation. Previously a workaholic, obsessed by running her business, she now became aware that in the space the last few minutes she undergone a surprising change of heart. She no longer cared about any of that. After all, what difference did it make, *really*? She felt free. She had not been conscious of the fact that her responsibilities had been chains restricting her life's journey. A wave of relief washed through her, as if cleaning away a clutter of petty concerns. She was here now and for the first time in her life she felt genuine love for a man, even though she had not known him long. There appeared to be an inexplicable bond created when their minds intermingled in this strange place. There seemed no question that from now on they would share a bed and their lives as soul mates, without even needing to discuss it. She could neither explain nor understand it but she knew it to be true. He too was enjoying the discovery of their mutual compatibility as they opened themselves to each other and their new experiences. These unfamiliar sensations, Adam thought to himself smiling, were a kind of "happy-ache".

Now, waking up to see the head of short spiky red hair resting on the pillow next to him, Adam still felt like he was dreaming, but recognised that it was a dream come true. He felt he could completely understand the phrase "died and gone to heaven". Rhona was lying on her side facing away from him, the covers rumpled at her waist and her bare back tantalisingly close. Sighing with happiness, he reached out to gently stroke her flawless skin with his fingers, and then placed a soft kiss on her shoulder. She stirred at the touch of his lips, wriggled a little and made contented mumblings before turning to face him and kiss him tenderly.

'Breakfast?' Adam asked, feeling a bit peckish.

'What's the hurry?' she said smiling coyly, and pulled him towards her.

A little later, when they sauntered happily into the common room, everyone else had already eaten. When Nick chirped, 'we know what *you've* been up to!' with a huge grin splitting his face, Adam felt no embarrassment and was glad to see his friend in good spirits again. Charlie was pleased for his brother too. Since he had left university, Adam had appeared discontented and directionless. Charlie's attempts to stay in contact became fewer as Adam became more distant in both character and location and they gradually drifted apart. It would be good to re-establish their relationship and get to know each other better. Also now that he had set aside his own misgivings, Charlie was anticipating an intriguing future. Atargatis had a heartening atmosphere of well-being and tranquillity, yet also harboured an industrious and enthusiastic population. It was almost like the perfect drug, which had been designed to provide just the right balance in a mixture of sedative and stimulant. Salamu explained to him that this was the result of his first experience of visiting a benign telepathic community and that this sensation would amplify as his own perceptions developed and improved.

By mid morning they were all ready to explore. Salamu guided them through a labyrinthine warren created by what seemed to be a haphazard arrangement of domes in varying sizes, towards the nearest of the circular towers. They encountered a few other people, mostly dressed in practical looking yet colourful tunics or coveralls, presumably dependent on the nature of their work, who greeted them warmly as they passed. Charlie looked up at the balcony that encircled the top of this unfeasibly thin, tall structure.

'That's where we are going,' announced their escort, 'it's the best place to get a view of the whole city. Then I can show you some of the details.'

The hundreds of steps that spiralled up the tight curve of the internal circumference were not so much of a slog as Charlie had been expecting them to be.

'We've seen that you have the technology to build elevators,' he said half way up, 'so why not here? Why all the steps?'

'What would be the purpose?' Salamu countered, 'besides, the exercise is beneficial.'

'Well, it would save a lot of time.'

'That is a commodity we are not short of. It is also an opportunity to reflect on one's thoughts. If we rush everywhere and fill every moment with actions and distractions, we do not have chance to think properly between our activities. This results in a restlessness of spirit that is all too common in modern societies. The value of time spent in contemplation cannot be underestimated.'

The view of the city from the top of the spire was even more astonishing than their first glimpse of the place. Now he could see the full extent of the conurbation it seemed even more improbable to Charlie that such a place could exist. About half a mile away in one direction, where the buildings ended, there were what appeared to be extensive gardens brightly lit by reflectors high on the cavern walls, giving the impression at ground level of almost normal daylight. Amongst the buildings were some smaller expanses of greenery that looked like parks for recreation and exercise. Salamu explained that a plentiful supply of water was obtained by collection of rain from the buildings above the surface and by extracting ground water from the rocks around them.

'How many people live here?' asked Charlie.

'At the moment,' replied Salamu, 'no more than one thousand, but once fully restored and recolonised, the capacity will be closer to ten times that.'

'Will the gardens be able to feed that many?' asked Bess.

'Not entirely, but our diet is supplemented by mycoprotein cultivation and fishing, so we should be able to be self-sufficient in food.'

'Are there many children here?' asked Lynn.

'There are a few dozen of various ages,' said their host, 'and several expectant mothers like yourself, so your baby will have no shortage of playmates.'

'I would love to see the gardens,' requested Bess.

'Of course, we'll go there next.'

As they approached the growing areas they could see that there were people scattered throughout, some walking slowly and some working diligently. When Bess' enthusiastic enquiries became ever more detailed, Salamu suggested that she remain and talk to one of the horticultural team, while the rest of the party continue on their way. Sonilla and Andor also decided to stay and learn more of the techniques employed here. They had both enjoyed gardening whilst at the foundation. Lynn was beginning to tire, so Nick volunteered to accompany her back to the dome. He had now completely overcome his sickness and petulance. He had admitted that he too had been having strange dreams over the last few weeks and had been becoming increasingly aware of the thoughts of those around him, but his ego and his fear had made him cling to the reality with which he felt safer. He apologised to everyone, but especially to Lynn and was quickly forgiven. In a cheerful state of heightened awareness his mood was buoyant and his manner jovial. It appeared to Adam as if Nick had dropped some Ecstasy but knew that wasn't the case. His friend was experiencing a euphoria induced by his own endorphins, revelling in the sensations of his recently liberated faculties. He was even confident of finding his way back through the confusing maze of the settlement to their lodgings, just using his newfound abilities. Rowan wanted to investigate something entitled "art play" with Lendi, from whom she was now inseparable. This enticing activity was something Lendi was familiar with and she was keen to share it with her new companion.

They skipped away hand-in-hand giggling like two happy and carefree ten year olds.

Charlie listened briefly to one of the gardeners explaining the methods of selective breeding used to propagate edible plants in conditions of low light, but then decided to follow Rhona and Adam, who were happy to continue on to what Salamu referred to as "the excavations", though whether these were of geological or historical significance was not clear. As they approached the site, Adam noticed that all the digging was being done by hand and recognised the layout as that normally used by archaeologists.

'There are parts of the city that are yet to be uncovered,' Salamu said, 'and records indicate that there should be additional caverns connected to the main one by tunnels through the rock. However, the city has been subjected to many land movements in the last thirty thousand years or so and although a great deal of it has remained remarkably intact, there is still a lot buried.'

'What are they looking for here?' asked Adam, 'anything in particular?'

'Yes actually. Something with which I'm sure both you and your brother are familiar. But first, there is someone here with whom you are acquainted and I'm sure he will be glad to see you.'

Adam was mystified. He couldn't imagine who on earth he would know who could be here. Full of curiosity, he followed Salamu through the excavations with Rhona and Charlie trailing behind them. They approached a slim figure bent double in a hole, poking at something with a trowel and completely absorbed in the task. Disturbed by the sound of their approach, he stood and turned to look at them. Adam had to do a double-take but recognised him immediately.

'Professor!' he exclaimed in surprise. 'How? I mean…what are you doing here. Blimey! It's good to see you!' He bent down smiling happily to enthusiastically shake the grimy hand offered by the older man who was still waist deep in his pit.

Tom Oakley grinned in return. 'Ah, Adam my boy! They told me you were coming...heard all about your adventures. My my, it seems you and your friends have had some rather remarkable experiences recently…but I bet I gave you a bit of a shock, eh? Sorry about our last meeting...I was a little overwrought to say the least...I imagine you thought I must have been incarcerated in an institution for the criminally insane!'

'Yeah. Last I knew you were being dragged off by the law. What happened to you?'

'Hmm, a most unpleasant experience too I can assure you,' the professor replied, 'framed for that bombing as I was by the "Everlords" for failing to play ball. But, as good fortune had it, I was rescued by my good friends here, who luckily also have connections in high places, and given sanctuary in this marvellous place. What do you think eh? Fascinating! It's good to be back, I can tell you.'

Adam was momentarily flabbergasted. 'Your friends...? You know people here? Back? You've been here before? But how? I mean when? I mean *what?*'

'It was Tom who first rediscovered this place,' Salamu told him.

Adam stood in stunned silence.

'Do you remember my expedition back in...oh it must have been eighty-nine or ninety?' Oakley asked him.

He nodded mutely.

'And the stones I gave you for safe keeping? I found them here, you know....,' he gestured with his right hand, which was still clutching the trowel. 'Have you brought them with you?' he added hopefully.

Adam's mind slipped back to his undergraduate days when he was Tom Oakley's keenest student. He particularly enjoyed the one-to-one tutorials with the professor – they both shared a passion for lost civilisations and Adam deduced that he was given more than his fair share of his teacher's time compared to that enjoyed by the other students. He was frequently invited back to Oakley's rooms where Tom would share his theories and show him artefacts he had found. He was free to browse the professor's library and they would often converse enthusiastically for hours into the night, oblivious to the passage of time. In the summer of 1990, Tom had announced that he was planning a trip to Orkney as a guest of Historic Scotland to study the Neolithic village of Skara Brae. Whilst on the islands it was his intention to explore another area on Hoy to investigate one of his own hypotheses. He had offered Adam a chance to join him as his assistant, but he had already arranged holiday work to help pay off his overdraft and as the position with Professor Oakley was unpaid, he was forced unwillingly to decline for financial reasons.

Eight weeks later, when Tom returned, he was full of excitement at his findings.

'I have found something *quite extraordinary,*' he announced to Adam in private, 'a sensational discovery that will completely overturn and *revolutionise* our knowledge and views of ancient history!'

'Why? What is it?' asked Adam eagerly.

'Can't tell you I'm afraid…not yet anyway my boy,' said the professor gravely, suddenly becoming serious. 'It seems that there are nefarious characters who would stop at nothing to get their hands on this information…and I don't want to put you in any danger. First of all, I need to make sure this discovery gets into the right hands…although I'm uncertain as yet to whom those hands belong…and where they might be…' he paused significantly and raised his left eyebrow as if this somehow would convey some meaning Adam was otherwise unlikely to construe. His student though, still felt completely in the dark.

'In the meantime,' continued Oakley, for some reason looking over his shoulder even though there was no one else in the room, 'I would like to put into your safe keeping, these extraordinary artefacts, for the time being.' He handed over a small but heavy Hessian sack and added, 'hide them well, show them to nobody and don't tell anyone about them. I'll come back for them soon.'

Opening the drawstring Adam looked in the bag and examined the contents. There were about a dozen highly polished bottle-green stones, resembling in size and form, large randomly shaped, slightly elongated potatoes. He picked one up to examine it more closely. It appeared to consist of hundreds of irregular crystals fused together in an intricate jigsaw that looked beyond the abilities of both humankind and nature to form. He suddenly felt an odd tingling sensation in his fingers that then pulsed to the top of his head through his spine and he thought he detected an almost imperceptible whispering of distant voices. He dropped the stone in fright.

'What the hell was that?' he asked putting his hand to his chest to still his trebling heartbeat.

'*Quite extraordinary* isn't it?' came the reply, 'outlandish to say the least. I've absolutely no idea what they are, but I found them at the site I was investigating. Now, get a move on, I've got to make myself scarce for a little while and I need to start packing. So, remember – keep them safe and don't tell a soul.'

He had kept the stones safe for the next few months, hidden under a panel in the bottom of the wardrobe in his digs. To begin with he had resisted the temptation to get them out for another look. He was fearful of the strange phenomenon that they had previously manifested and he was reluctant to repeat the experience. In the end, however, he gave in to the urge to examine the stones once more. Again he felt the same strange prickling sensation, like static electricity combined with pins and needles, but this time he did not let go. He heard the whispering more clearly this time but there were too many speaking at once to make out the words and even when he thought he could isolate a phrase it seemed to be in an unfamiliar, indecipherable language. A hot flush ran through his body followed by a shiver and simultaneously a snapshot image of buildings collapsing amid huge flames suddenly filled his awareness. The voices became louder and more distressed and as they did so, Adam felt his own emotions align with theirs. Panic, fear and sorrow filled his mind until he called out in anguish and dropped the stone. Panting and sweating he hurriedly replaced it with the others in the bag and returned it to its hiding place.

That was when the dreams started and they soon became nightmares, but not those haunted by demons or zombies or creatures of the night. These felt like very real catastrophes wherein he and his loved ones were imperilled by extreme natural disasters such as tsunamis, earthquakes and volcanoes in times of extreme cold and darkness. It was not long before he was reluctant to go to sleep at night and stayed up later and later hoping that if he was completely exhausted, he might be too tired to dream. When this failed he took to smoking a pipe of hash every night before going to bed in an attempt to quell the visions but this too was unsuccessful. The strain on his meagre student finances added worry to his fatigue and with the increased dope smoking affecting his ability to focus his studies began to suffer. When the professor returned after a four month "sabbatical" he seemed to be unwilling and unable to help. He said that until he had published his findings and needed to produce them as evidence he would not take the stones back.

Eventually, in desperation, Adam decided to conceal the troublesome burden at a great distance. With little more than a change of clothes he hitch-hiked to the North of Scotland to visit his brother. Charlie was both pleased and surprised to see him in the middle of an academic term, but despite misgivings about his brother's state of mind, he soon gave up trying to question him when his enquiries were curtly rebuffed. Unable to find a satisfactory tree under which to bury his bundle, Adam searched for a suitable wall, but the expansive and open terrain made him feel too vulnerable to potentially hostile eyes. The stiff-stemmed, desiccated grey skeletons of last year's thistles stood trembling in the strong, chill wind like ghostly victims of a nuclear nightmare. Everywhere he looked his mind's eye conjured up grim and threatening images. One night, demented by lack of sleep and with his wits crazed by horrific visions he ran to the beach and hurled the sack of rocks as far as he could into the middle of the estuary. Thus relieved but feeling a little guilty he went back to university and tried to return to relative normality. Distracted as he was by the threats and intimidation, Thomas Oakley did not ask about the stones again until he burst into Adam's flat on the night of his arrest.

'Adam?' prompted the Professor, raising his eyebrows quizzically and making a small circle in the air with his trowel as if this would help illicit a response. Adam broke out of his reverie and grimaced uncomfortably with his confession.

'I'm really sorry,' he said, also cringing inwardly, 'I er, lost...no, I actually threw them away years ago...I am *really* sorry....it's just I was getting all these nightmares and stuff...'

'Oh, don't worry my boy,' Oakley reassured him, 'there are plenty more where they came from now – we are finding more every day. There must be *thousands* of them.'

Adam sighed with relief, another guilty secret off his mind. Charlie reached into his jacket pocket and withdrew his own stone, avoiding skin contact by grasping it in his coat sleeve. He held it up for the old man to see. 'Is this one of them?' he asked.

'I say! Yes, it is,' affirmed the Professor, 'but where did *you* get it?'

'I found it on the beach.'

'It must be one of the ones I chucked,' said Adam, 'and when you found it and started having dreams....that was when my dreams came back too! There must have been some kind of psychic link because we're brothers...'

'Just exactly what *are* these stones anyway,' Charlie asked, 'and what have they got to do with the casket I was making?'

Salamu told him that these echo stones were synthesised from pizo-electric quartz and silicon in a process requiring enormous inputs of energy. They had been used since ancient times, before The Shift. Those who did not possess the faculties to continue as "ancestors" would store their memories and knowledge in these stones for the benefit of all, usually by thought transference at the time of death, but it could also be undertaken at other times too, such as when an important study had produced significant results. Thus was accumulated a vast portable "library" of experience and wisdom. For some of the people unsuitable for continuation this was not enough. They wished to retain their egos, identities and physical form, so devised a casket designed to mirror the energy flow of the life force in the body. By correctly siting a set of echo stones and other special gems of different vibrational frequencies in a matrix of gold and with someone to act as catalyst by guiding the energies, they were able to rejuvenate themselves in old age and gain another life span. The more times this was done, the longer lasting the body became and the less frequently the process was required. When those who disapproved of the practice destroyed a casket or none were available for some other reason, or a replacement could not be made in time, the most iniquitous amongst them chose to use "vessels".

'I'm afraid that this is where I must make a confession,' said the professor, finally clambering out of the excavations and brushing the soil from his trousers. 'It was I who set fire to the Belums' mansion....'

'What?' exclaimed Adam. He could not imagine any circumstances in which the aging academic would turn arsonist, until he remembered their last two encounters....

'Yes, you wouldn't think it of a harmless old soul such as myself, would you?' Oakley chuckled, but was obviously still embarrassed by his admission. 'But you see, you must understand what a desperate state I was in. My career and my reputation had been ruined, I *had* turned to alcohol and gambling and I really *was* being pursued by loan sharks. Eventually, I discovered the whereabouts of a couple of these so-called "Everlords", who I believed were at least partly responsible for my demise and in my deranged condition sought to wreak my revenge as an incendiary felon. Over the years I had become quite good at concealing myself from hostile forces, so to speak, and did so once more after this criminal act. That is when their network decided to frame me with the attack on the university, with a look-a-like visible to the security cameras, so that with the law enforcement agencies also on my tail, I might be easier to apprehend.'

Adam stood open-mouthed, staring at his old mentor with a mixture of shock and admiration.

'So you see,' continued Oakley, now looking a Charlie, 'as I was responsible for the destruction of the Belums' casket, it was I who unwittingly instigated the circumstances leading to your predicament vis-à-vis fashioning a replacement, which led to the kidnap of the young woman in Poland, your employer's niece and your wife. In all probability, without my thoughtless actions catalysing this complex and regrettable series of events, none of you would have been forced to flee here.'

Charlie didn't know what to say or feel. He couldn't blame the professor for everything that had happened since his arson attack. He could not have known what was going to happen as a result of his actions. Yet, here Charlie was, his life no longer what he chose and no longer in his control. He thought that maybe he *should* feel some resentment towards this eccentric character, but he merely felt numb. He had been through so much that his ability to react seemed to have been completely eroded.

'But there was the whole thing with the stones.....' muttered Adam, still both curious and fascinated by the revelations and their implications, 'if I hadn't chucked them in the sea and if Charlie hadn't picked one up, then he wouldn't have had those dreams...'

'None of us can undo the past,' said Charlie finally, 'although there's still a lot more I would like to understand about what is in the stones and why there are nightmares and bad visions triggered by them.'

Salamu tried to explain a little more. Another drawback with the stones that were used in the traumatic years of the shift was that they became imbued with the torment of the victims, hence the disagreeable nature of the dreams Charlie and Adam had experienced. Repeated use of these stones could lead the user to become indifferent to the suffering of others and in extreme cases to actually enjoy it. The Everlords had been known to use the stones as currency or even steal them from each other. They often fought amongst themselves, unable to unite into a cohesive force unless it served their own selfish desires.

'What about the field of monoliths that Bess and I dreamed about?' asked Charlie, 'the big ones like they found in Chile?'

'Before the shift, some cities had been continuous for several thousand years,' Salamu told him, 'so in these places they fashioned sets of larger echo stones for the population to enjoy as and when they wished. Most of these have been lost, so the recent find you referred to is extremely welcome news. We also suspect that there is such a grouping here in Atargatis too and hope that further excavations will reveal it soon.'

'There's one other thing that's been puzzling me,' admitted Charlie, 'how come so many of the dreams I had involved me making one of these caskets at various times throughout history? And why was it always involving the Belums?'

'The vibrations from the echo stones can stimulate your own genetic memories,' Salamu replied. 'Contrary to popular scientific theory – because they have not been looking and so have not yet learned how to detect them - your DNA contains energy imprints of your memories and those of your predecessors. That is why Asar and Ki chose you, because your ancestors had undertaken the work on many occasions, thereby imparting that skill to their descendants and so on to you.'

'So….are you saying that the reason I became a wood carver is because so many of my ancestors had been wood carvers? That it is "in my genes" and that I didn't really have an option? And that I was doomed to have those bastards as my "lords" in every incarnation?'

'Well, it is not predetermined but it would have had quite an influence on your choice of career. And it is certainly true that the same overlords would try to seek out your genetic line to get the best job done.'

Charlie had long wondered why working with wood had always felt so natural to him, he had even joked to Bess once that it felt like he had done it in a previous life. Now, it seemed like he was almost "fated" to follow this path and although he had always loved his craft, he felt slightly resentful in the knowledge that he was not so entirely in control of his own destiny as he had always imagined he was. Suddenly wishing to be alone with his thoughts for a while, he left the others to chat amongst themselves.

'There's one last question that's been on my mind,' said Adam, turning to Salamu, 'but with one thing and another, I haven't had a chance to ask. How come you were in the cellar in my dream putting stones in the Belums' casket? Was that an actual ancestral memory of a particular time and place...and were you really there?'

'The events you saw actually happened at the time of The Shift,' she began slowly, 'and ancestors of yours and Charlie's were present, but your mind reinterpreted everything in its dream state to create a collage of various realities. As for my own presence, no, that is not possible, but physical resemblances do recur repeatedly through genetic lines and I know from my own ancestral memories, that a forebear of mine did once serve the Belums, but that was before they became truly corrupted. However, it may be why I felt so repulsed by them when we met again. Perhaps knowledge of their actions stimulated an ancient mistrust in me from past betrayals….it is difficult to say and to be honest now largely irrelevant.'

The soothing ambience within the guest's dome was having a major influence on Nick's outlook. Having finally begun to accept the undeniable truth of the evidence around him, he was enthusiastically embracing this "new science". Lynn was reclined happily on a large and comfortable sofa, pleased to take the weight off her feet. She was starting to get sudden episodes of physical exhaustion, which she claimed must be "the little sproglet putting on a growth spurt.' Nick crouched on the floor next to her with his hands on her slowly swelling abdomen.

'Wow! It's bloody amazing to think that there's someone in there!' he declared in wonder. 'I can actually *sense* the little bugger somehow.... and now it looks like it's going to be born here, with all this crazy mind stuff going on...man, this kid is going to come out *tripping*!'

Lynn smiled to herself and put her hands on top of his. She was so glad that her man had at last come to terms with the changes within himself that he had previously denied. Her own pre-vision had developed in her teens and although Nick could not deny its existence, he had always belittled its significance or dismissed it as coincidence – a fact that had, despite her love for him, frequently niggled her. Over the last few weeks she had noticed an increase in her telepathic abilities too - a growing awareness of the emotions of those around her and some quite sudden insights into their thoughts. The most amazing thing for her though was the emergence of the daily strengthening bond she felt developing between her and the baby. She couldn't bring herself to think of it as a "foetus" or an "embryo" – it sounded so clinical, so impersonal. As soon as she was aware that she was pregnant, which was before the doctor confirmed it, she perceived that the budding life-form within her already had its own individual "essence", no matter how simple. Sighing contentedly, Lynn closed her eyes, knowing that she had a safe and secure place in which to give birth to her child.

'It's weird though...,' said Nick thoughtfully whilst gazing unseeingly at the wall, 'all that time I refused to think about what was going on with your paintings and you stuck by me. It must've really pissed you off when you knew there was something in it...you could have told me to sod off at any point, but you didn't...'

'That's because I love you Nick,' she mumbled sleepily. 'Even when you behave like an arsehole.'

'Yeah. And I love you too Lynn. And I'm sorry. It's funny to think of all that time I was into "facts" and "proof" that had to be presented in a particular way before I would believe anything. I thought I was open to new ideas and discoveries, yet there was stuff right in front of my own fucking eyes that I wouldn't look at. I was blinkered and I didn't even know it. Anyway, I have now been shown the error of my ways...'

Lynn had begun to snore.

The painting looked as happy as Rowan felt – it was after all a manifestation of her feelings whilst she was creating it. Huge round pink shapes seemed to bulge from the canvas as if floating on the bright orange background. Her broad and enthusiastic brush strokes had resulted in a surprisingly three-dimensional picture by the intuitive use of slightly varying shades and hues to produce the impression of a direction of light. She stood back and admired her work. She had never before enjoyed making artwork so much, or *"art play"* she corrected herself - and *that* was the difference. At school she always felt the expectations of the teachers and the judgement of her peers as an unwanted interference in the process that stifled her creativity. Even at home she knew that Rhona would appraise her efforts and say "that's nice" even though she didn't always mean it and this also affected her ability to reproduce her ideas. This new freedom to play and indulge her imagination fully, in a totally non-judgemental environment, released an artistic spirit that had been trapped within her like a caged bird of paradise, now liberated and so able to fly and sing with abandon.

She watched as Lendi worked on her own unfinished piece. At last, after several confusing, frustrating, unfulfilling years in attempts to overcome uncomfortable and disappointing encounters with boys, Rowan had discovered that a same sex romance was much more in harmony with her nature. She supposed that it took her so long to discover her orientation because her mind was always struggling to block out the unwanted thoughts of others and in so doing she had suppressed her own needs and desires. In addition to that, despite assertions of liberal leanings, the codes of behaviour underlying the culture in the Highlands were still very much embedded in Victorian moral principles and it was extremely rare to encounter anyone who would openly admit to being in anything other than a heterosexual relationship. Here and now though, her future seemed rosy indeed, but for the present she was extremely happy just to enjoy and live each moment to the full.

The park was asymmetrically laid out in a pleasing yet indiscernible pattern. Charlie wandered the curving paths amongst trees and bushes of familiar varieties but that had slight differences, presumably as a result of the adaptations required to make them more suited to the lower levels of sunlight. Coming to a bench of a design not dissimilar to what he imagined Gaudi might have devised, Charlie sat to rest his legs. It was fashioned from a material he couldn't identify, which certainly wasn't any kind of wood. He looked around. It seemed decidedly odd that there was no wind – not even a breeze. A few finches, tits and sparrows flitted and twittered about amongst the branches, giving the place a more natural feel.

Seeming to sense his desire for solitude, the passers-by greeted him politely and then left him in peace. Well, he thought, I could get used to people who could intuit my needs in this way. It would save awkwardness of apologies and false politeness. Although he hadn't yet perceived much difference in his own mental abilities, apart from with Bess, Salamu had assured him that it would come in time. Apparently different people developed at varying rates and acquired different strengths according to their own propensity. Charlie was a patient man though and was happy to let these things run their natural course. He glanced at the trees around him. None of them were very tall. He supposed that was also a consequence of the strange conditions here in this giant cave. He looked at the nearest tree, which he had identified as a kind of hawthorn, and noticed that its leaves were much larger and paler than he would have expected. He wondered what the timber would be like from these trees and whether or not they were actually allowed to harvest them. Come to think of it, he couldn't remember seeing anything made from wood since he had arrived in Atargatis. The thought then struck him that he may have to change the nature of his work as long as he was forced to dwell this underground city. He shrugged philosophically to himself. He'd had to adapt to numerous changes already in a very short space of time and felt sure he could cope with another. He looked up to the cavern roof high above, saw the openings of the light tunnels and huge convex mirrors reflecting the brightness of the day outside. It was very clever and very effective, but it just wasn't the same. He was looking up at a rock face, there were no clouds, no sun, no hills, no horizon. He might get used to living in this place eventually but there was one thing for certain – Charlie would miss the sky.

The End.

ACKNOWLEDGEMENTS

I am very grateful to all of the people who provided the invaluable help and information that assisted in the development and improvement of this book.

I would especially like to thank:

Fuggo (Fiona) King, Robert King, Kamila Lasu, Marion Macdonald, Christel Smeets, Pam Summers, Hilary Peters, Karen Atkinson and in particular my nephew Ben King.

Geoff King lives on a smallholding near the edge of the wilds in the North of Scotland with his wife, cats and chickens. Here he writes, walks to the beach, hand carves wooden jewellery and plants trees.

www.facebook.com/Geoff.F.King

Made in the USA
Charleston, SC
13 April 2015